THE MYSTERIOUS ISLAND

JULES VERNE

Translated by
DAVID PETAULT

ISBN: 9798340713872

INTRODUCTION

The Mysterious Island was published in 1875 as a serialized adventure in the *Magasin d'Éducation et de Récréation*. The novel is a compelling mix of adventure, science fiction, and mystery. It follows five Union prisoners from the American Civil War who escape in a hot air balloon and end up stranded on a remote, uncharted island in the Pacific. With limited resources, the men—led by the resourceful engineer Cyrus Smith—apply their knowledge of science and technology to survive and explore their new surroundings. What begins as a tale of survival evolves into a fascinating narrative of ingenuity, discovery, and intrigue as they unravel the island's hidden secrets.

The Mysterious Island was written during a period of great technological and scientific advancement in Europe, which deeply influenced Verne's work. The latter half of the 19th century saw significant breakthroughs in engineering, communication, and transportation, such as the construction of the Suez Canal, the expansion of railways, and the development of the telegraph. These developments sparked the imagination of writers and scientists alike, inspiring the themes of exploration and human achievement found in Verne's novels. The book also reflects the geopolitical tensions of its time. The characters' American Civil War background is a nod to contemporary events, while Verne's focus on survival and human resilience embodies the 19th-century optimism about progress and the power of human ingenuity.

Jules Verne (1828–1905) is widely regarded as one of the pioneers of the science fiction genre and one of the most influential writers of the 19th century. A French novelist and playwright, Verne's fascination with travel, exploration, and technology fueled his imaginative storytelling. His works often wove together scientific knowledge and adventure, captivating audiences around the world. Alongside *Journey to the Center of the Earth* (1864), *Twenty Thousand Leagues Under the Sea* (1870), and *Around the World in Eighty Days* (1872), *The Mysterious Island* remains one of his seminal contributions, establishing his legacy as a visionary and storyteller of grand speculative fiction.

This new translation seeks to preserve the richness and intensity of Verne's original prose while making the text more accessible for contemporary readers. Previous translations of *The Mysterious Island* often altered the tone, abridged sections, or rendered technical descriptions inaccurately, leading to inconsistencies and a dilution of Verne's meticulous attention to detail. Many earlier English versions of Verne's works were heavily abridged or "adapted" for younger audiences, often losing the technical depth and thematic nuances of the original. In contrast, this translation strives for fidelity to Verne's intent, maintaining the complex language and scientific references that make *The Mysterious Island* such a compelling read. Where older translations sometimes omitted entire passages or simplified character interactions, this version reinstates and accurately translates these segments, offering readers a fuller and more authentic experience of Verne's narrative.

The key differences from previous translations include the restoration of passages omitted in many English versions, which allows for a richer reading experience, and greater accuracy in scientific descriptions, ensuring that engineering and scientific explanations remain true to Verne's vision. The translation also captures the subtle nuances and distinct voices of each character, which were sometimes lost or flattened in earlier versions. Instead of modernizing the language, the translator has retained a period-specific tone, which preserves the historical context and flavor of the original work.

David Petault

❧ I ❧
THE AIR CASTAWAYS

$\mathfrak{H}$ I $\mathfrak{H}$

"Are we going up?

— No! On the contrary! We are going down!

— Worse than that, Mr. Cyrus! We are falling!

— For God's sake! Throw out ballast!

— Here's the last bag emptied!

— Is the balloon rising?

— No!

— I hear a splashing of waves!

— The sea is beneath the basket!

— It can't be five hundred feet below us!"

Then a powerful voice broke through the air, and these words echoed:

"Overboard everything that weighs!... everything! And may God help us!"

Such were the words that burst into the air above that vast water desert of the Pacific around four o'clock in the afternoon on March 23, 1865.

No one has likely forgotten the terrible northeast windstorm that erupted in the middle of the equinox that year, during which the barometric pressure dropped to seven hundred ten millimeters. It was a relentless hurricane that lasted from March 18 to 26. The devastation it caused was immense in America, Europe, and Asia, over a wide zone of eighteen hundred miles, stretching obliquely along the equator from the thirty-fifth parallel north to the fortieth parallel south!

Cities toppled, forests uprooted, shores devastated by walls of water crashing down like tidal waves, hundreds of ships thrown ashore, as reported by Bureau Veritas, entire territories leveled by whirlwinds that crushed everything in their path, several thousand people crushed on land or swallowed by the sea: such were the evidences left behind by this formidable hurricane. It surpassed in destruction the ones that ravaged Havana and Guadeloupe so fearfully, one on October 25, 1810, the other on July 26, 1825.

Now, at the very moment that so many catastrophes were occurring on land and at sea, a no less striking drama was unfolding in the disturbed skies. Indeed, a balloon, carried like a ball at the top of a waterspout, caught in the whirling motion of the column of air, was traveling through space at a speed of ninety miles an hour, spinning around itself, as if caught in some aerial maelstrom. Below the lower appendage of this balloon swayed a basket containing five passengers, barely visible amid the thick vapors, mingled with misty water, that trailed down to the surface of the Ocean.

Where had this aerostat come from, this true toy of the dreadful storm? From what point in the world had it launched? It obviously could not have taken off during the hurricane. Yet, the hurricane had already lasted five days, with its first signs appearing on the 18th. So it would have been reasonable to believe that this balloon had come from very far, as it could not have traveled less than two thousand miles in twenty-four hours; in any case, the passengers could not have had any means to estimate the distance covered since their departure, as they were lacking any reference point. It should even be noted that, caught in the midst of the storm's fury, they were not feeling its effects. They were moving, turning around themselves without sensing either this rotation or their horizontal movement. Their eyes could not pierce the thick fog that accumulated beneath the basket. Around them, everything was mist. The opacity of the clouds was such that they could not tell whether it was day or night. No reflection of light, no sound of inhabited lands, no roaring of the Ocean had reached them in this dark expanse, as long as they remained in the high altitudes. Their rapid descent alone had made them aware of the dangers they faced above the waves.

Meanwhile, the balloon, lightened of heavy objects like munitions, weapons, and provisions, had risen into the upper layers of the atmosphere, at a height of four thousand five hundred feet. The passengers, after realizing that the sea lay beneath the basket, finding the dangers less threatening above than below, had not hesitated to throw overboard even the most useful items, and they sought to lose nothing of this gas, this life of their apparatus, that held them above the abyss.

The night passed amid anxieties that would have been deadly for less strong souls. Then day returned, and with it, the hurricane showed signs of moderating. From the beginning of March 24, there were hints of calm. At dawn, the clouds, more wispy, had risen into the heights of the sky. Within hours, the waterspout had expanded and broken apart. The wind, shifting from hurricane force, changed to "strong breeze," meaning the speed of the atmospheric layers had decreased by half. It was still what sailors call "breeze with three reefs," but the improvement in the turbulent elements was nonetheless significant.

By eleven o'clock, the lower part of the air had notably cleared. The atmosphere exhibited that humid clarity seen and even felt after the passage of significant weather events. It seemed that the hurricane had not gone further west. It appeared to have extinguished itself. Perhaps it had dissipated in electric sheets after the waterspout broke, as sometimes happens with typhoons in the Indian Ocean.

But, around this time, it was noticeable again that the balloon was slowly descending, with a continuous motion, into the lower layers of air. It even seemed to be gradually deflating, its envelope stretching and shifting from a spherical to an oval shape.

By noon, the aerostat was floating only two thousand feet above the sea. It measured fifty thousand cubic feet, and, thanks to its capacity, it had obviously been able to stay aloft for quite a while, whether it had reached high altitudes or moved horizontally. At that moment, the passengers threw overboard the last items still weighing down the basket, the few supplies they had kept, everything, down to the small tools in their pockets, and one of them, having climbed onto the ring to which the net ropes were attached, tried to secure the lower appendage of the aerostat.

It was clear that the passengers could no longer keep the balloon in the high zones, and they lacked gas!

They were therefore doomed! For below them lay neither a continent nor even an island. The space offered no point of landing, no solid surface upon which their anchor could catch.

It was the immense sea, whose waves still crashed with incomparable violence! It was the boundless Ocean, with no visible limits, even for them, who looked down from high above and whose gaze extended over a span of forty miles! It was this liquid plain, mercilessly beaten, whipped by the hurricane, that must have appeared to them as a tumult of wild waves, thrown over which a vast network of white crests was cast! Not a land in sight, not a ship!

They needed, at all costs, to stop the downward movement to prevent the aerostat from being swallowed by the waves. And it was clearly this urgent operation that the passengers in the basket were engaged in. But despite their efforts, the balloon continued to descend while moving extremely fast in the direction of the wind, that is, from northeast to southwest.

A terrible situation was that of these unfortunate souls! They were obviously no longer in control of the aerostat. Their attempts could not succeed. The balloon's envelope continued to deflate increasingly. The gas escaped without any possibility of retaining it. The descent was visibly accelerating, and by one o'clock in the afternoon, the basket was not suspended more than six hundred feet above the Ocean.

And this was because, in fact, it was impossible to stop the gas from escaping through a tear in the apparatus. By lightening the basket of all the items it contained, the passengers had managed to prolong, for a few hours, their suspension in the air.

But the inevitable catastrophe could only be delayed, and if no land appeared before nightfall, passengers, basket, and balloon would definitively disappear beneath the waves.

The only maneuver left to make was carried out at that moment. The passengers of the aerostat were evidently energetic people who knew how to face death. Not a single murmur escaped their lips.

They were determined to fight until the last second, to do everything to delay their fall. The basket was just a kind of wicker box, unfit to float, and there was no way to keep it above the surface of the sea if it fell into it.

At two o'clock, the aerostat was barely four hundred feet above the waves. At that moment, a strong voice — that of a man whose heart was beyond fear — was heard. In response, voices as energetic replied.

"Is everything thrown out?

— No! There are still ten thousand francs in gold!"

A heavy bag immediately fell into the sea.

"Is the balloon rising?

— A little, but it won't be long before it falls again!

— What else is left to throw overboard?

— Nothing!

— Yes!... The basket!

— Let's cling to the net! and to the sea with the basket!"

That was, in fact, the only last means to lighten the aerostat. The ropes tying the basket to the ring were cut, and the aerostat, after its fall, rose by two thousand feet.

The five passengers had climbed into the net, above the ring, and held on in the mesh, looking into the abyss.

Everyone knows how sensitive aerostats are. Simply throwing the lightest object can cause a vertical displacement. The apparatus floats in the air like a mathematically precise balance. Therefore, it is understandable that when it is lightened of a relatively significant weight, its displacement is substantial and abrupt. This happened on this occasion.

However, after briefly balancing in the upper zones, the aerostat began to descend again.

The gas continued to escape through the tear that could not be repaired.

The passengers had done everything they could do. No human means could save them now. They could only rely on God's help.

At four o'clock, the balloon was only five hundred feet from the surface of the waters. A loud barking was heard. A dog accompanied the passengers and was clinging near its master in the netting.

"Top has seen something!" one of the passengers shouted.

Then, immediately, a strong voice rang out:

"Land! land!"

The balloon, which the wind was continuously driving toward the southwest, had, since dawn, covered a considerable distance, which amounted to hundreds of miles, and a fairly high land mass had indeed appeared in that direction.

But this land was still thirty miles downwind. It would take at least a full hour to reach it, and only on the condition that there would be no drift. One hour! Wouldn't the balloon, first, be emptied of all the gas it still held?

Such was the terrible question! The passengers clearly saw this solid point that had to be reached at all costs. They did not know what it was, an island or a continent, as they scarcely knew what part of the world the hurricane had carried them to! But this land, whether inhabited or not, whether hospitable or not, had to be reached!

But by four o'clock, it was clear that the balloon could no longer hold.

2

It skimmed the surface of the sea. Already the crest of the huge waves had licked the bottom of the net several times, weighing it down further, and the aerostat was rising only halfway, like a bird with lead in its wing. Half an hour later, the land was not more than a mile away, but the exhausted, flaccid balloon, stretched and wrinkled in large folds, retained only gas in its upper part. The passengers clinging to the net still weighed too much for it, and soon, half-submerged in the sea, they were battered by the furious waves. The envelope of the aerostat then pocketed, and the wind filled it, pushing it forward like a ship before the wind.

Perhaps it would reach the shore like that!

However, it was only two cable lengths away when terrible cries erupted from four throats simultaneously. The balloon, which seemed no longer able to rise, had just made another unexpected leap after being struck by a mighty wave. As if it had suddenly been lightened by a new part of its weight, it rose to a height of fifteen hundred feet, encountering a sort of wind swirl that caused it to follow a direction almost parallel instead of directly toward the shore. Finally, two minutes later, it approached obliquely, and it finally fell onto the sandy shore, beyond the reach of the waves.

The passengers, helping each other, managed to free themselves from the netting. The balloon, relieved of their weight, was caught by the wind, and like a wounded bird that recovers a moment of life, it disappeared into the sky.

The basket had held five passengers, plus a dog, and the balloon only threw four onto the shore.

8

The missing passenger had obviously been taken by the wave that had just struck the net, and it was this that had allowed the aerostat to rise one last time, then, moments later, to reach the land.

As soon as the four castaways — for we can give them that name — had set foot on the ground, all, thinking of the absent one, cried out: "He's maybe trying to swim ashore! Let's save him! save him!"

They were neither professional aeronauts nor enthusiasts of aerial expeditions, but rather, prisoners of war, whose audacity had pushed them to escape under extraordinary circumstances.

A hundred times they should have perished! A hundred times their ripped balloon should have sent them plunging into the abyss! But heaven reserved them for a strange fate, and on March 20, after fleeing from Richmond, besieged by the troops of General Ulysses Grant, they found themselves seven thousand miles from that capital of Virginia, the main stronghold of the separatists, during the terrible Civil War. Their aerial journey had lasted five days.

Here, in fact, are the curious circumstances under which the prisoners escaped — an escape that would lead to the known catastrophe.

In February 1865, during one of the raids that General Grant attempted, but in vain, to seize Richmond, several of his officers fell into enemy hands and were interned in the city. One of the most distinguished among those who were captured belonged to the federal staff and was named Cyrus Smith. Cyrus Smith, originally from Massachusetts, was an engineer and an outstanding scientist who was tasked by the Union government with overseeing the railroads during the war, which played a significant strategic role. A true Northerner, lean, bony, and lanky, about forty-five years old, he was already graying with short hair and a beard, of which he kept only a thick mustache. He had one of those handsome "numismatic" heads that seem meant to be minted into medals, with bright eyes, a serious mouth, and the face of a man of science in a militant school. He was one of those engineers who wanted to start by handling the hammer and pick, just like generals who wished to begin as simple soldiers. Thus, along with his ingenuity of mind, he possessed the supreme skill of hand. His muscles showed remarkable signs of tonicity. Truly a man of action as well as of thought, he acted effortlessly, under the influence of a vast vital expansion, having that lively persistence that defies all misfortune.

Highly educated, practical, and resourceful, to use a term from the French military language, he had a superb temperament, for despite remaining self-controlled regardless of the circumstances, he fully embodied the three conditions that together define human energy: activity of mind and body, impetuosity of desires, and willpower. His motto could have been that of William of Orange in the 17th century: "I do not need to hope in order to undertake, nor

9

to succeed in order to persevere." At the same time, Cyrus Smith was courage personified. He had fought in every battle during the Civil War. After starting under Ulysses Grant in the Illinois volunteers, he fought at Paducah, Belmont, Pittsburg Landing, the siege of Corinth, Port Gibson, the Black River, Chattanooga, Wilderness, on the Potomac, everywhere and valiantly, as a soldier worthy of the general who replied, "I never count my dead!" And a hundred times, Cyrus Smith should have been among those not counted by the feared Grant, but in those battles, where he hardly spared himself, luck always favored him, until the moment he was injured and captured on the battlefield of Richmond. Alongside Cyrus Smith, on the same day, another important figure fell into the hands of the Southerners. It was none other than the honorable Gédéon Spilett, a reporter for the New-York Herald, who had been tasked with following the events of the war amidst the Northern armies.

Gédéon Spilett was of the race of those remarkable English or American chroniclers, like Stanleys and others, who will go to any lengths to obtain accurate information and relay it to their newspaper as quickly as possible. The newspapers of the Union, such as the New-York Herald, were genuine powers, and their correspondents were representatives one could rely on. Gédéon Spilett stood at the forefront of these correspondents. A man of great merit, energetic, quick, and ready for anything, full of ideas, having traveled the entire world, soldier and artist, fervent in counsel and resolute in action, without counting the pains, fatigue, or dangers when it came to knowing everything, for himself first and for his newspaper afterward, a true hero of curiosity, information, the unpublished, the unknown, and the impossible, he was one of those fearless observers who write under fire, chronicle under cannonballs, and for whom all perils are good fortunes.

He too had been in all the battles, at the front line, revolver in one hand, notebook in the other, and the shrapnel did not shake his pencil. He did not waste wires on incessant telegrams, like those who speak when they have nothing to say, but each of his notes, short, clear, and precise, shed light on an important point. Moreover, he was not lacking in humor. It was he who, after the Black River affair, wanting at all costs to keep his place at the telegraphic office in order to inform his newspaper of the battle's outcome, telegraphed for two hours the first chapters of the Bible. This cost the New-York Herald two thousand dollars, but the New-York Herald was the first to be informed. Gédéon Spilett was tall. He was no more than forty years old. Blond sideburns tinged with red framed his face. His eye was calm, lively, and quick in its movements; it was the eye of a man accustomed to quickly perceiving all the details in a horizon. Solidly built, he had been tempered in every climate like a steel bar in cold water. For ten years, Gédéon Spilett had been the permanent reporter for the New-York Herald, enriching it with his chronicles and sketches, as he handled both pencil and pen equally well.

When he was captured, he was in the midst of describing and sketching the battle. The last words recorded in his notebook were: "A Southerner aims at me and..." And Gédéon Spilett was missed because, following his invariable habit, he escaped from that situation without a scratch. Cyrus Smith and Gédéon Spilett, who did not know each other except by reputation, were both transported to Richmond. The engineer quickly healed from his injury, and it was during his convalescence that he met the reporter. The two men liked each other and came to appreciate one another. Soon, their shared aim was nothing less than to escape, rejoin Grant's army, and fight again in its ranks for the federal unity.

The two Americans were therefore determined to seize any opportunity; but although they had been left free in the city, Richmond was so heavily guarded that an escape had to be viewed as impossible. Meanwhile, Cyrus Smith was joined by a devoted servant who was with him for life and death. This fearless man was a black man, born on the engineer's estate of enslaved parents, but whom Cyrus Smith, an abolitionist by reason and by heart, had freed long ago. The freedman did not want to leave his master. He loved him dearly. He was a thirty-year-old young man, strong, agile, skillful, intelligent, gentle, and calm, sometimes naïve, always smiling, helpful, and kind. His name was Nabuchodonosor, but he only answered to the shortened and familiar name of Nab. When Nab learned that his master had been captured, he left Massachusetts without hesitation, arrived in front of Richmond, and, through cunning and skill, after risking his life twenty times, managed to enter the besieged city. The joy of Cyrus Smith upon seeing his servant again and Nab's delight at reuniting with his master was beyond words.

But while Nab had managed to enter Richmond, it was much more difficult to get out again, as the federal prisoners were under very close surveillance. It would take an extraordinary opportunity to attempt an escape with any chance of success, and that opportunity was not only lacking, but it was also difficult to create. However, Grant continued his vigorous operations. The victory at Petersburg had cost him dearly. His forces, united with Butler's, were still making no headway before Richmond, and nothing suggested that the release of the prisoners would be imminent. The reporter, whose tedious captivity no longer provided him with any interesting details to note, could no longer stand it. He had but one idea: to get out of Richmond at all costs. More than once, he even attempted to venture outside, only to be stopped by insurmountable obstacles.

Meanwhile, the siege continued, and if the prisoners were eager to escape to rejoin Grant's army, certain besieged people were equally eager to flee to join the rebel army, including a certain Jonathan Forster, an enraged Southerner. The fact was that if the federal prisoners could not leave the city, the federals could not either, for the Northern army surrounded them. The governor of

Richmond had long been unable to communicate with General Lee, and it was of utmost importance to inform him of the city's situation to hasten the advance of the relief army. Jonathan Forster then had the idea of escaping in a balloon to cross the besieging lines and thus reach the camp of the rebels. The governor authorized the attempt. A balloon was constructed and made available to Jonathan Forster, who was to be followed into the air by five of his companions. They were equipped with weapons, in case they needed to defend themselves upon landing, and with provisions, in case their aerial voyage took longer than expected.

The balloon's departure was set for March 18. It was to take place during the night, and with a medium-strength northwesterly wind, the aeronauts hoped to reach Lee's headquarters within a few hours. However, this northwesterly wind was no mere breeze. By the 18th, it was evident that it was turning into a hurricane. Soon, the storm became so fierce that Forster's departure had to be postponed, as it was impossible to risk the balloon and those aboard it amid the unleashed elements. The balloon, inflated in Richmond's main square, was thus ready to depart at the first lull in the wind, and impatience was high in the city as no change in atmospheric conditions seemed to occur.

The 18th and 19th passed without any change in the storm. Great difficulties were faced in keeping the balloon, tied to the ground, that the gusts could lay flat against the ground. The night of the 19th to the 20th passed, but by morning, the hurricane was even more intense. Departure was impossible. That day, engineer Cyrus Smith was approached in one of the streets of Richmond by a man he did not recognize. This man was a sailor named Pencroff, aged about thirty-five to forty years, strongly built, very tanned, with bright eyes that blinked rapidly, but with a pleasant face. This Pencroff was a Northerner who had traveled all the oceans of the world, and everything that could happen extraordinarily to a two-legged creature without feathers had happened to him. It goes without saying that he had an enterprising nature, ready to risk everything, and was not easily astonished. At the beginning of this year, Pencroff had come to Richmond on business with a fifteen-year-old boy named Harbert Brown from New Jersey, the son of his captain, an orphan whom he loved as if he were his own child. Unable to leave the city before the first siege operations, he found himself trapped there, to his great dismay, and he too was left with just one idea: to escape by any means possible. He knew of engineer Cyrus Smith by reputation. He knew how impatient this determined man was becoming. So that day, he did not hesitate to approach him, saying without any preamble:

"Mr. Smith, are you tired of Richmond?"

The engineer stared at the man who spoke to him and who added in a low voice:

"Mr. Smith, do you want to flee?"

"When?" replied the engineer quickly, and it could be affirmed that this response escaped him because he had not yet fully examined the stranger addressing him. But after keenly observing the honest face of the sailor, he could not doubt that he was in front of a decent man.

"Who are you?" he asked brusquely.

Pencroff introduced himself.

"Alright," replied Cyrus Smith. "And how do you propose we flee?"

"By that lazy balloon just sitting there doing nothing, which seems to be waiting for us!"

The sailor did not need to finish his sentence. The engineer understood in one word. He seized Pencroff by the arm and pulled him to his home. There, the sailor elaborated on his plan, which was actually quite simple. One would only be risking their life to execute it.

The hurricane was indeed at its full force, but a skilled and bold engineer like Cyrus Smith would surely know how to handle a balloon. If he had known the maneuver, Pencroff would not have hesitated to depart—with Harbert, of course. He had seen much worse and was no stranger to storms!

Cyrus Smith listened to the sailor without saying a word, but his eyes shone. The opportunity was there. He was not someone to let it slip away. The project was very dangerous, thus it was executable.

At night, despite surveillance, one could approach the balloon, slip into the basket, and cut the ties holding it! Certainly, there was a risk of being killed, but on the other hand, success was possible, and without this storm... But without this storm, the balloon would already have taken off, and the long-sought opportunity would not present itself right now!

"I'm not alone!" Cyrus Smith finished by saying.

"How many people do you want to take with you?" asked the sailor.

"Two: my friend Spilett and my servant Nab."

"That makes three," replied Pencroff. "And with Harbert and me, that makes five. Now, the balloon could carry six..."

"That's enough. We will leave!" said Cyrus Smith.

This "we" committed the reporter, but the reporter was not someone to back down, and when the plan was conveyed to him, he wholeheartedly approved it. What surprised him was that such a simple idea had not occurred to him sooner. As for Nab, he would follow his master wherever his master wanted to go.

"See you tonight, then," said Pencroff. "We'll all five stroll around here as curious onlookers!"

"See you tonight at ten," replied Cyrus Smith, "and may heaven help that the storm does not calm down before our departure!"

Pencroff took his leave of the engineer and returned to his lodging, where young Harbert Brown was waiting. This brave boy knew the sailor's plan, and he awaited the outcome of the engineer's approach with a certain anxiety. As you can see, these were five determined men who were about to launch themselves into the storm, right into the heart of a hurricane!

No! The hurricane did not calm, and neither Jonathan Forster nor his companions could think of facing it in that frail nacelle! The day was dreadful. The engineer feared only one thing: that the balloon, held to the ground and laid flat against the wind, would tear to shreds. For several hours, he roamed the almost deserted square, watching the apparatus. Pencroff did the same from his side, hands in his pockets, yawning when necessary, like a man who does not know what to do to kill time, but also dreading that the balloon might tear or even break its ropes and escape into the air.

Evening arrived. Night fell very dark. Thick mist rolled in like clouds close to the ground. Rain mixed with snow fell. The weather was cold. A kind of fog hung over Richmond. It seemed that the violent storm had created a sort of truce between the besiegers and the besieged and that the cannon wished to fall silent before the fierce detonations of the hurricane. The streets of the city were deserted. It even seemed unnecessary, in such horrible weather, to guard the square where the balloon was struggling.

Everything clearly favored the prisoners' departure; but this journey amid the unleashed gusts!..."Bad tide!" thought Pencroff, securing his hat against the wind. "But oh well! We'll manage somehow!"

At half past nine, Cyrus Smith and his companions were sneaking into the square from different directions, which the gas lanterns, extinguished by the wind, left in deep darkness. They couldn't even see the enormous balloon, which was almost entirely deflated on the ground.

In addition to the ballast bags that held the net's ropes, the basket was secured by a strong cable tied to a ring set in the pavement, and its double was pulled aboard.

The five captives gathered near the basket. They had not been spotted, and the darkness was so thick that they couldn't see each other.

Without saying a word, Cyrus Smith, Gédéon Spilett, Nab, and Harbert climbed into the basket, while Pencroff, under the engineer's orders, detached the ballast bags one by one. It took only a few moments, and the sailor rejoined his companions.

At that point, the balloon was only held by the double cable, and Cyrus Smith just had to give the order to depart. At that moment, a dog jumped onto the basket.

It was Top, the engineer's dog, who had broken his chain and followed his master. Cyrus Smith, fearing the extra weight, wanted to send the poor animal away.

"Bah! One more won't hurt!" said Pencroff, unloading the basket of two sandbags.

Then, he let go of the double cable, and the balloon, taking off at an angle, disappeared after colliding with two chimneys, which it knocked down in its furious ascent.

The hurricane was raging with terrible force. The engineer could not think about descending during the night, and when daylight came, fog blocked all views of the land. Only five days later did a break in the gloom reveal the vast sea beneath the balloon, which the wind whisked away at terrifying speed!

It is known how, of those five men who departed on March 20, four were cast, on March 24, onto a deserted shore over six thousand miles from their homeland!

And the one who was missing, the one whom the four survivors of the balloon hurried to help first, was their natural leader, engineer Cyrus Smith!

3

The engineer, caught in the net's loosened strands, had been swept away by a wave.

His dog had also disappeared. The faithful animal had plunged into the water to save his master.

"Forward!" cried the reporter.

And the four of them—Gédéon Spilett, Harbert, Pencroff, and Nab—forgetting exhaustion and fatigue, began their search.

Poor Nab was crying with both rage and despair at the thought of losing everything he loved in the world.

Only two minutes had passed between the moment Cyrus Smith vanished and the time his companions landed. They might still hope to arrive in time to save him.

"Let's search! Let's search!" shouted Nab.

"Yes, Nab," replied Gédéon Spilett, "and we will find him!"

"Alive?"

"Alive!"

"Can he swim?" asked Pencroff.

"Yes!" replied Nab. "And besides, Top is here!"

The sailor, hearing the sea roar, shook his head!

It was to the north of the coast, about half a mile from where the castaways had just arrived, that the engineer had disappeared. If he could reach the closest point of the shore, it must be within half a mile from there.

It was nearly six o'clock then. The fog had just lifted and made the night very dark. The castaways walked northward along the eastern shore of this land on which chance had thrown them—a land unknown to them, whose geographic location they could not even guess. They treaded on a sandy ground mixed with stones, which seemed to have no vegetation.

This uneven, very rugged ground appeared to be riddled in some places with small holes, making walking very difficult. From these holes emerged heavy-flying large birds fleeing in all directions, invisible in the darkness. Others, more agile, flew up in flocks like clouds.

The sailor believed he recognized seagulls and gulls, whose sharp whistles battled with the roar of the sea. From time to time, the castaways stopped, called out loudly, and listened to see if any call could be heard from the Ocean.

They certainly thought that if they were near the spot where the engineer had landed, the barks of the dog Top, if Cyrus Smith was unable to signal, would reach them. But no sound broke through the crashing waves and the clattering of the surf. Then the small party resumed its march, searching every cranny of the shore.

After a twenty-minute trek, the four castaways were suddenly stopped by a frothing edge of waves. Solid ground was missing. They found themselves at the end of a sharp point, where the sea crashed violently.

"This is a promontory," said the sailor. "We must go back, keeping right, and we will reach the solid ground."

"But what if he is there!" responded Nab, pointing to the ocean, where the enormous waves were white in the shadows.

"Well then, let's call him!"

And all, joining their voices, sent out a strong call, but nothing responded. They waited for a lull. They called out again. Still nothing.

The castaways then turned back, following the opposite side of the promontory, walking on sandy, rocky ground again. However, Pencroff noticed that the coastline was steeper, that the ground was rising, and he guessed it must connect, by a long slope, to a high coast that loomed indistinctly in the darkness. The birds were less numerous on this part of the shore. The sea also was less turbulent, less noisy, and it was even noticeable that the agitation of the waves was noticeably decreasing. The sound of the surf was barely audible. This side of the promontory likely formed a semi-circular bay, protected from the swells of the open sea by its sharp point.

But by following this direction, they were heading south, moving away from the section of the coast where Cyrus Smith might have landed. After walking a mile and a half, the coastline still showed no curvature that would allow them to return north. Yet this promontory, which they had turned, must connect to solid land.

The castaways, though exhausted, continued to march bravely, hoping to find at every moment some sharp turn that would set them back on their original course. Their disappointment was great when, after walking about two miles, they found themselves once again stopped by the sea at a fairly high point made of slippery rocks.

"We're on an islet!" said Pencroff, "and we've walked its length from one end to the other!"

The sailor's observation was correct. The castaways had been thrown, not onto a continent, not even an island, but onto a islet that measured no more than two thousand feet in length, and whose width was evidently quite small.

Was this barren, stony, vegetation-free islet, a desolate refuge for some seabirds, connected to a larger archipelago? One could not say for certain. The balloon's passengers, when they glimpsed land through the fog from their basket, could not clearly recognize its significance. However, Pencroff, with his seaman's eyes accustomed to piercing the gloom, thought he could distinguish confused masses in the west, indicating an elevated coastline.

But, at that time, it was impossible to determine to what system—simple or complex—the islet belonged. They could also not leave, as the sea surrounded them. Therefore, they had to postpone the search for the engineer, who, alas! had not signaled his presence with any cries.

"Cyrus's silence doesn't prove anything," said the reporter. "He might be unconscious, injured, unable to respond at the moment, but let's not despair."

The reporter then suggested lighting a fire at some point on the islet that could serve as a signal for the engineer. But they searched in vain for wood or dry brush. All they found was sand and stones.

One can understand the grief of Nab and that of his companions, who had become deeply attached to the intrepid Cyrus Smith. It was all too evident that they were helpless to rescue him now. They would have to wait for daylight. Either the engineer had managed to get to safety on his own and had already found refuge on a part of the coast, or he was lost forever!

It was a long and torturous wait. The cold was sharp. The castaways suffered greatly, but hardly noticed it. They did not even think to take a moment's rest.

Forgetting themselves for their leader, hoping, wanting to hope always, they wandered about this barren islet, constantly returning to its northern point, where they should be closest to the place of the disaster. They listened, they shouted, they tried to catch any ultimate call, and their voices must have carried far, for a certain calm reigned in the atmosphere, and the sounds of the sea began to lessen with the swell. One of Nab's cries even seemed, at a certain moment, to echo back. Harbert pointed it out to Pencroff, adding:

"This suggests that there is a coast quite close to the west."

The sailor nodded in agreement. Besides, his eyes couldn't be deceived. If he had, even a little, discerned land, it meant land was there.

But that distant echo was the only response prompted by Nab's cries, and the vastness remained silent across the entire eastern part of the islet.

However, the sky gradually cleared. Around midnight, a few stars appeared, and if the engineer had been there, near his companions, he would have noticed that these stars were no longer those of the northern hemisphere. In fact, the North Star was not visible on this new horizon; the zenith constellations were no longer those he was used to observing in the northern part of the new continent, and the Southern Cross shone at the southern pole of the world.

The night passed. Around five in the morning, March 25, the heights of the sky lightened slightly. The horizon remained dark, but with the first rays of dawn, an opaque mist rose from the sea, obscuring visibility to no more than twenty steps. The fog rolled out in thick curls that moved sluggishly.

It was a setback. The castaways could see nothing around them. While Nab and the reporter scanned the Ocean, the sailor and Harbert searched for the coastline to the west. But not a speck of land was visible.

"Nonetheless," said Pencroff, "even if I can't see the coast, I can feel it... it's there... there... just as surely as we're not in Richmond anymore!"

But the fog would soon lift.

It was merely a haze from fair weather. A good sun was warming the upper layers, and this warmth filtered down to the surface of the islet. Indeed, around six-thirty, three quarters of an hour after sunrise, the mist became more transparent. It thickened at the top but dissolved below. Soon the entire islet appeared as if it had descended from a cloud; then the sea revealed itself in a circular expanse, infinite in the east, but bounded in the west by a high and steep coastline.

Yes! The land was there. There, salvation, at least temporarily assured. Between the islet and the coast, separated by a half-mile-wide channel, an extremely fast current surged with noise.

However, one of the castaways, only following his heart, immediately plunged into the current without consulting his companions, not even uttering a single word. It was Nab. He was eager to reach that coast and move northward along it. No one could stop him. Pencroff called him back, but in vain.

The reporter was getting ready to follow Nab.

Pencroff approached him:

"Do you want to cross this channel?" he asked.

"Yes," replied Gédéon Spilett.

"Well, wait, believe me," said the sailor. "Nab can manage to rescue his master. If we venture into this channel, we risk being swept out to sea by the current, which is extremely strong. If I'm not mistaken, it's a falling tide. Look, the tide is going out on the sand. So let's be patient, and at low tide, it's possible that we can find a fording point..."

"You're right," replied the reporter. "Let's separate as little as possible..."

Meanwhile, Nab fought vigorously against the current. He crossed at an oblique angle. His dark shoulders could be seen emerging with each stroke. He was being swept away with extreme speed, but he was also gaining on the shore. That half-mile separating the islet from the land took him more than half an hour to cross, and he only reached the shore several thousand feet from the point directly opposite the place he had departed from.

Nab landed at the foot of a tall granite wall and shook himself vigorously; then, running, he soon disappeared behind a rocky outcrop that jutted out to sea, roughly at the height of the northern end of the islet.

Nab's companions watched anxiously as he made his daring attempt, and when he was out of sight, they turned their eyes to that land they would soon seek refuge on, while munching on some shellfish scattered across the sand. It was a meager meal, but it was still a meal. The opposite shore formed a vast bay, ending in the south with a very sharp point, bare of any vegetation and looking very wild. This point joined the coastline with a rather whimsical shape and leaned against high granite rocks. In contrast, to the north, the bay spread out, creating a more rounded coast that ran from the southwest to the northeast and ended with a sharp cape. Between these two extreme points, which supported the arc of the bay, the distance was about eight miles. Half a mile from the shore, the small island occupied a narrow strip of sea and resembled a huge whale, its body greatly enlarged. Its widest point was no more than a quarter of a mile. In front of the island, the coastline consisted, in the foreground, of a sandy beach scattered with darkish rocks that were gradually reappearing as the tide went out. In the background, there was a sort of granite curtain, steeply cut, crowned by a whimsical ridge at least three hundred feet high. It stretched along a length of three miles and ended abruptly on the right with a cut section that looked as if it had been shaped by human hands. On the left, however, above the promontory, this irregular cliff, breaking into prismatic shards, made of compacted rocks and landslides, sloped down with a long incline that gradually blended with the rocks of the southern point. On the high plateau of the coast, there were no trees. It was a flat surface, like that above Cape Town at the Cape of Good Hope, but smaller in scale. At least, it seemed that way from the island. However, greenery was not lacking on the right, behind the cut section. One could easily make out the confused mass of large trees, their clustering extending beyond the limits of sight. This greenery delighted the eye, which was deeply saddened by the harsh lines of the granite cladding. Finally, in the background above the plateau, to the northwest, at least seven miles away, shone a white peak, struck by sunlight. It was a snowy cap crowning some distant mountain.

Thus, it was hard to determine whether this land formed an island or belonged to a continent. But, looking at those convulsed rocks piled up on the left, a geologist would not hesitate to attribute a volcanic origin to them, as they were undeniably the result of plutonic work. Gideon Spilett, Pencroff, and Harbert were closely observing this land, where they might live for many years, even die, if it was not on the route of ships!

"Well!" asked Harbert, "What do you say, Pencroff?"

"Well," replied the sailor, "there's good and bad, like everywhere. We'll see. But here comes the ebb tide. In three hours, we'll try to cross, and once there, we'll do our best to sort things out and find Mr. Smith!"

Pencroff had not been mistaken in his predictions.

Three hours later, at low tide, most of the sands forming the bed of the channel were uncovered. All that remained between the island and the coast was a narrow channel that would surely be easy to cross. Indeed, around ten o'clock, Gideon Spilett and his two companions stripped off their clothes, wrapped them on their heads, and ventured into the channel, which was no deeper than five feet. Harbert, for whom the water would have been too high, swam like a fish and did wonderfully. The three of them reached the opposite shore without difficulty. There, after quickly drying off in the sun, they put on their clothes, which they had kept away from the water, and held a council.

4

First, the reporter told the sailor to wait at that very spot, where he would join him, and without wasting a moment, he walked up the coastline in the direction that the black servant Nab had taken a few hours earlier. Then he quickly disappeared around a bend in the coast, eager to get news of the engineer.

Harbert had wanted to accompany him.

"Stay here, my boy," the sailor had said to him. "We need to set up a camp and see if we can find something more solid to eat than shells. Our friends will need to refuel upon their return. Everyone has their task."

"I'm ready, Pencroff," Harbert replied.

"Good! Let's proceed methodically. We are tired, cold, and hungry. So we need to find shelter, fire, and food. The forest has wood, the nests have eggs: now we just need to find a house."

"Well," Harbert answered, "I'll look for a cave in those rocks, and I'm sure I'll find a hole where we can hide!"

"That's it," Pencroff replied. "Let's go, my boy."

And off they went, both walking at the foot of the enormous wall, on the beach that the receding tide had exposed. Instead of heading north, however, they went south. Pencroff had noticed, just a few hundred paces below where they had landed, that the coast offered a narrow gap which, according to him, should lead to a river or creek.

Now, on one hand, it was important to settle near a source of drinkable water, and on the other hand, it was not impossible that the current had carried Cyrus Smith in that direction.

The tall wall, as stated, rose to a height of three hundred feet, but the mass was solid everywhere, and even at its base, barely lapped by the sea, it showed no fissure that could serve as a temporary shelter. It was a sheer wall made of very hard granite, which had never been eroded by waves. At the top was a whole world of waterbirds, particularly various species of the order of ducks, with elongated, compressed, and pointed beaks—very noisy birds, not easily frightened by the presence of a man who was, for the first time, disturbing their solitude. Among these ducks, Pencroff recognized several skuas, a type of seagull sometimes called stercorarii, and also small predatory gulls that nested in the granite crevices. A shot fired amidst this swarm of birds would have brought down many of them; however, to fire a shot, one needs a gun, and neither Pencroff nor Harbert had one.

Besides, these gulls and skuas are hardly edible, and even their eggs have a terrible taste.

However, Harbert, who had moved a bit further to the left, soon spotted some rocks covered with seaweed that the high tide would cover a few hours later. On these rocks, in the slippery kelp, there were plenty of bivalve shellfish that hungry people would not ignore. So Harbert called out to Pencroff, who hurried over.

"Hey! These are mussels!" exclaimed the sailor. "Here's something to replace the eggs we're missing!"

"They aren't mussels," replied young Harbert, who was carefully examining the mollusks clinging to the rocks, "they're lithodomes."

"And can you eat them?" Pencroff asked.

"Absolutely."

"Then let's eat lithodomes."

The sailor could trust Harbert. The young boy was very knowledgeable about natural history and had always had a real passion for this science. His father had encouraged him in this path by having him attend the courses of the best professors in Boston, who had taken a liking to him, an intelligent and hard-working child. Thus, his naturalist instincts would often be useful later on, and for his start, he did not make a mistake.

These lithodomes were elongated shellfish that were clustered and tightly attached to the rocks. They belonged to a type of burrowing mollusks that drill holes in the hardest stones, and their shells rounded at both ends, which is not the case with ordinary mussels.

Pencroff and Harbert fully enjoyed these lithodomes, which were half-open under the sun. They ate them like oysters and found them to have a distinctly peppery flavor, which removed all regret for lacking pepper or any other seasonings.

Their hunger was momentarily satisfied, but not their thirst, which grew after consuming these naturally spicy mollusks. Thus, it was imperative to find fresh water, and it was unlikely that there would be none in such a whimsically rugged area. Pencroff and Harbert, after taking care to gather a good supply of lithodomes, filling their pockets and handkerchiefs, returned to the base of the high land. Just two hundred paces away, they reached the gap through which, according to Pencroff's intuition, a small river should flow at full banks. At this point, the wall seemed to have been separated by some violent plutonic effort. At its base was a small cove, with a bottom that formed a rather sharp angle. The river measured a hundred feet in width at this point, and its banks on either side were just twenty feet wide.

The river flowed almost directly between the two granite walls that sloped down as it approached the mouth; then it turned sharply and disappeared under a thicket half a mile away.

"Here's water! Over there is wood!" said Pencroff. "Well, Harbert, all we need now is a house!"

The river water was clear. The sailor realized that at this time of the tide, that is, at low tide, when the rising tide did not push it, it was fresh. Establishing this important point, Harbert looked for some cavity that could serve as a retreat but did so in vain. Everywhere, the wall was smooth, flat, and sheer.

However, right at the mouth of the stream, above the reach of the high tide, the landslides had formed not a cave, but a pile of enormous rocks, like those often found in granite regions, and which are called "Chimneys."

Pencroff and Harbert ventured quite deep among the rocks, in these sandy corridors, where light was abundant, as it penetrated through the gaps left between the granites, some of which were only held up by a miracle of balance. But along with the light came the wind—a true corridor breeze—and with the wind, the sharp cold of the outside. However, the sailor thought that by blocking certain parts of these corridors and sealing some openings with a mix of stones and sand, they could make the "Chimneys" habitable. Their geometrical plan resembled the typographical character, which stands for and so on in abbreviated form. Now, by isolating the upper loop of the sign, through which the south and west winds rushed, it would likely be possible to utilize its lower section.

"Here's our plan," said Pencroff, "and if we ever see Mr. Smith again, he'll know how to make good use of this labyrinth."

"We will see him again, Pencroff!" exclaimed Harbert, "and when he returns, he must find here a fairly decent home. It will be if we can set up a hearth in the left corridor and keep an opening for the smoke."

"We will be able to, my boy," replied the sailor, "and these Chimneys— a name that Pencroff kept for this temporary shelter—will work for us. But first, let's go gather firewood. I imagine wood will be useful for blocking these openings through which the devil plays his trumpet!"

Harbert and Pencroff left the Chimneys, rounding the corner, and began to make their way up the left bank of the river. The current was quite swift and carried some driftwood. The rising tide—and it was already being felt at that moment—would forcefully push it back for a considerable distance. The sailor thus thought that they could use this ebb and flow for transporting heavy items.

After walking for a quarter of an hour, the sailor and the young boy arrived at the sharp bend that the river made as it veered left. From this point onward, its course continued through a forest of magnificent trees. These trees had retained their greenery despite the advanced season, as they belonged to the family of conifers that spread across all regions of the globe, from northern climates to tropical areas.

The young naturalist specifically recognized "deodars," a very numerous species in the Himalayan zone, releasing a pleasant aroma. Among these beautiful trees grew clusters of pines, whose opaque canopy spread wide. In the midst of the tall grass, Pencroff felt that his foot was crushing dried branches that crackled like fireworks.

"Good, my boy," he said to Harbert, "if I don't know the names of these trees, at least I can categorize them as "firewood," and right now, that's the only category we need!"

"Let's gather our supply!" replied Harbert, who immediately got to work.

The harvest was easy. It was not even necessary to prune the trees because enormous quantities of dead wood lay at their feet. But although fuel was plentiful, transport methods were wanting. This wood was very dry and would burn quickly. Hence, the need to bring back a considerable amount to the Chimneys, and two men would not suffice for the load. This was what Harbert pointed out.

"Hey! my boy," replied the sailor, "there must be a way to transport this wood. There's always a way to get things done! If only we had a cart or a boat, it would be too easy."

"But we have the river!" said Harbert.

"Exactly," replied Pencroff. "The river will be our self-moving path, and log trains weren't invented for nothing."

"Except," remarked Harbert, "our path currently goes in the opposite direction to ours, since the tide is rising!"

"We'll just have to wait for it to go back down," replied the sailor, "and it will carry our fuel back to the Chimneys. Let's prepare our train."

The sailor, followed by Harbert, headed toward the angle that the edge of the forest made with the river. Both carried, each in accordance with their strength, a load of wood, tied into bundles. Along the bank was also a large amount of dead branches, among these grasses where a human foot had probably never ventured. Pencroff immediately began to make his train.

In a sort of eddy created by a point of the shore that broke the current, the sailor and the young boy placed sufficiently large pieces of wood that they tied together with dry vines. Thus, a sort of raft was formed on which all their harvest was stacked successively, enough for at least twenty men. In an hour, the work was done, and the train, moored to the bank, had to wait for the tide to turn. There were a few hours to fill, and after discussing it, Pencroff and Harbert decided to climb to the upper plateau to explore the area more widely.

Exactly two hundred steps back from the angle formed by the river, the cliff, ending with a landslide, sloped gently down to the edge of the forest. It looked like a natural staircase. So, Harbert and the sailor began their ascent. Thanks to the strength in their legs, they quickly reached the ridge and took their position at the corner overlooking the river's mouth. Upon arrival, their first sight was the Ocean that they had just crossed under such terrible conditions! They looked at the northern part of the coast where the disaster had happened with emotion. This was where Cyrus Smith had disappeared. They scanned the horizon searching for any wreckage from their balloon that a person might still cling to. Nothing! The sea was just a vast desert of water. As for the coast, it was deserted as well. Neither the reporter nor Nab were visible. But it was possible that both were far enough away not to be seen.

"Something tells me," exclaimed Harbert, "that a man as resourceful as Mr. Cyrus wouldn't have just drowned like anyone else. He must have reached some point on the shore. Right, Pencroff?"

The sailor shook his head sadly. He didn't expect to see Cyrus Smith again; however, wanting to give Harbert a bit of hope, he said, "Of course, of course, our engineer is the type to save himself where anyone else would fail...!"

Meanwhile, he was observing the coast with great attention. Before them lay a sandy shore, limited on the right side of the river mouth by lines of breaking waves. These rocks, still above the water, resembled groups of amphibians resting in the surf. Beyond the band of rocks, the sea sparkled under the sunshine. To the south, a sharp point closed off the horizon, and it was unclear whether the land continued in that direction or if it veered southeast and southwest, which would make this coast a sort of very elongated peninsula. At the northern end of the bay, the shape of the coastline continued for a great distance in a more rounded line. Here, the shore was low, flat, without cliffs, with wide sandy banks exposed by the retreating tide.

Pencroff and Harbert then turned their gaze westward. Their eyes were immediately drawn to the snow-capped mountain rising six or seven miles away. From its lower slopes to two miles inland, vast stretches of forest extended, marked by large patches of green from evergreen trees. Then, from the edge of this forest to the coast itself, there was a wide plateau dotted with groups of trees placed in quirky arrangements. To the left, they could occasionally see the waters of the small river glistening through some clearings, and it seemed its winding course brought it back toward the foothills of the mountain, where it must originate. Where the sailor had left his wood train, it began to flow between the two high granite walls; but while the left bank remained steep and sheer, the right bank gradually sloped down, with large formations turning into isolated rocks, rocks into pebbles, and pebbles into gravel all the way to the tip.

"Are we on an island?" murmured the sailor.

"In any case, it seems quite large!" replied the young boy.

"An island, no matter how vast, is still just an island!" said Pencroff.

But this important question could not be resolved yet. They had to wait for another moment for an answer. As for the land itself—whether island or continent—it appeared fertile, pleasant in its appearance, and varied in its resources.

"That's fortunate," noted Pencroff, "and amidst our misfortune, we should thank Providence for it."

"May God be praised!" replied Harbert, whose devout heart was filled with gratitude for the Creator of all things.

For a long time, Pencroff and Harbert examined the region into which fate had thrown them, but it was difficult to envision what the future held after such a brief inspection.

Then they returned, following the southern edge of the granite plateau, lined with a long festoon of whimsical rocks that took on the most bizarre shapes. There, a few hundred birds lived, nesting in the crevices of the stone. As Harbert jumped on the rocks, he startled a whole flock of these birds.

"Ah!" he exclaimed, "those aren't seagulls or gulls!"

"What kind of birds are they?" asked Pencroff.

They look like, I swear, pigeons!

"Indeed, but they are wild pigeons, or rock pigeons," replied Harbert. "I recognize them by the double black band on their wings, their white rumps, and their blue-gray feathers. Now, if rock pigeon is good to eat, their eggs must be excellent, assuming they left any in their nests!"

"We won't give them time to hatch, unless in the form of an omelet!" replied Pencroff cheerfully.

"But how will you make your omelet?" asked Harbert. "In your hat?"

"Good one!" replied the sailor, "I'm not clever enough for that. So we'll stick to soft-boiled eggs, my boy, and I'll take care of finding the hardest ones!"

Pencroff and the young boy examined the crevices in the granite carefully, and, indeed, they found some eggs in certain hollows! They collected a few dozen, then placed them in the sailor's handkerchief, and as the time approached for the sea to be at full tide, Harbert and Pencroff began to head back toward the river.

When they arrived at the bend of the river, it was one o'clock in the afternoon.

The current was already shifting. They needed to take advantage of the retreating tide to bring the wood train to the mouth of the river. Pencroff had no intention of letting the wood train drift away without direction, and he also didn't want to board it to steer it. But a sailor is never at a loss when it comes to cables or ropes, and Pencroff quickly braided a rope several fathoms long from dry vines. This vegetable cable was tied to the back of the raft, and the sailor held it in his hand while Harbert, pushing the train with a long pole, kept it moving with the current.

The process worked perfectly. The huge load of wood, which the sailor controlled while walking along the shore, followed the current of the water. The bank was very steep, so there was no fear of the train running aground, and before two hours had passed, it reached the mouth, just a few steps from the Chimneys.

5

The first thing Pencroff did once the wood train was unloaded was to make the Chimneys livable by blocking off the corridors through which the draft entered. Sand, stones, intertwined branches, and wet dirt sealed the galleries, open to the southern winds, and isolated the upper loop. Only a single narrow, winding tunnel, which opened on the side, was left to allow smoke to escape and promote the draft of the hearth. Thus, the Chimneys were divided into three or four chambers, if one could even call them that, for they were dark dens only fit for a wild animal. But they were dry, and one could stand up in the main chamber, which occupied the center. Fine sand covered the floor, and all things considered, they could manage for now.

While working, Harbert and Pencroff talked.

"Maybe," said Harbert, "our companions have found a better place than ours?"

"That's possible," replied the sailor, "but in doubt, don't hold back! Better to have one too many strings to your bow than none at all!"

"Oh!" Harbert repeated, "if only they bring back Mr. Smith, if they find him, we'll have nothing left but to thank heaven!"

"Yes!" murmured Pencroff. "That man was something real!"

"It was..." said Harbert. "Do you despair of ever seeing him again?"

"God forbid!" replied the sailor.

The work of settling in was quickly done, and Pencroff declared himself very satisfied.

"Now," he said, "our friends can come back. They'll find enough shelter."

Next, they needed to set up the hearth and prepare the meal.

A simple and easy task in truth. Large flat stones were arranged at the back of the first left corridor, at the opening of the narrow tunnel left for smoke. Whatever heat the smoke didn't carry outside would certainly be enough to maintain a comfortable temperature inside. The wood supply was stored in one of the chambers, and the sailor placed a few logs, intermingled with twigs, on the hearth's stones.

The sailor was busy with this task when Harbert asked if he had any matches.

"Certainly," replied Pencroff, "and I'll add: Luckily, because without matches or tinder, we'd be in quite a bind!"

"We could always make a fire like the savages," responded Harbert, "by rubbing two dry sticks together?"

"Well! Try it, my boy, and let's see if you achieve anything beyond breaking your arms!"

"Yet, it's a very simple and commonly used method in the Pacific Islands."

"I'm not denying that," replied Pencroff, "but you have to believe that savages know how to do it or that they use a specific wood because I've wanted to make fire this way many times, and I've never succeeded! So I admit I prefer matches! Where are my matches?"

Pencroff searched his jacket for the box that never left him, as he was a dedicated smoker. He couldn't find it. He rummaged through his pants pockets and, to his great shock, he didn't find the box there either.

"Well, this is foolish, and more than foolish!" he said, looking at Harbert. "That box must have fallen from my pocket, and I've lost it! But you, Harbert, do you have anything, either a lighter or anything that could help make a fire?"

"No, Pencroff!"

The sailor went out, followed by the young boy, scratching his forehead vigorously. On the sand, in the rocks, near the riverbank, both searched with the greatest care, but to no avail. The box was made of copper and wouldn't have escaped their sight.

"Pencroff," asked Harbert, "did you not throw that box out of the balloon?"

"I made sure not to," replied the sailor. "But after being shaken up as we were, such a small item could have disappeared. Even my pipe left me! That cursed box! Where could it be?"

"Well, the tide is going out," said Harbert, "let's run back to where we landed."

It was unlikely they would find the box that the waves must have rolled into the pebbles at high tide, but it was worth considering that possibility. Harbert and Pencroff quickly headed toward the spot where they landed the day before, about two hundred steps from the Chimneys.

There, amid the pebbles, in the crevice of the rocks, the search was conducted thoroughly. No result. If the box had fallen in that spot, it must have been swept away by the waves. As the tide receded, the sailor searched every nook in the rocks without finding anything. It was a serious loss given the circumstances, and, for the moment, irreparable.

Pencroff did not hide his deep disappointment. His forehead wrinkled tightly. He didn't say a word. Harbert wanted to console him by pointing out that, very likely, the matches would have been wet from the seawater and would have been impossible to use.

"But no, my boy," replied the sailor. "They were in a copper box that was well-sealed! And now, what are we to do?"

"We will certainly find a way to make fire," said Harbert. "Mr. Smith or Mr. Spilett won't be as out of luck as we are!"

"Yes," replied Pencroff, "but in the meantime, we are without fire, and our friends will only find a dismal meal upon their return!"

"But," Harbert replied quickly, "it's not possible they have no tinder or matches!"

"I doubt it," replied the sailor, shaking his head. "Firstly, Nab and Mr. Smith don't smoke, and I fear Mr. Spilett would rather have kept his notebook than his box of matches!"

Harbert did not respond. The loss of the box was certainly a regrettable fact. However, the young boy was sure they would find a way to make fire somehow. Pencroff, more experienced and being the type who did not get bothered by little things or a lot, did not see it that way. In any case, there was only one course of action to take: wait for Nab and the reporter to return. But they had to give up the prospect of hard-boiled eggs he wanted to prepare for them, and the idea of eating raw meat didn't seem an appealing prospect for either them or himself.

Before returning to the Chimneys, the sailor and Harbert, in case fire was permanently out of reach, gathered some more lithodomes and silently made their way home.

Pencroff, his eyes fixed on the ground, continued to search for his elusive box. He even went back up the left bank of the river from its mouth to the corner where the wood train had been tied.

He returned to the upper plateau, traversed it in every direction, searched the tall grass on the edge of the forest—all in vain.

It was five o'clock in the evening when Harbert and he returned to the Chimneys. There was no need to say that the corridors were searched down to their darkest corners, and they had to resolve to give up.

Around six o'clock, just as the sun was setting behind the high lands to the west, Harbert, who was pacing back and forth on the shore, signaled the return of Nab and Gédéon Spilett.

They returned alone!... The young boy felt an indescribable tightening of his heart. The sailor had not been mistaken in his foreboding.

Engineer Cyrus Smith had not been found!

The reporter, upon arriving, sat on a rock, saying nothing. Exhausted from fatigue, dying of hunger, he lacked the strength to utter a word!

As for Nab, his reddened eyes showed how much he had cried, and the new tears he could not hold back made it clear that he had lost all hope!The reporter recounted the search efforts made to find Cyrus Smith. Nab and he had traveled along the coast for more than eight miles, well beyond the point where the balloon had last fallen, which was followed by the disappearance of the engineer and the dog Top. The shore was deserted. No trace, no footprint. Not a single stone that had been recently turned over, no sign in the sand, no mark of a human foot anywhere along this stretch of coastline. It was clear that no inhabitants frequented this part of the coast. The sea was as empty as the shore, and it was there, a few hundred feet off the coast, that the engineer had found his grave.

At this moment, Nab stood up and, with a voice displaying how much hope still lingered within him, exclaimed:

"No! he cried, no! He is not dead! No! that's not possible! Him! Come on! Me! any other person, maybe! but him! never. He's the kind of man who can come back from anything..."

Then, feeling weak, he murmured:

"Ah! I can't go on!"

Harbert rushed to him.

"Nab," said the young boy, "we will find him! God will bring him back to us! But in the meantime, you're hungry! Please eat a little!"

As he said this, he offered the poor Black man a few handfuls of shellfish, meager and insufficient food!

Nab hadn't eaten for many hours, but he refused. Without his master, Nab couldn't or didn't want to live anymore!

As for Gideon Spilett, he devoured the mollusks; then he lay down on the sand at the foot of a rock.

He was exhausted but calm.

Then, Harbert approached him and took his hand:

"Sir," he said, "we have found a shelter where you will be better than here. Night is coming. Come and rest! Tomorrow, we'll see…"

The reporter stood up, and guided by the young boy, he headed towards the Chimneys. At that moment, Pencroff approached him, and in the most natural tone, asked if he happened to have a match on him.

The reporter stopped, searched his pockets, found nothing, and said:

"I had some, but I must have thrown them all away…"

The sailor then called Nab and made the same request, receiving the same response.

"Damn it!" exclaimed the sailor, unable to hold back the curse.

The reporter heard him and went over to Pencroff:

"Not a match?" he asked.

"Not one, and therefore no fire!"

"Oh! cried Nab, if my master were here, he would know how to make one!"

The four castaways stood still and looked at each other, not without worry. It was Harbert who first broke the silence, saying:

"Mr. Spilett, you are a smoker; you always have matches on you! Maybe you didn't look well enough? Look again! Just one match would be enough for us!"

The reporter rummaged through his pants, waistcoat, and jacket pockets again, and finally, to the great joy of Pencroff, and his own immense surprise, he felt a small stick lodged in the lining of his waistcoat. His fingers grasped that little stick through the fabric, but they couldn't pull it out. Since it seemed to be a match, and just one, it was essential not to scrape off the phosphorus.

"Would you let me try?" said the young boy.

And very skillfully, without breaking it, he managed to pull out that little piece of wood, that miserable yet precious twig, which had such enormous importance for these poor souls! It was intact.

"A match!" exclaimed Pencroff. "Oh! it's like we have an entire cargo!"

He took the match, and, followed by his companions, he returned to the Chimneys.

That small piece of wood, which in populated areas is wasted so carelessly and has no value, had to be handled with extreme caution here. The sailor made sure it was completely dry. Then, when that was done:

"We need paper," he said.

"Here it is," replied Gideon Spilett, who, after a moment's hesitation, tore a page from his notebook.

Pencroff took the piece of paper that the reporter offered him and squatted in front of the hearth. There, a few handfuls of grasses, leaves, and dry moss were placed beneath the sticks, arranged so that air could circulate easily and ignite the dead wood quickly.

Then, Pencroff folded the piece of paper into a cone shape, as pipe smokers do in strong winds, and inserted it among the moss. Taking a slightly rough stone, he carefully wiped it and, with his heart pounding, gently rubbed the match, holding his breath.

The first strike didn't produce any effect.

Pencroff hadn't pressed hard enough, fearing he would scrape off the phosphorus.

"No, I can't do it," he said, "my hand is shaking... The match would fail... I can't... I won't!"

And standing up, he asked Harbert to take his place.

Certainly, the young boy had never been so moved in his life. His heart raced. Prometheus going to steal fire from the heavens could not have been more stirred! Yet, he did not hesitate and quickly rubbed the stone. A small crackling sound was heard, and a faint blue flame sprang up, producing a pungent smoke. Harbert gently turned the match to feed the flame, then slipped it into the paper cone.

The paper caught fire in seconds, and the moss immediately started burning. A few moments later, the dry wood crackled, and a joyous flame, fueled by the sailor's vigorous breath, roared amidst the darkness.

"Finally," exclaimed Pencroff as he stood up, "I've never been so moved in my life!"

Indeed, this fire was doing well on the flat stone hearth. The smoke was easily escaping through the narrow flue, the chimney was drawing well, and a pleasant warmth soon spread.

As for this fire, they had to make sure not to let it go out and to always keep some embers under the ashes. But that was just a matter of care and attention since wood was abundant, and provisions could always be renewed in time.

Pencroff first thought of using the hearth to prepare a supper more nourishing than a dish of lithodomes. Two dozen eggs were brought by Harbert. The reporter, leaning against a corner, watched the preparations without saying a word. A triplet of thoughts occupied his mind. Did Cyrus still live?

If he lived, where could he be? If he survived the fall, how could he explain not finding a way to signal his existence? Meanwhile, Nab loitered on the shore. He was nothing but a soulless body.

Pencroff, who knew fifty-two ways to cook eggs, had no choice at that moment. He had to settle for placing them in the warm ashes and letting them harden over a low fire. In a few minutes, they were cooked, and the sailor invited the reporter to take his share of the supper.

Such was the first meal of the castaways on this unknown coast. These hard-boiled eggs were excellent, and since the egg contains all the essential elements for human nourishment, these poor souls found them quite satisfying and felt comforted.

Ah! if one of them had not missed this meal! If all five prisoners who escaped from Richmond had been there, under those piled rocks, in front of that crackling and bright fire, on that dry sand, perhaps they would have had nothing but thanks to give to heaven! But the most ingenious, the most learned of them, the one who was their unquestioned leader, Cyrus Smith, was missing, alas! and his body had not even received a burial!

Thus passed the day of March 25. Night had fallen. Outside, the wind whistled and the monotonous surf beat against the coast. The pebbles, pushed and pulled by the waves, rolled with a deafening crash.

The reporter had retreated to a dark passageway after briefly noting the day's events: the first sighting of this new land, the engineer's disappearance, the exploration of the coast, the incident with the matches, etc.; and, fatigue helping, he managed to find some rest in sleep.

Harbert soon fell asleep. As for the sailor, keeping watch with one eye, he spent the night beside the hearth, pouring fuel into it. Only one of the castaways didn't rest in the Chimneys. It was the inconsolable, the despaired Nab, who, all night, and despite what his companions said to encourage him to rest, roamed the shore calling for his master!

6

The inventory of the items possessed by these air castaways, thrown onto a seemingly uninhabited coast, will be quickly established.

They had nothing except the clothes they were wearing at the time of the disaster. However, it should be noted that a notebook and a watch that Gideon Spilett had inadvertently kept, but not a weapon, not a tool, not even a pocket knife. The passengers of the car had thrown everything outside to lighten the balloon.

The fictional heroes of Daniel Defoe or Wyss, as well as Selkirk and Raynal, castaways on Juan Fernandez or the Auckland Islands, were never in such absolute poverty. They either drew abundant resources from their shipwreck —be it seeds, livestock, tools, or ammunition—or some wreckage arrived on the coast that allowed them to meet their basic needs. They were not left defenseless against nature from the start. But here, there was not a single instrument of any kind, not a utensil. They would have to create everything from nothing!

And if only Cyrus Smith had been with them, if the engineer could have put his practical science, his inventive mind, to use in this situation, perhaps all hope would not have been lost! Alas!

They could no longer count on seeing Cyrus Smith again.

The castaways had to expect nothing but from themselves and from that Providence which never abandons those whose faith is sincere.

But, above all, should they settle on this part of the coast without first seeking to know which continent it belonged to, whether it was inhabited, or if this shore was merely the edge of a deserted island?

It was an important question to resolve and to do so quickly. Its resolution would determine the measures to take. However, according to Pencroff's opinion, it seemed wise to wait a few days before undertaking an exploration. They needed, in fact, to prepare provisions and to procure a more fortifying diet than just eggs or mollusks. The explorers, exposed to long fatigue, without a shelter to rest their heads, had to, above all, restore their strength.

The Chimneys offered a sufficient temporary retreat. The fire was lit, and it would be easy to keep the coals. For the moment, there were plenty of shellfish and eggs in the rocks and on the beach. They would surely find a way to kill some of those pigeons that flew in hundreds at the plateau's crest, even if it meant hitting them with sticks or stones. Perhaps the trees in the nearby forest would offer edible fruits? Finally, fresh water was available. It was agreed, therefore, that for a few days they would stay at the Chimneys to prepare for an exploration, either along the coast or inland.

This plan particularly suited Nab. Stubborn in his ideas as well as in his intuitions, he was in no hurry to leave this section of the coast, site of the disaster. He did not believe, he did not want to believe, in the loss of Cyrus Smith.

No, it did not seem possible to him that such a man had come to such a common end, swept away by a wave, drowned in the currents, just a few hundred feet from shore! As long as the waves had not washed ashore the body of the engineer, as long as he, Nab, had not seen with his own eyes, touched with his hands, his master's corpse, he would not believe in his death!

And this idea rooted itself deeper than ever in his stubborn heart. An illusion perhaps, but a respectable illusion that the sailor did not want to destroy! For him, there was no longer any hope, and the engineer had truly perished in the waves, but with Nab, there was no arguing.

It was like the dog that cannot leave the spot where its master has fallen, and its pain was such that, probably, it would not survive him.

That morning, March 26, at dawn, Nab had returned to the coast heading north, back to where the sea had surely closed over the unfortunate Smith.

That day's lunch consisted solely of pigeon eggs and lithodomes. Harbert had found salt deposited in the rock crevices from evaporation, and this mineral substance came in very handy.

When that meal was finished, Pencroff asked the reporter if he wanted to accompany them into the forest, where Harbert and he were going to try hunting! But, upon reflection, it was necessary for someone to stay behind to keep the fire going, and in the unlikely event that Nab might need help. So the reporter stayed.

"Out hunting, Harbert," said the sailor. "We'll find ammunition on our way, and we'll carve our rifle in the forest."

But, just as they were about to leave, Harbert pointed out that since they lacked tinder, it might be wise to replace it with some other substance.

"Which one?" asked Pencroff.

"Burned linen," replied the young boy. "That can, if necessary, serve as tinder."

The sailor found the suggestion quite sensible. However, it had the drawback of requiring the sacrifice of a piece of handkerchief. Nevertheless, it was worth it, and Pencroff's checked handkerchief was soon partially reduced to a half-burned rag. This flammable material was placed in the main chamber, at the back of a small rock cavity, protected from wind and moisture.

It was then nine o'clock in the morning. The weather looked threatening, and the breeze blew from the southeast. Harbert and Pencroff turned the corner of the Chimneys, not without casting a glance at the smoke twisting from a rocky point; then, they ascended the left bank of the river.

Upon reaching the forest, Pencroff broke two sturdy branches from the first tree, which he transformed into clubs, and Harbert sharpened the tips on a rock. Ah! what he would have given for a knife! Then, the two hunters advanced into the tall grass, following the bank. From the bend that redirected its course southwest, the river gradually narrowed, and its banks formed a deep bed covered by the double arch of trees. Pencroff, in order not to get lost, decided to follow the waterway, which would always lead him back to his starting point. But the bank didn't lack some obstacles, here the trees whose flexible branches dipped down to the water's edge, there vines or thorns that had to be broken with sticks. Often, Harbert slipped between the broken stumps with the agility of a young cat and disappeared into the underbrush. But Pencroff immediately called him back, asking him not to wander.However, the sailor was carefully observing the layout and nature of the surroundings. On this left bank, the ground was flat and gradually rose inward. Sometimes damp, it took on a marshy appearance.

One could feel an underlying network of liquid streams that, through some underground fissure, must be flowing into the river. Occasionally, a stream ran through the thicket, which was easy to cross. The opposite bank seemed to be more rugged, and the valley, where the riverbed was, was more distinctly outlined there. The hill, covered with trees arranged in tiers, formed a curtain that concealed the view. On this right bank, moving would have been difficult, as the slopes descended sharply, and the trees, bent over the water, held on only by the strength of their roots.

It goes without saying that this forest, as well as the bank they had already traversed, was untouched by any human presence. Pencroff noticed only tracks of quadrupeds, fresh paths of animals whose species he could not identify. Very likely, — and Harbert agreed — some of these tracks had been left by formidable wild beasts that one would surely have to reckon with; but there was no mark of an axe on a tree trunk, no remains of a extinguished fire, nor footprint; which one might perhaps consider a blessing, for on this land, deep in the Pacific, the presence of man might have been more to fear than to desire.

Harbert and Pencroff, barely talking, as the difficulties of the route were great, were only making very slow progress, and after an hour of walking, they had barely covered a mile. Until then, the hunt had not been fruitful. However, some birds sang and flitted beneath the branches, appearing very timid, as if instinctively fearful of man. Among other birds, Harbert pointed out, in a marshy part of the forest, a bird with a long, pointed beak that anatomically resembled a kingfisher. However, it distinguished itself from the latter by its somewhat rough plumage, covered with a metallic sheen.

"It must be a jacamar," said Harbert, trying to get close enough to the animal.

"It would be a good opportunity to taste jacamar," replied the sailor, "if that bird was in the mood to be roasted!"

At that moment, a stone, skillfully and vigorously thrown by the young boy, struck the bird near the wing; but the blow was not sufficient, as the jacamar fled at full speed and disappeared in an instant.

"What a clumsy mistake!" shouted Harbert.

"Not at all, my boy!" replied the sailor. "The throw was well aimed, and more than one would have missed the bird. Come on! Don't be upset! We'll catch it another day!"

The exploration continued. As the hunters progressed, the trees became more spaced out and majestic, but none bore edible fruits. Pencroff was searching in vain for some of those precious palms that lend themselves to so many uses in domestic life, and whose presence has been noted as far north as the fortieth parallel in the northern hemisphere and only as far south as the thirty-fifth.

But this forest consisted only of conifers, such as deodars, already recognized by Harbert, "douglas" trees similar to those that grow on the northwest coast of America, and magnificent firs reaching a height of one hundred fifty feet. At that moment, a flock of small birds with lovely plumage, long and irides-cent tails, scattered among the branches, shedding their loosely attached feathers that covered the ground with fine down. Harbert picked up some of these feathers, and after examining them, said:

"They are couroucous," he said.

"I would prefer a guinea fowl or a grouse," replied Pencroff; "but anyway, if they're good to eat?..."

"They are good to eat, and even their meat is very delicate," Harbert responded. "Besides, if I'm not mistaken, they can be approached easily and killed with a stick."

The sailor and the young boy, sneaking through the grass, arrived at the foot of a tree whose low branches were covered with small birds. These couroucous were waiting for insects to pass by, which served as their food. You could see their feathered feet tightly gripping the medium branches that supported them.

The hunters then stood up, and with their sticks swung like a scythe, they took down entire rows of couroucous, which didn't think to fly away and stupidly let themselves be struck down. A hundred already littered the ground when the others decided to flee.

"Well," said Pencroff, "there's game that hunters like us can catch easily! You could almost take it by hand!"

The sailor strung the couroucous together like little birds using a flexible stick, and the exploration continued. They observed that the river took a slight curve, forming a hook toward the south, but this detour probably didn't extend far, as the river must have its source in the mountain and be fed by the melting snow that covered the slopes of the central cone.

The particular goal of this outing was, as is known, to provide the inhabitants of the Chimneys with as much game as possible. One could not say that the goal had been achieved so far. Thus the sailor continued his active search and grumbled when some animal, one he didn't even have time to recognize, fled among the tall grasses. If only he had had the dog Top!

But Top had disappeared along with his master and likely perished with him!

Around three in the afternoon, new flocks of birds were seen through certain trees, pecking at the aromatic berries, including some junipers. Suddenly, a real trumpet call resonated through the forest. These strange and sonorous fanfares were produced by the game birds known as "grouse" in the United States.

Soon they saw a few pairs, with varied plumage in tawny and brown, and brown tails. Harbert recognized the males by the two pointed winglets formed by the raised feathers on their necks. Pencroff deemed it essential to catch one of these game birds, about the size of a hen, and whose meat is worth that of a partridge. But it was difficult, as they wouldn't let themselves be approached. After several unsuccessful attempts, which had no other result than to scare the grouse away, the sailor said to the young boy:

"Since we can't catch them on the wing, we need to try to catch them by line."

"Like a carp?" exclaimed Harbert, very surprised by the suggestion.

"Exactly, like a carp," the sailor replied seriously.

Pencroff found in the grass half a dozen grouse nests, each containing two to three eggs. He was very careful not to touch these nests, from which their owners would surely return. It was around these that he planned to set his lines, — not snares, but real lines with hooks. He took Harbert some distance from the nests, and there he prepared his unusual tackle with the care that a disciple of Isaac Walton would have shown. Harbert followed this work with understandable interest, while doubting the success. The lines were made of thin vines, connected to one another and fifteen to twenty feet long. Strong, thick thorns with curved tips, provided by a bush of dwarf acacias, were tied to the ends of the vines as hooks. As for the bait, big red worms crawling on the ground served as it.

Once that was done, Pencroff, moving through the grass and concealing himself skillfully, went to place the end of his armed lines near the grouse nests; then he returned to take the other end and hid with Harbert behind a large tree. Both then waited patiently. Harbert, it must be said, didn't count much on the success of the inventive Pencroff. A good half hour passed, but, as the sailor had anticipated, several pairs of grouse returned to their nests. They hopped about, pecking at the ground, and did not in any way sense the presence of the hunters, who had, moreover, taken care to position themselves downwind of the game birds.

Certainly, the young boy felt very interested at that moment. He held his breath, and Pencroff, his eyes wide, mouth open, lips forward as if he were about to taste a piece of grouse, barely breathed.

However, the game birds wandered between the hooks, not too concerned. Pencroff then gave little shakes that stirred the baits as if the worms were still alive.

Undoubtedly, at that moment, the sailor felt an emotion much stronger than that of the fisherman, who does not see his prey approaching through the waters.

The shakes soon caught the attention of the game birds, and the hooks were attacked by pecks. Three grouse, very greedy no doubt, swallowed both the bait and the hook at once. Suddenly, with a sharp jerk, Pencroff "set" his gear, and the beating of wings indicated to him that the birds were caught.

"Hurrah!" he shouted as he rushed towards this game, quickly mastering it.

Harbert clapped his hands. It was the first time he had seen birds caught on a line, but the sailor, very modest, assured him that he wasn't trying it for the first time, and besides, he had no merit in the invention.

"And in any case," he added, "given our situation, we should expect to see many more!"

The grouse were tied by their legs, and Pencroff, happy not to return empty-handed and seeing the day beginning to wane, thought it advisable to return home.

The direction to follow was clearly indicated by the river, which they only had to descend, and around six o'clock, quite tired from their excursion, Harbert and Pencroff were returning to the Chimneys.

7

Gédéon Spilett, motionless, arms crossed, was on the shore, looking at the sea, where the horizon merged in the east with a large black cloud that was rapidly rising towards the zenith. The wind was already strong, and it was picking up with the decline of the day. The entire sky had a bad look, and the first symptoms of a storm were visibly manifesting.

Harbert entered the Chimneys, and Pencroff went toward the reporter. The latter, very absorbed, didn't see him coming.

"We are going to have a bad night, Mr. Spilett!" said the sailor. "Rain and wind to make the petrels happy!"

The reporter, turning around, saw Pencroff, and his first words were:

"How far from shore do you think the boat was when it took that wave that carried away our companion?"

The sailor was not expecting this question. He thought for a moment and answered:

"Two cable lengths at most."

"But what is a cable length?" asked Gédéon Spilett.

"About a hundred and twenty fathoms or six hundred feet."

"So," said the reporter, "Cyrus Smith would have disappeared at most twelve hundred feet from shore?"

"About that," replied Pencroff.

"And his dog too?"

"Also."

"What surprises me," added the reporter, "assuming our companion perished, is that Top also met his end, and that neither the body of the dog nor that of his master was washed ashore!"

"That's not surprising, with such rough seas," replied the sailor. "Moreover, it is possible that the currents carried them further along the coast."

"So it is your opinion that our companion has perished at sea?" the reporter asked again.

"That is my opinion."

"My opinion is," said Gédéon Spilett, "except for what I owe to your experience, Pencroff, that the absolute disappearance of both Cyrus and Top, alive or dead, is something inexplicable and implausible."

"I wish I could think like you, Mr. Spilett," replied Pencroff. "Unfortunately, I am convinced!"

Having said this, the sailor returned to the Chimneys. A good fire crackled in the hearth. Harbert had just thrown a bundle of dry wood on it, and the flame cast large lights into the dark parts of the corridor.

Pencroff immediately set about preparing dinner. He thought it appropriate to include some substantial dish in the menu, as everyone needed to recover their strength. The chains of couroucous were saved for the next day, but two grouse were plucked, and soon, speared on a stick, they were roasting in front of a blazing fire.

At seven in the evening, Nab had still not returned. This prolonged absence could only worry Pencroff about the negro. He must have feared either that something had happened to him on this unknown land or that the unfortunate man had made some desperate act. But Harbert drew very different conclusions from this absence. For him, if Nab had not returned, it was because some new circumstance had led him to extend his search. Now, everything new could only be to the advantage of Cyrus Smith.

Why hadn't Nab returned if no hope was keeping him? Perhaps he had found some clue, a footprint, a piece of wreckage that had put him on the trail? Maybe he was currently following a certain lead? Perhaps he was close to his master?

Thus the young boy reasoned. Thus he spoke.

His companions let him say. Only the reporter nodded in agreement. But for

Pencroff, what seemed probable was that Nab had gone further than the day before in his search along the coast, and that he could not yet be back.

However, Harbert, very agitated by vague premonitions, expressed several times his intention to go look for Nab. But Pencroff made him understand that this would be a fruitless trip, and that in this darkness and in such deplorable weather, he could not find Nab's tracks, and that it was better to wait. If Nab had not reappeared the next day, Pencroff would not hesitate to join Harbert in the search for Nab.

Gédéon Spilett agreed with the sailor's opinion that they should not separate, and Harbert had to abandon his plan; but two big tears fell from his eyes.

The reporter could not help but embrace the generous boy.

The bad weather had fully set in. A southeast gale was passing over the coast with unparalleled violence. One could hear the sea, which was then lowering, roaring against the edge of the first rocks, offshore from the coast. The rain, pulverized by the hurricane, lifted like a liquid fog.It looked like ragged clouds lingering over the coast, where the pebbles rattled violently, like carts dumping out stones. The sand, lifted by the wind, mixed with the rain, making the assault unbearable. There was as much mineral dust in the air as there was watery dust. Between the river's mouth and the wall, large whirlpools swirled, and the layers of air escaping from this maelstrom found no other outlet than the narrow valley, at the bottom of which the river rose, rushing violently into it. Consequently, the smoke from the fire, pushed back by the narrow passage, frequently retreated, filling the corridors and making them unlivable.

That's why, as soon as the grouse were cooked, Pencroff let the fire die down and kept only buried embers under the ash.

By eight o'clock, Nab had not yet returned; but it could now be assumed that this dreadful weather had been the only thing keeping him away, and he must have sought refuge in some hollow to wait for the storm to pass or at least for daylight to return. As for going out to find him, trying to track him down in these conditions was impossible.

The game formed the only dish for supper. They willingly ate this excellent meat.

Pencroff and Harbert, whose long outing had heightened their appetites, devoured it.

Then, everyone settled into the spot where they had rested the night before, and Harbert quickly fell asleep near the sailor, who had laid down along the fire. Outside, as night advanced, the storm grew more formidable. It was a windstorm comparable to the one that had carried prisoners from Richmond to this Pacific land. Frequent storms during these equinox times, fertile in disasters and especially terrible over this expansive area, which presented no barriers to their fury! So one can understand that a coast exposed like this to the east, directly facing the brunt of the hurricane, would be battered with a force that no description could convey.

Fortunately, the heap of rocks forming the Chimneys was solid. They were huge blocks of granite, some of which, however, seemed unsteadily balanced and appeared to tremble at their base. Pencroff sensed this, and beneath his hand, resting against the walls, rapid tremors ran. But still, he reminded himself, rightly, that there was nothing to fear and that his makeshift retreat wouldn't collapse.

However, he heard the sound of stones loosening from the top of the plateau, wrenched away by the wind's turbulence, falling onto the shore. Some even rolled down from the top of the Chimneys or shattered there when thrown perpendicular. Twice, the sailor got up and crawled to the corridor's entrance to look outside. But these minor landslides posed no danger, and he returned to his position in front of the fire, where the embers crackled under the ash.

Despite the hurricane's fury, the crash of the storm, the thunder of the tempest, Harbert slept soundly. Sleep eventually overtook Pencroff, who, as a sailor, was used to all these rough conditions. Only Gédéon Spilett stayed awake with worry. He reproached himself for not having accompanied Nab. It was clear that he hadn't given up hope. The premonitions that had troubled Harbert also continued to stir him. His thoughts were focused on Nab. Why hadn't Nab returned? He shifted on his bed of sand, barely paying attention to the elemental struggle outside.

Sometimes, his eyes, heavy with fatigue, closed for a moment, but some fleeting thought would almost immediately open them again.

Meanwhile, night wore on, and it could have been around two in the morning when Pencroff, soundly asleep at that moment, was shaken vigorously.

"What is it?" he exclaimed, waking up and regaining his thoughts with the quickness typical of sailors.

The reporter was leaning over him, saying, "Listen, Pencroff, listen!"

The sailor lent an ear and couldn't distinguish any noise other than the gusts.

"It's the wind," he said.

"No," replied Gédéon Spilett, listening again, "I thought I heard..."

"What?"

"The barking of a dog!"

"A dog!" cried Pencroff, springing up.

"Yes... barking..."

"That's impossible!" the sailor replied. "And besides, how, with the roaring of the storm..."

"Listen... listen..." said the reporter.

Pencroff listened more carefully and thought he truly heard distant barking during a moment of calm.

"Well!" said the reporter, clasping the sailor's hand.

"Yes... yes!" replied Pencroff.

"It's Top! It's Top!" cried Harbert, who had just woken up, and all three rushed to the entrance of the Chimneys.

They had a hard time getting out. The wind pushed them back. But finally, they managed to, and could only stand by leaning against the rocks.

They looked and couldn't speak.

The darkness was complete. The sea, sky, and land blended into equal intensities of darkness. It seemed that not a single speck of diffuse light was in the atmosphere.

For a few minutes, the reporter and his two companions remained there, as if crushed by the gusts, drenched by the rain, and blinded by the sand.

Then, they heard the barking again in a lull of the storm, and they recognized that it must be quite far.

It could only be Top barking like this!

But was he alone or with someone? It was more likely he was alone, for, assuming Nab was with him, Nab would have hurried towards the Chimneys.

The sailor squeezed the reporter's hand, unable to make himself heard, in a way that meant "Wait!" then he went back into the corridor. A moment later, he emerged with a burning bundle, threw it into the darkness, and emitted sharp whistles.

At that signal, which seemed to be anticipated, closer barking replied, and soon a dog rushed into the corridor.

Pencroff, Harbert, and Gédéon Spilett followed him in. A bunch of dry wood was thrown onto the coals. The corridor lit up with a bright flame.

"It's Top!" cried Harbert.

It was indeed Top, a magnificent Anglo-Norman, inheriting the speed of legs and the sharpness of scent from those two breeds, the two qualities par excellence of a hunting dog.

He was the engineer Cyrus Smith's dog.

But he was alone! Neither his master nor Nab accompanied him!

However, how could his instinct have led him to the Chimneys, which he did not know? That seemed inexplicable, especially in such a dark night and during such a storm! But, even more inexplicable, Top was neither tired, nor exhausted, nor even dirty from mud or sand!...

Harbert drew him close and pressed his head between his hands. The dog submitted and rubbed his neck against the boy's hands.

"If the dog has been found, the master will be found too!" said the reporter.

"God willing!" replied Harbert. "Let's go! Top will guide us!"

Pencroff didn't object. He felt that Top's arrival might disprove his worries.

"Let's go!" he said.

Pencroff carefully covered the fire's coals.

He placed some wood under the ashes so that they could have a fire again when they returned. Then, preceded by the dog, who seemed to urge him to follow with little barks, and followed by the reporter and the young boy, he dashed outside, after taking the remnants of their supper.

The storm was then at its full violence, perhaps even at its peak intensity. The new moon was in conjunction with the sun and did not allow a single ray of light to filter through the clouds. Following a straight path became difficult. The best option was to rely on Top's instinct. That's what they did. The reporter and the young boy walked behind the dog, with the sailor bringing up the rear. No exchange of words was possible. The rain was falling lightly, as it was scattered by the hurricane, but the hurricane was terrible.

However, one circumstance greatly favored the sailor and his two companions. The wind was blowing from the southeast, and thus, it pushed them along from behind. The sand it hurled with such force would have been unbearable, but they received it from behind, and as long as they didn't turn around, they were not bothered enough to hinder their pace. Overall, they went faster than they wanted, quickening their steps to avoid being knocked over, but a great hope doubled their strength, and this time they were not climbing the shore in futility. They had no doubt that Nab had found his master and sent back the faithful dog. But was the engineer alive, or was Nab only calling his companions to pay their last respects to the unfortunate Smith's corpse?

After passing the cut-off part of the high land they had cautiously steered clear of, Harbert, the reporter, and Pencroff stopped to catch their breath. The return of the rock sheltered them from the wind, and they breathed easier after this quarter-hour trek, which had been more of a run.

At that moment, they could hear, and the young boy, having spoken Cyrus Smith's name, found that Top barked in little bursts, as if he were saying that his master was safe.

"Safe, isn't he?" Harbert repeated, "safe, Top?"

And the dog barked as if to answer.

They resumed their march. It was around two-thirty in the morning. The sea began to rise, and pushed by the wind, this tide, which was a syzygy tide, threatened to be very strong. The large waves boomed against the edge of the reefs and assailed it with such violence that, very likely, they would pass over the islet, completely invisible at that time. Thus, this long barrier no longer covered the coast, which was now directly exposed to the shocks of the open sea.

As soon as the sailor and his companions moved away from the cut-off edge, the wind struck them with extreme fury again. Hunched over, turning their backs to the gusts, they walked very quickly, following Top, who did not hesitate on which way to take. They were heading north, with an endless crest of waves crashing to their right and an obscure land to their left, impossible to discern in appearance.

But they could sense that it must be relatively flat because the hurricane was now passing above them without striking back, which would happen when it hit the granite wall.

At four in the morning, one could estimate that a distance of five miles had been covered. The clouds had lifted slightly and no longer dragged along the ground. The gusts, less humid, spread in very brisk currents of air, drier and colder. Insufficiently sheltered by their clothing, Pencroff, Harbert, and Gédéon Spilett were suffering greatly, but not a complaint escaped their lips. They were determined to follow Top wherever the intelligent animal would lead them.

Around five o'clock, dawn began to break. First at the zenith, where the vapors were less thick, some grayish hues outlined the edges of the clouds, and soon, beneath an opaque band, a brighter line distinctly shaped the horizon of the sea. The crests of the waves were touched slightly by tawny glimmers, and the foam became white again. At the same time, to their left, the rugged parts of the coast began to blur indistinctly, but it was still just gray on black.

By six o'clock in the morning, it was daylight. The clouds raced with extreme speed in a relatively high zone. The sailor and his companions were about six miles from the Chimneys. They were following a very flat shore, bordered offshore by a fringe of rocks, the tops of which were just emerging at that time, as it was at high tide. To the left, the land, dotted with a few dunes covered in thorns, had a rather wild appearance of a vast sandy region. The coastline was not very indented and offered no other barrier to the Ocean than a somewhat irregular chain of mounds. Here and there, one or two trees grimaced, lying towards the west, their branches stretched in that direction. Further back, in the southwest, the edge of the last forest rounded. At that moment, Top showed unmistakable signs of excitement. He went ahead, returned to the sailor, and seemed to urge him to quicken his pace. The dog then left the shore and, driven by his admirable instinct, without showing any hesitation, headed between the dunes.

They followed him. The area seemed completely deserted. Not a living creature animated it.

The edge of the dunes, very wide, was made up of mounds and even of small hills very capriciously arranged. It was like a little Switzerland of sand, and it required nothing less than prodigious instinct to navigate it.

Five minutes after leaving the shore, the reporter and his companions arrived at a sort of excavation dug at the back of a high dune. There, Top stopped and let out a clear bark. Spilett, Harbert, and Pencroff entered the cave.

Nab was there, kneeling beside a body lying on a bed of grass...

This body was that of the engineer Cyrus Smith.

8

Nab did not move. The sailor only threw a word at him.

"Alive!" he cried.

Nab did not respond. Gédéon Spilett and Pencroff went pale. Harbert clasped his hands and stood frozen. But it was clear that the poor black man, absorbed in his grief, neither saw his companions nor heard the sailor's words.

The reporter knelt beside the motionless body and placed his ear on the engineer's chest, which he partly opened. A minute—an eternity!—passed as he tried to detect some heartbeat.

Nab had straightened up a bit and was looking without seeing.

Despair could not have altered a man's face more. Nab was unrecognizable, exhausted by fatigue, broken by grief. He believed his master was dead.

After a long and careful observation, Gédéon Spilett stood up.

"He lives!" he said.

Pencroff, in turn, knelt beside Cyrus Smith; his ear also caught a few beats, and his lips, some breath escaping from the engineer's mouth.Harbert, on a word from the reporter, dashed outside to find some water. He found a clear stream a hundred paces away, clearly swollen from the rain the day before, trickling through the sand. But there was nothing to hold the water, not even a shell in those dunes! The young boy had to settle for soaking his handkerchief in the stream, and he ran back to the cave.

Fortunately, this soaked handkerchief was enough for Gédéon Spilett, who only wanted to moisten the engineer's lips. The fresh water started to have an almost immediate effect. A sigh escaped from Cyrus Smith's chest, and it even seemed like he was trying to say a few words.

"We'll save him!" said the reporter.

Nab regained hope with these words. He undressed his master to see if there were any injuries on his body. Neither the head, nor the chest, nor the limbs had any bruises, not even any scrapes, which was surprising, since Cyrus Smith's body must have been rolled among the rocks; even his hands were intact, and it was hard to explain how the engineer had no signs of the effort he must have made to get past the reefs.

But the explanation for this situation would come later. When Cyrus Smith could talk, he would explain what had happened. For now, the goal was to bring him back to life, and it was likely that some rubbing would achieve this result.

That's what was done with the sailor's jacket.

The engineer, warmed by this vigorous massage, moved his arm slightly, and his breathing began to become more regular. He was dying from exhaustion, and surely, without the arrival of the reporter and his companions, it would have been the end for Cyrus Smith.

"You thought your master was dead, didn't you?" asked the sailor to Nab.

"Yes! Dead!" replied Nab, "and if Top hadn't found you, if you hadn't come, I would have buried my master and died next to him!"

You can see how close Cyrus Smith's life had come to being lost!

Nab then recounted what had happened. The day before, after leaving the Chimneys at dawn, he had walked along the coast heading north and reached a part of the shoreline he had already visited.

There, without any hope, he admitted, Nab had searched the shore, among the rocks, on the sand, for the slightest hint that could guide him.

He especially checked the part of the beach that high tide hadn't covered, because the tide would have washed away all traces at the edge. Nab no longer hoped to find his master alive. He was going in search of a corpse, a corpse he intended to bury with his own hands!

Nab searched for a long time. His efforts were fruitless. It didn't seem that this deserted coast had ever been frequented by human beings. The shells, those that the sea couldn't reach, — and which were found by the millions beyond the tidal points, —were intact. Not a single crushed shell. Over a stretch of two to three hundred yards, there was no trace of landings, neither old nor recent.

Nab decided to walk up the coast for a few miles. It was possible that the currents had carried a body to some further point.

When a corpse floats near a flat shore, it is rare that the tide doesn't wash it ashore sooner or later. Nab knew that, and he wanted to see his master one last time.

"I followed the coast for another two miles, I visited the whole line of the reefs at low tide, all the beach at high tide, and I was despairing of finding anything when yesterday, around five o'clock in the evening, I noticed footprints on the sand.

— Footprints? cried Pencroff.

— Yes! replied Nab.

— And these footprints started right at the reefs? asked the reporter.

— No, answered Nab, only at the tidal point, because the others must have been erased between the tidal points and the reefs.

— Go on, Nab, said Gédéon Spilett.

— When I saw these footprints, I went a bit crazy. They were very recognizable and were headed toward the dunes. I followed them for a quarter mile, running, but being careful not to erase them. Five minutes later, as night was falling, I heard the barking of a dog. It was Top, and Top led me right here, next to my master!"

Nab finished his story by saying how much pain he felt when he found the lifeless body. He had tried to sense some remnant of life in him!

Now that he had found him dead, he wanted him to be alive! All his efforts had been in vain! He no longer had anything to do but pay his last respects to the one he loved so much!

Nab then thought of his companions. They would surely want to see the unfortunate one one last time! Top was there. Couldn't he rely on the instinct of this faithful animal? Nab repeatedly called the reporter's name, the name of the engineer's companions that Top knew best. Then, he showed him the south of the coast, and the dog dashed off in the direction indicated.

It is known how, guided by an instinct that one might consider almost supernatural, for the animal had never been to the Chimneys, Top managed to get there.

Nab's companions listened to this account with extreme attention.

There was something inexplicable for them in how Cyrus Smith, after the efforts he must have made to escape the waves, crossing the reefs, showed no sign of a scratch. And what was even less explainable was that the engineer could have made it, over a mile from the coast, to this cave lost in the middle of the dunes.

"So, Nab," said the reporter, "it wasn't you who carried your master to this place?

— No, it wasn't me," replied Nab.

— It's quite clear that Mr. Smith came here on his own," said Pencroff.

— That's obvious, indeed," noted Gédéon Spilett, "but it's not believable!"

The explanation for this fact could only come from the engineer himself. For that, they had to wait until he could speak again. Fortunately, life was already returning to its course. The rubbing had restored blood circulation. Cyrus Smith moved his arms again, then his head, and a few incomprehensible words escaped once more from his lips.

Nab, leaning over him, called out to him, but the engineer didn't seem to hear, and his eyes were still closed. Life only revealed itself in him through movement. His senses were still not engaged.

Pencroff regretted not having a fire, or anything to get one, because he had unfortunately forgotten to bring the burnt cloth, which he could have easily ignited by striking two stones together. As for the engineer's pockets, they were completely empty, except for his vest pocket, which contained his watch. So they had to transport Cyrus Smith to the Chimneys, and as soon as possible. That was everyone's opinion.

However, the care given to the engineer should bring him back to consciousness sooner than expected. The water with which they moistened his lips gradually revived him. Pencroff also had the idea of mixing in with this water some juice from the grouse meat he had brought along. Harbert, having run down to the shore, returned with two large bivalve shells. The sailor made a kind of mixture and put it between the engineer's lips, who seemed to savor that mixture eagerly.

His eyes opened then. Nab and the reporter leaned over him.

"My master! My master!" cried Nab.

The engineer heard him. He recognized Nab and Spilett, then his other two companions, Harbert and the sailor, and his hand lightly squeezed theirs. A few words escaped from his mouth again—words he must have already uttered, indicating what thoughts were tormenting his mind even then. These words were understood this time.

"Island or continent?" he murmured.

"Ah!" exclaimed Pencroff, unable to hold back this exclamation. "For heaven's sake, we don't care, as long as you live, Mr. Cyrus! Island or continent? We'll find out later."

The engineer gave a slight affirmative sign and seemed to fall asleep.

They respected this sleep, and the reporter immediately made arrangements for the engineer to be transported in the best conditions. Nab, Harbert, and Pencroff left the cave and headed towards a tall dune topped with a few scraggly trees. And on the way, the sailor couldn't help repeating:

"Island or continent! To think about that when one has only breath left! What a man!"

When they reached the top of the dune, Pencroff and his two companions, with no other tools than their arms, stripped a rather scrawny tree of its main branches, a kind of maritime pine weakened by the winds; then, from those branches, they made a litter that, once covered with leaves and grass, would allow them to carry the engineer.

This took about forty minutes, and it was ten o'clock when the sailor, Nab, and Harbert returned to Cyrus Smith, whom Gédéon Spilett hadn't left.

The engineer was just waking from that sleep, or rather from the stupor in which he had been found. Color was returning to his cheeks, which until now had been pale as death. He sat up a bit, looked around him, and seemed to be asking where he was.

"Can you hear me without straining, Cyrus?" said the reporter.

"Yes," replied the engineer.

"I think," said the sailor then, "that Mr. Smith will hear you even better if he has that grouse jelly again—because it is grouse, Mr. Cyrus," he added, presenting a bit of that jelly, this time mixing in pieces of meat.

Cyrus Smith chewed the pieces of grouse, of which the remains were shared among his three companions, who were hungry and found the lunch rather meager.

"Good!" said the sailor, "the provisions are waiting for us at the Chimneys, for you should know, Mr. Cyrus, we have there, in the south, a house with rooms, beds, and a fireplace, and in the pantry, some dozens of birds that our Harbert calls couroucou. Your litter is ready, and as soon as you feel strong enough, we will carry you to our home."

"Thank you, my friend," replied the engineer, "just another hour or two, and we can leave... And now, speak, Spilett."

The reporter then recounted what had happened. He told him about the events that Cyrus Smith must have been unaware of, the final fall of the balloon, the landing on this unknown land, which seemed deserted, whatever it was, whether an island or a continent, the discovery of the Chimneys, the searches undertaken to find the engineer, Nab's dedication, all that was owed to the intelligence of faithful Top, etc.

"But," asked Cyrus Smith in a still weakened voice, "you didn't pick me up on the beach?

— No," replied the reporter.

— And it wasn't you who brought me to this cave?

— No.

— How far is this cave from the reefs?

— About half a mile," answered Pencroff, "and if you are surprised, Mr. Cyrus, we are no less astonished to see you here!

— Indeed," replied the engineer, gradually reviving and becoming interested in these details, "indeed, that is strange!

— But," the sailor resumed, "you must have been washed ashore and had the strength to walk here, since Nab found the footprints of your steps!

— Yes... it must be..." replied the engineer, thinking. "And you didn't see any signs of human beings on this coast?

— Not a trace," replied the reporter. "Besides, if by chance some savior had been there, right on time, why would he have left you after pulling you from the waves?

— You're right, my dear Spilett. — Tell me, Nab," the engineer added, turning to his servant, "it wasn't you who... you didn't have a moment of absence... during which... No, that's absurd... Are there still some of those footprints?" asked Cyrus Smith.

"Yes, my master," replied Nab, "look, at the entrance, right on the slope of that dune, in a place sheltered from the wind and rain. The others have been erased by the storm.

— Pencroff," replied Cyrus Smith, "would you take my shoes and see if they match those footprints exactly?"

The sailor did what the engineer asked. Harbert and he, guided by Nab, went to the place where the footprints were, while Cyrus Smith said to the reporter:

"There have been inexplicable things here!

— Inexplicable, indeed!" replied Gédéon Spilett.

— But let's not dwell on that right now, my dear Spilett, we'll discuss it later."

A moment later, the sailor, Nab, and Harbert returned.

There was no doubt. The engineer's shoes matched the footprints perfectly. So it was Cyrus Smith who had left them in the sand.

"Well," he said, "it must be I who experienced that hallucination, that absence that I attributed to Nab! I must have walked like a sleepwalker, without being aware of my steps, and it was Top who, by his instinct, brought me here after saving me from the waves... Come, Top! Come, my dog!"

The magnificent animal leaped to his master, barking, and he received plenty of affection.

It would be agreed that there was no other explanation for the facts that brought about the rescue of Cyrus Smith, and all the credit for the affair belonged to Top.

Around noon, Pencroff asked Cyrus Smith if he could be transported, to which Cyrus Smith, in response, and with an effort that showed the most vigorous will, got up.

But he had to lean on the sailor, for he would have fallen.

"Good! Good!" said Pencroff! "The engineer's litter."

The litter was brought. The cross branches had been covered with moss and long grass. Cyrus Smith was laid upon it, and they headed toward the coast, with Pencroff at one end of the stretcher and Nab at the other. There were eight miles to go, but since they couldn't move fast and would likely need to stop frequently, they anticipated it would take at least six hours before they reached the Chimneys.

The wind was still strong, but thankfully it wasn't raining anymore. Lying down, the engineer propped himself up on his arm and watched the coast, especially the part facing away from the sea. He didn't speak, but he observed, and surely the landscape with its rough terrain, forests, and various resources etched itself in his mind.

However, after two hours of travel, fatigue took over, and he fell asleep on the litter.

At five-thirty, the small group reached the bluff and, shortly after, arrived at the Chimneys.

Everyone stopped, and the litter was placed on the sand. Cyrus Smith was sleeping deeply and did not wake up.

To Pencroff's great surprise, he discovered that the dreadful storm from the previous night had changed the appearance of the area. Significant landslides had occurred. Large chunks of rock lay on the shore, and a thick mat of seagrass, kelp, and algae covered the entire coast. It was clear that the sea had surged over the islet, reaching the foot of the massive granite wall. In front of the Chimneys, the ground was deeply worn, having taken a violent battering from the waves.

Pencroff suddenly had a feeling of dread. He rushed into the corridor.

Almost immediately, he came out and stood still, looking at his companions...

The fire was out. The drowned ashes were nothing but sludge. The burned cloth, which should have served as tinder, had disappeared. The sea had flooded the corridors and completely disrupted everything inside the Chimneys!

9

In a few words, Gideon Spilett, Harbert, and Nab were informed of the situation. This accident, which could have very serious consequences—at least that's how Pencroff saw it—had various effects on the companions of the honest sailor.

Nab, overjoyed to have found his master, didn't listen or rather didn't want to be concerned about what Pencroff was saying.

Harbert seemed to share, to some extent, the sailor's worries.

As for the reporter, he simply replied to Pencroff's words:

"Honestly, Pencroff, I don't care!"

"But I tell you we have no fire left!"

"So what!"

"And we have no way to relight it."

"Whatever!"

"But, Mr. Spilett..."

"Isn't Cyrus here?" the reporter answered. "Isn't our engineer alive? He'll find a way to make us a fire!"

"And with what?"

"With nothing."

What could Pencroff have said? He wouldn't have replied because, deep down, he shared the confidence his companions had in Cyrus Smith. The engineer was for them a microcosm, a blend of all human science and intelligence! Being with Cyrus on a deserted island was worth more than being without him in the most bustling villa in the Union. With him, they could lack nothing.

With him, despair was unthinkable. They'd respond to these brave people saying that a volcanic eruption would annihilate their land, that the land would sink into the depths of the Pacific, and they would unwaveringly reply: "Cyrus is here! Look at Cyrus!"

Meanwhile, however, the engineer was still in a new stupor caused by the journey, and they couldn't appeal to his ingenuity at that moment. Dinner had to be quite scant. In fact, all the ptarmigan meat had been consumed, and there was no way to cook any game.

Moreover, the curlews that were meant to be a reserve had disappeared. They had to find a solution.

First, Cyrus Smith was carried into the central corridor. There, they managed to arrange a bed of seaweed and kelp that remained somewhat dry.

The deep sleep that had overtaken him could only quickly restore his strength, and likely even better than abundant food would have done.

Night fell, and with it, the temperature, changed by a shift in the wind from the northeast, cooled significantly. As the sea had destroyed the partitions set up by Pencroff in some areas of the corridors, drafts set in, making the Chimneys quite uncomfortable. The engineer would have been in pretty bad condition if his companions hadn't carefully covered him by taking off their vests or jackets.

That evening's dinner consisted only of those inevitable lithodomes, which Harbert and Nab gathered abundantly on the shore. However, the young boy also added a certain amount of edible seaweed, which he collected from high rocks that the sea would only wet during high tide. This seaweed, belonging to the family of fucaceae, was a type of sargassum that, when dried, provided a gelatinous matter quite rich in nutrients. The reporter and his companions, after consuming a considerable amount of lithodomes, then sucked on these sargassums, which they found had quite a palatable taste, and it must be said that, on the Asian coasts, they make up a significant part of the diet for the locals.

"Well! said the sailor, it's time for Mr. Cyrus to come to our aid."

Meanwhile, the cold became quite intense and unfortunately, there was no way to combat it.

The sailor, truly annoyed, searched by every possible means to get fire. Nab even helped him in this task. He found some dry moss, and by striking two pebbles together, he produced sparks; however, the moss wasn't flammable enough and didn't catch fire, plus these sparks, being only incandescent flint, didn't have the consistency of those from a piece of steel in a regular flint. The attempt was unsuccessful.

Pencroff, though lacking confidence in the method, then tried rubbing two pieces of dry wood against each other, as savages do. Certainly, the movement that Nab and he made, if turned into heat according to new theories, would have been enough to boil a steamer's kettle! The result was nothing. The pieces of wood heated up, that was all, and even less than the operators themselves.

After an hour of effort, Pencroff was sweating and he threw the wood pieces away in frustration.

"When someone convinces me that savages light fires this way," he said, "it'll be hot, even in winter! I'd rather light my arms by rubbing them together!"

The sailor was wrong to deny the method. It is true that savages ignite wood by rapid friction. But not every type of wood is suitable for this operation, and then there's the "right technique," as the saying goes, and it's likely that Pencroff didn't have "the right technique."

Pencroff's bad mood didn't last long. Those two pieces of wood that he discarded were picked up by Harbert, who enthusiastically continued trying to rub them together. The sturdy sailor couldn't hold back a laugh, watching the teenager's efforts to succeed where he had failed.

"Rub away, my boy, rub away!" he said.

"I'm rubbing," replied Harbert, laughing, "but I have no other aim but to warm myself instead of shivering, and soon I'll be as warm as you, Pencroff!"

And indeed, that happened. Whatever happened, they had to give up on getting fire that night.

Gideon Spilett repeated for the twentieth time that Cyrus Smith would not be stumped by such a small matter.

And in the meantime, he lay down in one of the corridors, on the bed of sand. Harbert, Nab, and Pencroff followed his lead while Top slept at his master's feet.

The next day, March 28, when the engineer woke up around eight in the morning, he saw his companions near him, eagerly awaiting his awakening. Just like the day before, his first words were:

"Island or continent?"

As you can see, it was his fixed idea.

"Well," replied Pencroff, "we don't know yet, Mr. Smith!"

"You still don't know?..."

"But we'll find out," Pencroff added, "when you guide us through this land."

"I believe I'm ready to try," replied the engineer, who stood up without too much effort.

"That's good!" shouted the sailor.

"I was especially dying of exhaustion," replied Cyrus Smith. "My friends, a bit of food, and I won't feel it anymore. — You have fire, right?"

This question didn't receive an immediate answer.

But after a few moments:

"Alas! we don't have fire," said Pencroff, "or rather, Mr. Cyrus, we don't have any left!"

And the sailor recounted what had happened the day before. He cheered the engineer by telling him the story of their only match, then his failed attempt to get fire the savage way.

"We'll figure something out," replied the engineer, "and if we can't find a substance similar to tinder..."

"Well?" the sailor asked.

"Well, we'll make matches."

"Chemical ones?"

"Chemical ones!"

"That's not any more difficult," shouted the reporter, patting the sailor on the shoulder.

The sailor didn't find it so simple, but he didn't protest. They all went out. The weather had become nice again. A bright sun rose on the horizon of the sea, shimmering like gold on the prismatic roughness of the enormous wall.

After quickly scanning his surroundings, the engineer sat on a chunk of rock. Harbert offered him some handfuls of mussels and sargassum, saying:

"This is all we have, Mr. Cyrus."

"Thank you, my boy," replied Cyrus Smith, "that will suffice — for this morning, at least."

And he ate eagerly this meager food, which he washed down with a bit of fresh water, drawn from the river in a large shell.

His companions watched him in silence. Then, after filling up as best as he could, Cyrus Smith, crossing his arms, said:

"So, my friends, you still don't know if fate has cast us onto a continent or an island?

"No, Mr. Cyrus," replied the young boy.

"We'll know tomorrow," the engineer continued. "Until then, there's nothing to be done."

"Yes, there is!" Pencroff retorted.

"What then?"

"Fire," said the sailor, who, too, had his fixed idea.

"We'll make some, Pencroff," replied Cyrus Smith. "While you were carrying me yesterday, didn't I see a mountain to the west that towers over this land?"

"Yes," replied Gideon Spilett, "a mountain that should be quite high..."

"Good," replied the engineer. "Tomorrow, we'll climb to its peak and see if this land is an island or a continent. Until then, I repeat, there's nothing to be done."

"Yes, fire!" insisted the stubborn sailor again.

"But we'll make fire!" retorted Gideon Spilett. "A little patience, Pencroff!"

The sailor looked at Gideon Spilett with an expression that seemed to say: "If only you could make some, we wouldn't taste roasted food anytime soon!" But he remained silent.

However, Cyrus Smith did not respond. He seemed very little concerned about the fire situation. For a few moments, he stayed absorbed in thought. Then, resuming his speech:

"My friends," he said, "our situation may be dire, but in any case, it's quite straightforward.

Either we are on a continent, and then, at the cost of more or less tiring efforts, we will reach some inhabited point, or we are on an island. In the latter case, it's two possibilities: if the island is inhabited, we will see how to deal with its inhabitants; if it is deserted, we'll figure out how to manage it ourselves.

"It's certainly no more complicated than that," replied Pencroff.

"But whether it's a continent or an island," asked Gideon Spilett, "where do you think, Cyrus, that this hurricane has thrown us?"

"Honestly, I can't tell," replied the engineer, "but the signs point to land in the Pacific. Indeed, when we left Richmond, the wind was blowing from the northeast, and its very strength proves that its direction likely hasn't changed. If this direction has remained from northeast to southwest, we have crossed the states of North Carolina, South Carolina, Georgia, the Gulf of Mexico, Mexico itself in its narrow part, and then a portion of the Pacific Ocean. I estimate the distance traveled by the balloon at no less than six to seven thousand miles, and, if the wind varied by even half a degree, it must have carried us either to the Mendanā archipelago, or to the Pomotou, or even, if it had a greater speed than I suppose, to the lands of New Zealand. If this last hypothesis came to be, our repatriation would be easy. English or Maori, we'd always find someone to talk to. If, on the contrary, this coast belongs to some deserted island in a Micronesian archipelago, perhaps we could recognize it from the top of that cone dominating the area, and then we would figure out how to settle here, as if we never meant to leave!"

"Never!" exclaimed the reporter. "You say never, my dear Cyrus?"

"It's better to expect the worst right from the start," replied the engineer, "and to reserve the surprise of the best."

"Well said!" replied Pencroff. "And let's hope that this island, if it is one, won't be precisely located outside the shipping route! That would truly be playing with misfortune!"

"We won't know what to make of it until after we've done, above all, the ascent of the mountain," replied the engineer.

"But tomorrow, Mr. Cyrus," asked Harbert, "will you be able to manage the exertion of this climb?"

"I hope so," replied the engineer, "but on the condition that you, Master Pencroff and you, my child, show yourselves to be intelligent and skillful hunters."

"Mr. Cyrus," replied the sailor, "since you mention game, if when I return, I were certain to roast it just as I am sure to bring it back..."

"Just bring it back, Pencroff," replied Cyrus Smith.

It was thus agreed that the engineer and the reporter would spend the day at the Chimneys, examining the coastline and the upper plateau. Meanwhile, Nab, Harbert, and the sailor would return to the forest, replenish their firewood supply, and seize any feathered or furry creature that crossed their path.

So they set off around ten in the morning, Harbert confident, Nab joyful, and Pencroff murmuring to himself:

"If I find fire at home when I return, it will be because Thunder himself came to light it!"

The three of them climbed up the bank, and when they reached the bend that the river made, the sailor stopped and said to his two companions:

"Are we starting as hunters or woodcutters?"

"Hunters," replied Harbert. "Look, Top is already on the hunt.""Let's go hunting then," the sailor replied; "afterward, we'll come back here to gather wood."

With that, Harbert, Nab, and Pencroff, after pulling three sticks from the trunk of a young fir tree, followed Top, who was bounding through the tall grass.

This time, instead of following the riverbank, the hunters plunged deeper into the heart of the forest. The same types of trees were everywhere, mostly belonging to the pine family. In some places, where they had more space, the isolated pines were massive, indicating that this area was situated at a higher latitude than the engineer had guessed. A few clearings, dotted with stumps worn down by time, were covered in dead wood, creating endless reserves of fuel. After passing these clearings, the undergrowth thickened and became nearly impenetrable.

Navigating through these dense trees without any trail was quite challenging. So, the sailor periodically marked their path by clearing a few branches for easy recognition. However, it might have been a mistake not to follow the river, as Harbert and he had done during their first outing, because after an hour of walking, not a single game animal had showed itself. Top, dashing under the low branches, only startled birds that could not be approached. Even the curassows were completely out of sight, so it was likely that the sailor would have to return to that marshy area of the forest where he had so successfully fished for the grouse.

"Hey, Pencroff," Nab said with a bit of sarcasm, "if this is all the game you promised to bring back to my master, there won't be much of a fire needed to roast it!"

"Patience, Nab," replied the sailor, "the game won't be lacking on the return journey!"

"Don't you trust in Mr. Smith?"

"I do."

"But you don't think he'll start a fire?"

"I'll believe it when I see the wood blazing in the fireplace."

"It will blaze, since my master said so!"

"We'll see!"

Meanwhile, the sun had not yet reached the highest point in its arc above the horizon.

The exploration continued, marked by the discovery Harbert made of a tree whose fruits were edible. It was the pigeon pine, which produces excellent almonds, highly esteemed in the temperate regions of America and Europe. These almonds were perfectly ripe, and Harbert pointed them out to his two companions, who enjoyed them.

"Alright," said Pencroff, "some seaweed for bread, raw mussels for meat, and almonds for dessert, what a meal for people who don't have a single match in their pockets!"

"We shouldn't complain," Harbert replied.

"I'm not complaining, my boy," Pencroff said. "I'm just saying that there isn't much meat in this kind of meal!"

"Top saw something!..." Nab exclaimed, running towards a thicket where the dog had disappeared while barking.

Top's barks were mixed with strange grunts.

The sailor and Harbert followed Nab. If there was game there, now was not the time to discuss how to cook it, but rather how to catch it.

As soon as they entered the thicket, they saw Top wrestling with an animal he had by one ear. This quadruped was a kind of pig, about two and a half feet long, with a dark brown color but a lighter belly, having coarse and sparse fur, and its toes, pressed firmly on the ground, appeared to be joined by membranes.

Harbert thought he recognized it as a capybara, one of the largest examples of the rodent order.

However, the capybara was not struggling against the dog. It simply rolled its large eyes, deeply set in a thick layer of fat. Perhaps it was seeing humans for the first time.

Just then, Nab, securing his stick in hand, was about to knock out the rodent when it broke free from Top's jaws, who only managed to keep a piece of its ear, uttered a powerful grunt, charged at Harbert, knocked him over, and disappeared into the woods.

"Ah, the rascal!" Pencroff shouted.

Immediately, all three took off after Top, and just as they were about to catch up with him, the animal vanished beneath the waters of a large pond, shaded by tall ancient pines.

Nab, Harbert, and Pencroff stopped, motionless. Top had jumped into the water, but the capybara, hiding at the bottom of the pond, was no longer visible.

"Let's wait," said the young boy, "because it will come to the surface to breathe soon."

"Won't it drown?" Nab asked.

"No," replied Harbert, "since it has webbed feet, it's almost amphibious. But let's keep an eye on it."

Top stayed afloat. Pencroff and his two companions positioned themselves along the bank to cut off the capybara's escape route, as the dog searched for it while swimming on the surface of the pond.

Harbert was right. After a few minutes, the animal surfaced. Top leaped onto it, preventing it from diving again. A moment later, the capybara, dragged to the bank, was knocked out by a blow from Nab's stick.

"Hurrah!" Pencroff shouted, happily using his usual cry of triumph. "Just a glowing ember, and this rodent will be gobbled to the bone!"

Pencroff hoisted the capybara onto his shoulder and, judging by the position of the sun, it was around two o'clock, so he signaled it was time to head back.

Top's instincts proved useful to the hunters, who, thanks to the intelligent dog, were able to find their way back. Half an hour later, they arrived at the bend of the river.

As he had done the first time, Pencroff quickly set up a wood train, even though it seemed useless without a fire, and following the line of the water, they returned toward the Chimneys.

But the sailor hadn't taken fifty steps when he stopped, let out another tremendous hurrah, and, pointing at the corner of the cliff, shouted:

"Harbert! Nab! Look!"

A plume of smoke was rising and swirling above the rocks!

10

A short while later, the three hunters found themselves in front of a crackling fire. Cyrus Smith and the reporter were there. Pencroff looked at both of them in silence, holding his capybara.

"Well, yes, my brave fellow," the reporter exclaimed. "A fire, a real fire, which will perfectly roast this magnificent game we will feast on shortly!"

"But who lit it?" asked Pencroff.

"The sun!"

Gédéon Spilett's answer was accurate. It was the sun that had provided the heat that astonished Pencroff. The sailor couldn't believe his eyes, and he was so stunned that he didn't think to ask the engineer.

"Did you have a lens, sir?" Harbert asked Cyrus Smith.

"No, my child," he replied, "but I made one."

And he showed the apparatus he had used as a lens. It was simply the two glasses he had taken from the reporter's and his own watch. After filling them with water and making their edges sticky with a bit of clay, he had thus created a true lens, which, concentrating the sun's rays on some dry moss, ignited it.

The sailor inspected the device, then looked at the engineer without saying a word. His expression spoke volumes! If, for him, Cyrus Smith wasn't a god, he was certainly more than just a man. Finally, he found his voice and shouted:

"Note that down, Mr. Spilett, write that on your paper!"

"It's noted," the reporter replied.

Then, with Nab's help, the sailor prepared the spit, and the properly cleaned capybara soon roasted, just like a simple piglet, before a bright, crackling flame.

The Chimneys had become more comfortable again, not only because the corridors were warming by the fire, but also because the walls of stone and sand had been repaired.

Clearly, the engineer and his companion had made good use of the day. Cyrus Smith had almost fully regained his strength and had ventured up to the upper plateau. From there, his trained eye, accustomed to estimating heights and distances, lingered on the cone that he aimed to reach the next day. The mountain, located about six miles northwest, seemed to rise three thousand five hundred feet above sea level. Therefore, an observer stationed at its summit could likely see the horizon in a radius of at least fifty miles.

It was thus probable that Cyrus Smith would easily resolve the "continent or island" issue he deemed more pressing than all others.

They had a suitable supper. The capybara meat was declared excellent. The sargassum and pine nuts completed this meal, during which the engineer spoke little. He was preoccupied with plans for the next day. Once or twice, Pencroff suggested what should be done, but Cyrus Smith, who was clearly a methodical thinker, merely shook his head.

"Tomorrow," he repeated, "we will know what to do and will act accordingly."

After dinner, more wood was thrown onto the fire, and the occupants of the Chimneys, including faithful Top, fell into a deep sleep. No incident disturbed this peaceful night, and the next day, March 29, refreshed and alert, they woke up, ready to embark on this expedition that would determine their fate.

Everything was ready for departure. The remains of the capybara could feed Cyrus Smith and his companions for another twenty-four hours. Furthermore, they hoped to resupply on the way. Since the glasses had been returned to the engineer and reporter's watches, Pencroff burned a bit of cloth which was to serve as tinder. As for flint, it should not be lacking in these volcanic soils.

It was seven thirty in the morning when the explorers, armed with sticks, left the Chimneys. Following Pencroff's advice, it seemed wise to take the same path they had traversed through the forest, planning to return via another route. It was also the most direct way to reach the mountain. They turned south and followed the left bank of the river, which they abandoned at the point where it bent to the southwest. The trail, already broken under the green trees, was rediscovered, and at nine o'clock, Cyrus Smith and his companions reached the western edge of the forest.

The ground, until then rather flat, marshy at first, then dry and sandy, showed a slight incline that rose from the coast toward the interior. A few very skittish animals were spotted under the foliage. Top would startle them quickly, but his master immediately called him back, as it wasn't the time to pursue them. They would see later. The engineer was not one to let himself be distracted from his main goal. One could even assert that he wasn't observing the land itself, neither in its shape nor in its natural resources. His sole focus was on the mountain he intended to climb, and he headed straight for it.

At ten o'clock, they took a short break. Upon leaving the forest, the orographic system of the area came into view. The mountain was composed of two cones. The first, truncated at an height of about two thousand five hundred feet, was supported by whimsical foothills that seemed to branch out like the claws of a massive claw resting on the ground. Nestled between these foothills were narrow valleys, dotted with trees, whose last clusters rose to the truncation of the first cone. However, the vegetation appeared less dense on the part of the mountain facing northeast, and there were deep streaks visible, which must have been lava flows. On the first cone rested a second, slightly rounded at its summit, which stood a bit tilted. It looked like a vast round hat placed on the ear. It seemed made of bare earth, pierced in many places by reddish rocks.

It was the summit of this second cone that they needed to reach, and the ridge of the foothills would offer the best path to get there.

"We are on volcanic terrain," Cyrus Smith had said, and his companions, following him, began to gradually ascend the flank of a foothill that led, via a winding route and therefore more easily crossed, to the first plateau.

The ground showed many bulges where the plutonic forces had obviously convulsed it. Here and there were erratic boulders, numerous fragments of basalt, pumice, and obsidian. Clusters of conifers sprouted isolated, which, several hundred feet lower, in the depths of narrow gorges, formed dense thickets, almost impenetrable to sunlight.

During the first part of the ascent on the lower slopes, Harbert pointed out some prints that indicated the recent passage of large animals, carnivorous or otherwise.

"Those beasts may not willingly yield their territory to us," said Pencroff.

"Well," replied the reporter, who had hunted tigers in India and lions in Africa, "we'll see about getting rid of them. But for now, let's stay alert!"

However, they continued to rise little by little. The path was long, filled with detours and obstacles that could not be crossed directly. Sometimes the ground would suddenly drop away, and they found themselves at the edge of deep chasms that had to be skirted. Going back to follow a passable route meant wasting time and enduring exhaustion. At noon, when the small group halted for lunch at the foot of a large clump of fir trees, near a small stream that cascaded down, they were still halfway to the first plateau, which they would likely not reach until nightfall. From this point, the horizon of the sea expanded more widely; however, to the right, the gaze, halted by the sharp promontory to the southeast, could not determine if the coast abruptly connected to any background land. To the left, the line of sight stretched a few miles to the north; however, from the northwest point where the explorers stood, it was abruptly cut off by the ridge of a strangely shaped foothill, forming like a powerful buttress of the central cone. They could thus not yet catch any hints of the question that Cyrus Smith wanted to resolve.

At one o'clock, they resumed their ascent. They had to veer southwest and engage once again in somewhat thick underbrush. There, under the cover of trees, several pairs of galliform birds from the pheasant family fluttered about. They were "tragopans," adorned with a fleshy wattle hanging from their throats, and two thin cylindrical horns planted behind their eyes. Among these pairs, rooster-sized, the female was uniformly brown, while the male shone under its reddish plumage sprinkled with small white teardrops.Gédéon Spilett, with a well-aimed stone, killed one of those tragopans that Pencroff, hungry from the fresh air, looked at with some desire.

After leaving the thicket, the climbers helped each other up a steep slope of a hundred feet and reached a higher level, sparsely populated with trees, where the ground had a volcanic appearance. They then had to head back east, making zigzags to make the slopes more passable, as they were very steep, and everyone had to carefully choose where to place their foot. Nab and Harbert led the way, while Pencroff brought up the rear; between them were Cyrus and the reporter. The animals that roamed these heights—there were plenty of tracks—must belong to those sure-footed and nimble species like chamois or ibex. They saw a few, but that wasn't what Pencroff called them. At one moment, he exclaimed, "Sheep!"

They all stopped fifty paces from a half-dozen large animals, with strong horns curved backward and flattened at the tips, covered in a woolly coat hidden under long silky tawny fur.

These were not ordinary sheep, but a species commonly found in moun-tainous regions of temperate zones, which Harbert called mouflons.

"Do they have legs and chops?" asked the sailor.

"Yes," replied Harbert.

"Well, then they're sheep!" said Pencroff.

The animals, standing still among the basalt debris, looked on in astonishment as if seeing humans for the first time. Then, startled, they disappeared, bouncing away over the rocks.

"Goodbye!" shouted Pencroff in such a funny tone that Cyrus Smith, Gédéon Spilett, Harbert, and Nab couldn't help but laugh.

The ascent continued. On certain slopes, they frequently noticed traces of lava, strikingly marked. Small fumaroles sometimes cut through their path, and they had to navigate carefully around them. At several points, sulfur had deposited in crystalline formations amid materials that typically precede lava flows, irregularly grainy and heavily toasted pozzolana, whitish ash made of countless tiny feldspar crystals. As they neared the first plateau formed by the truncation of the lower cone, the challenges of climbing became quite pronounced. By around four o'clock, they had surpassed the tree line. Only a few gaunt, twisted pines remained, which must have had a tough life resisting the strong winds at that height.

Fortunately for the engineer and his companions, the weather was beautiful, and the atmosphere calm, as a strong breeze at three thousand feet would have hindered their progress. The clarity of the sky at the zenith was felt through the air's transparency. Perfect calm surrounded them. They could no longer see the sun, which was hidden behind the vast screen of the upper cone, obscuring the half-horizon of the west, and whose enormous shadow stretched down to the coast, growing longer as the radiant star sank in its diurnal course. Some vapors, more mist than clouds, began to appear in the east, colored by the sunlight's rays in spectral hues.

They were only five hundred feet away from the plateau where they wanted to camp for the night, but those five hundred feet increased by over two miles due to the zigzagging they had to do. The ground, in a way, seemed lacking under their feet. The slopes often had such a gentle incline that they would slide on the lava flows when the worn ridges didn't provide enough grip. Eventually, evening fell, and it was almost night when Cyrus Smith and his companions, very tired after a seven-hour climb, reached the plateau of the first cone.

They then discussed setting up camp and recovering their strength, starting with dinner and then sleeping. This second level of the mountain rested on a rocky base, where they quickly found shelter. Firewood wasn't abundant, but they could get fire from the moss and dry brush scattered across parts of the plateau. While the sailor prepared his hearth with stones arranged for that use, Nab and Harbert gathered firewood.

They soon returned with their load of brush. The flint was struck, and the burning fabric caught the sparks from the flint, and with Nab's breath, a crackling fire quickly developed, sheltered by the rocks. This fire was only meant to combat the chill of the night, and it wasn't used to cook the pheasant, which Nab reserved for the next day. The remains of the capybara and a few dozen pine nuts made up their dinner. It was not yet six-thirty when everything was finished.

Cyrus Smith then thought of exploring, in the dim light, this wide circular base supporting the upper cone of the mountain. Before resting, he wanted to see if they could circle the cone at its base, in case the steep sides made it inaccessible to reach the summit. This question preoccupied him, as it was possible that on the side where the peak sloped, meaning north, the plateau might not be passable. If they couldn't reach the mountain's summit on one side, and if they couldn't go around the base of the cone on the other, examining the western part of the land would be impossible, and the purpose of their ascent would be partially unfulfilled.

So, the engineer, disregarding his fatigue and leaving Pencroff and Nab to set up their sleeping arrangements while Gédéon Spilett noted the day's events, began to follow the circular rim of the plateau heading north. Harbert accompanied him.

The night was fair and calm, and the darkness was still shallow. Cyrus Smith and the young boy walked side by side, silently. In certain places, the plateau opened wide before them, allowing them to pass unhindered. In others, blocked by debris, it offered only a narrow path where two people couldn't walk side by side. After walking for twenty minutes, Cyrus Smith and Harbert had to stop. From that point, the slopes of the two cones were just about level. There was no longer a ledge separating the two parts of the mountain. Going around on slopes inclined at nearly seventy degrees became impractical.

However, although the engineer and the young boy had to give up on following a circular path, they then had the chance to continue directly up the cone. Indeed, before them opened a deep breach in the mass. It was the opening of the upper crater, the neck, through which the liquid eruptive materials escaped when the volcano was still active. The hardened lava and crusty scoria formed a natural staircase with broad steps that would make reaching the summit easier. A glance was enough for Cyrus Smith to recognize this layout, and without hesitation, followed by the young boy, he entered the enormous crevice amid the growing darkness.

They still had a thousand feet to climb. Would the inner slopes of the crater be practical? They would see. The engineer would continue his ascent as long as he wasn't stopped. Fortunately, those slopes, very long and winding, formed a wide screw-like path inside the volcano, favoring upward movement.

As for the volcano itself, there was no doubt it was completely extinct. Not a wisp of smoke escaped from its flanks. No flame flickered in the deep cavities. No rumbling, murmur, or tremor emerged from this dark pit, which perhaps extended down to the Earth's core. The atmosphere inside this crater was not saturated with any sulfurous vapors. It was more than the sleep of a volcano; it was its complete extinction.

Cyrus Smith's attempt should succeed. Gradually, as Harbert and he ascended the internal walls, they saw the crater widen above their heads. The radius of that circular portion of the sky, framed by the edges of the cone, increased considerably. With every step, it seemed, new stars entered their field of view. The magnificent constellations of this southern sky shone brightly. At the zenith, the splendid Antares of the Scorpion glowed with pure brilliance, and nearby, the Centauri B, which is believed to be the nearest star to Earth. Then, as the crater expanded, Fomalhaut of the Fish and the Southern Triangle appeared, and finally, almost at the Antarctic pole, the sparkling Southern Cross, which replaces the North Star of the northern hemisphere.

It was close to eight o'clock when Cyrus Smith and Harbert set foot on the upper ridge of the mountain, at the top of the cone.

The darkness was complete then, preventing their sight from stretching two miles. Did the sea surround this unknown land, or was this land connected, to the west, to some continent of the Pacific? It was still impossible to tell. To the west, a band of clouds, sharply outlined on the horizon, deepened the darkness, and the eye could not discern whether the sky and water merged along a single circular line.

But at one point on the horizon, a faint light suddenly appeared, slowly descending as the cloud rose toward the zenith.

It was the delicate crescent of the moon, already near disappearance. But its light was enough to clearly outline the horizontal line, now detached from the cloud, and the engineer saw its trembling image reflected for a moment on a liquid surface.

Cyrus Smith took the young boy's hand and, in a serious voice, said, "An island!" just as the moonlight extinguished in the waves.

🏵 II 🏵

Half an hour later, Cyrus Smith and Harbert were back at the camp. The engineer limited himself to telling his companions that the land on which chance had thrown them was an island, and that they would make plans the next day. Then, everyone settled in as best as they could to sleep, and in this basalt hole, at a height of two thousand five hundred feet above sea level, on a peaceful night, "the islanders" enjoyed a deep rest.

The next day, March 30, after a light breakfast featuring the roasted tragopan, the engineer wanted to climb back up to the volcano's summit to observe closely the island where he and his crew were now trapped, perhaps for life, if this island were far from any land or if it wasn't on the shipping routes that visited the Pacific archipelagos. This time, his companions followed him on this new exploration. They too wanted to see this island on which they would depend for all their needs.

It must have been around seven in the morning when Cyrus Smith, Harbert, Pencroff, Gédéon Spilett, and Nab left the campsite. None of them seemed worried about their situation. They had faith in themselves, certainly, but it should be noted that the basis of this faith was not the same for Cyrus Smith as it was for his companions.

The engineer had confidence because he felt capable of extracting everything necessary for the life of his companions and himself from this wild nature, and they feared nothing precisely because Cyrus Smith was with them. This distinction is understandable. Pencroff, especially, since the incident of the rekindled fire, wouldn't have despaired for a moment, even if he found himself on a bare rock, as long as the engineer was there with him.

"Bah!" he said, "we left Richmond without permission from the authorities! It would be quite the devil if we couldn't manage to leave a place where no one will certainly hold us back!"

Cyrus Smith followed the same path as the day before. They went around the cone via the plateau that formed a shoulder until they reached the mouth of the enormous crack.

The weather was magnificent. The sun rose in a clear sky and bathed the eastern flank of the mountain in its rays.

They approached the crater. It was just as the engineer had recognized it in the shadow, that is to say, a vast funnel that widened to a height of a thousand feet above the plateau. At the bottom of the crevice, broad and thick lava flows wound down the flanks of the mountain and marked the route of erup-tive materials to the lower valleys that crisscrossed the northern part of the island.

The interior of the crater, whose incline did not exceed thirty-five to forty degrees, posed no difficulties or obstacles to climbing.

They noticed traces of very ancient lava, which probably flowed from the summit of the cone before this lateral crevice opened a new path for it.

As for the volcanic chimney that connected the underground layers to the crater, its depth could not be estimated by sight, as it disappeared into darkness. But there was no doubt about the complete extinction of the volcano.

Before eight o'clock, Cyrus Smith and his companions assembled at the summit of the crater, on a conical swell that bulged the northern edge.

"The sea! The sea everywhere!" they exclaimed, as if their lips could not hold back the word that made them islanders.

The sea, indeed, the vast circular body of water surrounding them! Perhaps, as Cyrus Smith ascended to the summit of the cone, he had hoped to discover some coast, some nearby island that he hadn't been able to see the day before during the darkness. But nothing appeared to the very edge of the horizon, that is, across more than fifty miles. No land in sight. Not a sail. All this vast-ness was deserted, and the island occupied the center of a circumference that seemed infinite. The engineer and his companions, silent and still, scanned all points of the Ocean with their eyes for several minutes. They searched the Ocean with their gaze up to its farthest limits. But Pencroff, who had an exceptional power of sight, saw nothing, and surely, if land had risen on the horizon, even if it had only appeared as an elusive mist, the sailor would undoubtedly have recognized it, as nature had given him two true telescopes set beneath his brow! From the Ocean, their gazes returned to the island below them, and the first question raised was by Gédéon Spilett, who asked, "What could be the size of this island?"

Truly, it did not seem large in the midst of this immense Ocean.

Cyrus Smith thought for a few moments; he carefully observed the island's perimeter, taking into account his elevated position; then he said:

"My friends, I don't believe I'm mistaken in estimating the island's coastline to be over a hundred miles long."

"And consequently, its area?...

"It's hard to assess," replied the engineer, "because its shape is too whimsically cut."

If Cyrus Smith was not mistaken in his assessment, the island was approximately the size of Malta or Zante in the Mediterranean; but it was much more irregular and less rich in caps, promontories, points, bays, inlets, or creeks. Its shape, truly strange, startled the eye, and when Gédéon Spilett, at the engineer's suggestion, sketched its outlines, it turned out to resemble some fantastic beast, a kind of monstrous pteropod, that had been sleeping on the surface of the Pacific.

Here is, indeed, the exact configuration of this island, which is important to reveal, and whose map was immediately drafted by the reporter with sufficient precision.

The eastern portion of the coastline, that is to say the one where the castaways had landed, widened greatly and bordered a vast bay, ending in the southeast with a sharp cape, hidden from Pencroff during his first exploration by a point. To the northeast, two other capes closed the bay, and between them was a narrow gulf that resembled the gaping jaw of some formidable shark.

From the northeast to the northwest, the coast rounded like the flattened skull of a beast, rising to form a sort of bulge that did not give a very defined shape to this part of the island, whose center was occupied by a volcanic mountain. From this point, the coastline ran fairly evenly north and south, carved, for two-thirds of its perimeter, by a narrow creek, from which it ended in a long tail, resembling the tail of a gigantic alligator.

This tail formed a true peninsula that extended over thirty miles into the sea, starting from the southeast cape of the island already mentioned, and it rounded off into a broad, open harbor, traced by the lower coastline of this strangely shaped land.

In its narrowest width, that is to say between the Chimneys and the creek on the corresponding western coast, the island measured only ten miles; but its greatest length, from the northeast jaw to the end of the southwest tail, was no less than thirty miles.

As for the interior of the island, its general appearance was as follows: very wooded throughout its southern portion from the mountain to the coastline, it was arid and sandy in the northern part. Between the volcano and the east coast, Cyrus Smith and his companions were quite surprised to see a lake, framed by its border of green trees, which they had not suspected existed. From this height, the lake seemed to be at the same level as the sea, but upon reflection, the engineer explained to his companions that the altitude of this small body of water must be three hundred feet, as the plateau that served as its basin was merely a continuation of that of the coast.

"So it's a freshwater lake?" asked Pencroff.

"Necessarily," replied the engineer, "as it must be fed by waters flowing down from the mountain."

"I see a small river flowing into it," said Harbert, pointing to a narrow stream that must have its source in the western foothills.

"Indeed," replied Cyrus Smith, "and since this stream feeds the lake, it is likely that there is an overflow drain on the sea side through which excess water escapes. We'll check on that when we return."

This small, quite winding stream and the already recognized river made up the hydrographic system, or at least that's how it developed in the explorers' eyes. However, it was possible that beneath the masses of trees that made up two-thirds of the island's vast forest, other streams flowed toward the sea. One had to assume so, given how fertile this region appeared and rich with the most magnificent samples of temperate zone flora. As for the northern part, there was no sign of flowing water; perhaps stagnant water in the marshy northeastern area, but that was all; overall, dunes, sand, a markedly arid landscape contrasted sharply with the richness of the soil in its larger expanse.

The volcano did not occupy the central part of the island. Instead, it arose in the northwest region and seemed to mark the boundary between the two zones. To the southwest, south, and southeast, the lower slopes disappeared under masses of greenery. To the north, however, one could follow their branches, which faded away into the sandy plains. It was also on this side that during eruptions, the flows had carved a path, and a wide lava highway extended all the way to this narrow jaw that formed the northeast gulf.

Cyrus Smith and his companions remained for an hour atop the mountain. The island unfolded beneath their gaze like a relief map with its varied hues, greens for the forests, yellows for the sands, blues for the waters. They took in the entirety of it, and the land hidden beneath the vast greenery, the thalweg of the shadowy valleys, the insides of the narrow gorges carved at the foot of the volcano, were the only parts that escaped their investigations.

A serious question remained to be solved that would significantly influence the future of the castaways.

Was the island inhabited?

It was the reporter who raised this question, to which it seemed they could already respond negatively, after the meticulous examination they had just performed of the various regions of the island.

Nowhere did they see the work of human hands. Not a cluster of huts, not a solitary cabin, not a fishing spot on the coast. No smoke rose in the air to betray the presence of man. True, a distance of about thirty miles separated the observers from the farthest points, that is to say, from the tail projecting to the southwest, and it would have been difficult, even for Pencroff's keen eyes, to discover a home there. One could also not lift the curtain of greenery that covered three-quarters of the island and see whether it harbored a village or not.

But generally, islanders in these narrow spaces emerging from the waves of the Pacific prefer to live on the coastline, and the coastline appeared to be absolutely deserted.

Until a more complete exploration, it could thus be assumed that the island was uninhabited.

But was it at least temporarily frequented by the natives of the neighboring islands? To this question, it was difficult to respond. No land appeared within a radius of about fifty miles. But fifty miles can be easily crossed, either by Malay praus or by large Polynesian canoes. Everything depended on the island's location, its isolation in the Pacific, or its proximity to the archipelagos.

Would Cyrus Smith later be able to determine his position in latitude and longitude without instruments? It would be difficult. In doubt, it was therefore wise to take certain precautions against a possible descent by neighboring natives.

The exploration of the island was completed, its configuration determined, its relief measured, its extent calculated, its hydrography and orography recognized. The layout of the forests and plains had been generally mapped out on the reporter's plan. All that was left was to descend the mountain slopes and to explore the land from the triple perspective of its mineral, vegetable, and animal resources.

But before giving his companions the signal to depart, Cyrus Smith told them in a calm and serious voice:

"Here, my friends, is the narrow piece of land on which the hand of the Almighty has thrown us. This is where we will live, perhaps for a long time. Perhaps also, unexpected help will come our way if a ship happens to pass by... I say 'happens,' because this island is not very significant; it doesn't even offer a port that could serve as a stop for ships, and it is to be feared that it is located outside the usual routes, that is to say, too far south for ships that visit the Pacific archipelagos, too far north for those headed to Australia rounding Cape Horn. I won't hide anything from you about the situation...

— And you're right, my dear Cyrus, replied the reporter promptly. You have made it clear to men. They trust you, and you can count on them. — Isn't that so, my friends?

— I will obey you in everything, Mr. Cyrus, said Harbert, grasping the engineer's hand.

— My master, now and always! cried Nab.

— As for me, said the sailor, may I lose my name if I sulk about the task, and if you will have it, Mr. Smith, we will make this island a little America! We will build cities, establish railways, set up telegraphs, and one fine day, when it is well transformed, well arranged, well civilized, we will offer it to the government of the Union! Only, I ask one thing.

— What is it? replied the reporter.

— It is to no longer consider us as castaways, but as colonists who have come here to colonize!"

Cyrus Smith could not help but smile, and the sailor's proposal was adopted. Then he thanked his companions and added that he counted on their energy and the help of heaven.

"Well then! Let's head for the Chimneys!" shouted Pencroff.

"A moment, my friends," replied the engineer, "I think it's good to give this island a name, as well as the capes, promontories, and waterways we have before us.

— Very good, said the reporter. This will simplify the instructions we may need to give or follow in the future.

— Indeed, replied the sailor, it's already something to be able to say where one is going and where one is coming from. At least, it gives the impression of being somewhere.

— The Chimneys, for example, said Harbert.

— Exactly! replied Pencroff. That name is already more convenient, and it came to me naturally. Shall we keep that name for our first camp, Mr. Cyrus?

— Yes, Pencroff, since you have given it that name.

— Good, as for the others, it will be easy, continued the sailor, who was getting into the spirit. Let's give them names like the Robinsons did, whose story Harbert has read to me more than once: "the Providence Bay," the "sperm whale point," the "cap of the mistaken Hope!"...

— Or rather the names of Mr. Smith, replied Harbert, of Mr. Spilett, of Nab!...

— My name! exclaimed Nab, showing his dazzling white teeth.

— Why not? replied Pencroff. "Port Nab" would sound very good! And "Cape Gédéon..."

— I'd prefer names taken from our country, replied the reporter, that would remind us of America.

— Yes, for the main ones, said Cyrus Smith then, for those of the bays or seas, I gladly agree. Let's give this vast bay in the east the name Union Bay, for example, to this wide indentation in the south the name Washington Bay, to the mountain that supports us at this moment the name Franklin Mountain, to the lake stretching beneath our gaze the name Grant Lake, nothing better, my friends. These names will remind us of our country and those great citizens who honored it; but for rivers, gulfs, capes, and promontories, which we can see from the top of this mountain, let's choose names that better reflect their particular configurations. They will stick better in our minds and will also be more practical. The shape of the island is strange enough that we won't be at a loss to imagine fitting names. As for the waterways we don't know yet, the various parts of the forest we will explore later, the creeks that will be discovered afterward, we will name them as they present themselves to us. What do you think, my friends?"

The engineer's proposal was unanimously accepted by his companions. The island lay before them like a map unfolded, and there was only one name to give to all its indents and projections, as well as to all its reliefs. Gédéon Spilett would inscribe them as they went, and the island's geographical nomenclature would be definitively adopted.

First, they named Union Bay, Washington Bay, and Franklin Mountain, the two bays and the mountain, just as the engineer had suggested.

"Now, said the reporter, for this peninsula that juts out to the southwest of the island, I would propose to name it Serpentine Peninsula, and call the curved tail ending it Reptile Cape, as it truly resembles a reptile's tail.

— Adopted, said the engineer.

— Now, said Harbert, this other end of the island, this gulf that resembles so strangely an open jaw, let's call it Shark Gulf.

— Well found! shouted Pencroff, and we will complete the image by naming the two parts of the jaw Mandible Cape.

— But there are two capes, the reporter pointed out.

— Well, replied Pencroff, we will have Mandible Cape North and Mandible Cape South.

— They are noted down, replied Gédéon Spilett.

— We need to name the point at the southeastern tip of the island, said Pencroff.

— That is to say the tip of Union Bay? replied Harbert.

— Claw Cape! shouted Nab immediately, who also wanted to be the godfather of some part of his domain.

And indeed, Nab had found an excellent name, as this cape truly represented the powerful claw of the fantastic creature that this strangely drawn island depicted.

Pencroff was delighted with how things were turning out, and the imaginations, a bit overly excited, soon gave:By the river that provided drinking water to the settlers, near which the balloon had dropped them, the name of Mercy —a true expression of gratitude to Providence; on the islet where the castaways first landed, the name of the Islet of Safety; on the plateau crowning the high granite wall above the Chimneys, where the view embraced the vast bay, the name of Great View Plateau; lastly, to the entire mass of impenetrable woods that covered the Serpentine peninsula, the name of Far-West Forests.

The naming of the visible and known parts of the island was thus complete, and later it would be filled in as new discoveries were made.

As for the orientation of the island, the engineer had roughly determined it by the height and position of the sun, placing the Union Bay and the whole Great View Plateau to the east. But the next day, by taking the exact time of sunrise and sunset and marking its position at half-time between the two, he planned to precisely fix the north of the island since, due to its location in the southern hemisphere, the sun, at the moment of its culmination, passed north and not south, as it seems to do for places in the northern hemisphere.

Everything was thus finished, and the settlers had only to descend Mount Franklin to return to the Chimneys when Pencroff exclaimed:

"Well! We are some real scatterbrains!

— Why's that? asked Gideon Spilett, who had closed his notebook and was getting ready to leave.

— And our island? What! We forgot to name it?"

Harbert was about to suggest naming it after the engineer, and all his companions would have cheered, when Cyrus Smith simply said:

"Let's call it after a great citizen, my friends, one who is now fighting to defend the unity of the American republic! Let's call it Lincoln Island!"

Three cheers were the response to the engineer's suggestion.

And that evening, before falling asleep, the new settlers talked about their distant country; they spoke of the terrible war staining it with blood; they couldn't doubt that the South would soon be subdued and that the North's cause, the cause of justice, would triumph, thanks to Grant, thanks to Lincoln!

Now, this was happening on March 30, 1865, and they had no idea that, sixteen days later, a horrific crime would be committed in Washington, and that on Good Friday, Abraham Lincoln would fall to the bullet of a fanatic.

12

The settlers of Lincoln Island took one last look around them, they went around the crater by its narrow ridge, and half an hour later, they had descended to the first plateau, to their campsite for the night.

Pencroff thought it was lunchtime, and this led to a discussion on setting the two watches of Cyrus Smith and the reporter.

It is known that Gideon Spilett's watch had been spared by saltwater since the reporter had been thrown first onto the sand, out of reach of the waves. It was an instrument made under excellent conditions, a real pocket chronometer, which Gideon Spilett had never forgotten to wind up carefully every day.

As for the engineer's watch, it had necessarily stopped during the time Cyrus Smith spent in the dunes.

The engineer therefore wound it up and, estimating by the height of the sun that it should be around nine o'clock in the morning, set his watch to that hour.

Gideon Spilett was about to follow suit when the engineer stopped him with his hand and said:

"No, my dear Spilett, wait. You've kept the time of Richmond, haven't you?

— Yes, Cyrus.

— Therefore, your watch is set to the meridian of that city, which is about the same as that of Washington?

— Of course.

— Well then, keep it that way. Just be sure to wind it very accurately, but don't touch the hands. It might be useful to us.

— What good will it do?" thought the sailor.

They ate, and so well that their stock of game and almonds was completely used up. But Pencroff was not at all worried. They would restock along the way. Top, whose share had been quite small, would surely find some new game under the cover of the bushes. Moreover, the sailor was thinking about simply asking the engineer to make some gunpowder, one or two hunting rifles, and he thought that wouldn't be a problem. As they left the plateau, Cyrus Smith proposed to his companions to take a new route to return to the Chimneys. He wanted to explore Grant Lake, so beautifully framed by its border of trees. They thus followed the ridge of one of the foothills, between which the creek that fed it likely originated. As they talked, the settlers now only used the proper names they had just chosen, which greatly facilitated the exchange of their ideas. Harbert and Pencroff—one young and the other a bit childish— were delighted, and while walking, the sailor said:

"Hey! Harbert! Look how well this is going! There's no way to get lost, my boy, because whether we follow the way to Grant Lake or join the Mercy through the Far-West woods, we'll surely arrive at the Great View Plateau, and consequently, to the Union Bay!"

It had been agreed that, without forming a compact group, the settlers would not stray too far from each other. Certainly, some dangerous animals lived in these thick island forests, and it was wise to stay on guard. Generally, Pencroff, Harbert, and Nab walked ahead, preceded by Top, who searched every nook. The reporter and the engineer walked together, Gideon Spilett ready to note any incident, the engineer mostly silent, only diverging from his path to gather sometimes one thing or another, mineral or plant substances, which he put in his pocket without making any remarks.

"What the devil is he picking up?" murmured Pencroff. "I look hard, and I see nothing worth bending down for!"

By ten o'clock, the small group was descending the last slopes of Mount Franklin. The ground was still only scattered with bushes and a few trees. They walked on a yellowish, scorched earth forming a plain about a mile long, which preceded the edge of the woods. Rough chunks of basalt, which, according to Bischof's studies, required three hundred and fifty million years to cool, littered the plain, very uneven in some places. However, there was no trace of the lava flows, which had particularly spilled out over the northern slopes.

Cyrus Smith believed he could reach, without incident, the course of the creek, which, according to him, should flow under the trees at the edge of the plain when he saw Harbert rush back while Nab and the sailor hid behind the rocks.

"What's the matter, my boy?" asked Gideon Spilett.

"A smoke," answered Harbert. "We saw smoke rising between the rocks, a hundred paces from us."

"Men in this area?" exclaimed the reporter.

"Let's avoid showing ourselves until we know who we're dealing with," replied Cyrus Smith. "I'm more afraid of natives, if there are any on this island, than I want them to be here. Where's Top?

— Top is ahead.

— And he's not barking?

— No.

— That's strange. Nevertheless, let's try to call him back."

In a few moments, the engineer, Gideon Spilett, and Harbert had rejoined their two companions, and like them, they slipped behind some basalt debris. From there, they clearly saw smoke swirling and rising into the air, with a very characteristic yellowish color.

Top, called back by a slight whistle from his master, returned, and the latter, signaling his companions to wait for him, slipped between the rocks.

The settlers stood still, waiting anxiously for the outcome of this exploration when an call from Cyrus Smith had them rushing over. They immediately joined him and were first struck by the unpleasant smell that permeated the atmosphere.

This smell, easily recognizable, had been enough for the engineer to guess what this smoke was that had initially worried him, and not without reason.

"This fire, or rather this smoke, is solely from nature. There's just a sulfur spring here, which will help us effectively treat our laryngitis.

— Good! exclaimed Pencroff. What a pity I'm not having a cold!"

The settlers then moved toward the source of the smoke. There, they saw a sodium-sulfur spring, flowing quite abundantly between the rocks, whose waters gave off a strong smell of hydrogen sulfide after absorbing oxygen from the air.

Cyrus Smith, dipping his hand in it, found the water to be smooth to the touch. He tasted it and found its flavor to be a bit sweet. As for the temperature, he estimated it to be around ninety-five degrees Fahrenheit (35 degrees Celsius). And when Harbert asked him how he based that estimation:

"Simply, my child," he said, "because when I put my hand in this water, I felt no sensation of cold or heat. Therefore, it is the same temperature as the human body, which is around ninety-five degrees."

Then, since the sulfur spring had no current use, the settlers headed towards the thick edge of the forest, which spread out a few hundred paces away.

There, as had been presumed, the creek carried its clear and lively waters between high banks of red earth, whose color revealed the presence of iron oxide. This color immediately led to naming this watercourse Creek-Red.

It was only a wide creek, deep and clear, formed by mountain waters, half stream, half torrent, here flowing peacefully over sand, there roaring over rocky heads or cascading down, running toward the lake over a length of a mile and a half and a variable width of thirty to forty feet. Its waters were sweet, which suggested that those of the lake were too. A fortunate circumstance in case they found a more suitable dwelling along its banks than the Chimneys.

As for the trees that shaded the creek banks a few hundred feet downstream, most belonged to the species abundant in the temperate zone of Australia or Tasmania, and no longer to those conifers that dotted the part of the island already explored a few miles from the Great View Plateau. At this time of year, at the beginning of April, which represents October in this hemisphere, that is, the start of autumn, the foliage was still present. They were particularly casuarinas and eucalyptus, some of which would provide next spring a sweet manna quite similar to the manna of the East. Clusters of Australian cedars also rose in the clearings, covered with that tall grass known as "tussock" in New Holland; but the coconut palm, so abundant in the Pacific islands, seemed to be missing from the island, whose latitude was likely too low.

"What a shame!" said Harbert, "such a useful tree with such beautiful nuts!"

As for the birds, they were abundant among the somewhat skimpy branches of the eucalyptus and casuarinas, which did not hinder the spread of their wings. Black, white, or gray cockatoos, parrots and parakeets, with plumage shaded in all colors, "kings," in bright green and crowned in red, blue lorikeets and "blues-mountains," seemed to only appear through a prism and flitted about in a deafening chatter.

Suddenly, a strange concert of discordant voices echoed from within a thicket. The settlers heard successively the singing of birds, the cries of quadrupeds, and a sort of clapping that they might have believed came from the lips of a native. Nab and Harbert had dashed toward the bush, forgetting the principles of the most elementary caution. Fortunately, there were neither fierce beasts nor dangerous natives there, but simply half a dozen of those mocking and singing birds, which were recognized to be "mountain pheasants." A few carefully delivered blows with a stick ended the scene of imitation, which provided excellent game for their evening dinner.

Harbert also spotted magnificent pigeons, with bronze wings, some topped with a superb crest, others draped in green, like their counterparts from Port Macquarie; but it was impossible to catch them, just as it was for the crows and magpies, which flew away in flocks. A shot with small shot would have made a heap of these birds, but the hunters were still limited, weapons of thrown were reduced to stones, and weapons of pole to sticks, and these primitive tools were still very insufficient.

Their insufficiency was made even clearer when a troop of quadrupeds, hopping, bouncing, making jumps of thirty feet, true flying mammals, fled over the bushes so swiftly and at such heights that one might have thought they were leaping from one tree to another like squirrels.

"Kangaroos!" cried Harbert.

"And can you eat that?" replied Pencroff.

"Prepared in stew, it's as good as the best venison!" responded the reporter..."

Gideon Spilett had not finished this exciting sentence when the sailor, followed by Nab and Harbert, had launched himself on the tracks of the kangaroos. Cyrus Smith called them back, in vain. But it must have been in vain also that the hunters pursued this elastic game, which bounced away like a ball. After five minutes of running, they were out of breath, and the band had disappeared into the thicket.

Top had not been more successful than his masters.

"Mr. Cyrus," said Pencroff, when the engineer and the reporter had caught up with him, "Mr. Cyrus, you see it's essential to make rifles. Will that be possible?

— Maybe, replied the engineer, but we will start by making bows and arrows, and I doubt you won't become as skilled in using them as Australian hunters.

— Arrows, bows!" said Pencroff with a disdainful grimace. "That's good for children!

— Don't be so proud, my friend Pencroff," replied the reporter. "Bows and arrows have been enough for centuries to stain the world with blood. Gunpowder is only yesterday, and war is as old as the human race—unfortunately!

— That's true, Mr. Spilett," replied the sailor, "and I often speak too hastily. You must excuse me!"

However, Harbert, engrossed in his favorite science, natural history, turned back to the kangaroos, saying:"Anyway, we encountered the toughest kind to catch. They were giants with long gray fur; but, if I'm not mistaken, there are black and red kangaroos, rock kangaroos, and rat kangaroos that are easier to catch. There are about a dozen species..."

— Harbert, the sailor replied solemnly, for me there's only one kind of kangaroo, the 'skewered kangaroo,' and that's precisely the one we won't have for dinner tonight!"

Everyone couldn't help but laugh at the new classification of Master Pencroff. The good sailor didn't hide his disappointment at having to settle for singing pheasants for dinner; however, fortune was about to be kind to him again. Indeed, Top, who knew his interests were at stake, was sniffing around enthusiastically with a fierce appetite. It was likely that if some piece of game fell into his path, there would be little left for the hunters, and that Top was hunting for himself; but Nab kept an eye on him, and he was right to do so.

Around three o'clock, the dog disappeared into the bushes, and soon deep growls indicated that he was engaged with some animal.

Nab rushed in and indeed saw Top greedily devouring a quadruped, which, ten seconds later, would have been impossible to identify in Top's stomach. But, very fortunately, the dog had stumbled upon a litter; he had made a triple catch, and two other rodents—belonging to that order—lay strangled on the ground.

Nab returned triumphantly, holding one of those rodents in each hand, which was larger than a hare. Their yellow fur was mixed with greenish spots, and their tails were barely formed. Citizens from the Union couldn't hesitate to give these rodents their proper name.

They were "maras," a type of agouti, slightly larger than their tropical counterparts, true American rabbits, with long ears and jaws equipped on each side with five molars, which is exactly what distinguishes them from agoutis.

"Hooray!" exclaimed Pencroff. "The roast is here! And now, we can go home!"

The march, temporarily interrupted, resumed. The Red Creek still rolled its clear waters under the arch of the casuarinas, banksias, and giant gum trees. Beautiful lilies rose to a height of twenty feet.

Other tree species, unknown to the young naturalist, leaned over the stream, which murmured beneath these green canopies.

Meanwhile, the watercourse visibly widened, and Cyrus Smith began to believe that they would soon reach its mouth. Indeed, after emerging from a thick cluster of fine trees, it suddenly appeared.

The explorers had arrived on the western shore of Lake Grant. The spot was worth looking at. This stretch of water, about seven miles in circumference and covering two hundred fifty acres, rested among a fringe of varied trees. To the east, through a picturesque curtain of greenery elevated in places, a sparkling horizon of sea appeared. To the north, the lake traced a gently concave curve, contrasting with the sharp design of its lower point. Numerous aquatic birds frequented the shores of this little Ontario, whose "thousand islands" of its American namesake were represented by a rock that emerged from its surface, a few hundred feet from the southern shore. There, various pairs of kingfishers lived in common, perched on some rock, grave, still, waiting for fish to pass by, then leaping, diving with a sharp cry, and reappearing with their catch in beak. Elsewhere, on the shores and on the islet, wild ducks, pelicans, moorhens, red-bills, and philodendrons, equipped with a brush-shaped tongue, strutted around, along with one or two specimens of those splendid menures, whose tail expands like the graceful columns of a lyre.

As for the waters of the lake, they were fresh, clear, a bit dark, and from certain bubbling and concentric circles crossing at the surface, one could not doubt that they were teeming with fish.

"It's truly beautiful! this lake," said Gideon Spilett. "One could live by its shores!"

"We will live there!" replied Cyrus Smith.

The colonists, wanting to return to the Chimneys by the shortest route, descended to the angle formed in the south by the junction of the shores of the lake. They struggled to carve a path through the thickets and brush that man's hand had never yet cleared, and they made their way towards the coast, aiming to arrive to the north of the Great View plateau. Two miles were crossed in this direction, and then, after the last screen of trees, the plateau appeared, covered with thick grass, and beyond, the infinite sea.

To return to the Chimneys, it was enough to cross the plateau diagonally over a mile and descend to the elbow formed by the first bend of the Mercy. However, the engineer wanted to find out how and where the overflow of the lake's waters drained, and the exploration was extended under the trees for a mile and a half towards the north. It was likely, in fact, that an outlet existed somewhere, and probably through a gap in the granite. This lake was, after all, just a huge basin that had gradually filled from the creek, and it had to overflow into the sea through some fall. If this was the case, the engineer thought it might be possible to make use of this fall and harness its power, which was currently being wasted without benefit to anyone. They thus continued to follow the shores of Lake Grant, climbing the plateau; but, after making another mile in this direction, Cyrus Smith had not been able to discover the outlet, which must exist.

It was half past four at that time. The dinner preparations required the colonists to return to their home. The small group retraced its steps, and, along the left bank of the Mercy, Cyrus Smith and his companions arrived at the Chimneys.

There, a fire was lit, and Nab and Pencroff, naturally assigned the roles of cooks, one in his capacity as a Black man, the other as a sailor, swiftly prepared grilled agoutis, which were greatly appreciated.

Once the meal was finished, as everyone was about to succumb to sleep, Cyrus Smith took out of his pocket small samples of different minerals and simply said: "My friends, this is iron ore, this is pyrite, this is clay, this is lime, this is coal. Here's what nature provides us, and here's her contribution to our common work! — tomorrow, it's our turn!"

13

"Well, Mr. Cyrus, where do we start?" asked Pencroff the next morning to the engineer.

"From the beginning," replied Cyrus Smith.

And indeed, it was from the "beginning" that these colonists would have to start. They didn't even have the tools necessary to make tools, and they weren't even in the same conditions as nature, which, "having time, economizes effort." They lacked time since they had to immediately meet their needs for existence, and while they had nothing to invent thanks to the experience they had gained, they had everything to manufacture.

Their iron, their steel were still in ore form, their pottery in clay, their linen and clothes in textile materials.

It should also be noted that these colonists were "men" in the beautiful and powerful sense of the word. Engineer Smith couldn't have been assisted by more intelligent companions, nor with more dedication and zeal. He had questioned them. He knew their abilities.

Gideon Spilett, a highly talented reporter, having learned everything to be able to speak on everything, would contribute greatly with both his head and his hands to colonizing the island. He would shy away from no task, and as a passionate hunter, he would make a profession out of what had only been a pastime until now.

Harbert, brave boy, already remarkably educated in the natural sciences, would provide serious support to the common cause.

Nab was the personification of dedication. Handy, intelligent, tireless, strong, with iron health, he had some knowledge of blacksmith work and could be very useful to the colony.

As for Pencroff, he had been a sailor on all oceans, a carpenter in the construction yards of Brooklyn, a tailor's assistant on state ships, a gardener, and a farmer during his leave, etc., and like sailors, good at everything, he knew how to do anything.

It would have been truly difficult to gather five men better suited to fight against fate, more assured of triumphing over it.

"From the beginning," Cyrus Smith had said. Now, this beginning the engineer spoke of was the construction of a device that could be used to transform natural substances. We know the role that heat plays in these transformations. Therefore, the fuel, whether wood or coal, was immediately usable. So, it was a matter of building a furnace to utilize it.

"What use is this furnace?" asked Pencroff.

"To make the pottery we need," replied Cyrus Smith.

"And how will we make the furnace?"

"With bricks."

"And the bricks?"

"With clay. On we go, my friends. To avoid transporting, we will set up our workshop right where the production is. Nab will bring provisions, and there will be no shortage of fuel for cooking the food.

— No," replied the reporter, "but what if the food runs out due to a lack of hunting tools?"

"Ah! if only we had a knife!" cried the sailor.

"Well?" asked Cyrus Smith.

"Well! I could quickly make a bow and arrows, and game would abound at the table!

— Yes, a knife, a sharp blade..." said the engineer, as if speaking to himself.

At that moment, his gaze turned to Top, who was wandering back and forth on the shore.

Suddenly, Cyrus Smith's expression brightened.

"Top, here!" he called.

The dog rushed at his master's call. He took Top's head in his hands, and unfastening the collar the animal wore around his neck, he broke it into two pieces, saying, "Here are two knives, Pencroff!" Two cheers from the sailor responded to him. Top's collar was made of a thin blade of tempered steel. It was enough to first sharpen it on a sandstone, to bring the edge to a fine angle, and then remove the burr on a finer sandstone. Now, this type of sandy rock was abundantly found on the shore, and, two hours later, the colony's tools consisted of two sharp blades that had been easily fitted into a solid handle.

The acquisition of this first tool was celebrated as a triumph. A valuable achievement indeed, and one that came just in time.

Off they went. Cyrus Smith's intention was to return to the western shore of the lake, where he had noticed the day before the clay land of which he had a sample. They followed the bank of the Mercy, crossed the Great View plateau, and after a walk of five miles at most, they arrived at a clearing located two hundred paces from Lake Grant.

Along the way, Harbert discovered a tree whose branches are used by the Indigenous people of South America to make their bows. It was the "crejim-ba," from the palm family, which does not bear edible fruit. Long, straight branches were cut, stripped, and shaped, thicker in the middle, weaker at the ends, and all that was left was to find a plant suitable for stringing the bow. This was a species belonging to the hibiscus family, a "hibiscus heterophyllus," which provided remarkably strong fibers that could be compared to animal tendons.

Pencroff thus made bows of considerable power, which only needed arrows. These were easy to make with straight, rigid branches, without knots, but the tips that would arm them, meaning a substance to replace iron, wouldn't be found so easily. However, Pencroff thought that since he had done his part in the work, luck would take care of the rest.

The colonists had arrived at the site they had scouted the day before. It consisted of that clay suitable for making bricks and tiles, clay that was there-fore very appropriate for the task at hand. The labor presented no difficulty. It was enough to temper this clay with sand, mold the bricks, and fire them to the heat of a wood fire.

Usually, bricks are pressed into molds, but the engineer was satisfied with making them by hand. The entire day and the next were spent on this work. The clay, soaked in water, was then kneaded with the feet and wrists of the workers and divided into prisms of equal size. An experienced worker can make up to ten thousand bricks in twelve hours without a machine; but during their two days of labor, the five brickmakers of Lincoln Island made no more than three thousand, which were stacked next to each other until their complete drying would allow for their firing, that is, in three or four days.

It was on April 2nd that Cyrus Smith focused on determining the island's orientation.

The day before, he had accurately noted the time at which the sun disappeared below the horizon, taking refraction into account. That morning, he noted no less accurately the hour at which it reappeared. Between this sunset and sunrise, twelve hours and twenty-four minutes had passed. Thus, six hours and twelve minutes after its rising, the sun would exactly cross the meridian that day, and the point in the sky it would occupy at that moment would be north.

At the appointed time, Cyrus marked this point, and by aligning two trees that would serve as landmarks with the sun, he thus established an unchanging meridian for his future operations.

During the two days preceding the firing of the bricks, they focused on gathering fuel. Branches were cut around the clearing, and all the wood that had fallen from the trees was collected. This was done not without some hunting in the vicinity, all the better since Pencroff now possessed a few dozen arrows armed with very sharp points. It was Top who provided these points by bringing back a porcupine, not the best game, but of undeniable value due to the quills it was covered in. These quills were securely attached to the ends of the arrows, which were directed with fletching from cockatoo feathers. The reporter and Harbert quickly became very skilled archers. Thus, hair and feathered game abounded at the Chimneys: capybaras, pigeons, agoutis, grouse, etc. Most of these animals were killed in the part of the forest located on the left bank of the Mercy, which was named Jacamar Woods, in memory of the bird Pencroff and Harbert had pursued during their first exploration. The game was eaten fresh, but the cabiai hams were preserved by smoking them over a fire of green wood, after being flavored with aromatic leaves. However, this very nourishing food always consisted of roasts upon roasts, and the guests would have been happy to hear a simple stew bubbling in the fireplace; but they had to wait for the pot to be made, and therefore, for the oven to be built.

During these outings, which only took place in a very limited area around the brickworks, the hunters noted the recent passage of large animals with powerful claws, the species of which they could not identify. Cyrus Smith therefore advised them to be extremely cautious, as it was likely that the forest contained some dangerous beasts. And he was right. Indeed, Gideon Spilett and Harbert spotted an animal that resembled a jaguar one day. Fortunately, this beast did not attack them, as they might not have escaped without some serious injury. But as soon as he had a proper weapon, meaning one of those rifles that Pencroff wanted, Gideon Spilett promised to wage a fierce war against the wild animals and cleanse the island of them.

The Chimneys didn't become more comfortable during those days, as the engineer planned to either discover or build, if necessary, a more suitable dwelling. They made do by laying down a refreshing bedding of mosses and dry leaves on the sand, and on these somewhat primitive beds, the exhausted workers slept soundly.

They also kept track of the days that had passed on Lincoln Island since the colonists had landed there, and they maintained a regular count from then on. On April 5, which was a Wednesday, it had been twelve days since the wind had thrown the shipwrecked survivors onto this shore.

On April 6, at dawn, the engineer and his companions gathered in the clearing where the brick-making would take place. Naturally, this operation had to be done outdoors, and rather, the assembly of the bricks would serve as one huge oven that would bake itself. The fuel, made of well-prepared bundles, was placed on the ground and surrounded by several rows of dried bricks, which soon formed a large cube, with vents constructed on the outside. This work lasted all day, and only in the evening did they set the bundles on fire.

That night, no one went to bed, and they were careful to ensure that the fire did not die down. The operation lasted forty-eight hours and was a complete success. They then had to allow the steaming mass to cool, and during that time, Nab and Pencroff, guided by Cyrus Smith, transported several loads of chalk, very common stones found abundantly north of the lake, on a stretcher made of intertwined branches. When decomposed by heat, these stones yielded a very rich quicklime that expanded a lot when extinguished, ultimately as pure as if it had been produced by calcining chalk or marble. Mixed with sand, which helps reduce shrinkage when the paste hardens, this lime provided excellent mortar.

From these various projects, by April 9, the engineer had a certain amount of prepared lime at his disposal and a few thousand bricks. So they began, without wasting a moment, the construction of a kiln, which would be used to fire the various pottery needed for domestic uses. They succeeded without too much difficulty. Five days later, the kiln was loaded with the coal that the engineer had discovered in an open pit near the creek's mouth, and the first smoke rose from a chimney about twenty feet high. The clearing had been transformed into a factory, and Pencroff was not far from believing that all the products of modern industry would come from this kiln. In the meantime, the first thing the colonists made was common pottery, but very well-suited for cooking food. The raw material was the clay from the soil itself, which Cyrus Smith mixed with a bit of lime and quartz. In reality, this paste constituted true "pipe clay," with which they made pots, cups that were molded on appropriately shaped pebbles, plates, large jars, and vats for holding water, etc.

These objects were awkwardly shaped and defective; however, after being fired at a high temperature, the kitchen of the Chimneys was provided with a number of utensils as valuable as if the finest kaolin had been included in their composition. It should be noted that Pencroff, eager to see if this clay justified its name of "pipe clay," made some rather crude pipes that he found charming, but sadly lacked tobacco! And it has to be said, this was a significant depriva-tion for Pencroff. "But tobacco will come, like everything else!" he repeated in fits of absolute confidence.

These works lasted until April 15, and it is understood that this time was employed consciously. The colonists, now potters, did nothing but make pottery. When Cyrus Smith deemed it appropriate to turn them into black-smiths, they would become blacksmiths. But since the next day was Sunday, and even Easter Sunday, everyone agreed to sanctify that day with rest. These Americans were religious men, scrupulous observers of the Bible's precepts, and their situation could only deepen their feelings of trust in the Creator of all things.

On the evening of April 15, they returned definitively to the Chimneys. The rest of the pottery was taken away, and the kiln was extinguished while awaiting a new purpose. The return was marked by a happy incident, the engi-neer's discovery of a substance suitable for replacing amadou. It is known that this spongy and velvety flesh comes from a certain fungus of the polypore kind. When properly prepared, it is extremely flammable, especially when saturated with gunpowder or boiled in a solution of nitrate or potassium chlo-rate. But until then, none of these polypores, nor any of the morels that could replace them, had been found. That day, the engineer recognized a certain plant belonging to the sagebrush genus, which includes such main species as wormwood, citronella, tarragon, and others; he uprooted several clumps and, presenting them to the sailor, said: "Here you go, Pencroff, this will please you."

Pencroff looked at the plant carefully, covered in silky, long hairs, with leaves draped in a cottony down. "Hey! What is this, Mr. Cyrus?" asked Pencroff. "Good heavens! Is it tobacco?" "No," replied Cyrus Smith, "it's wormwood, Chinese artemisia to the learned, and for us, it will be amadou." Indeed, this wormwood, when properly dried, provides a very flammable substance, espe-cially later when the engineer had soaked it in the potassium nitrate, of which the island had several layers, and which is nothing more than saltpeter.

That night, all the colonists, gathered in the central room, had a proper dinner. Nab had prepared a stew of agouti, a flavored cabiai ham, which was joined by boiled tubers of "caladium macrorhizum," a type of herbaceous plant belonging to the araceae family, which, under the tropical zone, would have taken on a tree-like form. These rhizomes had an excellent taste, were very nutritious, and were somewhat similar to the substance sold in England under the name of "Portland sago," and they could, to some extent, replace the bread, which the colonists on Lincoln Island were still missing.

Once dinner was finished, before heading off to sleep, Cyrus Smith and his companions went out for some fresh air on the shore. It was eight in the evening. The night was turning out beautifully. The moon, which had been full five days earlier, had not yet risen, but the horizon was already shimmering with those soft, pale shades that one might call the lunar dawn. In the southern zenith, the circumpolar constellations twinkled brightly, and among them, the Southern Cross that the engineer had saluted a few days earlier atop Mount Franklin.

Cyrus Smith watched this splendid constellation for a while, which has two first-magnitude stars at its top and bottom, a second-magnitude star on its left arm, and a third-magnitude star on its right. Then, after pondering a bit, he asked, "Harbert, are we not at April 15?" "Yes, Mr. Cyrus," answered Harbert. "Well, if I'm not mistaken, tomorrow will be one of the four days of the year for which true time matches mean time; that is to say, my child, that tomorrow, within a few seconds, the sun will cross the meridian exactly at noon by the clocks. So if the weather is clear, I believe I can determine the island's longitude with an approximation of a few degrees." "Without instruments, without a sextant?" asked Gideon Spilett. "Yes," replied the engineer. "Also, since the night is clear, I will try tonight to obtain our latitude by calculating the height of the Southern Cross, i.e., the south pole, above the horizon. You all understand, my friends, that before undertaking serious installation work, it is not enough to have established that this land is an island; it is necessary, as much as possible, to determine how far it is located from the American continent, the Australian continent, or the main archipelagos of the Pacific." "Indeed," said the reporter, "instead of building a house, we might be better off building a boat if we happen to be only a hundred miles from an inhabited coast." "That's why," Cyrus Smith replied, "I will try tonight to obtain the latitude of Lincoln Island, and tomorrow at noon, I will attempt to calculate its longitude."

If the engineer had had a sextant, an instrument that allows for precise measurement of the angular distance of objects by reflection, the operation would have posed no difficulty. That night, by the height of the pole, and the next day, by the sun's passage over the meridian, he would have obtained the island's coordinates. But lacking the device, he had to find a substitute. Cyrus Smith returned to the Chimneys. By the fire's light, he shaped two small flat sticks, connecting them by one of their ends to form something like a compass whose branches could spread apart or come together. The point of connection was fixed with a strong acacia thorn from the dead wood of the woodpile.

Once the instrument was completed, the engineer returned to the shore; but since he needed to take the height of the pole above a clearly defined horizon, that is, a sea horizon, and Cape Griffe obscured the southern horizon, he had to find a more suitable location. The best spot would have been the coastline facing directly south, but he would have had to cross the now deep Mercy, which posed a difficulty. Cyrus Smith decided, therefore, to go take his observation on the Grande-vue plateau, reserving the right to account for its height above sea level—a height that he intended to calculate the next day using a simple method of elementary geometry.

The colonists then made their way to the plateau, moving up the left bank of the Mercy, and they took position on the edge that aligned northwest to southeast, that is to say, on that line of whimsically shaped rocks bordering the river. This part of the plateau stood about fifty feet above the heights of the right bank, which sloped downwards in a twofold manner to the end of Cape Griffe and the southern coast of the island. No obstacle stopped their view, which encompassed the horizon over a half-circle, from the cape to the Reptile promontory. To the south, this horizon, illuminated from below by the first light of the moon, sharply outlined against the sky and could be aimed with a certain precision.

At that moment, the Southern Cross presented itself to the observer in an inverted position, with the alpha star marking its base, which is closer to the south pole. This constellation is not located as close to the Antarctic pole as the pole star is to the Arctic pole. The alpha star is about twenty-seven degrees away from it, but Cyrus Smith knew this and had to account for that distance in his calculations. He also made sure to observe it just as it passed over the meridian below the pole, which would simplify his operation.

Cyrus Smith directed one branch of his wooden compass toward the sea horizon and the other toward alpha, as he would have done with the circular repeaters' scopes, and the opening between the two branches gave him the angular distance separating alpha from the horizon. To firmly set the angle obtained, he pinned the two boards of his device with thorns to a third placed transversely, so that their spacing was maintained securely. Once that was done, he needed only to calculate the angle obtained, adjusting the observation to sea level to account for the horizon's depression, which required measuring the plateau's height. The value of that angle would thus give him the height of alpha, and consequently that of the pole above the horizon, that is to say, the island's latitude, since the latitude of a point on the globe is always equal to the height of the pole above that point's horizon.

These calculations would be postponed to the next day, and by ten o'clock, everyone was sound asleep.

❧ 14 ❧

The next day, April 16—Easter Sunday—the colonists emerged from the Chimneys at dawn and proceeded to wash their laundry and clean their clothes. The engineer planned to make soap as soon as he acquired the necessary raw materials for saponification, soda or potash, fat or oil. The important matter of renewing their clothing would also be addressed in due time. In any case, their clothes would last at least another six months, as they were sturdy and could withstand the rigors of manual work. But it all depended on the island's situation in relation to populated lands. This would be determined that day, if the weather allowed.

Now, the sun, rising over a clear horizon, announced a beautiful day, one of those lovely autumn days that are like warm season's last farewells. So they needed to complete the elements of the previous day's observations by measuring the height of the Grande-vue plateau above sea level. "Don't you need an instrument like the one you used yesterday?" asked Harbert of the engineer. "No, my child," he replied. "We will proceed differently, and in a manner that's about as precise."

Harbert, who loved to learn about everything, followed the engineer as he stepped away from the granite wall down to the shore. Meanwhile, Pencroff, Nab, and the reporter were busy with various tasks. Cyrus Smith had equipped himself with a sort of straight pole, about twelve feet long, which he had measured as accurately as possible, comparing it to his own height, which he knew to within a line. Harbert carried a plumb line that Cyrus Smith had given him, meaning a simple stone attached to the end of a flexible cord. When they arrived about twenty feet from the edge of the shore, and about five hundred feet from the granite wall, which stood upright, Cyrus

Smith drove the pole two feet into the sand, and by carefully stabilizing it, he managed, using a plumb line, to stand it upright to the level of the horizon.

After doing this, he stepped back far enough so that, lying on the sand, the line of sight from his eye grazed both the tip of the pole and the top of the wall.

Then he carefully marked this point with a stake.

Turning to Harbert, he asked,

"Do you know the basic principles of geometry?"

"A little, Mr. Cyrus," Harbert replied, not wanting to seem too confident.

"Do you remember what the properties of two similar triangles are?"

"Yes," Harbert answered. "Their corresponding sides are proportional."

"Well, my child, I just created two similar right triangles: the first, the smaller one, has as sides the vertical pole, the distance from the stake to the base of the pole, and my line of sight as the hypotenuse; the second has as sides the vertical wall, which we need to measure the height of, the distance from the stake to the base of this wall, and my line of sight also forming its hypotenuse —which happens to be the extension of that of the first triangle."

"Ah! Mr. Cyrus, I understand!" exclaimed Harbert. "Just as the distance from the stake to the pole is proportional to the distance from the stake to the base of the wall, the height of the pole is proportional to the height of this wall."

"That's exactly right, Harbert," the engineer replied, "and once we measure the first two distances, knowing the height of the pole, we'll just need to do a proportion calculation to get the height of the wall, avoiding the trouble of measuring it directly."

The two horizontal distances were recorded, using the pole, which stood exactly ten feet above the sand.

The first distance was fifteen feet from the stake to the point where the pole was planted in the sand.

The second distance, from the stake to the base of the wall, was five hundred feet.

Once these measurements were complete, Cyrus Smith and the young boy returned to the Chimneys.

There, the engineer took a flat stone he had brought back from his previous excursions, a kind of slate, on which it was easy to draw numbers with a sharp shell.

He accordingly established the following proportion:

15: 500:: 10: x   500 times 10 = 5000   5000 divided by 15 = 333.33.

Thus, it was determined that the granite wall measured three hundred thirty-three feet in height.

Cyrus Smith then took the instrument he had made the day before, where the two boards, due to their spacing, gave him the angular distance of the star alpha to the horizon. He measured the angle very precisely on a circle, which he divided into three hundred sixty equal parts. Now, by adding the twenty-seven degrees that separate alpha from the Antarctic pole, and adjusting the height of the plateau where the observation was made to sea level, this angle turned out to be fifty-three degrees. Subtracting these fifty-three degrees from ninety degrees—the distance from the pole to the equator—left thirty-seven degrees. Therefore, Cyrus Smith concluded that Lincoln Island was located at the thirty-seventh degree of southern latitude, or, accounting for a margin of error of five degrees due to imperfections in his calculations, it should be situated between the thirty-fifth and the fortieth parallels.

Next, they needed to determine the longitude to complete the coordinates of the island. That's what the engineer would try to figure out that same day, at noon, which was when the sun would pass over the meridian.

It was decided that this Sunday would be spent on a walk, or rather an exploration of the part of the island located between the north of the lake and the Shark Gulf, and if the weather permitted, they would push this reconnaissance to the northern slope of Cape Mandibule-Sud. They planned to have lunch on the dunes and return only in the evening.

At eight-thirty in the morning, the small group followed along the edge of the canal. On the other side, on Safety Island, many birds were walking about. They were divers, of the penguin kind, easily recognizable by their unpleasant cry, which resembles a donkey's bray.

Pencroff viewed them only as food, and learned with some satisfaction that their meat, while dark, is quite edible.

You could also see large amphibians, likely seals, crawling on the sand, which seemed to have chosen the islet as a refuge. It was hardly possible to evaluate these animals for food, as their oily flesh is terrible; however, Cyrus Smith observed them closely and, without revealing his thoughts, announced to his companions that they would soon pay a visit to the islet.

The shore, followed by the settlers, was littered with countless shells, some of which would have delighted a conchologist. Among others were phasianelles, terebratules, trigonies, etc. But what was likely to be more useful was a vast oyster bed discovered at low tide, which Nab pointed out among the rocks, about four miles from the Chimneys.

"Nab hasn't wasted his day," cried Pencroff, observing the bank of mollusks stretching offshore.

"It's a lucky discovery, indeed," said the reporter, "and if, as claimed, each oyster produces fifty to sixty thousand eggs a year, we'll have an inexhaustible supply here."

"Only, I believe that oysters aren't very nourishing," said Harbert.

"No," replied Cyrus Smith. "Oysters contain very little nitrogenous matter, so a person who would rely solely on them would need at least fifteen to sixteen dozen per day."

"Good!" replied Pencroff. "We'll be able to eat dozens upon dozens before we've depleted the bank. Shall we take some for our lunch?"

And without waiting for a response to his suggestion, knowing well that it would be approved, the sailor and Nab gathered a certain amount of these mollusks. They placed them in a sort of bag made of hibiscus fibers, which Nab had crafted and which already contained the meal. Then they continued making their way up the coast between the dunes and the sea. From time to time, Cyrus Smith checked his watch to prepare in time for the solar observation, which was to be done at noon sharp.

This part of the island was very arid up to the point that closed Union Bay, which had been named Cape Mandibule-Sud.

There was nothing but sand and shells, mixed with lava debris. A few seabirds frequented this desolate coast, gulls, large albatrosses, as well as wild ducks, which rightfully excited Pencroff's desire.

He tried to shoot them with arrows, but to no avail, as they rarely landed, and he would have needed to hit them while they were flying.

This led the sailor to reiterate to the engineer:

"You see, Mr. Cyrus, until we have one or two shotguns, our equipment will leave much to be desired!

"Indeed, Pencroff," replied the reporter, "but it's up to you! Get us iron for the barrels, steel for the locks, saltpeter, coal, and sulfur for the powder, mercury and nitric acid for the fulminate, and finally lead for the bullets, and Cyrus will make us first-class rifles."

"Oh!" replied the engineer, "we can surely find all those substances on the island, but a firearm is a delicate instrument that requires very precise tools. Anyway, we'll see about it later."

"Why did we have to throw overboard all those weapons the balloon carried with us, and our utensils, and even our pocket knives!" exclaimed Pencroff.

"But if we hadn't thrown them over, Pencroff, we would have been thrown into the sea by the balloon!" said Harbert.

"That's true what you're saying, my boy!" answered the sailor.

Then, moving on to another thought, he added, "But I just realized, what must have been the astonishment of Jonathan Forster and his companions when, the next morning, they found the place clean and the machine gone!"

"The last thing on my mind is to know what they could have thought!" said the reporter.

"It was me who had that idea!" said Pencroff with a satisfied air.

"A fine idea, Pencroff," laughed Gédéon Spilett, "and it got us where we are!"

"I'd rather be here than in the hands of the southerners!" shouted the sailor, especially since Mr. Cyrus was kind enough to come join us!

"And so would I, indeed!" replied the reporter. "Besides, what do we lack? Nothing!"

"If not... everything!" replied Pencroff, bursting into laughter and shaking his broad shoulders. "But one day or another, we'll find a way to get away!"

"And perhaps sooner than you imagine, my friends," said the engineer then, "if Lincoln Island is only an average distance from an inhabited archipelago or a continent. Before an hour, we will know. I don't have a chart of the Pacific, but my memory retains a very clear recollection of its southern portion. The latitude I obtained yesterday places Lincoln Island opposite New Zealand to the west and the coast of Chile to the east. But between those two lands, the distance is at least six thousand miles. What remains is to determine the exact point the island occupies in this vast expanse of sea, and that's what the longitude will give us shortly, with a sufficient approximation, I hope.

"Isn't it true," asked Harbert, "that the Pomotou archipelago is the closest to us in latitude?"

"Yes," replied the engineer, "but the distance that separates us is over twelve hundred miles."

"And over there?" said Nab, who was following the conversation with great interest, indicating the direction of the south with his hand.

"Over there, nothing," replied Pencroff.

"Nothing, indeed," added the engineer.

"Well then, Cyrus," asked the reporter, "if Lincoln Island is only two or three hundred miles from New Zealand or Chile?..."

"Well then," replied the engineer, "instead of building a house, we'll build a boat, and master Pencroff will take charge of navigating it...

"How so, Mr. Cyrus," shouted the sailor, "I'm ready to be captain... as soon as you find a way to construct a boat that can brave the sea!"

"We'll do it if necessary!" replied Cyrus Smith.

But while these men, truly undaunted, were talking, the moment was approaching for the observation to take place. How would Cyrus Smith manage to ascertain the sun's passage over the island's meridian without any instruments? This was something Harbert could not guess.

The observers were then six miles away from the Chimneys, near the part of the dunes where the engineer had been found after his mysterious rescue. They stopped in this spot, and everything was prepared for lunch as it was eleven-thirty. Harbert went to fetch fresh water from the stream that flowed nearby, and he brought it back in a jug that Nab had brought.

During these preparations, Cyrus Smith set everything up for his astronomical observation. He chose a very clear spot on the beach, perfectly leveled by the receding sea. This layer of very fine sand was smooth like a glass surface, with no grain protruding. It didn't matter that this layer was horizontal or not, nor did it matter that the stick, six feet tall, which was planted there stood upright. On the contrary, the engineer tilted it to the south, i.e., away from the sun, because it should not be forgotten that the colonists of Lincoln Island, since the island was located in the southern hemisphere, saw the radiant star arch its daily arc above the northern horizon, not above the southern horizon.

Harbert then understood how the engineer would proceed to establish the culmination of the sun, that is to say its passage over the island's meridian, or, in other words, midday in that location. It was through the shadow cast on the sand by the stick, a method that, in the absence of instruments, would give him an adequate approximation for the result he desired to obtain. Indeed, the moment when this shadow reached its minimum length would be precisely noon, and it would be enough to follow the end of this shadow to recognize the moment when, after gradually shortening, it would start getting longer again. By tilting his stick away from the sun, Cyrus Smith made the shadow longer, and consequently, it would be easier to observe its changes. Indeed, the larger the hand of a sundial, the easier it is to track the movement of its tip. The shadow of the stick was nothing but the hand of a sundial.

When he thought the moment had arrived, Cyrus Smith knelt on the sand and, using little wooden markers that he inserted into the sand, he began to mark the successive decreases of the shadow of the stick. His companions, leaning over him, watched the operation with great interest.

The reporter held his chronometer in hand, ready to record the time it would indicate when the shadow would be shortest. Furthermore, since Cyrus Smith was operating on April 16, a day when the true time and the mean time coincide, the time given by Gédéon Spilett would be the true time as it would be in Washington, which would simplify the calculation.

However, the sun was slowly advancing; the shadow of the stick gradually diminished, and when it seemed to Cyrus Smith that it was starting to grow again, he asked,

"What time is it?"

"Five hours and one minute," Gédéon Spilett immediately replied.

All that was left was to calculate the operation. Nothing could be easier. As we can see, there was a round difference of five hours between the meridian of Washington and that of Lincoln Island, meaning it was noon on Lincoln Island when it was already five o'clock in the evening in Washington. Now, the sun, in its apparent movement around the Earth, travels one degree in four minutes, or fifteen degrees per hour. Fifteen degrees multiplied by five hours yielded seventy-five degrees.

Thus, since Washington is at 77°3'11, which is to say seventy-seven degrees counted from the Greenwich meridian— which Americans use as the starting point for longitudes, along with the British—it followed that the island was located at seventy-seven degrees plus seventy-five degrees west of the Greenwich meridian, or at fifty-two degrees west longitude.Cyrus Smith shared this information with his companions, and considering the observational errors, as he had done for latitude, he believed he could assert that the location of Lincoln Island was between the thirty-fifth and thirty-seventh parallels, and between the one hundred fiftieth and one hundred fifty-fifth meridians west of the Greenwich meridian.

The possible margin of error he attributed to observational mistakes was, as one could see, five degrees in both directions, which, at sixty miles per degree, could lead to an error of three hundred miles in latitude or longitude for the precise bearing.

However, this error would not affect the decision that needed to be made. It was clear that Lincoln Island was so far from any land or archipelago that daring to cross this distance in a simple and fragile canoe would be unwise. Indeed, its bearing placed it at least twelve hundred miles from Tahiti and the islands of the Pomotou archipelago, more than eighteen hundred miles from New Zealand, and over four thousand five hundred miles from the American coast!

And when Cyrus Smith consulted his memories, he did not recall any island occupying the location assigned to Lincoln Island in this part of the Pacific.

❧   15   ❧

The next day, April 17, the first word from the sailor был to Gideon Spilett.

"Well, sir," he asked, "what shall we do today?"

"Whatever Cyrus decides," replied the reporter.

So, from being brickmakers and potters as they had been until then, the engineer's companions were going to become metallurgists.

The day before, after lunch, their exploration had reached the tip of Cape Mandible, nearly seven miles from the Chimneys. There, the long series of dunes ended, and the ground took on a volcanic appearance. It was no longer high walls, as on the Great View plateau, but a bizarre and capricious border framing the narrow gulf between the two caps, made of materials ejected by the volcano. Upon reaching that point, the settlers had turned back, and as night fell, they returned to the Chimneys, but they did not fall asleep before the question of whether to consider leaving Lincoln Island was definitively resolved.

The twelve hundred miles separating the island from the Pomotou archipelago was a considerable distance. A canoe would not suffice to cross it, especially with the bad season approaching.

Pencroff had stated this categorically. Now, building a simple canoe, even with the necessary tools, was a difficult task, and since the settlers had no tools, they would first have to make hammers, hatchets, drawknives, saws, augers, planes, etc., which would require some time. It was thus decided that they would winter on Lincoln Island and look for a more comfortable dwelling than the Chimneys to spend the winter months.

Before anything else, they needed to utilize the iron ore, some deposits of which the engineer had observed in the northwestern part of the island, and to convert this ore into either iron or steel.

The ground usually does not contain metals in pure form. Most are found combined with oxygen or sulfur.

Specifically, the two samples brought back by Cyrus Smith were one of magnetic iron, non-carbonated, and the other of pyrite, or iron sulfide. It was, therefore, the first, iron oxide, that needed to be reduced by coal, that is, stripped of oxygen to obtain it in pure form. This reduction is done by subjecting the ore in the presence of coal to high temperatures, either by the quick and easy "Catalan method," which has the advantage of transforming the ore directly into iron in a single operation, or by the blast furnace method, which first converts the ore into cast iron and then the cast iron into iron by removing three to four percent of the carbon combined with it.

However, what did Cyrus Smith need? Iron and not cast iron, and he had to look for the quickest reduction method. Moreover, the ore he had collected was already very pure and rich. It was this oxidized ore that, found in confused masses of dark gray, gives a black powder, crystallizes into regular octahedrons, provides natural magnets, and is used in Europe to make high-quality iron, of which Sweden and Norway are so abundantly supplied. Not far from this deposit were the deposits of coal already exploited by the settlers. Hence, great ease for processing the ore, since the materials for manufacturing were close by.

This is what contributes to the prodigious wealth of Britain's mines, where coal is used to make the metal extracted from the same ground at the same time.

"Then, Mr. Cyrus," said Pencroff, "are we going to work on the iron ore?"

"Yes, my friend," replied the engineer, "and to do that— which you will not dislike— we will start by sealing the island."

"The seal hunt!" exclaimed the sailor, turning to Gideon Spilett. "So we need seals to make iron?"

"Since Cyrus says so!" replied the reporter.

But the engineer had already left the Chimneys, and Pencroff prepared for the seal hunt, having received no further explanation.

Soon Cyrus Smith, Harbert, Gideon Spilett, Nab, and the sailor were gathered on the shore, at a point where the canal provided a sort of crossable passage at low tide. The tide was at its lowest ebb, and the hunters could cross the canal without getting wet above the knee.

Cyrus Smith was thus setting foot on the islet for the first time, and his companions for the second time, since it was where the balloon had dropped them initially.

As they landed, a few hundred penguins looked at them with innocent eyes. The settlers, armed with sticks, could have easily killed them, but they did not consider committing this unnecessary massacre again, as it was important not to scare the seals, which were lying on the sand a few cable lengths away. They also respected certain very innocent penguins, whose wings, reduced to stubs, flattened out like fins, covered in seemingly scaly feathers.

The settlers cautiously advanced toward the northern tip, walking on a ground riddled with small depressions that formed nests for waterfowl. At the edge of the islet, large black spots appeared floating on the surface of the water.

They looked like moving heads of rocks.

These were the seals to be captured.

They had to wait for them to come ashore, as with their narrow bodies, short, tightly-cropped fur, and streamlined shape, these seals, excellent swimmers, are difficult to catch in the sea, whereas on land, their short, webbed feet only allow for slow, crawling movements.

Pencroff was familiar with the habits of these seals, and he advised waiting for them to be sprawled out on the sand, under the rays of the sun, which would soon put them into a deep sleep.

They would maneuver to cut off their retreat and strike at their noses.

The hunters then concealed themselves behind the coastal rocks and waited silently. An hour passed before the seals came to frolic on the sand. There were about half a dozen of them. Pencroff and Harbert then moved out to circle the tip of the islet, so as to catch them in a flank and cut off their retreat. Meanwhile, Cyrus Smith, Gideon Spilett, and Nab, crawling along the rocks, slipped toward the future battlefield.

Suddenly, the tall figure of the sailor rose up.

Pencroff let out a cry. The engineer and his two companions rushed between the sea and the seals. Two of these animals, struck hard, lay dead on the sand, but the others managed to make it back to the sea and swim away.

"The seals you asked for, Mr. Cyrus!" said the sailor, moving towards the engineer.

"Good," replied Cyrus Smith. "We will make bellows from them!"

"Bellows!" cried Pencroff. "Well! those seals are lucky!"

Indeed, it was a blowing machine, necessary for processing the ore, that the engineer planned to make with the skins of these seals. They were of average size, as their length did not exceed six feet, and at the head, they resembled dogs.

As it was unnecessary to carry a weight as considerable as these two animals, Nab and Pencroff decided to skin them on the spot, while Cyrus Smith and the reporter would continue to explore the islet.

The sailor and the black man skillfully managed their task, and three hours later, Cyrus Smith had two seal skins at his disposal, which he planned to use as they were and without any tanning.

The settlers had to wait for the sea to lower again, and crossing the canal, they returned to the Chimneys.

Stretching these skins over wooden frames designed to maintain their spread and sewing them with fibers to store air without leaving too many leaks was no small feat. They had to try several times. Cyrus Smith only had the two steel blades from Top's collar at his disposal, and yet he was so skilled, with his companions helping him intelligently, that three days later, the small colony's tools had been increased by a blowing machine intended to inject air into the ore when it was treated by heat— a condition essential for the success of the operation.

It was on April 20, in the morning, that "the metallurgical period" began, as the reporter called it in his notes. The engineer was determined, as we know, to work directly on the coal and ore deposits. According to his observations, these deposits were located at the foot of the northeastern slopes of Mount Franklin, that is to say, six miles away. Thus, they could not think of returning to the Chimneys every day, and it was agreed that the small colony would camp under a hut of branches so that the important operation could be followed day and night.

With this plan set, they left in the morning. Nab and Pencroff dragged the blowing machine and a certain quantity of plant and animal provisions, which would be replenished on the way.

The route taken was through the Jacamar woods, which they crossed diagonally from southeast to northwest, and in its thickest part. They had to carve a path that would later form the most direct artery between the Great View plateau and Mount Franklin. The trees, belonging to already recognized species, were magnificent. Harbert pointed out new ones, among them dragon trees, which Pencroff whimsically called "pretentious leeks," because, despite their height, they belonged to the same lily family as onions, chives, shallots, or asparagus. These dragon trees could provide woody roots that, when cooked, are excellent, and that when subjected to certain fermentation, yield a very pleasant liquor. They gathered some of those.

This journey through the woods was long. It lasted the entire day, but it allowed for observing the fauna and flora. Top, especially in charge of fauna, ran through the grasses and brush, stirring up all kinds of game indistinctly. Harbert and Gideon Spilett killed two kangaroos with arrows, and also an animal that greatly resembled both a hedgehog and an anteater: to the first, because it curled up into a ball and bristled with spikes; to the second, because it had digging claws, a long, thin snout ending with a bird-like beak, and an extensible tongue covered in small spines that served to catch insects.

"And when it's in the stew pot," Pencroff naturally observed, "what will it look like?"

"Like a fine piece of beef," Harbert replied.

"We won't ask for anything more," replied the sailor.

During this excursion, they spotted a few wild boars that did not attempt to attack the small group, and it did not seem that they would encounter any formidable beasts, when, in a thick thicket, the reporter thought he saw, a few steps away from him, between the first branches of a tree, an animal he took for a bear and began to draw peacefully. Fortunately for Gideon Spilett, the animal in question did not belong to that fearsome family of bears. It was just a "koula," better known as "sloth," which had the size of a large dog, bristly, dirty-colored fur, and strong claws on its paws, allowing it to climb trees and feed on leaves. After confirming the identity of said animal, which they did not disturb from its activities, Gideon Spilett erased "bear" from the caption of his sketch, replaced it with "koula," and they resumed their journey.

At five in the evening, Cyrus Smith signaled a halt. He found himself outside the forest, at the base of these powerful slopes that supported Mount Franklin to the east. A few hundred steps away flowed the Creek-Rouge, and, therefore, potable water was not far off.

The campsite was quickly organized. In less than an hour, on the edge of the forest, between the trees, a hut made of intertwined branches and clay mud provided sufficient shelter. The geological searches were postponed until the next day. Dinner was prepared, a good fire blazed in front of the hut, the spit turned, and at eight o'clock, while one of the settlers kept watch to maintain the fire in case some dangerous beast wandered nearby, the others slept soundly.

The next day, April 21, Cyrus Smith, accompanied by Harbert, went to search for those ancient formation lands on which he had already found a sample of ore. He found the deposit just below the surface, almost at the springs of the creek, at the base of the lateral slope of one of those northeastern foothills.

This ore, very rich in iron, trapped in its fusible matrix, suited the method of reduction that the engineer planned to employ, that is, the Catalan method but simplified, as is used in Corsica. Indeed, the true Catalan method requires the construction of furnaces and crucibles in which the ore and coal, placed in alternating layers, are transformed and reduced. But Cyrus Smith intended to save on these constructions, wanting simply to form a cubic mass with the ore and coal, at the center of which he would direct the wind from his bellows. This was undoubtedly the process used by Tubal-Cain and the first metallurgists of the inhabited world. Therefore, what had succeeded with Adam's grandsons, what still produced good results in mineral-rich and fuel-abundant regions, could only succeed under the circumstances the settlers of Lincoln Island were in. Just like the ore, coal was harvested easily and not far from the surface of the ground. First, the ore was broken into small pieces and manually cleaned of the impurities that contaminated its surface. Then, coal and ore were piled in layers, just like a charcoal burner would do with the wood he wants to carbonize. This way, under the influence of air from the blowing machine, the coal was supposed to transform into carbon dioxide, then into carbon monoxide, which would reduce the iron oxide, releasing the oxygen.

This is how the engineer proceeded. The seal-skin bellows, fitted at its end with a refractory clay pipe made beforehand in a pottery kiln, was set up near the ore pile. Driven by a mechanism made of frames, fiber ropes, and counterweights, it blew a supply of air into the mass which, while raising the temperature, also contributed to the chemical transformation that would yield pure iron.

The operation was difficult. It took all the patience and ingenuity of the colonists to complete it successfully; but finally, it did succeed, and the end result was a lump of iron, reduced to a spongy state, that needed to be hammered and forged to remove the liquefied slag. It was evident that the first hammer was missing for these improvised blacksmiths; but, in the end, they found themselves in the same situation as the first metallurgist, and they did what he must have done.

The first lump, attached to a stick, served as a hammer to forge the second on a granite anvil, and they managed to obtain a rough, but usable metal. Finally, after much effort and fatigue, on April 25, several iron bars had been forged, which turned into tools, pincers, tongs, picks, shovels, etc., that Pencroff and Nab declared to be real treasures.

But this metal wasn't pure iron; it was much more useful in the form of steel. Steel is a combination of iron and carbon that can be derived either from cast iron by removing excess carbon or from iron by adding the needed carbon to it. The first type, obtained by decarburizing cast iron, yields natural or puddled steel; the second, produced by carburizing iron, gives cementation steel.

Thus, Cyrus Smith needed to focus on producing the latter, as he had pure iron at his disposal. He succeeded by heating the metal with powdered coal in a refractory clay crucible.

Then, he worked the steel, which is malleable when hot and cold, using a hammer. Nab and Pencroff, expertly guided, made the axe heads, which, when heated to red and immersed suddenly in cold water, acquired excellent tempering.

Other roughly shaped tools were also made, such as plane blades, axes, hatchets, strips of steel that were to be converted into saws, carpenter's chisels, as well as pickaxes, shovels, hammerheads, nails, etc. Finally, on May 5, the first metallurgical period was completed, and the blacksmiths returned to the Chimneys, ready for new work that would soon allow them to take on a new qualification.

16

It was May 6, a date that corresponds to November 6 in the northern hemisphere. The sky had been clouding over for a few days, and certain preparations were necessary for wintering. However, the temperature had not yet dropped significantly, and a centigrade thermometer moved to Lincoln Island still registered an average of ten to twelve degrees above zero. This average should not be surprising, since Lincoln Island, likely located between the thirty-fifth and fortieth parallels, would have similar climatic conditions in the southern hemisphere as Sicily or Greece in the northern hemisphere. But just as Greece or Sicily experience severe cold that produces snow and ice, Lincoln Island would also likely endure some drops in temperature during the most pronounced period of winter, necessitating preparations against it. In any case, even if the cold was not yet threatening, the rainy season was approaching, and on this isolated island, exposed to all the harsh weather of the open sea in the heart of the Pacific Ocean, bad weather was expected to be frequent and likely terrible.

The question of a more comfortable dwelling than the Chimneys had to be seriously considered and quickly resolved.

Pencroff, naturally, had some affection for this retreat he had discovered; but he understood that they needed to look for another one.

The Chimneys had already been visited by the sea in circumstances that were memorable, and they could not risk such an accident again.

"Besides," added Cyrus Smith, who was discussing these matters with his companions that day, "we have some precautions to take."

"Why? The island isn't inhabited," said the reporter.

"That's probable," replied the engineer, "even though we haven't fully explored it yet; but if there are no humans here, I fear there might be dangerous animals. So it's wise to protect ourselves from a possible attack and not strain one of us to keep a fire going every night. And then, my friends, we must plan for everything. We are here in a part of the Pacific that is often frequented by Malay pirates..."

"What? At such a distance from any land?" said Harbert.

"Yes, my child," replied the engineer. "These pirates are daring sailors as well as formidable criminals, and we must take measures accordingly."

"Well then," replied Pencroff, "we will fortify ourselves against wild animals, both two-legged and four-legged. But, Mr. Cyrus, wouldn't it be a good idea to explore the island thoroughly before undertaking anything?"

"That would be better," added Gideon Spilett. "Who knows if we might not find one of those caves on the opposite coast that we've been looking for in vain here?"

"That's true," replied the engineer, "but you're forgetting, my friends, that we need to settle near a water source, and that from the top of Mount Franklin, we didn't see any stream or river towards the west. Here, on the contrary, we are situated between the Mercy River and Grant Lake, which is a significant advantage that shouldn't be overlooked. Moreover, this east-facing coast is not exposed like the other to the trade winds blowing from the northwest in this hemisphere."

"Then, Mr. Cyrus," replied the sailor, "let's build a house by the lake. We have plenty of bricks and tools now."

After being brickmakers, potters, founders, and blacksmiths, we'll surely know how to be masons, for goodness' sake!

"Yes, my friend, but before making a decision, we must search. A dwelling that nature has already prepared for us would save us a lot of work, and it would likely offer us an even safer refuge, as it would be better defended from inside threats as well as those from outside."

"Indeed, Cyrus," replied the reporter, "but we have already examined all of this granite mass on the coast, and not a hole, not even a crack!"

"No, not a one!" added Pencroff. "Ah! If we could have carved a dwelling out of this wall at a certain height, so as to make it unreachable, that would have been ideal! I can picture it from here, on the face looking out to sea, five or six rooms..."

"With windows to let in light!" laughed Harbert.

"And a staircase to get up there!" added Nab.

"You're laughing," exclaimed the sailor, "and why? What's impossible about what I'm suggesting? Don't we have picks and shovels? Isn't Mr. Cyrus going to make gunpowder to blast the rock? Isn't that right, Mr. Cyrus, you'll make gunpowder on the day we need it?"

Cyrus Smith had listened to the enthusiastic Pencroff as he developed his slightly fanciful plans.

Assaulting this mass of granite, even with explosives, was a Herculean task, and it was indeed unfortunate that nature had not done the hardest part of the work. But the engineer replied to the sailor by proposing a more careful examination of the wall from the river mouth to the northern corner where it ended.

So they went out, and the exploration was carried out over approximately two miles with the utmost care. But at no point did the smooth, straight wall reveal any cavity. The nests of the rock pigeons that fluttered at its peak were, in reality, just holes bored at the very crest and along the irregularly cut edge of the granite.

This was an unfortunate circumstance, and to attack this mass, whether with picks or explosives, to create a large enough excavation was not something to consider. By chance, in all this coastal area, Pencroff had discovered the only temporarily habitable shelter, namely the Chimneys that they were yet ready to abandon.

After completing the exploration, the colonists found themselves at the northern corner of the wall, where it ended in sloping grounds leading down to the beach. From this spot to its extreme western limit, it formed only a kind of embankment, a thick agglomeration of stones, earth, and sand, intertwined with plants, shrubs, and grasses, sloping at only a forty-five-degree angle. Here and there, granite still protruded, extending in sharp points from this sort of cliff. Clusters of trees adorned its slopes, and fairly thick grass covered it. But the vegetation did not extend further, and a long expanse of sand stretched from the foot of the embankment to the seashore.

Cyrus Smith reasonably thought that this was likely where the overflow from the lake was spilling out in the form of a waterfall. Indeed, it was necessary that the excess water supplied by the Red Creek be lost at some point. However, the engineer had not yet found this point along any of the explored riverbanks, from the stream's mouth in the west to the Grand View plateau.

The engineer thus proposed to his companions to climb the slope they were observing and return to the Chimneys via higher ground, exploring the northern and eastern shores of the lake.

The proposal was accepted, and within minutes, Harbert and Nab reached the upper plateau. Cyrus Smith, Gideon Spilett, and Pencroff followed them at a more measured pace.

Two hundred feet up, through the foliage, the beautiful expanse of water sparkled in the sunlight.

The landscape was charming in this spot. The trees, with their yellowed tones, grouped together wonderfully for the delight of the eyes. Some old enormous trunks, toppled by age, contrasted with their dark bark against the green carpet covering the ground. A whole world of noisy cockatoos squabbled there, real mobile prisms, jumping from branch to branch. It seemed as if only decomposed light was entering through this peculiar foliage.

Instead of going directly to the north shore of the lake, the colonists skirted the edge of the plateau, aiming to reach the mouth of the creek on its left bank. It was a detour of at most a mile and a half. The walk was easy since the trees were widely spaced and left a clear passage between them. One could clearly sense that at this boundary, the fertile zone stopped, and the vegetation was less vigorous compared to the area between the creeks and the Mercy River.

Cyrus Smith and his companions walked with some caution on this new ground for them. Bows, arrows, and sticks with sharp iron tips were their only weapons.

However, no fierce animals appeared, and it was likely that these creatures preferred the thick forests to the south; but the colonists had the unpleasant surprise of seeing Top stop in front of a large snake, measuring fourteen to fifteen feet long. Nab knocked it out with a blow from his stick. Cyrus Smith examined the reptile and declared it non-venomous, as it belonged to the species of diamond snakes that the natives eat in New South Wales. But it was possible that there were others whose bite is deadly, such as those deaf vipers with forked tails, which rise beneath one's feet, or these winged snakes, equipped with two ear flaps that allow them to leap with great speed.

Top, after the initial moment of surprise, started hunting the reptiles with an eagerness that made his owner worry for him. So his master constantly called him back.

They soon reached the mouth of the Red Creek, where it flowed into the lake. The explorers recognized the opposite bank as the point they had already visited when coming down from Mount Franklin. Cyrus Smith noted that the water flow of the creek was quite substantial; therefore, it was essential that nature had provided a spillway for the lake's overflow at some point. It was this spillway that needed to be discovered, as it undoubtedly formed a water-fall whose mechanical power could be harnessed.

The colonists, walking freely but without straying too far from each other, began to circle the shore of the lake, which was quite steep.

The waters appeared to be extremely fish-rich, and Pencroff promised himself that he would make some fishing gear to exploit them.

They first needed to round the sharp point to the northeast. One might suppose that water was discharging there, as the end of the lake almost came to the edge of the plateau. But it was not the case, and the colonists continued to explore the shore, which, after a slight curve, descended parallel to the coast. On this side, the bank was less wooded, but some clumps of trees sprinkled here and there added to the picturesque quality of the landscape. Grant Lake then appeared in all its extent, and no breeze disturbed the surface of its waters. Top, rustling through the underbrush, startled flocks of various birds, which Gideon Spilett and Harbert greeted with their arrows. One of these birds was even skillfully hit by the young boy and fell amid the marshy grasses. Top rushed towards it and brought back a beautiful swimming bird, slate-colored, with a short beak, a well-developed frontal plate, and webbed toes bordered with a frilled edge, its wings edged with a white stripe. It was a "coot," the size of a large partridge, belonging to that group of macrodactyles which forms the transition between the wading bird order and that of the waterfowl. A rather sad game, overall, and one whose taste was likely to disappoint. But Top would probably not be as picky as his masters, and it was agreed that the coot would be served for his dinner. The colonists were then following the eastern shore of the lake, and they would soon reach the part that had already been explored. The engineer was quite surprised, as he saw no signs of overflow from the water. The reporter and the sailor were chatting with him, and he didn't hide his astonishment from them. At that moment, Top, who had been very calm until then, started showing signs of agitation.

The clever animal went back and forth on the shore, suddenly stopping to look at the water, one paw raised, as if he were on the scent of some invisible prey; then, he barked furiously, seemingly searching, and fell silent all of a sudden. Neither Cyrus Smith nor his companions initially paid much attention to Top's behavior; however, the dog's barking soon became so frequent that the engineer became concerned.

"What's wrong, Top?" he asked.

The dog leaped several times toward his master, visibly anxious, and then rushed again toward the shore. Then suddenly, he plunged into the lake.

"Here, Top!" shouted Cyrus Smith, who didn't want his dog to venture into the suspicious waters.

"What's going on down there?" Pencroff asked, examining the surface of the lake.

"Top must have sensed some amphibian," replied Harbert.

"An alligator, perhaps?" said the reporter.

"I don't think so," replied Cyrus Smith. "Alligators are only found in lower latitude regions."

Meanwhile, Top had come back at his master's call and had returned to the shore; but he couldn't stay still; he jumped among the tall grasses, and, guided by his instinct, it seemed he was tracking some invisible creature that had slipped under the lake's waters, along the edges. However, the water was calm, and not a ripple disturbed its surface. Several times, the colonists stopped on the shore and looked on with attention. Nothing appeared. There was some mystery here.

The engineer was greatly intrigued.

"Let's continue this exploration to the end," he said.

Half an hour later, they all arrived at the southeast corner of the lake and found themselves back on the Grande-vue plateau. At this point, the examination of the lake's shores should be considered complete, yet the engineer had not been able to discover where and how the water was being discharged.

"Still, this outflow exists," he repeated, "and since it's not external, it must be carved out inside the granite mass of the coast!"

"But why is it important for you to know this, my dear Cyrus?" asked Gideon Spilett.

"A fair amount," replied the engineer, "because if the drainage occurs through the massif, it's possible that there may be some cavity there that would have been easy to make habitable after diverting the water."

"But isn't it possible, Mr. Cyrus, that the water flows out through the very bottom of the lake?" said Harbert, "and that it goes to the sea through an underground channel?"

"That could indeed be," replied the engineer, "and if so, we will have to build our own house since nature hasn't made the initial layout."

The colonists were preparing to cross the plateau to return to the Chimneys, as it was five o'clock in the evening, when Top showed new signs of agitation. He barked with rage, and before his master could hold him back, he plunged a second time into the lake.

Everyone ran toward the shore. The dog was already over twenty feet out, and Cyrus Smith was calling him back urgently when a huge head emerged from the surface of the water, which didn't seem deep in this spot.

Harbert immediately recognized the type of amphibian to which this conical-headed creature with big eyes belonged, adorned with long silky-whiskers.

"A manatee!" he exclaimed.

It was not a manatee, but a specimen of this type, classified in the cetacean order, known as a "dugong," because its nostrils were opened at the top of its snout.

The enormous animal rushed toward the dog, who tried in vain to avoid it by returning to the shore. His master could do nothing to save him, and even before it crossed the minds of Gideon Spilett or Harbert to arm their bows, Top, seized by the dugong, disappeared beneath the water.

Nab, spear in hand, wanted to jump in to save the dog, determined to confront the formidable animal in its own element.

"No, Nab," said the engineer, holding back his brave servant.

However, a struggle was taking place beneath the water, an inexplicable struggle, as under those conditions, Top could obviously not resist, a struggle that must have been terrible, as evidenced by the bubbling on the surface, a struggle that could only end with the death of the dog! But suddenly, amidst a circle of foam, Top reappeared. Thrown into the air by some unknown force, he rose ten feet above the surface of the lake, fell back into the deeply disturbed waters, and soon reached the shore without serious injuries, miraculously saved.

Cyrus Smith and his companions looked on, bewildered. An equally inexplicable circumstance! It seemed as if the fight continued under the waters. Certainly, the dugong, attacked by some powerful creature, after letting go of the dog, was fighting for its own life.

But this didn't last long. The waters turned red with blood, and the body of the dugong, emerging from a scarlet pool that spread widely, soon washed ashore on a small beach at the southern tip of the lake.

The colonists ran toward that spot. The dugong was dead. It was a huge animal, fifteen to sixteen feet long, weighing between three and four thousand pounds. On its neck was a wound that seemed to have been made with a sharp blade. What sort of amphibian could have dealt the devastating blow to the formidable dugong? No one could say, and, quite preoccupied with this incident, Cyrus Smith and his companions returned to the Chimneys.

❧ 17 ❧

The next day, May 7, Cyrus Smith and Gideon Spilett, leaving Nab to prepare breakfast, climbed up the Grande-vue plateau, while Harbert and Pencroff went back up the river to replenish their supply of wood.

The engineer and the reporter soon arrived at the small beach located at the southern tip of the lake, where the amphibian had washed ashore. Large flocks of birds had already descended upon this meaty mass, and they had to be chased away with stones because Cyrus Smith wanted to keep the blubber from the dugong for the needs of the colony.

As for the animal's flesh, it would surely provide excellent food, since in some regions of Malaysia, it is specially reserved for the tables of indigenous princes. But that was Nab's business. At that moment, Cyrus Smith had other thoughts on his mind. The incident from the day before hadn't left his mind and continued to occupy him. He wanted to uncover the mystery of that under-water battle and know which relative of the mastodons or other sea monsters had inflicted such a strange wound on the dugong.

So he stood there on the edge of the lake, looking and observing, but nothing appeared beneath the tranquil waters, which sparkled in the early rays of the sun. On the little beach supporting the dugong's body, the waters were shallow; but from that point onward, the lake's bottom gradually dropped off, and it was likely that at the center, the depth was considerable. The lake could be seen as a large basin filled by the waters of the Red Creek.

"Well then, Cyrus," asked the reporter, "it seems these waters offer nothing suspicious?"

"No, my dear Spilett," replied the engineer, "and I really don't know how to explain yesterday's incident!"

"I admit," Gideon Spilett replied, "that the wound made to this amphibian is at least strange, and I can't explain how it could be that Top was thrown so vigorously from the water? It really seems as if a powerful arm threw him thus, and that this same arm, armed with a dagger, then dealt the death blow to the dugong!"

"Yes," replied the engineer, who had become thoughtful. "There is something here that I cannot comprehend. But do you understand better, my dear Spilett, how I was saved myself, how I could be pulled from the waves and transported onto the dunes? No, isn't it true? So I sense there is some mystery there that we will probably uncover one day. Let's observe, then, but let's not insist before our companions on these odd incidents. Let's keep our observations to ourselves and continue our work."

As you know, the engineer had still not been able to discover where the overflow from the lake was escaping, but as he hadn't seen any signs that it ever overflowed, it was necessary for an outflow to exist somewhere. Now, Cyrus Smith was rather surprised to notice a fairly strong current being felt in that area. He threw a few small pieces of wood and saw that they were heading toward the southern corner. He followed this current by walking along the shore and reached the southern tip of the lake.

There, a sort of depression of the waters occurred, as if they suddenly disappeared into some crack in the ground.

Cyrus Smith listened, putting his ear down to the lake, and he distinctly heard the sound of an underground waterfall.

"There it is," he said, standing up, "that's where the water is being discharged, there, no doubt, that through a channel carved into the granite massif, it leaves to join the sea, through some cavities that we could use to our advantage! Well! I'll find out!"

The engineer cut a long branch, stripped it of its leaves, and, dipping it at the angle of both banks, he recognized that there was a large hole located only a foot below the surface of the water. This hole was the outlet of the long-sought drain, and the strength of the current was such that the branch was pulled from the engineer's hands and disappeared.

"There is no doubt left now," repeated Cyrus Smith. "There is the outlet of the drain, and I will uncover that outlet."

— How?" asked Gideon Spilett.

— By lowering the water level of the lake by three feet.

— And how do we lower their level?

— By opening them a wider escape than this one.

— Where, Cyrus?

— On the part of the shore that comes closest to the coast.

— But that's a granite shore!" the reporter observed.

— Well then," replied Cyrus Smith, "I will blow up that granite, and the water, escaping, will lower enough to expose that outlet...

— And create a waterfall when falling onto the beach," the reporter added.

— A waterfall that we will use!" replied Cyrus. "Come, come!"

The engineer led his companion, whose confidence in Cyrus Smith was such that he had no doubt the undertaking would succeed. And yet, this granite shore, how to open it, how, without powder and with imperfect tools, to break apart those rocks? Wasn't this a task beyond his strength, to which the engineer was about to commit himself?

When Cyrus Smith and the reporter returned to the Chimneys, they found Harbert and Pencroff busy unloading their load of wood.

"The woodcutters are going to finish, Mr. Cyrus," the sailor said with a laugh, "and when you need bricklayers...

— Not bricklayers, but chemists," replied the engineer.

— Yes," added the reporter, "we're going to blow up the island...

— Blow up the island!" exclaimed Pencroff.

— Partially, at least!" replied Gideon Spilett.

"Listen to me, my friends," said the engineer.

And he told them the results of his observations. According to him, a more or less considerable cavity must exist in the granite mass supporting the Grande-vue plateau, and he intended to penetrate it.

To do this, it was first necessary to clear the opening through which the waters rushed, and consequently, to lower their level by providing them with a wider exit. Thus, there arose the need to create an explosive substance that could make a strong incision at another point along the shore. This was what Cyrus Smith was going to attempt with the minerals that nature provided him.

It goes without saying with what enthusiasm everyone, and more particularly Pencroff, greeted this project.

Using great means, blasting that granite, creating a waterfall, that appealed to the sailor! And he would be just as much a chemist as a bricklayer or shoemaker, since the engineer needed chemists. He would be everything they wanted, "even a dance and etiquette teacher," he told Nab, if that were ever necessary.

Nab and Pencroff were initially tasked with extracting the blubber from the dugong and preserving the flesh, which was destined for food. They set off immediately without even asking for more explanation. Their confidence in the engineer was absolute. Moments later, Cyrus Smith, Harbert, and Gideon Spilett, dragging the trellis and going up the river, headed toward the coal deposit where the pyritic schists abounded, which are indeed found in the most recent transitional formations, and of which Cyrus Smith had already brought back a sample.

The entire day was spent hauling a certain amount of these pyrites back to the Chimneys. By evening, there were several tons.

The next day, May 8, the engineer began his manipulations. These pyritic schists, composed mainly of coal, silica, alumina, and iron sulfide—of which there was an excess—needed to be isolated, and the iron sulfide turned into sulfate as quickly as possible. Once the sulfate was obtained, sulfuric acid would be extracted from it.

This was indeed the goal to achieve. Sulfuric acid is one of the most widely used agents, and the industrial importance of a nation can be measured by the consumption made of it. This acid would later prove extremely useful to the colonists for making candles, tanning hides, etc., but at this moment, the engineer reserved it for another use.

Cyrus Smith chose a spot behind the Chimneys where the ground was carefully leveled. On this ground, he placed a pile of branches and chopped wood, on which pieces of pyritic schists were arranged, leaning against one another; then, it was all covered with a thin layer of pyrites, previously reduced to the size of a walnut.

Once this was done, they lit the wood, whose heat transferred to the schists, which ignited since they contained coal and sulfur.

Then, new layers of crushed pyrites were arranged to form a huge pile, which was externally covered with earth and grasses, after vents were made, as if carbonizing a pile of wood to make charcoal.

Then they let the transformation take place, and it would take no less than ten to twelve days for the iron sulfide to turn into iron sulfate and the alumina into aluminum sulfate, two equally soluble substances, while the others, silica, burned coal, and ashes, were not.

While this chemical work was being carried out, Cyrus Smith proceeded with other operations. They put in more than just zeal. It was obsession.Nab and Pencroff had removed the fat from the dugong, which had been collected in large clay jars. They aimed to isolate one of its components, glycerin, through a process called saponification. To achieve this, it was enough to treat it with either sodium or lime. Indeed, either of these substances, after reacting with the fat, would form soap while isolating glycerin, which was exactly what the engineer wanted to obtain. Cyrus Smith had plenty of lime, as we know; however, using lime would only yield insoluble, useless lime soaps, while using sodium would produce a soluble soap that could be used for household cleaning.

As a practical man, Cyrus Smith needed to focus on obtaining sodium instead. Was it hard to find? No, because marine plants were abundant on the shore, such as samphire, ice plants, and all the wracks and kelps. So, they gathered a large quantity of these plants, dried them, and then burned them in open pits. The combustion of these plants was maintained for several days to heat the ashes to the point where they would melt into a compact gray mass, which has long been known as "natural soda."

With this result, the engineer treated the fat with sodium, yielding on one hand a soluble soap and on the other hand, the neutral substance glycerin. But that wasn't all. Cyrus Smith needed another substance, potassium nitrate, more commonly known as saltpeter, for his future preparations.

Cyrus Smith could have made this substance by treating potassium carbonate, which can easily be extracted from plant ashes, with nitric acid. But he didn't have nitric acid, and that was exactly the acid he wanted to obtain in the end. So, there was a vicious cycle he could never escape from.

Fortunately, nature was about to provide him with the saltpeter, without him having to do anything more than collect it. Harbert discovered a deposit in the northern part of the island, at the foot of Mount Franklin, and all that was left was to purify this salt.

These various tasks took about eight days. They were completed before the transformation of sulfide to iron sulfate was finished. In the days that followed, the colonists had time to make refractory pottery from plastic clay and to construct a specially designed brick furnace that would serve for the distillation of iron sulfate once it was obtained. All this was completed by May 18, around the time the chemical transformation was concluding. Gédéon Spilett, Harbert, Nab, and Pencroff, skillfully guided by the engineer, had become the most skilled workers in the world. Necessity, after all, is the greatest teacher, and the one you listen to the most.

When the pile of pyrites was completely burned, the operation resulted in iron sulfate, aluminum sulfate, silica, charcoal residue, and ash, which was deposited in a basin filled with water. They stirred the mixture, let it settle, then decanted it, obtaining a clear liquid that contained dissolved iron sulfate and aluminum sulfate, while the other materials remained solid since they were insoluble. Finally, as part of this liquid evaporated, iron sulfate crystals were formed, and the mother liquor, which contained aluminum sulfate, was discarded.

Cyrus Smith thus had a good amount of those iron sulfate crystals, from which he needed to extract sulfuric acid. In industrial practice, creating sulfuric acid is a costly process requiring significant facilities, special tools, platinum equipment, lead chambers that can withstand the acid, and other equipment where the transformation occurs, etc. The engineer had none of this equipment at his disposal, but he knew that sulfuric acid could be made in Bohemia through simpler means, which even had the advantage of producing it at a higher concentration.

This was how the acid known as Nordhausen acid was produced. To obtain sulfuric acid, Cyrus Smith had only one operation left to complete: to calcine the iron sulfate crystals in a closed vessel, so that sulfuric acid would distill into vapors, which would then condense into the acid.

Refractory pottery was used for this manipulation, in which the crystals were placed, and the furnace, whose heat would distill the sulfuric acid. The operation was perfectly executed, and by May 20, twelve days after commencing, the engineer possessed the agent he planned to utilize afterward in various ways.

So, why did he want this agent? Simply to produce nitric acid, which was easy since saltpeter, when treated with sulfuric acid, would yield exactly that acid through distillation. But in the end, what was he going to do with this nitric acid? His companions still didn't know, as he hadn't revealed the final step of his work.

However, the engineer was close to his goal, and one last operation provided him with the substance that had required so much manipulation. After obtaining nitric acid, he combined it with glycerin, which had been previously concentrated by evaporation in a water bath, and he produced several pints of an oily, yellowish liquid, even without using a refrigerant mix.

Cyrus Smith performed this last operation alone, away from the Cheminées, as it presented explosion hazards, and when he brought a flask of this liquid back to his friends, he simply said to them, "Here's nitroglycerin!" Indeed, it was that terrible product, whose explosive power is perhaps ten times that of ordinary gunpowder and has caused so many accidents! However, since a way had been found to transform it into dynamite, by mixing it with a solid, porous substance like clay or sugar to contain it, the dangerous liquid could be used more safely. But dynamite was not yet known at the time when the colonists were operating on Lincoln Island.

"And this stuff is going to blow up our rocks?" said Pencroff, sounding quite skeptical.

"Yes, my friend," replied the engineer, "and this nitroglycerin will be even more effective since this granite is extremely hard and will resist the explosion more."

"When will we see that, Mr. Cyrus?"

"Tomorrow, as soon as we've dug a mine hole," replied the engineer.

The next day, May 21, at dawn, the miners went to a point that formed the eastern shore of Lake Grant, just five hundred steps from the coast. At this spot, the plateau was lower than the waters, which were held back only by their granite frame. It was clear that if they broke this frame, the waters would escape through this outlet, creating a stream that, after flowing across the inclined surface of the plateau, would plunge down to the shore. Consequently, there would be a general lowering of the lake level, exposing the outlet, which was the final goal.

So, they needed to break the frame. Under the engineer's direction, Pencroff, armed with a pickaxe he skillfully wielded, attacked the granite from the outer surface. The hole they were going to drill began on a horizontal edge of the shore and had to slant downwards, reaching a level significantly lower than the lake waters. This way, the explosive force would, by pushing aside the rocks, allow the waters to flow freely outside, thus lowering the level sufficiently.

The work took a long time since the engineer, wanting to create a formidable effect, planned to use no less than ten liters of nitroglycerin for the operation. But Pencroff, who was relieved by Nab, managed so well that by around four o'clock in the evening, the mine hole was ready.

The only remaining question was how to ignite the explosive substance. Normally, nitroglycerin ignites through a detonator that, when it explodes, sets off the explosion. In fact, a shock is needed to trigger the explosion, and if ignited simply, the substance would burn without detonating.

Cyrus Smith could certainly have made a detonator. In the absence of fulminate, he could easily obtain a substance similar to gun cotton, as he had nitric acid available. This substance, pressed into a cartridge and placed within the nitroglycerin, would explode using a fuse and cause the explosive reaction.

But Cyrus Smith knew that nitroglycerin has the property of detonating upon impact. He decided to use this property, intending to employ another method if this one didn't work. Indeed, the impact of a hammer on a few drops of nitroglycerin spread on a hard stone surface is enough to cause the explosion.

However, the operator couldn't be there to strike the hammer without risking being caught in the operation.

Therefore, Cyrus Smith devised a plan where he would hang a mass of iron weighing several pounds from a post above the mine hole using a vegetable fiber. A long sulfur-coated fiber was attached to the middle of the first by one end, while the other end trailed on the ground several feet away from the mine hole. Once the fire was set to this second fiber, it would burn until it reached the first fiber. The first one would then catch fire, break, and drop the mass of iron onto the nitroglycerin.

So, this device was set up; then the engineer, after moving his companions away, filled the mine hole so that the nitroglycerin was level with the opening, and he dropped a few droplets onto the rock below the already hanging mass of iron.

This done, Cyrus Smith lit the end of the sulfur-coated fiber, then left the site and returned to his companions at the Cheminées. The fiber was supposed to burn for about twenty-five minutes, and indeed, twenty-five minutes later, an explosion occurred that defied description. It seemed as if the entire island was shaking on its base. A burst of stones shot into the air as if expelled by a volcano. The shockwave from the displaced air was so strong that the rocks of the Cheminées swayed. The colonists, though they were over two miles from the mine, were thrown to the ground.

They stood up, climbed back onto the plateau, and rushed to the spot where the lake's shore must have been blasted open by the explosion... A triple cheer erupted from their throats! The granite frame had split over a large area! A swift stream was gushing from it, rushing across the plateau, reaching the crest, and plunging three hundred feet down to the shore!

18

Cyrus Smith's project had succeeded; but, as was his habit, without showing any satisfaction, his lips pressed tight, his gaze fixed, he remained still. Harbert was thrilled; Nab was leaping with joy; Pencroff was nodding his big head and murmuring, "Well, our engineer is doing great!"

Indeed, the nitroglycerin had acted powerfully. The wound made to the lake was so significant that the volume of water now escaping through this new outlet was at least triple that which was previously flowing through the old one. Therefore, it was expected that shortly after the operation, the lake level would drop by at least two feet.

The colonists returned to the Cheminées to grab picks, iron-tipped spears, ropes made from fibers, a lighter, and tinder; then they went back to the plateau. Top was with them.

Along the way, the sailor couldn't help saying to the engineer:

"But do you realize, Mr. Cyrus, that with this lovely liquid you've made, you could blow up our entire island?"

"Without a doubt, the island, the continents, and the Earth itself," replied Cyrus Smith. "It's just a matter of quantity."

"Couldn't you use this nitroglycerin for loading firearms?" asked the sailor.

"No, Pencroff, because it's too explosive a substance. But it would be easy to make gun cotton or even ordinary gunpowder since we have nitric acid, salt-peter, sulfur, and charcoal. Unfortunately, what we lack are the weapons."

"Oh! Mr. Cyrus," replied the sailor, "with a bit of good will..."

Indeed, Pencroff had crossed out the word "impossible" from Lincoln Island's dictionary.

Once they reached the Grande-vue plateau, the colonists headed straight towards the point of the lake, close to where the outlet of the former drain was, which should now be exposed.

The outlet would, therefore, have become accessible, since the waters would no longer rush into it, and it would certainly be easy to identify its inner structure. In just a few moments, the colonists reached the lower angle of the lake, and one glance was enough to confirm that the desired result had been achieved. Indeed, in the granite wall of the lake, now above the water level, appeared the long-sought outlet. A narrow ledge, exposed by the retreat of the waters, allowed them access. This outlet measured about twenty feet in width but was only two feet high. It was like a sewer mouth at the edge of a sidewalk. This opening wouldn't have allowed easy passage for the colonists; but Nab and Pencroff took their pickaxes, and in less than an hour, they had made it tall enough.

The engineer then approached and saw that the walls of the drain, in its upper part, did not have a slope greater than thirty to thirty-five degrees. They were, therefore, passable, and as long as their steepness didn't increase, it would be easy to descend them to sea level. So, if, which was quite probable, there were some vast cavity inside the granite mass, they might find a way to use it.

"Well, Mr. Cyrus, what's stopping us?" asked the sailor, eager to venture into the narrow corridor. "You see Top has gone ahead of us!"

"Good," replied the engineer. "But we need to see clearly. — Nab, go cut some resinous branches."

Nab and Harbert ran to the shores of the lake, shaded by pines and other evergreen trees, and soon returned with branches that they arranged into torches. These torches were lit from the fire of the lighter, and with Cyrus Smith leading, the colonists entered the dark tunnel that the overflow of water had once filled.Contrary to what one might have assumed, the diameter of this tunnel widened as they descended, allowing the explorers to stand upright almost immediately. The granite walls, worn smooth by water over an endless time, were slippery, so they had to watch for falls. For this reason, the colonists tied themselves together with a rope, just like climbers do in the mountains. Fortunately, some ledges of granite formed real steps, making the descent less dangerous. Droplets still clinging to the rocks shimmered here and there in the light of the torches, and one could have believed that the walls were covered with countless stalactites.

The engineer examined the black granite. He saw not a single layer or crack. The mass was compact and had an extremely tight grain. This tunnel dated back to the very origin of the island. It was not the waters that had gradually worn it away. Pluto, not Neptune, had drilled it with his own hand, and one could see on the wall the traces of volcanic work that water erosion had not completely erased.

The colonists were descending very slowly. They felt a certain thrill venturing into the depths of this mass, which had clearly been visited by humans for the first time. They were silent, but they were thinking, and many must have wondered if some octopus or other gigantic cephalopod could occupy the internal cavities that were connected to the sea. They had to proceed with caution.

Moreover, Top was at the head of the small group, and they could rely on the dog's keen senses to alert them in case of danger.

After descending about a hundred feet along a rather winding path, Cyrus Smith, who was walking ahead, stopped, and his companions caught up with him. The spot where they halted was hollowed out, creating a small cave. Drops of water fell from its ceiling, but they didn't come from seepage through the mass. They were just the remnants left by the torrent that had roared through this cavity for so long, and the slightly damp air did not emit any foul smells.

"Well, my dear Cyrus?" said Gideon Spilett. "This is a well-hidden retreat deep in these depths, but ultimately, it is uninhabitable."

"Why uninhabitable?" asked the sailor.

"Because it's too small and too dark."

"Can't we enlarge it, dig it out, make openings for light and air?" replied Pencroff, who doubted nothing.

"Let's continue," replied Cyrus Smith, "let's continue our exploration. Perhaps further down, nature will have spared us this work."

"We're only about a third of the way down," Harbert observed.

"About a third, yes," Cyrus Smith replied, "since we have descended about a hundred feet from the opening, and it's not impossible that a hundred feet lower..."

"Where is Top...?" Nab asked, interrupting his master.

They searched the cave. The dog wasn't there.

"He probably continued on his way," said Pencroff.

"Let's go find him," replied Cyrus Smith.

They resumed their descent. The engineer carefully observed the deviations that the discharge was going through, and despite all the twists and turns, he could easily tell that its general direction was towards the sea.

The colonists had lowered themselves another fifty feet directly down when they were startled by distant sounds coming from the depths of the mass. They stopped and listened. These sounds, carried through the corridor like voices through an acoustic tube, arrived clearly to their ears.

"That's Top barking!" cried Harbert.

"Yes," replied Pencroff, "and our brave dog is barking with fury!"

"We have our iron-tipped spears," said Cyrus Smith. "Let's be on guard and move forward!"

"This is getting more and more interesting," murmured Gideon Spilett in the sailor's ear, who nodded in agreement.

Cyrus Smith and his companions hurried to help the dog. Top's barks grew increasingly audible. One could sense a strange rage in his staccato voice.

Was he indeed grappling with some animal he had disturbed? One could say that, without thinking of the danger they were putting themselves into, the colonists now felt an irresistible curiosity. They weren't just going down the corridor; they were almost sliding down its wall, and in a few minutes, they reached Top, who was sixty feet lower.

There, the corridor led to a vast and magnificent cavern. Top was running back and forth, barking furiously. Pencroff and Nab, shaking their torches, cast bursts of light on all the rough spots of the granite, while at the same time, Cyrus Smith, Gideon Spilett, and Harbert stood ready with their spears for any event.

The enormous cavern was empty. The colonists explored it in every direction. There was nothing, not a single animal or living being! And yet, Top continued to bark. Neither caresses nor threats could silence him.

"There must be some exit somewhere through which the waters of the lake flowed to the sea," said the engineer.

"Indeed," replied Pencroff, "and we should be careful not to fall into a hole."

"Go, Top, go!" shouted Cyrus Smith.

Excited by his master's words, the dog ran towards the back of the cavern, and there, his barking intensified.

They followed him, and in the light of the torches, they saw the opening of a true well in the granite. This was indeed where the waters that had once been trapped in the mass flowed out, and this time it wasn't an angled and navigable corridor but a vertical well, into which they couldn't venture.

The torches were held over the opening.

They saw nothing. Cyrus Smith broke off a flaming branch and threw it into the abyss. The bright resin, whose illuminating power increased due to the speed of its fall, lit up the interior of the well, but nothing appeared. Then, the flame extinguished with a slight flicker, indicating that it had reached the water layer, which meant it was at sea level.

The engineer, estimating the time taken for the fall, was able to measure the depth of the well, which turned out to be about ninety feet.

Thus, the floor of the cavern was positioned ninety feet above sea level.

"Here is our home," said Cyrus Smith.

"But it was occupied by some being," replied Gideon Spilett, who was not yet satisfied with his curiosity.

"Well, that being, whatever it was, has fled through this exit," replied the engineer, "and it has given us its place."

"Still, I would have liked to have been Top a quarter of an hour ago because after all, it's not without reason that he was barking!"

Cyrus Smith looked at his dog, and anyone of his companions who approached him would have heard him murmur these words: "Yes, I believe that Top knows more than we do about many things!"

However, the colonists' desires were largely fulfilled. Chance, aided by the incredible insight of their leader, had served them well. They now had access to a vast cavern, the capacity of which they could not yet estimate in the dim light of the torches, but which could certainly be divided into rooms using brick partitions and appropriated, if not as a complete house, at least as a spacious apartment. The waters had abandoned it and could no longer return.

The place was free.

There remained two difficulties: first, the possibility of lighting this excavation carved from a solid block; second, the need to make access easier. For lighting, they could not think about establishing it from above since a massive thickness of granite covered it; but perhaps could bore through the front wall, which faced the sea. Cyrus Smith, who had sufficiently approximated the angle and therefore the length of the discharge during the descent, was justified in believing that the front part of the wall would not be very thick. If lighting was obtained in this way, access would also be possible since it was as easy to make a door as it was to make windows and establish an outside ladder.

Cyrus Smith shared his ideas with his companions.

"Then, Mr. Cyrus, let's get to work!" replied Pencroff. "I have my pick, and I'll know how to break through this wall. Where should I strike?"

"Here," replied the engineer, indicating to the strong sailor a significant indentation in the wall, which would reduce its thickness.

Pencroff attacked the granite, and for half an hour, in the light of the torches, he sent chips flying all around him. The rock glittered under his pick. Nab relieved him, then Gideon Spilett took over after Nab.

This work had been going on for two hours already, so they began to worry that in this spot, the wall might exceed the length of the pick, when, with one last blow struck by Gideon Spilett, the tool pierced through the wall and fell outside.

"Hurrah! always hurrah!" shouted Pencroff.

The wall was only three feet thick in that spot.

Cyrus Smith leaned his eye against the opening, which rose eighty feet above the ground. Before him stretched the edge of the shore, the islet, and beyond that, the vast sea.

But through this wide opening, as the rock had disintegrated noticeably, light flooded in and produced a magical effect, illuminating this splendid cave! If on its left side it measured no more than thirty feet in height and width over a length of a hundred feet, on the right side, it was enormous, and its ceiling arched to more than eighty feet in height. In some places, unevenly placed granite pillars supported the vault like those in a cathedral nave.

Supported by types of lateral pillars, curving here into arches, rising there on pointed ribs, disappearing into dark vaults where whimsical arches could be glimpsed in the shadow, adorned profusely with projections that formed as many pendants, this vault presented a picturesque mix of everything that Byzantine, Romanesque, and Gothic architecture has produced by human hands. And yet, this was only the work of nature! She alone had carved this fairy-tale Alhambra out of a solid block of granite!

The colonists were stunned with admiration. Where they expected to find only a narrow cavity, they found a kind of wonderful palace, and Nab had taken off his hat as if he had been transported into a temple! Cries of admiration erupted from every mouth. The hurrahs echoed and faded away, ricocheted from one echo to another, all the way to the depths of the dark vaults.

"Ah! my friends, exclaimed Cyrus Smith, when we have thoroughly illuminated the interior of this mass, when we have arranged our rooms, our storerooms, and our offices in its left section, we will still have this splendid cavern, which we will use as our study room and our museum!"

"And we will call it...?" asked Harbert.

"Granite-House," replied Cyrus Smith, a name that his companions cheered with their hurrahs.

At that moment, the torches were almost entirely consumed, and since they had to return, they needed to go back up the corridor to reach the top of the plateau, it was decided to postpone the work related to the arrangement of their new home until the next day.

Before departing, Cyrus Smith leaned over the dark well that plunged perpendicularly down to sea level. He listened carefully. No sound emerged, not even the water, which the swells must occasionally have stirred in those depths. Another piece of burning resin was thrown in. The walls of the well illuminated for a moment but again, just like the first time, nothing suspicious revealed itself.

If some sea monster had been unexpectedly caught by the retreat of the waters, it must have returned to the open sea through the underground channel that extended beneath the shore, following the lake's overflow, before a new exit had been offered to it.

Meanwhile, the engineer, motionless, his ear attentive, his gaze fixed in the abyss, did not utter a single word.

The sailor approached him then, touching him on the arm: "Mr. Smith?" he said.

"What do you want, my friend?" replied the engineer, as if he had returned from the land of dreams.

"The torches will soon go out."

"Let's move!" responded Cyrus Smith.

The little group left the cavern and began their ascent through the dark drain. Top brought up the rear and continued making strange grumbles. The ascent was quite laborious. The colonists stopped for a few moments at the upper cave, which formed a kind of landing halfway up this long granite staircase. Then they began to climb again.

Soon a cooler breeze was felt. The droplets, dried by evaporation, no longer sparkled on the walls. The smoky brightness of the torches faded. The one Nab was carrying went out, and without wanting to venture into deep darkness, they had to hurry.

They did so, and just before four o'clock, as the sailor's torch was extinguished, Cyrus Smith and his companions emerged through the opening of the drain.

❧ 19 ❧

The next day, May 22, work began on the special adaptation of their new home. The colonists were eager to exchange their insufficient shelter of the Chimneys for this vast and healthy retreat carved into solid rock, protected from both the sea's waters and the sky. The Chimneys were not to be completely abandoned, however, and the engineer's plan was to make it a workshop for heavy work.

Cyrus Smith's first concern was to identify the exact point where the front of Granite-House was developing. He went to the shore, at the base of the enormous wall, and since the pick, which had slipped from the reporter's hands, must have fallen straight down, it was enough to find this pick to identify where the hole had been made in the granite.

The pick was easily found, and indeed, a hole opened vertically above the spot where it had lodged in the sand, about eighty feet above the shore. Some rock pigeons were already entering and exiting through this narrow opening. It really seemed like Granite-House had been discovered for them!

The engineer intended to divide the right side of the cavern into several rooms, preceded by an entrance hallway, and light it up with five windows and a door made in the façade.Pencroff accepted the five windows, but he couldn't see the point of having a door, since the old overflow provided a natural staircase that would always make it easy to access Granite-House.

"My friend," replied Cyrus Smith, "if it's easy for us to get to our home via the overflow, it will be just as easy for others to do the same. On the contrary, I plan to block this overflow at its opening and seal it tight."

"And how will we get in?" asked the sailor.

"Through an outside ladder," Cyrus Smith answered, "a rope ladder, which, once removed, will make our home inaccessible."

"But why all these precautions?" said Pencroff. "So far, the animals don't seem too threatening. As for being inhabited by natives, our island is not!"

"Are you sure about that, Pencroff?" asked the engineer, looking at the sailor.

"We won't be sure until we explore every part of it," replied Pencroff.

"Yes," said Cyrus Smith, "because we only know a small portion of it. However, if we don't have enemies inside, they could come from outside, as these Pacific waters are dangerous. So let's take precautions against any possibility."

Cyrus Smith spoke wisely, and without making further objections, Pencroff got ready to follow his orders.

The facade of Granite-House would be brightened by five windows and a door, serving what would be the "living area," along with a large bay window and portholes that would allow plenty of light into the wonderful hall that would serve as the main room. This facade, located eighty feet above the ground, faced east, and the rising sun greeted it with its first rays. It stretched across that part of the wall between the promontory by the mouth of the Mercy and a line drawn straight above the rock pile that formed the Chimneys.

Thus, the strong winds, specifically those from the northeast, only hit it at an angle, as it was protected by the very orientation of the promontory.

Moreover, while waiting for the window frames to be made, the engineer intended to cover the openings with thick shutters, which would prevent any wind or rain from entering and could be hidden if needed.

The first task was to block these openings. Using a pick on this hard rock would have been too slow, and it was known that Cyrus Smith preferred large-scale methods. He still had some nitroglycerin available, which he made good use of. The effect of the explosive was suitably localized, and under its force, the granite was blasted in the exact places chosen by the engineer. Then, with the pick and shovel, they completed the pointed shape of the five windows, the large bay window, the portholes, and the door, squaring the frames, which had rather whimsically chosen profiles, and a few days after starting the work, Granite-House was well lit by the light of the rising sun that penetrated deep into its most secret depths.

According to Cyrus Smith's plan, the living area was to be divided into five compartments overlooking the sea: on the right, an entrance served by a door leading to the ladder, followed by a first kitchen-room, thirty feet wide, a dining room measuring forty feet, a sleeping room of equal width, and finally a "guest room" requested by Pencroff, next to the large hall.

These rooms, or rather this suite of rooms that made up the Granite-House living area, were not meant to occupy the entire depth of the cavity. They were to be connected by a corridor located between them and a long storage room, where utensils, food supplies, and reserves would fit comfortably. All products gathered from the island, both flora and fauna, would be in excellent conditions for preservation and completely safe from moisture. There was plenty of space, and each item could be methodically organized. Additionally, the colonists still had access to the small cave above the large cavern, which would serve as the attic of the new home.

With this plan decided, they were left with just the task of putting it into action. The miners thus became brickmakers; the bricks were then brought and piled at the foot of Granite-House.

Until now, Cyrus Smith and his companions had accessed the cavern only via the old overflow. This method of communication required them to first climb to the Grande-vue plateau by taking a detour along the riverbank, then descend two hundred feet down the corridor, and then climb back up, which wasted time and was tiring. So, Cyrus Smith decided to immediately create a sturdy rope ladder, which, once pulled up, would make the entrance to Granite-House completely inaccessible.

This ladder was made with extreme care, and its posts, formed from braided fibers of "curry grass," were as strong as a heavy cable. The rungs came from a type of red cedar, with light and sturdy branches, and the apparatus was skillfully crafted by Pencroff.

Other ropes were also made from plant fibers, and a kind of crude block and tackle was installed at the door. This way, the bricks could be easily removed up to the level of Granite-House. The transport of materials was thus greatly simplified, and the actual interior setup began right away. There was no shortage of lime, and thousands of bricks were ready to use. The framework for the partitions was easily set up, quite rudimentary in design, and in a very short time, the living area was divided into rooms and a storage space according to the agreed plan.

These various tasks were carried out swiftly, under the engineer's guidance, who himself handled the hammer and trowel. No labor was foreign to Cyrus Smith, who thus set an example for intelligent and zealous companions. They worked with confidence, and even cheerfully, Pencroff always ready with a joke, sometimes as a carpenter, sometimes as a rope maker, sometimes as a mason, spreading his good humor to everyone around. His faith in the engineer was absolute. Nothing could disturb it.

He believed Cyrus capable of undertaking anything and succeeding at every-thing. The issue of clothing and shoes—undoubtedly a serious question—, matters of lighting during the winter nights, making use of fertile areas of the island, transforming this wild flora into cultivated flora, all seemed easy to him with Cyrus Smith's help, and everything would be accomplished in due time. He dreamed of canalized rivers, simplifying the transport of the land's wealth, of quarries and mines to exploit, of machines for all industrial practices, of railways, yes, railways! which would certainly one day cover Lincoln Island.

The engineer let Pencroff talk. He did not temper the exaggerations of the brave heart. He knew how contagious confidence could be; he even smiled to hear him speak and said nothing of the worries the future sometimes inspired in him. Indeed, in this part of the Pacific, aside from the passage of ships, he feared they might never be rescued. So, the colonists had to rely on them-selves, and only on themselves, as the distance from Lincoln Island to any other land was so great that venturing out on a necessarily flimsy boat would be a serious and perilous endeavor.

"But, as the sailor said, they were a hundred fathoms ahead of the Robinsons of old, for whom everything was a miracle to be accomplished."

And indeed, they "knew," and the man who "knows" succeeds where others would merely vegetate and inevitably perish.

During these works, Harbert distinguished himself. He was intelligent and active, quickly understanding and executing well, and Cyrus Smith grew increasingly fond of this boy. Harbert felt a strong and respectful friendship for the engineer. Pencroff noticed the close bond forming between the two but was not jealous.

Nab was Nab. He was what he would always be—courage, zeal, devotion, and selflessness embodied. He had the same faith in his master as Pencroff, but he expressed it less loudly. When the sailor got enthusiastic, Nab always seemed to respond: "But that's only natural." Pencroff and he were very fond of one another and quickly began to address each other informally.

As for Gideon Spilett, he contributed to the common work and was not the most clumsy one—which the sailor sometimes found surprising. A skilled "journalist," not only good at understanding everything but also at executing it!

The ladder was officially installed on May 28.

It had no less than a hundred rungs for that vertical height of eighty feet. Cyrus Smith had been able, fortunately, to divide it into two parts, taking advantage of a ledge on the wall that jutted out about forty feet above the ground. This ledge, carefully leveled with the pick, became a sort of landing where they attached the first ladder, thus cutting the swinging in half and allowing a rope to raise it to the level of Granite-House. The second ladder was anchored at both its lower end resting on the ledge and at its upper end connected to the door itself. Thus, climbing became noticeably easier.

In addition, Cyrus Smith planned to install a hydraulic lift later to avoid any fatigue and time loss for the inhabitants of Granite-House.

The colonists quickly got used to using this ladder. They were agile and skill-ful, and Pencroff, as a sailor used to running on the rigging, was able to give them lessons. But he also had to teach Top. The poor dog, with his four legs, wasn't built for this kind of exercise. But Pencroff was such an eager teacher that Top eventually managed to climb well, soon going up and down the ladder like dogs often do in circuses. If the sailor was proud of his pupil, it is hard to say. However, more than once, Pencroff carried him on his back, which Top never complained about.

It should be noted that during this period of active work, as the bad season approached, food supply was not neglected. Every day, the reporter and Harbert, now clearly the colony's providers, spent a few hours hunting. They had only explored the Jacamar woods on the left of the river so far, as they hadn't crossed the Mercy yet due to the lack of a bridge or canoe. Therefore, all those immense forests known as the Far-West woods had not been explored. They planned this important excursion for the first beautiful days of the following spring. But the Jacamar woods were rich in game; kangaroos and wild boars abounded, and the iron-tipped spears, bows, and arrows of the hunters worked wonders. Additionally, Harbert discovered, at the southwest corner of the lagoon, a natural warren, a slightly damp meadow covered with willows and aromatic herbs that perfumed the air, such as thyme, wild thyme, basil, savory—all fragrant members of the mint family, which rabbits are very fond of. Noting that since the table was set for rabbits, it would be surprising if no rabbits appeared, the two hunters carefully explored this warren. In any case, it produced abundant useful plants, and a naturalist would have found many specimens of the plant kingdom there to study. Thus, Harbert collected a fair amount of basil, rosemary, lemon balm, betony, etc., which have various therapeutic properties—some being good for the lungs, astringent, and fever-reducing, others being anti-spasmodic or anti-rheumatic. And later, when Pencroff asked what they would do with all these herbs,

"To take care of ourselves," replied the young boy, "to treat ourselves when we are sick."

"Why would we be sick when there are no doctors on the island?" Pencroff replied very seriously.

There was nothing to say to that, but the young boy nonetheless collected his herbs, which were very well received at Granite-House. Especially since he could add a notable amount of Monarda didyma, known in North America as

"Oswego tea," which makes an excellent drink. Finally, that day, by searching thoroughly, the two hunters arrived at the true location of the warren. The ground was perforated like a colander.

"Burrows!" shouted Harbert.

"Yes," replied the reporter, "I can see them well."

"But are they inhabited?"

"That's the question."

The question was soon resolved. Almost immediately, hundreds of small animals, similar to rabbits, fled in all directions, so quickly that even Top couldn't catch up with them. Hunters and dog ran after them, but these rodents easily escaped. However, the reporter was determined not to leave the site without capturing at least half a dozen of these quadrupeds. He wanted to stock the pantry first, intending to domesticate the ones they would catch later. With a few snares set at the entrances of the burrows, the operation should succeed. However, at that moment, there were no snares and nothing to make them with. So, they had to resign themselves to visiting each den, probing with a stick, and patiently doing what could not be done otherwise. Finally, after an hour of digging, four rodents were captured in their holes. They were rabbits quite similar to their European counterparts, and they are commonly known as "American rabbits."

Thus, the result of the hunt was brought back to Granite-House, and featured at the evening meal. The inhabitants of this warren were quite a catch, as they were delicious. This was a valuable resource for the colony that seemed inexhaustible.

On May 31, the partitions were finished. They only needed to furnish the rooms, which would take the long days of winter. A fireplace was built in the first room, which served as a kitchen. The chimney intended to carry smoke outside caused some work for the makeshift chimney sweeps. Cyrus Smith found it simpler to make it from brick that was molded; since it wouldn't be possible to give it an outlet at the upper plateau, they drilled a hole in the granite above the kitchen window, and this hole was where the pipe, angled, ended like that of a tin stove. Perhaps, most certainly even, due to the strong east winds that directly hit the facade, the chimney would smoke, but those winds were rare, and besides, master Nab, the cook, didn't mind it too much. When these interior improvements were finished, the engineer focused on blocking the opening of the old spillway leading to the lake to prevent any access through that route. Heavy rocks were rolled to the opening and cemented very securely. Cyrus Smith hadn't yet realized his plan to drown this opening under the lake's waters by bringing them back to their original level with a dam. Instead, he simply concealed the blockage with grass, shrubs, and brush that were planted in the crevices of the rocks, which the following spring was expected to grow abundantly.

However, he did make use of the spillway to bring a stream of fresh water from the lake to their new home. A small channel, dug below their level, achieved this result, and this diversion of a pure and inexhaustible source provided an output of twenty-five to thirty gallons per day.

So water would never be lacking at Granite-House. Finally, everything was completed, and it was just in time, as the bad season was approaching. Thick shutters allowed them to close the windows in front, while waiting for the engineer to have time to make glass panes.

Gédéon Spilett had artfully arranged around the windows, in the rock outcroppings, plants of various kinds along with long floating grasses, thus framing the openings with picturesque greenery that created a charming effect.

The residents of the solid, healthy, and safe home could only be delighted with their work. The windows allowed their gaze to stretch over an endless horizon, with the two capes Mandible closing in to the north and Cape Claw to the south.

The whole bay of Union unfolded magnificently before them. Yes, these brave settlers had every reason to be pleased, and Pencroff didn't hold back on the praises for what he humorously called "his apartment on the fifth floor above the ground floor!"

20

The winter season truly began with this month of June, which corresponds to December in the northern hemisphere. It started with showers and gusts of wind that followed one after another without letup. The inhabitants of Granite-House were able to appreciate the advantages of a home that the severe weather could not reach.

The shelter of the Chimneys would have been really insufficient against the rigors of a winter, and there was a fear that the high tides, driven by winds from the sea, could still break in there. Cyrus Smith even took some precautions, anticipating this possibility, to protect, as much as possible, the forge and the furnaces set up there.

Throughout June, the time was spent on various tasks, which included both hunting and fishing, and the stockpiles in the pantry were abundantly filled. Pencroff, as soon as he had the leisure, intended to set up traps from which he expected great benefit. He had made snare traps from fibrous materials, and there wasn't a day that the rabbit warren didn't provide its share of rodents. Nab spent almost all his time salting or smoking meats, ensuring excellent preserved food.

The question of clothing was then seriously discussed. The settlers had no other clothes than what they wore when the balloon dropped them on the island. These clothes were warm and sturdy; they had taken extreme care of them and their linens, keeping everything in perfect cleanliness, but it wouldn't be long before these would need replacing. Furthermore, if winter turned out to be harsh, the settlers would suffer greatly from the cold.

In this regard, Cyrus Smith's ingenuity was lacking. He had to deal with more pressing matters: creating a home, ensuring food supply, and the cold could catch him off guard before the clothing situation was resolved. Therefore, they had to resign themselves to getting through this first winter without too much complaint.

When the good season arrived, there would be serious hunting for those sheep whose presence had been noted during the exploration of Mount Franklin, and once the wool was collected, the engineer would know how to make warm and sturdy fabrics... How? He would think about it.

"Well, we'll just have to roast our legs at Granite-House!" said Pencroff. "The fuel is abundant, and there's no reason to spare it."

"Moreover," replied Gédéon Spilett, "Lincoln Island is not located at a very high latitude, and it is likely that the winters are not harsh. Didn't you tell us, Cyrus, that this thirty-fifth parallel corresponds to that of Spain in the other hemisphere?"

"Indeed," replied the engineer, "but some winters in Spain are very cold! There's snow and ice; nothing is missing, and Lincoln Island can also be harshly tested. However, it's an island, and as such, I hope that the temperature will be more moderate."

"And why is that, Mr. Cyrus?" asked Harbert.

"Because the sea, my child, can be seen as a huge reservoir that stores the summer's warmth. When winter comes, it releases this warmth, which gives nearby coastal regions a milder average temperature, lower in summer but not as low in winter."

"We'll see," replied Pencroff. "I ask to not worry about the cold, whether it's going to be severe or not. What is certain is that the days are already short and the evenings long. If we could tackle the issue of lighting."

"Nothing could be easier," replied Cyrus Smith.

"To tackle?" asked the sailor.

"To solve."

"And when do we begin?"

"Tomorrow, organizing a seal hunt."

"To make candles?"

"Goodness! Pencroff, candles."

Such was, indeed, the engineer's plan; a feasible plan since he had limestone and sulfuric acid, and the amphibians from the islet would provide the fat necessary for their production.

It was June 4. It was Pentecost Sunday, and there was unanimous agreement to celebrate the holiday. All work was suspended, and prayers were raised to the heavens. But these prayers were now acts of gratitude. The colonists of Lincoln Island were no longer the miserable shipwrecked people thrown onto the islet. They no longer asked for anything; they gave thanks.

The next day, June 5, in rather uncertain weather, they set out for the islet. They had to take advantage of the low tide to wade across the channel, and it was agreed that they would build, as best they could, a boat that would make communications easier and would also allow them to navigate up the Mercy during the great exploration of the southwest part of the island, which was to take place when the first nice days arrived.

The seals were numerous, and the hunters, armed with their iron-tipped spears, easily killed half a dozen. Nab and Pencroff skinned them and brought back only their fat and skin to Granite-House, the skin to be used for making sturdy shoes.

The result of this hunt was about three hundred pounds of fat that would be entirely used for making candles.

The operation was extremely simple, and while it didn't yield absolutely perfect products, they were usable. Cyrus Smith would have had to use sulfuric acid, heating it with neutral fatty substances—specifically seal fat—to isolate glycerin; then, from the new combination, he would easily have separated olein, margaric, and stearic acids using boiling water. However, to simplify the operation, he preferred to saponify the fat using lime.

In this way, he obtained a lime soap, easy to decompose by sulfuric acid, which precipitated the lime as sulfate and freed the fatty acids. From these three acids—oleic, margaric, and stearic—the first, being liquid, was expelled with sufficient pressure. The other two formed the very substance that would be used for molding the candles.

The operation lasted no more than twenty-four hours.

The wicks, after several trials, were made from plant fibers and, dipped in the liquefied substance, formed true stearin candles, molded by hand, which only needed whitening and polishing. They did not offer the advantage that wicks, impregnated with boric acid, have of vitrifying as they burn and consuming completely; but Cyrus Smith had made a fine pair of candle holders, and these candles were greatly appreciated during the evenings at Granite-House.

Throughout this month, there was no shortage of work inside the new home. Carpenters had plenty to do. They perfected the tools, which were very rudimentary. They also supplemented them. Scissors, among other things, were made, and the colonists could finally cut their hair, and if they couldn't shave, at least they could trim their beards to their liking.

Harbert didn't have any, Nab had hardly any, but their companions were bristling with hair that justified the making of said scissors.

Making a hand saw, of the type known as a panel saw, took infinite effort, but they finally obtained an instrument that, when wielded vigorously, could divide the woody fibers of the wood.

They made tables, chairs, and cabinets to furnish the main rooms, along with bed frames, all bedding consisting of seagrass mattresses. The kitchen, with its countertops where earthenware utensils rested, its brick stove, and its washing stone, looked very nice, and Nab operated there seriously, as if he were in a chemist's laboratory.

But soon the carpenters had to be replaced by the builders. Indeed, the new spillway, created with blasting, necessitated the construction of two culverts, one on the Grande-Vue plateau, the other right on the shore.

Now, the plateau and the shore were cut transversely by a stream which had to be crossed to reach the north side of the island. To avoid it, the colonists would have to make a considerable detour and go back west beyond the sources of the Red Creek. So, the simplest solution was to establish two culverts, twenty to twenty-five feet long, on the plateau and shore, using just a few trees squared only with an axe, which would form the entire framework. It took just a few days for this task.

Once the bridges were built, Nab and Pencroff took the opportunity to go all the way to the oyster beds discovered offshore from the dunes. They had dragged along a sort of crude cart that replaced the old, overly cumbersome sled, and they brought back several thousand oysters, which quickly acclimatized among these rocks, forming natural parks at the mouth of the Mercy. These mollusks were of excellent quality, and the colonists consumed them almost daily.

As can be seen, Lincoln Island, although its inhabitants had explored only a tiny portion of it, was already providing for almost all their needs. And it was likely that, if thoroughly searched through its most hidden corners, all this wooded area stretching from the Mercy to the promontory of the Reptile would yield new treasures. One deprivation still troubled the settlers on Lincoln Island. They lacked nitrogenous food, as well as the plant products to temper its use; the woody roots of the dragon trees, subjected to fermentation, gave them a sour drink, a kind of beer much better than pure water; they had even made sugar, without cane or beet, by collecting the liquid distilled from the "acer saccharinum," a type of maple from the acer family, which thrives in all temperate zones, and of which the island had a great number; they made a very pleasant tea using the monardas brought back from the rabbit warren; finally, they had an abundance of salt, the only mineral product entering into their diet... but they lacked bread.

Perhaps, later on, the settlers could replace this staple with some equivalent, such as sago flour or starch from the breadfruit tree. It was possible, indeed, that the southern forests contained these precious trees among their species, but so far they had not encountered them.

However, Providence would, in this particular circumstance, come directly to aid the settlers, albeit in an infinitesimal measure, it is true, but finally, Cyrus Smith, with all his intelligence and ingenuity, would never have been able to produce what, by the greatest chance, Harbert found one day in the lining of his jacket, which he was mending.

That day, — it was pouring rain — the settlers were gathered in the great room of Granite-House when the young boy suddenly exclaimed, "Look, Mr. Cyrus. A grain of wheat!"

And he showed his companions a grain, a unique grain that had slipped from his pocket into the lining of his jacket.

The presence of this grain was explained by Harbert's habit, back in Richmond, of feeding a few pigeons given to him by Pencroff.

"A grain of wheat?" quickly responded the engineer.

"Yes, Mr. Cyrus, but only one, just one!"

"Well, my boy," cried Pencroff, smiling, "this doesn't get us very far, honestly! What can we do with just one grain of wheat?"

"We'll make bread with it," replied Cyrus Smith.

"Bread, cakes, pies!" retorted the sailor. "Come on! The bread that this grain will provide won't choke us anytime soon!"

Harbert, placing little importance on his find, was about to throw the grain away, but Cyrus Smith took it, examined it, confirmed that it was in good condition, and looking directly at the sailor, asked, "Pencroff, do you know how many ears of grain one grain of wheat can produce?"

"One, I suppose!" replied the sailor, surprised by the question.

"Ten, Pencroff. And do you know how many grains are found on an ear?"

"Well, I don't know."

"On average, eighty," said Cyrus Smith. "So if we plant this grain, at the first harvest, we'll yield eight hundred grains, which at the second harvest could produce six hundred forty thousand, at the third five hundred twelve million, and at the fourth more than four hundred billion grains. That's the ratio."

Cyrus Smith's companions listened without responding. These figures astonished them. They were, however, correct.

"Yes, my friends," continued the engineer. "Such are the arithmetic progressions of bountiful nature. And again, how does this increase in wheat grains, of which the ear carries only eight hundred grains, compare to those poppy plants with thirty-two thousand seeds or those tobacco plants that produce three hundred sixty thousand? In just a few years, without the many destructive causes stopping their fertility, these plants would invade the entire earth."

But the engineer had not finished his little interrogatory.

"And now, Pencroff," he resumed, "do you know how many four hundred billion grains represent in bushels?"

"No," replied the sailor, "but what I know is that I'm just a fool!"

"Well, that would be more than three million, at one hundred thirty thousand per bushel, Pencroff."

"Three million!" exclaimed Pencroff.

"Three million."

"In four years?"

"In four years," replied Cyrus Smith, "and maybe in two years if, as I hope, we can produce two harvests a year in this latitude." In response, as was his habit, Pencroff believed he could only reply with a tremendous cheer.

"Thus, Harbert," added the engineer, "you have made a discovery of utmost importance for us. Everything, my friends, everything can be of use in the conditions we find ourselves in. Please, do not forget that.

— No, Mr. Cyrus, we won't forget, replied Pencroff, and if I ever find one of those tobacco seeds, which multiply by three hundred sixty thousand, I assure you I won't toss it to the wind! And now, do you know what we still have to do?

— We need to plant this seed, replied Harbert.

— Yes, added Gideon Spilett, with all the care it deserves, for it holds our future crops.

— Let's hope it grows! exclaimed the sailor.

— It will grow, replied Cyrus Smith.

It was June 20. The timing was therefore right to sow this unique and precious grain of wheat. They initially considered planting it in a pot; but after some thought, they decided to trust nature and plant it directly in the ground. This was done that very day, and it goes without saying that every precaution was taken to ensure the operation was successful.

The weather having cleared slightly, the colonists climbed the heights of Granite House. There, on the plateau, they chose a spot well sheltered from the wind, where the midday sun would shower all its warmth. The area was cleaned up, cultivated with care, even dug up to remove insects or worms; a layer of good soil mixed with a little lime was laid down; it was surrounded by a fence; then, the seed was buried in the damp layer.

Didn't it seem like these colonists were laying the first stone of a building? This reminded Pencroff of the day he lit his one match, and all the care he took in that operation. But this time, it was more serious. Indeed, the castaways would always have managed to get fire, one way or another, but no human power could replace that grain of wheat if, by misfortune, it were to perish!

🦎 2 1 🦎

From that moment on, not a single day passed without Pencroff visiting what he seriously called his "wheat field." And woe to the insects that dared to trespass there! They could expect no mercy.

Toward the end of June, after endless rain, the weather turned decidedly cold, and on the 29th, a Fahrenheit thermometer would certainly have registered only twenty degrees above zero (6.67 degrees Celsius below freezing).

The next day, June 30, which corresponds to December 31 in the Northern Hemisphere, was a Friday. Nab pointed out that the year ended on an unfortunate day; but Pencroff replied that naturally, the other would start on a good one—which was better. In any case, it began with a very sharp cold. Ice began to accumulate at the mouth of the Mercy, and the lake soon froze over completely.

They had to replenish their fuel supplies several times. Pencroff didn't wait for the river to freeze before hauling huge loads of wood to their destination. The current was an tireless engine, and it was used to carry driftwood until the cold came to chain it down. Along with the firewood provided so abundantly by the forest, they also brought several loads of coal, which had to be fetched from the foothills of Mount Franklin. The strong heat from the coal was greatly appreciated given the low temperature, which on July 4 fell to eight degrees Fahrenheit (13 degrees Celsius below zero). A second fireplace had been set up in the dining room, and there, they worked together.

During this cold spell, Cyrus Smith was grateful for having diverted a small stream from Lake Grant to Granite House. Taken from below the icy surface and then directed by the old outflow, the water remained liquid and reached an internal reservoir, which had been dug at the corner of the back store, and whose overflow flowed through the well to the sea.

Around this time, the weather being extremely dry, the colonists, dressed as warmly as they could, decided to dedicate a day to exploring the part of the island located in the southeast between the Mercy and Cape Griffe. It was a vast swampy area, and there might be some good hunting opportunities, as aquatic birds were bound to be plentiful there.

They needed to account for eight to nine miles each way, so the day would be well spent. Since it was also about exploring an unknown portion of the island, the whole colony had to participate. That's why, on July 5, at six in the morning, just as dawn was barely breaking, Cyrus Smith, Gideon Spilett, Harbert, Nab, and Pencroff, armed with poles, snares, bows and arrows, and equipped with sufficient provisions, left Granite House, preceded by Top, who bounded ahead of them.

They took the shortest route, which led them to cross the Mercy on the ice floes that were clogging it at the time.

"But, as the reporter rightly pointed out, this cannot replace a proper bridge!" Therefore, the construction of a "serious" bridge was noted among the upcoming projects.

It was the first time the colonists set foot on the right bank of the Mercy, venturing amid these large and magnificent conifers, now covered in snow.

But they hadn't gone half a mile before a thick thicket erupted, scattering a whole family of quadrupeds that had made it their home, and Top's barking sent them fleeing.

"Ah! They look like foxes!" exclaimed Harbert, as he saw the whole group scamper away.

They were indeed foxes, but of very large size, making a sort of barking sound that surprised even Top, who stopped chasing them and gave these fast animals time to escape.

The dog had a right to be surprised since he didn't know natural history. However, by their barking, these foxes, with reddish-gray fur and black tails tipped with a white tuft, revealed their identity. Thus, Harbert immediately named them by their true name, "culpeo." These culpeos are frequently found in Chile, the Falklands, and in all those American areas crossed by the thirtieth and fortieth parallels. Harbert regretted that Top couldn't catch one of these carnivores.

"Can you eat that?" asked Pencroff, who always regarded the island's wildlife from a special perspective.

"No," replied Harbert, "but zoologists haven't yet determined whether the pupils of these foxes are diurnal or nocturnal, and whether they should actually be classified within the dog family proper."

Cyrus Smith couldn't help but smile at the young boy's observation, which showed a serious mind. As for the sailor, as long as these foxes couldn't be classified as edible, he didn't care much. However, when a poultry yard would be established at Granite House, he noted that it would be wise to take some precautions against the likely visit from these four-legged thieves. No one disagreed with that.

After rounding the point of the wreck, the colonists found a long beach washed by the vast sea. It was then eight in the morning. The sky was very clear, as happens with prolonged severe cold; but warmed by their run, Cyrus Smith and his companions didn't feel too strongly the bites of the atmosphere.

Moreover, there was no wind, which made the significant drops in temperature infinitely more bearable. A brilliant sun, without any heating effect, was emerging from the Ocean, and its enormous disk was swinging at the horizon. The sea formed a tranquil blue expanse like that of a Mediterranean gulf when the sky is clear. Cape Griffe, curved like a yatagan, narrowed clearly about four miles to the southeast. To the left, the edge of the marsh was abruptly stopped by a small point drawn in a fiery line by the sun's rays.

Certainly, in this part of Union Bay, which was exposed to the ocean without any shelter, not even a sandbank, the ships, battered by the east winds, would find no refuge. The tranquility of the sea, which was undisturbed by any shallow waters, its uniform color untainted by any yellowish hue, and the absence of any reef confirmed that this coast was steep and that the Ocean covered profound depths there. Behind, to the west, the first lines of trees from the Far-West stretched out, but at a distance of four miles. One would almost think they were on the desolate coast of some island in the Antarctic regions that had been invaded by ice. The colonists paused at this spot to have lunch. A fire of dried brush and seaweed was lit, and Nab prepared a lunch of cold meat, which he accompanied with some cups of Oswego tea.

While eating, they looked around. This part of Lincoln Island was indeed barren and contrasted sharply with the entire western region. This led the reporter to reflect that if chance had initially thrown the castaways onto this beach, they would have formed a terrible idea of their future domain.

"I even believe we wouldn't have been able to reach it," replied the engineer, "because the sea is deep, and it offered us not a single rock to take refuge on. In front of Granite House, at least, there were some banks, an islet, which increased the chances of survival. Here, nothing but the abyss!"

— It's quite remarkable," remarked Gideon Spilett, "that this relatively small island presents such varied soil. This diversity of appearance logically belongs only to continents of a certain extent. It really seems as if the western part of Lincoln Island, so rich and fertile, is washed by the warm waters of the Gulf of Mexico, while its northern and southeastern shores stretch over a kind of Arctic sea.

— You're right, my dear Spilett," replied Cyrus Smith, "that's an observation I made as well. This island, in its shape and its nature, seems strange to me. It resembles a summary of all the aspects present in a continent, and I wouldn't be surprised if it had once been part of a continent.

— What! A continent in the middle of the Pacific?" exclaimed Pencroff.

— Why not?" replied Cyrus Smith. "Why would Australia, New Ireland, everything that English geographers call Australasia, combined with the Pacific archipelagos, not have formed a sixth part of the world, as important as Europe or Asia, Africa, or the two Americas? My mind does not refuse to accept that all the islands, emerging from this vast Ocean, are merely the summits of a continent now submerged, but which dominated the waters in prehistoric times.

— Like Atlantis once was," replied Harbert.

— Yes, my dear child... if it ever existed.

— And Lincoln Island would have been part of that continent?" asked Pencroff.

— It's probable," replied Cyrus Smith, "and that would sufficiently explain this diversity of productions visible on its surface.

— And the considerable number of animals that still inhabit it," added Harbert.

— Yes, my dear child," replied the engineer, "and you're providing me with a further argument to support my thesis. It is certain, based on what we have seen, that animals are abundant on the island, and what's more peculiar is that the species present are extremely varied. There is a reason for that, and for me, it's that Lincoln Island may have once been part of a vast continent that gradually sank below the Pacific.

— Then, one fine day," retorted Pencroff, who did not seem completely convinced, "what remains of that ancient continent may also disappear, and there will be nothing left between America and Asia?

— Yes," replied Cyrus Smith, "there will be new continents, which billions upon billions of microorganisms are currently working to build.

— And who are those builders?" asked Pencroff.

— The coral infusoria," replied Cyrus Smith. "They are the ones who have created, through continuous work, Clermont-Tonnerre Island, the atolls, and many other coral islands in the Pacific Ocean. It takes forty-seven million of these infusoria to weigh a grain, and yet, with the seawater salts they absorb, with the solid elements of water they assimilate, these microorganisms produce limestone, and this limestone forms enormous underwater structures, whose hardness and solidity equal those of granite. Once, in the earliest periods of creation, nature, employing fire, produced land by rising; but now she entrusts microscopic animals to replace this agent, whose dynamic power within the globe has obviously diminished—which is evidenced by the large number of extinct volcanoes currently found on the surface of the earth. And I truly believe that, with centuries succeeding centuries and infusoria following infusoria, this Pacific may one day transform into a vast continent, which new generations will inhabit and civilize in turn.

— That's going to take a long time!" said Pencroff.

— Nature has all the time in the world," replied the engineer.

— But what's the point of new continents?" asked Harbert. "It seems to me that the current extent of habitable lands is sufficient for humanity. Now, nature doesn't do anything in vain.

— Nothing in vain, indeed," resumed the engineer, "but here's how one could explain the future necessity for new continents, and specifically in this tropical zone occupied by the coral islands. At least, this explanation seems plausible to me.

— We're listening to you, Mr. Cyrus," replied Harbert.— Here's my thought: scientists generally agree that one day our planet will come to an end, or rather that animal and plant life will no longer be possible due to the intense cooling it will undergo. What they don't agree on is the cause of this cooling. Some believe it will come from a drop in the sun's temperature after millions of years; others think it results from the gradual extinction of the planet's internal fires, which have a more significant influence on it than is generally assumed. I lean towards the latter hypothesis, based on the fact that the moon is indeed a cooled sphere, which is no longer habitable, even though the sun continues to pour the same amount of heat onto its surface. So, if the moon has cooled, it's because those internal fires, to which it, like all the stars, owes its origin, have completely extinguished. Ultimately, regardless of the cause, our planet will cool one day, but this cooling will only happen gradually. What will happen then? The temperate zones, in a more or less distant future, will be no more habitable than the polar regions are now. Thus, human populations, like animal aggregations, will flow back towards the latitudes directly influenced by the sun. There will be a massive migration. Europe, Central Asia, and North America will gradually be abandoned, just like Australasia or the low parts of South America. Vegetation will follow human migration. The flora will retreat towards the equator simultaneously with the fauna. The central parts of South America and Africa will become the prime inhabited continents. The Laps and the Samoyeds will find the polar climatic conditions on the Mediterranean shores. Who's to say that by that time, the equatorial regions won't be too small to contain and sustain the human population? So, why wouldn't nature, in her foresightedness, lay the foundations for a new continent under the equator right now to give refuge to all that migrating vegetation and animals? Perhaps she charged the infusorials to construct it? I have often reflected on all these things, my friends, and I seriously believe that the appearance of our globe will one day be completely transformed, that, due to the emergence of new continents, the seas will cover the old ones, and that, in future centuries, explorers will go to discover the islands of Chimborazo, the Himalayas, or Mont Blanc, remnants of a submerged America, Asia, and Europe. Then finally, these new continents will themselves become uninhabitable; the heat will extinguish like the warmth of a body just abandoned by the soul, and life will disappear, if not permanently from the globe, at least temporarily. Perhaps, then, our spheroid will take a rest, reform itself in death, to one day be reborn in a higher condition! But all this, my friends, is the secret of the Author of all things, and regarding the work of the infusorials, I may have been led a bit too far in probing the secrets of the future.

— My dear Cyrus, replied Gédéon Spilett, these theories are, to me, prophecies, and they shall one day be fulfilled.

— It's God's secret, said the engineer.

— That's all well and good, said Pencroff, who had been listening attentively, but will you tell me, Mr. Cyrus, if Lincoln Island was built by your infusorials?

— No, replied Cyrus Smith, it is purely of volcanic origin.

— Then, will it one day disappear?

— It's likely.

— I certainly hope we won't be here to see it.

— No, don't worry, Pencroff, we won't be, since we don't want to die here, and we might eventually make it out.

— In the meantime, replied Gédéon Spilett, let's settle in as if for eternity. We should never do anything halfway.

This ended the conversation. Lunch was over. Exploration resumed, and the colonists reached the border where the marshy region began.

It was indeed a swamp, the extent of which could measure twenty square miles, reaching to the rounded coast that ended the island to the southeast.

The ground was made up of silty clay, mixed with numerous plant debris. Algae, reeds, sedges, bulrushes, and here and there some thick grass layers like a heavy carpet covered it. Some frozen puddles sparkled in many places under the sun's rays. Neither rain nor any river swollen by sudden floods had managed to form these water reserves. One could thus conclude that this marsh was fed by groundwater infiltration, and indeed, there was even a fear that the air would become charged with the miasmas that induce malarial fevers during the heat. Above the aquatic grasses, hovering over the stagnant waters was a world of birds.

Hunters in the marsh and professional birders could hardly miss a single shot. Wild ducks, pintails, teal, snipe lived there in flocks, and these not very fearful birds could be easily approached. A shotgun blast would certainly have hit dozens of these birds, given how closely packed they were. They had to be satisfied with hitting them with arrows. The result was less, but the silent arrow had the advantage of not scaring these birds, which the blast of a firearm would have scattered to all corners of the marsh. The hunters therefore settled for a dozen ducks this time, white bodies with a cinnamon stripe, green heads, black, white, and russet wings, with flattened beaks, which Harbert recognized as "tadornes."

Top skillfully assisted in capturing these birds, after which this part of the swamp got its name. The colonists thus had an abundant reserve of waterfowl. When the time came, it would only be a matter of exploiting it properly, and it was likely that several species of these birds could be acclimated, if not domesticated, in the lake's surroundings, which would bring them more directly into the reach of consumers.

Around five o'clock in the evening, Cyrus Smith and his companions took the path back home, crossing the Tadorn marsh (Tadorn's-fens), and they crossed the Mercy on the ice bridge.

At eight o'clock in the evening, everyone was back at Granite House.

✣ 22 ✣

These intense cold spells lasted until August 15, not exceeding, however, the maximum degrees Fahrenheit observed until then. When the atmosphere was calm, this low temperature was easily tolerated; but when the cold wind blew, it felt harsh for people inadequately dressed. Pencroff regretted that Lincoln Island didn't provide shelter for some families of bears, rather than for those foxes or seals, whose fur left much to be desired.

"The bears," he said, "are generally well clad, and I wouldn't mind borrowing the warm coat they have on their bodies for the winter.

— But," Nab laughed, "maybe those bears wouldn't agree to lend you their coat, Pencroff. They're not Saint Martins, those beasts!

— They would be made to agree, Nab, they would be made to agree," Pencroff replied in quite an authoritative tone. But those formidable carnivores did not exist on the island, or at least, they had not made their presence known until then.

However, Harbert, Pencroff, and the reporter set about making traps on the Grande-vue plateau and around the forest. According to the sailor's opinion, any animal, whatever it might be, would make a good catch, and rodents or carnivores that would try the new traps would be warmly welcomed at Granite House.

These traps, by the way, were extremely simple: pits dug into the ground, with a canopy of branches and grass obscuring the opening, some bait at the bottom whose smell could attract animals, and that was it. It should also be said that they had not been dug randomly, but in specific spots where numerous footprints indicated frequent crossings of quadrupeds. They were visited every day, and three times, in the first days, they found samples of those foxes that had already been seen on the right bank of the Mercy.

"Ah, is there really only foxes in this place!" exclaimed Pencroff the third time he pulled one of these animals from the pit where it was sitting very sheepishly. "Beasts that are worth nothing!

— But they are good for something!" said Gédéon Spilett.

— And what are they good for?

— For making bait to attract others!"

The reporter was right, and the traps were thus baited with the corpses of foxes.

The sailor had also made snares using fibers from the curry-rush, and the snares proved to be more profitable than the traps. It was rare for a day to go by without catching a rabbit from the warren. It was always rabbit, but Nab knew how to vary his sauces, and the diners did not think to complain.

However, once or twice during the second week of August, the traps delivered animals other than foxes, and more useful ones. These included a few of those wild boars that had already been reported to the north of the lake. Pencroff didn't need to ask if those beasts were edible. It was clear from their resemblance to the American or European pig.

"But they're not pigs," Harbert warned him, "I'm telling you, Pencroff.

— My boy," replied the sailor, bending over the trap and pulling out one of those representatives of the pig family by its small appendage that served as a tail, "let me believe they are pigs!

— And why?

— Because it pleases me!"

— So you really like pigs, Pencroff?

— I love pigs a lot," the sailor replied, "especially their feet, and if they had eight instead of four, I'd love them twice as much!"

As for the animals in question, they were peccaries belonging to one of the four genera in the family, and they were even the species known as "tajassous," recognizable by their dark color and lack of the long canines that arm the mouths of their relatives. These peccaries usually live in groups, and it was likely they were abundant in the wooded parts of the island. In any case, they were edible from head to toe, and that was all Pencroff needed.

Around August 15, the atmospheric state suddenly changed with a shift of wind from the northwest. Temperature rose a few degrees, and the vapors accumulated in the air quickly resolved into snow. The entire island became covered in a white layer, showing itself to its inhabitants in a new light. This snow fell abundantly for several days, and its thickness soon reached two feet.

The wind soon picked up extremely violently, and from the height of Granite House, one could hear the sea roaring on the reefs. At certain angles, rapid air eddies formed, and the snow, forming tall rotating columns in those spots, resembled those liquid funnels pirouetting on their base, which ships attack with cannon fire.

However, the hurricane, coming from the northwest, took the island from the rear, and the orientation of Granite House spared it a direct assault. But in the midst of this blizzard, as terrible as if it were happening in some polar region, neither Cyrus Smith nor his companions could, despite their desire, venture outside, and they remained confined for five days, from August 20 to 25. The storm could be heard raging in the Jacamar woods, which would surely suffer. Many trees would be uprooted, no doubt, but Pencroff consoled himself by thinking he wouldn't have to trouble himself with felling them.

"The wind can be the lumberjack; let it do the work," he repeated.

And, besides, there would have been no way to prevent it.

How much the inhabitants of Granite House must have thanked heaven for providing them with this solid and unshakable retreat! Cyrus Smith indeed deserved his fair share of the thanks, but ultimately, it was nature that had carved out this vast cavern, and he had merely discovered it. There, they were all safe, and the storm's blows could not reach them. Had they built a house of bricks and wood on the Grande-vue plateau, it certainly would not have withstood the fury of that hurricane. As for the Chimneys, just from the crash of the waves that echoed so forcefully, one would believe they were absolutely uninhabitable, as the sea, crashing over the islet, must have assaulted them furiously. But here at Granite House, amid this mass, against which neither water nor air could take hold, there was nothing to fear.

During those few days of seclusion, the colonists did not remain idle. There was no shortage of wood cut into planks in the store, and gradually, they completed the furnishings with solid tables and chairs, for the material was not spared. These pieces of furniture, a bit heavy, poorly justified their name, which makes their mobility an essential condition, but they were the pride of Nab and Pencroff, who wouldn't have changed them for Boule furniture.

Then, the carpenters turned into basket-makers, and they did quite well in this new craft. A fertile willow grove had been discovered near the point that the lake projected to the north, where many purple willows grew. Before the rainy season, Pencroff and Harbert had harvested these useful shrubs, and their branches, well separated then, could be effectively used. The first attempts were rudimentary, but thanks to the skill and intelligence of the workers, who consulted each other, recalling the models they had seen, competing among themselves, baskets and other containers of various sizes soon increased the colony's stock. The store was stocked with these, and Nab stored his collections of rhizomes, pine nuts, and dragon tree roots in special baskets.

During the last week of August, the weather changed once again. The temperature dropped slightly, and the storm calmed. The colonists rushed outside. There certainly was two feet of snow on the shore, but one could walk on the hardened surface of the snow without too much difficulty. Cyrus Smith and his companions climbed up to the Grande-vue plateau. What a change! Those woods, which they had left green, especially in the neighboring part dominated by conifers, now disappeared under a uniform color. Everything was white, from the summit of Mount Franklin to the coastline, the forests, the grasslands, the lake, the river, the shores. The water of the Mercy flowed under a vault of ice that broke apart with a loud crash with each ebb and flow. Numerous birds flitted above the solid surface of the lake—ducks, snipe, teal, and guillemots. There were thousands of them. The rocks between which the waterfall spilled at the edge of the plateau were covered with ice. It looked like the water was escaping from a monstrous gargoyle carved with all the creativity of a Renaissance artist. As for assessing the damage done to the forest by the hurricane, it couldn't be done yet; they had to wait for the immense layer of white to dissipate.

Gédéon Spilett, Pencroff, and Harbert took this opportunity to check their traps.

They didn't find them easily under the snow that covered them. They even had to be careful not to fall into one of them, which would have been both dangerous and humiliating: to get caught in one's own trap! But eventually, they avoided this mishap and found the traps perfectly intact. No animal had fallen into them, yet the footprints around were numerous, including some very clearly defined claw marks. Harbert had no hesitation in asserting that some carnivore of the feline kind had passed through, which justified the engineer's opinion about the presence of dangerous beasts on Lincoln Island. Certainly, these beasts usually lived in the thick forests of the Far West, but driven by hunger, they had ventured up to the Grand View plateau. Perhaps they could sense the inhabitants of Granite House?

"So, what are these felines?" asked Pencroff.

"They are tigers," replied Harbert.

"I thought those beasts only lived in warm countries?"

"On the new continent," the young boy replied, "they are seen from Mexico to the Pampas of Buenos Aires. Since Lincoln Island is roughly at the same latitude as the provinces of the Plate River, it's not surprising that some tigers could be found there."

"Well, we will keep an eye out," replied Pencroff.

However, the snow eventually melted due to the rising temperature. Rain began to fall, and, thanks to its dissolving action, the white layer faded away. Despite the bad weather, the colonists replenished their supplies of everything —pine nuts, dragon tree roots, rhizomes, maple syrup for the plant part; rabbits, agoutis, and kangaroos for the animal part. This required a few excursions into the forest, and they noticed that a certain number of trees had been knocked down by the last hurricane. The sailor and Nab even pushed the cart all the way to the coal deposit to bring back a few tons of fuel. They saw in passing that the chimney of the pottery kiln had been heavily damaged by the wind and had been knocked down by at least six feet. Along with the coal, the firewood supply was also replenished at Granite House, and they took advantage of the flow of the Mercy, which had become free again, to bring back several loads. It was possible that the period of extreme cold was not over yet. A visit had also been made to the Chimneys, and the colonists could only be glad they hadn't stayed there during the storm. The sea had left undeniable signs of its destruction.

Raised by the winds from the ocean and crashing over the islet, it had violently assaulted the corridors, which were half-filled with sand, and thick layers of seaweed covered the rocks. While Nab, Harbert, and Pencroff hunted or replenished their supplies of fuel, Cyrus Smith and Gédéon Spilett worked to clear the Chimneys, finding the forge and the furnaces almost intact, having been protected initially by the accumulation of sand.

The fuel reserve had proven useful. The colonists were not done with the harsh cold. It is known that, in the northern hemisphere, February is primarily marked by significant drops in temperature. The same must have been true in the southern hemisphere, and the end of August, which is February in North America, didn't escape this climatic law.

Around the 25th, after a new shift of snow and rain, the wind shifted to the southeast, and suddenly, the cold became extremely sharp. According to the engineer's estimate, the mercury column of a Fahrenheit thermometer must have registered no less than eight degrees below zero (22 degrees Celsius below freezing), and this intensity of cold, made even more painful by a sharp wind, lasted several days. The colonists had to return to living in Granite House, and since they had to seal all openings in the facade tightly, leaving only the strict passage for air renewal, the consumption of candles was considerable.

To conserve them, the colonists often lit only with the flames of the fires, where they didn't spare fuel. Several times, one or another went down to the beach, among the ice floes that the tide piled up during each flood, but they soon returned to Granite House, and it wasn't without effort and pain that their hands clung to the ladder rungs. In such intense cold, the rungs burned their fingers.

They also needed to occupy the leisure time that confinement had given the inhabitants of Granite House.

Cyrus Smith then undertook a project that could be done indoors.

It is known that the colonists had no other sugar available than the liquid substance they extracted from the maple tree by making deep incisions in it. They merely needed to collect this liquid in containers, and they used it in various culinary applications, especially since, as it aged, the liquid tended to whiten and take on a syrupy consistency.

But there was a better use to be made, and one day Cyrus Smith announced to his companions that they were going to become refiners.

"Refiners!" responded Pencroff. "That sounds like a very hot job!"

"Very hot!" replied the engineer.

"Then it's the right season!" retorted the sailor.

Let the word refining not bring to mind complicated factories filled with equipment and workers. No! To crystallize this liquid, it was enough to purify it through an extremely simple process. Placed over the fire in large earthen-ware vessels, it was simply subjected to a certain evaporation, and soon a froth rose to the surface. As soon as it began to thicken, Nab made sure to stir it with a wooden spatula, which would speed up its evaporation and prevent it from acquiring a burnt taste.

After several hours of boiling over a good fire, which was as beneficial for the operators as for the substance being processed, it transformed into a thick syrup. This syrup was poured into clay molds, made in the kitchen's very furnace and shaped into various forms. The next day, once cooled, this syrup had formed loaves and tablets. It was sugar, a little reddish in color, but almost transparent and with a perfect taste.

The cold continued until mid-September, and the inhabitants of Granite House were starting to find their confinement quite long. Almost every day, they attempted some outings that couldn't last long. They were therefore constantly working to improve their dwelling. They chatted while working.

Cyrus Smith taught his companions about everything, explaining mainly the practical applications of science. The colonists had no library available, but the engineer was like a book always ready, always open to the page that each one needed, a book that answered all their questions and that they often thumbed through. Time passed in this way, and these good people didn't seem to fear the future.

However, it was time for this confinement to end. Everyone was eager to see, if not the beautiful season, at least the end of the unbearable cold. If only they had been dressed in a way that allowed them to brave it, how many excursions they would have attempted, either to the dunes or to the Tadorn marsh! The game would have been easy to approach, and hunting would certainly have been fruitful. But Cyrus Smith insisted that no one compromise their health, since he needed all the hands, and his advice was followed.

But it must be said, the most impatient in this imprisonment, after Pencroff, was Top. The faithful dog felt very cramped in Granite House. He wandered from one room to another, expressing his boredom at being confined in his own way.

Cyrus Smith often noticed that when he approached the dark well that connected to the sea, whose opening was at the back of the storeroom, Top made peculiar growling sounds. Top circled this hole, which had been covered by a wooden panel. Sometimes he even tried to slide his paws under this panel, as if he wanted to lift it.

He barked in a particular way, indicating both anger and anxiety.

The engineer observed this behavior several times. What could possibly be in that abyss that so profoundly affected the intelligent animal? The well led to the sea, that was certain. Did it branch off into narrow tunnels through the island's structure?

Was it connected to some other inner cavities? Was some sea monster not occasionally coming to breathe at the bottom of this well? The engineer didn't know what to think, and couldn't help but dream of bizarre complications. Used to exploring far into the realm of scientific realities, he couldn't forgive himself for being drawn into the realm of the strange and almost supernatural; but how could he explain that Top, one of those sensible dogs who never wasted their time barking at the moon, continued to probe this abyss with his nose and ears if nothing was happening there to arouse his unease? Top's behavior puzzled Cyrus Smith more than it seemed reasonable for him to admit to himself. In any case, the engineer shared his impressions only with Gédéon Spilett, finding it unnecessary to introduce his companions to the involuntary thoughts that Top's behavior was raising in him, which might just be a whim of Top. At last, the cold ceased. There were rains, gusts mixed with snow, sudden showers, and windstorms, but these bad weather spells did not last. The ice had melted, the snow had disappeared; the beach, the plateau, the banks of the Mercy, the forest, had all become passable again. This return of spring delighted the inhabitants of Granite House, and soon they only spent their time there for rest and meals.

They hunted a lot in the second half of September, leading Pencroff to insist once again on the firearms that he claimed Cyrus Smith had promised.

The latter, knowing well that without specialized tools it would be almost impossible to make a gun that could be of any use, kept deferring the operation. Besides, he noted that Harbert and Gédéon Spilett had become skilled archers, that all sorts of excellent animals—agoutis, kangaroos, capybaras, pigeons, geese, wild ducks, snipe, in short, game of fur or feather—fell to their arrows, and therefore, there was no rush. But the stubborn sailor wasn't willing to accept that and wouldn't stop pestering the engineer until he got what he wanted. Gédéon Spilett also supported Pencroff on this matter.

"If the island, as can be doubted," he said, "contains fierce animals, we must think about fighting and exterminating them. A moment may come when it is our primary duty."

But at this time, Cyrus Smith was more preoccupied with the question of clothing than firearms. The clothes the colonists had endured the winter, but they wouldn't last until the next winter. Animal hides or wool from ruminants were what they needed to acquire at all costs, and since there were plenty of sheep, plans needed to be made to create a herd to be raised for the colony's needs. A pen for domestic animals, a yard arranged for fowl, in short, a kind of farm to be established somewhere on the island—these were the two important projects to be carried out during the beautiful season. Consequently, in view of these future establishments, it became urgent to explore the unknown part of Lincoln Island, that is, under the high forests extending on the right of the Mercy, from its mouth to the end of the Serpentine peninsula, as well as along the entire western coast.

But it needed favorable weather, and another month would have to pass before this exploration could be undertaken effectively.

So they waited with some impatience when an incident occurred that further heightened the colonists' desire to explore their domain entirely.

It was October 24. That day, Pencroff had gone to check the traps, which he always kept properly baited. In one of them, he found three animals that would be welcome for dinner. It was a female peccary and her two young ones.

So Pencroff returned to Granite House, delighted with his catch, and, as always, the sailor boasted about his hunt.

"Come on! We'll have a great meal, Mr. Cyrus!" he exclaimed. "And you too, Mr. Spilett, will eat some!"

"I'll gladly eat some," replied the reporter, "but what will I eat?"

"Roasted suckling pig."

"Ah really, suckling pig, Pencroff? From your tone, I thought you were bringing back a stuffed partridge!"

"What?!" exclaimed Pencroff. "Are you turning your nose up at suckling pig, perhaps?"

"No," replied Gédéon Spilett without showing any enthusiasm, "as long as it's not overdone..."

"That's enough, Mr. Journalist," replied the sailor, who didn't like hearing his catch downplayed. "Are you being picky? Seven months ago, when we landed on the island, you'd have been thrilled to come across such game!..."

"Well, well," replied the reporter. "Man is never perfect, nor satisfied."

"Anyway," resumed Pencroff, "I hope Nab will do well. Look! These two little peccaries are not even three months old! They will be tender as quails! Come on, Nab, let's go! I'll supervise their cooking myself."

And the sailor, followed by Nab, headed to the kitchen and immersed himself in his culinary tasks.

They let him do it his way. So, Nab and he prepared a magnificent meal—two little peccaries, a kangaroo stew, smoked ham, pine nuts, dragon tree drink, Oswego tea—in short, all the best they had; but among all the dishes, the savory peccaries stewed would certainly take center stage. At five o'clock, dinner was served in Granite-House. The kangaroo soup was steaming on the table. It was found to be excellent. After the soup came the peccaries, which Pencroff insisted on carving himself, serving monstrous portions to each of the guests.

These young pigs were truly delicious, and Pencroff was devouring his share with great enthusiasm when suddenly he let out a cry and a curse.

"What's wrong?" asked Cyrus Smith.

"It's... it's... I just broke a tooth!" replied the sailor.

"Ah! So there are stones in your peccaries?" said Gédéon Spilett.

"Must be," replied Pencroff, as he took the object that was costing him a molar!

It wasn't a stone... It was a pellet of lead.

❧ II ❧

THE ABANDONED

It had been exactly seven months since the balloon passengers were cast onto Lincoln Island. Since then, no human being had shown themselves to them despite their searches. Never had smoke betrayed the presence of man on the surface of the island.

Never had any manual work attested to man's passage, neither in ancient nor recent times. Not only did it seem uninhabited, but one would have to believe it had never been inhabited. And now, all of this scaffolding of deductions was falling apart because of a simple piece of metal found in the body of an innocent rodent!

Indeed, this lead had come from a firearm, and who else but a human could have used that weapon?

When Pencroff placed the pellet on the table, his companions looked at him with deep astonishment. All the implications of this incident, significant despite its apparent insignificance, suddenly struck their minds.

The sudden appearance of a supernatural being would not have impressed them more.

Cyrus Smith did not hesitate to formulate the hypotheses that this surprising and unexpected fact must provoke. He took the pellet, turned it over, felt it between his index finger and thumb. Then:

"Can you affirm," he asked Pencroff, "that the peccary, injured by this pellet, was no more than three months old?

"At most, Mr. Cyrus," replied Pencroff. "It was still suckling from its mother when I found it in the pit."

"Well," said the engineer, "this proves that a gunshot was fired on Lincoln Island no more than three months ago."

"And that a pellet of lead," added Gédéon Spilett, "hit but did not kill this little animal."

"That is undeniable," replied Cyrus Smith, "and here are the implications we must draw from this incident: either the island was inhabited before our arrival, or men have landed there in the last three months. Did these men arrive deliberately or accidentally, through a landing or a shipwreck? This point will only be clarified later. As for who they are, European or Malay, friends or foes of our race, nothing allows us to guess, and we do not know whether they still inhabit the island or have left. But these questions concern us too directly for us to remain longer in uncertainty.

"No! A hundred times no! A thousand times no!" exclaimed the sailor, getting up from the table. "There are no other men but us on Lincoln Island! What the hell!

The island isn't big, and if it had been inhabited, we would have seen some of its inhabitants by now!"

"On the contrary, that would indeed be very surprising," said Harbert.

"But it would be much more surprising, I suppose," observed the reporter, "if this peccary were born with a pellet in its body!"

"Unless," said Nab seriously, "Pencroff had ...

"Do you see that, Nab?" retorted Pencroff. "I've had a pellet in my jaw for five or six months without noticing it! But where would it have hidden?" the sailor added, opening his mouth to show off his magnificent thirty-two teeth. "Look closely, Nab, and if you find a cavity in that set of pearly whites, you can pull out half a dozen of them!"

"Nab's hypothesis is indeed inadmissible," replied Cyrus Smith, who, despite the seriousness of his thoughts, couldn't help but smile. "It is certain that a gunshot was fired on the island no more than three months ago. But I would tend to believe that the beings who landed on this coast are either very recent arrivals or have only passed through, for if the island had been inhabited when we explored it from Mount Franklin, we would have seen it or been seen. It is thus likely that in the past few weeks, shipwrecked people have been cast onto a part of the coast by a storm. In any case, it is important for us to be clear on this point."

"I think we should proceed cautiously," said the reporter.

"That is my opinion," replied Cyrus Smith, "as we must unfortunately fear that Malay pirates have landed on the island!

"Mr. Cyrus," asked the sailor, "would it be appropriate, before heading out to explore, to build a boat that would allow us to either go upriver or, if necessary, skirt the coast? We shouldn't find ourselves caught off guard."

"Your idea is good, Pencroff," replied the engineer, "but we cannot wait. It would take at least a month to build a boat..."

"A proper boat, yes," replied the sailor, "but we don't need a vessel meant for the open sea, and within five days at most, I can build a sufficient canoe to navigate on the Mercy."

"In five days!" shouted Nab. "Build a boat?"

"Yes, Nab, a boat a la mode indienne."

"Out of wood?" asked the Negro, looking unconvinced.

"Out of wood," replied Pencroff, "or rather out of bark. I tell you again, Mr. Cyrus, that in five days the job can be done!"

"In five days, so be it!" replied the engineer.

"But until then, we'd better stay extremely vigilant!" said Harbert.

"Very vigilant, my friends," replied Cyrus Smith, "and I'd ask you to limit your hunting excursions to the vicinity of Granite-House."

Dinner ended less cheerfully than Pencroff had hoped.

So then, the island was or had been inhabited by others besides the colonists. Since the incident of the lead pellet, this was now an undeniable fact, and such a revelation could only provoke strong unease among the colonists.

Cyrus Smith and Gédéon Spilett, before making themselves comfortable for the night, spoke at length about these matters.

They wondered if, by chance, this incident might have some connection with the inexplicable circumstances of the engineer's rescue and other strange details that had already struck them several times. However, Cyrus Smith, after discussing the pros and cons of the matter, finally stated:

"In short, do you want to know my opinion, my dear Spilett?

"Yes, Cyrus."

"Well, here it is: no matter how thoroughly we explore the island, we won't find anything!"

The next day, Pencroff got to work. The goal was not to build a boat with a frame and planking, but simply a flat-bottomed floating device that would be excellent for navigating the Mercy, especially near its sources where the water would be shallow. Pieces of bark sewn together would suffice to form the light-weight craft, and in case, due to natural obstacles, carrying it became necessary, it would neither be heavy nor cumbersome.

Pencroff planned to join the strips of bark using riveted nails, ensuring that their adherence would perfectly seal the craft.

The task, therefore, was to choose trees whose bark was supple and tough enough for this work.

Fortunately, the last storm had felled several Douglas firs that were perfect for this type of construction. Some of these firs lay on the ground, and all that was left was to strip off the bark, but this was the most difficult part due to the imperfect tools the colonists had. In any case, they managed to succeed.

While the sailor, aided by the engineer, busily worked without losing a minute, Gédéon Spilett and Harbert did not remain idle. They had taken on the role of suppliers for the colony. The reporter could not tire of admiring the young boy, who had developed remarkable skill in handling the bow or spear.

Harbert also showed great boldness, along with much of what could rightly be called "the reasoning of bravery." The two hunting companions, moreover, adhering to Cyrus Smith's instructions, no longer ventured more than two miles around Granite-House, but the first slopes of the forest provided a sufficient bounty of agoutis, capybaras, kangaroos, peccaries, etc., and although the catch from traps was minimal since the cold had ceased, at least the warren provided its usual share, which could feed the entire colony of Lincoln Island.

Often, during these hunts, Harbert discussed with Gédéon Spilett the incident of the lead pellet and the conclusions drawn by the engineer, and one day — it was October 26 — he said to him:

"But, Mr. Spilett, don't you find it very strange that if some shipwrecked people have landed on this island, they haven't shown themselves near Granite-House yet?

"Very surprising, if they are still there," replied the reporter, "but not surprising at all if they are no longer here!

"So, you think they may have already left the island?" Harbert responded.

"That's more than likely, my boy, for if their stay had been prolonged there, especially if they were still there, some incident would have revealed their presence by now.

"But if they were able to leave," the young boy pointed out, "they were not shipwrecked?

"No, Harbert, or at least, they were what I'd call provisional shipwrecked. It is very possible that a gust of wind threw them onto the island without displacing their vessel, and that once the storm passed, they got back to sea.

"We must admit one thing," said Harbert, "Mr. Smith has always seemed to fear rather than desire the presence of human beings on our island.

"Indeed," replied the reporter, "he sees hardly anyone but Malays as likely to frequent these waters, and those gentlemen are no good rogues that it's wise to avoid.

"It's not impossible, Mr. Spilett," Harbert continued, "that we might eventually find traces of their landing, and perhaps we will be settled regarding this?

"I won't say no, my boy. An abandoned camp, an extinguished fire could lead us in the right direction, and that's what we'll look for in our next exploration."

On the day the two hunters were talking like this, they were in a part of the forest near the Mercy that was remarkable for its beautiful trees. There, among others, rose several of those magnificent conifers that the natives call "kauris" in New Zealand, standing nearly two hundred feet above the ground.

"One idea, Mr. Spilett," said Harbert. "If I climbed to the top of one of these kauris, I might be able to survey the land over a fairly wide area?

"The idea is good," replied the reporter, "but will you be able to climb to the top of those giants?

"I'll give it a try," replied Harbert.

The young boy, agile and deft, leaped onto the first branches, whose arrangement made climbing the kauri relatively easy, and in a few minutes, he reached its summit, which emerged from the immense plain of greenery formed by the rounded canopies of the forest. From this high point, his gaze could extend over the entire southern portion of the island, from Cape Griffe in the southeast to the Reptile promontory in the southwest. In the northwest rose Mount Franklin, obscuring a large portion of the horizon.

But from his vantage point, Harbert could precisely view this still unknown portion of the island, which might have sheltered the foreigners suspected to be present.

The young boy looked with extreme attention. At sea, at first, nothing was in sight. Not a sail, neither on the horizon nor on the island's landings.

However, since the mass of trees concealed the coastline, it was possible that a ship, especially one stripped of its mast, could have approached very close to shore, and thus remained invisible to Harbert. Among the woods of the Far-West, nothing was visible either. The forest formed an impenetrable dome measuring several square miles, without a clearing, without an opening. It was even impossible to follow the course of the Mercy and identify the spot in the mountains where it originated.

Perhaps other creeks flowed westward, but nothing indicated that.

However, if all signs of a camp escaped Harbert's view, could he not catch sight of some smoke in the air that would reveal the presence of man? The atmosphere was clear, and the slightest vapor would have contrasted sharply against the sky's backdrop.

For a moment, Harbert thought he saw a thin wisp of smoke rising in the west, but a closer look revealed that he was mistaken. He scanned with great care, and his vision was excellent... no, there was definitely nothing.

Harbert climbed down from the kauri, and the two hunters returned to Granite-House. There, Cyrus Smith listened to the young boy's account, shook his head, and said nothing. It was clear that they could not draw any conclusions about this matter until a complete exploration of the island was conducted.

The day after, on October 28, another incident occurred, the explanation of which would still leave much to be desired. While roaming along the shore, two miles from Granite-House, Harbert and Nab were fortunate enough to capture a magnificent specimen of the order Chelonia. It was a green turtle of the type Mydas, whose shell had marvelous green reflections.

Harbert spotted this turtle slipping between the rocks to reach the sea.

"To me, Nab, to me!" he shouted.

Nab ran over.

"What a beautiful animal!" said Nab. "But how do we catch it?

"Nothing could be easier, Nab," replied Harbert. "We'll turn this turtle on its back, and it won't be able to bury itself. Grab your spear and follow my lead."

Sensing danger, the reptile had withdrawn its head and legs into its shell. Its head and limbs were out of sight, and it was as still as a rock.

Harbert and Nab then wedged their sticks under the animal's shell, and combining their efforts, they managed, with some difficulty, to turn it onto its back. This turtle, measuring three feet in length, must have weighed at least four hundred pounds."Good! exclaimed Nab, this will delight our friend Pencroff!" Indeed, Pencroff couldn't help but be delighted, because the flesh of these turtles, which feed on seagrass, is extremely tasty. At that moment, the turtle was showing only its small, flat head, but was greatly expanded at the back by large temporal fossae, hidden under a bony vault.

"And now, what will we do with our catch? said Nab. We can't drag it back to Granite House!

— Let's leave it here since it can't flip over, replied Harbert, and we'll come back for it with the cart.

— Agreed."

However, for extra caution, Harbert took the trouble, which Nab thought unnecessary, to prop the animal up with large pebbles. After that, the two hunters returned to Granite House, following the shore that the low tide had widely revealed.

Harbert, wanting to surprise Pencroff, said nothing about the "superb specimen of turtles" that he had left on the sand; but two hours later, Nab and he returned with the cart to the spot where they had left it. The "superb specimen of turtles" was gone.

Nab and Harbert looked at each other first, then looked around. It was definitely at this spot that the turtle had been left. The young boy even found the pebbles he had used, so he was sure he wasn't mistaken.

"Hey! said Nab, do these creatures actually flip over?

— It seems so, replied Harbert, who couldn't understand it and looked at the scattered pebbles on the sand.

— Well, Pencroff won't be happy!

— And Mr. Smith might be quite puzzled trying to explain this disappearance! thought Harbert.

— Well, said Nab, who wanted to hide his misadventure, let's not talk about it.

— On the contrary, Nab, we have to talk about it," replied Harbert.

And both, taking back the cart that they had brought uselessly, returned to Granite House.

Arriving at the workshop, where the engineer and the sailor were working together, Harbert recounted what had happened.

"Oh! What clumsiness! exclaimed the sailor. To have let go fifty soups at least!

— But, Pencroff, replied Nab, it's not our fault the beast escaped, since I told you we had flipped it over!

— Then, you didn't flip it over enough! retorted the stubborn sailor playfully.

— Not enough! shouted Harbert.

And he explained that he had carefully propped the turtle with pebbles.

JULES VERNE

"Then it's a miracle! replied Pencroff.

— I thought, Mr. Cyrus, said Harbert, that turtles, once placed on their backs, couldn't right themselves, especially when they are large?

— That's true, my child, replied Cyrus Smith.

— Then how could it happen...?

— How far from the sea did you leave this turtle? asked the engineer, who, having paused his work, was reflecting on this incident.

— About fifteen feet at most, replied Harbert.

— And the tide was low at that time?

— Yes, Mr. Cyrus.

— Well, replied the engineer, what the turtle couldn't do on the sand, it may have done in the water. It could have flipped over when the tide took it and swum back to the open sea peacefully.

— Ah! What clumsiness we are! cried Nab.

— That's precisely what I had the honor to tell you!" replied Pencroff.

Cyrus Smith had given this explanation, which was undoubtedly plausible. But was he truly convinced of its accuracy? That was uncertain.

2

On October 29, the canoe made of bark was completely finished. Pencroff had kept his promise, and a sort of pirogue, whose hull was reinforced with flexible crejimba sticks, was built in five days. A seat at the back, a second seat in the middle for stability, a third seat at the front, a gunwale to support the two oars, and a single oar for steering completed this vessel, which was twelve feet long and weighed less than two hundred pounds. As for launching it, that was extremely simple. The lightweight pirogue was carried to the sand at the edge of the shore, in front of Granite House, and the rising tide lifted it.

Pencroff, who immediately jumped in, maneuvered it with the single oar, and was able to confirm that it was very suitable for the intended use.

"Hooray! shouted the sailor, who did not hesitate to celebrate his own triumph this way. With this, one could go around...

— The world? asked Gideon Spilett.

— No, the island. A few stones for ballast, a mast up front, and a piece of sail that Mr. Smith will make for us one day, and we'll go far! Well! Mr. Cyrus, you, Mr. Spilett, you, Harbert, and you, Nab, aren't you coming to try out our new craft? Come on! We need to see if it can carry all five of us!"

Indeed, it was an experience to undertake. Pencroff, with a stroke of the oar, drove the vessel near the shore through a narrow passage between the rocks, and it was agreed that they would test the pirogue that very day, following the shoreline to the first point where the southern rocks ended. At the moment of boarding, Nab exclaimed:

"But your vessel takes on a lot of water, Pencroff!

— It's nothing, Nab, replied the sailor. The wood just needs to seal! In two days it won't be noticeable, and our pirogue won't have more water inside than there is in the stomach of a drunkard. Get on board!

So they got on, and Pencroff pushed off into the open water.

The weather was beautiful, the sea calm as if its waters were contained within the narrow banks of a lake, and the pirogue could handle it as safely as if it were paddling up the still current of the Mercy. Nab took one of the oars, Harbert the other, while Pencroff remained at the back of the vessel to steer with the single oar.

The sailor first crossed the channel and skimmed along the southern point of the islet. A light breeze blew from the south. No swell either in the channel or offshore. A few long swells that the pirogue barely felt, as it was heavily loaded, regularly rippled the surface of the sea. They moved about half a mile from the coast, enough to see the full view of Mount Franklin.

Then, Pencroff, changing course, returned towards the mouth of the river. The pirogue then followed the shoreline, which, curving toward the end, hid the entire marshy plain of the Tadornes.

This point, the distance of which was increased by the curvature of the coast, was about three miles from the Mercy. The colonists decided to go to its end and only move past it slightly to take a quick look at the coast up to Cape Griffe.

So the canoe followed the coast at a distance of no more than two cables, avoiding the obstacles strewn along these shores, which the rising tide was beginning to cover. The wall sloped down from the mouth of the river to the point. It was a pile of granite, whimsically distributed, very different from the curtain, forming the Grande-vue plateau, and had an extremely wild appearance.

It looked as if an enormous truckload of rocks had been dumped there. There was no vegetation on that very sharp promontory that extended two miles ahead of the forest, and this point resembled the arm of a giant emerging from a sleeve of greenery.

The canoe, propelled by the two oars, moved smoothly along. Gideon Spilett, with pencil in one hand and notebook in the other, sketched the coastline in broad strokes.

Nab, Pencroff, and Harbert chatted while observing this part of their domain that was new to their eyes, and as the pirogue continued south, the two Mandibule caps appeared to shift and close in more tightly on the Bay of Union.

As for Cyrus Smith, he said nothing; he watched, and from the suspicion expressed in his gaze, it always seemed as though he were observing some strange land.

However, after three-quarters of an hour of traveling, the pirogue had almost reached the tip of the point, and Pencroff was preparing to round it when Harbert, standing up, pointed out a dark patch, saying:

"What do I see over there on the shore?"

All eyes turned to the indicated spot.

"Indeed, said the reporter, there is something. It looks like a wreck half-buried in the sand.

— Ah! exclaimed Pencroff, I see what it is!

— What is it? asked Nab.

— Barrels, barrels that might be full! replied the sailor.

— To the shore, Pencroff! said Cyrus Smith.

In just a few strokes of the oar, the pirogue reached the bottom of a small cove, and its passengers leaped onto the shore.

Pencroff was not mistaken. Two barrels were there, half-buried in the sand, but still securely attached to a large crate which, supported by them, had floated until it came to rest on the shore.

"So there was a shipwreck near the island? asked Harbert.

— Obviously, replied Gideon Spilett.

— But what's in that crate? shouted Pencroff with understandable impatience. What's in that crate? It's closed, and there's nothing to break the lid! Well, let's break it open with rocks then..."

And the sailor, lifting a heavy block, was about to smash one of the sides of the crate when the engineer, stopping him:

"Pencroff, he said to him, can you control your impatience for just one hour?

— But, Mr. Cyrus, just think about it! There might be everything we're missing in there!

— We will find out, Pencroff, replied the engineer, but believe me, don't break this crate, which may be useful to us. Let's take it to Granite House, where we can open it more easily without damaging it. It's ready for the journey, and since it floated here, it will float well until we reach the mouth of the river.

— You're right, Mr. Cyrus, and I was wrong, replied the sailor, but one can't always master oneself!"

The engineer's advice was wise. In fact, the pirogue wouldn't have been able to hold the potentially heavy items inside the crate, as they had had to support it with two empty barrels. So, it was better to tow it like this until reaching the shore of Granite House.

And now, where did this wreck come from? That was an important question. Cyrus Smith and his companions carefully looked around and searched the shore over several hundred paces. No other debris came into view.

The sea was observed as well. Harbert and Nab climbed up a high rock, but the horizon was deserted. Nothing in sight, no damaged vessel, nor a sailing ship.

However, a shipwreck had indeed occurred; that was certain. Perhaps even this incident was linked to the incident with the lead grain? Maybe strangers had landed at another point on the island? Perhaps they were still there? But the reflection that naturally occurred to the colonists was that these strangers could not be Malay pirates, as the wreck clearly had an American or European origin.

They all returned to the crate, which measured five feet long and three feet wide. It was made of oak, very carefully closed, and covered with a thick skin held in place with copper nails. The two large barrels, hermetically sealed but felt empty upon being struck, were attached to its sides with strong ropes tied with knots that Pencroff easily recognized as "marine knots." It appeared to be in perfect condition, which could be explained by the fact that it had washed up on a sandy shore and not on reefs. It could even be said, upon closer examination, that its time spent in the sea had not been long and that its arrival on this shore was recent. Water did not seem to have penetrated inside, and the items it contained must be intact.

It was evident that this crate had been thrown overboard from a storm-damaged ship headed toward the island, and in the hope it would reach the shore where they could later find it, passengers had taken the precaution of lightening it with a floating device.

"We're going to tow this wreck to Granite House, said the engineer, and we'll take inventory; then, if we discover any survivors from this presumed shipwreck on the island, we will return it to those whom it belongs. If we find no one...

— We'll keep it for ourselves! shouted Pencroff. But, for heaven's sake, what could possibly be in there!"

The tide was already beginning to reach the wreck, which would surely float at high tide. One of the ropes that attached the barrels was partially unrolled and was used as a tie to secure the floating device to the canoe. Then, Pencroff and Nab dug into the sand with their oars to ease the movement of the crate, and soon the pirogue, towing the crate, began to round the point, which was named Wreck Point (flotson-point). The tow was heavy, and the barrels barely kept the crate above water. The sailor feared at any moment that it might detach and sink to the bottom. But, fortunately, his fears did not materialize, and an hour and a half after leaving—it had taken all that time to cover the three miles—the pirogue landed on the shore in front of Granite House.

The canoe and wreck were then dragged onto the sand, and as the sea was already receding, they quickly remained dry. Nab went to get tools to open the crate, so as to minimize damage, and they proceeded with their inventory.

Pencroff did not hide that he was extremely moved.

The sailor first detached the two barrels, which, being in very good condition, could certainly be used. Then, the locks were forced with a pair of pliers, and the lid immediately came off. A second layer of zinc lined the inside of the crate, which had been obviously prepared so that the items it contained would be safe from moisture under all circumstances.

"Ah! exclaimed Nab, could there be preserved goods in there!

— I certainly hope not, replied the reporter.

— If only there were... said the sailor softly.

— What is it? Nab asked, hearing him.

— Nothing!"The zinc sheet was split across its width and then folded down over the sides of the crate, and gradually various items of very different nature were pulled out and placed on the sand. With each new item, Pencroff let out new cheers, Harbert clapped his hands, and Nab danced... like a jolly fellow. There were books that would have made Harbert overjoyed and cooking utensils that Nab would have covered in kisses!

Furthermore, the colonists had every reason to be extremely satisfied, as this crate contained tools, weapons, instruments, clothing, books, and here is the exact list, as recorded in Gédéon Spilett's notebook:

Tools: 3 multi-bladed knives.

2 axe forgers.

2 carpenter's axes.

Tools: 3 planes.

2 chisels.

1 spokeshave.

6 cold chisels.

2 files.

3 hammers.

3 drills.

2 augers.

10 bags of nails and screws.

3 saws of various sizes.

Tools: 2 boxes of needles.

Weapons: 2 flint rifles.

2 caplock rifles.

2 centerfire carbines.

5 machetes.

4 boarding swords.

2 kegs of powder, each able to hold twenty-five pounds.

12 boxes of blasting caps.

Instruments: 1 sextant 1 pair of binoculars.

Instruments: 1 telescope.

1 box of compasses.

1 pocket compass.

1 Fahrenheit thermometer 1 aneroid barometer.

1 box containing a complete photographic apparatus, lens, plates, chemicals, etc.

Clothing: 2 dozen shirts made from a special fabric that looked like wool, but whose origin was clearly vegetable.

3 dozen socks made from the same fabric.

Utensils: 1 iron cooking pot.

6 tinned copper pans.

3 iron plates.

10 aluminum cutlery sets.

2 kettles.

1 small portable stove.

6 table knives.

Books: 1 Bible containing the Old and New Testaments.

1 atlas.

1 dictionary of various Polynesian dialects.

1 dictionary of natural sciences, in six volumes.

3 reams of white paper.

2 registers of blank pages.

"I must admit," said the reporter, after the inventory was completed, "that the owner of this crate was a practical man! Tools, weapons, instruments, clothing, utensils, books, everything is here! It really seems he expected to shipwreck and prepared for it in advance!"

"Everything is indeed here," murmured Cyrus Smith thoughtfully.

"And surely," added Harbert, "the ship that carried this crate and its owner was not a Malay pirate!"

"Unless," said Pencroff, "this owner had been captured by pirates..."

"That's unlikely," replied the reporter. "It's more probable that an American or European vessel got caught in these waters, and that passengers, wanting to save at least the essentials, prepared this crate and tossed it into the sea."

"Is that your opinion, Mr. Cyrus?" asked Harbert.

"Yes, my child," replied the engineer, "that could have happened. It's possible that at the moment, or in anticipation of a shipwreck, they gathered together various useful items in this crate, to find them at some point on the shore..."

"Even the box with the photography equipment!" observed the sailor, sounding quite skeptical.

"As for that device," replied Cyrus Smith, "I don't really see its usefulness, and it would have been better for us, as for all other shipwrecked people, to have a more complete assortment of clothing or more abundant ammunition!"

"But is there no mark, no address on these instruments, tools, or books that could help us recognize their origin?" asked Gédéon Spilett.

That remained to be seen. Each item was thus examined carefully, especially the books, instruments, and weapons. Neither the weapons nor the instruments, contrary to what usually happens, bore the manufacturer's mark; they were, moreover, in perfect condition and did not seem to have been used. The same was true for the tools and utensils; everything was new, which proved that these items were not randomly taken to toss into this crate but, on the contrary, that the selection of these items had been deliberate and their arrangement done with care. This was also indicated by the second metal envelope that had kept them free from moisture and could not have been sealed in a moment of haste.

As for the dictionaries of natural sciences and Polynesian dialects, both were in English but bore no publisher's name or publication date. The same was true for the Bible, printed in English, remarkable typographically, and which appeared to have been frequently opened.

The atlas was a magnificent work, including maps of the whole world and several world maps created according to Mercator's projection, and whose nomenclature was in French, — but which also bore no publication date or publisher's name.

Thus, there were no clues on these various items that could indicate their origin, and nothing, therefore, to raise suspicions about the nationality of the ship that must have recently passed through these waters. But wherever this crate came from, it made the colonists of Lincoln Island wealthy.

Until then, by transforming the products of nature, they had created everything by themselves, and thanks to their intelligence, they had managed to get by.

But didn't it seem that providence wanted to reward them by sending them these various products of human industry? Their thanks rose unanimously to the heavens.

However, one of them was not completely satisfied.

That was Pencroff. It seemed that the crate did not contain one thing that he seemed to care about greatly, and as the items were taken out, his cheers diminished in intensity, and when the inventory was finished, he was heard murmuring these words:

"All this is nice and good, but you'll see that there will be nothing for me in this box!"

This prompted Nab to say to him:

"Well now! My friend Pencroff, what were you expecting?"

"A half-pound of tobacco!" replied Pencroff seriously, "and nothing would have been lacking for my happiness!"

Everyone couldn't help but laugh at the sailor's remark.

But the discovery of the wreck made it now, more than ever, necessary to carry out a serious exploration of the island. It was therefore agreed that the next day, at dawn, they would set off, going up the Mercy, so as to reach the western coast.

If any castaways had landed at some point on this coast, it was to be feared that they were without resources, and they needed to help them without delay.

During that day, the various items were transported to Granite House and methodically arranged in the great hall.

That day—October 29—was exactly a Sunday, and, before going to bed, Harbert asked the engineer if he would read them a passage from the Gospel.

"Gladly," replied Cyrus Smith.

He took the sacred book and was about to open it when Pencroff, stopping him, said:

"Mr. Cyrus, I am superstitious. Open at random and read us the first verse that falls under your eyes. We'll see if it applies to our situation."

Cyrus Smith smiled at the sailor's reflection, and, complying with his wish, he opened the Gospel exactly at a place where a bookmark separated the pages.

Suddenly, his gaze was caught by a red cross, which, drawn in pencil, was placed before verse 8 of chapter VII of the Gospel of Saint Matthew.

And he read this verse, which went: "Everyone who asks receives, and whoever seeks finds."

ᘓ 3 ᘏ

The next day—October 30—everything was ready for the planned exploration, which recent events made so urgent. Indeed, things had turned out such that the colonists of Lincoln Island could imagine themselves no longer asking for help, but rather being able to offer it.

It was agreed that they would ascend the Mercy as far as the river's current would allow. A large part of the route would thus be done without fatigue, and the explorers could transport their supplies and weapons to a forward point in the island's west.

They had to think not only about the items they were taking, but also about what they might possibly bring back to Granite House. If there had been a shipwreck on the coast, as everything suggested, the remains would be plentiful and good finds. In this expectation, a cart would have suited better than the fragile canoe; however, this cart, heavy and crude, needed to be dragged, making its use less convenient, which led Pencroff to express regret that the crate hadn't contained, along with "his half-pound of tobacco", a pair of those sturdy New Jersey horses, which would have been very useful to the colony!

The supplies, already loaded by Nab, consisted of canned meat and some gallons of beer and fermented liquor, that is to say, enough to sustain them for three days—the maximum time Cyrus Smith allotted for the exploration. Moreover, they expected, if necessary, to replenish supplies on the way, and Nab made sure not to forget the small portable stove. In terms of tools, the colonists took the two axe forgers, which were to be used to clear a path through the thick forest, and in terms of instruments, the telescope and pocket compass.

186

For weapons, they chose the two flint rifles, more useful in this island than cartridge rifles, as the former used only flint, easy to replace, while the latter required blasting caps, which frequent use would quickly deplete. However, they also took one of the carbines and some cartridges. As for the powder, which the kegs contained about fifty pounds of, they had to carry a sufficient supply, but the engineer planned to manufacture an explosive substance that would allow them to conserve it. Along with the firearms, they added the five well-sheathed machetes, and in these conditions, the colonists could venture into this vast forest with some chance of making it back.

It's unnecessary to add that Pencroff, Harbert, and Nab, thus armed, were at the height of their wishes, even though Cyrus Smith had made them promise not to fire a shot without necessity.

At six in the morning, the canoe was pushed into the sea. Everyone embarked, including Top, and headed towards the mouth of the Mercy.

The tide had been rising for only half an hour. There were still a few hours of flooding left to take advantage of, as later, the ebb would make it difficult to ascend the river. The tide was already strong since the moon was to be full three days later, and the canoe, which only needed to be kept in the current, moved quickly between the two high banks, without needing to increase its speed with the help of paddles. In a few minutes, the explorers arrived at the bend that the Mercy formed, and precisely at the angle where, seven months earlier, Pencroff had set up his first wood pile.

After this rather sharp angle, the river rounded and curved towards the south-west, its course unfolding beneath the shade of tall conifers with evergreen foliage.

The view of the banks of the Mercy was magnificent.

Cyrus Smith and his companions could only admire without reservation the beautiful effects that nature so easily achieves with water and trees.

As they advanced, the forest species changed. On the right bank of the river stood beautiful samples of the ulmaceae, these valuable elms, so sought after by builders, which have the property of lasting a long time in water. Then there were many groups belonging to the same family, including hackberries, whose nuts produce a very useful oil. Further along, Harbert noticed some lardizabalas, whose flexible branches, soaked in water, provide excellent ropes, and two or three trunks of ebony trees, which displayed a beautiful black color streaked with whimsical veins. From time to time, at certain spots where landing was easy, the canoe stopped.

Then Gédéon Spilett, Harbert, and Pencroff, rifle in hand and preceded by Top, scoured the bank. Not counting game, they might find some useful plant not to be dismissed, and the young naturalist was well served, as he discovered a type of wild spinach from the Chenopodiaceae family and many samples of crucifers, belonging to the cabbage genus, which could certainly be "civilized" by transplanting; they were watercress, horseradish, turnips, and finally small woody stems, slightly hairy, a meter high, that produced almost brown seeds.

"Do you know what that plant is?" asked Harbert of the sailor.

"Tobacco!" shouted Pencroff, who obviously had only ever seen his favorite plant in the bowl of his pipe.

"No! Pencroff!" replied Harbert, "it's not tobacco, it's mustard."

"Let it be mustard!" replied the sailor, "but if, by chance, a tobacco plant turns up, my boy, please do not overlook it."

"We'll find one day!" said Gédéon Spilett.

"Surely!" exclaimed Pencroff. "Well, on that day, I really don't know what will be missing from our island!"

These various plants, carefully uprooted, were transported in the canoe, which Cyrus Smith never left, always absorbed in his thoughts.

The reporter, Harbert, and Pencroff thus landed several times, sometimes on the right bank of the Mercy, and sometimes on its left bank. The latter was less steep, but the former was more wooded. The engineer was able to ascertain, by consulting his pocket compass, that the direction of the river since the first bend was significantly southwest and northeast, and almost straight for a length of about three miles. But it was assumed that this direction changed further on and that the Mercy continued northwest, towards the foothills of Mount Franklin, which should feed it with their waters.

During one of these excursions, Gédéon Spilett managed to catch two pairs of live game birds. They were birds with long, slender beaks, elongated necks, short wings, and no visible tails. Harbert rightly named them "tinamous", and it was decided that they would make the first guests of the future poultry yard.

But until then, the rifles had not fired, and the first shot that echoed in this Far-West forest was caused by the appearance of a beautiful bird that anatomically resembled a kingfisher.

"I recognize it!" cried Pencroff, and it can be said that his shot went off before he knew it.

"What do you recognize?" asked the reporter.

"The bird that escaped us on our first outing and that we named this part of the forest after."

"A jacamar!" cried Harbert. It was indeed a jacamar, a beautiful bird with rather coarse plumage that shone with a metallic luster. Some lead shot had brought it down, and Top carried it back to the boat along with a dozen "touracos-loris," types of climbers about the size of a pigeon, all painted green, with part of their wings crimson and a straight crest edged with white. The young boy received the honor of this fine shot, and he was quite proud of it. The loris made for better game than the jacamar, whose flesh is somewhat tough, but it would have been hard to convince Pencroff that he had not killed the king of edible birds.

It was ten o'clock in the morning when the canoe reached a second bend of the Mercy, about five miles from its mouth. They stopped there to have lunch, and this break, sheltered by large, beautiful trees, lasted half an hour. The river was still sixty to seventy feet wide, and its bed was five to six feet deep. The engineer noted that many tributaries were increasing its flow, but these were just small, unnavigable streams. As for the forest, under both the name of Jacamar Woods and Far-West Forest, it stretched as far as the eye could see. Nowhere, neither under the tall trees nor along the banks of the Mercy, was there any sign of human presence. The explorers could not find any suspicious traces, and it was clear that the woodcutter's axe had never marked these trees, that the pioneer's knife had never cut these vines stretched from trunk to trunk amidst the thick underbrush and long grasses. If some shipwrecked people had landed on the island, they had not yet left the shore, and it was not under this thick cover that they needed to search for the presumed survivors of the shipwreck.

The engineer therefore showed a certain eagerness to reach the western coast of Lincoln Island, which he estimated to be at least five miles away. Navigation resumed, and although the Mercy seemed to flow not toward the coast but rather toward Mount Franklin by its current direction, it was decided to use the canoe as long as there was enough water beneath it to float. It saved them considerable fatigue and time since they would have had to hack a path through thick brush.

But soon the current ran almost dry, either because the tide was falling—and indeed it was supposed to lower at this time—or because it was no longer felt at this distance from the mouth of the Mercy. They then had to row. Nab and Harbert took their places on the bench, Pencroff took the oars, and they continued upstream.

It then seemed that the forest was starting to thin out on the Far-West side. The trees were less crowded and often stood alone. But precisely because they were more spaced out, they enjoyed more fully the free, pure air circulating around them, and they were magnificent. What splendid examples of flora from this latitude! Surely, their presence would have been enough for a botanist to confidently name the parallel that crossed Lincoln Island!

"Eucalyptus!" exclaimed Harbert.

Indeed, these were these magnificent plants, the last giants of the extra-tropical zone, relatives of the eucalyptus from Australia and New Zealand, both located at the same latitude as Lincoln Island. Some stood two hundred feet tall. Their trunks measured twenty feet around at the base, and their bark, marked with networks of fragrant resin, was up to five inches thick. Nothing was more marvelous, but also more peculiar, than these enormous specimens of the myrtaceae family, whose foliage presented itself side-on to the light and allowed sunlight to reach the ground! At the foot of these eucalyptus, fresh grass covered the ground, and from the midst of the clumps flew out small birds that sparkled in the sunlight like winged jewels.

"Those are trees!" cried Nab, "but are they good for anything?"

"Bah!" replied Pencroff. "Giant plants are like giant humans. They're hardly good for anything except showing off at fairs!"

"I think you're mistaken, Pencroff," replied Gédéon Spilett, "and that eucalyptus wood is becoming very useful in woodworking."

"And I'll add," said the young boy, "that these eucalyptus belong to a family that includes many useful members: the guava tree, which produces guavas; the clove tree, which yields cloves; the pomegranate tree, which bears pomegranates; the 'eugenia cauliflora,' whose fruits are used to make a passable wine; the myrtle 'ugni,' which contains an excellent alcoholic liqueur; the myrtle 'caryophyllus,' whose bark forms valued cinnamon; the 'eugenia pimenta,' which provides Jamaica pepper; the common myrtle, whose berries can replace pepper; the 'eucalyptus robusta,' which produces an excellent manna; the 'eucalyptus gunei,' whose sap ferments into beer; and finally, all these trees known as 'trees of life' or 'ironwood,' which belong to this myrtaceae family, which counts forty-six genera and one thousand three hundred species!"

They let the young boy go on, who delivered his little botany lecture with great enthusiasm.

Cyrus Smith listened to him with a smile, and Pencroff with an impossible-to-describe feeling of pride.

"Well, Harbert," replied Pencroff, "but I'd bet that all those useful examples you just mentioned aren't giants like these!"

"Indeed, Pencroff."

"That supports what I said," replied the sailor, "namely, that giants are good for nothing!"

"That's where you're mistaken, Pencroff," said the engineer then, "and precisely these gigantic eucalyptus that shelter us are good for something."

"And what might that be?"

"To purify the land they inhabit. Do you know what they are called in Australia and New Zealand?"

"No, Mr. Cyrus."

"They're called 'fever trees.'"

"Because they give it?"

"No, because they prevent it!"

"Good. I'll note that," said the reporter.

"Do note it, my dear Spilett, for it seems proven that the presence of eucalyptus is enough to neutralize malarial miasmas. This natural preservative has been tried in certain regions of southern Europe and northern Africa, where the soil was absolutely unhealthy, and in which the health of the inhabitants gradually improved. No more intermittent fevers in the areas covered by these myrtaceae forests. This fact is now beyond doubt, and it is a happy circumstance for us, colons of Lincoln Island."

"Ah! What an island! What a blessed island!" shouted Pencroff! "I'm telling you, it lacks nothing... Except..."

"That will come, Pencroff, it will be found," replied the engineer; "but let's resume our navigation and go as far as the river will carry our canoe!"

So the exploration continued for at least two miles, through an area covered with eucalyptus, which dominated all the woods in that part of the island. The space they covered extended beyond the limits of sight on either side of the Mercy, whose fairly winding bed now lay between high, green banks. This bed was often obstructed by tall grasses and even sharp rocks that made navigation quite difficult. The action of the oars was hindered, and Pencroff had to push with a pole. They also felt that the bottom was gradually rising, and that the moment was not far off when the boat, lacking water, would have to stop. The sun was already setting on the horizon and casting the immense shadows of trees on the ground. Seeing that he would not be able to reach the western coast of the island that day, Cyrus Smith decided to camp right where, due to lack of water, navigation would inevitably stop. He estimated they were still about five or six miles from the coast, and that distance was too great to attempt to cross in the dark through these unfamiliar woods.

The boat was therefore pushed relentlessly through the forest, which gradually became denser and seemed more inhabited as well, for, if the sailor's eyes did not deceive him, he thought he caught sight of bands of monkeys running under the bushes. Sometimes even, two or three of these animals stopped at a distance from the canoe and watched the colonists without showing any fear, as if, seeing humans for the first time, they had not yet learned to dread them. It would have been easy to shoot these primates, but Cyrus Smith opposed this unnecessary massacre that tempted the eager Pencroff a little. Besides, it was prudent because these monkeys, strong and incredibly agile, could be formidable, and it was better not to provoke them with a perfectly inopportune attack.

It is true that the sailor viewed the monkey from a purely dietary perspective, and indeed, these animals, which are strictly herbivorous, make excellent game; but since provisions were plentiful, it was unnecessary to waste ammunition for no reason.

Around four o'clock, navigating the Mercy became very difficult because its course was blocked by aquatic plants and rocks. The banks rose more and more, and the riverbed was already sinking among the first foothills of Mount Franklin. Its sources could not be far away since they fed off all the waters from the southern slopes of the mountain.

"Within fifteen minutes," said the sailor, "we will be forced to stop, Mr. Cyrus."

"Well, we will stop, Pencroff, and we will set up camp for the night."

"How far can we be from Granite-House?" asked Harbert.

"About seven miles," replied the engineer, "but taking into account the meanders of the river that have taken us northwest."

"Shall we continue forward?" asked the reporter.

"Yes, as long as we can," replied Cyrus Smith. "Tomorrow at dawn, we will leave the canoe behind, and I hope we will cover the distance separating us from the coast in two hours, and we'll have most of the day to explore the shore."

"Forward!" replied Pencroff.

But soon the canoe scraped the rocky bottom of the river, which then was no more than twenty feet wide. A thick arch of greenery rounded overhead and enveloped it in half-darkness. They could also hear the pronounced sound of a waterfall, indicating, a few hundred steps upstream, the presence of a natural dam.

And indeed, at a last bend of the river, a waterfall appeared through the trees. The canoe hit the bottom of the stream, and moments later, it was tied to a trunk near the right bank.

It was around five o'clock. The last rays of the sun slipped under the thick foliage and struck obliquely at the small fall, whose damp mist sparkled with the colors of the prism. Beyond, the bed of the Mercy disappeared under the thickets, where it drew from some hidden spring. The various streams flowing into it made it a real river lower down, but at that moment, it was nothing more than a clear, shallow brook.

They camped right at that charming spot. The colonists disembarked, and a fire was soon lit under a clump of large micocouliers, among the branches of which Cyrus Smith and his companions would have, if needed, found shelter for the night.

Dinner was quickly devoured, for they were hungry, and soon the only thing on their minds was to sleep. However, when a few suspicious growls were heard at dusk, the fire was stoked for the night, so as to protect the sleepers from its crackling flames. Nab and Pencroff even took turns keeping watch and did not spare the fuel. Perhaps they were not mistaken when they thought they saw some shadows of animals roaming around the camp, either under the thicket or between the branches; but the night passed without incident, and the next day, October 31, at five in the morning, everyone was up and ready to leave.

4

It was six in the morning when the colonists, after a light breakfast, set out again, intending to make their way to the western coast of the island by the shortest route. How long would it take them to reach it? Cyrus Smith had said two hours, but that obviously depended on the nature of the obstacles that would present themselves. This part of the Far-West seemed packed with woods, like an immense thicket made of extremely varied species. It was therefore likely that they would need to hack their way through grasses, bushes, and vines, and walk with axes in hand—and the rifle too, no doubt, if they relied on the cries of wild animals heard at night.

The exact position of the campsite had been determined by the location of Mount Franklin, and since the volcano rose to the north less than three miles away, they simply needed to head straight southwest to reach the western coast.

They set off after carefully securing the canoe. Pencroff and Nab carried provisions that would be enough to feed the small group for at least two days.

There was no longer any question of hunting, and the engineer even advised his companions to avoid any untimely detonations so as not to signal their presence near the coast.

The first blows of the axe were struck in the brush, among lentisk bushes, a little above the waterfall, and with his compass in hand, Cyrus Smith indicated the route to follow.

The forest then consisted of trees that most had already been recognized around the lake and the Grande-Vue plateau. They were deodars, douglas firs, casuarinas, gum trees, eucalyptus, dragon trees, hibiscus, cedars, and other species, generally of medium height since their number had hindered their growth. The colonists could only progress slowly on this route they were clearing as they walked, which, in the engineer's mind, should later be connected to that of the Creek-Rouge. Since their departure, the colonists had been descending the low slopes that made up the island's orographic system, and on very dry land, but whose lush vegetation suggested either the presence of a hydrographic network beneath the ground or the upcoming flow of some brook.

However, Cyrus Smith did not recall, during his excursion to the crater, recognizing any other watercourses than those of Creek-Rouge and Mercy. During the first hours of the excursion, they saw groups of monkeys that seemed to be quite surprised by the sight of these men, who were new to them. Gédéon Spilett jokingly asked if these agile and sturdy primates considered him and his companions as degenerate brothers! And honestly, ordinary pedestrians, hindered at every step by the underbrush, held back by vines, and blocked by tree trunks, did not shine compared to these nimble animals that jumped from branch to branch without anything stopping them. These monkeys were numerous, but fortunately, they showed no signs of hostility.

They also spotted a few wild boars, agoutis, kangaroos, and other rodents, as well as two or three koulas, which Pencroff would gladly have shot.

"But," he said, "the hunting season isn't open. So frolic away, my friends, jump and fly in peace! We'll have a few words with you on the way back!"

At nine-thirty in the morning, the path, which directly headed southwest, was suddenly blocked by an unknown watercourse, about thirty to forty feet wide, with a strong current, caused by the slope of its bed and broken up by numerous rocks, rushing forward with a loud roar.

This creek was deep and clear, but it was absolutely unnavigable.

"We're cut off!" shouted Nab.

"No," replied Harbert, "it's just a stream, and we can easily cross it by swimming."

"What's the point?" Cyrus Smith responded. "It's clear this creek flows to the sea. Let's stay on its left bank, follow its shore, and I'll be very surprised if it doesn't lead us quickly to the coast. Let's go!"

"Wait a minute," said the reporter. "And what about the name of this creek, my friends? Let's not leave our geography incomplete."

"Good point!" said Pencroff.

"Name it, my boy," said the engineer, addressing the young boy.

"Isn't it better to wait until we've seen it down to its mouth?" Harbert suggested.

"Alright," replied Cyrus Smith. "Let's follow it without stopping."

"One more moment!" said Pencroff.

"What is it?" the reporter asked.

"If hunting is forbidden, fishing is allowed, I suppose," said the sailor.

"We don't have time to waste," replied the engineer.

"Oh! Just five minutes!" Pencroff insisted. "I only ask for five minutes for the sake of our lunch!"

And Pencroff, lying down on the bank, plunged his arms into the rushing water and soon pulled out several dozen beautiful crayfish that were swarming between the rocks.

"That'll be great!" Nab exclaimed, coming to help the sailor.

"When I tell you that, aside from tobacco, there's everything in this island!" Pencroff murmured with a sigh.

It took less than five minutes for a miraculous catch, as the crayfish were plentiful in the creek. From these crustaceans, which had a cobalt blue shell and a rostrum armed with a small tooth, they filled a bag, and then resumed their journey. Since they had been following the bank of this new watercourse, the colonists walked more easily and quickly. Moreover, the banks were untouched by any human imprint. Occasionally, they spotted some tracks left by large animals that usually came to quench their thirst at this stream, but nothing more, and it was still not in this part of the Far West that the peccary had received the bullet that cost Pencroff a dog.

However, considering the fast current flowing toward the sea, Cyrus Smith began to suspect that he and his companions were much farther from the western coast than they had thought. And indeed, at this hour, the tide was rising on the shore and should have reversed the flow of the creek if its mouth was just a few miles away.

However, this effect was not happening, and the stream followed the natural slope of its bed. The engineer must have been very surprised, and he frequently consulted his compass to ensure that some twist of the river was not pulling him back inland into the Far West.

Meanwhile, the creek gradually widened, and its waters became less turbulent. The trees on the right bank were as dense as those on the left, and it was impossible to see beyond; but these woodland masses were certainly deserted because Top was not barking, and the intelligent animal would have missed signaling the presence of any stranger near the watercourse.

At ten-thirty, to Cyrus Smith's great surprise, Harbert, who had moved slightly ahead, suddenly stopped and shouted: "The sea!"

And moments later, the colonists, paused on the edge of the forest, saw the western shore of the island unfold before their eyes.

But what a contrast between this coast and the east coast, where chance had first cast them! No more granite walls, no reefs offshore, not even a sandy beach. The forest formed the coastline, and its last trees, battered by the waves, leaned over the waters. This was not a coastline, as nature usually creates it, either by spreading vast carpets of sand or by grouping rocks, but an admirable edge made up of the most beautiful trees in the world. The bank was elevated enough to rise above the level of the largest seas, and on this lush ground, supported by a granite base, the splendid forest species seemed to be as firmly anchored as those growing deeper in the island.

The colonists found themselves at the mouth of a small insignificant creek, which could barely hold two or three fishing boats and which served as a funnel for the new creek; however, oddly enough, its waters, instead of flowing into the sea through a gently sloping mouth, fell from a height of over forty feet— which explained why, at high tide, it had not felt any effects upstream. Indeed, the tides of the Pacific, even at their highest point, should never reach the level of this river, whose bed formed a higher pool, and millions of years would likely pass before the water had eroded this granite bottom and carved a navigable mouth. Thus, it was agreed upon to name this watercourse "Falls River." Beyond, to the north, the edge formed by the forest stretched for about two miles; then the trees became sparser, and beyond them, very picturesque heights drew an almost straight line running north to south. In contrast, all along the coastline between Falls River and Reptile Point, it was nothing but wooded masses, magnificent trees, some upright, others leaning, whose long undulation of the sea came to bathe their roots. It was towards this side, that is to say, along the entire Serpentine Peninsula, that the exploration should continue, as this part of the coastline offered shelters that the other, arid and wild, would obviously deny to any castaways.

The weather was nice and clear, and from the top of a cliff where Nab and Pencroff set up lunch, the view could extend far.

The horizon was perfectly clear, and there wasn't a sail offshore. As far as the eye could see along the coast, there wasn't a vessel, not even a wreck. But the engineer would not feel well assured in that regard until he had explored the coast to the very end of the Serpentine Peninsula.

Lunch was quickly wrapped up, and at eleven-thirty, Cyrus Smith signaled for departure. Instead of following either the edge of a cliff or a sandy beach, the colonists had to navigate through the cover of trees to stay along the coastline.

The distance from the mouth of Falls River to Reptile Point was about twelve miles. In four hours, on a walkable beach, and without hurrying, the colonists could have covered this distance; but it took them double that time to reach their goal because the trees to navigate around, the underbrush to clear, the vines to break, constantly impeded their progress, and the numerous detours significantly lengthened their route.

Additionally, there was nothing indicating a recent shipwreck along this coastline. It is true, as Gédéon Spilett pointed out, that the sea could have swept everything out to sea, and one shouldn't conclude that just because no traces were found, no ship had been wrecked on this part of Lincoln Island.

The reporter's reasoning was sound, and moreover, the incident involving the bullet proved indisputably that, no more than three months ago, a gunshot had been fired on the island.

It was already five o'clock, and the tip of the Serpentine Peninsula was still two miles from where the colonists were. It was clear that after reaching Reptile Point, Cyrus Smith and his companions would not have time to return before sunset to the camp that had been set up near the sources of the Mercy. Therefore, they needed to spend the night at the promontory itself. But they had plenty of provisions, which was fortunate because large game was no longer appearing along this edge, which was merely a coastline, after all. On the other hand, birds were teeming there: jacamars, couroucous, tragopans, grouse, loris, parrots, cockatoos, pheasants, pigeons, and a hundred other species. Not a single tree was without a nest, not a nest that wasn't filled with flapping wings!

Around seven o'clock in the evening, the colonists, exhausted from fatigue, reached Reptile Point, a strangely shaped outcropping jutting into the sea. Here, the riverside forest of the peninsula ended, and the coastline, in its southern part, regained the usual appearance of a shore, with its rocks, reefs, and beaches. It was therefore possible that a ship might have washed up on this part of the island, but night was falling, and they had to postpone exploration until the next day.

Pencroff and Harbert immediately hurried to find a suitable spot to set up camp. The last trees of the Far West forest came to an end at this point, and among them, the young boy recognized thick clumps of bamboo.

"Good!" he said, "that's a valuable discovery."

"Valuable?" replied Pencroff.

"Of course," Harbert continued. "I'm not going to tell you, Pencroff, that the bark of bamboo, cut into flexible strips, is used to make baskets or containers, that this bark, reduced to pulp and soaked, is used to make Chinese paper, that the stems provide, depending on their thickness, canes, pipe stems, and conduits for water; that the large bamboos make excellent materials for construction, lightweight and strong, which are never attacked by insects. I won't even add that by sawing the joints of bamboos and keeping some of the transverse partition that forms the node for the base, you obtain solid and convenient vessels which are very commonly used by the Chinese! No! That wouldn't satisfy you. But...

"But?..."

"But I will tell you, if you don't know, that in India, people eat these bamboos like asparagus."

"Asparagus of thirty feet!" exclaimed the sailor. "And they're good?"

"Excellent," Harbert replied. "However, it's not the thirty-foot stems you eat, but the young shoots of bamboo."

"Perfect, my boy, perfect!" responded Pencroff.

"I'll also add that the soft inner part of the new stems, preserved in vinegar, makes a highly prized condiment."

"Better and better, Harbert."

"And finally that these bamboos exude a sweet liquid between their knots, which can make a very pleasant drink."

"Is that all?" the sailor asked.

"That's all!"

"And it can't be smoked, by chance?"

"It can't be smoked, my poor Pencroff!"

Harbert and the sailor didn't have to look long for a favorable spot to spend the night. The shoreline rocks—very jagged, as they must be violently battered by the sea due to winds from the southwest—had cavities that would allow them to sleep protected from the elements. However, just as they were about to enter one of these recesses, formidable roars stopped them.

"Back!" shouted Pencroff. "We only have small shot in our rifles, and beasts that roar like that wouldn't care about it a bit!"

And the sailor, grabbing Harbert by the arm, pulled him to safety behind the rocks, just as a magnificent animal appeared at the entrance of the cave.

It was a jaguar, measuring at least as much as its Asian counterparts, meaning it was over five feet from the tip of its head to the base of its tail. Its tawny coat was highlighted by several rows of regularly spaced black spots and contrasted with the white fur of its belly. Harbert recognized this fierce rival of the tiger, far more dangerous than the cougar, which is just a rival of the wolf!

The jaguar approached and looked around, its fur bristled, eyes ablaze, as if it had never sensed a human before. At that moment, the reporter turned around the high rocks, and Harbert, thinking he hadn't seen the jaguar, was about to rush towards it; but Gédéon Spilett waved his hand at him and kept walking. He was no stranger to tigers, and getting within ten steps of the animal, he stood still, rifle at the shoulder, without a muscle twitching.

The jaguar, crouched low, lunged at the hunter, but just as it leaped, a bullet struck it between the eyes, and it fell dead.

Harbert and Pencroff rushed towards the jaguar. Nab and Cyrus Smith came running over, and they stayed for a moment to contemplate the animal, stretched out on the ground, whose magnificent pelt would adorn the great hall of Granite House.

"Ah! Mr. Spilett! How I admire and envy you!" exclaimed Harbert in a rush of well-deserved enthusiasm.

"Easy there, my boy," replied the reporter, "you would have done the same."

"Me! Such composure! ..."

"Imagine, Harbert, a jaguar is a hare, and you'll shoot it most calmly."

"There you have it!" replied Pencroff. "It's not more complex than that!"

"And now," said Gédéon Spilett, "since this jaguar has vacated its lair, I don't see, my friends, why we shouldn't occupy it for the night."

"But others might return!" said Pencroff.

"It will be enough to light a fire at the entrance of the cave," said the reporter, "and they won't dare cross the threshold."— "Back to the jaguar's home, then!" replied the sailor, dragging the animal's corpse behind him.

The colonists headed towards the abandoned lair, and there, while Nab was skinning the jaguar, his companions piled a large amount of dry wood at the cave's entrance, which the forest provided abundantly.

But Cyrus Smith, having spotted a bunch of bamboo, went to cut some, which he mixed with the fuel for the fire.

With that done, they settled into the cave, which was strewn with bones; the guns were loaded just in case of a sudden attack; they had dinner, and then, when it was time to rest, the pile of wood at the cave's entrance was set on fire. Immediately, a real explosion burst into the air! It was the bamboo, caught by the flames, exploding like fireworks!

That noise alone would have been enough to frighten the most daring wild beasts!

And this method of provoking loud explosions was not invented by the engineer, for, according to Marco Polo, the Tartars have been using it successfully for centuries to keep the fierce beasts of Central Asia away from their camps.

Cyrus Smith and his companions slept like innocent marmots in the cave that the jaguar had so politely left at their disposal. At sunrise, they were all on the shore, at the very tip of the promontory, gazing once more at the horizon, which was visible for two-thirds of its circumference. One last time, the engineer was able to confirm that no sails or shipwrecks appeared on the sea, and the telescope did not discover any suspicious point.

Nothing, either, on the coastline, at least in the straight part forming the southern shore of the promontory for three miles, for beyond that, a depression in the land hid the rest of the coast, and even from the end of Serpentine Peninsula, one could not see Cape Griffe, hidden by high rocks.

So, the southern shore of the island remained to be explored. Should they attempt to undertake this exploration immediately and dedicate this day, November 2, to it?

This did not fit into the original plan. Indeed, when the canoe was abandoned at the sources of Mercy River, it had been agreed that after observing the west coast, they would go back to retrieve it and return to Granite House via the Mercy route. Cyrus Smith then believed that the western shore could offer refuge, either for a distressed vessel or for a ship on a regular route; but since this coastline presented no landing, they had to search on the south side of the island for what they couldn't find on the west.

It was Gédéon Spilett who proposed to continue the exploration so that the issue of the presumed shipwreck would be completely resolved, and he asked how far Cape Griffe could be from the tip of the peninsula.

"About thirty miles," replied the engineer, "if we take the curves of the coast into account."

"Thirty miles!" echoed Gédéon Spilett. "That's quite a long day's walk. Still, I think we should return to Granite House by following the southern shore."

"But," Harbert pointed out, "from Cape Griffe to Granite House, you'll need to count on another ten miles at least."

"Let's say forty miles in total," replied the reporter, "and let's not hesitate to cover them. At least, we'll explore this unknown coastline, and we won't have to do this exploration again."

"Very true," said Pencroff then. "But what about the canoe?"

"The canoe has been left alone for a day at the sources of Mercy," replied Gédéon Spilett, "it can very well stay there for two days! So far, we can't really say that the island is infested with thieves!"

"However," said the sailor, "when I think about the tortoise story, I don't have much trust."

"The tortoise! The tortoise!" replied the reporter. "Don't you know it was the sea that turned it over?"

"Who knows?" murmured the engineer.

"But..." said Nab.

Nab had something to say, that was evident, as he opened his mouth to speak but didn't say anything.

"What do you want to say, Nab?" the engineer asked him.

"If we go back along the shore to Cape Griffe," replied Nab, "after rounding that cape, we'll be blocked..."

"By the Mercy! Indeed," Harbert responded, "and we won't have a bridge or boat to cross it!"

"Well, Mr. Cyrus," Pencroff replied, "with a few floating logs, we won't have any trouble getting across that river!"

"Regardless," said Gédéon Spilett, "it will be useful to build a bridge if we want to have easy access to the Far West!"

"A bridge!" exclaimed Pencroff! "Well, isn't Mr. Smith an engineer by trade? He'll build us a bridge when we want one! As for getting you across to the other side of Mercy tonight without getting a thread of your clothes wet, I'm on it. We still have a day's worth of food, that's all we need, and besides, game may not be lacking today as it was yesterday. Let's go!"

The reporter's proposal, strongly supported by the sailor, received general approval, as everyone wanted to put their doubts to rest, and by returning by Cape Griffe, the exploration would be complete. But there was not a moment to lose, for a forty-mile hike was long, and they could not expect to reach Granite House before nightfall.

At six in the morning, the little group set off. In anticipation of possible encounters with two or four-legged animals, the rifles were loaded with bullets, and Top, who was to lead the way, was given orders to patrol the edge of the forest.

From the end of the promontory that formed the tail of the peninsula, the coast curved over a distance of five miles, which was quickly crossed, without the most thorough investigations revealing the slightest trace of a past or recent landing, nor a wreck, nor any remnants of encampment, nor the ashes of a fire, nor a footprint!

The colonists, arriving at the corner where the curvature ended to follow the northeast direction forming Washington Bay, could then take in the entire southern coastline of the island. At twenty-five miles, the coast ended at Cape Griffe, which barely faded into the morning mist, and a mirage effect heightened it, as if it were suspended between land and water. Between the spot occupied by the colonists and the back of the vast bay, the shoreline consisted first of a wide, very flat beach bordered by a line of trees in the background; then afterward, the coastline, becoming quite irregular, jutted sharp points into the sea, and finally, some dark rocks were piled in a picturesque disorder to end at Cape Griffe.

Such was the layout of this part of the island, which the explorers beheld for the first time and which they scanned at a glance after stopping for a moment.

"A ship that ventured here would inevitably be lost," said Pencroff. "Sandbanks extend offshore, and beyond them, reefs! Bad waters!"

"But at least, there would be something left of that ship," the reporter pointed out.

"There would be pieces of wood on the reefs, and nothing on the sands," replied the sailor.

"Why not?"

"Because those sands, more dangerous than the rocks, swallow everything that thrown upon them, and just a few days are enough for the hull of a ship of several hundred tons to completely disappear!"

"So, Pencroff," asked the engineer, "if a vessel was lost on these banks, it would not be surprising that there would be no trace left now?"

"No, Mr. Smith, with the help of time or a storm. However, it would be surprising, even in that case, if pieces of masts or spars had not been washed ashore beyond the reach of the sea."

"Let's continue our search then," replied Cyrus Smith.

At one o'clock in the afternoon, the colonists had arrived at the back of Washington Bay, and at that moment, they had covered a distance of twenty miles.

They stopped to have lunch.

There began an irregular coast, bizarrely jagged and covered by a long line of those reefs that followed the sandbanks and which the tide, calm at this moment, would soon reveal. The soft waves of the sea, breaking on the tips of the rocks, unfurled into long foamy fringes. From this point to Cape Griffe, the beach was narrow and confined between the line of reefs and the line of trees.

The walk was becoming more difficult, as countless fallen rocks cluttered the shore.

The granite wall also tended to rise higher, and from the trees that crowned it in the back, only the green treetops, stirred by no breath of air, were visible.

After half an hour's rest, the colonists resumed their walk, and their eyes missed not a single point along the reefs and the beach. Pencroff and Nab even ventured among the reefs whenever something caught their attention. But there was no wreck, and they were misled by some bizarre rock formations. They did, however, confirm that edible shells abounded on this beach, but it could only be profitably exploited when a communication had been established between the two banks of the Mercy River, and also when the means of transport were improved.

So, nothing related to the presumed shipwreck appeared on this coastline, and yet an object of some importance, the hull of a vessel for example, would have been visible by then, or its debris would have been washed ashore, just like that crate found less than twenty miles away. But there was nothing.

Around three o'clock, Cyrus Smith and his companions arrived at a narrow, well-closed creek, which had no watercourse leading to it. It formed a true little natural harbor, invisible from the sea, which had a narrow pass made between the reefs. At the back of this creek, some violent upheaval had torn the rocky edge, and a gradual slope led to the upper plateau, which could be less than ten miles from Cape Griffe, and thus, four miles in a straight line from the Grande-vue plateau.

Gédéon Spilett suggested that his companions take a break at this spot. They agreed, as the walk had whetted each one's appetite, and although it was not dinner time, no one refused a bite of venison to refresh themselves. This lunch was meant to keep them until supper at Granite House. A few minutes later, the colonists, seated at the foot of a magnificent cluster of maritime pines, devoured the provisions that Nab had taken from his backpack.

The place was elevated about fifty to sixty feet above sea level. The view was thus quite extensive, and soaring over the last rocks of the cape, it reached out to the Bay of Union. But neither the islet nor the Grande-vue plateau were visible and could not be at that moment, as the terrain's relief and the curtain of tall trees abruptly masked the northern horizon.

Needless to say, despite the broad stretch of sea the explorers could survey, and although the engineer's telescope had scanned point by point along the circular outline where sky and water converged, no ship was sighted. Likewise, throughout all this part of the coastline that still remained to be explored, the telescope was moved with the same care from the shore to the reefs, and no wreck appeared in the field of the instrument.

"Well," said Gédéon Spilett, "we must make peace with this and console ourselves by thinking that no one will dispute us the possession of Lincoln Island!"

"But after all, that lead shot! Surely, it's not an illusion!" said Harbert.

"A thousand devils, no!" exclaimed Pencroff, thinking of his missing jawbreaker.

"Then what can we conclude?" asked the reporter.

"This," replied the engineer: "it's that three months ago at most, a ship landed, voluntarily or not..."

"What! You would accept, Cyrus, that it sank without leaving any trace?" cried the reporter.

"No, my dear Spilett, but note that if it is certain that a human being set foot on this island, it seems no less certain that they have now left it."

"So, if I understand you correctly, Mr. Cyrus," said Harbert, "the ship would have set sail again?..."

"Obviously."

"And we would have lost an opportunity to return?" said Nab.

"Without a return, I'm afraid."

"Well! Since the opportunity is lost, let's get moving," said Pencroff, who was already missing Granite House.

But hardly had he stood up when Top's barks rang out loudly, and the dog emerged from the woods, holding a muddy piece of cloth in his mouth.

Nab snatched the piece of fabric from the dog's mouth.

It was a piece of strong canvas.

Top continued to bark, and by his way back and forth, he seemed to invite his master to follow him into the woods.

"There's something here that could very well explain my lead shot!" exclaimed Pencroff.

"A shipwrecked person!" replied Harbert.

"Injured, maybe!" said Nab.

"Or dead!" replied the reporter.

And all rushed to follow the dog's tracks amidst the tall pines that formed the first curtain of the forest. Just in case, Cyrus Smith and his companions had prepared their weapons.

They had to advance quite deeply into the woods; but, to their great disappointment, they still saw no footprint. The underbrush and vines were intact, and they even had to cut through them with an axe, just as they had done in the thickest parts of the forest. It was thus difficult to believe that a human creature had passed through there, and yet Top moved back and forth, not like a dog searching at random, but like a being with a will following an idea.

After seven or eight minutes of walking, Top stopped.

Arriving at a sort of clearing, bordered by tall trees, the colonists looked around and saw nothing, neither under the brush nor between the tree trunks.

"But what's wrong, Top?" said Cyrus Smith.

Top barked louder, jumping at the foot of a gigantic pine.

Suddenly, Pencroff exclaimed:

"Ah! Good! Oh! Perfect!

— What is it? asked Gédéon Spilett.

— We're looking for a wreck at sea or on land!

— Well?

— Well, it's up in the air!"

And the sailor pointed to a sort of large whitish rag caught in the top of the pine, of which Top had brought back a fallen piece.

"But that's not a wreck!" cried Gédéon Spilett.

"Beg your pardon!" replied Pencroff.

"What? Is it?...

— It's all that's left of our airship, our balloon that got stranded up there, at the top of that tree!"Pencroff was not mistaken, and he let out a magnificent cheer, adding:

"Now that's some good fabric! This will give us enough linen for years! We can make handkerchiefs and shirts! What do you say, Mr. Spilett, about an island where shirts grow on trees?"

It was truly a fortunate circumstance for the settlers of Lincoln Island that the balloon, after making its last leap into the air, had fallen back onto the island, giving them the chance to recover it.

They could either keep the envelope as it was if they wanted to make another escape by air, or they could use this beautiful quality cotton fabric, once it was freed from its varnish, for many purposes. As you can imagine, Pencroff's joy was shared unanimously and enthusiastically.

But they needed to remove the envelope from the tree it was hanging on to store it safely, and that was no small task. Nab, Harbert, and the sailor climbed to the top of the tree and had to show incredible skill to detach the massive deflated balloon.

The operation took nearly two hours, and not only the envelope with its valve, springs, copper fittings, but also the net, which included a substantial amount of ropes and cords, the retaining ring, and the balloon's anchor were now on the ground. The envelope, except for one tear, was in good condition, with the only damage being to its lower appendage.

It was a windfall that had fallen from the sky.

"All the same, Mr. Cyrus," said the sailor, "if we ever decide to leave the island, it won't be by balloon, right? Air ships don't go where you want them to, and we know that! If you take my advice, we'll build a good boat of about twenty tons, and you'll let me cut out a mainsail and a jib from this fabric. The rest will help us get dressed!"

"We'll see, Pencroff," replied Cyrus Smith, "we'll see."

"In the meantime, we need to put all of this away safely," said Nab. Indeed, it was unthinkable to transport this load of fabric and ropes to Granite House due to its considerable weight, and while waiting for a suitable vehicle, it was important not to leave these treasures at the mercy of the next storm. The settlers, gathering their efforts, managed to haul everything to the shore, where they discovered a fairly large rock cavity that neither the wind, nor the rain, nor the sea could reach, thanks to its orientation.

"We needed a cupboard, and we have one," said Pencroff; "but since it doesn't have a lock, it would be wise to hide the opening. I'm not saying this for the two-legged thieves, but for the four-legged ones!"

By six in the evening, everything was stored away, and after naming the small inlet "Balloon Port," they headed back towards Cape Griffe. Pencroff and the engineer talked about various plans that needed to be executed as soon as possible. First, they had to build a bridge over the Mercy to establish a quick route to the south of the island; then, the cart would return to pick up the balloon since the canoe wouldn't be able to carry it; then, they would build a decked boat; then, Pencroff would rig it as a ketch, and they could set off on travel... around the island; then, etc.

Meanwhile, night fell, and the sky was already dark when the settlers reached the point of the wreck, exactly where they had discovered the valuable crate. However, just like at other locations, there was no sign indicating that a ship-wreck had ever occurred, and they had to return to the conclusions previously drawn by Cyrus Smith. From the wreck to Granite House, there were still four miles to cover, and they crossed them quickly; however, it was after midnight when, having followed the shoreline to the mouth of the Mercy, they arrived at the first bend formed by the river.

There, the riverbed measured about eighty feet wide, which was difficult to cross, but Pencroff took it upon himself to overcome this challenge, and he was prompted to do so.

They had to admit that the settlers were exhausted.

The journey had been long, and the balloon incident hadn't allowed their legs and arms to rest. They were eager to get back to Granite House for supper and sleep; if the bridge had been built, they would have been home in a quarter of an hour.

The night was very dark. Pencroff then prepared to keep his promise by making a sort of raft to assist with crossing the Mercy. Nab and he, armed with axes, chose two neighboring trees by the riverbank, which they planned to turn into a kind of raft, and they started chopping them down at the base.

Cyrus Smith and Gideon Spilett, sitting on the bank, waited for the moment to help their companions, while Harbert came and went, not straying too far.

Suddenly, the young boy, who had gone upstream, rushed back and shouted, pointing to the Mercy:

"What's that drifting up there?"

Pencroff stopped his work, and he saw a moving object appearing vaguely in the darkness.

"A canoe!" he said.

Everyone rushed over and, to their great surprise, saw a boat following the current.

"Oh! a canoe!" shouted the sailor from a remaining professional habit, not thinking it might have been better to remain silent.

No response. The boat continued to drift, and it was only a few steps away when the sailor exclaimed:

"But it's our canoe! It broke free from its mooring and is following the current! I must admit it's just in time!"

"Our canoe?..." murmured the engineer.

Pencroff was right. It was indeed the canoe, whose mooring had likely broken, and which was now returning by itself from the sources of the Mercy! It was crucial to grab it before it was swept away by the strong river current, beyond its mouth, which is exactly what Nab and Pencroff did skillfully with a long pole.

The canoe reached the shore. The engineer was the first to board, secured the mooring, and confirmed by touch that the mooring had indeed worn down from rubbing against the rocks.

"There you go," he said quietly to the reporter, "this is what you could call a coincidence..."

"Strange!" replied Cyrus Smith.

Strange or not, it was a fortunate turn of events! Harbert, the reporter, Nab, and Pencroff boarded in turn. They had no doubt that the mooring had worn thin; but the most astonishing thing was that the canoe had arrived just when the settlers were there to catch it, because fifteen minutes later, it would have been lost at sea.

Had they been in the age of genies, this incident might have led one to think that the island was haunted by a supernatural being who was using its power to assist castaways! With a few strokes of the oars, the settlers arrived at the mouth of the Mercy. The canoe was dragged onto the shore near the Chimneys, and everyone headed towards the ladder of Granite House.

But at that moment, Top barked angrily, and Nab, who was looking for the first rung, let out a cry... the ladder was gone.

$$\text{❧} \quad 6 \quad \text{❧}$$

Cyrus Smith stopped, speechless. His companions searched in the darkness, both on the wall in case the wind had moved the ladder, and near the ground in case it had come loose... but the ladder had completely vanished. As for determining whether a gust had pulled it up to the first landing, halfway up the wall, it was impossible in that deep night.

"If this is a joke," shouted Pencroff, "it's a bad one! Arriving home and not finding a ladder to get to your room isn't something to amuse tired people!"

Nab was also lost in exclamations!

"But it hasn't been windy!" Harbert noted.

"I'm starting to think strange things are happening on Lincoln Island!" Pencroff said.

"Strange?" replied Gideon Spilett, "No, Pencroff, nothing could be more natural. Someone came during our absence, took possession of the house, and removed the ladder!"

"Someone!" shouted the sailor. "And who would that be?..."

"Well, the hunter with the lead pellet," replied the reporter. "What else could explain our misadventure?"

"Well, if there's someone up there," Pencroff responded, swearing as impatience began to get to him, "I'll call him out, and he'll have to answer."

And with a thunderous voice, the sailor let out a prolonged "ho!" that echoed back loudly.

The settlers listened closely and thought they heard some sort of chuckle coming from the height of Granite House, though they could not identify its source.

But no voice replied to Pencroff's call, which he repeated in vain.

There was definitely enough there to astonish even the most indifferent people, and the settlers could not afford to be indifferent. Given their situation, every incident carried weight, and certainly, in the seven months they had lived on the island, none had been of such a surprising nature.

In any case, forgetting their fatigue and overwhelmed by the peculiarity of the event, they stood at the foot of Granite House, not knowing what to think, not knowing what to do, questioning themselves without being able to answer, multiplying hypotheses that were all more far-fetched than the last. Nab lamented, very disappointed that he could not get back into his kitchen, especially since their travel provisions were exhausted and he had no means to replenish them at the moment.

"My friends," said Cyrus Smith, "we have only one thing to do, wait for dawn, and then act according to the circumstances. But to wait, let's go to the Chimneys. There, we will be sheltered, and while we may not be able to have supper, at least we can sleep."

"But what kind of audacity has played this trick on us?" asked Pencroff once again, unable to accept the situation.

Whatever the audacity, the only thing to do was, as the engineer said, to head back to the Chimneys and wait for dawn. However, orders were given for Top to remain under the windows of Granite House, and when Top receives an order, he follows it without question. The brave dog stayed at the foot of the wall while his master and companions took refuge in the rocks. To say that the settlers slept well on the sand of the Chimneys, despite their exhaustion, would be untrue. Not only were they anxious to understand the importance of this new incident—whether it resulted from a chance occurrence whose natural causes would appear in the morning, or whether it was the work of a human being—but they were also quite uncomfortable. In any case, one way or another, their home was occupied at that moment, and they could not re-enter it.

Granite House was more than just their home; it was their storehouse. All the equipment of the colony was there: weapons, tools, instruments, ammunition, food reserves, etc. If all of this were to be plundered, the settlers would have to start over with their setup, remaking weapons and tools. A serious issue! Therefore, yielding to anxiety, one or the other would occasionally go out to see if Top was keeping a good watch. Only Cyrus Smith remained with his usual patience, although his persistent reason was aggravated by facing an absolutely inexplicable fact, and he felt indignation thinking that around him, perhaps above him, some influence was at work that he couldn't name. Gideon Spilett completely shared his opinion on this matter, and the two of them discussed several times—though in hushed tones —the inexplicable circumstances that were baffling their insight and experience. There was undoubtedly a mystery on this island, and how could they penetrate it? Meanwhile, Harbert could only imagine and wished to question Cyrus Smith.

As for Nab, he ended up telling himself that all of this did not concern him, that it was for his master to worry about, and if he hadn't feared to displease his companions, the brave Black man would have slept that night just as soundly as if he were resting on his cot in Granite House! Finally, more than anyone, Pencroff was fuming, and he was genuinely very angry.

"This is a joke," he said, "this is a prank someone played on us! Well, I don't like jokes, and whoever the joker is, they'd better not cross my path!"

As soon as the first light of dawn rose in the east, the settlers, properly armed, made their way to the shore, at the edge of the reefs.

Granite House, struck directly by the rising sun, would soon be illuminated by the dawn's light, and indeed, before five o'clock, the windows, whose shutters were closed, appeared through their leafy curtains. From that side, everything was in order, but a cry escaped the settlers when they saw the door wide open, which they had, however, closed before their departure. Someone had entered Granite House. There was no doubt about that.

The upper ladder, usually stretched from the landing to the door, was in place; but the lower ladder had been removed and raised to the threshold. It was evident that the intruders had wanted to protect themselves from any surprises.

As for recognizing their type and number, that wasn't possible yet since none of them showed themselves.

Pencroff called out again.

No response.

"The scoundrels!" shouted the sailor. "They must be sleeping peacefully, as if they were at home! Oh! Pirates, bandits, privateers, sons of John Bull!"

When Pencroff, as an American, had referred to someone as a "son of John Bull," he had reached the highest limits of insult.

At that moment, daylight fully broke, and the facade of Granite House lit up under the sun's rays. But inside, as well as outside, everything was silent and calm.

The settlers were left wondering whether Granite House was occupied or not, and yet the position of the ladder suggested it was, and it was even certain that the occupants, whoever they were, could not have fled! But how to reach them?

Harbert then had the idea of tying a rope to an arrow and launching it so that it would pass between the first rungs of the ladder, which hung at the threshold of the door. They could then use the rope to lower the ladder to the ground and re-establish communication between the ground and Granite House.

There was evidently no other option, and with a little skill, this method should succeed. Fortunately, bows and arrows had been left in a corridor of the Chimneys, where there were also several tens of feet of a light hibiscus rope. Pencroff unrolled this rope, fixing one end to a well-fletched arrow. Then, Harbert, after placing the arrow on his bow, carefully aimed at the dangling end of the ladder.

Cyrus Smith, Gédéon Spilett, Pencroff, and Nab had stepped back to observe what would happen at the windows of Granite-House. The reporter, rifle on his shoulder, prepared to aim at the door.

The bowstring snapped, the arrow whistled, pulling the rope, and passed between the last two rungs of the ladder.

The operation succeeded. Immediately, Harbert grabbed the end of the rope; but just as he gave a tug to bring down the ladder, a hand shot quickly between the wall and the door, seized it, and pulled it back inside Granite-House.

"Curse you!" cried the sailor. "If a bullet can make you happy, you won't have to wait long!"

"But who is it?" asked Nab.

"Who? Didn't you recognize?..."

"No."

"But it's a monkey, a macaque, a sapajou, a guenon, an orangutan, a baboon, a gorilla, a sagouin! Our home has been invaded by monkeys who climbed in the ladder during our absence!"

And, at that moment, as if to confirm the sailor's words, three or four primates appeared at the windows, having pushed aside the shutters, greeting the real owners of the place with a thousand contortions and grimaces.

"I knew it was just a prank!" shouted Pencroff, "but one of these pranksters will pay for the others!"

The sailor, aiming his rifle, quickly shot one of the monkeys. They all disappeared except one, which, mortally wounded, tumbled onto the shore.

This monkey, tall and of the first order of primates, was unmistakably so. Whether it was a chimpanzee, an orangutan, a gorilla, or a gibbon, it ranked among these anthropoids, so named due to their resemblance to humans. Moreover, Harbert declared it was an orangutan, and it is known that the young boy was knowledgeable in zoology.

"What a magnificent beast!" exclaimed Nab.

"Magnificent, if you want!" replied Pencroff, "but I still don't see how we can get back home!"

"Harbert is a good shot," said the reporter, "and his bow is there! Let him try again..."

"Good! These monkeys are clever!" shouted Pencroff, "and they won't return to the windows, and we can't kill them, and when I think of the damage they can do in the rooms, in the store..."

"Patience," replied Cyrus Smith. "These animals cannot hold us off for long!"

"I won't be sure until they're down," replied the sailor. "And first of all, do you know, Mr. Smith, how many dozens of those pranksters are up there?"

It would have been difficult to answer Pencroff, and as for letting the young boy try again, that was not easy, because the lower end of the ladder had been pulled back inside the door, and when they tried to pull on the rope again, it broke, and the ladder did not fall.

The situation was indeed awkward. Pencroff was fuming. The situation had a certain comical aspect, which he did not find funny at all, on his part.

It was clear that the colonists would eventually reclaim their home and drive out the intruders, but when and how? That was something they could not determine. Two hours passed during which the monkeys avoided showing themselves; but they were still there, and three or four times, a snout or a paw slipped through the door or the windows, receiving rifle shots in return.

"Let's hide," said the engineer. "Maybe the monkeys will think we've left and will show themselves again. But let Spilett and Harbert position themselves behind the rocks, and fire at anything that appears."

The engineer's orders were followed, and while the reporter and the young boy, the two best shots in the colony, took up positions within range but out of sight of the monkeys, Nab, Pencroff, and Cyrus Smith climbed the plateau and headed to the forest to hunt some game, as it was lunch time, and there was nothing left in terms of food. After half an hour, the hunters returned with a few rock pigeons, which they managed to roast. Not a single monkey had reappeared.

Gédéon Spilett and Harbert went to have their share of lunch while Top kept watch under the windows. Then, after eating, they returned to their position. Two hours later, the situation had not changed at all. The primates did not show any signs of existence, leading them to believe they had vanished; but what seemed most likely was that, frightened by one of their own being killed, terrified by the gunshots, they were hiding in the depths of Granite-House's rooms, or even in the store. And when they thought of the riches contained in that store, the patience so often recommended by the engineer eventually turned into violent irritation, and frankly, there was reason for that.

"Really, it's too ridiculous," finally said the reporter, "and there's really no reason for this to go on!"

"We have to drive those scoundrels out!" cried Pencroff. "We could manage it even if there were twenty of them, but for that, we need to fight them up close! Is there really no way to get to them?"

"Yes," replied the engineer, as an idea crossed his mind.

"One?" said Pencroff. "Well, it's the only good one since there are no others! And what is it?"

"Let's try to go back to Granite-House through the old lake outlet," replied the engineer.

"Oh! A thousand devils!" cried the sailor. "And I didn't think of that!"

That was indeed the only way to enter Granite-House to confront the gang and drive them out. The outlet was, indeed, blocked by a wall of cemented stones that would need to be sacrificed, but it could be rebuilt later. Fortunately, Cyrus Smith had not yet carried out his plan to conceal this opening by flooding it under the lake's waters, as that would have taken some time.

It was already past noon when the colonists, well-armed and equipped with picks and shovels, left the Chimneys, passed under the windows of Granite-House after instructing Top to stay on his post, and prepared to ascend the left bank of the Mercy to reach the Grande-vue plateau.

But they hadn't taken fifty steps in that direction when they heard the furious barking of the dog. It was like a desperate call.

They stopped.

"Let's run!" said Pencroff.

And all of them raced down the bank.

Once they reached the turn, they saw that the situation had changed. The monkeys, suddenly seized by an inexplicable fear, were trying to flee. Two or three were running and jumping from one window to another with a clownish agility. They didn't even try to bring the ladder back, which would have made it easy for them to descend, and in their panic, perhaps they had forgotten that escape route. Soon, five or six were in position to be shot, and the colonists, aiming with ease, fired. Some, wounded or killed, fell back inside the rooms, letting out sharp cries. Others, thrown outside, broke their fall, and moments later, it could be assumed that there was not a single living primate left in Granite-House.

"Hurrah!" shouted Pencroff, "Hurrah! Hurrah!"

"Not so many hurrahs!" said Gédéon Spilett.

"Why? They're all dead," replied the sailor.

"Agreed, but that doesn't give us a way to get back home."

"Let's go to the outlet!" replied Pencroff.

"Of course," said the engineer. "However, it would have been better…"

At that moment, as if in answer to Cyrus Smith's remark, the ladder was seen sliding across the threshold of the door, then unfolding and falling down to the ground.

"Ah! A thousand pipes! How is that possible?" exclaimed the sailor, looking at Cyrus Smith.

"Too much so!" murmured the engineer, who rushed first onto the ladder.

"Be careful, Mr. Cyrus!" cried Pencroff, "if there are still some of those monkeys…"

"We'll see," replied the engineer without stopping.

All his companions followed him, and in a minute, they reached the doorstep.

They looked around. No one in the rooms, nor in the store which had been left untouched by the monkey gang.

"Hey, what about the ladder?" cried the sailor. "Who's the gentleman who returned it to us?"

But at that moment, a cry was heard, and a large monkey, which had taken refuge in the corridor, rushed into the room, pursued by Nab.

"Ah! The bandit!" yelled Pencroff.

With an axe in hand, he was about to split the animal's head when Cyrus Smith stopped him and said:

"Spare it, Pencroff."

"Should I spare this brute?"

"Yes! It's the one who threw the ladder to us!"

And the engineer said this in such a peculiar voice that it was hard to tell if he was serious or not.

Nevertheless, they rushed at the monkey, which, after bravely defending itself, was subdued and tied up.

"Phew!" exclaimed Pencroff. "And what will we do with it now?"

"A servant!" replied Harbert.

And in saying this, the young boy was not entirely joking, as he knew the potential of this intelligent race of primates.

The colonists then approached the monkey and examined it closely. It indeed belonged to the species of anthropoids whose facial angle is not significantly less than that of Australians and Hottentots. It was an orangutan, which, as such, had neither the ferocity of a baboon, nor the thoughtlessness of a macaque, nor the uncleanliness of a sagouin, nor the nervousness of a macaque, nor the bad instincts of a cynocephalus. It is from this anthropoid family that many traits indicate in these animals a nearly human intelligence. Used in homes, they can serve at the table, clean rooms, take care of clothes, polish shoes, adeptly handle knives, spoons, and forks, and even drink wine... just as well as the best two-legged featherless servant. It is known that Buffon had one of these monkeys, which served him for a long time as a faithful and zealous servant.

The one who was currently tied up in the Granite-House room was a tall fellow, six feet high, with a perfectly proportioned body, a broad chest, a medium-sized head, a facial angle reaching sixty-five degrees, a rounded skull, a prominent nose, and skin covered with a smooth, soft, and shiny fur—finally, a perfect example of anthropoids. His eyes, slightly smaller than human eyes, shone with intelligent liveliness; his white teeth gleamed under his mustache, and he sported a small, curly beard of hazel color.

"A handsome guy!" said Pencroff. "If only we knew his language, we could talk to him!"

"So, is this serious, my master?" asked Nab. "Are we going to take him as a servant?"

"Yes, Nab," replied the engineer with a smile. "But don't be jealous!"

"And I hope he will make an excellent servant," added Harbert. "He seems young, his education will be easy, and we won't have to use force to make him submit, nor pull out his canines, as is usually done in such circumstances! He can only become attached to masters who will be kind to him."

"And we will be," said Pencroff, who had forgotten all his grudge against "the pranksters."

Then, approaching the orangutan:

"Well, my boy," he asked, "how's it going?"

The orangutan replied with a little grunt that didn't show much annoyance.

"So, you want to be part of the colony?" asked the sailor. "Are you going to come serve Mr. Cyrus Smith?"

New approving grunt from the monkey.

"And we'll make do with our food for payment?"

Third affirmative grunt.

"His conversation is a bit monotonous," observed Gédéon Spilett.

"Good!" replied Pencroff, "the best servants are the ones that talk the least. And besides, no wages! — you hear me, my boy? To start, we won't give you any wages, but we'll double them later if we're happy with you!"

That's how the colony gained a new member, who would be of great service to them.

As for the name they would call him, the sailor suggested that, in memory of another monkey he had known, he should be called Jupiter, or Jup for short.

And that's how, without further fuss, Master Jup was settled into Granite-House.

7

The colonists of Lincoln Island had thus reclaimed their home, without having to follow the old outlet, which spared them masonry work. It was truly fortunate that just as they were about to do so, the band of monkeys had been gripped by a sudden and inexplicable fear that drove them from Granite-House. Did these animals somehow sense that a serious assault was about to be made against them through another route? That's about the only way to interpret their retreat.

During the last hours of that day, the bodies of the monkeys were transported to the woods, where they were buried; then the colonists set about restoring the disorder caused by the intruders — disorder and not damage, as while they had overturned the furniture in the rooms, they had broken nothing.

Nab rekindled his stoves, and the supplies from the pantry provided a substantial meal that everyone enjoyed. Jup was not forgotten, and he eagerly ate pine nuts and rhizome roots of which he was abundantly supplied. Pencroff had untied his arms, but he deemed it wise to keep the restraints on his legs until he could count on his compliance.

Then, before going to bed, Cyrus Smith and his companions, seated around the table, discussed some urgent projects that needed to be executed.

The most important and pressing were the establishment of a bridge over the Mercy, to connect the southern part of the island with Granite-House, and the foundation of a corral, intended for housing sheep or other wool-bearing animals that they needed to capture.

As can be seen, these two projects aimed to solve the issue of clothing, which was then the most serious. Indeed, the bridge would facilitate the transport of the balloon envelope, which would supply the linen, and the corral was to provide the wool harvest, which would yield the winter clothing.As for this corral, Cyrus Smith's intention was to establish it at the very sources of the Creek-Rouge, where the grazing animals would find fresh and abundant pastures. The path between the Grande-vue plateau and the springs was already partially cleared, and with a better-equipped cart than the first one, transport would be easier, especially if they succeeded in capturing a draft animal.

But while there was no issue with the corral being far from Granite-House, the same could not be said for the chicken coop, which Nab drew the colonists' attention to. The birds indeed needed to be within reach of the cook, and no spot seemed more suitable for the chicken coop than the portion of the lake's shore near the old drain. The waterfowl would thrive there just as well as the others, and the pair of tinamous caught during the last excursion would serve for a first attempt at domestication.

The next day, November 3, the new work began with the construction of the bridge, and everyone was needed for this important task.

Saws, axes, chisels, and hammers were loaded onto the backs of the colonists, who, turned into carpenters, made their way down to the shore.

There, Pencroff made a remark:

"What if, while we're away, Mr. Jup decides to take back that ladder he so gallantly sent us back yesterday?"

"Let's secure it by its lower end," replied Cyrus Smith.

This was done using two stakes, firmly driven into the sand. Then, the colonists, moving up the left bank of the Mercy, soon reached the bend created by the river.

There, they stopped to examine whether the bridge should be built at this spot. The location seemed suitable. Indeed, from this point to Port Ballon, which they discovered the day before on the southern coast, it was only a distance of three and a half miles, and from the bridge to the port, it would be easy to clear a usable road, facilitating communication between Granite-House and the southern part of the island.

Cyrus Smith then shared with his companions a project that was both very simple to execute and very advantageous, which he had been considering for some time.

It was to completely isolate the Grande-vue plateau to protect it from any attacks by quadrupeds or quadrumana. This way, Granite-House, the Chimneys, the chicken coop, and the entire upper part of the plateau designated for sowing, would be shielded from the depredations of animals.

Nothing could be easier to execute than this plan, and here's how the engineer planned to carry it out.

The plateau was already defended on three sides by waterways, either artificial or natural: to the northwest, by the bank of Lake Grant, from the angle supported at the mouth of the old drain to the cut made at the east bank of the lake for water drainage; to the north, from this cut to the sea, by the new waterway that had dug its bed on the plateau and on the shore, upstream and downstream of the waterfall, and it sufficed to dig the bed of this creek to make passage impossible for animals; along the entire eastern edge, by the sea itself, from the mouth of the aforementioned creek to the mouth of the Mercy; finally, to the south, from this mouth to the bend of the Mercy where the bridge was to be established.

This left the western part of the plateau, located between the bend of the river and the southern tip of the lake, less than a mile away, open to all comers. But nothing was easier than digging a wide and deep ditch that would be filled by the waters of the lake, and which, when overflowing, would flow through a second fall into the bed of the Mercy. The level of the lake would undoubtedly lower slightly due to this new drainage of its waters, but Cyrus Smith had noticed that the flow of the Creek-Rouge was significant enough to allow for the execution of his plan.

"So, added the engineer, the Grande-vue plateau will truly be an island, surrounded by water on all sides, and it will communicate with the rest of our domain only through the bridge we are going to build over the Mercy, the two culverts already established upstream and downstream of the fall, and finally two other culverts to be built, one over the ditch I propose to dig, and the other on the left bank of the Mercy. Now, if these bridge and culverts can be raised at will, the Grande-vue plateau will be protected from any surprise."

Cyrus Smith, to make himself better understood by his companions, had drawn a map of the plateau, and his project was immediately grasped in its entirety. Thus, a unanimous opinion approved it, and Pencroff, brandishing his carpenter's axe, shouted:

"To the bridge, first!"

It was the most urgent work. Trees were chosen, felled, stripped of branches, and cut into beams, planks, and boards. This bridge, fixed at the point resting on the right bank of the Mercy, was to be movable in the part that would connect to the left bank, allowing it to be raised using counterweights, like certain lock bridges.

Understandably, this was considerable work, and while it was skillfully executed, it still took some time, as the Mercy was about eighty feet wide. It was therefore necessary to drive stakes into the riverbed to support the fixed deck of the bridge and set up a bell to act on the heads of the stakes, which would thus form two arches and allow the bridge to support heavy loads.

Fortunately, there were no shortages of tools for working the wood, fittings to reinforce it, the ingenuity of a man who was wonderfully skilled at these tasks, and finally the zeal of his companions, who had necessarily gained considerable skill during the past seven months.

And it must be said that Gédéon Spilett was not the most clumsy and vied in skill with the sailor himself, "who would never have expected so much from a mere journalist!"

The construction of the Mercy bridge lasted three weeks, which were very productively occupied. They had lunch right at the worksite, and with the weather being magnificent at the time, they only returned to Granite-House for supper.

During this time, it was noticeable that Mr. Jup was adapting easily and becoming familiar with his new masters, whom he still looked at with great curiosity. However, as a precaution, Pencroff did not yet give him full freedom of movement, wisely wanting to wait until the plateau's boundaries had been made impassable due to the planned works. Top and Jup got on very well and played happily together, but Jup remained serious.

On November 20, the bridge was completed. Its movable part, balanced by counterweights, pivoted easily, needing only a light effort to lift; there was a gap of twenty feet between its hinge and the last beam it rested on when it was closed, which was sufficiently wide for animals not to cross it.

Then, the discussion arose about going to retrieve the envelope of the aerostat, which the colonists were eager to secure; but to transport it, they needed to drive a cart to Port Ballon, and therefore had to clear a path through the thick masses of the Far-West. This took some time. So Nab and Pencroff first scouted their way to the port, and as they found that the "stock of fabric" had suffered no damage in the cave where it had been stored, it was decided that the works relating to the Grande-vue plateau would continue without interruption.

"This," Pencroff pointed out, "will allow us to set up our chicken coop under better conditions, since we won't have to fear visits from foxes or attacks from other harmful beasts."

"Not to mention," added Nab, "that we can clear the plateau and transplant wild plants there..."

"And prepare for our second wheat field!" shouted the sailor with a triumphant expression.

The fact is that the first wheat field, sown with only one grain, had thrived wonderfully, thanks to Pencroff's care. It had produced the ten ears promised by the engineer, and with each ear bearing eighty grains, the colony ended up with eight hundred grains—in just six months—promising a double harvest each year.

These eight hundred grains, minus about fifty which were reserved for safety, were to be sown in a new field, with just as much care as the single grain.

The field was prepared and then surrounded by a strong, high, pointed palisade, which quadrupeds would have a hard time crossing. As for the birds, loud turnstiles and frightening scarecrows, courtesy of Pencroff's imaginative design, sufficed to keep them at bay. The seven hundred fifty grains were then sown in well-ordered little furrows, and nature would take care of the rest.

On November 21, Cyrus Smith began to sketch the ditch that would close off the plateau to the west, from the southern tip of Lake Grant to the bend of the Mercy. There was two to three feet of topsoil, and beneath it, granite. Therefore, they needed to produce nitro-glycerin again, and the nitro-glycerin did its usual job. In less than fifteen days, a ditch twelve feet wide and six feet deep was dug into the hard ground of the plateau. A new cut was similarly made at the rocky edge of the lake, and the waters rushed into this new bed, forming a small watercourse named "Creek-Glycérine," which became a tributary of the Mercy. As the engineer had predicted, the level of the lake dropped, but in an almost imperceptible manner. Finally, to complete the enclosure, the bed of the creek on the shore was significantly widened, and the sands were held in place with a double palisade.

By the first half of December, these works were definitively completed, and the Grande-vue plateau, which was an irregular pentagon with a perimeter of about four miles, surrounded by a liquid belt, was absolutely safe from any aggression.

During this December, the heat was very intense. However, the colonists did not want to suspend the execution of their projects, and since it became urgent to organize the chicken coop, they proceeded with its organization.

Needless to say, since the complete closure of the plateau, Mr. Jup had been set free. He no longer left his masters and showed no desire to escape. He was a gentle animal, although very strong, and surprisingly agile. Ah! When it came to climbing the ladder of Granite-House, no one could rival him. He was already being employed for some tasks: he was hauling loads of wood and carrying stones that had been extracted from the bed of the Creek-Glycérine.

"He's not yet a mason, but he's already a monkey!" joked Harbert, referring to the nickname "monkey" that masons give their apprentices. And if ever a name was justified, it was certainly that one!

The chicken coop occupied an area of two hundred square yards, chosen on the southeast shore of the lake.

It was surrounded by a palisade, and various shelters were built for the animals that would inhabit it. These were small huts made of branches, divided into compartments, which soon awaited their guests.

The first inhabitants were the pair of tinamous, who quickly produced many chicks. They were accompanied by half a dozen ducks, familiar to the lake's banks. Some belonged to the Chinese breed, whose wings fan out, and which, with the brightness and vividness of their plumage, rival golden pheasants. A few days later, Harbert caught a pair of round-tailed, long-feathered fowl, magnificent "alectors," that quickly became tame. As for the pelicans, king-fishers, and moorhens, they came on their own to the shore of the chicken coop, and this little community, after a few squabbles, cooing, chirping, and clucking, ended up getting along and increased in a reassuring proportion for the future nourishment of the colony.

Cyrus Smith, also wanting to complete his work, set up a pigeon loft in a corner of the chicken coop.

He housed a dozen of the pigeons that frequented the high rocks of the plateau. These birds quickly got accustomed to return every evening to their new home and showed more inclination to domestication than the wild rock pigeons, which, by the way, only reproduce in the wild. Finally, the time had come to utilize the envelope of the aerostat for making linen, for keeping it in that form and risking a hot air balloon to leave the island above a virtually limitless sea would only be acceptable for those lacking everything, and Cyrus Smith, a practical mind, could not entertain such thoughts.

So, it was about bringing the envelope back to Granite-House, and the colonists worked to make their heavy cart more manageable and lighter. But while the vehicle was available, the power source still needed to be found! Was there really no draft animal of an indigenous species in the island that could replace a horse, donkey, ox, or cow? That was the question.

"Indeed," said Pencroff, "a draft animal would be very useful while Mr. Cyrus is willing to build a steam cart, or even a locomotive, for certainly, one day we will have a railway from Granite-House to Port Ballon, with a branch to Mount Franklin!"

And the honest sailor, speaking this way, believed what he said! Oh! Imagination, when faith is involved!

But to not exaggerate, a simple draft quadruped would have easily sufficed for Pencroff, and as Providence had a soft spot for him, she did not keep him waiting long. One day, December 23, both Nab cried out and Top barked enthusiastically. The colonists, busy at the Chimneys, rushed over, fearing some unfortunate incident. What did they see? Two beautiful large animals that had ventured unwisely onto the plateau, where the culverts had not been closed. They looked like two horses, or at least two donkeys, a male and a female, with slender shapes, tawny coats, white legs and tail, striped with black lines on their head, neck, and body. They advanced calmly, showing no signs of alarm, and looked at these men with bright eyes, not yet able to recognize them as masters.

"They're onaggas!" exclaimed Harbert, quadrupeds that lie between the zebra and the quagga!

"Why not donkeys?" asked Nab.

"Because they don't have long ears and their forms are more graceful!"

"Donkeys or horses," retorted Pencroff, "they're 'motors,' as Mr. Smith would say, and as such, good to capture!"

Without scaring the two animals, the sailor slipped through the grass to the culvert of the Creek-Glycérine, tipped it, and captured the onaggas.

Now, would they seize them through violence and subject them to forced domestication? No. It was decided that for a few days, they would be allowed to roam freely on the plateau, where grass was abundant, and immediately the engineer had a stable built near the henhouse, where the onaggas could find refuge at night with good bedding.

Thus, this magnificent pair was completely free to move around, and the colonists even avoided scaring them by getting too close. However, several times the onaggas seemed to feel the need to leave this plateau, too restricted for them, as they were used to wide open spaces and deep forests. You could see them following the water's edge, which posed an insurmountable barrier, letting out sharp brays, then galloping through the grass, and when calm returned, they would spend entire hours gazing at those great woods that were forever closed to them!

Meanwhile, harnesses and traces made of vegetable fibers had been created, and a few days after capturing the onaggas, not only was the cart ready to be hitched, but also a straight path, or rather a cut, had been made through the Far-West forest, from the bend of the Mercy to Ballon port. So they could pull the cart there, and it was towards the end of December that the onaggas were tested for the first time.

Pencroff had already managed to coax these animals enough for them to eat from his hand, and they allowed him to approach without difficulty, but once hitched, they reared up, and it took great effort to contain them. However, they would soon have to submit to this new service, as the onagga, less rebellious than the zebra, is frequently harnessed in the mountainous regions of southern Africa, and it has even been acclimatized in Europe under relatively cold zones.

That day, the whole colony, except for Pencroff, who walked ahead with his animals, climbed into the cart and set off for Ballon port. If they were jolted along this barely made road, that goes without saying; but the vehicle arrived without any problems, and on the same day, they were able to load the envelope and various gear of the aerostat.

At eight in the evening, after crossing the bridge over the Mercy, the cart went down the left bank of the river and stopped on the shore. The onaggas were unharnessed and then taken back to their stable, and Pencroff, before going to sleep, let out a sigh of satisfaction that echoed loudly in Granite-House.

8

The first week of January was dedicated to making laundry for the colony. The needles found in the box worked between strong, if not delicate, fingers, and one can say that whatever was sewn was done solidly.

There was no shortage of thread, thanks to Cyrus Smith's idea to reuse the thread that had already been used for sewing the bands of the aerostat. These long bands were patiently unraveled by Gédéon Spilett and Harbert, as Pencroff had to give up this task, which annoyed him greatly; but when it came to sewing, he had no equal. After all, it is well known that sailors have a remarkable aptitude for sewing.

The fabrics that made up the aerostat's envelope were later degreased using soda and potash obtained by burning plants, so that the cotton, stripped of its varnish, regained its natural suppleness and elasticity; then, when exposed to the decolorizing effect of the atmosphere, it achieved perfect whiteness. A few dozen shirts and socks—these not knitted, of course, but made from sewn fabric—were thus prepared. It was such a joy for the colonists to finally wear white clothing—clothing that was very rough, undoubtedly, but they were not worried about such trifles—and to sleep between sheets that transformed the Granite-House beds into quite serious sleeping arrangements.

Around this time, shoes made of seal leather were also fashioned, appropriately replacing the shoes and boots brought from America. One can say that these new shoes were wide and long and never bothered the feet of the walkers!

With the beginning of the year 1866, the heat was persistent, but hunting in the woods did not stop. Agoutis, peccaries, capybaras, kangaroos, fur and feathered game were truly plentiful, and Gédéon Spilett and Harbert were too good marksmen to miss a single shot.

Cyrus Smith always advised them to be sparing with ammunition, and he took steps to replace the powder and lead found in the box, which he wanted to reserve for the future. Did he know where chance might one day throw him and his people, in case they had to leave their domain? Therefore, provisions had to be made for all necessities of the unknown, conserving ammunition while substituting other easily renewable substances.

To replace lead, of which Cyrus Smith found no trace on the island, he used iron shot instead, which was easy to make. These pellets were not as heavy as lead pellets, so he had to make them larger, and each charge contained less, but the hunters' skill made up for this deficiency. As for the powder, Cyrus Smith could have made it since he had access to saltpeter, sulfur, and charcoal; however, this preparation requires extreme care, and without special tools, it is difficult to produce it in good quality.

Cyrus Smith therefore preferred to manufacture pyroxyl, that is to say, nitro-cotton, a substance in which cotton is not essential, as it only serves as cellulose. Now, cellulose is nothing more than the elementary tissue of plants, and it is found almost in a state of purity, not only in cotton but also in the textile fibers of hemp and linen, in paper, old linen, elder pith, etc. And indeed, elder trees abounded on the island, near the mouth of Creek-Rouge, and the colonists were already using the berries of these shrubs, which belong to the honeysuckle family, as coffee.

Thus, to obtain this elder pith, that is, cellulose, it was merely necessary to collect it, and regarding the other substance necessary for making pyroxyl, it was only fuming nitric acid.

Now, Cyrus Smith, having sulfuric acid at his disposal, had already been able to easily produce nitric acid by treating the saltpeter that nature had provided him. He therefore resolved to manufacture and use pyroxyl, while acknowledging some serious disadvantages, such as a significant variability in effect, excessive flammability, since it ignites at one hundred seventy degrees instead of two hundred forty, and finally a too-instantaneous detonation that could damage firearms. Conversely, the advantages of pyroxyl consisted in that it did not deteriorate with moisture, it did not foul the barrels of rifles, and its propulsive power was four times that of ordinary powder.

To make pyroxyl, it suffices to soak cellulose in fuming nitric acid for a quarter of an hour, then wash it thoroughly and dry it. As one can see, nothing could be simpler.

Cyrus Smith only had regular nitric acid at his disposal, not fuming nitric acid or monohydrate, which means acid that emits whitish vapor upon contact with moist air; but by substituting ordinary nitric acid, mixed in the ratio of three volumes to five volumes of concentrated sulfuric acid, the engineer obtained the same result, and he did achieve it. Thus, the island's hunters soon had a perfectly prepared substance available to them, and when used discreetly, it yielded excellent results.

Around this time, the colonists cleared three acres of the Grande-vue plateau, while leaving the rest as prairies for the care of the onaggas. Several excursions were made into the forests of Jacamar and Far-West, and they returned with a true harvest of wild plants, such as spinach, watercress, horseradish, and turnips, which intelligent cultivation would soon modify, helping to temper the nitrogen-rich diet to which the colonists of Lincoln Island had hitherto been subjected. They also moved notable quantities of wood and coal. Each excursion was, at the same time, a means to improve the roads, which were gradually compacted under the wheels of the cart.

The rabbit warren continued to supply its share of rabbits for the Granite-House kitchens. Since it was situated a little outside the point where Creek-Glycerine was announced, its inhabitants could not enter the reserved plateau, thus not ravaging the newly planted crops. As for the oyster bed, located among the rocks on the beach and whose products were frequently renewed, it provided excellent mollusks on a daily basis. Moreover, fishing, either in the lake's waters or in the current of the Mercy, did not take long to be fruitful, as Pencroff had set up bottom lines armed with iron hooks, which frequently caught beautiful trout and certain fish, extremely tasty, whose silver sides were sprinkled with small yellowish spots. Thus, Master Nab, in charge of culinary duties, was able to pleasantly vary the menu of each meal. Only bread was still missing from the colonists' table, and, as it has been said, it was a deprivation they really felt.

Around this time, sea turtle hunting was also undertaken along the beaches of Cape Mandible. Here, the shore was dotted with small swellings, containing perfectly spherical eggs, with a white and hard shell, and whose albumin does not coagulate like that of bird eggs. It was the sun that took care of hatching them, and their number was naturally very considerable, since each turtle can lay up to two hundred fifty eggs annually.

"A real field of eggs," Gédéon Spilett remarked, "and all we have to do is collect them."

But they did not stop at just gathering the products; they also hunted the producers, which allowed them to bring back a dozen of these chelonians, truly prized from a nutritional standpoint, to Granite-House. Turtle broth, seasoned with aromatic herbs and enhanced with a few cruciferous vegetables, often drew well-deserved praise to Master Nab, its preparer.

We must also mention a fortunate occurrence that allowed for new reserves for winter. Salmon came in schools to venture into the Mercy and swam upstream for several miles. It was the season when the females, seeking suitable places to spawn, led the males and made quite a commotion in the fresh waters. A thousand of these fish, measuring up to two and a half feet long, thus surged into the river, and it was sufficient to establish a few barriers to trap a large quantity. They caught several hundred in this way, which were salted and stored for the time when winter would freeze the waterways, making fishing impractical.

Around this time, the very intelligent Jup was promoted to the role of chamberlain. He was dressed in a jacket, short white pants, and an apron whose pockets brought him joy, as he stuffed his hands into them and didn't allow anyone to rummage in them. The clever orangutan had been wonderfully styled by Nab, and it seemed that the black man and the monkey understood each other when they talked together. Jup had, besides, a real fondness for Nab, and Nab returned the sentiment. Unless someone needed his services, either to carry wood or to climb to the top of a tree, Jup spent most of his time in the kitchen, trying to imitate Nab in everything he saw him do. The master showed, moreover, extreme patience and even zeal in teaching his pupil, and the pupil displayed remarkable intelligence in benefiting from the lessons given by his master.

One can imagine the satisfaction Master Jup gave to the diners at Granite-House one day when, with a napkin over his arm, he came to serve them at the table without them having been warned. Skillful and attentive, he carried out his duties with perfect ease, changing plates, bringing dishes, pouring drinks, all with a seriousness that greatly amused the colonists and delighted Pencroff.

"Jup, some soup!

— Jup, a bit of agouti!

— Jup, a plate!

— Jup! Brave Jup! Honest Jup!"

That was all they heard, and Jup, never flustered, responded to everything, kept an eye on everything, and nodded his intelligent head when Pencroff, repeating his first day's joke, told him, "Definitely, Jup, we'll have to double your wages!"

Needless to say, the orangutan was now fully acclimated to Granite-House, and he often accompanied his masters into the forest without ever showing any desire to escape. You had to see him walking in the most amusing way, with a cane Pencroff had made for him, which he carried over his shoulder like a rifle! If you needed to pick some fruit from the top of a tree, he was up there in no time! If the cart's wheel got stuck, what strength Jup used, with one strong shoulder, to get it back on track!

"What a guy!" Pencroff often exclaimed. "If he were as bad as he is good, there'd be no way to handle him!"

It was towards the end of January that the colonists undertook major work in the central part of the island. It was decided that, near the sources of Creek-Rouge, at the foot of Mount Franklin, a corral would be established to contain the ruminants, whose presence would have been troublesome at Granite-House, particularly the sheep, which were to provide wool for making winter clothing.

Every morning, the whole colony, sometimes entirely, but most often represented only by Cyrus Smith, Harbert, and Pencroff, went to the creek's sources, and with the help of the onaggas, it was now just a five-mile stroll under a dome of greenery along this newly carved road, which was named the "Corral Road."

There, a vast area had been chosen, at the very back of the southern slope of the mountain. It was a meadow, dotted with clusters of trees, located at the foot of a foothill that enclosed it on one side. A small stream, born on its slopes, after watering it diagonally, flowed into the Creek-Rouge. The grass was fresh, and the trees growing here and there allowed air to circulate freely at its surface. Therefore, it was just necessary to surround this meadow with a circular fence, which would lean against each end of the foothill and be high enough so that animals, even the most agile, could not jump over it. This enclosure could hold, along with about a hundred animals with horns, wild sheep or goats, the young ones that would be born later on.

The perimeter of the corral was therefore marked out by the engineer, and they were to proceed with cutting down the necessary trees for constructing the fence; but as the opening of the road had already required the sacrifice of a certain number of trunks, they were used, providing about a hundred posts, which were firmly planted in the ground.At the front of the palisade, a wide entry was made and closed with a double door made of strong planks, which were reinforced with outer bars.

Building this corral took at least three weeks, because in addition to the palisade work, Cyrus Smith constructed large wooden sheds under which the grazing animals could take shelter.

Moreover, it was essential to establish these structures with extreme sturdiness, as the rams are strong animals, and their initial aggression was to be feared. The stakes, sharpened at their upper ends and hardened by fire, were linked together with bolted crosspieces, and at intervals, braces ensured the overall stability.

With the corral completed, the task was to perform a significant drive at the foot of Mount Franklin, in the pastures frequented by the grazing animals. This operation took place on February 7, on a beautiful summer day, with everyone participating. The two onagers, already well-trained and ridden by Gédéon Spilett and Harbert, were very helpful in this situation.

The maneuver involved simply herding the rams and goats, gradually tightening the circle around them. Cyrus Smith, Pencroff, Nab, and Jup positioned themselves at various points in the woods while the two riders and Top galloped within a half-mile radius around the corral.

Rams were abundant in this part of the island. These beautiful animals, as large as deer, with stronger horns than those of a ram, and a grayish fleece mixed with long hairs, resembled argalis.

It was a tiring day of hunting! So much running back and forth, so many chases and counter-chases, and so many shouts! Of about a hundred rams that were driven, more than two-thirds escaped the herders; however, in the end, about thirty of these ruminants and ten wild goats, gradually pushed toward the corral with its open door seemingly offering them an exit, rushed in and were captured. Overall, the result was satisfactory, and the colonists had nothing to complain about. Most of these rams were females, some of which would soon give birth. It was therefore certain that the herd would thrive, and that not only wool but also skins would be abundant in the near future.

That evening, the hunters returned exhausted to Granite-House. However, the next day, they still went to visit the corral. The prisoners had tried to knock down the palisade, but they had not succeeded, and they soon settled down more quietly.

During this month of February, nothing of great importance occurred. Daily work continued methodically, and while the roads to the corral and Balloon Port were improved, a third road was started, leading from the enclosure toward the western coast. The still-unknown portion of Lincoln Island was always the vast woods that covered the Serpentine Peninsula, where the wild beasts, which Gédéon Spilett intended to eradicate from his domain, took refuge.

Before the cold season returned, meticulous care was also given to the cultivation of wild plants that had been transplanted from the forest to the Grandevue plateau. Harbert hardly returned from an excursion without bringing back some useful plants. One day, it was samples from the chicory family, whose seeds could yield excellent oil when pressed; another day, it was common sorrel, whose anti-scurvy properties were not to be underestimated; then, some of those precious tubers that have been cultivated throughout South America, those potatoes, of which there are now over two hundred varieties. The vegetable garden, now well-maintained, well-watered, and defended against birds, was divided into small squares, where lettuce, vitelottes, sorrel, turnips, horseradish, and other crucifers grew. The soil on this plateau was remarkably fertile, and it was hoped that the harvests would be abundant.

Various drinks were also plentiful, and as long as nobody demanded wine, the picky ones had no reason to complain. In addition to Oswego tea made from the Monarda didyma, and the fermented liquor extracted from dragonnier roots, Cyrus Smith had added a real beer; he made it with the young shoots of "abies nigra," which, after boiling and fermenting, produced this pleasant and particularly healthy drink that Anglo-Americans call "spring-berr," meaning fir beer.

Towards the end of summer, the farmyard had a beautiful pair of bustards, which belonged to the "houbara" species, characterized by a kind of feathered mantle, a dozen shovelers, whose upper bill was extended on either side by a membranous appendage, and magnificent roosters, black in crest, caruncle, and skin, resembling Mozambique roosters, which strutted along the lake shore.

Thus, everything succeeded due to the efforts of these brave and intelligent men. Providence did a lot for them, doubtless; but, faithful to the great principle, they helped themselves first, and then heaven helped them.

After those hot summer days, in the evenings, when the work was done, as the sea breeze began to rise, they liked to sit on the edge of the Grande-vue plateau, under a sort of veranda covered in climbing plants that Nab had built with his own hands. There, they talked, educated each other, made plans, and the jolly demeanor of the sailor constantly delighted this small group, in which perfect harmony had never ceased to reign.

They also talked about the country, about dear old America. What was happening with the civil war?

It couldn't have dragged on! Richmond had surely fallen quickly into General Grant's hands! The capture of the Confederate capital must have been the last act of this disastrous struggle! Now, the North had triumphed for the good cause. Ah! How welcome a newspaper would have been for the exiles of Lincoln Island! It was now eleven months since all communication between them and the rest of humanity had been interrupted, and soon, on March 24, the anniversary would arrive of the day when the balloon dropped them on this unknown coast! They had then been mere castaways, unsure if they could even fight the elements for their miserable lives! And now, thanks to their leader's knowledge, and their own intelligence, they were genuine colonists, armed with weapons, tools, and instruments, who had learned to transform to their advantage the animals, plants, and minerals of the island, which meant the three kingdoms of nature!

Yes! They often discussed all these things and formed many future plans!

As for Cyrus Smith, most of the time silent, he listened to his companions more than he spoke. Sometimes he smiled at a comment from Harbert or a jest from Pencroff, but always, everywhere, he thought about those inexplicable events, that strange riddle whose secret still eluded him!

ঙ্গ 9 ঞ্চ

The weather changed during the first week of March.

There had been a full moon at the beginning of the month, and the heat was still excessive. The atmosphere felt charged with electricity, and a longer or shorter period of stormy weather was genuinely to be feared. Indeed, on the 2nd, the thunder roared with extreme violence. The wind blew from the east, and hail directly struck the front of Granite-House, cracking like a volley of gunfire. They had to seal the door and window shutters tightly; otherwise, everything inside the rooms would have been flooded. Seeing the hailstones, some as large as pigeon eggs, Pencroff had only one thought: that his wheat field was in serious danger.

And immediately he ran to his field, where the ears were already starting to lift their little green heads, and with a large canvas, he managed to protect his crop. He was pelted with hailstones, but he didn't complain about it.

This bad weather lasted eight days, during which the thunder continued to rumble in the depths of the sky. Between storms, it could still be heard rumbling softly beyond the horizon, then it would return with renewed fury. The sky was streaked with lightning, and lightning struck several trees on the island, including a huge pine that stood near the lake at the edge of the forest. Two or three times, too, the shore was struck by the electrical current, which melted the sand and vitrified it. Upon finding these fulgurites, the engineer was led to believe that it would be possible to fit the windows with thick and sturdy glass that could withstand wind, rain, and hail.

The colonists, having no urgent work to do outside, took advantage of the bad weather to work inside Granite-House, whose layout improved and completed day by day. The engineer installed a lathe, which allowed him to turn out some toilet or kitchen utensils, and especially buttons, which were in high demand. A rack had been set up for the weapons, which were maintained with extreme care, and neither shelves nor cupboards left anything to be desired. They sawed, planed, filed, turned, and throughout this period of bad weather, all that could be heard was the creaking of the tools or the rumbling of the lathe, responding to the thunder's growl.

Master Jup had not been forgotten and was occupying a separate room near the general store, a sort of cabin always filled with good bedding, which suited him perfectly.

"With this good Jup, never any complaints," Pencroff often repeated, "never any inappropriate responses! What a servant, Nab, what a servant!

— My student," Nab replied, "and soon my equal!

— Your superior," the sailor retorted laughingly, "because after all, Nab, you talk, and he doesn't!"

It goes without saying that Jup was now well-acquainted with the service. He beat the clothes, turned the spit, swept the rooms, served at the table, stacked the wood, and – a detail that delighted Pencroff – he never went to bed without tucking the worthy sailor in.

As for the health of the colony's members, whether bipeds or bimanuals, quadrumanes or quadrupeds, it left nothing to be desired. With this life in the open air, on this healthy ground, under this temperate zone, working with head and hands, they could hardly believe that illness could ever reach them.

Everyone was indeed in wonderful health.

Harbert had already grown two inches in a year. His features were forming and becoming more masculine, and he promised to be a man as accomplished physically as morally. Moreover, he took advantage of every opportunity left for him by manual work to educate himself; he read the few books found in the crate and, after the practical lessons resulting from the very necessity of his position, he found in the engineer a teacher for sciences, and in the reporter a teacher for languages, who were pleased to complete his education.

The engineer's fixed idea was to pass on to the young boy everything he knew, to instruct him by example as much as by words, and Harbert took full advantage of his professor's lessons.

"If I die," Cyrus Smith thought, "he will replace me!"

The storm ended around March 9, but the sky remained covered with clouds throughout the last month of summer. The atmosphere, violently disturbed by these electrical commotions, could not regain its previous clarity, and almost invariably there were rains and fog, except for three or four beautiful days that favored all sorts of excursions.

Around this time, the female onager gave birth to a young one of the same sex as its mother, which was very well. In the corral, there was a similar increase in the flock of rams, and several lambs were already bleating under the sheds, much to the delight of Nab and Harbert, each of whom had their favorite among the newborns.

They also attempted a domestication trial for the peccaries, which was fully successful. A stable was built near the farmyard and soon housed several young ones being civilized, that is to say, fattened under Nab's care.

Master Jup, tasked with bringing them daily food, dishwater, kitchen scraps, etc., diligently fulfilled his duty. Sometimes, he mischievously teased his little charges and pulled their tails, but it was mischief and not malice, as those little twisted tails amused him like a toy, and his instinct was that of a child. One day in March, Pencroff, talking with the engineer, reminded Cyrus Smith of a promise he had not yet had time to fulfill.

"You had mentioned a device that would eliminate the long ladders of Granite-House, Mr. Cyrus," he said. "Won't you set it up someday?

— You mean some sort of elevator!" replied Cyrus Smith.

— Let's call it an elevator if you want," replied the sailor. "The name doesn't matter, as long as it lifts us comfortably to our home.

— Nothing could be easier, Pencroff, but is it truly necessary?

— Certainly, Mr. Cyrus. After we've taken care of the essentials, let's think a bit about comfort. For people, it will be luxury, if you like; but for things, it's essential! It's not that easy to climb a long ladder when heavily loaded!

— Well then, Pencroff, we shall try to satisfy you," replied Cyrus Smith.

— But you don't have a machine at your disposal.

— We'll make one.

— A steam machine?

— No, a water machine."

And indeed, to operate his device, a natural force was available to the engineer that he could use without great difficulty.

For this, it was sufficient to increase the flow of the small diversion made at the lake that provided water to the interior of Granite-House. The opening between the stones and the grass at the upper end of the spillway was therefore enlarged, creating a strong drop at the end of the corridor, from which the overflow poured into the interior well. Below this drop, the engineer installed a paddle wheel cylinder that connected to the outside with a wheel wrapped with a strong cable supporting a bucket. In this way, using a long rope that fell to the ground and allowed for engaging or disengaging the hydraulic motor, one could rise in the bucket to the door of Granite-House.

It was on March 17 that the elevator functioned for the first time, to everyone's satisfaction.

From then on, all loads, wood, coal, provisions, and the colonists themselves were lifted by this simple system, replacing the primitive ladder, which nobody thought to regret. Top was particularly delighted with this improvement, as he did not have, and could not have, Master Jup's skill for climbing the steps, and many times he had to ascend to Granite-House on Nab's back, or even on that of the orangutan.

Around this time too, Cyrus Smith tried to make glass, and first had to adapt the old pottery kiln for this new purpose. This was quite challenging; but after several unsuccessful attempts, he finally succeeded in setting up a glass-making workshop, which Gédéon Spilett and Harbert, the engineer's natural assistants, did not leave for several days.

As for the materials used to make glass, they consisted solely of sand, chalk, and soda (carbonate or sulfate). The shore provided sand, lime provided chalk, sea plants provided soda, pyrites supplied sulfuric acid, and the soil provided coal to heat the furnace to the required temperature. Therefore, Cyrus Smith was in the right conditions to proceed.

The tool that proved most difficult to make was the glassblower's "pipe," a five to six-foot-long iron tube, used to gather molten material at one end. However, using a long, thin iron strip rolled like a rifle barrel, Pencroff managed to create this pipe, and it was soon ready for use.

On March 28, the furnace was heated vigorously. One hundred parts of sand, thirty-five of chalk, forty of sodium sulfate, mixed with two or three parts of powdered coal, made up the substance, which was placed in refractory clay crucibles. Once the high temperature of the furnace melted it into a liquid or rather a paste, Cyrus Smith "gathered" a certain amount of this paste with the pipe; he spun and turned it on a metal plate prepared beforehand to shape it appropriately for blowing; then he handed the pipe to Harbert, telling him to blow into the other end.

"Like blowing soap bubbles?" asked the young boy.

"Exactly," replied the engineer.

And Harbert, puffing out his cheeks, blew into the pipe so skillfully while continually turning it that his breath expanded the glassy mass.

More amounts of molten material were added to the first batch, and soon a bubble measuring one foot in diameter formed. Then Cyrus Smith took the pipe back from Harbert and, swinging it like a pendulum, stretched the pliable bubble to give it a conical cylindrical shape.

Thus, the blowing process created a glass cylinder topped with two hemispherical caps, which were easily removed using a sharp iron dampened with cold water; then, through the same method, the cylinder was split lengthwise, and after being made pliable with a second heating, it was rolled out on a plate and flattened using a wooden roller.

The first pane of glass was thus made, and it was just a matter of repeating the operation fifty times to have fifty panes. Soon the windows of Granite-House were fitted with translucent sheets, perhaps not very white but sufficiently transparent.

As for the glassware, glasses, and bottles, it was just child's play. They accepted them as they came from the end of the pipe. Pencroff had requested the chance to "blow" in his turn, and it was a joy for him, but he blew so hard that his products took on the most amusing shapes, which filled him with admiration.

During one of the excursions made at this time, a new tree was discovered, whose products further increased the food resources of the colony.

Cyrus Smith and Harbert, while hunting, had ventured one day into the Far-West forest, to the left of the Mercy, and, as usual, the young boy asked a thousand questions of the engineer, to which he responded wholeheartedly. But hunting is like any other endeavor on this earth, and when one is not sufficiently eager, there are many reasons for failure.

Since Cyrus Smith was not a hunter and, on the other hand, Harbert was talking chemistry and physics, that day many kangaroos, capybaras, or agoutis passed within good range yet escaped the young boy's rifle. This meant that, with the day already advanced, the two hunters were at risk of having made an unproductive excursion, when Harbert stopped and, with a cry of joy, exclaimed, "Ah! Mr. Cyrus, do you see that tree?"

And he pointed to a shrub rather than a tree, for it consisted only of a single stem covered with scaly bark, bearing leaves streaked with small parallel veins.

"And what is this tree that looks like a small palm?" asked Cyrus Smith.

"It's a 'cycas revoluta,' whose picture I have in our natural history dictionary!"

"But I don't see any fruit on this shrub?"

"No, Mr. Cyrus," replied Harbert, "but its trunk contains flour that nature provides already ground."

"So it's the bread tree?"

"Yes! The bread tree."

"Well, my child," replied the engineer, "this is a precious discovery, while we wait for our wheat harvest. To work, and may heaven grant that you are not mistaken!"

Harbert was not mistaken. He broke off the stem of a cycas, which was made of glandular tissue and contained a certain amount of floury pith, crossed by woody bundles separated by rings of the same substance arranged concentrically. This starch was mixed with a slimy juice of an unpleasant taste, but which could easily be eliminated by pressure. This cellular substance formed a real flour of superior quality, extremely nutritious, and whose exportation was once prohibited by Japanese law.

Cyrus Smith and Harbert, after studying the area of the Far-West where these cycads grew, took some reference points and returned to Granite-House, where they shared their discovery.

The next day, the colonists went to harvest, and Pencroff, increasingly enthusiastic about his island, said to the engineer, "Mr. Cyrus, do you think there are islands for castaways?"

"What do you mean by that, Pencroff?"

"Well, I mean islands created specifically so that people can conveniently shipwreck on them, where poor souls can always manage to survive!"

"That's possible," replied the engineer, smiling.

"That's certain, sir," replied Pencroff, "and it is equally certain that Lincoln Island is one of them!"

They returned to Granite-House with an ample yield of cycas stems. The engineer set up a press to extract the slimy juice mixed with the starch, and he obtained a considerable quantity of flour, which, under Nab's hands, was transformed into cakes and puddings. It wasn't quite the real wheat bread yet, but it was very close.

At that time, the onagras, goats, and sheep from the corral provided the daily milk needed for the colony. Thus, the cart—or rather a kind of light cart that had replaced it—made frequent trips to the corral, and when it was Pencroff's turn to make the rounds, he took Jup and made him drive, which Jup did, cracking his whip and performing his usual intelligent duties.

Everything was thriving both in the corral and at Granite-House, and truly the colonists, except for being far from their homeland, had no complaints. They were so accustomed to this life, so familiar with this island, that they would not have left its hospitable ground without regret!

And yet, as much as love for one's homeland is held in the heart of a person, if any ship had unexpectedly appeared in sight of the island, the colonists would have signaled to it, attracted it, and they would have left!... In the meantime, they lived this happy existence, having more fear than desire that any event might interrupt it.

But who could flatter themselves with ever having fixed their fortune and being safe from its reverses!

Anyway, this Lincoln Island, which the colonists had already inhabited for more than a year, was often the subject of their conversations, and one day an observation was made that would later lead to serious consequences.

It was on April 1st, a Sunday, Easter Day, which Cyrus Smith and his companions had sanctified with rest and prayer. The day had been beautiful, like an October day in the northern hemisphere.

All of them, towards the evening after dinner, were gathered under the veranda at the edge of the Grande-vue plateau, watching the night rise on the horizon. A few cups of elderberry seed infusion, replacing coffee, had been served by Nab. They were discussing the island and its isolated position in the Pacific when Gédéon Spilett was led to say:

"My dear Cyrus, since you have had that sextant found in the box, have you taken another observation of our island's position?"

"No," replied the engineer.

"But it might be wise to do so, with this instrument which is more accurate than the one you used before.

"What good would that do?" asked Pencroff. "The island is where it is!"

"Of course," continued Gédéon Spilett, "but it's possible that the imperfection of the devices has affected the accuracy of the observations, and since it is easy to verify their accuracy..."

"You're right, my dear Spilett," replied the engineer, "and I should have made this verification earlier, although if I made any error, it shouldn't exceed five degrees in longitude or latitude."

"Who knows?" replied the reporter, "who knows if we're not much closer to inhabited land than we think?"

"We will know tomorrow," replied Cyrus Smith, and without so many occupations that have left me no leisure, we would already know.

"Good!" said Pencroff, "Mr. Cyrus is too good an observer to have made a mistake, and if it hasn't moved, the island is where he said it is!"

"We shall see."

So the next day, using the sextant, the engineer made the necessary observations to verify the coordinates he had already obtained, and here were the results of his operation: his first observation had given the position of Lincoln Island: in western longitude: from 150 degrees to 155 degrees; in southern latitude: from 30 degrees to 35 degrees.

The second one gave exactly: in western longitude: 150 degrees 30 minutes; in southern latitude: 34 degrees 57 minutes.

Thus, despite the imperfection of his devices, Cyrus Smith had operated so skillfully that his error did not exceed five degrees.

"Now," said Gédéon Spilett, "since we have both a sextant and an atlas, let's see, my dear Cyrus, the exact position that Lincoln Island occupies in the Pacific."

Harbert went to fetch the atlas, which, as we know, had been published in France, and whose nomenclature was therefore in the French language.

The map of the Pacific was unfolded, and the engineer, compass in hand, prepared to determine its location.

Suddenly, the compass stopped in his hand, and he said:

"But there is already an island in this part of the Pacific!"

"An island?" cried Pencroff.

"Our island, no doubt?" replied Gédéon Spilett.

"No," replied Cyrus Smith. "This island is located at 153 degrees longitude and 37 degrees 11 minutes latitude, that is, two and a half degrees further west and two degrees further south than Lincoln Island."

"And what is this island?" asked Harbert.

"Tabor Island."

"An important island?"

"No, a lost islet in the Pacific, that may have never been visited!"

"Well, we will visit it," said Pencroff.

"We?"

"Yes, Mr. Cyrus. We will build a decked boat, and I will take charge of navigating it. — How far are we from Tabor Island?

"About one hundred and fifty miles northeast," replied Cyrus Smith.

"One hundred and fifty miles! What's that?" replied Pencroff. "In forty-eight hours and with a good wind, we can do it!"

"But what for?" asked the reporter.

"We don't know. We'll see!"

And on this response, it was decided that a boat would be built, so that they could set sail around the coming October, at the return of the fine season.

❧ 10 ❧

Once Pencroff set his mind to a project, he wouldn't rest until it was executed. Now, he wanted to visit Tabor Island, and since a reasonably sized boat was necessary for this journey, that boat had to be built.

Here was the plan agreed upon by the engineer and the sailor.

The boat would measure thirty-five feet long and nine feet wide, which would make it a good runner if its bottom and water lines were done right, and it should not draw more than six feet, sufficient water depth to keep it from drifting. It would be decked the whole length, pierced with two hatches giving access to two chambers separated by a partition, and rigged as a sloop, with brigantine, staysail, foresail, mainsail, and a very manageable sail setup, good for handling in heavy weather, and very favorable for sailing upwind. Finally, its hull would be built with flush sides, meaning that the planks would be flush rather than overlapping, and for its framing, heat would be applied after fitting the planks that would be mounted on false frames. What wood would be used for the construction of this boat? Elm or spruce, both plentiful on the island? They decided on pine, slightly "checked," in the language of carpenters, but easy to work with and as durable as elm in water immersion.

With these details settled, it was agreed that since the return of the fine weather wouldn't happen for another six months, Cyrus Smith and Pencroff would work alone on the boat. Gédéon Spilett and Harbert would continue hunting, and neither Nab nor master Jup, his assistant, would abandon their assigned domestic duties. As soon as the trees were chosen, they were felled, cut down, and sawn into boards, as any sawyers would have done. Eight days later, in the recess between the Chimneys and the wall, a worksite was prepared, and a keel, thirty-five feet long, equipped with a stern post at the rear and a bow at the front, lay on the sand.

Cyrus Smith hadn't gone into this new task blindly. He understood ship-building like almost everything else, and it was on paper that he first sought the template for his boat. Moreover, he was well served by Pencroff, who, having worked a few years in a shipyard in Brooklyn, knew the practical side of the trade. So it was only after careful calculations and mature reflections that the false frames were attached to the keel.

Pencroff, as you might believe, was all fired up to see this new undertaking succeed, and he wouldn't have wanted to abandon it for an instant. Only one operation managed to pull him away, but just for a day, from his construction site. This was the second wheat harvest, which took place on April 15. It had succeeded as well as the first and yielded the expected proportion of grains.

"Five bushels! Mr. Cyrus," said Pencroff, after carefully measuring his riches.

"Five bushels," replied the engineer, "and at one hundred thirty thousand grains per bushel, that makes six hundred fifty thousand grains."

"Well! We will sow all of it this time, said the sailor, but we'll keep a small reserve!— Yes, Pencroff, and if the next harvest yields a proportional amount, we will have four thousand bushels.

— And we will eat bread?

— We will eat bread.

— But we will need to make a mill?

— We will make a mill.

The third wheat field was therefore incomparably larger than the first two, and the soil, prepared with extreme care, received the precious seed. With that done, Pencroff returned to his work.

Meanwhile, Gédéon Spilett and Harbert were hunting nearby, and they ventured quite deep into the still-unknown parts of the Far-West, their rifles loaded and ready for any danger. It was an impenetrable tangle of magnificent trees, pressed closely together as if space were limited. Exploring these wooded masses was extremely difficult, and the reporter never dared venture without carrying a pocket compass, as the sun barely pierced the thick branches, making it hard to find one's way back. Naturally, game was rarer in these areas, where it wouldn't have had enough freedom of movement. However, three large herbivores were killed during this last fortnight of April. They were koulas, which the colonists had previously seen a sample of north of the lake, and they were stupidly killed among the thick branches of the trees where they sought refuge. Their skins were brought back to Granite-

House, and with the help of sulfuric acid, they were subjected to a sort of tanning that made them usable. A valuable discovery from another perspective was also made during one of these excursions, and that was thanks to Gédéon Spilett.

It was April 30. The two hunters had gone deep into the southwest of the Far-West when the reporter, ahead of Harbert by about fifty paces, arrived in a kind of clearing, where the trees were more spaced out, allowing some rays of light to penetrate.

Gédéon Spilett was initially surprised by the smell emitted by certain straight, cylindrical, and branching plants that produced flowers arranged in clusters and very small seeds. The reporter pulled up one or two of these stems and returned to the young boy, saying:

"Look at this, Harbert?

— And where did you find this plant, Mr. Spilett?

— Over there, in a clearing, where it grows very abundantly.

— Well then! Mr. Spilett, said Harbert, this is a discovery that guarantees you all the rights to Pencroff's gratitude!

— So it's tobacco?

— Yes, and even if it's not first quality, it's still tobacco!

— Ah! That good Pencroff! He's going to be so happy! But he won't smoke it all, for goodness' sake! He'll surely leave us our share!

— Ah! I have an idea, Mr. Spilett, replied Harbert. Let's not tell Pencroff anything, let's take the time to prepare these leaves, and one fine day, we'll present him with a fully stuffed pipe!

— Agreed, Harbert, and on that day our worthy companion will have nothing left to desire in this world!"

The reporter and the young boy made a good supply of the precious plant and returned to Granite-House, where they "smuggled" it in, being as cautious as if Pencroff were the strictest customs officer.

Cyrus Smith and Nab were let in on the secret, and the sailor suspected nothing during the long enough time it took to dry the thin leaves, chop them, and roast them on hot stones. This took two months; but all these manipulations could be done without Pencroff knowing, as he was busy constructing the boat and only returned to Granite-House at rest time.

Once again, however, despite everything, his favorite work was interrupted on May 1 by a fishing adventure that all the colonists had to participate in. For a few days, an enormous animal had been observed at sea, two or three miles offshore, swimming in the waters of Lincoln Island. It was a whale of the largest size, which was likely of the southern species known as the "Cape whale."

"What good fortune it would be to take it! exclaimed the sailor. Ah! If we only had a suitable boat and a good harpoon, I would say: 'Let's go after the beast, for it's worth it!'

— Hey! Pencroff, said Gédéon Spilett, I would have liked to see you manage the harpoon. It must be interesting!

— Very interesting and not without danger, said the engineer; but since we don't have the means to attack this animal, it's useless to concern ourselves with it.

— I'm surprised, said the reporter, to see a whale under this relatively high latitude.

— Why so, Mr. Spilett? replied Harbert. We are precisely in this part of the Pacific that English and American fishermen call the "whale-field," and it is here, between New Zealand and South America, that the whales of the southern hemisphere are found in larger numbers.

— Nothing could be more true, replied Pencroff, and what surprises me is that we haven't seen more of them. After all, since we can't approach them, it doesn't matter!"

And Pencroff returned to his work, not without a sigh of regret, for in every sailor, there is a fisherman, and if the pleasure of fishing is directly proportional to the size of the animal, one can imagine what a whaler feels in the presence of a whale!

And if it had been only for pleasure! But one couldn't ignore that such prey would have been very profitable for the colony, as the oil, fat, and baleen could be used for many things!

Now, this happened: the observed whale seemed unwilling to leave the waters of the island. So, whether from the windows of Granite-House or from the Heights, Harbert and Gédéon Spilett, when they were not hunting, Nab, while watching his stoves, kept the telescope trained on it and observed all the movements of the animal. The cetacean, deeply engaged in the vast Union Bay, swiftly traversed it from Mandible Point to Claw Point, driven by its tremendously powerful tail fin, on which it supported itself and moved in bursts with a speed that sometimes reached twelve miles per hour. Sometimes it also approached so close to the islet that it could be fully distinguished.

It was indeed the southern whale, which is entirely black, and its head is more flattened than that of northern whales.

It could also be seen ejecting through its blowholes, and at great height, a cloud of vapor... or water, for—however strange it may seem—naturalists and whalers still do not agree on this matter.

Is it air, is it water that is expelled? It is generally accepted that it is vapor, which suddenly condenses in contact with cold air, falling back as rain.

However, the presence of this marine mammal concerned the colonists. It especially annoyed Pencroff and provided him with distractions during his work.

He began to desire that whale like a child desires something forbidden. At night, he dreamed about it aloud, and certainly, if he had had the means to attack it, if the dinghy had been fit to brave the sea, he wouldn't have hesitated to pursue it.

But what the colonists could not do, chance did for them, and on May 3, Nab's cries from the window of his kitchen announced that the whale had washed ashore on the island's coast.

Harbert and Gédéon Spilett, who were about to leave for hunting, abandoned their rifles, Pencroff threw down his axe, and Cyrus Smith and Nab joined their companions, and all quickly headed towards the stranding location.

This stranding occurred on the beach near the wreck's point, three miles from Granite-House and at high tide. It was therefore likely that the cetacean could not free itself easily. In any case, they needed to hurry, so as to cut off its retreat if necessary. They ran with picks and iron-tipped spears, crossed the Mercy Bridge, went down the right bank of the river, took to the beach, and within less than twenty minutes, the colonists were beside the enormous animal, which was already swarmed by a multitude of birds.

"What a monster!" cried Nab.

And the expression was correct, for it was a southern whale, eighty feet long, a giant of the species, weighing no less than one hundred fifty thousand pounds!

However, the monster, stranded as it was, did not move and did not seek to struggle back to the water while the sea was still high.

The colonists soon understood the reason for its immobility when, at low tide, they walked around the animal.

It was dead, and a harpoon was sticking out of its left flank.

"So there are whalers around here?" said Gédéon Spilett immediately.

— Why do you say that? asked the sailor.

— Since this harpoon is still here...

— Hey! Mr. Spilett, that doesn't prove anything, replied Pencroff. We've seen whales swim thousands of miles with a harpoon in their flank, and this one could have been struck in the North Atlantic and come to die in the South Pacific; it wouldn't be surprising!

— However... said Gédéon Spilett, Pencroff's assertion did not satisfy him.

— That is perfectly possible, replied Cyrus Smith; but let's examine this harpoon. Perhaps, according to a common practice, the whalers have engraved the name of their ship on it?"

Indeed, Pencroff, having pulled out the harpoon that the animal had in its flank, read this inscription: Maria-Stella Vineyard.

"A ship from Vineyard! A ship from my home!" he exclaimed. "The Maria-Stella! A fine whaler, my word! And I know it well! Ah! My friends, a vessel from Vineyard, a whaling ship from Vineyard!"

And the sailor, brandishing the harpoon, repeated with emotion the name that meant so much to him, the name of his homeland!

But, since they couldn't wait for the Maria-Stella to come claim the animal it had harpooned, they decided to proceed with the butchering before decomposition set in. The predatory birds, which had been watching this rich prey for several days, wanted to claim it without delay, and they had to be driven away with gunshots.

This whale was a female, whose udders produced a large amount of milk that, according to the naturalist Dieffenbach, could pass for cow's milk, and indeed, it did not differ in taste, color, or density.

Pencroff had formerly served on a whaling ship, and he was able to methodically lead the butchering operation—quite an unpleasant task that lasted three days, but none of the colonists were deterred, not even Gédéon Spilett, who, according to the sailor, would eventually make "a very good castaway."

The lard, cut into parallel slices two and a half feet thick and then divided into chunks weighing about a thousand pounds each, was melted down in large earth pots brought to the butchering site—because they didn't want to foul the area around the Heights—and in this melting, it lost about a third of its weight. But there was plenty: just the tongue alone yielded six thousand pounds of oil and the lower lip four thousand. Then, with this fat, which was sure to provide a long-term supply of stearin and glycerin, there were also the baleen plates, which would surely find use, even though they had neither umbrellas nor corsets at Granite-House. The upper part of the cetacean's mouth was indeed equipped, on both sides, with eight hundred horn plates, very elastic, fibrous in texture, and tapered at their edges like two large combs, whose teeth, six feet long, serve to catch the thousands of small animals, fish, and mollusks that the whale feeds on.

Once the operation was complete, to the great satisfaction of the operators, the remains of the animal were left to the birds, who would presumably remove every last vestige, and the daily work resumed at Granite-House.

However, before returning to the construction site, Cyrus Smith had the idea to make certain devices that piqued the curiosity of his companions. He took a dozen whale baleen plates, cut them into six equal parts, and sharpened their ends.

"And this, Mr. Cyrus, asked Harbert, when the operation was finished, will this serve?...

— To kill wolves, foxes, and even jaguars, replied the engineer.

— Now?

— No, this winter, when we'll have ice available.

— I don't understand... replied Harbert.

— You will understand, my child, replied the engineer. This device is not my invention, and it's commonly used by Aleutian hunters in Russian America. These baleen plates that you see, my friends, well! When it freezes, I will bend them, I will sprinkle them with water until they are entirely covered with a layer of ice that will maintain their curvature, and I will spread them on the snow after having previously concealed them under a layer of grease. Now, what will happen if a starving animal swallows one of these baits? The heat of its stomach will melt the ice, and the baleen will then spring back and pierce it with its sharpened ends.

— That's clever! said Pencroff.

— And it will save powder and bullets, replied Cyrus Smith.

— That's better than traps! added Nab.

— Let's wait for winter then!

— Let's wait for winter."

Meanwhile, the construction of the boat was progressing, and by the end of the month, it was halfway done. One could already recognize that its shape would be excellent for holding steady at sea.

Pencroff worked with unparalleled zeal, and it took his robust nature to withstand this fatigue; but his companions secretly prepared a reward for him for all his hard work, and on May 31, he was about to experience one of the greatest joys of his life.

That day, at the end of dinner, at the moment when he was about to leave the table, Pencroff felt a hand rest on his shoulder.

It was Gédéon Spilett's hand, who said to him:

"One moment, Master Pencroff, you can't leave like that! And what about the dessert you're forgetting?

— Thank you, Mr. Spilett, the sailor replied, I'm going back to work.

— Well then, how about a cup of coffee, my friend?

— Not even that.

— A pipe, then?"

Pencroff suddenly stood up, and his good, hearty face paled when he saw the reporter presenting him with a fully stuffed pipe, and Harbert with a glowing ember.

The sailor wanted to say something but couldn't manage to; instead, grabbing the pipe, he brought it to his lips; then, applying the ember, he took five or six quick puffs. A bluish, fragrant cloud billowed out, and from the depths of that cloud, a delirious voice could be heard repeating:

"Tobacco! Real tobacco!

— Yes, Pencroff, replied Cyrus Smith, and even excellent tobacco!— Oh! Divine providence! Sacred creator of all things! shouted the sailor. So, nothing is missing from our island!

And Pencroff kept smoking, smoking, smoking!

"And who made this discovery?" he finally asked. "You, I suppose, Harbert?"

— No, Pencroff, it's Mr. Spilett.

— Mr. Spilett! exclaimed the sailor, hugging the reporter, who had never experienced such a squeeze.

— Phew! Pencroff, replied Gideon Spilett, catching his breath, which had been momentarily compromised. Make sure to share your gratitude with Harbert, who identified this plant, with Cyrus, who prepared it, and with Nab, who worked hard to keep the secret!

— Well then, my friends, I'll repay you someday! replied the sailor. Now, it's a matter of life and death!

11

Meanwhile, winter was arriving with this June, which is December in the northern zones, and the main task became making warm and sturdy clothing.

The sheep in the corral had been sheared of their wool, and this precious textile was now to be transformed into fabric.

It goes without saying that since Cyrus Smith had no carders, combers, finishers, stretchers, spinners, or looms to work with the wool, he had to proceed in a simpler way to save on spinning and weaving. Indeed, he intended to utilize the property of wool fibers, which when pressed in every direction, tangle together and form the fabric known as felt through their simple interlacing. This felt could thus be obtained through a straightforward fulling process, which, while reducing the fabric's flexibility, notably increased its heat retention properties. Now, the wool provided by the sheep was made of very short strands, which is a good condition for felting.

The engineer, aided by his companions, including Pencroff—who had to abandon his boat once again—began the preliminary operations aimed at removing the oily and greasy substance known as suint from the wool. This degreasing was done in tubs filled with water, which were heated to seventy degrees, and in which the wool soaked for twenty-four hours; then it underwent a thorough washing using soda baths; after that, the wool, once sufficiently dried by pressing, was ready to be felted, that is, to produce a solid fabric, coarse perhaps and of no value in an industrial center of Europe or America, but one which would be highly valued on the "markets of Lincoln Island."

It is understood that this type of fabric must have been known since ancient times, and indeed, the first woolen fabrics were made using the very method Cyrus Smith was about to employ.

Where his quality as an engineer was very useful was in constructing the machine designed to felt the wool, as he cleverly took advantage of the unused mechanical force from the waterfall on the shore to operate a fulling mill.

Nothing could be more rudimentary. A tree, equipped with cams that lifted and dropped vertical hammers alternately, troughs to hold the wool inside which the hammers fell, and a strong timber frame containing and connecting the entire system: such was the machine in question, and such it had remained for centuries, until the idea of replacing the hammers with roller compresses and subjecting the material not to beating but to actual rolling came about.

The operation, well directed by Cyrus Smith, was a complete success. The wool, previously soaked in a soapy solution, designed to facilitate its sliding, compressing, and softening, while also preventing it from being damaged by the beating, emerged from the mill in the form of a thick sheet of felt. The ridges and roughness naturally present on the wool fibers had so well hooked and intertwined with one another that they formed a fabric suitable for making clothes or blankets. It was obviously neither merino, nor muslin, nor cashmere, nor any of the other fine fabrics! It was "Lincoln felt," and Lincoln Island had gained another industry.

The settlers thus had good clothing and thick blankets, allowing them to face the winter of 1866-67 without fear.

The severe cold began to be felt around June 20, and much to his regret, Pencroff had to suspend building the boat, which could not fail to be completed by next spring.

The sailor's fixed idea was to explore Tabor Island, even though Cyrus Smith did not approve this trip, which was purely one of curiosity since there could obviously be no help to find on that deserted, half-arid rock. A journey of one hundred and fifty miles on a relatively small boat, in the midst of unknown seas, naturally caused him some apprehension. If the vessel, once at sea, were unable to reach Tabor and could not return to Lincoln Island, what would become of it in the middle of that Pacific, so ripe with disasters?

Cyrus Smith often discussed this plan with Pencroff, finding in the sailor a peculiar stubbornness in wanting to undertake this journey, a stubbornness perhaps not fully recognized by him.

"For after all," the engineer said one day, "I must point out to you, my friend, that after praising Lincoln Island so much, after so many times expressing regret at having to abandon it, you're the first one to want to leave."

— Leave for just a few days, replied Pencroff, just a few days, Mr. Cyrus! Long enough to go and come back, to see what that is like over there!

— But it can't be as good as Lincoln Island!

— I'm sure of it in advance!

— Then why venture?

— To see what's happening on Tabor Island!

— But nothing is happening there! It can't possibly be!

— Who knows?

— And what if you are caught in a storm?

— That's not likely in the good season, replied Pencroff. But, Mr. Cyrus, as it's necessary to foresee everything, I will ask your permission to take only Harbert with me on this trip.

— Pencroff, the engineer replied, placing his hand on the sailor's shoulder, if something were to happen to you and that child, whom chance has made our son, do you think we could ever console ourselves?

— Mr. Cyrus, replied Pencroff with unshakeable confidence, we won't cause you that grief. Besides, we will talk more about this trip when the time comes. Then, I imagine that once you've seen our boat well rigged and equipped, once you've observed how it behaves at sea, once we've circled our island— because we will do that together—I imagine, I say, that you won't hesitate to let me go! I won't hide from you that it will be a masterpiece, your boat!

— At least say: our boat, Pencroff! replied the engineer, temporarily disarmed.

The conversation ended thus to begin again later, without convincing either the sailor or the engineer.

The first snows fell towards the end of June. Before that, the corral had been sufficiently stocked and no longer needed daily visits, but it was decided that they would never let a week pass without checking in.

The traps were set once more, and they tested the devices made by Cyrus Smith. The curved whalebones, trapped in a sheath of ice and covered with a thick layer of fat, were placed on the edge of the forest, where animals commonly passed on their way to the lake.

To the great satisfaction of the engineer, this renewed invention of the Aleutian fishermen worked perfectly. A dozen foxes, some wild boars, and even a jaguar were caught, and these animals were found dead, their stomachs pierced by the released whalebones.

Here we find an attempt worth mentioning because it was the first time the settlers tried to communicate with their fellow humans.

Gideon Spilett had already thought several times about throwing a notice into the sea in a bottle that the currents might carry to an inhabited coast, or entrusting it to pigeons. But how could one seriously hope that pigeons or bottles could cover the distance between the island and any land, a distance of twelve hundred miles?

That would have been sheer madness.

But on June 30, they captured, not without difficulty, an albatross that Harbert had slightly injured in the leg with a gunshot. It was a magnificent bird from the family of those large gliders, with wings that span ten feet, and which can cross seas as wide as the Pacific.

Harbert would have liked to keep this splendid bird, whose wound healed quickly and claimed to tame it, but Gideon Spilett made him understand that they couldn't miss the opportunity to try to communicate with the lands of the Pacific using this messenger, and Harbert had to concede since if the albatross had come from some inhabited region, it would certainly return there as soon as it was free.

Perhaps, deep down, Gideon Spilett, who sometimes had the chronicler's urge, was not unhappy to toss a charming article narrating the adventures of the settlers of Lincoln Island! What a success for the assigned reporter of the New-York Herald, and for the issue that would contain the column, if it ever reached the desk of its director, the honorable John Bennett!

Gideon Spilett thus wrote a succinct notice that was placed in a bag of strong waxed fabric, with an urgent request to anyone who found it to deliver it to the New-York Herald offices.

This little bag was strapped to the albatross's neck, not its leg, because these birds are accustomed to resting on the surface of the sea; then, they set the speedy messenger free, and it was not without some emotion that the settlers watched it disappear into the mist of the west.

"Where is it going?" asked Pencroff.

— To New Zealand, replied Harbert.

— Safe travels! exclaimed the sailor, who did not expect much result from this method of communication.

With winter, work resumed inside Granite-House, repairing clothes, making various items, and among other things, the sails for the boat, which were cut from the endless fabric of the balloon...

During July, the cold was intense, but they spared neither wood nor coal.

Cyrus Smith had installed a second chimney in the great room, and it was there that long evenings were spent. Conversations while working, reading when hands remained idle, and time passed productively for everyone.

It was a true delight for the settlers when, in this well-lit room filled with candles, well-heated with coal, after a comforting dinner, steaming elderberry coffee in their cups, and pipes puffing fragrant smoke, they heard the storm howling outside! They would have experienced complete well-being if well-being could ever exist for someone who is far from their fellow humans and without any possible communication with them! They always spoke about their homeland, the friends they had left behind, the greatness of the American republic, whose influence could only grow, and Cyrus Smith, who had been deeply involved in the affairs of the Union, thoroughly engaged his listeners with his stories, insights, and predictions.

One day, it happened that Gideon Spilett was led to say to him:

"But after all, my dear Cyrus, all this industrial and commercial movement that you predict will progress steadily, isn't it at risk of being completely halted eventually?

— Halted! And by what?

— But by the lack of this coal, which one can rightly call the most precious of minerals!

— Yes, indeed, the most precious, replied the engineer, and it seems that nature wanted to prove it by making the diamond, which is solely pure crystallized carbon.

— You don't mean, Mr. Cyrus, replied Pencroff, that we will burn diamonds instead of coal in the boilers?

— No, my friend, replied Cyrus Smith.

— However, I insist, continued Gideon Spilett. You don't deny that one day coal will be entirely consumed?

— Oh! The coal deposits are still considerable, and the one hundred thousand workers who annually extract one hundred million metric quintals are not about to exhaust them!

— With the growing proportion of coal consumption, replied Gideon Spilett, it can be foreseen that these one hundred thousand workers will soon be two hundred thousand and that extraction will double?

— Of course; but after the deposits in Europe, which new machines will soon allow us to exploit more thoroughly, the coal mines of America and Australia will continue to supply the industry for a long time yet.

— How long? asked the reporter.

— At least two hundred fifty or three hundred years.

— That's reassuring for us, replied Pencroff, but worrying for our great-great-grandchildren!

— They will find something else, said Harbert.

— We must hope so, replied Gideon Spilett, because without coal, no machines, and without machines, no railroads, no steam boats, no factories, none of what modern life requires!

— But what will they find? asked Pencroff. Can you imagine it, Mr. Cyrus?

— Pretty much, my friend.

— And what will they burn in place of coal?

— Water, replied Cyrus Smith.

— Water, shouted Pencroff, water to heat steam boats and locomotives, water to heat water!

— Yes, but water decomposed into its constituent elements, replied Cyrus Smith, and indeed decomposed by electricity, which will then have become a powerful and manageable force, for all great discoveries, by an inexplicable law, seem to coincide and complement each other at the same moment. Yes, my friends, I believe that water will one day be used as fuel, that hydrogen and oxygen, which constitute it, used separately or simultaneously, will provide an inexhaustible source of heat and light with an intensity that coal cannot achieve. One day, the holds of steamers and the tenders of locomotives will be charged, instead of coal, with these two compressed gases, which will burn in the furnaces with enormous heat power. So, there is nothing to fear. As long as this earth is inhabited, it will supply the needs of its inhabitants, and they will never lack for light or heat, nor for the products of the vegetable, mineral, or animal kingdoms. I therefore believe that when the coal deposits are exhausted, we will heat and warm ourselves with water. Water is the coal of the future.

— I would like to see that, said the sailor.

— You got up too early, Pencroff, replied Nab, who only intervened with these words in the discussion.However, it was not Nab's words that ended the conversation, but rather the barking of Top, which erupted again with that strange tone that had already concerned the engineer. At the same time, Top began circling around the opening of the well, which was located at the end of the inside corridor.

"What is Top barking about now?" asked Pencroff.

"And Jup growling like that?" added Harbert.

Indeed, the orangutan, joining the dog, showed unmistakable signs of agitation, and, interestingly, these two animals appeared to be more anxious than irritated.

"It's clear," said Gideon Spilett, "that this well is directly connected to the sea, and that a sea creature comes down here to breathe from time to time."

"That makes sense," replied the sailor, "and there's no other explanation for it... Come on, be quiet, Top," Pencroff added, turning to the dog, "and you, Jup, back to your room!"

The monkey and the dog fell silent. Jup went back to lie down, but Top stayed in the living room, continuing to make low growls throughout the evening.

The incident was not mentioned again, although it darkened the engineer's brow.

For the rest of July, there were alternating spells of rain and cold. The temperature didn't drop as low as the previous winter, with its maximum not exceeding eight degrees Fahrenheit (13.33 degrees Celsius below zero). However, although this winter was less cold, it was more disturbed by storms and winds. There were still violent assaults from the sea, which endangered the Chimneys more than once. It was as if a tidal wave, caused by some underwater disturbance, lifted these monstrous waves and hurled them against the wall of Granite-House.

When the colonists leaned out of their windows to observe these enormous masses of water crashing before their eyes, they could only admire the magnificent sight of the ocean's powerless fury. The waves rebounded in dazzling foam, the entire shore disappeared under this raging flood, and the massif seemed to emerge from the sea itself, with spray rising more than a hundred feet high.

During these storms, it was difficult to venture into the island's paths, even dangerous, as fallen trees were common.

Nevertheless, the colonists didn't let a week go by without visiting the corral. Fortunately, this enclosure, sheltered by the southeast slope of Mount Franklin, didn't suffer too much from the hurricane's violence, which spared its trees, sheds, and fence. But the poultry yard, established on the Grande-vue plateau, and therefore directly exposed to the eastern winds, sustained rather considerable damages. The dovecote was blown off twice, and the fence also collapsed. All of this needed to be rebuilt more solidly, as it was clear that Lincoln Island was situated in one of the worst areas of the Pacific. It truly seemed to be the central point of vast cyclones, which whipped it like the whip of a top.

Only here, the top was stationary, and the whip was spinning.

During the first week of August, the gusts gradually calmed, and the atmosphere regained a tranquility it seemed to have lost forever. With the calm came a drop in temperature; the cold became very sharp, and the thermometer fell to eight degrees Fahrenheit below zero (22 degrees Celsius below freezing).

On August 3rd, an excursion that had been planned for a few days took place in the southeast of the island, towards the pond of the tadornes. The hunters were tempted by all the waterfowl that were making their winter quarters there. Wild ducks, snipe, teal, grebes, were abundant, and it was decided that a day would be dedicated to an expedition against these birds.

Not only Gideon Spilett and Harbert, but also Pencroff and Nab participated in the expedition. Only Cyrus Smith, claiming some work, did not join them and remained at Granite-House.

The hunters took the road to Balloon Port to get to the marsh, after promising to return by evening. Top and Jup accompanied them. As soon as they crossed the Mercy Bridge, the engineer raised it and returned, planning to carry out a project for which he wanted to be alone.

Now, this project was to thoroughly explore this inner well whose opening was level with the corridor of Granite-House, and which connected with the sea since it once served as a passage for the lake's waters.

Why did Top circle around this opening so often? Why did he let out such strange barks when a sort of anxiety brought him back to this well? Why did Jup join Top in a common anxiety? Did this well have other connections besides the vertical one with the sea? Did it branch out towards other parts of the island? That was what Cyrus Smith wanted to know, and first of all, he wanted to be the only one to know. He had therefore resolved to explore the well while his companions were away, and the opportunity presented itself to do so.

It was easy to descend to the bottom of the well using the rope ladder that hadn't been used since the installation of the elevator, and which was long enough. This is what the engineer did. He dragged the ladder to the hole, which measured about six feet in diameter, and let it unfurl after securely attaching its upper end. Then, having lit a lantern, taken a revolver, and strapped a machete to his belt, he began to descend the first rungs.

Everywhere, the wall was solid; but some rocky projections stood out from time to time, and using these ledges, it could actually be possible for an agile being to climb back up to the opening of the well.

This was a remark made by the engineer; however, as he carefully moved his lantern over these ledges, he found no prints, no breaks, that would suggest they had been used for climbing, either recently or in the past.

Cyrus Smith descended further, illuminating all points of the wall. He saw nothing suspicious.

When the engineer reached the last rungs, he felt the surface of the water, which was perfectly calm at that moment. Neither at his level nor in any other part of the well did any side corridors open that could branch out inside the massif. The wall, which Cyrus Smith struck with the handle of his machete, sounded solid. It was compact granite, through which no living being could make its way. To reach the bottom of the well and then rise back to its opening, one necessarily had to go through this submerged canal, which connected it to the sea through the rocky subsoil of the shore, and this was only possible for marine animals. As for the question of where this canal led, at what point of the coast and how deep beneath the waves, it could not be resolved.

Thus, Cyrus Smith, having finished his exploration, came back up, removed the ladder, covered the opening of the well, and returned, deep in thought, to the great room of Granite-House, saying to himself: "I saw nothing, and yet there is something!"

12

That very evening, the hunters returned, having had a good hunt, literally loaded with game, carrying everything that four men could manage.

Top had a string of teal around his neck, and Jup had snipe belts around his waist.

"Here you go, my master," shouted Nab, "this is enough to keep us busy! Canned goods, pies, we'll have a nice reserve! But I need someone to help me. I'm counting on you, Pencroff."

"No, Nab," replied the sailor. "The rigging on the boat calls for me, and you'll have to do without me."

"And you, Mr. Harbert?

"Me, Nab, I must go to the corral tomorrow," replied the young boy.

"So it will be you, Mr. Spilett, who will help me?"

"To oblige you, Nab," replied the reporter, "but I warn you that if you reveal your recipes to me, I'll publish them."

"As you wish, Mr. Spilett," replied Nab, "as you wish!"

And that's how, the next day, Gideon Spilett, becoming Nab's assistant, was set up in his culinary laboratory. But beforehand, the engineer had informed him of the results of the exploration he had conducted the day before, and in this regard, the reporter shared Cyrus Smith's opinion that, although he had found nothing, a secret remained to be discovered!

The cold persisted for another week, and the colonists did not leave Granite-House except for tending the poultry yard. The home was filled with the delightful aromas emitted by Nab's and the reporter's clever manipulations; however, not all the game from the marsh hunt was turned into canned goods, and as the game, due to the intense cold, kept perfectly, wild ducks and others were eaten fresh and declared superior to all other waterfowl in the known world.

During that week, Pencroff, helped by Harbert, who skillfully handled the sewing of the sails, worked so hard that the sails of the boat were finished. There was no lack of hemp rope, thanks to the rigging found with the balloon's envelope. The cables, the net lines, all of this was made from excellent cable, which the sailor made good use of. The sails were lined with strong edges, and there was still enough material to make the halyards, shrouds, sheets, etc. As for the pulley system, following Pencroff's advice and using the lathe he had set up, Cyrus Smith made the necessary pulleys. It happened that the rigging was fully prepared well before the boat was finished. Pencroff even made a blue, red, and white flag, the colors of which came from certain dye plants that were very abundant on the island. However, instead of the thirty-seven stars representing the thirty-seven states of the union that shine on the American yacht flags, the sailor added an extra thirty-eighth star, the star of "the state of Lincoln," as he considered his island already linked to the great republic.

"And," he said, "it is in spirit, even if not yet in fact!" Meanwhile, this flag was hoisted at the central window of Granite-House, and the colonists greeted it with three cheers.

However, as the end of the cold season approached, it seemed that this second winter was going to pass without serious incident, when, in the night of August 11th, the Grande-vue plateau was threatened with complete devastation.

After a busy day, the colonists were sound asleep when, around four in the morning, they were suddenly awakened by Top's barking.

This time, the dog wasn't barking near the opening of the well, but at the threshold of the door, and he was throwing himself against it as if he wanted to break it down. Jup, for his part, was letting out sharp cries.

"Well, Top!" cried Nab, who was the first to wake.

But the dog continued barking with even more fury.

"What is it?" asked Cyrus Smith.

And all, hastily dressed, rushed to the windows of their room, which they opened.

Before their eyes lay a layer of snow that barely looked white in the very dark night. The colonists saw nothing but heard strange barks erupting in the shadows. It was clear that the shore had been invaded by a number of animals that couldn't be distinguished.

"What is it?" exclaimed Pencroff.

"Wolves, jaguars, or monkeys!" replied Nab.

"Damn! But they could reach the top of the plateau!" said the reporter.

"And our poultry yard!" cried Harbert, "and our crops?..."

"How did they get through?" asked Pencroff.

"They must have crossed the culvert at the shore," replied the engineer, "which one of us must have forgotten to close."

"Indeed," said Spilett, "I remember leaving it open..."

"What a fine move you made there, Mr. Spilett!" exclaimed the sailor.

"What's done is done," replied Cyrus Smith. "Let's think about what we need to do!"

These were the questions and answers that were quickly exchanged between Cyrus Smith and his companions. It was certain that the culvert had been crossed, that the shore was overrun by animals, and that these, whatever they were, could, moving up the left bank of the Mercy, reach the Grande-vue plateau. Therefore, they needed to get the upper hand and fight them, if necessary.

"But what kind of beasts are they?" was asked a second time, as the barking grew louder.

These barks made Harbert start, and he remembered hearing them before during his first visit to the sources of the red creek.

"They are culpeos, they are foxes!" he said.

"Let's go!" shouted the sailor.

And all, arming themselves with axes, rifles, and revolvers, rushed into the elevator hatch and stepped onto the shore.

These culpeos are dangerous animals when they are in large numbers and hunger drives them.

Nevertheless, the colonists did not hesitate to throw themselves into the midst of the pack, and their first revolver shots, sending bright flashes into the darkness, pushed back the initial assailants.

What mattered most was to prevent these raiders from reaching the Grande-vue plateau, as the crops and the poultry yard would have been at their mercy, and immense damages, perhaps irreparable, especially regarding the wheat field, would inevitably occur.

But since the invasion of the plateau could only happen via the left bank of the Mercy, it was enough to oppose an insurmountable barrier to the culpeos on this narrow portion of the bank between the river and the granite wall.

This was understood by everyone, and at Cyrus Smith's command, they moved to the designated spot while the team of culpeos leaped in the shadows.

Cyrus Smith, Gideon Spilett, Harbert, Pencroff, and Nab positioned themselves to form an impassable line. Top, his formidable jaws wide open, led the colonists, followed by Jup, armed with a knotted club that he wielded like a mace.

The night was extremely dark. It was only in the light of the gunshots, each one sending a ray ahead, that the assailants could be seen, who numbered at least a hundred, their eyes gleaming like embers.

"They must not pass!" shouted Pencroff.

"They will not pass!" replied the engineer.

But if they didn't pass, it wasn't for lack of trying. The rear ranks were pushing the front ones, and it was an unending battle of revolver shots and axe blows. Many culpeo corpses must already have littered the ground, but the pack did not seem to diminish, and it was as if it renewed itself unceasingly through the culvert at the shore.Soon, the settlers had to fight hand to hand, and fortunately they had only received a few light injuries. Harbert had, with a gunshot, freed Nab, who had just been knocked down by a huge beast that had pounced on him like a tiger cat. Top fought with genuine ferocity, jumping at the foxes and strangling them outright. Jup, armed with his stick, was swinging it like a madman, and it was in vain to try to make him stay back. Gifted, no doubt, with a vision that allowed him to pierce the darkness, he was always in the thick of the fight and occasionally let out a sharp whistle, which marked his extreme excitement. At one point, he even advanced so far that, illuminated by a gunshot, he was seen surrounded by five or six large beasts, which he faced with remarkable composure.

However, the fight was to end in favor of the settlers, but only after they had resisted for two full hours! The first light of dawn must have prompted the retreat of the assailants, who scampered off to the north, crossing the culvert that Nab immediately ran to reset.

When day had sufficiently illuminated the battlefield, the settlers could count about fifty corpses scattered on the shore.

"And Jup! shouted Pencroff. Where's Jup?"

Jup had disappeared. His friend Nab called for him, and for the first time, Jup did not respond to his friend's call.

Everyone began searching for Jup, fearing that he would be counted among the dead. They cleared away the area of corpses, which stained the snow with their blood, and Jup was found in the middle of a true heap of beasts, whose shattered jaws and broken backs testified that they had faced the terrible club of the fearless animal. The poor Jup still held the broken piece of his stick in his hand; but deprived of his weapon, he had been overwhelmed by the numbers, and deep wounds marred his chest.

"He's alive!" cried Nab, who leaned over him.

"And we will save him," replied the sailor, "we will care for him as one of us!"

It seemed that Jup understood because he rested his head on Pencroff's shoulder as if to thank him.

The sailor was injured himself, but his wounds, as well as those of his companions, were minor, because, thanks to their firearms, they had almost always been able to keep the attackers at bay. Therefore, it was only the orangutan whose condition was serious.

Jup, carried by Nab and Pencroff, was taken to the lift, and he barely let out a weak groan. They gently raised him to Granite-House. There, he was laid on one of the mattresses borrowed from one of the bunks, and his wounds were cleaned with the utmost care.

It did not seem that they had affected any vital organs, but Jup had been greatly weakened by blood loss, and a fever developed to a considerable degree.

They lay him down after dressing his wounds, imposed a strict diet on him, "just like for a natural person," said Nab, and they made him drink a few cups of refreshing herbal tea, the ingredients for which were provided by the plant pharmacy of Granite-House.

Jup fell asleep, at first with an agitated sleep; but gradually his breathing became more regular, and they left him to rest in the greatest calm. From time to time, Top, walking, one might say "on tiptoe," would come to visit his friend and seemed to approve of all the care given to him. One of Jup's hands hung outside the bed, and Top licked it with a look of sorrow.

That very morning, they proceeded to bury the dead, who were dragged to the Far-West forest and buried deeply.

This attack, which could have had such serious consequences, was a lesson for the settlers, and from then on, they did not go to bed without one of them ensuring that all bridges were raised and that no invasion was possible.

Meanwhile, Jup, after worrying everyone for a few days, reacted vigorously against the illness. His constitution prevailed, the fever gradually decreased, and Gédéon Spilett, who was somewhat of a doctor, soon considered him out of danger. On August 16, Jup began to eat. Nab prepared him some sweet treats that the sick one savored with delight, because if he had a cute flaw, it was being a bit of a glutton, and Nab had never done anything to correct him of that flaw.

"What can you do?" he said to Gédéon Spilett, who sometimes reproached him for spoiling him, "he has no other pleasure than that of the mouth, poor Jup, and I'm just so happy to recognize his services like this!"

Ten days after taking to bed, on August 21, master Jup got up. His wounds had healed, and it was clear that he would soon recover his usual flexibility and strength. Like all convalescents, he was then struck by a ravenous hunger, and the reporter let him eat as he pleased, because he trusted that instinct which often is lacking in rational beings and which should protect the orangutan from all excess. Nab was delighted to see his pupil's appetite return.

"Eat, my Jup," he said, "and don't hold back! You shed your blood for us, and it's the least I can do to help you get it back!"

Finally, on August 25, they heard Nab's voice calling his companions.

"Mr. Cyrus, Mr. Gédéon, Mr. Harbert, Pencroff, come! Come!"

The settlers, gathered in the main room, stood up at Nab's call, who was then in the room reserved for Jup.

"What is it?" asked the reporter.

"Look!" replied Nab, bursting into a wide laugh.

And what did they see? Master Jup, who was smoking, calmly and seriously, squatting like a Turk at the door of Granite-House!

"My pipe!" shouted Pencroff. "He took my pipe! Ah! My brave Jup, it's a gift from me! Smoke, my friend, smoke!"

And Jup was blowing thick puffs of tobacco seriously, which seemed to bring him unmatched pleasures.

Cyrus Smith did not appear otherwise surprised by the incident, and he cited several examples of tame monkeys, for whom the use of tobacco had become familiar.

From that day on, master Jup had his own pipe, the former pipe of the sailor, which was hung in his room next to his supply of tobacco. He filled it himself, lit it with a glowing charcoal, and seemed to be the happiest of four-handed creatures. You can imagine that this shared taste only tightened the close bonds of friendship that already united the worthy monkey and the honest sailor.

"He might be a man," Pencroff sometimes said to Nab. "Wouldn't it surprise you if one day he started talking to us?"

"Not at all," Nab replied. "What surprises me is rather that he doesn't talk, because after all, he's only missing the speech!"

"It would still amuse me," resumed the sailor, "if one fine day he said to me: 'What if we changed pipes, Pencroff!'"

"Yes," Nab replied. "What a pity he was born mute!"

With the month of September, winter was completely over, and work resumed with enthusiasm.

The construction of the boat advanced rapidly. It was already fully planked, and they were assembling it internally to connect all parts of the hull, with frames softened by steam that adapted to all the requirements of the shape.

Since there was no shortage of wood, Pencroff suggested to the engineer to line the inside of the hull with waterproof sheathing, which would completely ensure the boat's sturdiness.

Cyrus Smith, not knowing what the future held, approved the sailor's idea to make his vessel as solid as possible.

The sheathing and deck of the boat were fully completed by around September 15. To caulk the seams, they made oakum from dry eelgrass, which was hammered between the planks of the hull, sheathing, and deck; then, these seams were covered with boiling pitch, generously supplied by the pine trees in the forest.

The equipment of the boat was very simple.

It had initially been weighted down with heavy pieces of granite, set in a bed of lime, totaling about twelve thousand pounds. A deck was placed over this ballast, and the interior was divided into two cabins, along which two benches extended to serve as chests. The foot of the mast was to support the partition separating the two cabins, which could be accessed through two hatches, opened on the deck and fitted with covers.

Pencroff had no trouble finding a suitable tree for the mast. He chose a young fir, straight, with no knots, which he only had to square at its base and round at its head. The fittings for the mast, those for the rudder, and those for the hull had been coarsely but solidly made at the forge of the chimneys. Finally, yardarms, the bowsprit, boom, spars, oars, etc., were all completed in the first week of October, and it was agreed that they would test the boat in the vicinity of the island to see how it performed at sea and how much trust they could place in it.

During all this time, the necessary works had not been neglected. The corral was rearranged because the herd of sheep and goats had several young ones that needed shelter and food. The settlers had not neglected visits to the oyster park, the rabbit warren, the coal and iron deposits, and to some areas of the Far-West forests that had not yet been explored and were quite game-rich.

Some indigenous plants were discovered, and if they had no immediate utility, they helped to diversify the plant reserves of Granite-House. These were species of iceplants, some similar to those of the Cape, with edible fleshy leaves, others producing seeds that contained a kind of flour.

On October 10, the boat was launched into the sea. Pencroff was radiant. The operation was a success.

The fully rigged vessel, having been pushed on rollers to the edge of the shore, was caught by the rising tide and floated to the cheers of the settlers, especially Pencroff, who showed no modesty on this occasion. Moreover, his pride was bound to survive the completion of the boat since, after having built it, he would be called upon to command it. The rank of captain was bestowed upon him with the agreement of all.

To please Captain Pencroff, they first had to name the vessel, and after several long discussions on various proposals, the votes converged on the name Bonadventure, which was the first name of the honest sailor.

As soon as the Bonadventure was lifted by the rising tide, it was evident that it was sitting perfectly in the water, and that it should sail properly under all conditions.

In addition, the trial was to be conducted that very day during an excursion off the coast. The weather was beautiful, the breeze fresh, and the sea easy, especially along the southern shore, as the wind had been blowing from the northwest for an hour already.

"Let's board! Let's set sail!" cried Captain Pencroff.

But they needed to have lunch before leaving, and it even seemed wise to bring provisions on board, in case the excursion extended into the evening.

Cyrus Smith was also eager to try this boat, the plans of which had come from him, although, on the sailor's advice, he had often modified some parts; but he did not have the confidence in it that Pencroff expressed, and since the latter was no longer mentioning the trip to Tabor Island, Cyrus Smith even hoped that the sailor had given it up. He would have disliked seeing two or three of his companions venture far out in that small boat, which only measured about fifteen tons.

At ten-thirty, everyone was on board, including Jup and Top. Nab and Harbert raised the anchor that was biting the sand near the mouth of the Mercy, the mainsail was hoisted, the Lincoln flag flew at the top of the mast, and the Bonadventure, steered by Pencroff, set off into the open sea.

To leave Union Bay, they first had to sail downwind, and it was clear that under this course, the speed of the vessel was satisfactory.

After rounding the point of the wreck and Bluff Cape, Pencroff had to sail as close as possible to extend the southern coast of the island, and after running a few courses, he noticed that the Bonadventure could sail about five points off the wind and was holding well against the drift. It tacked very well close-hauled, having good "speed," as sailors say, and even gained in its tacking.

The passengers of the Bonadventure were truly delighted. They had a good vessel that, in case of need, could serve them greatly, and in this fine weather, with this pleasant breeze, the ride was charming.

Pencroff set off to sea, three or four miles from the coast, across from Balloon Harbor. The island then appeared in all its extent and under a new aspect, with the varied panorama of its coastline from Bluff Cape to Reptile Promontory, its first stretches of forests where the conifers stood out against the young foliage of other barely budding trees, and that Mount Franklin, which dominated the whole, with a few snows whitening its peak.

"How beautiful it is!" exclaimed Harbert.

"Yes, our island is beautiful and good," replied Pencroff. "I love it as I loved my poor mother! It welcomed us, poor and lacking everything, and what do these five children who fell from heaven lack?

"Nothing!" replied Nab, "nothing, Captain!"

And the two brave men let out three mighty cheers in honor of their island!

Meanwhile, Gédéon Spilett, leaning against the foot of the mast, was sketching the panorama that unfolded before his eyes.

Cyrus Smith watched in silence.

"Well, Mr. Cyrus," asked Pencroff, "what do you think of our boat?

"It seems to be behaving well," replied the engineer.

"Good! And do you believe now that it could undertake a journey of some length?

"What journey, Pencroff?

"That of Tabor Island, for example?

"My friend," replied Cyrus Smith, "I believe that, in an urgent case, we should not hesitate to trust the Bonadventure, even for a longer crossing; but, as you know, I would be sorry to see you leave for Tabor Island, since nothing compels you to go there.

"It's nice to know your neighbors," replied Pencroff, who clung to his idea. "Tabor Island is our neighbor, and it's the only one! Politeness demands that we at least pay it a visit!

"Good heavens!" said Gédéon Spilett, "our friend Pencroff is strict about etiquette!

"I'm not strict at all," replied the sailor, slightly vexed by the engineer's opposition but who wouldn't want to cause him any trouble.

"Remember, Pencroff," replied Cyrus Smith, "that you cannot go to Tabor Island alone.

"A companion will suffice for me."— So be it, replied the engineer. Are you really willing to deprive the colony on Lincoln Island of two out of five colonists?

— Six! responded Pencroff. You're forgetting Jup.

— Seven! added Nab. Top is worth as much as anyone!

— There's no risk, Mr. Cyrus, Pencroff insisted.

— That's possible, Pencroff; but I repeat, it's exposing yourself unnecessarily!

The stubborn sailor said nothing more and let the conversation drop, determined to pick it up again later. But he had no idea that an incident was about to help him and turn what was merely a whim, albeit a debatable one, into an act of humanity. Indeed, after staying offshore, the Bonadventure had just come closer to the coast, heading for Ballon Port. It was important to check the channels made between the sandbanks and reefs, marking them if necessary, since this little cove was to be the anchorage for the boat.

They were only half a mile from the coast and had to sail close-hauled against the wind. The speed of the Bonadventure was very moderate at that moment because the breeze, partly blocked by the high land, barely filled its sails, and the sea, smooth as glass, only rippled under the breath of the capricious gusts.

Harbert stood at the bow, indicating the route to follow through the channels, when he suddenly shouted, "Land, Pencroff, land."

— What is it? the sailor answered, getting up. A rock?

— No... wait, said Harbert... I can't see well... more land... okay... come a bit closer...

And saying this, Harbert, lying along the edge, quickly plunged his arm into the water and came up saying, "A bottle!"

He held in his hand a sealed bottle that he had just grabbed a few cables from the shore.

Cyrus Smith took the bottle. Without saying a word, he popped the cork and pulled out a wet paper that read:

Shipwrecked... Tabor Island: 153 degrees o. longitude — 37 degrees 11 south latitude.

13

"A shipwrecked person!" exclaimed Pencroff, abandoned a few hundred miles from us on Tabor Island! Ah! Mr. Cyrus, you're not going to oppose my travel plan now!

— No, Pencroff, answered Cyrus Smith, and you will leave as soon as possible.

— Tomorrow?

— Tomorrow."

The engineer held the paper he had pulled from the bottle in his hand. He pondered it for a few moments, then spoke again:

"From this document, my friends, he said, from the very form in which it is presented, we must first conclude this: firstly, that the shipwrecked person on Tabor Island is someone who has advanced knowledge of navigation, since he provides the latitude and longitude of the island, matching the ones we found, to within a minute of approximation; secondly, that he is either English or American, since the document is written in English.

— This makes perfect sense, replied Gideon Spilett, and the presence of this shipwrecked person explains the arrival of the crate on the shores of the island. There was a shipwreck since there is a shipwrecked person. As for him, whoever he is, he is lucky that Pencroff had the idea to build that boat and test it today, because a day's delay and that bottle could have broken on the reefs.

— Indeed, said Harbert, it's a lucky chance that the Bonadventure passed by just when that bottle was still floating!

— And doesn't that seem strange to you? asked Cyrus Smith of Pencroff.

— It seems fortunate to me, that's all, replied the sailor. Do you find anything extraordinary about it, Mr. Cyrus? That bottle had to go somewhere, and why not here as well as anywhere?

— You may be right, Pencroff, replied the engineer, but still...

— But, observed Harbert, nothing proves that this bottle has been floating at sea for a long time.

— Nothing, replied Gideon Spilett, and even the document seems to have been recently written. What do you think, Cyrus?

— That is difficult to verify, and besides, we'll find out!" replied Cyrus Smith.

During this conversation, Pencroff had not remained idle. He had tacked, and the Bonadventure, with a full sail, sped quickly toward Cape Griffe. Each person was reflecting on this shipwrecked individual from Tabor Island. Was it still time to save him? A major event in the lives of the colonists!

They themselves were mere castaways, but it was to be feared that another might not have been as fortunate as they, and their duty was to face misfortune head on.

They rounded Cape Griffe, and the Bonadventure dropped anchor around four o'clock at the mouth of the Mercy.

That very evening, details regarding the new expedition were settled. It seemed appropriate that Pencroff and Harbert, who were familiar with handling a boat, should be the only ones undertaking this journey. Departing the following day, October 11, they could arrive on the 13th during the day, for with the wind that prevailed, it would take no more than forty-eight hours to cover the one hundred fifty miles. One day on the island, three or four days for the return, they could therefore expect to be back on Lincoln Island by the 17th. The weather was fine, the barometer rising steadily, the wind seemed stable, all the chances were therefore in favor of these brave people, whom a duty of humanity was going to lead far from their island.

Thus, it was agreed that Cyrus Smith, Nab, and Gideon Spilett would stay at Granite House; but there was an objection, and Gideon Spilett, who did not forget his job as a reporter for the New-York Herald, declared that he would swim rather than miss such an opportunity, so he was allowed to join the voyage.

The evening was spent loading the Bonadventure with some bedding, utensils, weapons, ammunition, a compass, and enough food for eight days, and, once this loading was accomplished quickly, the colonists returned to Granite House.

The next day, at five in the morning, farewell was said, not without some emotion on both sides, as Pencroff, unfurling his sails, headed toward Cape Griffe, which he would round before taking the direct route southwest.

The Bonadventure was already a quarter mile from the shore when its passengers spotted two men on the heights of Granite House waving goodbye. It was Cyrus Smith and Nab.

"Our friends!" shouted Gideon Spilett. "This is our first separation in fifteen months!"

Pencroff, the reporter, and Harbert waved one last goodbye, and Granite House soon disappeared behind the high rocks of the cape.

Throughout the early hours of the day, the Bonadventure stayed in constant view of the southern coast of Lincoln Island, which soon appeared only as a green basket, with Mount Franklin rising above it. The heights, diminished by distance, made it look less inviting for ships attempting to land there.

The promontory of the reptile was passed around one o'clock, but at ten miles offshore. From this distance, it was no longer possible to distinguish anything on the western coast stretching towards Mount Franklin's slopes, and three hours later, all that was Lincoln Island had disappeared below the horizon.

The Bonadventure was sailing perfectly. It rose easily to the waves and made quick progress. Pencroff had rigged his triangular sail, and, with everything set, he was heading straight on, following the course indicated by the compass. From time to time, Harbert took over at the helm, and the young boy's hand was so steady that the sailor had nothing to fault him for.

Gideon Spilett chatted with one, then the other, and, when needed, helped with the maneuvering. Captain Pencroff was absolutely satisfied with his crew, and wasn't talking of anything less than rewarding them "with a quart of wine per shift"! In the evening, the crescent moon, which was not supposed to reach its first quarter until the 16th, emerged in the solar twilight and soon vanished. The night was dark but very starry, and another beautiful day was expected the following day.

As a precaution, Pencroff lowered the triangular sail, not wanting to risk being caught by a gust of wind with sail up. Perhaps it was too cautious for such a calm night, but Pencroff was a careful sailor, and he could not be blamed.

The reporter slept part of the night. Pencroff and Harbert took turns every two hours at the helm. The sailor trusted Harbert as he would trust himself, and his trust was justified by the young boy's calmness and reasoning. Pencroff directed him like a commander to his helmsman, and Harbert kept the Bonadventure on a straight course.

The night passed well, and the day of October 12 unfolded under the same conditions. The south-west direction was strictly maintained throughout the day, and if the Bonadventure didn't fall victim to some unknown currents, it should land right on Tabor Island.

As for the sea that the boat was navigating, it was completely deserted. Occasionally, a large bird, either an albatross or a frigate, would pass within shooting range, and Gideon Spilett wondered if it had been one of those powerful flyers he had entrusted his last article to for the New-York Herald. These birds were the only beings that seemed to frequent this part of the ocean between Tabor Island and Lincoln Island.

"And yet," noted Harbert, "we are in the season when whalers usually head towards the southern Pacific. Truly, I don't believe there is a more deserted sea than this one!"

— It's not so deserted as that! replied Pencroff.

— How do you mean? asked the reporter.

— But since we're here! Do you take our boat for a wreck and us for porpoises?"

And Pencroff laughed at his own joke. In the evening, based on estimates, they figured the Bonadventure had covered a distance of one hundred twenty miles since leaving Lincoln Island, which meant thirty-six hours ago, giving a speed of three and a third miles an hour. The breeze was weak and tending to calm. However, they hoped that the following day, at dawn, if the estimates were accurate and if the direction had been correct, they would spot Tabor Island. So, neither Gideon Spilett nor Harbert nor Pencroff slept during the night of October 12 to 13. Anticipating the next day, they could not help but be very emotional. There were so many uncertainties in the venture they were attempting! Were they close to Tabor Island? Was the island still inhabited by this shipwrecked person they were heading to rescue? Who was this man? Would his presence bring any trouble to the little colony that had been so united until now?

Furthermore, would he agree to trade his prison for another? All these questions, which would surely be resolved the next day, kept them awake, and at the first light of dawn, they successively fixed their gazes on all points of the western horizon.

"Land!" shouted Pencroff around six in the morning.

And since it was unthinkable for Pencroff to have made a mistake, it was clear that land was ahead. Just imagine the joy of the little crew of the Bonadventure! In a few hours, they would be on the coastline of the island!

Tabor Island, a low-lying coast barely emerging from the waves, was no more than fifteen miles away. The bow of the Bonadventure, which was somewhat south of the island, was headed straight for it, and as the sun rose in the east, a few peaks began to appear here and there.

"This island is just a much smaller islet than Lincoln Island," noted Harbert, "likely caused by some underwater uplift, just like it."

By eleven o'clock in the morning, the Bonadventure was only two miles away, and Pencroff, searching for a channel to land, was now proceeding with utmost caution over these unknown waters.

They could see the islet as a whole, with clumps of green gum trees and a few other large trees similar to those found on Lincoln Island. But, strangely enough, not a single wisp of smoke rose indicating that the islet was inhabited, and no signal appeared at any point along the shoreline!

And yet the document was clear: there was a shipwrecked person, and that person should have been on the lookout!

However, the Bonadventure was venturing between some rather unpredictable passes left by the reefs, and Pencroff was observing every curve with extreme care. He had placed Harbert at the helm, and stationed at the bow, he examined the waters, ready to lower the sail, of which he kept the halyard in hand. Gideon Spilett, with his spyglass to his eyes, scanned the entire shoreline without spotting anything. Finally, around noon, the Bonadventure ran aground on a sandy beach. The anchor was dropped, the sails lowered, and the crew of the small boat disembarked.

And there was no doubt that this was indeed Tabor Island, since, according to the most recent maps, there were no other islands in that part of the Pacific between New Zealand and the American coast.

The boat was securely tied up, so that the ebbing tide could not carry it away; then, Pencroff and his two companions, after arming themselves well, climbed the shore to reach a sort of cone, two hundred fifty to three hundred feet high, which rose half a mile away.

"From the top of this hill," said Gideon Spilett, "we will surely have a general view of the islet, which will facilitate our search.

— It's just like what Mr. Cyrus did first on Lincoln Island when he climbed Mount Franklin," replied Harbert.

— Exactly," replied the reporter, "and it's the best way to proceed!"

While chatting, the explorers advanced along the edge of a meadow that ended at the foot of the cone itself. Flocks of rock pigeons and sea swallows, similar to those from Lincoln Island, flew before them. In the woods lining the meadow to the left, they heard rustlings in the underbrush, they caught glimpses of moving grasses indicating the presence of very wary animals; but nothing so far indicated that the islet was inhabited.

Upon reaching the foot of the cone, Pencroff, Harbert, and Gideon Spilett climbed it in no time, and their gazes swept across the horizon.

They were indeed on an islet measuring no more than six miles in circumference, with a perimeter that was little fringed with caps or promontories, not much indented by bays or creeks, giving it the shape of an elongated oval. All around, the sea, completely deserted, extended to the horizons. There was not a piece of land, not a sail in sight! This small island, covered entirely in forest, didn't have the varied appearance of Lincoln Island, which was dry and wild in some parts but fertile and rich in others. Here, it was a uniform mass of greenery, dominated by two or three low hills. A stream flowed diagonally through a wide meadow and emptied into the sea on the western coast through a narrow outlet.

"The area is small," said Harbert.

"Yes," replied Pencroff, "it would be a bit small for us!"

"And on top of that," said the reporter, "it seems uninhabited."

"Indeed," replied Harbert, "there's nothing here to indicate the presence of humans."

"Let's go down," said Pencroff, "and look around."

The sailor and his two companions returned to the shore at the spot where they had left the Bonadventure. They decided to walk around the island before venturing inland, so as not to miss any spot in their investigation.

The shore was easy to follow, and only in a few places were large rocks in their way, which could be easily navigated around. The explorers headed south, causing flocks of water birds and herds of seals to rush into the sea as soon as they spotted them.

"Those creatures," observed the reporter, "aren't seeing humans for the first time. They're scared of us, so they know us."

An hour after setting off, the three arrived at the southern tip of the island, finished off by a sharp cape, and they headed north along the western coast, which was also made of sand and rocks, bordered in the background by thick woods.

There was no sign of habitation anywhere, no footprint of a human, and after four hours of walking, they had completely circled the island. It was quite extraordinary and made one wonder if Tabor Island was not, or was no longer, inhabited. Perhaps, after all, the document was several months or even years old, and in that case, it was possible that the castaway had been rescued or had died from misery.

Pencroff, Gideon Spilett, and Harbert, forming more or less plausible hypotheses, quickly dined aboard the Bonadventure, so as to resume their excursion and continue until nightfall. They did so at five o'clock in the evening, at which time they ventured into the woods. Many animals fled at their approach, mainly, one could say exclusively, goats and pigs, which, it was easy to see, belonged to European species. Surely some whaling ship had dropped them off on the island, where they had quickly multiplied.

Harbert promised himself to catch one or two pairs alive to take back to Lincoln Island.

It was thus no longer in doubt that humans had visited this island at some point. This became even more evident when they saw paths cleared through the forest, tree trunks felled by an axe, and everywhere the signs of human work; but those trees, rotting away, had been down for many years, the axe marks velvety with moss, and tall, thick grass grew through the paths, making them difficult to recognize.

"But," observed Gideon Spilett, "this proves that not only humans have landed on this island, but that they lived here for some time. Now, who were these people? How many were there? How many are left?"

"The document," said Harbert, "only mentions a single castaway."

"Well, if he's still on the island," replied Pencroff, "it's impossible that we won't find him!"

The exploration continued. The sailor and his companions naturally followed the path that cut diagonally across the island, and thus they came to the stream that headed toward the sea.

If the European animals and some signs of human handiwork undeniably demonstrated that man had already come to this island, several samples of the plant kingdom did not prove any less. In certain places, in the middle of clearings, it was evident that the land had been planted with vegetable crops long ago. So, what joy Harbert felt when he recognized potatoes, chicory, sorrel, carrots, cabbages, and turnips, from which it would be enough to gather seeds to enrich the soil of Lincoln Island!

"Good! Great!" replied Pencroff. "This will suit Nab and us just fine. So, if we don't find the castaway, then at least our trip won't have been useless, and God will have rewarded us!"

"Of course," replied Gideon Spilett; "but looking at the state of these fields, one can fear that the island has not been inhabited for a long time."

"Indeed," replied Harbert, "a resident, whoever he was, would not have neglected such an important cultivation!"

"Yes!" said Pencroff, "this castaway is gone! ... that's to be assumed..."

"So we must accept that the document is already dated?"

"Clearly."

"And that this bottle only arrived at Lincoln Island after having floated at sea for a long time?"

"Why not?" replied Pencroff. "— but look, night is coming," he added, "and I think it's better to suspend our search."

"Let's go back aboard, and tomorrow we'll start again," said the reporter.

That was the wisest course to take, and the advice was about to be followed when Harbert, pointing to a confusing mass among the trees, exclaimed, "A dwelling!" Immediately, the three headed toward the indicated dwelling. In the twilight, it was possible to see that it had been built of planks covered with a thick tarred cloth.

The half-closed door was pushed open by Pencroff, who entered quickly ... the dwelling was empty!

🦋 14 🦋

Pencroff, Harbert, and Gideon Spilett remained silent in the darkness.

Pencroff called out loudly. No reply came.

The sailor then struck a match and lit a twig. This light briefly illuminated a small room, which seemed to be completely abandoned. At the back was a rough fireplace, with some cold ashes supporting a bundle of dry wood. Pencroff tossed the burning twig into it, the wood crackled, and gave a bright glow.

Then the sailor and his two companions saw a messy bed, with damp and yellowed blankets proving that it hadn't been used in a long time; in one corner of the fireplace, two kettles covered in rust and an overturned pot; a cupboard with a few half-moldy sailor clothes; on the table, a tin plate and a bible ruined by dampness; in a corner, a few tools, a shovel, a pick, a chisel, two hunting rifles, one of which was broken; on a board serving as a shelf, a barrel of powder still intact, a lead barrel, and several boxes of ammunition; all covered by a thick layer of dust, perhaps accumulated over many years.

"There's no one here," said the reporter.

"No one!" replied Pencroff.

"This room hasn't been inhabited in a long time," noted Harbert.

"Yes, a long time!" replied the reporter.

"Mr. Spilett," then said Pencroff, "instead of returning aboard, I think it's better to spend the night in this dwelling."

"You're right, Pencroff," replied Gideon Spilett, "and if its owner comes back, well! He may not complain to find his space taken!"

"He won't come back!" said the sailor, shaking his head.

"Do you think he left the island?" asked the reporter.

"If he had left the island, he would have taken his weapons and tools," replied Pencroff. "You know the value castaways place on these items, which are the last remnants of a shipwreck. No! no!" repeated the sailor with conviction, "no! He hasn't left the island! If he'd escaped on a boat made by him, he would have abandoned these essentials even less! No, he is on the island!"

"Alive?" asked Harbert.

"Alive or dead. But if he is dead, he didn't bury himself, I suppose," replied Pencroff, "and we will at least find his remains!"

It was agreed to spend the night in the abandoned dwelling, as a supply of wood found in one corner would allow for adequate warmth. With the door closed, Pencroff, Harbert, and Gideon Spilett, sitting on a bench, remained there, talking little but thinking a lot. They were in a state of mind to assume everything, as to await everything, and they listened intently to the sounds outside. If the door had suddenly opened and a man had appeared before them, they would not have been any less surprised, despite everything this place revealed of abandonment, and they had their hands ready to shake hands with this man, this castaway, this unknown friend whom friends awaited!

But no sound was heard, the door did not open, and the hours passed in this manner. How long that night seemed to the sailor and his two companions! Only Harbert had slept for two hours, for at his age, sleep is a need. All three were eager to resume their exploration from the previous day and to search this island down to its deepest corners! The conclusions drawn by Pencroff were absolutely correct, and it was almost certain that, since the house was abandoned and the tools, utensils, and weapons were still there, this resident had succumbed. Therefore, it was appropriate to search for his remains and at least give him a Christian burial.

Daylight appeared. Pencroff and his companions immediately set about examining the dwelling. It had indeed been built in a fortunate location, at the foot of a small hill sheltered by five or six magnificent gum trees. In front of its facade and through the trees, an axe had cleared a large opening, allowing the gaze to stretch over the sea. A small lawn, surrounded by a decaying wooden fence, led to the shore, where the stream opened on the left.

This dwelling had been constructed from planks, and it was easy to see that these planks came from the hull or deck of a ship. It was therefore likely that a disabled vessel had run aground on the island, that at least one member of the crew had been saved, and that with the ship's debris and tools at his disposal, this man had built this home.

This became even clearer when Gideon Spilett, after walking around the dwelling, saw on a board—probably one of those that formed the sides of the shipwreck—these letters already half-faded: Br.tan.. a

"Britannia!" cried Pencroff, whom the reporter had called to, "that's a name common to many ships, and I couldn't say whether this one was English or American!"

"Doesn't matter, Pencroff!"

"Doesn't matter, indeed," replied the sailor, "and if the survivor of its crew is still alive, we will save him, whatever country he comes from! But before we resume our exploration, let's return to the Bonadventure first!"

A sort of anxiety had taken hold of Pencroff regarding his boat. What if the island was inhabited, and some resident had seized it... but he shrugged at this implausible assumption.

Still, the sailor was not displeased to go have lunch aboard. The route, already marked, was not long—barely a mile.

They set off again, keeping an eye out through the woods and thickets, through which goats and pigs fled by the hundreds.

Twenty minutes after leaving the dwelling, Pencroff and his companions saw the eastern coast of the island and the Bonadventure, safely anchored, firmly biting into the sand. Pencroff could not contain a sigh of satisfaction.

After all, this boat was his child, and a father's right is to be more anxious than necessary.

They went back aboard, had lunch, aiming to need only a late dinner; then, after the meal, the exploration was resumed and conducted with the utmost care.

In summary, it was very probable that the only inhabitant of the island had perished. Therefore, it was rather a dead man than a living one whom Pencroff and his companions sought to find traces of! But their searches were in vain, and for half the day they searched in vain through those masses of trees that covered the island. They had to admit that, if the castaway had died, there was no longer any trace of his corpse, and that some beast, no doubt, had devoured him down to the last bone.

"We will set off tomorrow at dawn," said Pencroff to his two companions, who, around two o'clock in the afternoon, lay down in the shade of a cluster of pines to rest for a while.

"I believe we can without scruple take the utensils that belonged to the cast-away, right?" added Harbert.

"I think so too," replied Gideon Spilett, "and these weapons and tools will complete the supplies at Granite House. If I'm not mistaken, the reserve of powder and lead is significant."

"Yes," replied Pencroff, "but let's not forget to capture one or two pairs of those pigs, of which Lincoln Island is devoid…"

"Nor to gather these seeds," added Harbert, "which will give us all the vegetables from both the old and new continents."

"It might be advisable then," said the reporter, "to stay one more day on Tabor Island to collect everything that may be useful to us."

"No, Mr. Spilett," replied Pencroff, "and I'll ask you to leave at dawn. The wind seems to be tending toward the west, and after having favorable winds to come here, we'll have favorable winds to leave."

"Then let's not waste time!" said Harbert, getting up.

"Let's not waste time," replied Pencroff. "You, Harbert, take care of collecting those seeds, which you know better than we do. Meanwhile, Mr. Spilett and I will go hunting for pigs, and even in Top's absence, I hope we'll manage to catch a few!"

Harbert headed off along the path that would bring him back to the cultivated part of the island, while the sailor and the reporter went directly into the forest.

Many samples of the pig species fled before them, and these animals, remarkably agile, did not seem inclined to let themselves be approached.

However, after half an hour of chasing, the hunters managed to catch a pair that had hidden in a thick thicket when cries echoed a few hundred steps to the north of the island. These cries were mingled with horrible croaks that had nothing human about them.

Pencroff and Gideon Spilett stood up, and the pigs took advantage of this movement to flee just as the sailor was preparing ropes to tie them.

"That's Harbert's voice!" said the reporter.

"Let's run!" cried Pencroff.

And immediately the sailor and Gideon Spilett set off at full speed toward the source of those cries. They were right to hurry because, at the bend of the path near a clearing, they saw a young boy overpowered by a wild being, probably a giant monkey, who was going to harm him.

To jump on the monster, tackle it in turn, wrench Harbert away, and then hold him tightly; it took only a moment for Pencroff and Gédéon Spilett. The sailor had Herculean strength, and the reporter was also very sturdy. Despite the monster's resistance, it was securely tied up so it could no longer move.

"Are you hurt, Harbert?" Gédéon Spilett asked.

"No! No!"

"Ah! If that monkey had hurt you!" Pencroff exclaimed.

"But it's not a monkey!" Harbert replied.

At these words, Pencroff and Gédéon Spilett then looked at the strange being lying on the ground. In truth, it was not a monkey! It was a human creature; it was a man! But what a man! A savage, in the most horrible sense of the word, and all the more terrifying because it seemed to have fallen to the lowest degree of stupidity!

With bristling hair, an unkempt beard reaching down to his chest, a nearly naked body except for a tattered piece of covering around his waist, fierce eyes, enormous hands, excessively long nails, skin as dark as mahogany, feet hardened as if made of horn: such was the miserable creature who, despite everything, had to be called a man!

But one really had the right to wonder if there was still a soul in that body, or if only the common instinct of a beast had survived in him!

"Are you sure he's a man, or that he ever was?" Pencroff asked the reporter.

"Alas! There's no doubt about it," he replied.

"So this must be the castaway?" Harbert suggested.

"Yes," Gédéon Spilett answered, "but the unfortunate man is no longer human!"

The reporter was right. It was clear that if the castaway had ever been a civilized being, isolation had turned him into a savage, and worse, perhaps a true wild man. Harsh sounds emerged from his throat between teeth that were sharp like those of carnivores, made only for tearing raw flesh. Memory must have abandoned him long ago, and for a long time, he no longer knew how to use his tools or his weapons; he no longer knew how to make fire! It was evident that he was agile and flexible, but that all his physical qualities had developed at the expense of moral qualities!

Gédéon Spilett spoke to him. He did not seem to understand, nor even to hear... Yet, looking closely into his eyes, the reporter thought he saw that all reason was not extinguished in him.

However, the prisoner did not struggle, nor did he try to break his bonds. Was he paralyzed by the presence of these men who had once been like him? Was he recalling some fleeting memory in a corner of his brain that was bringing him back to humanity? If free, would he have tried to escape, or would he have stayed? No one knew, but they did not put it to the test, and after observing the miserable creature with great care:

"Whoever he is, Gédéon Spilett said, whatever he has been and whatever he may become, our duty is to bring him back with us to Lincoln Island!"

"Yes! Yes!" agreed Harbert, "and maybe with care we'll awaken some spark of intelligence in him!"

"The soul does not die," the reporter said, "and it would be a great satisfaction to rescue this creature of God from his degradation!"

Pencroff shook his head in doubt.

"We have to try, at any rate," the reporter replied, "and humanity commands us to do so."

It was indeed their duty as civilized and Christian beings. All three understood this, and they knew well that Cyrus Smith would approve of their actions.

"Shall we leave him bound?" the sailor asked.

"Maybe he would walk if we untied his feet?" Harbert suggested.

"Let's try," Pencroff replied.

The ropes that bound the prisoner's feet were untied, but his arms remained firmly secured. He stood up by himself and showed no desire to flee. His dry eyes shot an intense look at the three men walking beside him, and nothing indicated that he remembered being similar to them or even that he ever had been. A continuous whistling escaped from his lips, and his appearance was fierce, but he did not attempt to resist. On the reporter's advice, this unfortunate man was taken back to his home. Perhaps the sight of the objects that belonged to him would make some impression on him!

Perhaps all it would take was a spark to revive his obscured thoughts, to rekindle his extinguished soul!

The dwelling was not far. In a few minutes, they all arrived, but there, the prisoner recognized nothing, and it seemed he had lost awareness of everything! What could one conjecture about the degree of degradation to which this miserable being had fallen, except that his imprisonment on the islet had been long-standing, and that after arriving there in a rational state, isolation had reduced him to such a condition?

The reporter then had the idea that seeing fire might have an effect on him, and in an instant, one of those beautiful flames that attract even animals lit up the hearth.

The sight of the flame seemed initially to capture the attention of the unfortunate man, but soon he recoiled, and his unseeing gaze extinguished.

Evidently, there was nothing to be done for the moment, at least, except to take him back on board the Bonadventure, which was done, and there he remained under Pencroff's watch.

Harbert and Gédéon Spilett returned to the islet to finish their operations, and a few hours later, they returned to the shore carrying utensils, weapons, a harvest of vegetable seeds, some pieces of game, and two pairs of pigs. Everything was loaded, and the Bonadventure was ready to set sail as soon as the tide rose the next morning.

The prisoner had been placed in the fore cabin, where he remained calm, silent, deaf, and mute all at once.

Pencroff offered him food, but he rejected the cooked meat that was presented to him and that undoubtedly no longer suited him. Indeed, when the sailor showed him one of the ducks that Harbert had killed, he lunged at it with bestial greed and devoured it.

"Do you think he will recover?" Pencroff said, shaking his head.

"Maybe," the reporter replied. "It's not impossible that our care will eventually have an effect on him, because it is isolation that has made him what he is, and he will no longer be alone from now on!"

"Surely the poor man has been in this state for a long time!" said Harbert.

"Perhaps," Gédéon Spilett replied.

"How old can he be?" the young boy asked.

"That is hard to say," the reporter answered, "because it is impossible to see his features under the thick beard covering his face, but he is no longer young, and I suppose he must be at least fifty."

"Did you notice, Mr. Spilett, how deeply his eyes are set under their brow?" the young boy asked.

"Yes, Harbert, but I add that they look more human than one would be tempted to believe from his appearance."

"Anyway, we will see," replied Pencroff, "and I am curious to learn what Mr. Smith will think of our savage. We went to find a human creature, and we are bringing back a monster! Well, we do what we can!"

The night passed, and whether the prisoner slept or not is unknown, but in any case, although he had been untied, he did not move. He was like those wild animals who are overwhelmed in the early moments of captivity and who later rage. At dawn the next day — October 15 — the change in weather that Pencroff had predicted occurred. The wind had shifted to the northwest, favoring the return of the Bonadventure; but at the same time, it was getting colder and would make navigation more difficult.

At five in the morning, the anchor was lifted. Pencroff took in a reef in his main sail and set course to east-northeast, aiming to sail directly towards Lincoln Island.

The first day of the crossing was uneventful. The prisoner remained calm in the forward cabin, and since he had been a sailor, it seemed that the movements of the sea had a sort of beneficial reaction on him.

Could some memory of his former occupation be returning to him? In any case, he was quiet, more astonished than beaten.

The next day — October 16 — the wind picked up considerably, moving further north, and therefore in a direction less favorable to the Bonadventure's journey, which was bouncing on the waves. Pencroff soon had to sail as close as possible, and without saying anything, he began to worry about the state of the sea, which was crashing violently against the front of his vessel.

Certainly, if the wind did not change, it would take longer to reach Lincoln Island than it had taken to reach Tabor Island. Indeed, by the morning of the 17th, it had been forty-eight hours since the Bonadventure had set out, and there was no indication that it was near the island. It was impossible, moreover, to estimate the route covered, as the direction and speed had been too erratic.

Twenty-four hours later, there was still no land in sight. The wind was completely against them then and the sea terrible. They had to maneuver rapidly the sails of the boat, which were covered by large waves, take in reefs, and often change courses, going from tack to tack. It even happened that on the 18th, the Bonadventure was completely swamped by a wave, and if its passengers had not taken the precaution to tie themselves on deck in advance, they would have been swept away.

On this occasion, Pencroff and his companions, very busy freeing themselves, received unexpected help from the prisoner, who rushed up through the hatch as if his instinct as a sailor took over, and broke the guardrails with a strong swing of a spar to let the water draining faster off the deck; then, once the boat was cleared, without saying a word, he returned to his cabin.

Pencroff, Gédéon Spilett, and Harbert, absolutely amazed, left him to act.

However, the situation was dire, and the sailor had reason to believe he was lost on this vast sea, with no possibility of finding his way!

The night of the 18th to the 19th was dark and cold. However, around eleven o'clock, the wind calmed, the swell subsided, and the Bonadventure, no longer shaking, gained more speed. Besides, it had remarkably weathered the storm.

Neither Pencroff, nor Gédéon Spilett, nor Harbert thought of taking even an hour of sleep. They remained alert with extreme care because either Lincoln Island could not be far away, and they would know at daybreak, or the Bonadventure, carried by currents, had drifted downwind, making it almost impossible to correct its course.

Pencroff, extremely worried, did not, however, despair, for he had a strong spirit, and while seated at the helm, he stubbornly sought to pierce the thick darkness that enveloped him.

Around two in the morning, he suddenly stood up:

"A fire! A fire!" he shouted.

And indeed, a bright light appeared twenty miles to the northeast. Lincoln Island was there, and this light, evidently lit by Cyrus Smith, showed the way to follow.

Pencroff, who was far too far north, adjusted his course and set a heading toward the fire that shone above the horizon like a bright star.

❧ 15 ❧

The next day — October 20 — at seven in the morning, after four days of travel, the Bonadventure gently grounded on the shore at the mouth of the Mercy.

Cyrus Smith and Nab, very worried about the bad weather and the prolonged absence of their companions, had climbed to the Grande Vue plateau at dawn, and had finally spotted the boat that had taken so long to return!

"Thank God! They're here!" Cyrus Smith exclaimed.

As for Nab, in his joy, he started dancing, spinning around clapping his hands and shouting: "Oh! My master!" a more touching pantomime than the most beautiful speech!

The first thought of the engineer, when counting the people he could see on the Bonadventure's deck, was that Pencroff had not found the castaway from Tabor Island or that, at least, this unfortunate man had refused to leave his island and change his prison for another.

And indeed, Pencroff, Gédéon Spilett, and Harbert were the only ones on the Bonadventure's deck. When the boat docked, the engineer and Nab awaited them on the shore, and before the passengers had jumped onto the sand, Cyrus Smith said to them:

"We have been very worried about your delay, my friends! Did something happen to you?"

"No," replied Gédéon Spilett, "and everything went wonderfully, on the contrary. We will tell you all about it."

"However," the engineer continued, "you failed in your search, since it's just the three of you as when you set off?"

"Excuse me, Mr. Cyrus," replied the sailor, "we are four!"

"You found that castaway?"

"Yes."

"And you brought him back?"

"Yes."

"Alive?"

"Yes."

"Where is he? What is he like?"

"It's," the reporter replied, "or rather it was a man! That's all we can tell you, Cyrus!"

The engineer was immediately briefed on what had happened during the journey. They told him under what conditions the search had been conducted, how the only dwelling on the islet had been long abandoned, and finally how they had captured a castaway who seemed no longer to belong to the human species.

"And it is to such a point," Pencroff added, "that I don't know if we did the right thing bringing him here."

"Certainly, you did the right thing, Pencroff!" the engineer replied swiftly.

"But this poor man has lost his reason?"

"Now, it's possible," Cyrus Smith replied, "but just a few months ago, this unfortunate was a man like you and me. And who knows what the last survivor of us would become after a long solitude on that island? Woe to the one who is alone, my friends, and we must believe that isolation can quickly destroy reason, since you found this poor being in such a state!"

"But, Mr. Cyrus," Harbert asked, "what leads you to believe that the degradation of this unfortunate has only been recent?"

"Because the document we found had been written recently," the engineer replied, "and that only the castaway could have written that document."

"Unless," Gédéon Spilett pointed out, "it was written by a companion of that man, who has since died."

"That is impossible, my dear Spilett."

"Why so?" asked the reporter.

"Because the document would have mentioned two castaways," Cyrus Smith replied, "and it only speaks of one."Harbert quickly summarized the events of the crossing and emphasized the curious fact of a sort of temporary resurrection that had occurred in the prisoner's mind when, for a moment, he had reverted to being a sailor in the midst of the storm.

"Well, Harbert," replied the engineer, "you're right to place great importance on this fact. This unfortunate person must not be beyond hope, and it's despair that has made him what he is. But here, he will find his kind, and since he still has a soul within him, we will save that soul!"

The shipwrecked man from Tabor Island, to the great pity of the engineer and the astonishment of Nab, was then taken out of the cabin he occupied at the front of the Bonadventure, and once on the ground, he initially showed a desire to flee.

But Cyrus Smith approached him, placing a hand on his shoulder with a gesture of authority, and looked at him with infinite kindness. Immediately, the unfortunate man, feeling an instant of domination, gradually calmed down, his eyes lowered, his forehead bowed, and he no longer offered any resistance.

"Poor abandoned soul!" murmured the engineer.

Cyrus Smith had observed him closely. Judging by his appearance, this miserable creature seemed no longer human, yet Cyrus Smith, just as the reporter had before, noticed a fleeting glimmer of intelligence in his gaze.

It was decided that the abandoned man, or rather the stranger, as his new companions would now call him, would remain in one of the rooms of Granite House, where he could not escape anyway. He allowed himself to be led there without difficulty, and with good care, it was hoped that one day he would become another companion for the settlers of Lincoln Island.

During lunch, which Nab had hurried, as the reporter, Harbert, and Pencroff were famished, Cyrus Smith asked to hear all the details of the incidents that had marked the exploration trip to the islet.

He agreed with his friends on the point that the stranger must be either English or American, as the name Britannia suggested, and moreover, through his wild beard and shaggy hair, the engineer thought he recognized the distinctive features of an Anglo-Saxon.

"But, by the way," said Gideon Spilett to Harbert, "you didn't tell us how you met this savage; and we know nothing except that he would have strangled you if we hadn't arrived in time to save you!"

"Indeed," replied Harbert, "I would be hard-pressed to recount what happened. I was, I believe, occupied with my plant gathering when I heard what sounded like an avalanche falling from a very tall tree. I barely had time to turn around... this poor man, who was probably hiding in a tree, had leaped at me in less time than it takes to tell you, and if Mr. Spilett and Pencroff hadn't..."

"My child!" said Cyrus Smith, "you faced a real danger, but perhaps without that, this poor being would have always eluded your searches, and we would not have one more companion."

"So you hope, Cyrus, to make him a man again?" asked the reporter.

"Yes," replied the engineer.

Once lunch was over, Cyrus Smith and his companions left Granite House and returned to the shore.

Then the unloading of the Bonadventure took place, and after examining the weapons and tools, the engineer saw nothing that would help him identify the stranger.

The capture of the pigs on the islet was viewed as very beneficial for Lincoln Island, and these animals were taken to the stables, where they were expected to acclimate easily.

The two barrels containing powder and lead, as well as the packets of fuses, were well received. They even agreed to establish a small powder magazine, either outside Granite House or in the upper cave, where there would be no risk of explosion. However, the use of pyroxyl should continue, as this substance yielded excellent results, and there was no reason to replace it with ordinary powder.

When the unloading of the boat was finished:

"Mr. Cyrus," said Pencroff, "I think it would be wise to put our Bonadventure in a safe place."

"Isn't it properly at the mouth of the Mercy?" asked Cyrus Smith.

"No, Mr. Cyrus," replied the sailor. "Half the time, it's stuck in the sand, and that's tiring for it. It's a good boat, you see, and it performed admirably during that storm that hit us so violently on the return."

"Can't we keep it afloat in the river itself?"

"Of course, Mr. Cyrus, we could, but this mouth offers no shelter, and with east winds, I believe the Bonadventure would suffer greatly from the waves."

"Well, where do you want to put it, Pencroff?"

"At Balloon Port," replied the sailor. "This little creek, sheltered by the rocks, seems to me just the harbor it needs."

"Isn't it a bit far?"

"Nonsense! It's no more than three miles from Granite House, and we have a lovely straight road to take us there!"

"Go ahead, Pencroff, and take your Bonadventure," replied the engineer, "but I would prefer it under our more immediate supervision. It will need a little port when we have time."

"Great!" exclaimed Pencroff. "A port with a lighthouse, a pier, and a dry dock! Ah! Truly, with you, Mr. Cyrus, everything becomes too easy!"

"Yes, my brave Pencroff," replied the engineer, "but on the condition that you help me, because you're pretty much three-quarters of all our work!"

Harbert and the sailor then reboarded the Bonadventure, its anchor was raised, the sail was hoisted, and the offshore wind quickly guided it to Grip Cape. Two hours later, it rested on the calm waters of Balloon Port.

During the first days that the stranger spent at Granite House, did he show any signs that his wild nature had changed? Was there a more intense light shining from the depths of his clouded mind? Was his soul, at last, returning to his body?

Yes, surely, to such an extent that Cyrus Smith and the reporter wondered if the unfortunate man's reason had ever been completely extinguished.

At first, accustomed to the open air and the limitless freedom he enjoyed on Tabor Island, the stranger exhibited some violent outbursts, and it had to be feared that he might throw himself out of one of the windows of Granite House. But gradually, he calmed down, and they were able to allow him some freedom of movement.

There was thus hope, and much of it. Already, forgetting his predatory instincts, the stranger accepted a less savage food than he had consumed on the islet, and cooked meat no longer produced the feeling of disgust in him as it had aboard the Bonadventure.

Cyrus Smith had taken advantage of a moment while he was sleeping to cut his wild hair and beard, which formed a sort of mane and gave him such a savage appearance. He also dressed him more appropriately after removing the rag of fabric that covered him.

As a result, thanks to this care, the stranger regained a human appearance, and it even seemed that his eyes had returned to a softer state. Certainly, when intelligence had once illuminated his face, this man must have had a certain kind of beauty.

Every day, Cyrus Smith made it a task to spend a few hours in his company. He would work near him and engage him in various activities to capture his focus.

It could indeed be enough, with just a flash, to rekindle that soul or a memory to traverse that brain to recall reason. They had seen this clearly during the storm aboard the Bonadventure!

The engineer also made sure to speak aloud, aiming to reach the depths of that dazed intelligence through both hearing and sight. Sometimes one of his companions would join him, sometimes another, and occasionally all of them together. They mostly talked about things related to the sea, which were meant to touch a sailor's heart more deeply. At times, the stranger seemed to lend a vague attention to what was being said, and the settlers soon came to the belief that he partially understood them. Sometimes even the expression on his face was profoundly painful, a sign that he suffered internally; for his countenance could not deceive that much; yet he did not speak, although on various occasions, it seemed that some words were about to escape his lips.

In any case, the poor being remained calm and sad! But was his calm merely an appearance?

Was his sadness simply the consequence of his confinement? Nothing could be affirmed yet.

Seeing only certain objects and in a limited field, constantly in contact with the settlers to whom he would eventually get used, having no desires to satisfy, better nourished, better clothed, it was natural that his physical nature would gradually change; but had he immersed himself in a new life, or to use a term that could rightly apply to him, had he merely been tamed like an animal towards its master? This was an important question that Cyrus Smith was eager to resolve, yet he did not want to hasten his patient!

To him, the stranger was just a sick man! Would he ever be a convalescent? Thus, the engineer observed him at all times!

How he watched for his soul, if one could put it that way!

How ready he was to seize it!

The settlers followed with sincere emotion all the phases of this cure undertaken by Cyrus Smith.

They also helped him in this act of humanity, and all, except perhaps the skeptical Pencroff, soon began to share his hope and faith.

The stranger's calm was deep, as mentioned, and he showed a kind of attachment to the engineer, whose influence he was visibly under.

Cyrus Smith thus resolved to test him by moving him to a different environment, in front of that ocean that his eyes had once been accustomed to gaze upon, on the edge of those forests that should remind him of those where he had spent so many years of his life!

"But," said Gideon Spilett, "can we hope that if set free, he won't escape?"

"It's an experiment to be made," replied the engineer.

"Good!" said Pencroff. "When that fella gets some space before him and feels the open air, he'll take off in a flash!"

"I don't think so," replied Cyrus Smith.

"Let's try," said Gideon Spilett.

"Let's try," replied the engineer.

That day was October 30, and thus the shipwrecked man from Tabor Island had been imprisoned at Granite House for nine days. It was warm, and a beautiful sun was shining on the island.

Cyrus Smith and Pencroff went to the room occupied by the stranger, whom they found lying by the window, gazing at the sky.

"Come on, my friend," said the engineer.

The stranger immediately got up. His eyes fixed on Cyrus Smith, and he followed him, while the sailor walked behind him, quite unsure of the outcome of the experiment.

Arriving at the door, Cyrus Smith and Pencroff placed him in the elevator, while Nab, Harbert, and Gideon Spilett waited for them at the bottom of Granite House. The basket descended, and within moments, they were all united on the shore.

The settlers moved slightly away from the stranger so as to give him some space.

He took a few steps toward the sea, and his gaze sparkled with intense animation, but he made no attempt to escape. He watched the small waves that, broken by the islet, came to die on the sand.

"It's still only the sea," observed Gideon Spilett, "and it's possible that it doesn't inspire him with the desire to flee!"

"Yes," replied Cyrus Smith, "we need to take him to the plateau, at the edge of the forest. There, the experience will be more telling.

"Besides, he won't be able to escape," Nab noted, "since the bridges are up."

"Oh!" exclaimed Pencroff, "that's a man to be troubled by a creek like the glycerine creek! He could easily jump over it in a single bound!"

"We'll see," was all Cyrus Smith replied, his eyes never leaving the stranger's.

The stranger was then led to the mouth of the Mercy, and all of them, walking up the left bank of the river, made their way to the Grande-vue plateau.

Upon reaching the spot where the first beautiful trees of the forest grew, and with the breeze gently stirring the foliage, the stranger seemed to drink in with delight the penetrating scent that filled the air, and a long sigh escaped from his chest!

The settlers stood back, ready to restrain him if he made a move to escape!

And indeed, the poor soul was about to leap into the creek that separated him from the forest, and his legs relaxed for a moment like a spring... but almost immediately, he folded back into himself, sagged halfway down, and a large tear rolled from his eyes!

"Ah!" cried Cyrus Smith, "so you have become a man again, for you weep!"

16

Yes! The unfortunate man had cried! Some memory, no doubt, had crossed his mind, and, in Cyrus Smith's words, he had returned to being a man through tears.

The settlers left him on the plateau for some time and even moved a bit away to give him a sense of freedom; but he did not think at all of taking advantage of this freedom, and Cyrus Smith soon decided to take him back to Granite House. Two days after this scene, the stranger seemed to want to gradually blend into common life. It was evident that he heard and understood, but equally evident that he displayed a strange stubbornness in not speaking to the settlers, for one evening, Pencroff, listening at the door of his room, heard him mutter: "No! Here! Me! Never!"

The sailor reported these words to his companions.

"There's a painful mystery there!" said Cyrus Smith.

The stranger had begun to use gardening tools and was working in the vegetable garden. When he paused in his work, which happened often, he remained as if concentrated within himself; however, on the engineer's recommendation, they respected the isolation he seemed to want to maintain. If one of the settlers approached him, he would retreat, and sobs would rise in his chest, as if it were too full!

Could it be that remorse was weighing so heavily on him?

One could believe so, and Gideon Spilett could not help but make this observation one day:

"If he doesn't speak, it's because he has, I believe, things that are too serious to say!"

Patience was necessary, and one had to wait. A few days later, on November 3, the stranger, working on the plateau, had stopped after letting his spade fall to the ground, and Cyrus Smith, who was observing him from a short distance, once again saw tears streaming from his eyes. An irresistible feeling of pity led him towards him, and he lightly touched his arm.

"My friend?" he said. The stranger tried to avoid him, and when Cyrus Smith reached out to take his hand, he quickly stepped back.

"My friend," Cyrus Smith said firmly, "look at me, I command you!"

The stranger looked at the engineer and seemed to be under his influence, like a person under hypnosis. He wanted to escape. But then there was a transformation in his expression. His eyes flashed with intensity. Words struggled to escape his lips. He could no longer contain himself!... finally, he crossed his arms and in a low voice asked,

"Who are you?" he asked Cyrus Smith.

"We are shipwrecked like you," the engineer replied, deeply moved. "We brought you here, among your kind."

"My kind!... I have none!"

"You are among friends..."

"Friends!... To me! Friends!" the stranger cried, covering his head with his hands... no... never... let me be! Let me be!"

Then he fled toward the plateau overlooking the sea, where he remained motionless for a long time.

Cyrus Smith rejoined his companions and told them what had just happened.

"Yes! There is a mystery in the life of this man," said Gideon Spilett, "and it seems that he has returned to humanity only through remorse."

"I don't quite know what kind of man we've brought back," said the sailor. "He has secrets..."

"Which we will respect," Cyrus Smith replied. "If he has committed some fault, he has cruelly atoned for it, and in our eyes, he is absolved."

For two hours, the stranger remained alone on the beach, obviously under the influence of memories that were bringing back his past — a wretched past, no doubt — and the colonists, without losing sight of him, did not attempt to disturb his solitude.

However, after two hours, he seemed to reach a decision and came to find Cyrus Smith. His eyes were red from the tears he had shed, but he was no longer crying. His whole demeanor was marked by profound humility. He appeared timid and ashamed, trying to make himself small, and his gaze was constantly turned down towards the ground.

"Sir," he said to Cyrus Smith, "are you and your companions English?"

"No," replied the engineer, "we are Americans."

"Ah!" said the stranger, and he murmured,

"I prefer that!

"And you, my friend?" asked the engineer.

"English," he replied hastily.

And as if those few words weighed heavily on him, he walked away from the shore, traversing it from the waterfall to the mouth of the Mercy, in a state of extreme agitation.

Then, at one point, he passed by Harbert, stopped, and in a strangled voice asked,

"What month is it?"

"December," replied Harbert.

"What year?"

"1866."

"Twelve years! Twelve years!" he exclaimed.

Then he abruptly left him.

Harbert reported back to the colonists the questions and responses he had received.

"This unfortunate man," noted Gideon Spilett, "has not been in tune with the months or the years!

"Yes," added Harbert, "and he has already been on the islet for twelve years when we found him there!"

"Twelve years!" replied Cyrus Smith. "Ah! Twelve years of isolation, after perhaps a cursed existence, can certainly affect a man's reason!"

"I tend to believe," then said Pencroff, "that this man did not arrive on Tabor Island by shipwreck, but that following some crime, he was abandoned there."

"You must be right, Pencroff," replied the reporter, "and if that's the case, it's not impossible that those who left him on the island might come back for him one day!"

"And they won't find him," said Harbert.

"But then," Pencroff replied, "we would have to return, and..."

"My friends," said Cyrus Smith, "let's not discuss this question until we know what we are dealing with. I believe this poor man has suffered, that he has atoned for his faults, whatever they may be, and that the need to pour out his heart is overwhelming him. Let's not provoke him into telling us his story! He will tell us in time, and when we know it, we will see what action is best to take. Only he can tell us if he has kept more than hope — the certainty of being repatriated one day, but I doubt it!"

"And why is that?" asked the reporter.

"Because if he were sure of being rescued in a set amount of time, he would have waited for the hour of his deliverance and would not have thrown that document into the sea. No, it's more probable that he was condemned to die on that islet and was never meant to see his kind again!"

"But," the sailor observed, "there's one thing I cannot explain."

"What is it?"

"If this man has been abandoned on Tabor Island for twelve years, one can well suppose that he has been in that state of savagery for several years before we found him!"

"That is probable," replied Cyrus Smith.

"So there would then be several years during which he would have written that document!

"Of course..., and yet the document seemed recently written!..."

"Moreover, how can we accept that the bottle containing the document took several years to travel from Tabor Island to Lincoln Island?

"It's not absolutely impossible," replied the reporter. "Couldn't it have been in the vicinity of the island for a long time already?"

"No," Pencroff replied, "because it was still floating. We can't even suppose that after having stayed on the shore for more or less time, it could have been taken back by the sea, as that coastline is all rocks and it would have surely been smashed!"

"Indeed," replied Cyrus Smith, who remained pensive.

"And besides," added the sailor, "if the document was dated several years back, if it had been inside that bottle for several years, it would have been damaged by humidity. And yet, that was not the case, and it was found in perfect condition."

The sailor's observation was very astute, and there was an incomprehensible fact because the document seemed to have been written recently when the colonists found it in the bottle. Moreover, it provided the position of Tabor Island in latitude and longitude with precision, which implied that its author had quite extensive knowledge of hydrography, which a simple sailor could not have.

"There's once again something inexplicable here," said the engineer, "but let's not provoke our new companion into speaking. When he wishes to, my friends, we will be ready to listen!"

In the days that followed, the stranger did not speak a word and did not leave the plateau's premises even once. He worked the land without losing a moment, without taking a break, but always apart. During meal times, he did not come up to Granite House, even though he was invited several times, and he contented himself with eating a few raw vegetables. When night came, he did not return to the room assigned to him, but remained there, under some cluster of trees, or, when the weather was bad, he huddled into some rocky crevice. Thus, he continued to live as he had when he had no other shelter than the forests of Tabor Island, and all insistence to make him change his way of life having been in vain, the colonists waited patiently. But the moment was finally approaching when, compelled and almost involuntarily pushed by his conscience, terrible confessions would escape him.

On November 10, around eight o'clock in the evening, as darkness began to set in, the stranger unexpectedly appeared before the colonists, who were gathered under the veranda. His eyes shone strangely, and he had regained the fierce appearance of his bad days.

Cyrus Smith and his companions were shocked to see that, under the sway of intense emotion, his teeth were chattering like those of a feverish person.

What was wrong with him? Was the sight of his kind unbearable to him? Had he had enough of this life among honest people? Was the nostalgia for numbness overtaking him again? One had to believe so, when they heard him express himself in incoherent phrases:

"Why am I here?... by what right have you dragged me from my islet?... can there be any link between you and me?... do you know who I am... what I have done... why I was over there... alone? And who tells you that I wasn't abandoned there... that I wasn't condemned to die there?... do you know my past?... do you know if I have not stolen, murdered... if I am not a wretch... a cursed being... fit to live like a wild beast... away from everyone... tell me... do you know?"

The colonists listened without interrupting the wretched man, from whom these half-confessions escaped almost despite himself. Cyrus Smith then tried to calm him by approaching him, but he stepped back quickly.

"No! No!" he cried. "Just one word... am I free?"

"You are free," replied the engineer.

"Then farewell!" he exclaimed, and he ran away like a madman.

Nab, Pencroff, and Harbert immediately rushed toward the edge of the woods... but they returned alone.

"We must let him be!" said Cyrus Smith.

"He will never come back," exclaimed Pencroff.

"He will come back," replied the engineer.

And many days passed since then; but Cyrus Smith — was it a kind of premonition? — persisted in the unwavering belief that the unfortunate man would return sooner or later.

"This is the last rebellion of that tough nature," he said, "that remorse has touched and that a new isolation would terrify."

Meanwhile, work of all kinds was continued, both on the Grande-vue plateau and in the corral, where Cyrus Smith intended to build a farm. It goes without saying that the seeds collected by Harbert on Tabor Island had been carefully sown.

The plateau then formed a vast, well-designed, well-maintained garden, which kept the colonists' hands busy. There was always work to do there. As the vegetable plants multiplied, it became necessary to enlarge the simple plots, which were starting to resemble real fields and to replace the meadows. But the forage was abundant in the other parts of the island, and the onagers need not fear ever being rationed. Furthermore, it was better to convert the Grande-vue plateau into a garden, protected by its deep belt of creeks, and to push out the meadows which did not need to be shielded from the ravages of primates and quadrupeds. By November 15, the third harvest was made. Here was a field that had increased in size, since eighteen months had passed since the first grain of wheat had been sown! The second crop of six hundred thousand grains produced this time four thousand bushels, or more than five hundred million grains! The colony was rich in wheat since it sufficed to sow ten bushels for the harvest to be ensured every year, allowing both men and beasts to feed on it.

The harvest was completed, and the last two weeks of November were dedicated to bread-making work. Indeed, they had grain but not flour, and setting up a mill was necessary. Cyrus Smith could have used the second drop that poured over the Mercy to set up his engine, the first already being occupied in moving the hammers of the fulling mill; but after discussion, it was decided to set up a simple windmill on the heights of Grande-vue. Building one was no more difficult than building the other, and on the other hand, they were sure that the wind would not be lacking on this plateau, exposed to the breezes from the sea.

"Not to mention," said Pencroff, "that this windmill will be more cheerful and will look good in the landscape!"

So work began by choosing timber for the cage and the mechanisms of the mill. Some large granite stones located in the north of the lake could easily be turned into grinding stones, and as for the sails, the inexhaustible fabric of the balloon would provide the necessary cloth.

Cyrus Smith made the plans, and the location of the mill was chosen a bit to the right of the barn, near the bank of the lake. The entire cage was to rest on a pivot held in sturdy frames, so that it could turn along with all the mechanism it contained according to the wind's demands.

This work was completed quickly. Nab and Pencroff had become very skilled carpenters and only had to follow the templates provided by the engineer. Thus, a sort of cylindrical lookout, a real pepper pot, topped with a pointed roof, quickly rose at the designated spot. The four frames that formed the sails had been securely embedded in the main post, creating a certain angle with it, and they were fixed with iron tenons. As for the various parts of the internal mechanism — the box intended to hold the two stones, the bedstone and the runner stone, the hopper, a sort of large square trough, wide at the top, narrow at the bottom, which was to allow the grains to fall onto the stones, the oscillating spout intended to regulate the flow of grain, which earned its perpetual ticking the nickname of "chatterbox," and finally the sifter, which, through the process of sifting, separates the bran from the flour — all of this was made without difficulty. The tools were good, and the work was not very hard, because, in the end, the mechanisms of a mill are very simple. It was only a matter of time.

Everyone had worked on the construction of the mill, and by December 1, it was finished.

As always, Pencroff was delighted with his work, and he had no doubt that the device was perfect.

"Now, a good wind," he said, "and we will beautifully grind our first harvest!

"A good wind, fine," replied the engineer, "but not too much wind, Pencroff.

"Bah! Our mill will just turn faster!

"It's not necessary for it to turn that fast," replied Cyrus Smith. "Experience shows that the greatest amount of work is produced by a mill when the number of revolutions made by the sails in one minute is six times the number of feet traveled by the wind in one second. With a medium breeze, which gives twenty-four feet per second, it will turn the sails sixteen times in one minute, and that will be enough.

"Exactly!" exclaimed Harbert, "there's a nice northeast breeze blowing that will suit us perfectly!"

There was no reason to delay the inauguration of the mill, as the colonists were eager to taste the first loaf of bread from Lincoln Island. So that day, in the morning, two to three bushels of wheat were ground, and the next day at breakfast, a magnificent loaf, perhaps a bit dense, although risen with brewer's yeast, graced the table of Granite House. Everyone bit into it eagerly, and with what pleasure, as one can imagine!

However, the stranger had not reappeared. Gideon Spilett and Harbert had searched the forest around Granite House several times without encountering him or finding any trace of him. They were seriously worried about his extended disappearance. Certainly, the former savage of Tabor Island could not be troubled by living in these game-rich forests of the Far West, but was it not to be feared that he might return to his old habits and that this independence might rekindle his wild instincts?

Nevertheless, Cyrus Smith, perhaps prompted by a sense of premonition, always insisted that the fugitive would return. "Yes, he will come back!" he repeated with a confidence that his companions could not share. When this unfortunate man was on Tabor Island, he knew he was alone! Here, he knows that his peers are waiting for him! Since he has only partially talked about his past life, this poor penitent will come back to tell it all, and on that day, he will be ours!"

The event would prove Cyrus Smith right.

On December 3, Harbert had left the Grande-vue plateau and had gone fishing on the southern shore of the lake. He was unarmed, and until now, there had been no precautions to take, since dangerous animals had not appeared in this part of the island.

Meanwhile, Pencroff and Nab were working in the poultry yard, while Cyrus Smith and the reporter were busy at the chimneys making soda, as their soap supply had run out.

Suddenly, cries echoed:

"Help! Help!"

Cyrus Smith and the reporter, too far away, could not hear these cries. Pencroff and Nab, abandoning the poultry yard in a hurry, rushed to the lake.

But before them, the unknown man, whose presence nobody could have suspected in this spot, crossed the creek-glycerine, which separated the plateau from the forest, and leaped onto the opposite shore.

There, Harbert faced a formidable jaguar, similar to the one that had been killed at the reptile promontory. Caught by surprise, he stood against a tree, while the animal, crouched and prepared to pounce... but the unknown, armed only with a knife, rushed at the fearsome beast, which turned against this new adversary.

The struggle was brief. The unknown was extraordinarily strong and skilled. He grabbed the jaguar by the throat with one hand, powerful as a pair of shears, undeterred by the beast's claws sinking into his flesh, and with the other, he plunged his knife into its heart.

The jaguar fell. The unknown kicked it away, and he was about to flee when the colonists arrived at the scene of the struggle, and Harbert, clinging to him, shouted:

"No! No! You won't leave!"

Cyrus Smith approached the unknown, whose brows furrowed when he saw him coming closer. Blood was running down his shoulder under his torn jacket, but he paid no attention.

"My friend," said Cyrus Smith, "we owe you a debt of gratitude. To save our child, you risked your life!

— My life! murmured the unknown. What is it worth? Less than nothing!

— Are you hurt?

— It doesn't matter.

— Will you give me your hand?"

And as Harbert tried to take this hand, which had just saved him, the unknown crossed his arms, his chest puffed up, his gaze clouded, and he seemed about to flee; but making a violent effort, and in a brusque tone:

"Who are you?" he asked, "and what do you intend to be to me?"

This was the story of the colonists that he was asking for, and for the first time. Perhaps, once he told that story, he would share his own? In a few words, Cyrus Smith recounted everything that had happened since their departure from Richmond, how they had managed to survive, and what resources were now at their disposal.

The unknown listened with extreme attention.

Then the engineer mentioned who they all were—Gédéon Spilett, Harbert, Pencroff, Nab, and himself—and he added that the greatest joy they had felt since arriving on Lincoln Island was on their return from the islet when they could count one more companion.

At these words, the unknown flushed, his head lowered to his chest, and a sense of confusion painted his whole being.

"And now that you know us," added Cyrus Smith, "will you give us your hand?

— No," replied the unknown in a dull voice, "no! You are honest people! And I..."

17

These last words justified the colonists' feelings. There was something sinister in this man's past, perhaps atoned for in the eyes of men, but not yet absolved in his conscience. In any case, the guilty one had remorse, he was repentant, and although they would have warmly accepted the hand he was asked for, he did not feel worthy of extending it to honest people! However, after the jaguar incident, he did not return to the forest, and from that day on, he no longer left the confines of Granite-House. What was the mystery of this existence? Would the unknown man speak one day? Only time would tell. In any case, it was well agreed that his secret would never be asked, and they would live with him as if they suspected nothing.

For a few days, common life continued as it had been. Cyrus Smith and Gédéon Spilett worked together, sometimes as chemists, sometimes as physicists. The reporter only left the engineer to hunt with Harbert, for it would not have been wise to let the young boy wander alone in the forest, and one needed to stay alert.

As for Nab and Pencroff, one day they worked in the stables, another in the poultry yard, and yet another in the corral, not to mention the tasks at Granite-House; they never lacked for work.

The unknown worked off to the side, and he had resumed his usual existence, not attending meals, sleeping under the trees on the plateau, and never mingling with his companions. It genuinely seemed that the company of those who had saved him was unbearable to him!

"But then," Pencroff remarked, "why did he call for the aid of his peers? Why did he throw that document into the sea?

— He'll tell us," Cyrus Smith would invariably respond.

— When?

— Perhaps sooner than you think, Pencroff."

And indeed, the day of revelations was near.

On December 10, a week after his return to Granite-House, Cyrus Smith saw the unknown come toward him, who, in a calm voice and humble tone, said:

"Sir, I have a request to make of you.

— Go ahead," replied the engineer; "but first, let me ask you a question."

At these words, the unknown flushed and almost retreated. Cyrus Smith understood what was happening in the soul of the guilty man, who undoubtedly feared that the engineer would question him about his past!

Cyrus Smith held him back by the hand:

"Comrade," he said, "not only are we your companions, but we are friends. I wanted to tell you that, and now I am listening."

The unknown wiped his eyes. He was trembling somewhat, and remained for a few moments unable to articulate a word.

"Sir, he finally said, I come to ask you for a favor.

— Which one?

— You have, about four or five miles from here, at the foot of the mountain, a corral for your domestic animals. These animals need to be cared for. Will you allow me to live there with them?"

Cyrus Smith looked at the unfortunate man for a few moments with a deep sense of compassion. Then:

"My friend," he said, "the corral has only stables, hardly suitable for animals...

— That will be good enough for me, sir.

— My friend," Cyrus Smith replied, insisting purposely on this friendly term, "you will let us decide what we should do about that!

— Thank you, sir," replied the unknown as he withdrew.

The engineer immediately informed his companions of the proposal that had been made to him, and it was decided to build a wooden house at the corral that would be made as comfortable as possible.

On the same day, the colonists went to the corral with the necessary tools, and within a week, the house was ready to receive its occupant. It had been built about twenty feet above the stables, and from there, it would be easy to supervise the flock of sheep, which then numbered over eighty heads. A few pieces of furniture—a bed, table, bench, cupboard, chest—were made, and weapons, ammunition, and tools were transported to the corral.

The unknown, moreover, had not gone to see his new home, and he had left the colonists to work without him, while he busied himself on the plateau, likely wanting to finish his work. And indeed, thanks to him, all the lands were plowed and ready to be seeded as soon as the moment came.

It was December 20 when the preparations at the corral were completed. The engineer announced to the unknown that his home was ready to receive him, and the latter replied that he would go there to sleep that very night.

That evening, the colonists were gathered in the great hall of Granite-House. It was then eight o'clock—the time when their companion should have left them. Not wanting to burden him by imposing farewells that might have cost him, they had left him alone and had gone back to Granite-House.

Now, they had been talking in the great hall for a few moments when a light knock was heard at the door. Almost immediately, the unknown entered, and without any preamble:

"Gentlemen," he said, "before I leave you, it's good that you know my story. Here it is."

These simple words left a very strong impression on Cyrus Smith and his companions.

The engineer stood up.

"We ask nothing of you, my friend," he said. "It is your right to remain silent...

— It is my duty to speak.

— Then please, sit down.

— I will remain standing.

— We are ready to listen to you," replied Cyrus Smith.

The unknown stood in a corner of the room, somewhat protected by the dim light. He was bareheaded, with his arms crossed over his chest, and in this posture, in a dull voice, speaking as if forcing himself to talk, he recounted the following story, which his listeners did not interrupt even once:

"On December 20, 1854, a pleasure yacht, the Duncan, belonging to the Scottish laird, Lord Glenarvan, anchored at Cape Bernouilli, on the western coast of Australia, at the latitude of the thirty-seventh parallel. On board this yacht were Lord Glenarvan, his wife, a major of the English army, a French geographer, a young girl, and a young boy. The latter two were the children of Captain Grant, whose ship, the Britannia, had been lost with all hands, a year prior. The Duncan was commanded by Captain John Mangles and crewed by fifteen men.

"Here's why this yacht was there at that time on the coasts of Australia.

"Six months before, a bottle containing a document written in English, German, and French, had been found in the Irish Sea and picked up by the Duncan. This document stated, in essence, that there were still three survivors of the shipwreck of the Britannia, that these survivors were Captain Grant and two of his men, and that they had found refuge on land whose latitude was given, but whose longitude, washed away by seawater, was no longer legible.

"This latitude was that of 37°11' south. Therefore, with the longitude unknown, if one followed this thirty-seventh parallel across continents and seas, one would be certain to arrive at the land inhabited by Captain Grant and his two companions.

"The British admiralty having hesitated to undertake this search, Lord Glenarvan resolved to do everything in his power to find the captain. Mary and Robert Grant had been put in contact with him. The yacht, the Duncan, was equipped for a long expedition in which the lord's family and the captain's children wanted to participate, and the Duncan, leaving Glasgow, headed into the Atlantic, rounded the Strait of Magellan, and then up the Pacific to Patagonia, where, following an early interpretation of the document, it was thought that Captain Grant was being held by native people.

"The Duncan landed its passengers on the western coast of Patagonia and returned to pick them up on the eastern coast at Cape Corrientes.

"Lord Glenarvan crossed Patagonia, following the thirty-seventh parallel, and, having found no trace of the captain, he reembarked on November 13 to continue his search across the ocean.

"After unsuccessfully visiting Tristan da Cunha and Amsterdam islands along its route, the Duncan, as I said, arrived at Cape Bernouilli on the Australian coast on December 20, 1854.

"Lord Glenarvan's intention was to cross Australia as he had crossed America, and he disembarked. A few miles from the shore was a farm owned by an Irishman, who offered hospitality to the travelers. Lord Glenarvan explained to this Irishman the reasons that had brought him to this area and asked if he had any knowledge of an English three-masted ship, the Britannia, that had been lost less than two years ago on the west coast of Australia.

"The Irishman had never heard of that shipwreck; however, to everyone's great surprise, one of the Irishman's servants, intervening, said:

— My lord, praise and thank God. If Captain Grant is still alive, he is alive on Australian soil.

— Who are you? asked Lord Glenarvan.

— A Scotsman like you, my lord, replied the man, and I am one of Captain Grant's companions, one of the survivors of the Britannia."

"This man was named Ayrton. He was indeed the mate of the Britannia, as his papers attested. But separated from Captain Grant at the moment the ship broke on the reefs, he had thought until then that his captain had perished along with the entire crew, and that he, Ayrton, was the sole survivor of the Britannia.

— Only, he added, it's not on the west coast, but on the east coast of Australia that the Britannia sank, and if Captain Grant is still alive, as indicated in his document, he is a prisoner of the Australian natives, and we must search for him on the other coast."

"This man, speaking in this way, had a frank voice, a confident look. One could not doubt his words. The Irishman, who had had him in his service for over a year, confirmed this. Lord Glenarvan believed in that man's loyalty, and thanks to his advice, he resolved to cross Australia following the thirty-seventh parallel. Lord Glenarvan, his wife, the two children, the major, the Frenchman, Captain Mangles, and a few sailors made up the small group led by Ayrton, while the Duncan, under the orders of the second-in-command, Tom Austin, would go to Melbourne, where it would await instructions from Lord Glenarvan.

"They departed on December 23, 1854.

"It is time to say that this Ayrton was a traitor. He was indeed the mate of the Britannia; but after disputes with his captain, he had tried to lead his crew into mutiny and seize the ship, and Captain Grant had left him ashore on April 8, 1852, on the western coast of Australia, and then sailed away, abandoning him— which was only just."So, this miserable man knew nothing about the wreck of the Britannia. He had just learned about it from Glenarvan's account! Since his abandonment, he had become, under the name of Ben Joyce, the leader of escaped convicts, and if he shamelessly claimed the wreck happened on the east coast, if he pushed Lord Glenarvan to head in that direction, it was because he hoped to separate him from his ship, seize the Duncan, and turn that yacht into a pirate ship of the Pacific."

At this point, the unknown man paused for a moment. His voice trembled, but he continued:

"The expedition set out and made its way through the Australian land. It was naturally unfortunate since Ayrton, or Ben Joyce as he preferred, was directing it, sometimes leading, sometimes followed by his band of convicts, who had been alerted to the plan in advance.

"Meanwhile, the Duncan had been sent to Melbourne for repairs. The objective was to convince Lord Glenarvan to order the ship to leave Melbourne and go to the east coast of Australia, where it would be easy to seize it. After bringing the expedition close to that coast amid vast forests where all resources were scarce, Ayrton obtained a letter which he was to deliver to the second-in-command of the Duncan, a letter instructing the yacht to go immediately to the east coast, to Twofold Bay, which was just a few days from where the expedition had stopped. That was where Ayrton had arranged to meet his accomplices.

"At the moment the letter was to be delivered to him, the traitor was unmasked and had no choice but to flee. However, he had to secure that letter which would deliver the Duncan into his hands at all costs. Ayrton managed to seize it, and two days later he arrived in Melbourne.

"Up until then, the criminal had succeeded in his vile plans. He was soon able to lead the Duncan to Twofold Bay, where it would be easy for the convicts to capture it, and with the crew massacred, Ben Joyce would become the master of those seas... But God was meant to stop him at the culmination of his disastrous plans.

"Ayrton, arriving in Melbourne, delivered the letter to the second-in-command, Tom Austin, who read it and set sail immediately; but imagine Ayrton's disappointment and anger when, the day after setting sail, he learned that the second was taking the ship, not to the east coast of Australia, to Twofold Bay, but to the east coast of New Zealand. He tried to oppose it, but Austin showed him the letter!... And indeed, due to a fortunate error from the French geographer who drafted the letter, the east coast of New Zealand was indicated as the destination.

"All of Ayrton's plans had failed! He wanted to revolt. He was imprisoned. Thus, he was taken to the coast of New Zealand, no longer knowing what would become of his accomplices or Lord Glenarvan.

"The Duncan remained cruising along that coast until March 3rd. On that day, Ayrton heard explosions. It was the cannon of the Duncan firing, and soon afterward, Lord Glenarvan and all his party boarded.

"This is what had happened.

"After enduring a thousand hardships and dangers, Lord Glenarvan had managed to complete his journey and arrive at the east coast of Australia, at Twofold Bay. No Duncan! He telegraphed to Melbourne. They replied: 'Duncan left on the 18th for an unknown destination.'

"Lord Glenarvan could think of nothing but that the honest yacht had fallen into the hands of Ben Joyce and was now a pirate ship!

"However, Lord Glenarvan did not want to abandon his quest. He was a brave and generous man. He boarded a merchant ship, had himself taken to the west coast of New Zealand, crossed it at the thirty-seventh parallel, without finding any trace of Captain Grant; but on the other coast, to his great surprise, and by the will of heaven, he found the Duncan, under the command of the second, who had been waiting for five weeks!

"It was March 3, 1855. Lord Glenarvan was therefore aboard the Duncan, but Ayrton was too. He faced the lord, who wanted to extract from him every-thing the bandit could know about Captain Grant. Ayrton refused to speak. Lord Glenarvan then told him that at the first stop, he would be handed over to the English authorities. Ayrton remained silent.

"The Duncan resumed its route along the thirty-seventh parallel. Meanwhile, Lady Glenarvan took it upon herself to overcome the bandit's resistance. Finally, her influence prevailed, and in exchange for what he could tell, Ayrton proposed to Lord Glenarvan to be abandoned on one of the Pacific islands instead of being delivered to the English authorities. Lord Glenarvan, deter-mined to do anything to learn what concerned Captain Grant, agreed.

"Ayrton then recounted his entire life, and it became clear that he knew nothing since the day Captain Grant had landed him on the Australian coast.

"Nevertheless, Lord Glenarvan kept the promise he had made. The Duncan continued its journey and arrived at Tabor Island. This was where Ayrton was meant to be dropped off, and it was also here that, by a true miracle, Captain Grant and his two men were found, precisely on that thirty-seventh parallel. The convict was to replace them on that deserted islet, and here, at the moment he left the yacht, were the words spoken by Lord Glenarvan: '— Here, Ayrton, you will be far from any land and without any possible commu-nication with your kind. You will not be able to escape this islet where the Duncan leaves you. You will be alone, under the eye of a God who sees into the depths of hearts, but you will neither be lost nor forgotten as Captain Grant was. As unworthy as you may be of men's remembrance, men will remember you. I know where you are, Ayrton, and I know where to find you. I will never forget it!'

"And the Duncan, setting sail, soon disappeared.

"It was March 18, 1855.

"Ayrton was alone, but he lacked neither ammunition, weapons, tools, nor seeds. The convict had at his disposal the house built by the honest Captain Grant. He merely had to let himself live and atone for the crimes he had committed in isolation.

"Gentlemen, he repented, felt shame for his crimes and he was very unhappy! He thought that if men came to seek him one day on that islet, he must be worthy of returning among them! How he suffered, the wretched man! How he worked to redeem himself through labor! How he prayed to regenerate himself through prayer!

"For two years, three years, it was so; but Ayrton, crushed by isolation, always looking to see if a ship would not appear on the horizon of his island, wondering if the time of atonement was nearly complete, suffered as one has never suffered before! Ah! how hard is that solitude, for a soul tormented by remorse!

"But surely heaven did not find him punished enough, the unfortunate man, because he gradually felt himself becoming a savage! He gradually felt dullness overtaking him! He cannot tell you if it was after two or four years of abandonment, but in the end, he became the miserable person you found!

"I don't need to tell you, gentlemen, that Ayrton or Ben Joyce and I are one!"

Cyrus Smith and his companions had stood up at the end of this tale. It is hard to describe how deeply they were moved! So much misery, so much pain and despair laid bare before them!

"Ayrton," Cyrus Smith then said, "you were a great criminal, but heaven must certainly find you have atoned for your crimes! It proved that by bringing you back among your kind. Ayrton, you are forgiven! And now, do you want to be our companion?"

Ayrton stepped back.

"Here is my hand!" said the engineer.

Ayrton rushed toward the hand extended by Cyrus Smith, and big tears flowed from his eyes.

"Do you want to live with us?" asked Cyrus Smith.

"Mr. Smith, give me a little more time," replied Ayrton, "leave me alone in this corral house!"

"As you wish, Ayrton," replied Cyrus Smith.

Ayrton was about to withdraw when the engineer addressed him with one last question:

"One more thing, my friend. Since your intention was to live in isolation, why did you throw that document into the sea which put us on your trail?"

"A document?" replied Ayrton, seeming not to understand what they were talking about.

"Yes, the document enclosed in a bottle that we found, which gave the exact location of Tabor Island!"

Ayrton rubbed his forehead. Then, after thinking:

"I never threw a document into the sea!" he replied.

"Never?" exclaimed Pencroff.

"Never!"

And Ayrton, bowing, went back toward the door and left.

18

"The poor man!" said Harbert, who, after rushing to the door, returned after seeing Ayrton slide down the elevator rope and disappear into the darkness.

"He will come back," said Cyrus Smith.

"By the way, Mr. Cyrus," shouted Pencroff, "what does that mean? So, it wasn't Ayrton who threw that bottle into the sea? But who then?"

Surely, if any question needed to be asked, it was that one!

"It's him," Nab replied, "only the poor man was already half mad."

"Yes!" said Harbert, "and he had lost all awareness of what he was doing."

"That can only be explained that way, my friends," Cyrus Smith replied quickly, "and I now understand how Ayrton could indicate the exact location of Tabor Island, since the very events that preceded his abandonment on the island made it known to him.

"However," Pencroff pointed out, "if he was not a brute when he wrote his document, and if he threw it into the sea seven or eight years ago, how was it that the paper was not damaged by moisture?"

"That proves," replied Cyrus Smith, "that Ayrton was only deprived of his wits at a much more recent time than he believes."

"It must be so," replied Pencroff; otherwise, the thing would be inexplicable.

"Inexplicable, indeed," replied the engineer, who seemed unwilling to prolong this conversation.

"But did Ayrton tell the truth?" asked the sailor.

"Yes," replied the reporter. "The story he recounted is true in every respect. I remember very well that the newspapers reported on the attempt made by Lord Glenarvan and the outcome he had achieved."

"Ayrton told the truth," added Cyrus Smith, "don't doubt it, Pencroff, for it was cruel enough to him. One speaks truly when one accuses oneself like that!"

The next day—December 21—the colonists went down to the shore, and having climbed the plateau, they found no Ayrton. Ayrton had gone during the night to his corral house, and the colonists thought it best not to intrude on him. Time would surely do what encouragement had failed to achieve.

Harbert, Pencroff, and Nab then resumed their usual activities. Precisely that day, the same tasks brought Cyrus Smith and the reporter together at the chimney workshop.

"Do you know, my dear Cyrus," said Gideon Spilett, "the explanation you gave yesterday regarding that bottle did not satisfy me at all! How can we accept that this poor man could write that document and throw that bottle into the sea, without retaining any memory of it?

"Thus it is not he who threw it," my dear Spilett.

"So, you still believe..."

"I believe nothing, I know nothing!" replied Cyrus Smith, interrupting the reporter. "I simply categorize that incident among those I have not been able to explain until today!"

"Indeed, Cyrus," said Gideon Spilett; "these things are incredible! Your rescue, the box washed up on the sand, Top's adventures, that bottle finally... will we never find the key to these mysteries?

"Yes!" the engineer replied quickly, "yes, if I have to dig this island down to its very roots!

"Perhaps chance will give us the key to this mystery!"

"Chance! Spilett! I don't believe much in chance, nor in mysteries in this world. There is a cause for everything inexplicable that happens here, and I will discover that cause. But for now, let us observe and work."

January arrived. It was the year 1867 that began. Summer work was carried out diligently. In the days that followed, Harbert and Gideon Spilett, having gone toward the corral, were able to confirm that Ayrton had taken possession of the house that had been prepared for him. He was taking care of the numerous herd entrusted to him, and he would spare his companions the fatigue of having to visit the corral every two or three days.

However, so as not to leave Ayrton alone for too long, the colonists visited him fairly often. It wasn't indifferent either—given certain suspicions that the engineer and Gideon Spilett shared—that this part of the island was under some surveillance, and Ayrton, should any incident arise, would not neglect to inform the inhabitants of Granite House.

However, it could happen that the incident might be sudden and require swift communication to the engineer. Beyond all facts related to the mystery of Lincoln Island, many others could occur, which might call for prompt intervention from the colonists, such as the appearance of a ship passing offshore and in sight of the western coast, a shipwreck on the western landings, the possible arrival of pirates, etc. Thus, Cyrus Smith resolved to establish instant communication between the corral and Granite House.

It was on January 10 that he shared his plan with his companions.

"By the way! How do you plan to do this, Mr. Cyrus?" asked Pencroff. "Are you perhaps thinking about setting up a telegraph?"

"Precisely," replied the engineer.

"An electric one?" exclaimed Harbert.

"Electric," replied Cyrus Smith. "We have all the necessary elements to make a battery, and the most difficult part will be to stretch wires, but with a die, I believe we will manage it.

"Well, after that," retorted the sailor, "I no longer despair of seeing us one day rolling on a railroad!"

So they got to work, starting with the most difficult part, that is to say, the making of wires, because if they failed, it would become unnecessary to make the battery and other accessories.

The iron from Lincoln Island, as we know, was of excellent quality, and thus very suitable for stretching. Cyrus Smith began by making a die, which is a steel plate that was drilled with conical holes of various diameters that would successively reduce the wire to the desired thickness. This piece of steel, after being tempered, "as hard as it can be," as they say in metallurgy, was fixed firmly on a frame solidly embedded in the ground, just a few feet from the great waterfall, which the engineer would still use for power. Indeed, there was the fulling mill, which was not in operation at that time, but whose shaft, driven with extreme power, could serve to stretch the wire by winding it around itself.

The operation was delicate and required much care.Iron, first prepared into long, thin rods with tapered ends, was introduced into the large die and stretched by the spool unit, rolled out to a length of twenty-five to thirty feet, then unwound and presented successively to the smaller diameters! Eventually, the engineer obtained wires that were forty to fifty feet long, which were easy to connect and stretch across the five miles that separated the corral from the Granite-House enclosure.

It only took a few days to complete this task, and as soon as the machine was running, Cyrus Smith let his companions take on the task of drawing the wire while he focused on making his battery.

The goal was to create a constant current battery. It is known that the elements of modern batteries typically consist of carbon, zinc, and copper. The engineer had completely run out of copper and, despite his search, had not found any trace of it on Lincoln Island, so he had to make do without it. The carbon, specifically the hard graphite found in gasworks, could have been produced, but it would have required setting up special equipment, which would have been a large job. As for zinc, it was remembered that the box found at the tip of the wreck was lined with a cover of this metal, which couldn't have been better used at this time.

After careful thought, Cyrus Smith resolved to make a very simple battery, similar to the one Becquerel invented in 1820, which used only zinc. As for the other substances, nitric acid and potash were readily available to him.

Thus, this is how the battery was composed, with the effects produced by the reaction of the acid and potash on one another. A number of glass flasks were made and filled with nitric acid. The engineer sealed them with a stopper, which had a glass tube running through it, closed on the lower end, intended to dip into the acid using a clay tamp held by cloth. In this tube, through its upper end, he poured a solution of potash that he had previously obtained by burning various plants, allowing the acid and potash to react through the clay.

Cyrus Smith then took two zinc plates, one of which was dipped in the nitric acid, while the other was dipped into the potash solution. Immediately, a current was generated, flowing from the plate in the flask to the one in the tube, and these two plates were connected by a metal wire, with the tube plate becoming the positive pole and the flask plate becoming the negative pole of the device.

Each flask thus produced a current, which, when combined, should be sufficient to generate all the phenomena of electric telegraphy.

This was the clever and simple device that Cyrus Smith built, a device that would allow him to set up a telegraphic communication between Granite-House and the corral.

On February 6, the planting of the posts began, equipped with glass insulators, intended to support the wire that would run to the corral. A few days later, the wire was stretched, ready to produce the electrical current that would travel back to its origin point at a speed of one hundred thousand kilometers per second. Two batteries were made, one for Granite-House and the other for the corral because if the corral was to communicate with Granite-House, it was also useful for Granite-House to communicate with the corral.

As for the receiver and the manipulator, they were very simple. At both stations, the wire wrapped around an electromagnet—a piece of soft iron surrounded by wire. When communication was established between the two poles, the current would travel from the positive pole, through the wire, into the electromagnet, temporarily magnetizing it, and returning to the negative pole through the ground. When the current was interrupted, the electromagnet lost its magnetism immediately. So, it was sufficient to place a piece of soft iron in front of the electromagnet, which, attracted during the current's passage, would fall when the current was cut off. With this movement of the plate, Cyrus Smith could easily attach a needle placed on a dial, which displayed the letters of the alphabet, allowing them to correspond from one station to the other.

Everything was fully installed by February 12. That day, Cyrus Smith, after sending the current through the wire, asked if everything was okay at the corral and received a satisfactory response from Ayrton a few moments later.

Pencroff was overjoyed, and every morning and evening, he sent a telegram to the corral, which was never left unanswered.

This method of communication had two real advantages: first, it confirmed Ayrton's presence at the corral, and secondly, it prevented him from being completely isolated. Moreover, Cyrus Smith never let a week go by without visiting him, and Ayrton occasionally came to Granite-House, where he was always warmly welcomed.

The beautiful season passed in the midst of regular work. The colony's resources, particularly in vegetables and cereals, grew day by day, and the plants brought from Tabor Island had thrived. The Grande-vue plateau had a very reassuring appearance. The fourth wheat harvest had been outstanding, and, of course, no one thought to count whether the four hundred billion grains made it to the harvest. However, Pencroff had considered doing so, but when Cyrus Smith informed him that even if he managed to count three hundred grains per minute, or nine thousand an hour, it would take him about five thousand five hundred years to finish, the brave sailor thought it best to give it up.

The weather was magnificent, with very hot temperatures during the day; but in the evening, breezes from the sea tempered the heat of the atmosphere and provided cool nights for the inhabitants of Granite-House. There were, however, a few storms that, while not lasting long, struck Lincoln Island with extraordinary force. For a few hours, the lightning lit up the sky continuously, and the rumblings of thunder did not stop.

Around this time, the small colony was extremely prosperous. The farmyard animals were multiplying, and there was an excess that urgently needed to be brought down to a more manageable number. The pigs had already produced piglets, and it was understood that caring for these animals took up a large portion of Nab and Pencroff's time. The onagers, which had given birth to two lovely beasts, were often ridden by Gédéon Spilett and Harbert, now an excellent rider under the reporter's guidance, and they were also hitched to the cart to transport wood and coal to Granite-House, or various mineral products that the engineer used.

Several exploratory expeditions took place around this time, deep into the forests of the Far West. The explorers could venture there without fearing extreme temperatures, as the sun's rays barely penetrated the thick foliage above them. They visited the entire left bank of the Mercy, bordered by the road leading from the corral to the mouth of the river of the falls.

However, during these excursions, the settlers took care to be well armed, as they frequently encountered some very wild and fierce wild boars, against which they had to fight seriously.

During this season, a fierce war was also waged against the jaguars. Gédéon Spilett had a special hatred for them, and his pupil Harbert was a great help. Armed as they were, they did not fear encountering one of these beasts.

Harbert's boldness was impressive, and the reporter's composure was remarkable. Already twenty magnificent skins adorned the main hall of Granite-House, and if this continued, the jaguar population would soon be eradicated on the island, which was the purpose the hunters were pursuing.

The engineer sometimes took part in various explorations in the unknown portions of the island, which he observed with meticulous attention. He was looking for other traces than those of animals in the densest parts of these vast woods, but nothing suspicious ever came to his attention. Neither Top nor Jup, who accompanied him, showed any signs of there being anything unusual, and yet, more than once, the dog barked at the opening of the well that the engineer had explored without finding anything.

Around this time, Gédéon Spilett, with Harbert's help, took several pictures of the most picturesque parts of the island using the camera that had been found in the box, which had not been used until then.

This camera, equipped with a powerful lens, was very complete. Necessary substances for photographic reproduction, collodion to prepare the glass plate, silver nitrate to sensitize it, sodium hyposulfite to fix the image obtained, ammonium chloride for soaking the paper meant for positive prints, sodium acetate and gold chloride to impregnate the latter—nothing was missing. Even the papers were there, all chlorinated, and before placing them in the chassis for the negative prints, it was enough to soak them for a few minutes in a solution of silver nitrate diluted with water.

The reporter and his assistant quickly became skilled operators, obtaining beautiful prints of landscapes, such as a view of the entire island taken from the Grande-vue plateau with Mount Franklin on the horizon, the mouth of the Mercy, so picturesquely framed by its tall rocks, the clearing and the corral backed up against the foothills of the mountain, and the fascinating development of Cape Claw, the point of the wreck, etc.

The photographers didn't forget to take portraits of all the inhabitants of the island, leaving no one out.

"That fills up the place," said Pencroff.

And the sailor was delighted to see his image, faithfully reproduced, adorn the walls of Granite-House, stopping gladly in front of this display as he would have done at the richest showcases of Broadway.

But it must be said, the best portrait was undoubtedly that of Master Jup. Master Jup posed with an indescribable seriousness, and his image was quite expressive!

"It looks like he's going to make a face!" shouted Pencroff.

And if Master Jup hadn't been pleased, it would have been quite difficult; but he was, and he gazed at his image with a sentimental look that revealed a slight touch of vanity.

The intense heat of summer ended with the month of March. There were sometimes rainy days, yet the atmosphere was still warm. This March, which corresponded to September in the northern latitudes, was not as beautiful as one might have hoped. Perhaps it heralded an early and harsh winter.

One morning, on the 21st, it seemed that the first snow had appeared. Indeed, Harbert, having gotten up early at one of the windows of Granite-House, exclaimed:

"Look! The islet is covered with snow!"

"Snow at this time?" replied the reporter, who had joined the young boy.

Soon their companions were near them, and they could only confirm one thing: not only the islet, but the entire beach at the foot of Granite-House was covered with a uniformly spread white layer on the ground.

"It really is snow!" said Pencroff.

"Or it's pretty similar!" answered Nab.

"But the thermometer reads fifty-eight degrees (14 degrees Celsius above zero)!" observed Gédéon Spilett.

Cyrus Smith watched the white blanket without saying a word, for he truly did not know how to explain this phenomenon at this time of year and under such temperature.

"A thousand devils!" shouted Pencroff, "our crops are going to freeze!"

And the sailor was preparing to go down when he was preceded by the agile Jup, who let himself drop to the ground.

But the orangutan had barely touched the ground when the huge layer of snow rose and scattered into the air in such countless flakes that the sunlight was obscured for a few minutes.

"Birds!" shouted Harbert.

Indeed, they were swarms of sea birds, with brilliantly white plumage. They had descended by the hundreds of thousands onto the islet and coast, and they disappeared far off, leaving the settlers astonished as if they had witnessed a transformation from summer to winter in a scene from a fairytale. Unfortunately, the change had been so sudden that neither the reporter nor the young lad managed to shoot one of these birds, which they could not identify.

A few days later, on March 26, it was two years since the airship castaways had been thrown onto Lincoln Island!

❧ 19 ❧

Two years already! And for two years the settlers had had no communication with their fellow humans! They were without news from the civilized world, lost on this island, just as if they had been on some tiny asteroid in the solar world! What was happening back in their country? The image of their homeland was always in their minds, that homeland torn apart by civil war, at the time they had left and which the southern rebellion was perhaps still bloodily affecting! This was a great distress for them, and they often discussed these matters, without ever doubting that the Northern cause would triumph for the honor of the American Confederation.

During these two years, not a ship had passed in sight of the island, or at least not a sail had been spotted. It was clear that Lincoln Island was out of the usual shipping routes and was even unknown—as proven by the maps— because in the absence of a port, its water supply should have attracted ships seeking to renew their supply. But the sea surrounding it was always deserted as far as the eye could see, and the settlers should hardly count on anyone but themselves to get home.

However, there was a chance of salvation, and this chance was precisely discussed one day in the first week of April by the settlers, who were gathered in the hall of Granite-House.

It was precisely about America, and they spoke of their homeland, which they had so little hope of seeing again.

"Ultimately, we will have only one way," said Gédéon Spilett, "one way to leave Lincoln Island, and that is to build a vessel large enough to brave the sea for a few hundred miles. It seems to me that once you've made a small boat, you can certainly build a ship!"

"And you can definitely go to the Pomotou, added Harbert, since you went to Tabor Island!"

"I'm not saying no," replied Pencroff, who always had a decisive voice on maritime matters, "I'm not saying no, although it's not quite the same thing to go nearby as it is to go far! If our small boat had been threatened by some bad weather during the journey to Tabor Island, we knew that the port was not far either way; but twelve hundred miles to cover is quite a distance, and the nearest land is at least that far away!"

"Well, if it comes to that, Pencroff, wouldn't you try your luck?" asked the reporter.— I will try whatever you want, Mr. Spilett, replied the sailor, and you know I'm not the kind to back down!

— Besides, notice that we have one more sailor among us, Nab pointed out.

— Who? asked Pencroff.

— Ayrton.

— That's right, replied Harbert.

— If only he would agree to come! Pencroff observed.

— Well! said the reporter, do you really think that if Lord Glenarvan's yacht had shown up at Tabor Island while he was still living there, Ayrton would have refused to leave?

— You forget, my friends, Cyrus Smith then said, that Ayrton wasn't in his right mind during the last years of his stay. But that's not the point. The question is whether we should count this return of the Scottish vessel among our chances of salvation. Now, Lord Glenarvan promised Ayrton he would come back to pick him up at Tabor Island when he judged his crimes sufficiently atoned for, and I believe he will return.

— Yes, the reporter said, and I would add that he will return soon, since it's been twelve years since Ayrton was abandoned!

— Ah! replied Pencroff, I fully agree that the lord will come back, and soon, too. But where will he land? At Tabor Island, not Lincoln Island.

— That is even more certain, Harbert replied, since Lincoln Island isn't even marked on the map.

— So, my friends, the engineer continued, we must take the necessary precautions to ensure our presence and that of Ayrton on Lincoln Island is reported to Tabor Island.

— Obviously, the reporter replied, and there's nothing easier than to leave a notice in that cabin, which was home to Captain Grant and Ayrton, indicating the location of our island, a notice that Lord Glenarvan or his crew will surely find.

— It's even unfortunate, the sailor observed, that we forgot to take this precaution during our first trip to Tabor Island.

— And why would we have taken it? Harbert replied. We didn't know Ayrton's story at that time; we had no idea someone would need to come rescue him one day, and when we learned the story, the season was too far along to allow us to return to Tabor Island.

— Yes, Cyrus Smith replied, it was too late, and we must postpone this crossing until next spring.

— But what if the Scottish yacht comes before then? Pencroff said.

— That's unlikely, replied the engineer, because Lord Glenarvan wouldn't choose the winter season to venture into those distant seas. Either he has already returned to Tabor Island since Ayrton has been with us, that is to say, for the past five months, and he has left again, or he will come later, and it will be time, as the first beautiful days of October arrive, to go to Tabor Island and leave a notice there.

— I must admit, Nab said, it would be very unfortunate if the Duncan had reappeared in these seas only a few months ago!

— I hope that's not the case, Cyrus Smith replied, and that heaven hasn't taken away the best chance we have left!

— I believe, the reporter observed, that in any case we will know where we stand when we return to Tabor Island, because if the Scots have returned, they will have necessarily left some traces of their passage.

— That is clear, replied the engineer. So, my friends, since we have this chance of being rescued, let's wait patiently, and if it is taken from us, we will see what we should do then.

— In any case, said Pencroff, it is understood that if we leave Lincoln Island one way or another, it won't be because we are unhappy there!

— No, Pencroff, the engineer replied, it will be because we are far from every-thing a person should cherish most in the world: family, friends, and homeland!»

With things decided this way, there was no longer any talk of building a ship large enough to venture either to the archipelagos in the north or to New Zealand in the west, and they focused only on the usual work in preparation for a third winter at Granite-House.

However, it was also decided that the boat would be used, before the bad weather set in, to make a trip around the island. A complete survey of the coasts had not yet been completed, and the colonists only had an imperfect idea of the coastline to the west and north, from the mouth of the waterfall river to the mandibule caps, as well as the narrow bay that lay between them like a shark's jaw.

The project for this excursion was proposed by Pencroff, and Cyrus Smith fully agreed, as he wanted to see for himself all this part of his domain.

The weather was variable at that time, but the barometer was not fluctuating abruptly, so one could count on manageable weather.

Specifically, during the first week of April, after a sharp drop in barometric pressure, the rise was marked by a strong westerly wind that lasted five to six days; then the needle of the instrument became stationary at a height of twenty-nine inches and nine tenths (759.45 mm), and the conditions seemed favorable for exploration.

The departure date was set for April 16, and the Bonadventure, anchored in Balloon Port, was stocked for a trip that could last a while.

Cyrus Smith informed Ayrton of the planned expedition and invited him to join; however, since Ayrton preferred to stay on shore, it was decided he would come to Granite-House during his companions' absence. Master Jup was to keep him company and made no complaints.

On the morning of April 16, all the colonists, accompanied by Top, boarded. The wind was blowing from the southwest, with a nice breeze, and the Bonadventure had to tack leaving Balloon Port in order to head for Reptile Promontory. Of the ninety miles that measured the island's perimeter, the southern coast accounted for about twenty from the port to the promontory. From there, it was necessary to cover the last twenty miles as closely as possible since the wind was directly against them.

It took the entire day to reach the promontory, as the boat, upon leaving the port, found only two hours of ebb tide and, on the contrary, had six hours of flood tide that were very difficult to manage. It was already night when they rounded the promontory.

Pencroff then proposed to the engineer to continue at a slow speed, with two reefs in the sail. But Cyrus Smith preferred to anchor a short distance from shore in order to revisit this part of the coast during the day. It was even agreed that, since it was a detailed exploration of the island's coastline, they would not navigate at night and that, once evening came, they would drop anchor close to shore as long as the weather allowed.

The night therefore passed at anchor under the promontory, and as the wind died down with the mist, the silence was undisturbed. The passengers, with the exception of the sailor, might have slept a little less well aboard the Bonadventure than they would have in their rooms at Granite-House, but they did sleep.

The next day, April 17, Pencroff set sail at daybreak, and with a broad reach and port tack, he could hug the western coast very closely.

The colonists were familiar with this magnificent wooded coast since they had already walked along its edge, yet it still excited all their admiration. They sailed close to land as much as possible, moderating their speed in order to observe everything, being careful only not to hit some tree trunks that floated here and there.

Several times, they even dropped anchor, and Gédéon Spilett took photographic views of this superb coastline.

Around noon, the Bonadventure arrived at the mouth of the waterfall river. Beyond, on the right bank, the trees reappeared, but more sparse, and three miles further on, they formed only isolated clusters among the western foothills of the mountain, whose barren ridge extended down to the coastline. What a contrast between the southern part and the northern part of this coast! As lush and green as the former was, the latter was rough and wild! It looked like one of those "iron coasts," as they are called in certain places, and its tortured structure seemed to indicate that a true crystallization had occurred abruptly in the still boiling basalt of geological eras. A heap of a terrifying aspect, which would have frightened the colonists at first, if chance had thrown them on this part of the island! When they were on the summit of Mount Franklin, they could not recognize the deeply sinister appearance of this shore, as they were too high above it; but viewed from the sea, this coastline presented a strangeness that perhaps had no equal anywhere else in the world.

The Bonadventure passed before this coast, keeping a half-mile distance. It was easy to see that it consisted of blocks of all sizes, from twenty feet to three hundred feet high, and of all shapes, cylindrical like towers, prismatic like steeples, pyramidal like obelisks, conical like factory chimneys. An ice floe from the icy seas could not have been arranged more capriciously in its sublime horror! Here, bridges thrown from one rock to another; there, arches arranged like those of a nave, whose depth was invisible; in one place, wide excavations, whose vaults had a monumental appearance; in another, a genuine hubbub of peaks, pyramids, and spires like none ever seen in a Gothic cathedral. All of nature's whims, even more varied than those of the imagination, shaped this grand coastline, which stretched for a length of eight to nine miles.

Cyrus Smith and his companions looked on in astonishment bordering on shock.

But while they remained silent, Top did not hesitate to bark, his barks echoing off the basalt wall. The engineer even noticed that these barks had something unusual about them, just like those the dog made at the mouth of the well at Granite-House.

"Let's approach," he said.

And the Bonadventure came as close as possible to the rocks along the shoreline. Perhaps there existed some cave that needed to be explored? But Cyrus Smith saw nothing—not a cavern, not a crevice that could serve as a refuge for any beings, as the base of the rocks washed directly in the surf of the waters. Soon Top's barking ceased, and the boat pulled back a few cables from the shore.

In the northwest part of the island, the shore became flat and sandy. A few sparse trees loomed above a low, marshy land that the colonists had already glimpsed, and in stark contrast to the other desolate coast, life manifested itself in the presence of a myriad of water birds.

That evening, the Bonadventure anchored in a slight cove of the shoreline, in the northern part of the island, close to shore, for the waters were deep in that spot.

The night passed peacefully, as the breeze seemed to die down along with the last light of day, and it only returned with the first hints of dawn.

As it was easy to approach the shore that morning, the designated hunters of the colony, namely Harbert and Gédéon Spilett, went for a two-hour walk and came back with several strings of ducks and snipe.

Top had performed wonderfully, and not a single game was lost, thanks to his zeal and skill.

At eight in the morning, the Bonadventure set sail again and sped quickly toward the mandibule north cape, as it had a following wind, and the breeze seemed to be freshening.

"Besides," said Pencroff, "I wouldn't be surprised if a storm from the west were brewing. Yesterday, the sun set over a very red horizon, and look, this morning, there are 'cat's tails' that don't bode well."

These cat's tails were thin cirrus clouds scattered in the zenith, which are never less than five thousand feet above sea level. They looked like light pieces of cotton, and their presence usually heralds some imminent trouble in the elements.

"Well then," Cyrus Smith said, "let's hoist as much sail as we can carry and seek refuge in Shark Gulf. I think the Bonadventure will be safe there.

— Perfectly," Pencroff replied, "and besides, the northern coast is made only of dunes that aren't very interesting to consider.

— I wouldn't mind, the engineer added, spending not only the night but even the whole of tomorrow in this bay, which deserves to be explored carefully.

— I think we will be forced to do so, whether we want to or not," Pencroff replied, "as the horizon is starting to look threatening in the west. Look how murky it's getting!

— In any case, we have a good wind to reach the mandibule cape," the reporter pointed out.

— A very good wind," the sailor replied; "but for entering the gulf, we will have to tack, and I would like to see clearly in these parts that I don't know!

— Areas that must be strewn with reefs," added Harbert, "if we judge by what we saw on the southern coast of Shark Gulf.

— Pencroff," said Cyrus Smith, "do your best, we are relying on you.

— Don't worry, Mr. Cyrus," the sailor replied, "I won't expose myself needlessly! I would prefer a knife in my vital parts to a rock hitting my Bonadventure!"

What Pencroff called vital parts referred to the submerged portion of his boat's hull, and he cared more for it than for his own skin!

"What time is it?" Pencroff asked.

— Ten o'clock, Gédéon Spilett replied.

— And how far do we have to go to reach the cape, Mr. Cyrus?

— About fifteen miles, the engineer answered.

— That's about two and a half hours," said the sailor, "and we will be off the cape between noon and one o'clock. Unfortunately, the tide will turn at that time, and the ebb will flow out of the gulf. So I fear it will be difficult to enter, battling both wind and sea.

— Especially since it's a full moon today," Harbert pointed out, "and the tides in April are very strong.

— Well then, Pencroff," Cyrus Smith asked, "can't you anchor at the tip of the cape?

— Anchor close to shore, with bad weather on the horizon? exclaimed the sailor. Are you serious, Mr. Cyrus? That would be like willingly running aground!

— Then, what will you do?

— I will try to hold off until the flood tide, meaning until around seven in the evening, and if there is still a bit of daylight, I will attempt to enter the gulf; otherwise, we'll have to sail back and forth all night, and we will enter tomorrow at daybreak.

— I told you, Pencroff, we are relying on you," Cyrus Smith replied.

— Ah! said Pencroff, if only there were a lighthouse on this coast, it would be easier for navigators!

— Yes," Harbert replied, "and this time, we won't have a handy engineer lighting a fire to guide us into port!

— By the way, my dear Cyrus," Gédéon Spilett said, "we never thanked you, but honestly, without that fire, we would never have been able to reach...— A fire...? asked Cyrus Smith, very surprised by the reporter's words.

— What we mean, Mr. Cyrus, replied Pencroff, is that we were very troubled onboard the Bonadventure during the last hours before our return, and that we would have drifted past the island if it weren't for your foresight in lighting a fire on the Granite-House plateau on the night of October 19 to 20.

— Yes, yes!... that was a great idea I had! said the engineer.

— And this time, added the sailor, unless the thought comes to Ayrton, there won't be anyone to do us that little favor!

— No! No one! replied Cyrus Smith.

And a few moments later, finding himself alone at the front of the boat with the reporter, the engineer leaned closer to his ear and said:

"If there's one thing certain in this world, Spilett, it's that I never lit a fire on the night of October 19 to 20, neither on the Granite-House plateau nor anywhere else on the island!"

Things went exactly as Pencroff had predicted, because his instincts could not be wrong. The wind grew stronger, and from a good breeze, it became a gale, meaning it reached a speed of forty to forty-five miles per hour, and a ship in open sea would have been in serious trouble with its sails furled. Now, as it was around six o'clock when the Bonadventure was at the entrance of the gulf, and at that moment the ebb tide was being felt, it was impossible to enter. They had to stay offshore, because even if he wanted to, Pencroff wouldn't have been able to reach the mouth of the Mercy. So, after setting his foresail on the main mast as a storm sail, he waited, aiming the bow toward land.

Fortunately, although the wind was very strong, the sea, sheltered by the coast, did not become too rough. Therefore, there were no worries about breaking waves, which are a great danger for small boats.

The Bonadventure would probably not capsize, because it was well ballasted; however, huge amounts of water crashing onboard could have compromised it if the hatches hadn't held. Pencroff, being a skilled sailor, prepared for all events. Certainly! He had extreme confidence in his boat, but he still awaited the dawn with some anxiety.

During that night, Cyrus Smith and Gédéon Spilett did not have the opportunity to talk together, yet the phrase whispered to the reporter by the engineer deserved to be discussed once again regarding the mysterious influence that seemed to prevail over Lincoln Island. Gédéon Spilett kept pondering this new and inexplicable incident, the appearance of a fire on the island's coast. He had truly seen that fire! His companions, Harbert and Pencroff, had seen it just like he had! This fire had helped them recognize the island's location during that dark night, and they could not doubt that it was the engineer's hand that had lit it, and yet Cyrus Smith was now declaring firmly that he had done nothing of the sort!

Gédéon Spilett promised himself to return to this incident as soon as the Bonadventure returned, and to urge Cyrus Smith to inform his companions about these strange events. Perhaps they would then decide to conduct a thorough investigation of all parts of Lincoln Island together.

In any case, that evening no fire was lit on those unknown shores that formed the entrance of the gulf, and the small boat remained offshore throughout the night.

When the first light of dawn appeared on the eastern horizon, the wind, which had calmed slightly, turned by two points and allowed Pencroff to more easily enter the narrow entrance of the gulf. By around seven in the morning, the Bonadventure, after holding its course toward the northern cap, cautiously entered the passage and ventured into these waters, framed by the strangest lava formations.

"Look, said Pencroff, that's a stretch of sea that would make an admirable harbor, where fleets could maneuver at ease!

— What's particularly curious, observed Cyrus Smith, is that this gulf was formed by two lava flows from the volcano that built up during successive eruptions. Therefore, this gulf is completely sheltered on all sides, and it's likely that even in the worst winds, the sea is calm here like a lake.

— Certainly, replied the sailor, since the wind can only enter through this narrow gap carved between the two caps, and even then, the northern cap shields the southern one, making it very difficult for gusts to get in. In truth, our Bonadventure could stay here all year round without even straining at its anchors!

— That's a bit too big for it! the reporter remarked.

— Oh, Mr. Spilett, replied the sailor, I agree it's too big for the Bonadventure, but if the Union fleets need a safe harbor in the Pacific, I believe they won't find a better one than this harbor!

— We're in the mouth of a shark, then, Nab pointed out, referring to the shape of the gulf.

— Right in its mouth, my brave Nab! replied Harbert, but you're not afraid it will close on us, are you?

— No, Mr. Harbert, replied Nab, yet I must admit I'm not too fond of this gulf! It has a nasty look about it!

— Well! exclaimed Pencroff, here's Nab denigrating my gulf, just when I'm thinking of presenting it to America!

— But at least are the waters deep? asked the engineer, because what is enough for the Bonadventure's keel wouldn't be enough for our armored ships.

— Easy to check, replied Pencroff.

And the sailor sent down a long rope he used as a sounding line, which had a weight attached to it. The line measured about fifty fathoms and unrolled completely without hitting the bottom.

"All right, said Pencroff, our ships can come here! They won't run aground!

— Indeed, said Cyrus Smith, this gulf is a true abyss; but, taking into account the plutonic origin of the island, it is not surprising that the sea floor offers such depressions.

— It looks like, remarked Harbert, that those walls have been cut straight down, and I believe that at their base, even with a five or six times longer sounding line, Pencroff wouldn't find a bottom.

— That's all well and good, then said the reporter, but I will point out to Pencroff that something important is missing from his harbor!

— And what is that, Mr. Spilett?

— A cut, some kind of trench that provides access to the interior of the island. I don't see a single place where we can land!"

And indeed, the high lava cliffs, very steep, offered no spot along the entire perimeter of the gulf conducive to landing. It was an unpassable curtain, reminiscent—though even more barren—of the fjords of Norway. The Bonadventure, skimming these high walls as if to touch them, didn't find even a protrusion that would allow the passengers to leave the boat.

Pencroff consoled himself by saying that, when the time came, they would surely find a way to breach this wall using mining methods, and since there was clearly nothing to be done in this gulf, he directed his boat toward the gap and set out around two in the afternoon.

"Phew!" said Nab, sighing with satisfaction.

It truly did seem that the brave black man was not comfortable in that enormous jaw!

From the northern cap to the mouth of the Mercy, there was hardly more than eight miles. They then set sail for Granite-House, and the Bonadventure, with a favorable wind in its sails, extended its course along the coast at a mile's distance. Soon, enormous lava rocks gave way to those whimsical dunes, among which the engineer had been so unusually found, and which were frequented by hundreds of seabirds.

Around four o'clock, Pencroff, leaving the tip of the isle on his left, entered the channel that separated him from the shore, and at five o'clock, the anchor of the Bonadventure bit into the sandy bottom at the mouth of the Mercy.

It had been three days since the colonists had left their home. Ayrton awaited them on the shore, and master Jup joyfully came to meet them, sounding happy grunts of satisfaction.

The complete exploration of the island's coasts was therefore accomplished, and no suspicious trace had been observed.

If any mysterious being resided there, it could only be hidden under the impenetrable woods of the snake-like peninsula, where the colonists had not yet conducted their investigations.

Gédéon Spilett discussed these matters with the engineer, and it was agreed they would draw their companions' attention to the strange nature of certain incidents that had occurred on the island, the most recent being one of the most inexplicable. So Cyrus Smith, returning to the matter of the fire lit by an unknown hand along the coastline, couldn't help but say once more to the reporter:

"But are you sure you saw correctly? Couldn't it have been a partial eruption of the volcano, or some meteor?

— No, Cyrus, replied the reporter, it was certainly a fire lit by human hands. Besides, question Pencroff and Harbert. They saw it just as I did myself, and they will confirm my words."

Thus, it followed that a few days later, on April 25, during the evening when all the colonists were gathered on the Grand View plateau, Cyrus Smith spoke up, saying:

"My friends, I feel I must draw your attention to certain facts that have occurred on the island, and I would very much like your opinion on them. These facts are, so to speak, supernatural...

— Supernatural! exclaimed the sailor, blowing out a puff of tobacco. Could it be that our island is supernatural?

— No, Pencroff, but certainly mysterious, replied the engineer, unless you can explain what Spilett and I have been unable to understand up to now.

— Go on, Mr. Cyrus, replied the sailor.

— Well! Do you understand, said the engineer, how it could be that after falling into the sea, I was found a quarter of a mile inside the island, and without being conscious of that movement?

— Unless you were unconscious... said Pencroff.

— That's not acceptable, replied the engineer. But never mind. Do you understand how Top was able to find your refuge, five miles from the cave where I was lying?

— The dog's instinct... replied Harbert.

— Odd instinct! observed the reporter, since, despite the rain and wind raging that night, Top arrived at the chimneys dry and with no mud on him!

— Let's move on, the engineer continued. Have you understood how our dog was so strangely cast out of the waters of the lake after his fight with the dugong?

— No! Not really, I admit, replied Pencroff, and the wound the dugong had on its side, a wound that seemed to have been made with a sharp instrument, makes no more sense.

— Let's move on again, Cyrus Smith continued. Have you understood, my friends, how this lead pellet ended up in the body of the young peccary, how this crate washed ashore so conveniently, without there being any signs of a shipwreck, how this bottle containing the document presented itself so opportunely during our first sea excursion, how our boat, having broken its mooring, came to join us in the current of the Mercy precisely when we needed it, how, after the monkeys invaded us, the ladder was returned so conveniently from the heights of Granite-House, how finally, the document that Ayrton claimed he never wrote ended up in our hands?"

Cyrus Smith had just listed, without leaving any out, the strange events that had occurred on the island. Harbert, Pencroff, and Nab looked at one another, unsure how to respond, because the succession of these incidents, grouped together for the first time, struck them with the highest surprise.

"By my faith, finally said Pencroff, you are right, Mr. Cyrus, and it's difficult to explain these things!

— Well then, my friends, replied the engineer, one final fact has been added to those, and it is no less incomprehensible than the others!

— Which one, Mr. Cyrus? Harbert eagerly asked.

— When you returned from Tabor Island, Pencroff, the engineer continued, did you say that a fire appeared on Lincoln Island?

— Certainly, replied the sailor.

— And you are certain you saw that fire?

— As sure as I see you.

— You too, Harbert?

— Oh! Mr. Cyrus, cried Harbert, that fire shone like a first-magnitude star!

— But could it not have been a star? insisted the engineer.

— No, replied Pencroff, for the sky was covered with heavy clouds, and in any case, a star would not have been that low on the horizon. But Mr. Spilett saw it like we did, and he can confirm our words!

— I will add, said the reporter, that the fire was very bright and projected like an electric sheet.

— Yes! Yes! Perfectly... replied Harbert, and it was certainly placed on the heights of Granite-House.

— Well then, my friends, replied Cyrus Smith, during that night of October 19 to 20, neither Nab nor I lit a fire along the coast.

— You didn't?... exclaimed Pencroff, overwhelmed with astonishment, unable even to finish his sentence.

— We didn't leave Granite-House, replied Cyrus Smith, and if a fire appeared on the coast, it was another hand than ours that lit it!"

Pencroff, Harbert, and Nab were astounded. There could be no possible illusion, and a fire had indeed struck their eyes during that night of October 19 to 20!

Yes! They had to admit it, a mystery existed! An inexplicable influence, clearly favorable to the colonists, but very irritating to their curiosity, was felt and seemed timely on Lincoln Island. Was there some hidden being in its deepest retreats? That was something they had to find out at all costs!

Cyrus Smith also reminded his companions of the strange behavior of Top and Jup when they were lurking at the mouth of the well that connected Granite-House to the sea, and he told them he had explored the well without discovering anything suspicious. Finally, the conclusion of this conversation was a determination made by all the members of the colony to thoroughly search the island as soon as the nice weather returned.

But since that day, Pencroff appeared to be troubled.

This island, which he had made his personal property, suddenly seemed less entirely his, and he felt he was sharing it with another master, to whom, willingly or not, he felt subject.

Nab and he often talked about these inexplicable things, and both, very inclined to the marvelous by their nature, were not far from believing that Lincoln Island was under the influence of some supernatural power.

Meanwhile, the bad days had arrived with May—November in the northern zones. Winter seemed likely to be harsh and early. So, the preparations for winterizing were undertaken without delay. Moreover, the colonists were well prepared for the harsh winter that lay ahead. They had plenty of felt clothing, and the numerous sheep at the time had provided an abundance of wool necessary for making this warm fabric.

It goes without saying that Ayrton had been supplied with these comfortable clothes. Cyrus Smith invited him to spend the cold season at Granite-House, where he would be housed better than in the corral, and Ayrton promised to do so as soon as the final work on the corral was completed, which he did around mid-April. Since then, Ayrton shared communal life and was useful on every occasion; but, always humble and sad, he never took part in the pleasures of his companions!

During most of the third winter that the colonists spent on Lincoln Island, they remained confined to Granite-House. There were very severe storms and terrible gusts of wind that seemed to shake the rocks down to their base. Huge tidal waves threatened to cover the island entirely, and certainly, any ship moored along the shore would have been lost completely. Twice, during one of these storms, the Mercy swelled to such an extent that there was a fear the bridge and the culverts would be swept away, and it was even necessary to reinforce those on the shore, which were disappearing under layers of water when the sea battered the coastline.

It is easy to imagine that such storms, comparable to waterspouts, where rain and snow mingled, caused damage on the Grande-vue plateau. The mill and the poultry yard particularly suffered. The colonists often had to make urgent repairs there, without which the existence of the birds would have been seriously threatened.

During these severe weather conditions, a few pairs of jaguars and bands of four-handed creatures ventured close to the edge of the plateau, and there was always a fear that the most agile and daring, driven by hunger, would manage to cross the stream, which, by the way, offered an easy passage when frozen. Plants and domestic animals would have been certainly destroyed then without constant vigilance, and often it was necessary to fire shots to keep these dangerous visitors at a respectful distance. Thus, there was no shortage of work for the winter dwellers, as besides external care, there were always a thousand tasks to improve Granite-House.

There were also some excellent hunts conducted during the cold spells in the vast marshes of the shelducks. Gédéon Spilett and Harbert, aided by Jup and Top, did not miss a single shot amidst these myriads of ducks, snipe, teal, and plovers. Access to this game-rich territory was easy, whether one went there by the balloon port road, after crossing the Mercy bridge, or by going around the rocks at the point of the wreck, and the hunters never strayed more than two or three miles from Granite-House.

Thus passed the four months of winter, which were truly harsh, namely June, July, August, and September. However, overall, Granite-House did not suffer too much from the harsh weather, and the same was true for the corral, which, being less exposed than the plateau and largely covered by Mount Franklin, only received remnants of wind blasts already broken by the forests and high coastal rocks. The damage was therefore minimal, and Ayrton's active and skillful hands quickly repaired it when, in the second half of October, he returned to spend a few days at the corral.

During this winter, no new inexplicable incidents occurred. Nothing strange happened, even though Pencroff and Nab were on the lookout for even the most insignificant events that they could link to a mysterious cause. Top and Jup themselves no longer roamed around the well and showed no signs of concern. It seemed that the series of supernatural incidents had come to a halt, although they were often discussed during the evenings at Granite-House, and it was well agreed that the island would be searched even in its hardest-to-explore parts. But a highly serious event, whose consequences could be disastrous, temporarily diverted Cyrus Smith and his companions from their plans.

It was now October. The beautiful season was approaching quickly. Nature was reviving under the rays of the sun, and amidst the persistent foliage of the conifers that formed the edge of the woods, the new foliage of the hackberry trees, banksias, and deodars was already appearing.

Remember that Gédéon Spilett and Harbert had, on several occasions, taken photographic views of Lincoln Island. Well, on this day, October 17, around three in the afternoon, Harbert, captivated by the clarity of the sky, thought of capturing the entire Union Bay facing the Grande-vue plateau, from Mandible Cape to Claw Cape.

The horizon was beautifully defined, and the sea, undulating under a soft breeze, presented the stillness of a lake's waters in the background, dotted here and there with bright spots. The lens had been placed at one of the windows of the great room of Granite-House, and therefore, it overlooked the shore and the bay. Harbert proceeded as he usually did, and, having obtained the image, he went to fix it with the substances kept in a dark alcove of Granite-House.

Returning to the light, while examining it carefully, Harbert noticed a tiny almost imperceptible spot marring the horizon of the sea. He tried to wash it away repeatedly but could not succeed. "It's a defect in the glass," he thought.

And then he had the curiosity to examine this defect with a strong lens he unscrewed from one of the binoculars. But as soon as he looked, he let out a cry, and the image nearly slipped from his hands.

Rushing immediately to the room where Cyrus Smith was, he handed the image and lens to the engineer, pointing out the little spot. Cyrus Smith examined this point; then, grabbing his telescope, he rushed to the window. The telescope, after slowly scanning the horizon, finally stopped on the suspicious point, and Cyrus Smith, lowering it, uttered just one word: "Ship!"

And indeed, a ship was in sight of Lincoln Island!

III

THE SECRET OF THE ISLAND

I

For two and a half years, the balloon castaways had been thrown onto Lincoln Island, and so far, no communication had been established between them and their fellow humans. Once, the reporter had tried to connect with the inhabited world by entrusting a bird with a note that contained the secret of their situation, but that was a chance upon which one could not seriously count. Only Ayrton, in the known circumstances, had joined the small colony members. Now, on this very day, — October 17, — other men suddenly appeared in sight of the island, on this always deserted sea!

There was no doubt about it! A ship was there!

But would it pass by, or would it anchor? In a few hours, the colonists would definitely know what to think.

Cyrus Smith and Harbert, having immediately called Gédéon Spilett, Pencroff, and Nab into the great room of Granite-House, informed them of what was happening. Pencroff, grabbing the telescope, quickly scanned the horizon, and stopping on the indicated point, which was the one that made the imperceptible spot on the photographic image: "A thousand devils! It's definitely a ship!" he said in a voice that did not exhibit extraordinary satisfaction.

"Is it coming toward us?" asked Gédéon Spilett.

"Impossible to affirm anything yet," replied Pencroff, "for only its masts appear above the horizon, and we cannot see a piece of its hull!"

"What should we do?" said the young boy.

"Wait," replied Cyrus Smith.

And for quite a long time, the colonists remained silent, engaged in all the thoughts, emotions, fears, and hopes that this incident — the most serious that had occurred since their arrival on Lincoln Island — could arouse in them.

Certainly, the colonists were not in the situation of those castaways abandoned on a barren isle, struggling for their miserable existence against a cruel nature and incessantly consumed by the need to see inhabited lands again. Pencroff and Nab, especially, who found themselves at once so happy and so rich, would not have left their island without regret. They had, moreover, become accustomed to this new life amidst this domain that their intelligence had virtually civilized! But still, this ship represented, at any rate, news from the continent, and perhaps a piece of their homeland coming toward them! It carried beings like them, and one can understand that their hearts would have leapt at the sight of it!

From time to time, Pencroff would take the telescope and position himself at the window. From there, he closely examined the vessel that was twenty miles away to the east. The colonists still had no way of signaling their presence. A flag would not have been seen; a gunshot would not have been heard; a fire would not have been visible.

However, it was certain that the island, dominated by Mount Franklin, could not have escaped the gaze of the ship's lookouts. But why would this vessel land there? Was it not a mere coincidence that brought it to this part of the Pacific, where the maps mentioned no land except for Tabor Isle, which itself was outside the usual routes taken by long-distance ships from the Polynesian archipelagos, New Zealand, and the American coast?

To this question that everyone was asking, Harbert suddenly provided an answer.

"Could it be the Duncan?" he exclaimed.

The Duncan, one remembers, was Lord Glenarvan's yacht that had left Ayrton on the islet and was supposed to return for him one day. Now, the islet was not that far from Lincoln Island, that a ship sailing towards one could not happen to pass in view of the other. Only one hundred fifty miles separated them in longitude, and seventy-five miles in latitude.

"We must inform Ayrton," said Gédéon Spilett, "and call him immediately. He alone can tell us if it is indeed the Duncan."

That was the consensus, and the reporter, going to the telegraphic device that connected the corral and Granite-House, sent this telegram: "Come quickly."

A few moments later, the bell rang.

"I'm coming," Ayrton replied.

Then the colonists continued to observe the ship.

"If it's the Duncan," said Harbert, "Ayrton will easily recognize it, since he sailed on board for some time.

"And if he recognizes it," added Pencroff, "it will be quite an emotional moment for him!

"Yes," replied Cyrus Smith, "but now, Ayrton is worthy of returning to board the Duncan, and may heaven grant that it is indeed Lord Glenarvan's yacht because any other ship would seem suspect to me! These seas are treacherous, and I always fear for our island's visit from some Malay pirates.

"We would defend it!" cried Harbert.

"Of course, my child," replied the engineer, smiling, "but it's better not to have to defend it."

"One simple observation," said Gédéon Spilett. "Lincoln Island is unknown to navigators, for it isn't even shown on the most recent maps. Don't you think, Cyrus, that this is a reason for a ship that unexpectedly finds itself in sight of this new land to seek to visit it rather than to flee from it?

"Certainly," replied Pencroff.

"I think so too," added the engineer. "One can even argue that it is a captain's duty to signal and therefore to come to recognize any land or island not yet cataloged, and Lincoln Island is in that case."

"Well, then," said Pencroff, "let's assume this ship lands, that it anchors there, a few cables away from our island, what will we do?"

This question, suddenly posed, initially remained unanswered. But Cyrus Smith, after reflecting, replied in his usual calm tone:

"What we will do, my friends, what we must do, is this: we will communicate with the ship, we will take passage on board, and we will leave our island after taking possession of it in the name of the Union States. Then we will return with all those who want to follow us to colonize it definitively and provide the American republic with a useful station in this part of the Pacific Ocean!

"Hurray!" shouted Pencroff, "and it won't be a small gift that we give to our country! The colonization is already almost complete, the names are assigned to all parts of the island, there's a natural harbor, a freshwater source, roads, a telegraph line, a shipyard, a factory, and we'll just have to get Lincoln Island included on the maps!

"But what if someone takes it while we are away?" Gédéon Spilett observed.

"A thousand devils!" cried the sailor, "I'd rather stay alone to guard it, and by

Pencroff's faith, they wouldn't steal it from me like a watch from a tourist's pocket!"

For an hour, it was impossible to say for certain whether the indicated vessel was heading toward or away from Lincoln Island. It had approached, however, but at what speed was it sailing? That was something Pencroff could not determine. However, since the wind blew from the northeast, it was likely to assume that this ship was sailing with a starboard tack. Besides, the breeze was good to push it toward the shores of the island, and with the calm sea, it had no fear of approaching, though the soundings were not indicated on the map.

Around four o'clock, — an hour after he was called, — Ayrton arrived at Granite-House. He entered the great room, saying: "At your service, gentlemen." Cyrus Smith extended his hand to him, as he usually did, and, leading him to the window: "Ayrton," he said, "we asked you to come for a serious reason. A ship is in sight of the island."

Ayrton initially paled slightly, and his eyes blurred for a moment. Then, leaning out of the window, he scanned the horizon, but saw nothing.

"Take this telescope," said Gédéon Spilett, "and look closely, Ayrton, for it is possible that this ship is the Duncan, come to these seas to bring you back."

"The Duncan!" murmured Ayrton. "Already!"

That last word slipped involuntarily from Ayrton's lips, who let his head drop into his hands.

Twelve years of abandonment on a deserted islet did not seem a sufficient expiation to him? Did the repentant guilty party not still feel forgiven, either in his own eyes or in the eyes of others?

"No," he said, "no! It cannot be the Duncan."

"Look, Ayrton," said the engineer, "for it is important that we know in advance what to think."

Ayrton took the telescope and directed it toward the indicated direction. For several minutes, he observed the horizon without moving, without uttering a single word. Then: "Indeed, it is a ship," he said, "but I do not believe it is the Duncan.— Why wouldn't it be him? asked Gideon Spilett.

— Because the Duncan is a steam yacht, and I don't see any trace of smoke, either above or near that ship.

— Maybe it's just sailing? Pencroff suggested. The wind is favorable for the course it's taking, and it must be trying to save its coal, being so far from land.

— It's possible you're right, Mr. Pencroff, Ayrton replied, and that ship has put out its fires. Let's let it reach the shore, and we will soon know what to think.

That said, Ayrton went to sit in a corner of the great hall and remained silent. The settlers continued to discuss the unknown ship, but Ayrton did not participate in the conversation.

They were all in a state of mind that wouldn't allow them to continue their work. Gideon Spilett and Pencroff were unusually anxious, pacing back and forth, unable to sit still. Harbert felt more curious. Nab, alone, maintained his usual calm.

Wasn't his country wherever his master was?

As for the engineer, he remained absorbed in his thoughts, and deep down, he feared more than he wanted the arrival of this ship.

Meanwhile, the vessel had come a little closer to the island. With the help of the telescope, it became possible to recognize that it was a long-distance ship, and not one of those Malay praos usually used by Pacific pirates. It could then be believed that the engineer's fears were unfounded, and that the presence of this ship in the waters of Lincoln Island did not pose a danger to it. After careful observation, Pencroff believed he could affirm that this ship was rigged as a brig and was heading obliquely toward the coast, on a starboard tack, under its lower sails, topsails, and jibs. This was confirmed by Ayrton.

But at this pace, it would soon disappear behind the point of Cape Griffe, as it was heading southwest, making it necessary to go up to the heights of Washington Bay, near Port Balloon, to observe it. A troublesome circumstance, since it was already five o'clock in the evening, and dusk would soon make any observation very difficult.

"What will we do when night falls?" asked Gideon Spilett. "Shall we light a fire to signal our presence on this shore?"

This was a serious question, and yet, despite some premonitions the engineer had, it was resolved positively. During the night, the ship could disappear, move away forever, and once this ship was gone, would another return to the waters of Lincoln Island? Who could predict what the future held for the settlers?

"Yes," said the reporter, "we must let this ship, whatever it is, know that the island is inhabited. Neglecting the opportunity presented to us would only lead to future regrets!"

It was decided that Nab and Pencroff would go to Port Balloon, and that there, once night fell, they would light a big fire whose brightness would necessarily attract the attention of the brig's crew.

But just as Nab and the sailor were preparing to leave Granite House, the ship changed its course and headed directly toward the island, steering toward Union Bay. This brig was a fast mover, as it quickly approached.

Nab and Pencroff then suspended their departure, and the telescope was put in Ayrton's hands so he could definitively identify whether this ship was the Duncan or not. The Scottish yacht was also rigged as a brig. The question was whether a chimney rose between the two masts of the observed vessel, which was now only ten miles away.

The horizon was still very clear. The verification was easy, and Ayrton soon let his telescope drop, saying:

"It's not the Duncan! It couldn't be him!..."

Pencroff once again framed the brig in the sight of the telescope and recognized that this brig, with a tonnage of three to four hundred tons, beautifully streamlined, boldly rigged, and superbly built for sailing, must be a fast sea runner. But to what nation did it belong? That was hard to tell.

"And yet," the sailor added, "a flag is flying at its bow, but I can't make out the colors.

— In half an hour, we'll know about that," replied the reporter. "Besides, it's clear that the captain of this ship intends to land, and therefore, if not today, tomorrow at the latest, we will meet him.

— Whatever! said Pencroff. It's better to know who we're dealing with, and I wouldn't mind recognizing his colors, especially that guy!"

And as he spoke, the sailor did not take his eyes off the telescope.

The day was starting to fade, and with it, the offshore wind was dying down too. The brig's flag, less taut, was getting tangled in the rigging, and it was becoming more difficult to observe.

"That's not an American flag," Pencroff said from time to time, "nor an English one, whose red would be easy to spot, nor French or German colors, nor the white flag of Russia, nor Spain's yellow... it looks like it's a solid color... let's see... in these seas... what more commonly would we find?... the Chilean flag? But it's tricolored... Brazilian? It's green... Japanese? It's black and yellow... whereas this one..."

At that moment, a breeze unfurled the unknown flag.

Ayrton, grabbing the telescope that the sailor had let drop, applied it to his eye and, in a low voice, cried out:

"The black flag!"

Indeed, a dark fabric was unfurling at the brig's bow, and it was only right that now it could be considered a suspicious vessel!

Had the engineer been right in his hunches? Was it a pirate ship? Was it prowling those low waters of the Pacific, competing with the Malay praos that still infest them? What could it want on the shores of Lincoln Island? Did it see an unknown land, unrecognized, suitable for becoming a hideout for stolen cargo? Was it asking these shores for a port of refuge for the winter months? Was the honest domain of the settlers destined to transform into a infamy refuge—a sort of capital of Pacific piracy?

All these thoughts instinctively came to the settlers' minds. There was no doubt, in any case, about the meaning to attach to the color of the flag displayed. It was indeed that of sea robbers! It was what the Duncan would have flown if the convicts had succeeded in their criminal plans!

There was no time to waste in discussion.

"My friends," said Cyrus Smith, "perhaps this ship just wants to observe the island's coastline? Maybe its crew won't land? That's a chance. Whatever happens, we must do everything to hide our presence here. The mill, set up on the Grande-Vue plateau, is too easily recognizable. Let Ayrton and Nab take down its sails. Let's also disguise the windows of Granite House under thicker foliage. Let all fires be put out. Let nothing finally betray the presence of man on this island!

— What about our boat? Harbert asked.

— Oh!" replied Pencroff, "it's sheltered in Port Balloon, and I dare those scoundrels to find it there!"

The engineer's orders were immediately carried out. Nab and Ayrton went up to the plateau and took necessary measures to hide any signs of habitation. While they were working on this task, their companions went to the edge of the Jacamar woods and brought back a large quantity of branches and vines, which at a distance would resemble natural foliage and sufficiently cover the openings in the granite wall. At the same time, the ammunition and weapons were arranged so they could be used at a moment's notice, in case of an unexpected attack.

When all these precautions had been taken:

"My friends," said Cyrus Smith—and his voice showed that he was moved—"if these wretches want to seize Lincoln Island, we will defend it, won't we?

— Yes, Cyrus," replied the reporter, "and if necessary, we will all die to defend it!"

The engineer extended his hand to his companions, who clasped it warmly.

Only Ayrton, still in his corner, had not joined the settlers. Perhaps he, the former convict, still felt unworthy!

Cyrus Smith understood what was happening in Ayrton's soul and, going to him:

"And you, Ayrton," he asked him, "what will you do?

— My duty," Ayrton replied.

Then he went to position himself by the window and gazed through the foliage.

It was half past seven. The sun had disappeared about twenty minutes ago behind Granite House. Consequently, the eastern horizon was gradually darkening. Meanwhile, the brig continued to approach Union Bay. It was no more than eight miles away, right opposite the Grande-Vue plateau, as after rounding Cape Griffe, it had gained a lot of ground to the north, aided by the rising tide. One could even say that, at that distance, it had already entered the vast bay, since a straight line drawn from Cape Griffe to Cape Mandibule remained to its west, on its starboard side.

Would the brig sink into the bay? That was the first question. Once in the bay, would it anchor? That was the second.

Would it only be satisfied, after observing the coastline, to move offshore again without landing its crew? They would find out within an hour. The settlers had no choice but to wait.

Cyrus Smith had not seen without deep anxiety the suspicious ship flying the black flag.

Wasn't it a direct threat against the work that his companions and he had accomplished so far? The pirates—there was no doubt that the crew of this brig were indeed such—had they already visited this island since they were raising their colors after landing?

Had they conducted any raid before, which would explain certain peculiarities that had remained unexplained until then? Was there in its uncharted areas some accomplice ready to communicate with them?

To all these questions he silently asked himself, Cyrus Smith had no answers; but he felt that the situation of the colony could only be very seriously compromised by the arrival of this brig.

However, his companions and he were resolved to resist to the last extremity. Were these pirates numerous and better armed than the settlers?

That was certainly a key question!

But how to find out?

Night had fallen. The new moon, swept away in the solar rays, had disappeared. A profound darkness enveloped the island and the sea. The clouds, heavy and piled up on the horizon, let no light filter through. The wind had completely died down with dusk. Not a leaf stirred in the trees, and not a wave murmured on the shore. Nothing could be seen from the ship; all its lights were extinguished, and if it were still in sight of the island, it was impossible to even determine its position.

"Hey! Who knows?" Pencroff then said. "Maybe that damned ship has sailed during the night, and we won't find it anymore at dawn?"

As if in response to the sailor's remark, a bright flash shot out to sea, and a cannon shot echoed.

The ship was still there, and there were artillery pieces aboard.

Six seconds had passed between the flash and the shot.

Thus, the brig was about a mile and a quarter from the coast.

At the same time, a sound of chains was heard grinding through the hawse pipes.

The ship had anchored in sight of Granite House!

2

There was no longer any doubt about the pirates' intentions. They had anchored at a short distance from the island, and it was clear that, the next day, using their boats, they planned to land on the shore!

Cyrus Smith and his companions were ready to act, but as resolute as they were, they had to remember to be cautious. Perhaps their presence could still be concealed, in case the pirates were content to land along the coastline without moving further into the island. It was possible, after all, that they had no other plan than to gather water at the Mercy watering place, and it wasn't unlikely that the bridge, one and a half miles from the mouth, and the improvements to the chimneys, might escape their notice.

But why fly that flag at the brig's bow?

Why that cannon shot? Pure bravado, no doubt, unless it was a sign of a takeover! Cyrus Smith now knew that the ship was heavily armed. Now, to respond to the cannon of the pirates, what did the settlers of Lincoln Island have? Just a few rifles.

"However," Cyrus Smith pointed out, "we are here in an impregnable situation. The enemy cannot discover the opening of the outlet, now that it is concealed under reeds and grasses, and therefore, it is impossible for them to penetrate Granite House.

— But our plantations, our poultry yard, our corral, everything in fact! they can ravage everything in a matter of hours! Pencroff exclaimed, stamping his foot.

— Everything, Pencroff," Cyrus Smith replied, "and we have no means to prevent them from doing so.

— Are they numerous? That's the question," the reporter then said. "If there are only a dozen, we know how to stop them, but what if there are forty, fifty, maybe even more!

— Mr. Smith," Ayrton then said, stepping toward the engineer, "would you grant me permission?

— Which one, my friend?

— The leave to go to the ship to assess the strength of its crew.

— But, Ayrton...," the engineer replied hesitantly, "you'll be risking your life...

— Why not, sir?

— That's more than your duty, you know.

— I have more than my duty to fulfill," Ayrton replied.

— Would you swim to the ship? Gideon Spilett asked.

— No, sir, but I will swim. The pirogue wouldn't be able to go where a man can slip through the water.

— Do you realize that the brig is a mile and a quarter from the coast? Harbert said.

— I'm a good swimmer, Mr. Harbert.

— It's risking your life, I tell you," the engineer reiterated.

— It doesn't matter," Ayrton replied. "Mr. Smith, I ask this as a favor. Perhaps this is a way for me to redeem myself in my own eyes!

— Go, Ayrton," the engineer replied, who well understood that a refusal would deeply sadden the former convict, who had become an honest man.

— I will accompany you," said Pencroff.

— You doubt me!" Ayrton replied sharply.

Then, more humbly:

"Alas!

— No! No!" Cyrus Smith replied excitedly, "No, Ayrton! Pencroff does not doubt you! You have misinterpreted his words.— Indeed, replied the sailor, I suggest to Ayrton that I accompany him only to the islet. It's possible, though unlikely, that one of those scoundrels has landed, and two men will not be too many, in that case, to prevent him from raising the alarm. I will wait for Ayrton on the islet, and he can go to the ship alone, as he has offered to do."

With this plan agreed upon, Ayrton made his preparations for departure. His project was bold, but it could succeed, thanks to the darkness of the night. Once he reached the vessel, with his grip on either the stays or the shrouds, Ayrton could assess the number and possibly catch the intentions of the convicts.

Ayrton and Pencroff, followed by their companions, descended to the shore. Ayrton undressed and rubbed himself with grease, so as to suffer less from the cold water, which was still chilly. He might indeed have to stay in it for several hours.

Meanwhile, Pencroff and Nab went to fetch the canoe, tied a few hundred paces up the Mercy River, and when they returned, Ayrton was ready to depart. A blanket was thrown over Ayrton's shoulders, and the colonists came to shake his hand.

Ayrton boarded the canoe with Pencroff. It was half-past ten at night when they both vanished into the darkness. Their companions returned to wait for them at the chimneys.

The canal was easily crossed, and the canoe came to shore on the opposite side of the islet. This was done with some caution, in case pirates were lurking in the area. But after observing, it seemed certain that the islet was deserted. So, Ayrton, followed by Pencroff, crossed it quickly, startling the birds nesting in the rock crevices; then, without hesitating, he dove into the sea and swam silently towards the ship, whose lights, having been recently lit, indicated its exact location.

As for Pencroff, he settled into a nook on the shore and waited for his companion's return.

Meanwhile, Ayrton swam with strong strokes, gliding through the water without causing even the slightest ripple. His head barely broke the surface, and his eyes were fixed on the dark mass of the brig, whose lights were reflecting on the sea.

He thought only of the duty he had promised to carry out and didn't even consider the dangers he faced, not just on board the ship, but also in these waters frequently frequented by sharks. The current was carrying him away, and he was quickly distancing himself from the coast. A half-hour later, without being seen or heard, Ayrton glided through the water, approached the ship, and grasped the bow's stays. He then took a breath, and, hoisting himself onto the chains, managed to reach the end of the bowsprit. There were some sailor pants drying there.

He put one on. Then, having secured himself firmly, he listened.

People were not sleeping on board the brig. On the contrary. They were talking, singing, laughing. And here are the words, accompanied by curses, that particularly struck Ayrton:

"Good acquisition, our brig!

— She sails well, the speedy! She deserves her name!

— All the navy of Norfolk can follow her! Get after her!

— Hooray for her captain!

— Hooray for Bob Harvey!"

What Ayrton felt when he heard this fragment of conversation can be understood when one learns that in this Bob Harvey, he recognized one of his former companions from Australia, a bold sailor who had taken up his criminal projects. Bob Harvey had seized this brig in the waters near Norfolk Island, which was loaded with weapons, ammunition, and all kinds of tools intended for one of the Sandwich Islands. His entire gang had boarded, and, having turned pirates after being convicts, these wretches roamed the Pacific, destroying ships and massacring crews, more ferocious than the Malays themselves!

These convicts were speaking loudly, recounting their exploits while drinking excessively, and this is what Ayrton was able to understand:

The current crew of the speedy consisted solely of English prisoners who had escaped from Norfolk.

Now, here is what Norfolk is.

At 29.2 degrees south latitude and 165.42 degrees east longitude, in the eastern part of Australia, lies a small island six leagues around, dominated by Mount Pitt, which rises eleven hundred feet above sea level. This is Norfolk Island, the site of a settlement where the most unyielding condemned prisoners from English penitentiaries are held. There are five hundred of them, subjected to harsh discipline, facing terrible punishments, guarded by one hundred and fifty soldiers and one hundred and fifty staff members under the orders of a governor. It would be hard to imagine a worse gathering of scoundrels. Sometimes—even though it is rare—despite the excessive surveillance they are under, several manage to escape by seizing ships they surprise, and they then run through the Polynesian archipelagos.

This is what Bob Harvey and his companions had done.

This is what Ayrton had once wanted to do. Bob Harvey had seized the brig the speedy, anchored near Norfolk Island; the crew had been massacred, and, for a year, this ship, having turned into a pirate vessel, had been roaming the

Pacific, under the command of Harvey, once a long-haul captain, now a sea marauder, whom Ayrton knew well!

The convicts were mostly gathered on the quarterdeck, at the back of the ship, but a few, sprawled on the deck, were talking loudly.

As the conversation continued amidst shouts and drinking, Ayrton learned that it was only by chance that the speedy had come into view of Lincoln Island. Bob Harvey had never set foot there, but as Cyrus Smith had suspected, finding this unknown land, which was not marked on any map, in his path, he had formed the plan to visit it, and, if necessary, if it suited him, to make it the brig's port of call.

As for the black flag flying at the stern of the speedy and the cannon fire that had been shot, like warships when they lower their colors, it was pure pirate bravado.

It was not a signal, and no communication yet existed between the escapees from Norfolk and Lincoln Island.

Thus, the colonists' domain was threatened by immense danger. Obviously, the island, with its easy water source, its small port, its resources of all kinds so well developed by the colonists, its hidden depths of Granite House, could only suit the convicts; in their hands, it would become an excellent refuge, and by virtue of its being unknown, it would ensure them, perhaps for a long time, impunity and security.

It was also clear that the colonists' lives would not be respected, and the first concern of Bob Harvey and his accomplices would be to massacre them without mercy.

Cyrus Smith and his group therefore had no option to flee, to hide on the island, since the convicts planned to reside there, and since, in the event that the speedy left for an expedition, it was probable that a few men from the crew would remain onshore to settle there. Thus, fighting was necessary, they had to destroy these wretches, unworthy of pity, and against whom any means would be justified.

That's what Ayrton thought, and he knew very well that Cyrus Smith would share his point of view.

But was resistance, and ultimately victory, possible? That depended on the armament of the brig and the number of men on board. This was what Ayrton resolved to ascertain at all costs, and as, an hour after his arrival, the shouting had begun to calm down, and many of the convicts were already plunged into the sleep of drunkenness, Ayrton did not hesitate to venture onto the deck of the speedy, which the extinguished lanterns left in profound darkness.

He climbed up to the bowsprit, and from there, he made his way to the fore-deck of the brig. Slipping between the convicts sprawled here and there, he took a tour of the vessel and recognized that the speedy was armed with four cannons, which were capable of launching eight to ten-pound projectiles. He even checked, by touching them, that these cannons loaded from the breech. They were therefore modern pieces, easy to use, and with a terrible effect.

As for the men lying on the deck, there were about ten of them, but it was likely that more, possibly many more, were sleeping inside the brig. Moreover, by listening, Ayrton believed he understood that there were about fifty of them on board. That was a lot for the six colonists of Lincoln Island! But finally, thanks to Ayrton's dedication, Cyrus Smith would not be caught off guard; he would know the strength of his adversaries and take his measures accordingly.

So, all that was left for Ayrton was to return and report to his companions about the mission he had undertaken, and he prepared to head back towards the front of the brig to slip back into the sea.

But, at that moment, a heroic thought struck this man who wanted — as he had said — to do more than his duty. It was to sacrifice his life, but he would save the island and the colonists. Cyrus Smith would obviously not be able to resist fifty armed bandits, who, either by breaking into Granite House force-fully, or by starving the besieged, would overcome them. And then he pictured his saviors, those who had made him a man and an honest man, to whom he owed everything, killed mercilessly, their work destroyed, their island turned into a pirate den! He told himself that, in the end, he, Ayrton, was the original cause of so many disasters, since his former companion, Bob Harvey, had merely realized his own plans, and a sense of horror seized all of his being. And then he was overtaken by an irresistible urge to blow up the brig, taking with it all who were aboard. Ayrton would perish in the explosion, but he would do his duty.

Ayrton didn't hesitate. Getting to the powder magazine, which is always located at the back of a ship, was easy. The powder should not be lacking on a vessel engaged in such business, and it would take just a spark to annihilate it in an instant.

Ayrton carefully lowered himself into the between-decks, littered with numerous sleepers, whom drunkenness, more than sleep, kept heavy. A lantern was lit at the foot of the main mast, around which was hung a rack filled with all kinds of firearms.

Ayrton detached a revolver from the rack and ensured that it was loaded and cocked. That was all he needed to carry out the act of destruction.

He then slithered towards the back, so as to arrive under the brig's quarter-deck, where the magazine must be.

However, it was difficult to crawl without bumping into some half-asleep convict in this almost dark between-deck. Thus, there were curses and blows. More than once, Ayrton was forced to pause his progress. But finally, he arrived at the bulkhead closing the aft compartment, and found the door that should open onto the magazine itself.

Ayrton, having to force it open, got to work.

It was a difficult task to accomplish quietly, as it involved breaking a padlock. But under Ayrton's strong hand, the padlock sprang open, and the door was opened... at this moment, an arm rested on Ayrton's shoulder.

"What are you doing there?" demanded a tall man in a harsh voice, who, rising from the shadows, abruptly shone a lantern in Ayrton's face.

Ayrton recoiled. In a brief flash of the lantern, he recognized his former accomplice, Bob Harvey, but he could not be recognized by him, as he was supposed to believe Ayrton was dead long ago.

"What are you doing there?" said Bob Harvey, grabbing Ayrton by the waist-band of his pants.

But Ayrton, without answering, forcefully pushed off the convict's leader and tried to leap into the magazine. A shot from his revolver among those barrels of powder, and everything would have been over!...

"Help me, boys!" Bob Harvey shouted. Two or three pirates, awakened by his voice, rose up, and throwing themselves on Ayrton, they tried to bring him down. The strong Ayrton shook off their grips. Two shots from his revolver rang out, and two convicts fell; but a knife blow he could not block cut into his shoulder flesh.

Ayrton understood well that he could no longer carry out his plan. Bob Harvey had closed the magazine door, and a movement was taking place in the between-deck, indicating a general awakening of the pirates.

Ayrton had to reserve himself to fight alongside Cyrus Smith. He had no choice but to flee!

But was escape still possible? It was doubtful, although Ayrton was determined to try everything to rejoin his companions.

He had four shots left. Two then fired, one of which aimed at Bob Harvey, did not hit him, at least not badly, and Ayrton, taking advantage of a movement backward from his opponents, rushed towards the hatch ladder in an effort to reach the deck of the brig. As he passed near the lantern, he smashed it with the butt of his weapon, plunging everything into deep darkness, which would favor his escape. Two or three pirates awakened by the noise were now descending the ladder. A fifth shot from Ayrton's revolver knocked one down the steps, and the others disappeared, not understanding what was happening. Ayrton, in two jumps, was on the deck of the brig, and three seconds later, after firing his revolver one last time at the face of a pirate who had just grabbed him by the neck, he vaulted over the bulwarks and plunged into the sea.

Ayrton had not traveled six fathoms when bullets zipped around him like hail. What must have been the emotions of Pencroff, sheltered under a rock on the islet, those of Cyrus Smith, the reporter, Harbert, and Nab, huddled in the chimneys, when they heard these explosions aboard the brig. They had rushed to the shore, their rifles ready, poised to repel any aggression.

For them, there was no doubt!

Ayrton, caught by the pirates, had been slaughtered by them, and perhaps these wretches were going to take advantage of the night to launch an assault on the island! Half an hour passed amidst mortal dread. However, the sounds of gunfire had ceased, and neither Ayrton nor Pencroff had reappeared. Was the islet then overrun? Should they rush to the aid of Ayrton and Pencroff? But how?

The sea, high at that moment, made the canal impassable. The canoe was no longer there! Just imagine the horrible anxiety that seized Cyrus Smith and his companions!

Finally, around twelve-thirty, a canoe carrying two men reached the shore. It was Ayrton, slightly wounded in the shoulder, and Pencroff, safe and sound, whom their friends received with open arms. Immediately, they all took refuge in the chimneys. There, Ayrton recounted what had happened and did not hide his plan to blow up the brig that he had attempted to execute. All hands reached out to Ayrton, who did not hide how serious the situation was.

The pirates were alert. They knew that Lincoln Island was inhabited. They would only land in large numbers and well-armed. They would show no mercy.

If the colonists fell into their hands, they should expect no pity!

"Well! We will know how to die!" said the reporter.

"Let's go back and keep watch," replied the engineer.

"Do we have any chance of getting out of this, Mr. Cyrus?" asked the sailor.

"Yes, Pencroff."

"Hmm! Six against fifty!"

"Yes! Six!... not counting..."

"Who else?" asked Pencroff.

Cyrus didn't answer, but pointed to the sky with his hand.

3

The night passed without incident. The colonists stayed vigilant and did not abandon their post at the chimneys. The pirates, for their part, did not seem to have made any attempt to land. Since the last shots had been fired at Ayrton, there had been no detonations or even noise to reveal the presence of the brig on the island's shore. One might have thought that it had weighed anchor, thinking it faced too strong a foe, and had moved away from the area.

But that was not the case, and when dawn began to appear, the colonists could see a vague mass in the morning mist. It was the speedy.

"Here, my friends," said the engineer, "are the plans I think we should make before this fog completely lifts. It hides us from the pirates, and we can act without alerting them. What is important, above all, to let the convicts believe, is that the island's inhabitants are many and, therefore, capable of resisting them. I propose that we divide into three groups: the first at the chimneys, the second at the mouth of the Mercy. As for the third, I believe it would be wise to place it on the islet, to prevent or at least delay any attempt at landing. We have two rifles and four guns at our disposal. Each of us will be armed, and since we are well supplied with powder and bullets, we won't spare our shots. We have nothing to fear from their guns, nor even from the brig's cannons. What could they do against these rocks? And since we won't be firing from the windows of Granite House, the pirates won't think to send shells that could cause irreparable damage. What we must fear is the need to come to hand-to-hand combat since the convicts have the numbers on their side. Therefore, we must try to oppose any landing without revealing ourselves. So let's not save the ammunition. Let's shoot often, but shoot accurately. Each of us has eight or ten enemies to kill, and they must be killed!"

Cyrus Smith had clearly outlined the situation while speaking in the calmest voice, as if he were directing a project instead of organizing a battle. His companions approved the plan without uttering a word. It was now just a matter of taking their positions before the fog completely lifted.

Nab and Pencroff quickly returned to Granite House and brought back enough ammunition. Gideon Spilett and Ayrton, both very good shots, were armed with the two precision rifles that could hit nearly a mile away. The four other guns were distributed among Cyrus Smith, Nab, Pencroff, and Harbert.

Here's how the posts were formed.

Cyrus Smith and Harbert stayed hidden at the chimneys, thus commanding the shore at the foot of Granite House over a wide radius.

Gideon Spilett and Nab went to hide among the rocks at the mouth of the Mercy—where the bridge and culverts had been raised—to prevent any passage by boat and even any landing on the opposite shore.

As for Ayrton and Pencroff, they pushed the canoe into the water and prepared to cross the channel to occupy two separate positions on the islet. In this way, gunfire exploding from four different points would lead the convicts to think that the island was both sufficiently populated and strongly defended. If a landing were to occur and they couldn't prevent it, and even if they saw themselves about to be outflanked by some boat from the brig, Pencroff and Ayrton were to return with the canoe to gain a foothold on the shore and move toward the most threatened spot.

Before going to their posts, the colonists shook hands one last time. Pencroff managed to control his emotions enough to embrace Harbert, his child!... and they parted. A few moments later, Cyrus Smith and Harbert on one side, the reporter and Nab on the other, had disappeared behind the rocks, and five minutes later, Ayrton and Pencroff, having successfully crossed the channel, landed on the islet and hid in the recesses of its eastern shore. None of them could be seen, as they barely distinguished the brig through the fog.

It was six-thirty in the morning.

Soon, the fog gradually tore apart in the upper layers of air, and the tops of the brig's masts emerged from the mist. For a few moments, thick steam swirled above the surface of the sea; then a breeze sprang up, quickly dispersing this mass of mist.

The speedy appeared in full, anchored by two anchors, heading north, and presenting its port side to the island. As Cyrus Smith had estimated, it was no more than a mile and a quarter from the shore.

The sinister black flag waved at its corner.

The engineer, with his binoculars, could see that the four cannons making up the ship's artillery had been pointed toward the island. They were clearly ready to fire at the first signal.

However, the speedy remained silent. About thirty pirates were seen moving back and forth on deck. A few had climbed onto the quarterdeck; two others, stationed on the topsail yard and equipped with telescopes, were observing the island with extreme attention.

Certainly, Bob Harvey and his crew could hardly comprehend what had transpired during the night aboard the brig.

This half-naked man, who had just broken down the door of the powder magazine and against whom they had struggled, who had fired his revolver six times at them, who had killed one of their own and injured two others—had he escaped their bullets? Had he managed to swim back to shore? Where had he come from? What was he doing aboard? Had his plan really been to blow up the brig, as Bob Harvey thought? All of this must have been quite confusing in the convicts' minds. But what they could no longer doubt was that the unknown island before which the speedy had anchored was inhabited and that there was perhaps a whole colony ready to defend it. And yet, no one was showing themselves, neither on the shore nor on the heights. The coast seemed absolutely deserted. In any case, there was no trace of habitation. Had the inhabitants fled inland?

This was what the pirate chief must have been wondering, and undoubtedly, as a prudent man, he was looking to scout the area before committing his gang.

For an hour and a half, there were no signs of attack or landing aboard the brig. It was clear that Bob Harvey was hesitating. His best glasses, no doubt, had not allowed him to spot a single one of the colonists hiding among the rocks. It wasn't even likely that his attention had been drawn to the veil of green branches and vines that concealed the windows of Granite House and contrasted with the bare wall. Indeed, how could he have imagined that a dwelling was excavated, at that height, in the granite massif? From Cape Claw to Mandible Cap, along the entire perimeter of Union Bay, nothing had informed him that the island was or could be occupied.

At eight o'clock, however, the colonists noticed a certain movement taking place aboard the speedy. They were hauling on the tackles of the boats, and a canoe was lowered into the water.

Seven men descended into it. They were armed with rifles; one took the helm, four took the oars, and the other two, crouched at the bow, ready to shoot, were examining the island. Their purpose was undoubtedly to conduct a preliminary reconnaissance but not to land, since in that case they would have come in greater numbers.

The pirates, perched in the rigging up to the topsail yard, had evidently been able to see that an islet covered the coast and that it was separated from it by a channel about half a mile wide. However, it soon became clear to Cyrus Smith, observing the direction taken by the canoe, that it would not initially attempt to enter this channel, but would approach the islet, a measure of caution justified, in any case.

Pencroff and Ayrton, each hiding on either side in narrow crevices of rock, saw it coming directly toward them, and they waited until it was within good range.

The canoe advanced with extreme caution.

The oars only dipped into the water at long intervals. One could also see that one of the convicts placed at the bow held a sounding line in hand and was attempting to gauge the channel carved by the current of the Mercy. This indicated Bob Harvey's intention to move his brig closer to the coast. About thirty pirates, scattered in the shrouds, were watching every movement of the canoe and noting certain landmarks that would allow them to land safely.

The canoe was only two cables away from the islet when it stopped. The man at the helm, standing, was looking for the best point to approach. In an instant, two gunshots rang out. A small cloud of smoke swirled above the rocks of the islet. The helmsman and the look-out fell back into the canoe. The bullets from Ayrton and Pencroff had struck them both at the same time.

Almost immediately, a louder blast was heard, a glaring jet of steam burst from the side of the brig, and a cannonball, striking the top of the rocks that sheltered Ayrton and Pencroff, shattered them to pieces, but the two shooters were unscathed.

Horrible curses erupted from the canoe, which immediately resumed its course. The helmsman was quickly replaced by one of his companions, and the oars plunged vigorously into the water.

However, instead of returning aboard, as one might have expected, the canoe continued along the shore of the islet, aiming to turn it by its southern point. The pirates were rowing with all their strength to get out of reach of the bullets.

They advanced this way until five cables from the indented part of the coast that ended at the point of the wreck, and after rounding it in a semicircular line, still protected by the brig's cannons, they headed toward the mouth of the Mercy.

Their obvious intention was to penetrate into the channel and take the colonists who were posted on the islet in a rear attack, so that they, regardless of their numbers, would be caught between the fires of the canoe and the fires of the brig, and would find themselves in a very disadvantageous position. A quarter of an hour passed this way as the canoe moved in this direction. Absolute silence, complete calm in the air and on the waters.

Pencroff and Ayrton, even though they understood they were at risk of being outflanked, did not abandon their post, whether because they did not yet want to reveal themselves to the attackers and expose themselves to the speedy's cannons, or because they were counting on Nab and Gideon Spilett, watching at the mouth of the river, and on Cyrus Smith and Harbert, hidden in the rocks of the chimneys.

Twenty minutes after the first gunshots, the canoe was across from the Mercy and less than two cables away. As the tide began to rise with its usual strength, provoked by the narrowness of the strait, the convicts felt themselves being pulled toward the river, and it was only with great effort that they kept themselves in the middle of the channel. But as they passed within good range of the mouth of the Mercy, two bullets greeted them on their way, and two of their number fell in the boat.

Nab and Spilett hadn't missed their shot. Immediately, the brig fired a second cannonball at the position betrayed by the smoke of firearms, but with no other result than chipping some rocks. At this moment, the canoe contained only three able-bodied men. Caught in the current, it shot into the channel like an arrow, passing before Cyrus Smith and Harbert, who, deeming it not within range, stayed silent; then, turning around the northern point of the islet with the two remaining oars, it prepared to regain the brig.

So far, the colonists had no cause for complaint.

The game was not going well for their adversaries. They already counted four men seriously injured, perhaps dead; they, on the other hand, had not been wounded and hadn't lost a bullet. If the pirates continued to assault them this way, if they renewed any attempt at landing with the canoe, one by one they could be destroyed.

One can understand how advantageous the engineer's plans were. The pirates could believe they were dealing with numerous and well-armed adversaries, whom they would not easily defeat. A half-hour passed before the canoe, which had to struggle against the current from the open sea, rejoined the speedy. Terrible cries resounded when it returned aboard with the wounded, and three or four cannon shots were fired that could yield no result.

But then other convicts, mad with anger and perhaps still from the revelry of the previous day, jumped into the boat, numbering about a dozen. A second canoe was also launched into the sea in which eight men took place, and while the first was heading straight for the islet to flush out the colonists, the second maneuvered to force the entrance to the Mercy.

The situation was clearly becoming very perilous for Pencroff and Ayrton, and they understood they had to regain solid ground.

However, they still waited for the first canoe to be within good range, and two bullets, skillfully aimed, again disrupted its crew. Then, Pencroff and Ayrton, abandoning their post—though not without enduring about ten rifle shots—ran across the islet with all the speed their legs could muster, threw themselves into the canoe, crossed the channel just as the second canoe reached its southern tip, and rushed to hide at the chimneys; they had barely rejoined Cyrus Smith and Harbert when the islet was overrun and the pirates from the first boat were searching it in every direction.

Almost at the same moment, new detonations exploded at the Mercy post, to which the second canoe had quickly approached. Two, out of eight, of the men aboard were mortally struck by Gideon Spilett and Nab, and the boat itself, irresistibly carried onto the reefs, was smashed at the mouth of the Mercy. But the six survivors, raising their weapons above their heads to keep them away from the water, managed to get a foothold on the right bank of the river. Then, seeing themselves too exposed to the fire from the post, they fled as fast as they could towards the tip of the wreck, out of range of the bullets.

The current situation was therefore this: on the islet, twelve convicts, some of whom were likely injured, but still having a boat at their disposal; on the island, six landed, but unable to reach Granite-House because they couldn't cross the river, as the bridges were up.

"Alright! said Pencroff as he rushed into the chimneys, it's alright, Mr. Cyrus! What do you think?

"I think," replied the engineer, "that the fight is going to take a new form, because we can't assume these convicts are foolish enough to continue under such unfavorable conditions!

"They still can't cross the channel," said the sailor. "Ayrton's and Mr. Spilett's rifles are there to prevent that. You know they reach more than a mile!

"Certainly," replied Harbert, "but what can two rifles do against the cannons of the brig?

"Hey! The brig isn't in the channel yet, I suppose!" replied Pencroff.

"And what if it comes in?" said Cyrus Smith.

"That's impossible; it would risk grounding and getting lost in there!

"It's possible," Ayrton replied. "The convicts could take advantage of the high tide to enter the channel, even if they end up grounding at low tide, and then, under fire from their cannons, our posts wouldn't be defensible anymore.

"By the thousand devils of hell!" cried Pencroff, "it seems, really, that those scoundrels are preparing to weigh anchor!

"Perhaps we will be forced to take refuge in Granite-House?" Harbert pointed out.

"Let's wait!" replied Cyrus Smith.

"But Nab and Mr. Spilett?..." said Pencroff.

"They will know how to join us in time. Be ready, Ayrton. It's your rifle and Spilett's that need to speak now."

It was all too true! The brig was beginning to turn on its anchor and showed its intention to move closer to the islet. The sea would still rise for another hour and a half, and the flood current was already broken, making it easy for the brig to maneuver. But as for entering the channel, Pencroff, contrary to Ayrton's opinion, could not believe it would dare to attempt it.

Meanwhile, the pirates occupying the islet had gradually moved towards the opposite shore, and they were no longer separated from the land except by the channel. Armed only with rifles, they could do no harm to the colonists, who were hidden either in the chimneys or at the mouth of the Mercy; but not knowing they were armed with long-range rifles, they also believed they weren't exposed themselves. So they were walking openly across the islet and patrolling its edge.

Their illusion was short-lived. Ayrton's and Gideon Spilett's rifles then spoke and probably said unpleasant things to two of those convicts, as they fell backwards.

It was a general panic. The other ten didn't even take the time to gather their injured or dead companions; they hurried back to the other side of the islet, jumped into the boat that had brought them, and rowed back to shore.

"Eight less!" cried Pencroff. "It's as if Mr. Spilett and Ayrton are coordinating to operate together!

"Gentlemen," said Ayrton while reloading his rifle, "this is going to get serious. The brig is setting sail!

"The anchor's up!... cried Pencroff.

"Yes, and it's already slipping."

Indeed, the distinct clatter of the pawl striking the windlass could be heard as the brig's crew maneuvered. The brig had first come to the call of its anchor; then, once it had been pulled from the bottom, it began to drift towards the shore. The wind was blowing from the sea; the large foresail and the small topsail were raised, and the ship gradually neared the land. From the two positions at Mercy and the chimneys, they watched it maneuvering without showing any sign of life, but not without some emotion. It would be a terrible situation for the colonists when they would be exposed, at close range, to the brig's cannon fire, without being able to respond effectively. How could they then keep the pirates from landing?

Cyrus Smith realized this and wondered what could be done. Soon, he would have to make a decision. But what decision?

To shut themselves inside Granite-House, be besieged there, endure for weeks, even months, since there was plenty of food? Good! But then? The pirates would still be masters of the island, which they would ravage at will, and eventually, they would defeat the prisoners in Granite-House.

However, one chance remains: that Bob Harvey would not dare to take his ship into the channel and would stay outside the islet. Half a mile would still separate him from the shore, and at that distance, his shots might not be extremely harmful.

"Never," repeated Pencroff, "never will this Bob Harvey, since he's a good sailor, enter the channel! He knows well that it would risk the brig if the sea turned rough! And what would happen to him without his ship?"

Meanwhile, the brig had approached the islet, and it was clear that it was trying to reach its lower end. The breeze was light, and since the current had lost much of its strength, Bob Harvey was absolutely in control of how to maneuver.

The path previously followed by the boats had allowed him to recognize the channel, and he had boldly engaged in it. His plan was all too clear: he wanted to ground in front of the chimneys and from there respond with shells and cannonballs to the bullets that had so far decimated his crew.

Soon the brig reached the tip of the islet; it turned it with ease; the brigantine was then unfurled, and the brig, close-hauled, found itself abeam of the Mercy.

"The bandits! They're coming!" cried Pencroff.

At that moment, Cyrus Smith, Ayrton, the sailor, and Harbert were joined by Nab and Gideon Spilett.

The reporter and his companion had deemed it appropriate to leave the Mercy post, from which they could no longer do anything against the ship, and they had acted wisely. It was better for the colonists to be together at a time when a decisive action was likely about to take place. Gideon Spilett and Nab had arrived, slipping behind the rocks, but not without enduring a hail of bullets that did not hit them.

"Spilett! Nab!" cried the engineer. "Are you unhurt?

"No!" replied the reporter, "just a few bruises from ricochets! But that damn brig is entering the channel!

"Yes!" replied Pencroff, "and in less than ten minutes, it will be anchored in front of Granite-House!

"Do you have a plan, Cyrus?" asked the reporter.

"We need to take refuge in Granite-House while there's still time and the convicts can't see us.

"I agree," responded Gideon Spilett; "but once we're locked in...

"We'll take our advice from the circumstances," replied the engineer.

"Let's go then, and hurry!" said the reporter.

"Would you rather, Mr. Cyrus, that Ayrton and I stay here?" asked the sailor.

"What's the point, Pencroff?" replied Cyrus Smith. "No. Let's not separate!"

There was no time to lose. The colonists left the chimneys. A little turn of the curtain prevented them from being seen from the brig; but two or three detonations and the sound of cannonballs striking the rocks told them that the brig was now only a short distance away.

They rushed into the lift, hoisted themselves up to the door of Granite-House, where Top and Jup had been locked up since the day before, and dashed into the large room in no time.

It was just in time, as the colonists, through the branches, saw the brig surrounded by smoke, darting into the channel. They even had to step aside, as the discharges were incessant, and the cannonballs from the four cannons struck blindly both the Mercy post, though it was no longer occupied, and the chimneys. The rocks were shattered, and cheers accompanied each detonation.

However, there was hope that Granite-House would be spared, thanks to the precaution Cyrus Smith had taken to hide its windows, when a cannonball, grazing the door bay, penetrated the corridor.

"Cursed! Are we discovered?" cried Pencroff.

Maybe the colonists had not been seen, but it was certain that Bob Harvey deemed it appropriate to send a projectile through the suspicious foliage that concealed this part of the tall wall.

Soon enough, he redoubled his shots when another cannonball, having cut through the curtain of foliage, revealed a gaping hole in the granite.

The situation of the colonists was desperate. Their retreat was discovered. They could oppose no obstacle to these projectiles nor protect the stone, of which the splinters were flying around them like shrapnel.

They only had to take refuge in the upper corridor of Granite-House and abandon their home to all the devastation, when a dull sound was heard, followed by terrible cries!

Cyrus Smith and his companions rushed to one of the windows...

The brig, irresistibly lifted on a sort of watery vortex, had just split in two, and within less than ten seconds, it was sunk along with its criminal crew!

🜲 4 🜲

"They have jumped!" cried Harbert.

"Yes! Jumped as if Ayrton had set fire to the powder!" replied Pencroff as he jumped into the lift, along with Nab and the young boy.

"But what just happened?" asked Gideon Spilett, still stunned by this unex-pected outcome.

"Ah! This time we will know!... replied the engineer eagerly.

"What will we know?...

"Later! Later! Come on, Spilett. The important thing is that these pirates have been wiped out!"

And Cyrus Smith, pulling the reporter and Ayrton along, joined Pencroff, Nab, and Harbert on the shore.

The brig was no longer visible, not even its masts.

After being lifted by this vortex, it had capsized and sunk in that position, probably due to some enormous breach. But as the channel at this point did not measure more than twenty feet deep, it was certain that the submerged sides of the brig would reappear at low tide. Some debris floated on the sea's surface.

There was a whole assortment of masts and spare spars, hen coops with their still-living fowl, crates and barrels that were gradually rising to the surface after having escaped through the hatches; but there were no floating wreckage, no deck planks, no hull boards—which made the sudden sinking of the speedy rather inexplicable.

Nevertheless, the two masts that had been broken a few feet above the stern, after having snapped struts and shrouds, soon rose to the canal's waters, with their sails, some of which were unfurled and others furled. But they couldn't let the ebb have time to carry all these riches away, and Ayrton and Pencroff jumped into the canoe with the intention of mooring all this debris either on the island's coastline or on the islet's coastline.

But just as they were about to board, a thought from Gideon Spilett stopped them.

"And the six convicts who landed on the right bank of the Mercy?" he said.

Indeed, one must not forget that the six men whose boat had broken on the rocks had landed at the tip of the wreck.

They looked in that direction. None of the fugitives were visible. It was likely that after seeing the brig sink beneath the waters of the channel, they had fled deeper into the island.

"Later, we'll deal with them," then said Cyrus Smith. "They could still be dangerous, as they are armed, but still, six against six, the odds are equal. Let's focus on the most urgent."

Ayrton and Pencroff boarded the canoe and vigorously swam towards the debris.

The sea was calm then, and very high, as the moon had been new two days earlier. At least another hour was likely to pass before the brig's hull would emerge from the waters of the canal.

Ayrton and Pencroff had time to moor the masts and spars using ropes, the ends of which were brought to the shore of Granite-House. There, the colonists, combining their efforts, managed to haul these debris ashore. Then the canoe collected everything that was floating, hen coops, barrels, crates, which were immediately transported to the chimneys.

Some corpses were also floating. Among others, Ayrton recognized the body of Bob Harvey, and he pointed it out to his companion, saying in an emotional voice:

"What I have been, Pencroff!"

"But what you are no longer, brave Ayrton!" replied the sailor.

It was quite peculiar that the bodies which were floating were so few in number. There barely counted five or six, which the ebb was already beginning to take towards the open sea.

Most likely, the convicts, surprised by the sinking, had not had time to flee, and the ship, having tipped over, most had remained trapped under the bulwarks. Now, the ebb, which would take the corpses of those wretches out to sea, would spare the colonists the sad task of burying them somewhere on their island.

For two hours, Cyrus Smith and his companions were solely occupied with hauling the spars onto the sand and unshackling, then drying the sails, which were perfectly intact. They spoke little, so engrossed were they in their work, but countless thoughts crossed their minds! It was a fortune to possess this brig, or rather everything it contained. Indeed, a ship is like a small complete world, and the colony's supplies would increase with numerous useful items. This would be, "on a grand scale," the equivalent of the box found at the tip of the wreck.

"And besides," thought Pencroff, "why would it be impossible to refloat this brig? If it only has one breach, it can be plugged, a breach, and a ship of three to four hundred tons is a real ship compared to our Bonadventure! And you can go far with that! And you can go wherever you want! It will require that Mr. Cyrus, Ayrton, and I examine the matter! It's worth it!"

Indeed, if the brig was still seaworthy, the chances of repatriating the colonists of Lincoln Island would be significantly increased.

But to resolve this important question, it was necessary to wait until the sea was completely low so that the brig's hull could be inspected in all its parts.Once the wrecks were secured on the shore, Cyrus Smith and his companions took a moment to have lunch. They were literally starving. Fortunately, the kitchen was not far away, and Nab could easily manage as a quick cook. So they ate by the fireplaces, and during this meal, it's easy to imagine, they only talked about the unexpected event that had miraculously saved the colony.

"Miraculously is the right word," Pencroff repeated, "because we must admit that those scoundrels blew up just at the right moment! Granite-House was starting to become quite uninhabitable!"

"Can you imagine, Pencroff?" the reporter asked, "how it happened and who could have caused the brick to explode?"

"Hey! Mr. Spilett, it's nothing simpler," Pencroff replied. "A pirate ship isn't protected like a warship! Convicts aren't sailors! It's certain that the hold of the brick was open, since we were being shelled without pause, and it would only have taken one careless or clumsy person to blow up the engine!"

"Mr. Cyrus," said Harbert, "what surprises me is that this explosion didn't have more effect. The blast wasn't strong, and, overall, there are only a few wreckage and planks torn off. It seems like the ship sank instead of blowing up."

"Does that surprise you, my child?" asked the engineer.

"Yes, Mr. Cyrus."

"And I'm also surprised, Harbert," replied the engineer, "but when we visit the hull of the brick, we will probably get an explanation for this fact."

"Hey! Mr. Cyrus," said Pencroff, "are you seriously saying that the speedy simply sank like a ship that runs into a reef?"

"Why not?" Nab pointed out, "if there are rocks in the channel?"

"Come on! Nab," Pencroff replied. "You didn't open your eyes at the right moment. Just before sinking, the brick, I clearly saw it, rose on a huge wave, and it fell over on its left side. Now, if it had just brushed against something, it would have sunk quietly, like an honest ship going down."

"That's precisely because it wasn't an honest ship!" Nab replied.

"Well, we'll see, Pencroff," the engineer resumed.

"We'll see," added the sailor, "but I'd bet my head there are no rocks in the channel. Come on, Mr. Cyrus, honestly, do you think there's anything miraculous about this event?"

Cyrus Smith did not respond.

"In any case," said Gédéon Spilett, "whether from a shock or an explosion, you must agree, Pencroff, that it happened just in time!"

"Yes!... yes!..." answered the sailor, "but that's not the point. I'm asking Mr. Smith if he sees anything supernatural in all this."

"I won't make a judgment, Pencroff," said the engineer. "That's all I can tell you."

A response that did not satisfy Pencroff at all. He maintained it was "an explosion," and he would not back down. He would never agree to admit that there could be an unknown reef in the channel, formed of a bed of fine sand like the shore itself, and that he had often crossed at low tide. Besides, at the moment the brick sank, the sea was high, meaning there was more water than needed to pass safely over any rocks that would not be exposed at low tide. Therefore, there could not have been a collision. Thus, the ship did not touch. Therefore, it blew up.

And it must be said that the sailor's reasoning was not without a certain logic.

Around one-thirty, the colonists boarded the canoe and went to the site of the wreck. It was regrettable that the two boats from the brick could not be salvaged; one, as was known, had been broken at the mouth of Mercy and was utterly useless; the other had vanished in the sinking of the brick, and, undoubtedly crushed by it, had not reappeared.

At that moment, the hull of the speedy began to emerge above the water. The brick was more than tipped on its side, as after breaking its masts under the weight of its ballast displaced by the fall, it was almost keel-up. It had truly been turned upside down by the inexplicable yet dreadful underwater action, which at the same time manifested itself through the displacement of an enormous whirlpool.

The colonists circled the hull, and as the sea lowered, they could recognize, if not the cause that had provoked the catastrophe, at least the effect produced. On the front, on both sides of the keel, seven or eight feet before the bow, the sides of the brick were frightfully torn over a length of at least twenty feet. There were two large openings through which water could freely enter, which would have been impossible to seal. Not only had the copper sheathing and planking disappeared, reduced to dust no doubt, but also there was no trace of the very framework, iron bolts, and the strakes that held it together. All along the hull, up to the stern's stern walk, the planks, shredded, no longer held. The false keel had been separated with inexplicable violence, and the keel itself, torn from the frames in several places, was broken along its entire length.

"A thousand devils!" exclaimed Pencroff. "Here's a ship that will be difficult to salvage!"

"It will even be impossible," said Ayrton.

"In any case," Gédéon Spilett pointed out to the sailor, "the explosion, if there was an explosion, caused some strange effects! It breached the hull in its lower parts instead of blowing off the deck and the upper structures! Those large openings seem to have been made by a shock against a reef rather than by an explosion in a hold!"

"There are no reefs in the channel!" the sailor retorted. "I accept everything you want, except for the collision with a rock!"

"Let's try to get inside the brick," said the engineer. "Perhaps we'll discover what we can make of the cause of its destruction."

This was the best course of action, and it was, moreover, appropriate to inventory all the treasures contained on board and to organize everything for their recovery.

Access to the interior of the brick was easy at that time.

The water was still lowering, and the underside of the deck, now the top due to the hull's overturning, was passable. The ballast, made of heavy iron weights, had smashed through in several places. The sound of the sea could be heard murmuring as it flowed through the cracks in the hull.

Cyrus Smith and his companions, axe in hand, proceeded onto the half-broken deck. It was cluttered with all sorts of crates, and since they had only languished in the water for a very limited time, perhaps their contents were not spoiled.

They then set about putting all this cargo in a safe place. The water wouldn't return for a few hours, and these hours were used most profitably. Ayrton and Pencroff had secured a hoist at the opening they made in the hull, which was used to raise the barrels and crates. The canoe received them and immediately transported them to the beach. They took everything, indiscriminately, intending to sort through these items later. In any case, the colonists could immediately note with extreme satisfaction that the brick held a very varied cargo, an assortment of items of all kinds, utensils, manufactured products, tools, like those loaded on ships that do long coastal trade in Polynesia. It was likely they would find a bit of everything, and it must be agreed that this was precisely what the colony of Lincoln Island needed.

However, — and Cyrus Smith noted this in silent astonishment, — not only had the hull of the brick, as mentioned, suffered greatly from whatever shock had caused the catastrophe, but the fittings were devastated, especially towards the front. Bulkheads and beams were broken as if some formidable shell had exploded inside the brick. The colonists were able to move easily from the front to the back after moving the crates which were extracted piece by piece. These were not heavy bales, which would have been difficult to move, but simple packages, whose stowage, moreover, was no longer recognizable.

The colonists then reached the rear of the brick, in that part which was once topped by the poop deck. This is where, following Ayrton's indication, they were to search for the powder room. Cyrus Smith thought that it had not blown up, so it was possible that a few barrels could be salvaged and that the powder, which is usually enclosed in metal containers, had not suffered from contact with water.

Indeed, that was exactly what had happened. They found, amid a large quantity of projectiles, about twenty barrels, which were lined with copper, and which were carefully extracted.

Pencroff convinced himself with his own eyes that the destruction of the speedy could not be attributed to an explosion. The portion of the hull where the hold was located was precisely the part that had suffered the least damage.

"Possible!" replied the stubborn sailor, "but as for a rock, there are no rocks in the channel!"

"Then what happened?" Harbert asked.

"I don't know," replied Pencroff, "Mr. Cyrus doesn't know, and no one knows and will ever know anything!"

During these various searches, several hours had passed, and the tide was starting to come in. They had to suspend the salvage work.

Moreover, there was no fear that the wreck of the brick would be carried away by the sea, as it was already stuck, and just as securely fixed as if it had been anchored to its moorings.

They could therefore wait for the next low tide to resume operations without any inconvenience. But, as for the ship itself, it was definitely doomed, and they would even need to hurry to save the remnants of the hull, as it was soon to disappear in the shifting sands of the channel.

It was five o'clock in the evening. The day had been tough for the workers. They ate with great appetite, and, no matter how exhausted they were, they did not resist the desire, after their dinner, to explore the crates that made up the cargo of the speedy.

Most contained ready-made clothes, which, it is easy to imagine, were well received. There was enough there to clothe an entire colony, from everyday linen to shoes for all types of feet.

"We're too rich now!" Pencroff exclaimed. "But what are we going to do with all this?"

And at every moment, jubilant cheers erupted from the joyful sailor when he recognized barrels of rum, sacks of tobacco, firearms and bladed weapons, bales of cotton, farming tools, carpenter's tools, blacksmith's tools, and crates of seeds of all kinds, which their short stay in the water had not damaged. Ah! Two years earlier, how timely these things would have been! But still, even now that these industrious colonists had equipped themselves, this wealth would find its use.

There was no shortage of space in the stores of Granite-House; but, that day, there was not enough time to store everything. They should not forget, however, that six survivors of the crew of the speedy had landed on the island, that they were probably top-tier rascals, and that they needed to watch out for them. Although the bridge over Mercy and the culverts had been raised, those convicts would not be deterred by a river or a stream, and, driven by despair, such scoundrels could be dangerous.

What action should be taken regarding them would be sorted out later; but, for now, it was necessary to keep an eye on the crates and packages piled up by the fireplaces, and this is what the colonists did throughout the night, taking turns.

The night passed, however, without the convicts attempting any aggression. Master Jup and Top, keeping watch at the foot of Granite-House, would have quickly alerted them.

The next three days, October 19, 20, and 21, were spent salvaging anything that could have value or utility, either from the cargo or from the rigging of the brick. At low tide, they cleared out the hold. At high tide, they stored the rescued items. A large part of the copper sheathing could be torn off the hull, which, each day, sank deeper. But before the sands submerged the heavy objects that had sunk to the bottom, Ayrton and Pencroff, having dived several times down to the riverbed, found the chains and anchors of the brick, the heavy weights, and even the four cannons, which, assisted by empty barrels, could be brought ashore.

As we can see, the colony's arsenal gained just as much from the salvage as the offices and stores of Granite-House. Pencroff, ever enthusiastic in his projects, was already talking about building a battery to command the channel and the mouth of the river. With four cannons, he promised to prevent any fleet, "no matter how powerful," from venturing into the waters of Lincoln Island! In the meantime, when only a useless carcass remained of the brick, bad weather came along to finish its destruction. Cyrus Smith had intended to blow it up to gather the wreckage on the shore, but a strong north-easterly wind and rough seas allowed him to save his powder. Indeed, during the night from the 23rd to the 24th, the hull of the brick was completely dismantled, and part of the wreckage washed up on the shore.

As for the ship's papers, needless to say that, although he searched meticulously through the cupboards of the poop deck, Cyrus Smith found no trace. The pirates had evidently destroyed everything relating to either the captain or the owner of the speedy, and since the name of its home port was not displayed on the stern, nothing could suggest its nationality. However, by certain shapes of its bow, Ayrton and Pencroff seemed to believe that this brick was of English construction.

Eight days after the catastrophe, or rather after the fortunate yet inexplicable outcome that had saved the colony, nothing of the ship could be seen, even at low tide. Its wreckage had been scattered, and Granite-House was rich in almost everything it had contained.

However, the mystery surrounding its strange destruction would likely never have been clarified if, on November 30, Nab, wandering on the shore, had not found a piece of a thick iron cylinder, which showed signs of explosion. This cylinder was twisted and torn at its edges, as if it had been subjected to the action of an explosive substance.

Nab brought this piece of metal to his master, who was then busy with his companions in the workshop by the fireplaces.

Cyrus Smith examined the cylinder closely, then turned to Pencroff:

"Do you still insist, my friend," he said, "that the speedy did not perish due to a collision?"

"Yes, Mr. Cyrus," replied the sailor. "You know as well as I do that there are no rocks in the channel."

"But what if it had bumped into this piece of iron?" said the engineer, pointing to the broken cylinder.— What, this piece of pipe? Pencroff exclaimed in complete disbelief.

— My friends, Cyrus Smith replied, do you remember that before sinking, the brig was caught at the top of a real waterspout?

— Yes, Mr. Cyrus! Harbert answered.

— Well, do you want to know what caused that waterspout? It was this, said the engineer, pointing at the broken tube.

— This? Pencroff retorted.

— Yes! This cylinder is all that remains of a torpedo!

— A torpedo! cried the engineer's companions.

— And who put this torpedo there? asked Pencroff, unwilling to give in.

— All I can tell you is that it wasn't me! replied Cyrus Smith, but it was there, and you have seen its incredible power!

So, everything was explained by the underwater explosion of this torpedo. Cyrus Smith, who had had the opportunity to experiment with these terrible destruction devices during the Civil War, could not be mistaken. It was under the action of this cylinder, loaded with an explosive substance—nitroglycerin, picrate, or something similar—that the water in the canal rose like a water-spout, that the brig, struck at its hull, sank instantly, and that is why it was impossible to raise it, given the significant damage suffered by its hull. A torpedo that could destroy an armored frigate just as easily as a simple fishing boat, the speedy could not withstand!

Yes! Everything was explained, everything... except for the presence of this torpedo in the canal's waters!

"My friends," Cyrus Smith then said, "we can no longer doubt the existence of a mysterious being, a shipwrecked person like us perhaps, abandoned on our island, and I say this so that Ayrton is aware of what strange events have happened in the past two years. Who is this benevolent unknown whose inter-vention, so fortunate for us, has manifested itself on many occasions? I can't imagine. What interest does he have in acting this way, in hiding after providing so many services? I can't understand. But his services are none the less real, and they are of the kind that only a man with extraordinary power could provide us. Ayrton is indebted to him just like us, because if it was the unknown who saved me from the waves after the balloon's fall, it was obvi-ously him who wrote the document, who placed this bottle on the canal's path and informed us of our companion's situation. I will add that this box, so conveniently provided with everything we were missing, it was he who deliv-ered and stranded at the wreck's point; that this fire placed on the heights of the island, which allowed you to land, it was he who lit; that this lead pellet found in the body of the peccary, it was he who shot; that this torpedo that destroyed the brig, it was he who submerged it in the canal; in short, all these inexplicable facts, which we could not account for, are due to this mysterious being. So, whoever he is, whether shipwrecked or exiled on this island, we would be ungrateful if we thought we were free of all gratitude towards him. We have incurred a debt, and I hope that we will pay it one day.

— You're right to say that, my dear Cyrus, replied Gédéon Spilett. Yes, there is a being, almost all-powerful, hiding somewhere on the island, whose influence has been remarkably beneficial to our colony. I will add that this unknown seems to possess means of action that might verge on the supernatural, if the supernatural were acceptable in practical life. Is it him who secretly communicates with us through the Granite-House well, and thus knows all our plans? Is it him who handed us this bottle when the canoe made its first excursion at sea? Is it him who cast Top from the waters of the lake and killed the dugong? Is it him, as everything suggests, who saved you from the waves, Cyrus, in circumstances where anyone else who was merely human could not have acted? If it is him, he thus possesses a power that renders him master of the elements."

The reporter's observation was accurate, and everyone felt it.

"Yes," Cyrus Smith replied, "if the intervention of a human being is no longer doubtful for us, I agree that he has at his disposal means of action that go beyond those of humanity. That remains another mystery, but if we discover the man, the mystery will also be revealed. So the question is: should we respect this generous being's anonymity, or should we do everything possible to reach him? What is your opinion on this matter?

— My opinion," Pencroff replied, "is that, whoever he is, he is a good man, and he has my respect!

— Fair enough," Cyrus Smith replied, "but that doesn't answer the question, Pencroff.

— My master," said Nab, "I have the idea that we could search for as long as we want for the gentleman in question, but we will only discover him when it pleases him.

— That's not a bad thought, Nab," replied Pencroff.

— I agree with Nab," Gédéon Spilett responded, "but that's no reason not to attempt the adventure. Whether we find this mysterious being or not, we will have at least fulfilled our duty towards him.

— And you, my child, give us your opinion," the engineer said, turning to Harbert.

— Ah! cried Harbert, his eyes lighting up, I would like to thank the one who saved you first and then saved us!

— Not disheartened, my boy," Pencroff retorted, "and me too, and all of us! I'm not curious, but I'd willingly give one of my eyes to see that particular fellow face to face! I imagine he must be handsome, tall, strong, with a beautiful beard, hair like rays, and he must be lying on clouds, holding a big ball in his hand!

— Well, Pencroff," replied Gédéon Spilett, "you're drawing the portrait of God the Father there!

— Possible, Mr. Spilett," replied the sailor, "but that's how I picture him!

— And you, Ayrton?" the engineer asked.

— Mr. Smith," Ayrton replied, "I can't really give you my opinion in this circumstance. What you decide will be well decided. When you want to include me in your searches, I will be ready to follow you.

— Thank you, Ayrton," Cyrus Smith replied, "but I would like a more direct response to the request I made to you. You are our companion; you have devoted yourself several times for us, and, like everyone here, you should be consulted when an important decision needs to be made. So speak up.

— Mr. Smith," Ayrton replied, "I think we must do everything possible to find this unknown benefactor. Perhaps he is alone? Perhaps he is suffering? Perhaps it's a life worth renewing? I too, as you said, have a debt of gratitude to him. It is he, it can only be him who came to Tabor Island, who found the wretched man you knew, who made you aware that there was a poor soul to be saved!... it is therefore thanks to him that I have become a man again. No, I will never forget him!

— It's decided then," said Cyrus Smith. "We will begin our search as soon as possible. We will not leave any part of the island unexplored. We will search it down to its most secret retreats, and may this unknown friend forgive us for our intention!"

For several days, the colonists worked hard on hay-making and harvesting. Before putting their plan to explore the still unknown parts of the island into action, they wanted to make sure that all essential tasks were finished. It was also the time to harvest the various vegetables from the plants of Tabor Island. Everything needed storing, and luckily, there was no shortage of space at Granite-House, where they could store all the island's riches. The colony's products were there, methodically arranged, and in a safe place, you can believe, as much protected from beasts as from men. No humidity was to be feared in the midst of this thick mass of granite.

Several of the natural excavations located in the upper corridor were enlarged or hollowed out, either with picks or mine tools, and Granite-House became a general warehouse containing supplies, ammunition, spare tools, in a word, all the materials of the colony.

As for the cannons from the brig, they were fine pieces made of cast steel that, at Pencroff's insistence, were hoisted by means of pulleys and cranes to the landing of Granite-House; embrasures were made between the windows, and soon they could see them extending their gleaming muzzles through the granite wall. From this height, these cannon mouths truly commanded the entire Union Bay. It was like a small Gibraltar, and any ship that dared to anchor off the islet would have been inevitably exposed to the fire from this aerial battery.

"Mr. Cyrus," one day Pencroff said—it was November 8—"now that this armament is complete, we must try out the range of our pieces.

— Do you think that's useful?" the engineer replied.

— It's more than useful, it's necessary! Otherwise, how will we know the distance to which we can send one of those lovely cannonballs we are stocked with?

— Then let's try," replied the engineer. "However, I think we should conduct the test using not ordinary powder, which I want to keep intact, but pyroxylin, of which we will never run out.

— Can these cannons withstand the explosion of pyroxylin?" asked the reporter, who was just as eager as Pencroff to test out the artillery of Granite-House.

— I believe so. Besides, the engineer added, we will act prudently."

The engineer had reason to believe that these cannons were excellently made, and he was knowledgeable about them. Made of forged steel and loading from the breech, they should therefore withstand a considerable load, and consequently have an enormous range. Indeed, from the perspective of useful effect, the trajectory traced by the cannonball must be as flat as possible, and this flatness can only be achieved on the condition that the projectile is given a very high initial speed.

"Now," Cyrus Smith said to his companions, "the initial speed is proportional to the amount of powder used. The whole issue in the manufacture of the pieces boils down to the use of a metal that is as strong as possible, and steel is undoubtedly the metal that resists best. I have reason to believe that our cannons will safely withstand the expansion of the gases from the pyroxylin and will give excellent results.

— We will be all the more certain once we've tried!" replied Pencroff.

It goes without saying that the four cannons were in perfect condition. Since they had been pulled from the water, the sailor had made it his task to polish them conscientiously. How many hours he had spent scrubbing them, greasing them, polishing them, cleaning the mechanism of the breech, the lock, the pressure screw! And now these pieces were as shiny as if they had been on board a frigate of the United States Navy.

So that day, in front of the entire colony staff, including Jup and Top, the four cannons were tested in succession. They were loaded with pyroxylin, taking into account its explosive power, which, as mentioned, is four times that of ordinary powder; the projectile they were to launch was cylindrical-conical.

Pencroff, holding the fuse cord, was ready to fire. At a signal from Cyrus Smith, the shot was fired. The cannonball, aimed at the sea, sailed over the islet and disappeared offshore at a distance which could not be accurately assessed.

The second cannon was aimed at the farthest rocks of the wreck's point, and the projectile, striking a sharp stone nearly three miles from Granite-House, shattered it to pieces.

It was Harbert who had aimed and fired the cannon, and he was very proud of his test shot.

Only Pencroff was prouder than he! Such a shot, the honor of which belonged to his dear boy!

The third projectile, launched this time at the dunes forming the upper coast of Union Bay, struck the sand at a distance of at least four miles; then, having ricocheted, it was lost at sea in a cloud of foam.

For the fourth piece, Cyrus Smith slightly increased the load to test its maximum range. Then, each person moved away in case it might burst, and the fuse was ignited with a long cord. A violent explosion was heard, but the piece had withstood, and the colonists rushed to the window to see the projectile strike the rocks of the Mandible Cape, nearly five miles from Granite-House, and disappear in Shark Gulf.

"Well, Mr. Cyrus," Pencroff shouted, whose cheers could have competed with the sounds of the detonations, "what do you say about our battery? All the pirates of the Pacific can come forward before Granite-House! Not one will land now without our permission!

— If you ask me, Pencroff," replied the engineer, "it's better not to test it.

— By the way," the sailor continued, "what are we going to do about those six scoundrels lurking on the island? Are we going to let them roam our forests, our fields, our meadows? Those pirates are like real jaguars, and it seems to me that we shouldn't hesitate to treat them as such? What do you think, Ayrton?" Pencroff added, turning to his companion.

Ayrton hesitated at first to respond, and Cyrus Smith regretted that Pencroff had rather thoughtlessly asked this question. He felt very moved when Ayrton humbly replied:

"I was one of those jaguars, Mr. Pencroff, and I have no right to speak..."

And with slow steps, he walked away.

Pencroff understood.

"Confounded fool that I am!" he cried. "Poor Ayrton! He has just as much right to speak here as anyone else!

— Yes," said Gédéon Spilett, "but his reserve honors him, and it is appropriate to respect this feeling he has regarding his sad past.

— Understood, Mr. Spilett," replied the sailor, "and I won't be caught doing that again! I'd rather swallow my tongue than cause Ayrton any distress! But let's return to the matter at hand. It seems to me that these bandits deserve no pity, and we must rid the island of them as soon as possible.

— Is that really your opinion, Pencroff?" the engineer asked.

— Absolutely my opinion.

— And before pursuing them mercilessly, wouldn't you wait for them to make another act of hostility against us?

— Isn't what they have done enough?" asked Pencroff, who didn't understand this hesitation.

— They may come to different feelings!" said Cyrus Smith, and perhaps they may repent...

— Repent, them!" the sailor exclaimed, shrugging his shoulders.

— Pencroff, think of Ayrton!" Harbert then said, taking the sailor's hand. "He has become an honest man again!"Pencroff looked at each of his companions one by one. He never expected that his suggestion would raise any hesitation. His tough nature couldn't accept that they would make deals with the crooks who had landed on the island, with Bob Harvey's accomplices, the murderers of the Speedy's crew, and he viewed them as wild beasts that needed to be destroyed without hesitation and without remorse.

"Look! Everyone is against me! You want to be generous with those rascals! Fine. Let's hope we won't regret it!

— What's the danger we face, said Harbert, if we are careful and keep our guard up?

— Hmm! said the reporter, who wasn't too sure. There are six of them and they're well armed. If any one of them hides in a spot and shoots at one of us, they'll soon take control of the colony!

— Why haven't they done that? replied Harbert. Surely because it wouldn't be in their interest. Besides, we are six too.

— Good! Good! replied Pencroff, who could be convinced by no reasoning. Let those fine folks go about their little activities, and let's not think about them anymore!

— Come on, Pencroff, said Nab, don't be so mean! If one of those poor souls was here in front of you, within easy range of your rifle, you wouldn't shoot him...

— I'd shoot him like a rabid dog, Nab, replied Pencroff coldly.

— Pencroff, said the engineer, you have often shown great respect for my advice. Would you be willing to rely on me in this situation again?

— I'll do as you wish, Mr. Smith, replied the sailor, who was not at all convinced.

— Well then, let's wait, and we'll only fight back if we're attacked."

So it was decided how to handle the pirates, although Pencroff had no good feeling about it.

They wouldn't attack, but they would stay alert. After all, the island was large and fertile. If these wretches had any sense of honor left in their souls, perhaps they could improve. Their interest—of course—was it not, given their living conditions, to create a new life for themselves? In any case, if only out of humanity, they should wait. The colonists might no longer have the same ease to come and go without suspicion as before.

Until now, they had only to guard against wild animals, and now six convicts, perhaps of the worst kind, were roaming their island. This was serious, of course, and for less brave people, their safety would have been lost.

Nevertheless! At the present moment, the colonists were right against Pencroff. Would they be right in the future? Only time would tell.

6

Meanwhile, the colonists' main concern was to carry out the complete exploration of the island that had been decided upon, an exploration that would now have two objectives: to first discover the mysterious being whose existence was no longer in question, and at the same time, to determine what had become of the pirates, what retreat they had chosen, what kind of life they were leading, and what threats they might pose.

Cyrus Smith wanted to set out without delay; however, since the expedition would last several days, it seemed wise to load the cart with various camping gear and utensils that would facilitate organizing their stops. At this moment, one of the onagers, injured in the leg, could not be harnessed; it needed a few days of rest, so they felt they could delay their departure by a week, that is, until November 20. The month of November, in this latitude, corresponds to May in the northern regions. Thus, it was the beautiful season. The sun was crossing the Tropic of Capricorn and bringing the longest days of the year. The time would therefore be quite favorable for the planned expedition, which, even if it did not achieve its primary goal, could yield many discoveries, especially regarding natural resources, since Cyrus Smith intended to explore the dense forests of the Far West, which extended to the very tip of the serpentine peninsula.

During the nine days leading up to the departure, it was agreed that they would finish the last works on the Grande-vue plateau.

Meanwhile, it was necessary for Ayrton to return to the corral, where the domestic animals needed his care. It was decided that he would spend two days there and would not come back to Granite House until he had fully stocked the stables. Just as he was about to leave, Cyrus Smith asked him if he wanted one of them to accompany him, pointing out that the island was less safe than before.

Ayrton replied that it wasn't necessary, that he could handle the task, and that he wasn't afraid of anything. If any incident occurred at the corral or in the surrounding area, he would immediately alert the colonists via telegram addressed to Granite House.

Ayrton set off on the morning of the 9th at dawn, taking the cart, which was harnessed to only one onager, and two hours later, the electric bell rang, announcing that everything was in order at the corral.

During those two days, Cyrus Smith worked on a project that would definitively protect Granite House from any surprises. It involved completely hiding the upper opening of the old overflow, which had already been walled up and was half concealed under grass and plants at the southern corner of Lake Grant. It was quite easy, as all that needed to be done was to raise the water level of the lake by two to three feet, under which the opening would then be completely submerged.

To raise this level, all they needed to do was build a dam at the two outlets made to the lake, which supplied the Glycerine Creek and the Great Fall Creek. The colonists were called to this task, and the two dams, which, moreover, did not exceed seven to eight feet in width and three in height, were quickly constructed using well-cemented rock blocks.

Once this work was completed, it was impossible to suspect that there was an underground conduit at the lake's tip through which the overflow of the waters had once drained.

It goes without saying that the small diversion that served to supply Granite House's reservoir and to operate the elevator had been carefully preserved, and there would be no shortage of water in any case.

Once the elevator was raised, this safe and comfortable retreat defied any surprise or attack.

This work had been quickly completed, and Pencroff, Gédéon Spilett, and Harbert found time to make a quick trip to Port Balloon.

The sailor was very eager to know if the little cove where the Bonadventure was anchored had been visited by the convicts.

"Precisely," he noted, "those gentlemen landed on the southern coast, and if they followed the coastline, it is to be feared they discovered the little port; in that case, I wouldn't give half a dollar for our Bonadventure."

Pencroff's concerns were not without some foundation, and a visit to Port Balloon seemed quite timely.

So the sailor and his companions set out on the afternoon of November 10, and they were well armed. Pencroff, ostentatiously slipping two bullets into each barrel of his rifle, shook his head, which boded ill for anyone who got too close, "beast or man," he said.

Gédéon Spilett and Harbert took their rifles as well, and around three o'clock, the three of them left Granite House.

Nab accompanied them as far as the bend in the Mercy, and after their passage, he raised the bridge. It was agreed that a gunshot would announce the return of the colonists, and that Nab, at this signal, would come back to restore communication between the two banks of the river.

The small group moved directly along the road to the port towards the southern coast of the island. It was only a distance of three and a half miles, but Gédéon Spilett and his companions took two hours to cover it. They had also searched the entire edge of the road, both on the side of the dense forest and on the side of the marsh of the tadornes. They found no trace of the escapees, who, doubtlessly, not yet settled on the number of colonists and the means of defense at their disposal, must have retreated to the least accessible parts of the island.

Upon arriving at Port Balloon, Pencroff saw with extreme satisfaction the Bonadventure quietly anchored in the narrow creek. Moreover, Port Balloon was so well hidden among the high rocks that it could not be discovered from the sea or the land unless you were right on top of it or inside.

"Well," said Pencroff, "those scoundrels haven't come here yet. The tall grasses are better suited for reptiles, and it's obviously in the Far West that we will find them again.

— And that's a good thing, because if they had found the Bonadventure," added Harbert, "they would have seized it to escape, which would have prevented us from returning to Tabor Island anytime soon.

— Indeed," replied the reporter, "it will be important to take a document there that informs them of the situation on Lincoln Island and Ayrton's new residence, in case the Scottish yacht comes to retrieve him.

— Well, the Bonadventure is still there, Mr. Spilett!" replied the sailor. Her crew and she are ready to leave at the first signal!

— I think, Pencroff, that we should do that as soon as our expedition on the island is finished. It's possible, after all, that this unknown, if we manage to find him, knows a lot about both Lincoln Island and Tabor Island. Let's not forget he is the undeniable author of the document, and he might know what's going on with the yacht's return!

— A thousand devils! exclaimed Pencroff, who can it possibly be? This person knows us, and we don't know him! If he's just a simple castaway, why is he hiding? We are good people, I suppose, and the company of good people is unpleasant to no one! Did he come here voluntarily? Can he leave the island if he wishes? Is he still here? Is he no longer here?..."

While talking like this, Pencroff, Harbert, and Gédéon Spilett had boarded and were walking around the deck of the Bonadventure. Suddenly, the sailor, having examined the bitt on which the anchor cable was wound:

"Ah! For example! he exclaimed. This is very strange!

— What is it, Pencroff? asked the reporter.

— It's that I didn't make this knot!"

And Pencroff pointed to a rope that tied down the cable on the bitt itself, to prevent it from slipping.

"What, you didn't? asked Gédéon Spilett.

— No! I would swear to it. This is a flat knot, and I'm used to making two half-hitches.

— You must be mistaken, Pencroff.

— I'm not mistaken! The sailor asserted. You do it by hand, naturally, and the hand doesn't make mistakes!

— Then, the convicts must have come aboard? asked Harbert.

— I don't know, replied Pencroff, but what is certain is that someone raised the Bonadventure's anchor and dropped it again! And look! Here's another piece of evidence. They let out some anchor cable, and its equipment is no longer on the line from the hawsehole. I repeat, someone used our boat!

— But if the convicts used it, they would have either looted it or fled...

— Fled!... where to?... to Tabor Island?... replied Pencroff! Do you think they would risk going to sea on a boat of such small tonnage?

— Besides, it should be assumed that they knew about the islet, replied the reporter.

— Regardless, said the sailor, as sure as I am Bonadventure Pencroff from the Vineyard, our Bonadventure sailed without us!"

The sailor was so certain that neither Gédéon Spilett nor Harbert could contest his claim.

It was evident that the boat had been moved to some extent since Pencroff had brought it back to Port Balloon. For the sailor, there was no doubt that the anchor had been raised and then dropped back to the bottom. Now, why these two maneuvers if the boat hadn't been used for some expedition?

"But how could we not have seen the Bonadventure pass offshore from the island?" observed the reporter, who wanted to articulate all possible objections.

— Eh! Mr. Spilett, replied the sailor, all it takes is to leave at night with a good breeze, and in two hours, you're out of sight of the island!

— Well then, Gédéon Spilett replied, I ask again, for what purpose would the convicts have used the Bonadventure, and why, after using it, would they have brought it back to port?

— Eh! Mr. Spilett, replied the sailor, let's count this among the inexplicable things, and let's not think about it anymore! The important thing is that the Bonadventure is here, and she is. Unfortunately, if the convicts visited her a second time, she might not be found in her place!

— Then, Pencroff, said Harbert, perhaps it would be wise to bring the Bonadventure back in front of Granite House?

— Yes and no, replied Pencroff, or rather no. The mouth of the Mercy is a bad spot for a boat, and the sea is rough there.

— But by pulling her onto the sand, right up to the foot of the chimneys?...

— Maybe... yes..., replied Pencroff. In any case, since we are going to leave Granite House for a significant expédition, I think the Bonadventure will be safer here during our absence, and that we would do well to leave her there until the island is cleared of these rascals.

— I agree, said the reporter. At least, in case of bad weather, she won't be exposed like she would be at the mouth of the Mercy.

— But what if the convicts go to visit her again! said Harbert.

— Well then, my boy, replied Pencroff, not finding her here, they would quickly search for her near Granite House, and during our absence, nothing would stop them from seizing her! So I think, like Mr. Spilett, that we should leave her at Port Balloon. But when we get back, if we haven't cleared the island of those rascals, it would be prudent to bring our boat back to Granite House until there's no longer any risk of a bad visit.

— It's agreed. Let's go!" said the reporter.

When Pencroff, Harbert, and Gédéon Spilett returned to Granite House, they informed the engineer about what had happened, and he approved their arrangements for both the present and the future. He even promised the sailor that he would study the section of the canal between the islet and the coast to see if it would be possible to create an artificial port there using dams. In this way, the Bonadventure would always be within reach, under the colonists' eyes, and if necessary, under lock and key.

That very evening, a telegram was sent to Ayrton asking him to bring back a couple of goats from the corral that Nab wanted to acclimate on the meadows of the plateau. Oddly enough, Ayrton didn't acknowledge receipt of the message, as he was accustomed to doing. This surprised the engineer. But it was possible that Ayrton wasn't at the corral at the moment, or that he was on his way back to Granite House. Indeed, two days had passed since his departure, and it had been decided that he would be back either on the evening of the 10th or by the morning of the 11th at the latest. The colonists waited for Ayrton to appear on the heights of Grande-vue. Nab and Harbert even kept watch near the bridge, ready to lower it as soon as their friend showed up.

However, by around ten o'clock at night, there was still no sign of Ayrton. They decided it was best to send another telegram, asking for an immediate response.

Granite-House remained silent.

Then the colonists became very concerned. What had happened? Was Ayrton no longer at the corral, or if he was still there, had he lost his freedom of movement? Should they go to the corral on this dark night?

They debated. Some wanted to leave, while others preferred to stay.

"But," said Harbert, "maybe something went wrong with the telegraph and it's not working anymore?"

"That's possible," said the reporter.

"Let's wait until tomorrow," replied Cyrus Smith. "It's possible Ayrton hasn't received our telegram, or even that we haven't received his."

They waited, and understandably, not without some anxiety.

As soon as dawn broke, on November 11, Cyrus Smith tried sending an electrical current through the wire again, but received no response.

He tried again: the same result.

"Let's head to the corral!" he said.

"And well-armed!" added Pencroff.

It was quickly decided that Granite-House would not be left alone and that Nab would stay there. After escorting his companions to the glycerin creek, he would raise the bridge and hide behind a tree, watching for either their return or Ayrton's. If the pirates showed up and tried to cross, he would attempt to stop them with his rifle, and ultimately, he could retreat to Granite-House, where he would be safe once the lift was raised.

Cyrus Smith, Gédéon Spilett, Harbert, and Pencroff were to head straight for the corral and, if they didn't find Ayrton there, search the surrounding woods.

By six o'clock in the morning, the engineer and his three companions had crossed the glycerin creek, and Nab was positioned behind a slight rise topped with a few tall dragon trees on the left bank of the stream.

The colonists, after leaving the Grande-vue plateau, immediately took the path toward the corral.

They carried their rifles at the ready, prepared to fire at the slightest sign of danger. Both carbines and rifles had been loaded with bullets. The thicket on either side of the path was dense and could easily hide malefactors who, armed, would have been truly formidable.

The colonists moved quickly and quietly. Top led the way, running on the path or making little detours through the woods, but always silent and showing no signs of sensing anything unusual.

And one could count on the faithful dog not being caught off guard and barking at the first sign of danger. Along with the path, Cyrus Smith and his companions followed the telegraph wire connecting the corral and Granite-House. After walking for about two miles, they still hadn't seen any breaks in the line. The poles were in good condition, the insulators intact, the wire properly tensioned. However, from this point, the engineer noticed that the tension seemed less complete, and finally, upon arriving at pole No. 74, Harbert, who was leading the way, stopped and shouted, "The wire is broken!"

His companions quickened their pace and reached the spot where the boy had stopped.

There, the fallen pole lay across the path. The break in the wire was thus confirmed, and it was evident that the messages from Granite-House hadn't reached the corral, nor those from the corral to Granite-House.

"It's not the wind that knocked this pole down," observed Pencroff.

"No," replied Gédéon Spilett. "The ground has been dug out at its base, and it's been uprooted by human hands."

"Moreover, the wire is broken," added Harbert, showing the two ends of the wire that had been violently snapped.

"Is the break fresh?" asked Cyrus Smith.

"Yes," answered Harbert, "and it's clear that the break happened very recently."

"To the corral! To the corral!" shouted the sailor.

The colonists were then halfway between Granite-House and the corral. They still had two and a half miles to go. They broke into a run, fearing that something serious might have happened at the corral. Surely, Ayrton could have sent a telegram that hadn't arrived, and that wasn't the only reason to worry, but even stranger, Ayrton, who had promised to return the night before, had not reappeared. After all, there was a reason why all communication between the corral and Granite-House had been interrupted, and who but the convicts would benefit from cutting off that communication?

So the colonists ran, their hearts tight with emotion. They had sincerely grown fond of their new companion. Would they find him struck down by the very hands of those who had once been his subordinates?

Soon they reached the place where the road ran alongside a small stream flowing from the red creek, which irrigated the corral meadows. They slowed their pace in order not to tire themselves just as a struggle might be necessary. The rifles were no longer resting; they were readied. Each watched a side of the forest. Top let out some low growls that weren't reassuring. Finally, the palisaded enclosure appeared through the trees. There was no sign of damage. The gate was closed as usual. A profound silence reigned in the corral. Neither the usual bleating of the sheep nor Ayrton's voice could be heard.

"Let's go in!" said Cyrus Smith.

And the engineer moved forward, while his companions, keeping watch twenty paces behind him, were ready to fire.

Cyrus Smith lifted the inner latch of the door, and he was about to push one of the leaves open when Top barked violently. A shot rang out above the palisade, and a cry of pain answered it.

Harbert had been struck by a bullet and lay on the ground!

❧ 7 ❧

At Harbert's cry, Pencroff, dropping his weapon, rushed toward him.

"They've killed him!" he cried! "Him, my boy! They've killed him!"

Cyrus Smith and Gédéon Spilett rushed toward Harbert. The reporter listened to see if the poor child's heart was still beating.

"He's alive," he said. "But we need to move him..."

"To Granite-House? That's impossible!" replied the engineer.

"To the corral, then!" shouted Pencroff.

"One moment," said Cyrus Smith.

And he darted to the left to go around the enclosure. There, he encountered a convict who, aiming at him, shot through his hat. A few seconds later, before he even had time to fire his second shot, he fell, struck in the heart by Cyrus Smith's dagger, which was even more reliable than his rifle.

Meanwhile, Gédéon Spilett and the sailor climbed to the corners of the palisade, they vaulted over the top, jumped into the enclosure, knocked down the braces holding the door closed from inside, and rushed into the empty house. Soon, poor Harbert lay on Ayrton's bed. A few moments later, Cyrus Smith was by his side.

Seeing Harbert lifeless, the sailor's pain was terrible. He sobbed, he cried, he wanted to smash his head against the wall. Neither the engineer nor the reporter could calm him. The emotion nearly suffocated them as well. They couldn't speak.

Nevertheless, they did everything they could to fight death for the poor child who was gasping before their eyes. Gédéon Spilett, after so many incidents in his life, was somewhat experienced in common medicine.

He knew a little about everything, and there had already been many situations where he had to care for wounds caused either by knives or firearms. With Cyrus Smith's help, he proceeded to care for Harbert's injuries.

At first, the reporter was struck by the general stupor that overwhelmed him, whether due to blood loss or even a concussion, if the bullet had hit a bone with enough force to cause a violent shock.

Harbert was extremely pale, and his pulse was so weak that Gédéon Spilett could only feel it beat at long intervals, as if it were about to stop. At the same time, there was nearly a total loss of sensation and consciousness. These symptoms were very serious.

Harbert's chest was exposed, and after stopping the blood with handkerchiefs, it was washed with cold water.

The bruise, or rather the contused wound, appeared. An oval hole existed on his chest between the third and fourth rib. That's where the bullet had struck Harbert.

Cyrus Smith and Gédéon Spilett then rolled the poor boy over, who let out a groan so faint that one might have thought it was his last breath. Another contused wound stained Harbert's back, and the bullet that had hit him immediately escaped.

"God be praised!" said the reporter, "the bullet hasn't stayed in his body, and we won't need to extract it."

"But the heart..." asked Cyrus Smith.

"The heart hasn't been touched, otherwise Harbert would be dead!"

"Dead!" cried Pencroff, who let out a growl!

The sailor had only heard the last words spoken by the reporter.

"No, Pencroff," replied Cyrus Smith, "no! He's not dead. His pulse is still beating! He even let out a groan. But for your son's sake, calm yourself. We need all our composure. Don't make us lose it, my friend."

Pencroff fell silent, but feeling a reaction within him, big tears streamed down his face.

Meanwhile, Gédéon Spilett was trying to recall his memories and proceed methodically. From his observations, it was clear to him that the bullet, having entered from the front, had exited from the back.

But what damage had that bullet caused in its passage? Which vital organs were affected? That was something even a professional surgeon might scarcely be able to say at that moment, let alone the reporter.

Still, he knew one thing: he had to prevent inflammatory strangulation of the injured parts and then combat the local inflammation and fever that would result from this injury—a potentially fatal one! So, which topical treatments, which anti-inflammatory agents should be used? By what means could he divert this inflammation? In any case, what was important was that both wounds be dressed without delay. Gédéon Spilett did not think it necessary to provoke a new blood flow by washing them with warm water and compressing their lips. The bleeding had been quite abundant, and Harbert was already too weakened by blood loss.

The reporter believed he should therefore be content to wash both wounds with cold water.

Harbert was positioned on his left side and kept in that position.

"He must not move," said Gédéon Spilett. "He is in the most favorable position for the wounds on his back and chest to drain easily, and absolute rest is necessary."

"What! We can't take him to Granite-House?" asked Pencroff.

"No, Pencroff," replied the reporter.

"Cursed be it!" shouted the sailor, his fist raised to the sky.

"Pencroff!" said Cyrus Smith.

Gédéon Spilett had resumed examining the injured child with great care. Harbert remained so terrifyingly pale that the reporter felt unsettled.

"Cyrus," he said, "I'm not a doctor... I'm in terrible peril... you must help me with your advice and experience!...

"Calm yourself..., my friend," replied the engineer, squeezing the reporter's hand... "stay cool-headed... think only of this: we must save Harbert!"

These words restored Gédéon Spilett's composure, which, in a moment of discouragement, the strong sense of responsibility had made him lose. He sat down next to the bed.

Cyrus Smith stood. Pencroff had torn his shirt and, mechanically, was making lint.

Gédéon Spilett then explained to Cyrus Smith that he believed he had to stop the bleeding first, but not to close the two wounds or provoke their immediate healing, because there had been internal perforation and he didn't want pus to accumulate in the chest.

Cyrus Smith fully agreed, and it was decided that they would dress the two wounds without trying to close them immediately. Fortunately, it didn't seem they needed to be debrided.

And now, to react against any inflammation that might arise, did the colonists have an effective agent?

Yes! They had one, because nature generously provides it. They had cold water, which is the most powerful sedative available for treating wound inflammation, the most effective therapeutic agent in serious cases, and which is now adopted by all doctors. Cold water also has the advantage of leaving the wound in absolute rest and protecting it from any premature dressing, which is a considerable benefit, since experience has shown that contact with air is harmful during the first few days.

Gédéon Spilett and Cyrus Smith reasoned in this way with their simple common sense, and they acted as the best surgeon would. Compresses of cloth were applied to the two wounds of poor Harbert and had to be kept constantly soaked in cold water.

The sailor had initially started a fire in the fireplace of the house, which lacked nothing essential for life. Maple sugar and medicinal plants—those the young boy had collected on the banks of Lake Grant—were used to make some refreshing teas, which they gave him without him realizing it. His fever was extremely high, and the whole day and night passed without him regaining consciousness. Harbert's life hung by a thread, and that thread could snap at any moment.

The next day, November 12, Cyrus Smith and his companions regained some hope. Harbert had come out of his long stupor. He opened his eyes, recognized Cyrus Smith, the reporter, and Pencroff. He uttered two or three words. He didn't know what had happened. They explained it to him, and Gédéon Spilett urged him to keep absolute rest, telling him that his life was not in danger and that his wounds would heal in a few days. Moreover, Harbert was hardly suffering, and the cold water, which they were constantly pouring on them, was preventing any inflammation of the wounds. Suppuration was developing regularly, his fever was not increasing, and they could hope that this terrible injury wouldn't lead to any catastrophe. Pencroff felt his heart gradually lighten. He was like a charity sister, like a mother at her child's bedside.

Harbert fell asleep again, but his sleep seemed to be better. "Repeat to me that you hope, Mr. Spilett!" said Pencroff. "Repeat to me that you will save Harbert!

— Yes, we will save him! replied the reporter. The injury is severe, and perhaps the bullet has even pierced the lung, but a wound to that organ isn't necessarily fatal.

— May God hear you!" Pencroff echoed.

As you can imagine, since they had been at the corral for twenty-four hours, the colonists had been solely focused on taking care of Harbert. They were not concerned about the danger that could threaten them if the convicts returned, nor about the precautions they needed to take for the future.

But that day, while Pencroff stood by the sickbed, Cyrus Smith and the reporter discussed what needed to be done.

First, they surveyed the corral. There was no sign of Ayrton. Had the poor man been taken by his former accomplices? Had he been caught by them in the corral? Had he fought and succumbed in that battle? That last scenario was all too likely. Gideon Spilett, at the moment he scaled the palisade, had clearly seen one of the convicts fleeing down the southern slope of Mount Franklin, towards which Top had rushed. This was one of those whose boat had smashed against the rocks at the mouth of the Mercy. Additionally, the one Cyrus Smith had killed, whose body was found outside the enclosure, indeed belonged to Bob Harvey's gang.

As for the corral, it had suffered no devastation. The gates were closed, and the domesticated animals had not been able to scatter into the forest. There were also no signs of a struggle, no damage either to the dwelling or the palisade.

Only the ammunition that Ayrton had stocked had vanished along with him.

"The poor man must have been caught by surprise," Cyrus Smith said, "and, since he was someone who would have fought back, he likely fell in that fight.

— Yes! That is to be feared!" replied the reporter. "And, presumably, the convicts settled in the corral, where they found everything in abundance, and only fled when they saw us arriving. It is quite clear that at that moment, Ayrton, dead or alive, was no longer here.

— We need to search the forest," said the engineer, "and rid the island of these wretches. Pencroff's intuition was correct when he wanted us to hunt them down like wild beasts. That would have spared us many troubles!

— Yes," replied the reporter, "but now we have every right to be ruthless!

— In any case," said the engineer, "we are forced to wait a bit and stay at the corral until we can safely transport Harbert to Granite House.

— But what about Nab? asked the reporter.

— Nab is safe.

— And what if, worried about our absence, he takes the risk of coming here?

— He must not come!" Cyrus Smith replied sharply. "He would be murdered on the way!

— It is highly likely that he will try to join us!

— Ah! If only the telegraph were still working, we could warn him! But that is impossible now! As for leaving Pencroff and Harbert alone here, we can't do that!... well, I will go alone to Granite House.

— No, no! Cyrus," replied the reporter, "you must not put yourself at risk! Your bravery would be of no use. These scoundrels are clearly watching the corral; they are hiding in the thick woods surrounding it, and if you leave, we would soon regret having two misfortunes instead of just one!

— But Nab?" the engineer repeated. "It has been twenty-four hours since he has heard from us! He will want to come!

— And since he will be even less cautious than we would be ourselves," replied Gideon Spilett, "he would be struck!...

— Is there no way to warn him?"

While the engineer was deep in thought, his gaze fell on Top, who was pacing back and forth, seemingly saying, "Am I not here?"

"Top!" Cyrus Smith exclaimed.

The animal leaped at the sound of his master's voice.

"Yes, Top can go!" said the reporter, understanding the engineer. "Top will pass where we could not! He will bring news from the corral to Granite House, and then he will bring back news from Granite House to us!

— Quick!" replied Cyrus Smith. "Quick!"

Gideon Spilett quickly tore a page from his notebook and wrote the following lines:

"Harbert injured. We are at the corral. Stay alert. Do not leave Granite House. Have the convicts appeared nearby? Reply through Top."

This brief note contained everything Nab needed to know and simultaneously asked him for all the information that was important to the colonists. It was folded and attached to Top's collar in a very conspicuous way.

"Top! My dog," the engineer said, patting the animal, "Nab, Top! Nab! Go! Go!"

Top jumped upon hearing those words. He understood, he sensed what was expected of him. The route to the corral was familiar to him. In less than half an hour, he could have crossed it, and it was hoped that where neither Cyrus Smith nor the reporter could have safely ventured, Top, running through the grass or under the forest's edge, would go unnoticed.

The engineer went to the corral door and pushed one of its panels open.

"Nab! Top, Nab!" the engineer called out once again, extending his hand towards Granite House.

Top sprang out and disappeared almost immediately.

"He will arrive!" said the reporter.

— Yes, and he will return, the faithful animal!

— What time is it?" asked Gideon Spilett.

— Ten o'clock.

— In an hour he could be here. We will watch for his return."

The corral door was closed. The engineer and the reporter went back into the house. Harbert was then deeply asleep. Pencroff maintained his compresses in a permanently moist state.

Gideon Spilett, seeing that there was nothing to be done at the moment, occupied himself with preparing some food, while carefully monitoring the part of the enclosure next to the foothills, through which an attack could occur.

The colonists waited anxiously for Top's return. A little before eleven o'clock, Cyrus Smith and the reporter, rifle in hand, stood behind the door, ready to open it at the first bark of their dog. They had no doubt that if Top had successfully reached Granite House, Nab would have immediately sent him back.

They had been standing there for about ten minutes when a gunshot rang out, immediately followed by repeated barking.

The engineer opened the door, and seeing still a trace of smoke one hundred paces away in the woods, he fired in that direction.

Almost immediately, Top bounded into the corral, and the door was quickly closed behind him.

"Top, Top!" exclaimed the engineer, taking the dog's big, warm head in his arms. A note was attached to his neck, and Cyrus Smith read these words, written in Nab's large handwriting:

"No pirates around Granite House. I will not move. Poor Mr. Harbert!"

❧ 8 ❧

So, the convicts were still lurking around, watching the corral, and determined to kill the colonists one by one! They could only be treated like wild beasts. But great precautions needed to be taken, as these wretches currently had the advantage since they could see without being seen, able to attack suddenly without fear of being surprised.

Cyrus Smith arranged to live at the corral, which, by the way, could supply enough provisions for quite some time. Ayrton's house had been stocked with everything necessary for life, and the convicts, being frightened by the arrival of the colonists, did not have time to plunder it. It was likely, as Gideon Spilett observed, that events unfolded as follows: the six convicts, having landed on the island, followed its southern coast and, after traversing the dual shore of the serpentine peninsula, not being inclined to venture into the woods of the Far West, reached the mouth of the waterfall river. Once there, while climbing the right bank of the stream, they arrived at the foothills of Mount Franklin, where it was natural for them to look for some refuge, and they must not have taken long to discover the corral, which was then uninhabited. There, they had presumably settled while waiting to execute their heinous plans.

Ayrton's arrival must have taken them by surprise, but they had managed to capture the unfortunate man, and... the rest was easy to guess!

Now, the convicts — reduced to five, it is true, but well-armed — roamed the woods, and venturing there was exposing oneself to their shots, without the possibility of parrying or warning.

"Wait! There is nothing else to do!" repeated Cyrus Smith. "Once Harbert is healed, we can organize a full sweep of the island and deal with these convicts. That will be the objective of our big expedition, at the same time...

— As the search for our mysterious protector," added Gideon Spilett, completing the engineer's sentence. "Ah! I must admit, my dear Cyrus, that this time his protection has failed us, exactly when it was most needed!

— Who knows!" replied the engineer.

— What do you mean?" asked the reporter.

— That we are not yet at the end of our troubles, my dear Spilett, and that the powerful intervention might still have the opportunity to exert itself. But that is not what matters. Harbert's life comes first."

That was the colonists' most painful concern. A few days passed, and thankfully the condition of the poor boy had not worsened. Now, gaining time against the illness was a lot. The cold water, consistently kept at the right temperature, had absolutely prevented inflammation of the wounds. The reporter even thought that this water, a little sulfurous — which was explained by the proximity of the volcano — had a more direct effect on healing. The pus was much less abundant, and thanks to the constant care he received, Harbert was coming back to life, and his fever was beginning to subside. He was also on a strict diet, and consequently, his weakness was and must be extreme; but herbal teas were plentiful, and complete rest did him the greatest good.

Cyrus Smith, Gideon Spilett, and Pencroff had become quite adept at bandaging the young wounded man. All the linen in the house had been sacrificed. Harbert's wounds, covered with compresses and lint, were not wrapped too tightly or too loosely, in order to promote their healing without causing inflammatory reactions. The reporter took extreme care with these bandages, fully understanding their importance, and repeating to his companions what most doctors will gladly acknowledge: that it is perhaps rarer to see a well-done bandage than a well-done operation. After ten days, on November 22nd, Harbert was noticeably better. He had begun to eat a little. Colors returned to his cheeks, and his kind eyes smiled at his caretakers. He chatted a bit, despite Pencroff's efforts, who spoke all the time to keep him from speaking and told the most unbelievable stories.

Harbert had asked him about Ayrton, whom he was surprised not to see by his side, thinking he must be at the corral. But the sailor, not wanting to distress Harbert, had simply replied that Ayrton had joined Nab to protect Granite House.

"Hah! he exclaimed, those pirates! They are gentlemen who have lost all rights to any consideration! And Mr. Smith, who wanted to appeal to their feelings! I will send them some sentiment, yes, but with good lead!

— And we haven't seen them again?" asked Harbert.

— No, my child," replied the sailor, "but we will find them, and when you are healed, we will see if those cowards, who strike from behind, dare to attack us face to face!

— I am still very weak, my poor Pencroff!

— Hey! Your strength will gradually return! What is a bullet through the chest? Just a little joke! I've seen much worse, and I'm none the worse for it!"

Finally, things seemed to be improving, and as long as no complication arose, Harbert's recovery could be considered assured. But what would have been the situation of the colonists had his condition worsened, if, for example, the bullet had remained in his body, if his arm or leg had to be amputated!

"No," Gideon Spilett said more than once, "I have never thought about such a possibility without shuddering!

— And yet, had action been required," Cyrus Smith replied one day, "you wouldn't have hesitated?

— No, Cyrus!" said Gideon Spilett, "but may God be blessed for sparing us that complication!"

As in so many other situations, the colonists had appealed to the straightforward logic that had served them so well in the past, and once again, thanks to their general knowledge, they had succeeded! But would there not come a time when all their learning would fail them? They were alone on this island. Men complement each other through the structure of society; they are necessary to one another. Cyrus Smith knew this well, and sometimes he wondered if some circumstance would not arise that they would be powerless to overcome!

He even felt that his companions and he, so far so fortunate, had entered a negative phase. For more than two and a half years since they had escaped from Richmond, you could say that everything had gone their way. The island had abundantly provided them with minerals, flora, fauna, and while nature had constantly blessed them, their knowledge had succeeded in making the most of what it offered. The material well-being of the colony was practically complete. Furthermore, at certain moments, some inexplicable influence had come to their aid!... but all this couldn't last forever!

In short, Cyrus Smith believed he was noticing that fortune seemed to be turning against them. Indeed, the convicts' ship had appeared in the waters of the island, and although these pirates had been almost miraculously destroyed, at least six of them had escaped destruction. They had landed on the island, and the five who survived were practically elusive.

Ayrton had undoubtedly been killed by these miscreants, who possessed firearms, and at the very first use they made of them, Harbert fell, struck almost fatally. Were these the first blows that bad fortune aimed at the colonists? That is what Cyrus Smith wondered! That is what he often repeated to the reporter, and they both felt that this strange but effective intervention, which had helped them so much until now, was now absent. That mysterious being, whatever he may be, whose existence they could not deny, had he then abandoned the island? Had he succumbed as well?

To these questions, no answer was possible. But one should not think that Cyrus Smith and his companion, just because they were discussing these matters, were people to lose hope! Quite the opposite. They faced the situation head-on, analyzed their chances, prepared for any event, stood firm and upright before the future, and if adversity were to strike them, it would find in them men ready to fight back.

The young patient's recovery was progressing steadily. The only thing left to wish for was that his condition allowed him to return to Granite-House. No matter how well-equipped and stocked the corral's dwelling was, it couldn't provide the comfort of the solid granite home. Moreover, it didn't offer the same security, and its occupants, despite their watchfulness, were always under threat from gunfire from the convicts. Over there, on the other hand, in the middle of that impregnable and inaccessible massif, they would have nothing to fear, and any attempt against them would surely fail. They were therefore impatiently awaiting the moment when Harbert could be moved safely, and they were determined to carry out this transport, even though traversing the jacamar woods was quite challenging.

They hadn't heard from Nab but were not worried about him. The brave black man, well secured in the depths of Granite-House, wouldn't be caught off guard. Top had not been sent back to him, and it seemed unnecessary to expose the loyal dog to any gunfire that could deprive the settlers of their most useful ally.

So they waited, but the settlers were eager to reunite at Granite-House. It troubled the engineer to see his forces divided, as it played into the pirates' hands. Since Ayrton's disappearance, they were only four against five, as Harbert was still unable to count. This was a concern for the brave child, who understood the troubles he had caused!

The question of how they would act against the convicts under the current conditions was thoroughly discussed on November 29 between Cyrus Smith,

Gideon Spilett, and Pencroff, at a moment when Harbert was dozing and couldn't hear them.

"My friends," said the reporter, after they talked about Nab and the impossibility of communicating with him, "I believe, like you, that venturing out on the road to the corral would be risking a gunshot without being able to return fire. But don't you think that what we should do now is to hunt down these wretches?"

"That's what I was thinking," replied Pencroff. "We aren't, I suppose, afraid of a bullet, and for my part, if Mr. Cyrus approves, I'm ready to charge into the woods! What the devil! A man is as good as another!"

"But is one as good as five?" asked the engineer.

"I will join Pencroff," replied the reporter, "and the two of us, well-armed, accompanied by Top..."

"My dear Spilett, and you too, Pencroff," Cyrus Smith interjected, "let's reason calmly. If the convicts were holed up somewhere on the island, if we knew where that was, and if it were simply a matter of flushing them out, I would understand a direct attack. But isn't there reason to fear that they would be ready to take the first shot?"

"Come on, Mr. Cyrus," Pencroff exclaimed, "a bullet doesn't always hit its target!"

"The one that hit Harbert didn't miss, Pencroff," the engineer replied. "Besides, note that if the two of you left the corral, I would be left alone to defend it. Do you really think the convicts wouldn't see you abandoning it, that they wouldn't prevent you from entering the forest, and that they wouldn't attack while you were gone, knowing that all that would be left here is an injured child and one man?"

"You're right, Mr. Cyrus," replied Pencroff, whose chest was swelling with suppressed anger, "you're right. They will do everything to retake the corral, which they know is well stocked! And alone, you couldn't hold against them! Ah! If only we were at Granite-House!"

"If we were at Granite-House," the engineer replied, "the situation would be very different! There, I wouldn't be afraid to leave Harbert with one of us, and the other three could search the island's forests. But we are at the corral, and we must stay here until we can leave all together!"

There was nothing to respond to Cyrus Smith's reasoning, and his companions understood this well.

"If only Ayrton were still with us!" said Gideon Spilett. "Poor man! His return to social life was only brief!"

"What if he's dead?" added Pencroff in a rather peculiar tone.

"Do you really think these scoundrels would have spared him?" asked Gideon Spilett.

"Yes! If it benefitted them to do so!"

"What! You would suppose that Ayrton, finding his former accomplices, forgetting all that he owes us..."

"What do we know?" replied the sailor, who hesitated to voice this troubling doubt.

"Pencroff," said Cyrus Smith as he took the sailor's arm, "you have a bad thought there, and I would be very distressed if you persisted in speaking that way! I guarantee Ayrton's loyalty!"

"So do I!" the reporter added quickly.

"Yes... yes!... Mr. Cyrus... I was wrong," replied Pencroff. "It's indeed a bad thought I had, and nothing justifies it! But what do you want? I'm not quite in my right mind. This confinement in the corral weighs heavily on me, and I've never been so on edge!"

"Be patient, Pencroff," replied the engineer.

"In how long, my dear Spilett, do you think Harbert could be transported to Granite-House?"

"That's hard to say, Cyrus," the reporter replied. "For imprudence could lead to disastrous consequences. But his recovery is going well, and if in eight days he recovers his strength, well then, we will see!"

Eight days! That pushed the return to Granite-House to the early days of December only.

By that time, spring had already been going for two months. The weather was nice, and the heat was beginning to become strong. The island's forests were in full leaf, and the time was approaching when the usual harvests should be gathered. The return to the Grande-vue plateau would therefore be followed by major agricultural work, interrupted only by the planned expedition on the island.

One can understand how this confinement at the corral must have affected the settlers. But while they were forced to bend to necessity, they were not doing so without impatience. Once or twice, the reporter ventured onto the path and circled the palisade. Top accompanied him, and Gideon Spilett, with his rifle loaded, was ready for anything.

He encountered no danger and found no suspicious traces. His dog would have warned him of any threat, and since Top didn't bark, one could conclude that there was nothing to fear, at least at that moment, and that the convicts were busy elsewhere on the island.

However, during his second outing on November 27, Gideon Spilett, who had ventured into the woods for a quarter of a mile south of the mountain, noticed that Top was sensing something.

The dog no longer exhibited his indifferent demeanor; he was going back and forth, nosing through the grass and brambles, as if his sense of smell revealed some suspicious object.

Gideon Spilett followed Top, encouraging him, urging him with his voice, while keeping a watchful eye, his rifle poised, and using the cover of the trees for protection. It was unlikely that Top had sensed the presence of a man, as in that case he would have announced it with half-contained barks and a kind of subdued anger. Since he made no growl, it meant the danger was neither immediate nor close.

About five minutes passed in this way, Top probing, the reporter following him cautiously, when suddenly the dog dashed toward a thick bush and pulled out a piece of cloth.

It was a rag of clothing, stained, torn, which Gideon Spilett immediately brought back to the corral.

There, the settlers examined it, and they recognized it as a piece of Ayrton's jacket, a piece of the felt made only in the workshop at Granite-House.

"You see, Pencroff," Cyrus Smith pointed out, "there was a struggle on the part of the unfortunate Ayrton. The convicts took him against his will! Do you still doubt his honesty?"

"No, Mr. Cyrus," replied the sailor, "and I've long since overcome my brief moment of suspicion! But it seems to me there's a conclusion to be drawn from this fact."

"What is that?" the reporter asked.

"It's that Ayrton wasn't killed at the corral! That he was taken alive, since he resisted! Now, he might still be alive!"

"Perhaps, indeed," replied the engineer, who remained thoughtful.

There was a glimmer of hope for Ayrton's companions. In fact, they must have believed that caught at the corral, Ayrton had fallen to some bullet, just as Harbert had. But if the convicts hadn't killed him right away, if they had taken him alive to some other part of the island, could it not be supposed that he was still their prisoner? Perhaps one of them had even recognized in Ayrton an old companion from Australia, Ben Joyce, the leader of the escaped convicts?

And who knows if they didn't harbor the impossible hope of bringing Ayrton back to them!

He would have been so useful to them if they could make a traitor of him!

This incident was therefore interpreted favorably at the corral, and it no longer seemed impossible that Ayrton could be found. On his part, if he was only a prisoner, Ayrton would surely do everything to escape from the hands of those bandits, and he would be a powerful ally for the settlers!

"In any case," Gideon Spilett pointed out, "if, by some chance, Ayrton manages to escape, he will go directly to Granite-House, for he doesn't know about the murder attempt that Harbert suffered, and consequently, he cannot believe that we are imprisoned at the corral."

"Oh! I wish he were there, at Granite-House!" Pencroff exclaimed, "and that we were too! Because, after all, if the scoundrels can't do anything against our home, they can at least ravage the plateau, our crops, our poultry!"

Pencroff had become a true farmer, deeply attached to his harvests. But it must be said that Harbert was more than anyone impatient to return to Granite-House, for he understood how necessary the presence of the settlers was there. And it was he who was holding them back at the corral! Therefore, this singular idea occupied his mind: leaving the corral, leaving no matter what! He believed he could endure the transport to Granite-House. He insisted that his strength would return faster in his room with the air and the view of the sea!

Several times he pressed Gideon Spilett, but the latter, reasonably fearing that Harbert's poorly healed wounds could reopen on the way, did not give the order to depart.

However, an incident occurred that led Cyrus Smith and his two friends to yield to the young boy's wishes, and God knows what pains and remorse this decision could cause them!

It was November 29. It was seven in the morning. The three settlers were talking in Harbert's room when they heard Top barking vigorously.

Cyrus Smith, Pencroff, and Gideon Spilett grabbed their rifles, always ready to fire, and they stepped outside the house.

Top, having rushed to the foot of the palisade, was jumping and barking, but it was in joy, not anger.

"Someone's coming!

"Yes!

"It's not an enemy!

"Nab, maybe?

"Or Ayrton?"

Barely had these words been exchanged between the engineer and his two companions when a figure jumped over the palisade and landed on the ground of the corral.

It was Jup, master Jup himself, to whom Top gave a true friendly welcome!

"Jup!" exclaimed Pencroff.

"It's Nab who sent him!" said the reporter.

"Then," replied the engineer, "he must have some message for us."

Pencroff rushed toward the orangutan. Obviously, if Nab had something important to convey to his master, he couldn't have employed a more reliable and faster messenger who could pass where neither the settlers nor even Top himself might have been able to.

Cyrus Smith was not mistaken. Around Jup's neck hung a small bag, and inside this bag was a note written by Nab. Just think of Cyrus Smith's and his companions' despair when they read these words:

"Friday, 6 a.m. 'Plateau invaded by convicts! Nab.'"

They looked at each other without saying a word, then they went back inside the house. What were they to do?

The convicts at the Grande-vue plateau meant disaster, devastation, ruin!

Harbert, seeing the engineer, the reporter, and Pencroff return, understood that the situation had worsened, and when he spotted Jup, he no longer doubted that calamity threatened Granite-House.

"Mr. Cyrus," he said, "I want to leave. I can endure the journey! I want to leave!"

Gideon Spilett approached Harbert. Then, after looking at him,

"Let's leave then!" he said.

The question was quickly decided as to whether Harbert would be transported on a stretcher or in the cart that Ayrton had brought to the corral. The stretcher would have provided smoother movements for the injured, but it required two bearers, meaning two rifles would be missing for defense if an attack occurred on the way.

Could they not, on the other hand, using the cart, leave all arms available? Was it really impossible to place the mattresses on which Harbert rested in the cart and advance with such caution as to avoid any jolts? They could do that.

The cart was brought up. Pencroff hitched up the onagga.

Cyrus Smith and the reporter lifted Harbert's mattresses and placed them at the bottom of the cart between the two sideboards.

The weather was nice. Bright rays of sunlight were filtering through the trees.

"Are the weapons ready?" asked Cyrus Smith.

They were ready. The engineer and Pencroff, each armed with a double-barreled rifle, and Gideon Spilett, holding his carbine, were only left to leave.

"Are you alright, Harbert?" asked the engineer.

"Ah! Mr. Cyrus," replied the young boy, "don't worry, I won't die on the way!"

In saying this, it was clear that the poor child was calling on all his energy, and that, by a supreme will, he was holding back his strength, which was ready to fade.

The engineer felt his heart tighten painfully.

He hesitated again to give the signal to leave. But it would have been to despair Harbert, perhaps to kill him.

"Let's go!" said Cyrus Smith.

The gate of the corral was opened. Jup and Top, who knew how to keep quiet at the right moment, rushed ahead. The cart exited, the gate was closed, and the onagga, guided by Pencroff, moved forward at a slow pace.Surely, it would have been better to take a different route than the one that went directly from the corral to Granite-House, but the cart would have faced great difficulties moving through the woods. Therefore, they had to follow this path, even though it was likely known to the convicts.

Cyrus Smith and Gédéon Spilett walked on either side of the cart, ready to respond to any attack. However, it was unlikely that the convicts had abandoned the raised area. Nab's note had obviously been written and sent as soon as the convicts had shown themselves there. This note was dated six o'clock in the morning, and the agile orangutan, accustomed to frequently visiting the corral, had taken barely three-quarters of an hour to cover the five miles to Granite-House. The route should therefore be safe at this moment, and if there was to be any gunfire, it would likely only happen near Granite-House.

However, the colonists remained very vigilant. Top and Jup, the latter armed with his stick, alternated between leading ahead and beating the brush on the sides of the path, signaling no danger.

The cart moved slowly under Pencroff's direction. They had left the corral at seven-thirty. An hour later, four miles had been covered without any incident occurring.

The road was deserted like the whole part of the wood that stretched between the Mercy and the lake. There was no alarm. The underbrush seemed as deserted as on the day the colonists landed on the island.

They were approaching the plateau. One more mile, and they would see the culvert of the glycerin creek. Cyrus Smith had no doubt that the culvert was in place, whether the convicts had entered through that spot or, after crossing one of the waterways that formed the enclosure, they had taken the precaution to lower it, to secure an escape route. Finally, the gap between the last trees revealed the horizon of the sea. But the cart continued its march, for none of its defenders could think of abandoning it. At that moment, Pencroff stopped the onager, and in a terrible voice:

"Ah! The wretches!" he exclaimed.

And he pointed with his hand at a thick smoke swirling above the mill, the stables, and the buildings of the poultry yard. A man was moving in the midst of these vapors.

It was Nab.

His companions shouted. He heard them and ran to them...

The convicts had abandoned the plateau about half an hour earlier, after devastating it!

"And Mr. Harbert?" cried Nab.

Gédéon Spilett returned to the cart at that moment.

Harbert had lost consciousness!

✣ I O ✣

There was no longer any talk of the convicts, the dangers threatening Granite-House, or the ruins that covered the plateau. Harbert's condition overshadowed everything. Had the transport been fatal for him, causing some internal injury? The reporter could not say, but he and his companions were desperate.

The cart was brought to the bend of the river. There, a few branches arranged like a stretcher received the mattresses on which Harbert lay unconscious. Ten minutes later, Cyrus Smith, Gédéon Spilett, and Pencroff were at the foot of the wall, leaving Nab to guide the cart back to the Grande-vue plateau.

The lift was set in motion, and soon Harbert was stretched out on his bed in Granite-House.

The care given to him brought him back to life. He smiled for a moment upon finding himself in his room, but he could barely murmur a few words, so great was his weakness.

Gédéon Spilett checked his wounds. He feared that they might have reopened, having been imperfectly healed... but they had not.

So where was this prostration coming from? Why had Harbert's condition deteriorated?

The young boy then fell into a sort of feverish sleep, and the reporter and Pencroff remained by his bedside.

Meanwhile, Cyrus Smith brought Nab up to speed on what had happened at the corral, and Nab recounted to his master the events that had just taken place on the plateau.

It was only the previous night that the convicts had shown themselves at the edge of the forest, near the glycerin creek. Nab, who had been watching near the poultry yard, had not hesitated to fire at one of those pirates, who was about to cross the river; but, in that rather dark night, he could not tell if that wretch had been hit. In any case, it had not been enough to deter the gang, and Nab had only had time to return to Granite-House, where at least he was safe.

But then, what to do? How to prevent the devastation that the convicts threatened on the plateau? Did Nab have a way to warn his master? And besides, what situation were they themselves in as the occupants of the corral?

Cyrus Smith and his companions had left on November 11, and it was now the 29th. So Nab had not had any news for nineteen days other than what Top had brought him, disastrous news: Ayrton missing, Harbert seriously injured, the engineer, the reporter, and the sailor, so to speak, trapped in the corral! What to do? the poor Nab wondered. For himself personally, he had nothing to fear, as the convicts could not reach him in Granite-House.

But the constructions, the crops, all these arrangements were at the mercy of the pirates! Shouldn't Cyrus Smith be allowed to judge what he would have to do, and at least be warned of the dangers threatening him?

Nab then thought of using Jup and entrusting him with a note. He knew the orangutan's remarkable intelligence, which had been tested many times. Jup understood the word "corral," which had often been said in front of him, and it should be recalled that he had often led the cart along with Pencroff. The day had not yet dawned. The agile orangutan would surely be able to go unnoticed in those woods, which the convicts would likely believe him to be one of its natural inhabitants.

Nab did not hesitate. He wrote the note, attached it to Jup's neck, brought the monkey to the door of Granite-House, from which he let a long rope unroll down to the ground; then, repeatedly, he called out:

"Jup! Jup! Corral! Corral!"

The animal understood, grabbed the rope, slid quickly down to the shore, and vanished into the shadows without attracting the attention of the convicts at all.

"You did well, Nab," replied Cyrus Smith, "but by not warning us, perhaps you could have done even better!"

And, speaking like this, Cyrus Smith was thinking of Harbert, whose transport appeared to have so severely compromised his recovery.

Nab finished his account. The convicts had not appeared on the shore. Not knowing the number of the island's inhabitants, they could assume that Granite-House was defended by a significant group. They must remember that during the attack on the brig, many shots had greeted them, both from the lower rocks and the upper ones, and they probably did not want to expose themselves. But the Grande-vue plateau was open to them and was not covered by the fires of Granite-House. They therefore indulged their instincts for plunder, looting, burning, doing harm for the sake of harm, and they left barely half an hour before the colonists arrived, whom they must still have believed to be confined in the corral.

Nab had rushed out of his hiding place. He had climbed up to the plateau, risking being hit by a bullet, tried to put out the fire that was consuming the buildings of the poultry yard, and had fought, but in vain, against the flames, until the cart appeared at the edge of the woods.

Such had been these grave events. The presence of the convicts constituted a permanent threat for the once-happy colonists of Lincoln Island, who might expect even greater misfortunes ahead!

Gédéon Spilett stayed at Granite-House near Harbert and Pencroff, while Cyrus Smith, accompanied by Nab, went to assess the extent of the disaster for himself.

It was fortunate that the convicts had not advanced to the foot of Granite-House. The chimney workshops would not have escaped devastation. But after all, that damage might have been more easily reparable than the ruin accumulated on the Grande-vue plateau!

Cyrus Smith and Nab made their way toward the Mercy and walked up the left bank without encountering any trace of the convicts' passage. On the other side of the river, in the thickness of the woods, they did not see any suspicious signs either.

Moreover, this is what could be inferred with a reasonable degree of probability: either the convicts knew of the colonists' return to Granite-House, as they could have seen them pass along the road from the corral; or after the devastation of the plateau, they had plunged into the jacamar woods, following the course of the Mercy, and were unaware of this return.

In the first case, they must have returned to the corral, now defenseless, which contained precious resources for them.

In the second, they had likely returned to their camp and were waiting there for some opportunity to restart the attack.

There would therefore be grounds to warn them; but any endeavor to rid the island of them was still contingent on Harbert's condition. Indeed, Cyrus

Smith would not have all his strength, and no one could, at that moment, leave Granite-House.

The engineer and Nab arrived at the plateau. It was a wreck. The fields had been trampled. The ears of grain, which were about to be harvested, lay on the ground. The other crops had suffered just as much. The vegetable garden was overturned.

Fortunately, Granite-House had a reserve of seeds that would allow them to repair this damage.

As for the mill and the buildings of the poultry yard, as well as the stables for the onagas, fire had destroyed everything. A few frightened animals wandered across the plateau. The birds, having taken refuge during the fire on the waters of the lake, were already returning to their usual places and were dabbling on the shores. There, everything would have to be redone.

The look on Cyrus Smith's face, paler than usual, indicated an inner anger he struggled to control, but he did not utter a word.

One last time he looked at his devastated fields, the smoke still rising from the ruins, then he returned to Granite-House.

The days that followed were the saddest the colonists had ever spent on the island! Harbert's weakness was visibly increasing. It seemed that a more serious illness, a consequence of the profound physiological disturbance he had undergone, threatened to break out, and Gédéon Spilett sensed such a worsening in his condition that he would be powerless to fight against it! Indeed, Harbert remained in a kind of continuous stupor, and some symptoms of delirium began to manifest. Refreshing herbal teas were the only remedies available to the colonists. The fever was not yet very strong, but soon it seemed to want to establish itself through regular bouts.

Gédéon Spilett recognized it on December 6. The poor child, whose fingers, nose, and ears became extremely pale, first experienced light chills, irritation, and tremors.

His pulse was small and irregular, his skin dry, and he had intense thirst. Soon after this period came a period of heat; his face animated, his skin reddened, his pulse quickened; then an abundant sweat appeared, after which the fever seemed to diminish. The access had lasted about five hours.

Gédéon Spilett did not leave Harbert, who was now suffering from intermittent fever, it was all too certain, and this fever had to be cut off at all costs before it became more serious.

"And to cut it off," Gédéon Spilett said to Cyrus Smith, "we need a fever reducer."

"A fever reducer!" replied the engineer. "We have neither quinine nor sulfate of quinine!"

"No," said Gédéon Spilett, "but there are willows by the lake, and willow bark can sometimes replace quinine."

"Let's try it without losing a moment!" replied Cyrus Smith.

Willow bark has indeed been recognized as a substitute for quinine, just like the Indian chestnut, holly leaves, snake root, etc. It was evident they had to try this substance, although it was not as good as quinine, and they had to use it in its natural state since they lacked the means to extract its alkaloid, which is salicin.

Cyrus Smith personally went to cut some pieces of bark from a kind of black willow; he brought them back to Granite-House, powdered them, and this powder was administered to Harbert that very evening.

The night passed without any serious incidents. Harbert had some delirium, but the fever did not return that night, nor did it come back the next day.

Pencroff regained some hope. Gédéon Spilett said nothing. It could well be that the intermittent fever was not daily, that the fever was tertian, in short, and that it would return the next day. Thus, they awaited that next day with the keenest anxiety.

It could also be noted that during the apyrexial period, Harbert remained as if broken, with a heavy head and prone to dizziness. Another symptom greatly frightened the reporter: Harbert's liver was beginning to become congested, and soon a more intense delirium showed that his brain was also affected.

Gédéon Spilett was devastated by this new complication. He took the engineer aside.

"This is a pernicious fever!" he told him.

"A pernicious fever!" exclaimed Cyrus Smith. "You are mistaken, Spilett. A pernicious fever does not arise spontaneously. One must have had the germ!"

"I am not mistaken," the reporter replied. "Harbert must have contracted this germ in the marshes of the island, and that is enough. He has already experienced a first bout. If a second bout occurs, and if we do not succeed in stopping the third... he is lost!"

"But this willow bark?"

"It is insufficient," the reporter replied, "and a third bout of pernicious fever that is not stopped with quinine is always fatal!"

Fortunately, Pencroff had not heard any of this conversation. He would have gone mad.

One can understand the worries that the engineer and the reporter experienced during that day of November 7 and during the night that followed.

Around the middle of the day, the second bout struck. The crisis was terrible. Harbert felt lost! He reached out his arms to Cyrus Smith, to Spilett, to Pencroff! He did not want to die!... this scene was heart-wrenching. Pencroff had to be sent away.

The bout lasted five hours. It was clear that Harbert could not endure a third.

The night was dreadful. In his delirium, Harbert said things that broke the hearts of his companions! He raved, fought against the convicts, called for Ayrton! He begged this mysterious being, this protector, now vanished, and whose image haunted him... Then he would fall back into a profound prostration that completely annihilated him... Several times, Gédéon Spilett thought that the poor boy was dead!The next day, December 8, was nothing but a series of weaknesses. Harbert's thin hands tightened around his sheets. They had given him more doses of crushed bark, but the reporter no longer expected any results from it.

"If we don't give him a stronger fever reducer by tomorrow morning," said the reporter, "Harbert will be dead!"

Night fell—likely the last night for this brave, kind, intelligent boy who was so far beyond his years, and whom everyone loved as their own son! The only remedy that existed against this terrible pernicious fever, the only specific that could conquer it, could not be found on Lincoln Island!

During the night of December 8 to 9, Harbert fell into an even more intense delirium. His liver was horrifically congested, his brain was affected, and it was already impossible for him to recognize anyone.

Would he survive until the next day, until the third attack that would inevitably take him? It was no longer likely. His strength was exhausted, and in the intervals between fits, he lay as if lifeless.

Around three in the morning, Harbert let out a terrifying scream. He seemed to twist in a final convulsion. Nab, who was near him, terrified, rushed into the next room where his companions were keeping watch!

At that moment, Top barked in a strange way...

They all rushed back in and managed to hold the dying boy down, who was trying to throw himself out of bed, while Gideon Spilett, taking his arm, felt his pulse gradually rising...

It was five o'clock in the morning. The first rays of the rising sun began to slip into the rooms of Granite House. A beautiful day was on the horizon, and this day would be poor Harbert's last!... A ray of light slipped onto the table near the bed.

Suddenly, Pencroff, letting out a cry, pointed to an object on that table... it was a small oblong box, with the words written on the lid: sulphate of quinine.

Gideon Spilett took the box and opened it. It contained about two hundred grains of a white powder, of which he brought a few particles to his lips. The extreme bitterness of this substance could not deceive him. It was indeed the precious alkaloid from cinchona, the ultimate anti-periodic.

There was no hesitation; this powder had to be administered to Harbert. How it had ended up there could be discussed later.

"Coffee," asked Gideon Spilett.

A moment later, Nab brought a cup of lukewarm infusion. Gideon Spilett added about eighteen grains of quinine to it, and they managed to get Harbert to drink this mixture.

It was still time, for the third attack of the pernicious fever had not yet shown itself!

And, it should be said, it would not return!

Moreover, it must also be said that everyone had regained hope. The mysterious influence had once again exerted itself, and at a critical moment, when they had almost given up hope!... After a few hours, Harbert was resting more peacefully. The colonists were then able to discuss this incident. The intervention of the unknown was more evident than ever. But how had he managed to penetrate into Granite House during the night?

It was utterly inexplicable, and indeed, the way the "genius of the island" operated was no less strange than the genius himself.

Throughout this day, and every three hours or so, the sulphate of quinine was administered to Harbert.

By the next day, Harbert was feeling somewhat better. Certainly, he was not cured, and intermittent fevers are prone to frequent and dangerous relapses, but he was not lacking care. And besides, the specific was there, and not far away, surely, the one who had brought it! Finally, immense hope returned to everyone's heart.

This hope was not unfounded. Ten days later, on December 20, Harbert began his recovery. He was still weak, and a strict diet had been imposed on him, but there had been no further attacks. And besides, the obedient child gladly complied with all the prescriptions imposed upon him! He was so eager to get well!

Pencroff was like a man pulled from the depths of an abyss. He had fits of joy that bordered on delirium. After the moment of the third attack had passed, he had hugged the reporter so tightly he could barely breathe. Since then, he had only referred to him as Dr. Spilett.

Now, the real doctor needed to be discovered.

"We'll find him!" the sailor kept repeating.

And certainly, this man, whoever he was, should expect a hearty embrace from the worthy Pencroff!

December came to a close, and with it the year 1867, which had been so harsh for the colonists of Lincoln Island. They entered the year 1868 with magnificent weather, beautiful warmth, and tropical temperatures, happily refreshed by the sea breeze.

Harbert was reviving, and from his bed by one of the windows of Granite House, he breathed in the healthy air filled with saline emanations that were restoring his health. He began to eat, and God knows what delicious, light, and tasty dishes Nab was preparing for him!

"It would make you wish you had been dying!" Pencroff would say.

Throughout this period, the convicts had not shown themselves anywhere near Granite House. No news of Ayrton, and while the engineer and Harbert still held some hope of finding him, their companions no longer doubted that the poor man had succumbed. Nevertheless, these uncertainties couldn't last, and as soon as the young boy was healthy again, the expedition, whose outcome would be so significant, would take place. But they would have to wait a month, perhaps, as it would take all the forces of the colony to deal with the convicts.

Moreover, Harbert was getting better and better. The congestion in his liver had cleared up, and his injuries could be considered definitively healed.

In that month of January, important work was done on the Grande-vue plateau; but it only consisted of saving what could still be salvaged from the devastated crops, whether wheat or vegetables. The seeds and plants were collected so as to provide a new harvest for the next half-season.

As for reconstructing the buildings of the barnyard, the mill, and the stables, Cyrus Smith preferred to wait.

While he and his companions would be pursuing the convicts, they might well make another visit to the plateau, and it was best not to give them reason to resume their plundering and arson ways. Once the island had been cleared of these criminals, they would see about rebuilding.

The young convalescent began to get up during the second half of January, starting with one hour a day, then two, then three. His strength was rapidly returning, as his constitution was vigorous. He was eighteen at the time. He was tall and promised to grow into a man of noble and fine stature.

From that moment on, his recovery, although still requiring some care—and Dr. Spilett was quite strict—progressed steadily.

By the end of the month, Harbert was already roaming the Grande-vue plateau and the shores. A few sea baths he took with Pencroff and Nab did him a world of good. Cyrus Smith thought it might be possible to set the departure date for February 15. The nights, very clear at this time of year, would be ideal for the searches they were to conduct across the island.

The preparations needed for this exploration were thus started, and they would be significant, as the colonists had vowed not to return to Granite House until their dual purpose was accomplished: to destroy the convicts and find Ayrton if he was still alive, and to discover who had been so effectively overseeing the colony's fate.

From Lincoln Island, the colonists knew the entire eastern coast from Cap Griffe to Cap Mandibules, the vast marshes of tadornes, the areas around Lake Grant, the jacamar woods between the road to the corral and the Mercy, the courses of the Mercy and the Red Creek, and finally the foothills of Mount Franklin, where the corral had been established.

They had explored but imperfectly the vast coastline of Washington Bay from Cap Griffe to the Reptile Promontory, the forested and marshy edge of the western coast, and those interminable dunes that ended at the gaping mouth of Shark Gulf.

But they had not in any way recognized the large wooded areas that covered the serpentine peninsula, the entire right bank of Mercy, the left bank of the falls river, and the entanglement of foothills and valleys that held up three-quarters of the base of Mount Franklin to the west, north, and east, where so many deep retreats undoubtedly existed. Thus, several thousand acres of the island still eluded their investigations.

It was therefore decided that the expedition would proceed into the Far-West, so as to encompass the entire area situated to the right of the Mercy.

Perhaps it would have been better to first head for the corral, where they should fear that the convicts had again taken refuge, either to plunder it or to settle there. But either the devastation of the corral was now a done deal, and it was too late to prevent it, or the convicts had found it better to retreat there, and it would always be possible to chase them out of their hideout later.

So, after discussion, the initial plan was maintained, and the colonists resolved to make their way through the woods to the Reptile Promontory. They would walk with axes and thus lay the first trace of a road connecting Granite House to the end of the peninsula over a length of sixteen to seventeen miles.

The cart was in perfect condition. The onagers, well-rested, could provide a long haul.

Food, camping gear, portable cooking equipment, various utensils were loaded onto the cart, as well as carefully chosen weapons and ammunition from the now-complete arsenal at Granite House. But they could not forget that the convicts might be lurking in the woods, and that, amidst these thick forests, a gunshot could be quickly fired and received. Therefore, it was necessary for the small group of colonists to stay together and not to split up for any reason.

It was also decided that no one would stay at Granite House. Top and Jup were also to take part in the expedition. The inaccessible dwelling could protect itself.

February 14, the day before departure, was a Sunday.

It was dedicated entirely to rest and sanctified by the thanksgiving that the colonists offered to the Creator. Harbert, fully recovered but still a bit weak, would have a reserved place on the cart.

The next day, at dawn, Cyrus Smith took the necessary measures to protect Granite House from any invasion. The ladders that had once been used to ascend were brought to the chimneys and deeply buried in the sand, so they could be used for the return, since the lift drum had been taken down, leaving no communication between the upper level and the shore. Pencroff was the last to leave Granite House to finish this task, and he descended using a rope that was doubled and held at the bottom, and once it was returned to the ground, it left no communication between the upper level and the shore.

The weather was magnificent.

"What a hot day is coming!" said the reporter joyfully.

"Bah! Dr. Spilett," replied Pencroff, "we'll be walking in the shade of the trees and won't even see the sun!"

"Let's go!" said the engineer.

The cart was waiting on the shore, in front of the chimneys. The reporter insisted that Harbert take a seat there, at least for the first hours of the journey, and the young boy had to comply with his doctor's orders.

Nab took the lead with the onagers. Cyrus Smith, the reporter, and the sailor went ahead. Top danced about joyfully. Harbert offered a spot to Jup in his vehicle, and Jup accepted without hesitation. The moment of departure had arrived, and the small group set off.

The cart first rounded the corner of the mouth, then, after traveling one mile up the left bank of the Mercy, it crossed the bridge at the end of which the road to Port-Ballon began, where the explorers, leaving this road on their left, started to delve into the vast woods that formed the region of the Far-West.

During the first two miles, the trees, widely spaced, allowed the cart to move freely; occasionally it was necessary to cut through some vines and thickets, but no serious obstacle stopped the colonists' progress.

The thick foliage of the trees maintained a cool shade on the ground. Deodars, Douglas firs, casuarinas, banksias, eucalyptus, dracaenas, and other already recognized species succeeded each other beyond the limits of sight. The world of the usual birds found on the island was fully represented, including partridges, jacamars, pheasants, lories, and the entire chattering family of cockatoos, parakeets, and parrots. Agoutis, kangaroos, and capybaras darted between the grasses, all of which reminded the colonists of the first excursions they had made upon arriving on the island.

"However," noted Cyrus Smith, "I notice that these animals, both quadrupeds and birds, are more skittish than before. These woods must have been recently traversed by the convicts, of whom we must surely find traces."

And indeed, in many places, they were able to recognize the more or less recent passage of a group of men: here, breakages made in the trees, perhaps to mark the path; there, ashes of a dead fire, and footprints retained by some clayey portions of the ground. But, after all, nothing indicated a permanent camp.

The engineer had advised his companions to refrain from hunting. The gunshots could alert the convicts, who might be prowling in the forest. Besides, hunters would necessarily be lured some distance away from the cart, and it was strictly prohibited to walk alone.

During the second part of the day, about six miles from Granite House, the passage became quite difficult. In order to get through certain thickets, it was necessary to cut down trees and create a path. Before they engaged, Cyrus Smith took care to send Top and Jup into the thick underbrush, who conscientiously performed their task, and when the dog and the orangutan returned without signaling anything, it meant there was nothing to fear, either from the convicts or from any wild animals—two types of beings from the animal kingdom that their fierce instincts placed on equal footing.

On the evening of this first day, the colonists camped about nine miles from Granite House, on the bank of a small tributary of the Mercy, whose existence they were unaware of, and which was to link to the hydrographic system that gave this land its remarkable fertility.

They had a hearty supper, as the colonists had a strong appetite, and measures were taken to ensure the night passed without incident. If the engineer had only to deal with wild animals, like jaguars or others, he would have simply lit fires around his camp, which would have been enough to protect it; but the convicts would have been more attracted than deterred by those flames, and it was better, in this case, to encircle themselves with deep darkness. The surveillance was, moreover, strictly organized. Two of the colonists had to keep watch together, and every two hours, it was agreed that they would be relieved by their comrades. However, since Harbert was excused from guard duty despite his protests, Pencroff and Gédéon Spilett, on one side, and the engineer and Nab, on the other, took turns watching the approaches to the camp.

In fact, there were barely a few hours of night. The darkness was mainly due to the thickness of the foliage rather than the disappearance of the sun. The silence was only slightly disturbed by the harsh howls of jaguars and the screams of monkeys, which seemed to particularly annoy Master Jup.

The night passed without incident, and the next day, February 16, they resumed their march, which was slow rather than difficult, through the forest. That day, they could only cover six miles because constantly they had to clear a path with an axe. Like true settlers, the colonists spared the large, beautiful trees, whose cutting would have cost them great effort, and sacrificed the smaller ones; but this meant the path took a winding direction with many detours.

During this day, Harbert discovered new tree species that had not yet been reported on the island, such as tree ferns with drooping fronds that seemed to spill like water from a basin, carob trees, whose onaggas eagerly munched on the long pods and produced sweet pulp of excellent taste. There, the colonists also found magnificent kauris, arranged in groups, with their cylindrical trunks topped with a cone of greenery reaching a height of two hundred feet. These were indeed the royal trees of New Zealand, as famous as the cedars of Lebanon.

As for the fauna, there were no other samples than those that the hunters had encountered before. However, they caught a glimpse, but could not get close to, a pair of those large birds native to Australia, akin to cassowaries, called emus, which stand five feet tall and are brown-feathered, belonging to the wading bird order. Top dashed after them with all his speed, but the emus easily outpaced him, so great was their speed.

Regarding the traces left by the convicts in the forest, a few were still collected. Near a fire that seemed to have been recently extinguished, the colonists noticed footprints that were examined with great care. Measuring them one by one for length and width, they easily found the trace of five men's feet. The five convicts had clearly camped there; however—and that's what warranted such meticulous examination!—they could not find a sixth footprint, which would have belonged to Ayrton.

"Ayrton was not with them!" said Harbert.

"No," replied Pencroff, "and if he wasn't with them, it means those miserable wretches have already killed him! Don't they have a den where we can track them down like tigers?"

"No," replied the reporter. "It's more likely they wander aimlessly, and it's in their interest to roam about until they are masters of the island."

"Masters of the island!" exclaimed the sailor. "Masters of the island!" he repeated, and his voice was strangled as though a iron hand had grasped his throat.

Then in a calmer tone: "Do you know, Mr. Cyrus, what bullet I loaded into my rifle?"

"No, Pencroff!"

"It's the bullet that went through Harbert's chest, and I promise you it won't miss its mark!"

But this just retribution could not bring Ayrton back to life, and from the examination of the footprints left on the ground, they had to conclude, alas! that there was no longer any hope of ever seeing him again!

That evening, the camp was set up fourteen miles from Granite-House, and Cyrus Smith thought they couldn't be more than five miles from the reptile promontory. And indeed, the next day, they reached the tip of the peninsula and crossed the forest entirely; but no sign had led them to find the retreat where the convicts had taken refuge, nor the equally secret one sheltering the mysterious stranger.

12

The following day, February 18, was dedicated to exploring the wooded area that formed the coastline from the reptile promontory to the waterfall river. The colonists were able to thoroughly search this forest, which varied in width from three to four miles, as it was situated between the two shores of the serpentine peninsula. The trees, with their towering height and thick foliage, testified to the vegetation's power of the soil, more astonishing here than in any other part of the island. It looked like a piece of those virgin forests from America or Central Africa, transported to this temperate zone. This suggested that these magnificent plants found in this soil, moist at the surface but warmed inside by volcanic fires, heat that could not belong to a temperate climate. The dominant species were precisely those kauris and eucalyptus that reached gigantic sizes.

But the colonists' aim was not to admire these botanical marvels. They already knew that, in this regard, Lincoln Island deserved to be ranked among the Canary Islands, whose first name was the Fortunate Islands. Now, alas! their island no longer wholly belonged to them; others had taken possession, scoundrels were trampling its soil, and they needed to eliminate them entirely. Along the western coast, they found no traces, no matter how careful they searched. No more footprints, no more broken branches, no more cooled ashes, no more abandoned camps.

"That doesn't surprise me," said Cyrus Smith to his companions. "The convicts landed near the wreck's point and immediately dived into the forests of the Far West after crossing the marsh of the tadornes. They thus followed roughly the route we took leaving Granite-House. That's what explains the traces we recognized in the woods. But, once they reached the coastline, the convicts surely understood they wouldn't find a suitable refuge there, and that's when, having moved up north, they discovered the corral..."

"Where they may have returned..." said Pencroff.

"I don't think so," replied the engineer, "because they must realize our search will be directed that way. The corral is for them merely a supply place, not a permanent camp."

"I agree with Cyrus," said the reporter, "and I believe the convicts must have sought a hideout among the foothills of Mount Franklin."

"Then, Mr. Cyrus, right to the corral!" exclaimed Pencroff. "It's time to finish this, and we have lost enough time up to now!"

"No, my friend," replied the engineer. "You forget that we had a vested interest in knowing whether the forests of the Far West concealed any habitation. Our exploration has a dual purpose, Pencroff. If on one hand we must punish the crime, on the other we have a reconnaissance mission to accomplish!"

"That's well said, Mr. Cyrus," replied the sailor. "Still, I think we won't find that gentleman unless he's willing!"

And indeed, Pencroff was merely expressing the opinion of all. It was likely that the mysterious stranger's hideout was no less secretive than he was!

That evening, the carriage stopped at the mouth of the waterfall river. The camp was set up as usual, and the usual precautions were taken for the night. Harbert, back to being the strong and healthy boy he was before his illness, was making the most of this outdoor life, between the ocean breezes and the invigorating atmosphere of the forests. His place was no longer on the wagon but at the head of the caravan.

The next day, February 19, the colonists, leaving the coastline, where beyond the mouth lay basalt formations piled up so picturesquely, ascended the river along the left bank. The route was partially cleared due to previous excursions made from the corral to the west coast. The colonists then found themselves six miles from Mount Franklin.

The engineer's plan was to carefully observe the entire valley, whose thalweg formed the riverbed, and cautiously approach the area around the corral; if the corral was occupied, to take it by storm; if not, to take refuge there and make it the center of operations aimed at exploring Mount Franklin.

This plan was unanimously approved by the colonists, and they were eager to fully regain possession of their island!

So they traveled through the narrow valley separating two of the strongest foothills of Mount Franklin. The trees, pressed against the riverbanks, thinned out towards the higher areas of the volcano. It was a mountainous terrain, quite rugged, very suited for ambushes, and they only ventured forward with extreme caution. Top and Jup walked ahead as scouts, darting left and right into the thick undergrowth, competing in intelligence and skill. But nothing indicated that the banks of the stream had been recently frequented; nothing suggested the presence or proximity of the convicts.

Around five in the evening, the carriage stopped about six hundred paces from the palisaded enclosure. A semi-circular curtain of large trees still concealed it.

The task was to scout the corral to see if it was occupied. Going openly, in broad daylight, would expose them to an ambush, just as had happened to Harbert. It would be better to wait for nightfall.

However, Gédéon Spilett wanted to scout the approaches to the corral without delay, and Pencroff, out of patience, offered to accompany him.

"No, my friends," replied the engineer. "Wait for nightfall. I won't let any of you expose yourselves in broad daylight."

"But, Mr. Cyrus..." retorted the sailor, not inclined to obey.

"Please, Pencroff," said the engineer.

"Very well!" replied the sailor, who redirected his anger by hurling the worst remarks from the maritime repertoire at the convicts.

Thus, the colonists stayed around the carriage and carefully watched the nearby parts of the forest.

Three hours passed this way. The wind had died down, and an absolute silence reigned under the tall trees. The breaking of the smallest branch, the sound of footsteps on the dry leaves, the rustle of a body moving through the grass would have been easily heard. Everything was quiet. Moreover, Top, lying on the ground with his head resting on his paws, showed no sign of concern.

By eight o'clock, night seemed advanced enough for a reconnaissance to be carried out under good conditions. Gédéon Spilett declared he was ready to go, accompanied by Pencroff. Cyrus Smith consented. Top and Jup had to stay with the engineer, Harbert, and Nab, as it was necessary that no barking or cries, launched inopportunely, would give them away.

"Don't engage recklessly," recommended Cyrus Smith to the sailor and the reporter. "You don't need to take possession of the corral, but only to find out if it's occupied or not."

"Agreed," replied Pencroff.

And the two set off.

Under the trees, thanks to the thickness of their foliage, a certain darkness already made objects invisible beyond a range of thirty to forty feet. The reporter and Pencroff, stopping whenever any noise seemed suspicious, advanced only with the utmost precautions.

They walked somewhat apart from each other, to be less exposed to gunfire. And honestly, they expected a shot to ring out at any moment.

Five minutes after leaving the carriage, Gédéon Spilett and Pencroff reached the edge of the woods, in front of the clearing where the palisaded enclosure stood.

They stopped. A few vague lights still bathed the treeless meadow. Thirty paces away stood the door of the corral, which appeared to be closed. These thirty paces they needed to cross between the forest's edge and the enclosure represented the dangerous zone, to borrow a term from ballistics. In fact, one or more bullets from the top of the palisade would have taken down anyone daring to enter this zone.

Gédéon Spilett and the sailor were not the type to back down, but they knew that any recklessness on their part, for which they would be the first victims, would then fall back on their companions. If they were killed, what would happen to Cyrus Smith, Nab, and Harbert?

But Pencroff, agitated by being so close to the corral, where he assumed the convicts had taken refuge, was about to push forward when the reporter held him back with a firm grip.

"In a few moments, it will be completely dark," whispered Gédéon Spilett into Pencroff's ear, "and that will be the time to act."

Pencroff, gripping the stock of his rifle tightly, held himself back while muttering.

Soon, the last glimmers of twilight completely faded. The shadow that seemed to emerge from the thick forest engulfed the clearing. Mount Franklin rose like a giant screen against the horizon of the setting sun, and darkness rapidly fell, as happens in regions already low in latitude. It was time.

The reporter and Pencroff, since they had positioned themselves at the edge of the woods, had not lost sight of the palisaded enclosure. The corral seemed completely deserted. The top of the palisade formed a line slightly darker than the surrounding shadow, and nothing obscured its clarity.

However, if the convicts were there, they must have posted one of their own to prevent any surprise.

Gédéon Spilett squeezed his companion's hand, and they both crawled towards the corral, their rifles ready to fire.

They reached the door of the enclosure without the shadow having been pierced by a single beam of light.

Pencroff tried to push the door, which, as the reporter and he had assumed, was closed. However, the sailor was able to confirm that the outer bars had not been placed.

One could conclude that the convicts were occupying the corral and had probably secured the door so that it could not be forced open.

Gédéon Spilett and Pencroff listened carefully.

No sound inside the enclosure. The sheep and goats, presumably asleep in their stalls, did not disturb the calm of the night.

The reporter and the sailor, hearing nothing, wondered if they should scale the palisade and enter the corral. Which was against Cyrus Smith's instructions.It's true that the operation could succeed, but it could fail too. However, if the convicts had no idea what was happening, if they were unaware of the expedition being attempted against them, and if there was a chance to surprise them, should one jeopardize that chance by recklessly crossing the palisade?

The reporter did not think so. He believed it was reasonable to wait until all the settlers were gathered before trying to enter the corral. What was certain was that one could approach the palisade without being seen, and it didn't seem to be guarded. With that established, all that was left to do was return to the cart and come up with a plan.

Pencroff likely agreed with this view, as he had no hesitation in following the reporter when he stepped back into the woods. A few minutes later, the engineer was briefed on the situation.

"Well," he said after thinking, "I now have reason to believe that the convicts are not in the corral."

"We'll find out," Pencroff replied, "when we climb the enclosure."

"To the corral, my friends!" Cyrus Smith urged.

"Should we leave the cart in the woods?" Nab asked.

"No," replied the engineer, "it's our wagon for supplies and ammunition, and if necessary, it will serve as a defense."

"Let's move then!" Gédéon Spilett said.

The cart emerged from the woods and began to roll silently toward the palisade. The darkness was deep, and the silence was as complete as when Pencroff and the reporter had crawled away on the ground. The thick grass completely muffled any sound of footsteps.

The settlers were ready to fire. Jup, under Pencroff's orders, stayed back. Nab led Top by a leash so that he wouldn't rush ahead.

The clearing soon appeared. It was deserted.

Without hesitation, the small group moved toward the enclosure. In a short time, they crossed the dangerous area. Not a shot had been fired. When the cart reached the palisade, it stopped. Nab remained at the front of the onagers to keep them contained. The engineer, the reporter, Harbert, and Pencroff then made their way to the gate to see if it was barricaded from the inside... one of the doors was open!

"But what do you say?" asked the engineer as he turned to the sailor and Gédéon Spilett.

Both were stunned.

"Upon my word," said Pencroff, "that door was shut just now!"

The settlers hesitated. Were the convicts in the corral when Pencroff and the reporter conducted their reconnaissance? It couldn't be doubted, since the door, which had been closed before, could only have been opened by them! Were they still inside, or had one of them just come out?

All these questions rushed into everyone's mind, but how could they be answered? At that moment, Harbert, who had stepped a few paces inside the enclosure, suddenly jumped back, grabbing Cyrus Smith's hand.

"What's wrong?" asked the engineer.

"A light!"

"In the house?"

"Yes!"

All five advanced toward the door, and indeed, through the window panes facing them, they saw a faint glow flickering.

Cyrus Smith quickly made up his mind.

"This is a unique opportunity," he said to his companions, "to find the convicts locked in that house, not expecting anything! They belong to us! Forward!"

The settlers slipped into the enclosure, their rifles ready to fire. The cart had been left outside under the watch of Jup and Top, who had been tied there for safety.

Cyrus Smith, Pencroff, and Gédéon Spilett on one side, Harbert and Nab on the other, moved along the palisade, watching the completely dark and deserted area of the corral. In moments, everyone was near the house, in front of the closed door.

Cyrus Smith signaled his companions with a hand gesture to stay still and approached the window, which was now dimly lit from inside.

He peered into the only room making up the ground floor of the house. On the table, a lit lantern shone. Next to the table was the bed that had once belonged to Ayrton.

On the bed lay the body of a man.

Suddenly, Cyrus Smith recoiled, and in a muffled voice exclaimed, "Ayrton!" Immediately, the door was more burst open than opened, and the settlers rushed into the room.

Ayrton appeared to be sleeping. His face showed that he had suffered greatly and for a long time. His wrists and ankles bore large bruises.

Cyrus Smith leaned over him.

"Ayrton!" cried the engineer, grabbing the arm of the man he had found in such unexpected circumstances.

At his call, Ayrton opened his eyes and looked at Cyrus Smith, then at the others: "You?" he cried out.

"Ayrton! Ayrton!" Cyrus Smith repeated.

"Where am I?"

"In the corral house!"

"Alone?"

"Yes!"

"But they will come!" Ayrton shouted. "Defend yourselves! Defend yourselves!"

And Ayrton collapsed, exhausted.

"Spilett," the engineer said, "we could be attacked at any moment. Get the cart into the corral. Then barricade the door and come back here."

Pencroff, Nab, and the reporter hurried to carry out the engineer's orders. There was no time to waste. Perhaps the cart was already in the hands of the convicts! In a flash, the reporter and his two companions crossed the corral and reached the palisade gate, behind which Top was growling softly.

The engineer, leaving Ayrton for a moment, stepped out of the house ready to fire. Harbert was at his side. Both were watching the ridge that overlooked the corral. If the convicts were hidden there, they could strike the settlers one by one. At that moment, the moon rose in the east above the black curtain of the forest, and a white sheet of light spread inside the enclosure.

The corral lit up entirely with its clumps of trees, the little stream that flowed through it, and its wide carpet of grass. On the mountain side, the house and part of the palisade stood out in white. On the opposite side, toward the gate, the enclosure remained dark. Soon a black mass appeared. It was the cart entering the circle of light, and Cyrus Smith could hear the sound of the door that his companions were closing and securing tightly from the inside.

But at this moment, Top, breaking free from his leash, started barking furiously and dashed toward the back of the corral, to the right of the house.

"Watch out, my friends, and get ready to fire!" Cyrus Smith shouted.

The settlers had shouldered their rifles and were waiting for the moment to shoot. Top continued barking, and Jup, running toward the dog, made sharp whistling sounds.

The settlers followed and reached the edge of the little stream, shaded by large trees.

And there, in full light, what did they see?

Five bodies lying on the bank!

They were those of the convicts who had landed on Lincoln Island four months ago!

13

What had happened? Who had struck the convicts?

Could it have been Ayrton? No, since just a moment ago he had feared their return!

But Ayrton was then under the spell of a deep slumber from which it was no longer possible to rouse him. After the few words he had spoken, a heavy stupor had seized him, and he had fallen back on his bed, motionless.

The settlers, overwhelmed by a thousand confusing thoughts and under the influence of intense excitement, waited all night, not leaving Ayrton's house, not returning to the place where the bodies of the convicts lay. Regarding the circumstances of their deaths, it was likely that Ayrton could tell them nothing, since he didn't even know he was in the corral house. But at least he would be in a position to recount the events that preceded this terrible execution.

The next day, Ayrton emerged from his stupor, and his companions expressed their joy at seeing him again, nearly safe and sound, after one hundred four days apart.

Ayrton then briefly recounted what had happened, or at least what he knew.

The day after his arrival at the corral, November 10, at nightfall, he was surprised by the convicts, who had scaled the enclosure.

They bound and gagged him; then he was taken to a dark cave at the foot of Mount Franklin, where the convicts had sought refuge.

His death had been decided, and the next day he was to be killed, when one of the convicts recognized him and called him by the name he had used in Australia. These wretches wanted to massacre Ayrton! They spared Ben Joyce!

But from that moment, Ayrton was subject to the obsession of his former accomplices. They wanted to draw him back to them and counted on him to seize Granite-House, to penetrate this inaccessible home, to become masters of the island after murdering the settlers!

Ayrton resisted. The repentant and forgiven former convict would rather die than betray his companions.

Ayrton, bound, gagged, and kept under supervision, lived in that cave for four months.

Meanwhile, the convicts discovered the corral shortly after their arrival on the island, and since then, they had lived off its supplies, but hadn't settled there. On November 11, two of these bandits, unexpectedly surprised by the arrival of the settlers, fired at Harbert, and one of them returned boasting that he had killed one of the island's inhabitants, but he came back alone. His companion, as we know, had fallen under Cyrus Smith's dagger. Imagine Ayrton's anxiety and despair when he learned of Harbert's death! The settlers were left with only four and were practically at the mercy of the convicts!

Following this event, and for the entire time that the settlers, delayed by Harbert's illness, stayed at the corral, the pirates didn't leave their cave, and even after pillaging the Grande-vue plateau, they didn't think it wise to abandon it.

The mistreatment of Ayrton then increased. His hands and feet still bore the bloody marks of the bonds that restrained him day and night. Every moment he awaited a death from which it seemed he could not escape.

This continued until the third week of February. The convicts, always looking for a favorable opportunity, rarely left their hideout and only made a few hunting excursions, either on the island or to the southern coast. Ayrton had received no news of his friends and had lost hope of ever seeing them again! Finally, the unfortunate man, weakened by the mistreatment, fell into a deep prostration that left him unable to see or hear. Thus, from that moment, which was two days ago, he could hardly say what had happened.

"But, Mr. Smith," he added, "since I was imprisoned in that cave, how is it that I find myself in the corral?"

"How is it that the convicts lie there, dead, in the middle of the enclosure?" replied the engineer.

"Dead!" exclaimed Ayrton, who, despite his weakness, sat up halfway.

His companions supported him. He wanted to rise, and they let him, and all moved toward the little stream.

It was bright daylight.

There, on the bank, in the position where death had struck them with a sudden blow, lay the five corpses of the convicts!

Ayrton was distraught. Cyrus Smith and his companions watched him without saying a word. At a signal from the engineer, Nab and Pencroff examined these bodies, already stiffened by the cold.

They bore no visible signs of injury.

Only, after carefully examining them, Pencroff noticed on one's forehead, on another's chest, on the back of one, and on the shoulder of another, a tiny red spot, a barely visible bruise, and it was impossible to identify the source.

"That's where they were struck!" said Cyrus Smith.

"But with what weapon?" exclaimed the reporter.

"A deadly weapon whose secret we do not know!"

"And who struck them?" asked Pencroff.

"The island's avenger," replied Cyrus Smith, "the one who brought you here, Ayrton, the one whose influence has just manifested again, the one who does for us all that we cannot do ourselves, and who, having done so, vanishes from our sight."

This invisible protection, which rendered their own actions null, irritated and moved the engineer at the same time. The relative inferiority it implied could be something a proud soul might feel wounded by. A generosity that evades any sign of gratitude revealed a sort of disdain for those who owe a debt, which somewhat spoiled, in Cyrus Smith's eyes, the value of the benefaction.

"Let's search," he said again, "and may God allow us one day to prove to this haughty protector that he is not dealing with ingrates! What wouldn't I give to repay him, by giving him in turn, even at the cost of our lives, some great service!"

From that day on, this search became the sole concern of the inhabitants of Lincoln Island. Everything drove them to uncover the answer to this mystery, an answer that could only be the name of a man endowed with a truly inexplicable and somewhat superhuman power.

After a few moments, the settlers returned to the corral house, where their care quickly restored Ayrton's moral and physical strength.

Nab and Pencroff carried the convicts' bodies into the forest, some distance from the corral, and buried them deeply.

Then, Ayrton was informed of the events that had taken place during his confinement. He learned of Harbert's adventures and the series of trials the settlers had endured. As for them, they had no longer hoped to see Ayrton and feared that the convicts had mercilessly slaughtered him.

"And now," said Cyrus Smith, concluding his narrative, "we have a duty to fulfill. Half of our task is complete, but even if the convicts are no longer a threat, we must not take credit for having regained control of the island."

"Well," replied Gédéon Spilett, "let's search this entire labyrinth of the foothills of Mount Franklin! Let's leave no excavation or hole unexplored! Ah! If any reporter has ever faced an exciting mystery, it's me speaking to you, my friends!"

"And we will not return to Granite-House," replied Harbert, "until we have found our benefactor."— Yes! said the engineer, we'll do everything humanly possible to find him... but, I repeat, we will only locate him if he allows it!

— Are we staying at the corral? asked Pencroff.

— Let's stay here, replied Cyrus Smith, the supplies are abundant, and we are right in the center of our investigation area. Besides, if necessary, the cart will quickly go to Granite House.

— Alright, replied the sailor. Just one observation.

— Which one?

— The beautiful season is approaching, and we must not forget that we have a crossing to make.

— A crossing? said Gédéon Spilett.

— Yes! The crossing of Tabor Island, replied Pencroff. It's necessary to place a notice indicating the location of our island, where Ayrton is currently, in case the Scottish yacht comes to pick him up. Who knows if it's already too late?

— But, Pencroff, asked Ayrton, how do you plan to make this crossing?

— On the Bonadventure!

— The Bonadventure! exclaimed Ayrton... it no longer exists.

— My Bonadventure no longer exists! shouted Pencroff, jumping up.

— No! replied Ayrton. The convicts found it in its small harbor just eight days ago, they took to sea, and...

— And? said Pencroff, whose heart was racing.

— And, lacking Bob Harvey to maneuver, they ran aground on the rocks, and the boat was completely destroyed!

— Ah! The wretches! The bandits! The despicable scoundrels! cried Pencroff.

— Pencroff, said Harbert, taking the sailor's hand, we'll build another Bonadventure, a bigger one! We have all the hardware and rigging from the brig at our disposal!

— But do you know, replied Pencroff, that it takes at least five to six months to build a vessel of thirty to forty tons?

— We'll take our time, replied the reporter, and we'll give up the crossing to Tabor Island this year.

— What can you do, Pencroff, we have to resign ourselves, said the engineer, and I hope this delay won't be detrimental to us.

— Ah! My Bonadventure! my poor Bonadventure!" cried Pencroff, genuinely distressed over the loss of his vessel, which he was so proud of!

The destruction of the Bonadventure was obviously a regrettable event for the colonists, and it was agreed that this loss should be rectified as soon as possible. With this established, they focused solely on successfully completing the exploration of the island's most secret portions. Searches began the same day, February 19, and lasted a full week. The base of the mountain, between its foothills and their numerous branches, formed a maze of valleys and ravines laid out very whimsically. It was clearly in the depths of these narrow gorges, perhaps even within the massif of Mount Franklin, that they ought to continue their search. No part of the island would have been better suited to hide a dwelling whose occupant wanted to remain unknown. But such was the tangle of the foothills that Cyrus Smith had to explore them with a strict methodology.

The colonists first visited the entire valley that opened to the south of the volcano and that collected the first waters of the falling river. It was here that Ayrton showed them the cave where the convicts had taken refuge and where he had been held until his transfer to the corral. This cave was exactly as Ayrton had left it. They found a certain amount of ammunition and provisions that the convicts had taken with the intention of creating a reserve.

The entire valley leading to the cave, a valley shaded by beautiful trees, among which the conifers predominated, was explored with extreme care, and once the southwestern foothill was rounded at its tip, the colonists entered a narrower gorge that commenced at the picturesque pile of coastal basalts.

Here, the trees were scarcer. The stone replaced the grass. Wild goats and sheep frolicked among the rocks. This marked the beginning of the island's arid part. It could already be recognized that of the many valleys branching from the base of Mount Franklin, only three were wooded and rich in pastures like the one at the corral, which bordered the valley of the falling river to the west and the valley of the red creek to the east. These two streams, which further downstream became rivers due to the absorption of some tributaries, were formed by all the waters from the mountain and thus determined the fertility of its southern part. As for the Mercy, it was more directly fed by abundant springs hidden under the cover of the jacamar woods, and it was also sources of this nature that, spilling out through a thousand rivulets, watered the soil of the serpentine peninsula.

Now, of these three valleys where water was plentiful, one could have served as a retreat for some hermit who might find all the necessities of life there. But the colonists had already explored them, and nowhere had they been able to confirm the presence of a person.

Could it then be at the bottom of these arid gorges, among the rock debris, in the harsh ravines of the north, between the lava flows, where this retreat and its occupant could be found?

The northern part of Mount Franklin consisted solely at its base of two valleys, wide, shallow, and devoid of greenery, scattered with erratic blocks, streaked with long moraines, paved with lava, dotted with large mineral protrusions, dusted with obsidian and labradorite. This part required long and difficult explorations.

There, a thousand cavities were hollowed out, rather uncomfortable no doubt, but completely hidden and with difficult access. The colonists even visited dark tunnels dating from the plutonian era, still blackened by the passage of ancient fires, that extended into the massif of the mountain. They traversed these dark galleries, lit them with burning resins, searched every nook, probed every depth. But everywhere silence, darkness. It didn't seem like a human being had ever stepped into these ancient corridors, or that their arms had ever moved a single one of these blocks. They were as they were, as the volcano had hurled them above the waters at the time of the island's emergence.

However, if these structures seemed completely deserted, if darkness reigned there, Cyrus Smith was forced to acknowledge that absolute silence was not in control.

Upon reaching the bottom of one of these dark cavities, which extended for several hundred feet into the mountain, he was surprised to hear distant rumblings, whose resonance was amplified by the rocks.

Gédéon Spilett, who accompanied him, also heard these distant murmurs, which indicated a revival of the underground fires. Several times, they both listened and agreed that some chemical reaction was taking place in the earth's core.

"The volcano is not completely extinguished then? said the reporter.

— It's possible that since our exploration of the crater, replied Cyrus Smith, some activity has occurred in the lower layers. Every volcano, even when considered extinct, can obviously re-ignite.

— But if an eruption of Mount Franklin is preparing, asked Gédéon Spilett, wouldn't there be a risk for Lincoln Island?

— I don't think so, replied the engineer. The crater, that is to say the safety valve, exists, and the overflow of vapors and lavas will escape, as it used to, through its usual outlet.

— Unless these lavas find a new path to the fertile parts of the island!

— Why, my dear Spilett, replied Cyrus Smith, why wouldn't they follow the route that is naturally mapped out for them?

— Hey! Volcanoes are capricious! replied the reporter.

— Note, continued the engineer, that the slope of the entire massif of Mount Franklin favors the spillage of materials toward the valleys we are currently exploring. A landslide would have to change the mountain's center of gravity for this spillage to be altered.

— But an earthquake is always to be feared under these conditions, observed Gédéon Spilett.

— Always, replied the engineer, especially when the underground forces start to awaken and the earth's core risks being obstructed after a long rest. Thus, my dear Spilett, an eruption would be a serious event for us, and it would be much better if this volcano had no inclination to wake up. But we can't do anything about it, can we? In any case, whatever happens, I don't believe that our domain of Great View can be seriously threatened. Between it and the mountain, the ground is noticeably depressed, and if the lavas ever took the path to the lake, they would be redirected onto the dunes and nearby portions of Shark Gulf.

— We haven't seen any smoke indicating a possible eruption at the top of the mountain, said Gédéon Spilett.

— No, replied Cyrus Smith, not a vapor escapes from the crater, which I precisely observed yesterday. But it is possible that, at the lower part of the chimney, time has accumulated rocks, ashes, hardened lavas, and that this valve I was talking about is temporarily overloaded. But with the first serious effort, all obstacles will disappear, and you can be sure, my dear Spilett, that neither the island, which is the boiler, nor the volcano, which is the chimney, will explode under the pressure of the gases. Nevertheless, I repeat, it would be better if there were no eruption.

— And yet we are not mistaken, replied the reporter. Distant rumblings can indeed be heard from the very belly of the volcano!

— Indeed, replied the engineer, listening again with great attention, there is no mistaking it... a reaction is taking place whose significance and ultimate result we cannot evaluate."

Cyrus Smith and Gédéon Spilett, after exiting, rejoined their companions and informed them of this situation.

"Well! exclaimed Pencroff, this volcano that might want to cause trouble! But let it try! It will find its master!...

— Who's that? asked Nab.

— Our genius, Nab, our genius, who will gag its crater if it dares to open it!"

You see, the sailor's confidence in the special god of his island was absolute, and indeed, the hidden power that had so far manifested itself through so many inexplicable acts seemed limitless; but, also, it managed to escape the meticulous searches of the colonists, for despite all their efforts, more than their zeal, their tenacity in their exploration, the strange retreat could not be discovered.

From February 19 to 25, the circle of investigations was expanded to the entire northern region of Lincoln Island, where the most secret spots were rummaged through. The colonists began to probe every rocky wall, as agents would in a suspect building. The engineer even took a very precise survey of the mountain, and he extended his searches down to the last layers supporting it.

It was explored right up to the height of the truncated cone that capped the first tier of rocks, then up to the upper ridge of this enormous hat at the bottom of which the crater opened.

More so, they visited the abyss, still dormant, but in the depths of which distinct rumblings could be heard. However, not a single puff of smoke, not a whiff of vapor, not a warming of the wall indicated an imminent eruption. But neither there nor in any other part of Mount Franklin did the colonists find any trace of the one they were searching for.

The investigations were then directed toward the entire dune region. They carefully visited the high lava walls of Shark Gulf, from base to crest, although it was extremely difficult to reach the very level of the gulf. No one! Nothing!

Ultimately, these two words summarized so many efforts wasted, so much obstinacy yielding no results, and there was a sort of anger in the disappointment of Cyrus Smith and his companions.

Thus, they had to think about returning, as these searches could not continue indefinitely. The colonists had every right to believe that the mysterious being did not reside on the island's surface, and then the wildest hypotheses haunted their overactive imaginations. Pencroff and Nab, in particular, were no longer satisfied with the strange and let themselves be swept away into the realm of the supernatural.

On February 25, the colonists returned to Granite House, and with the help of the double rope, which an arrow brought back to the door ledge, they re-established communication between their domain and the ground. One month later, on March twenty-fifth, they celebrated the third anniversary of their arrival on Lincoln Island!

$$\bigstar \quad I4 \quad \bigstar$$

Three years had passed since the prisoners from Richmond had escaped, and how many times, during these three years, they spoke of their homeland, always present in their thoughts!

They did not doubt that the civil war was now over, and it seemed impossible to them that the just cause of the North had not triumphed. But what had been the incidents of this terrible war? How much blood had it cost? What friends of theirs had perished in the struggle? That was often what they talked about, without yet seeing the day when they would be given the chance to see their country again. To return, even just for a few days, to reconnect socially with the inhabited world, to establish a communication between their homeland and their island, and then to spend perhaps the longest, best part of their lives in this colony they had founded and which would then belong to the metropolis; was that then an unreachable dream?

But this dream could only be realized in two ways: either a ship would appear one day in the waters of Lincoln Island, or the colonists would build for themselves a vessel sturdy enough to sail to the nearest lands.

"Unless, said Pencroff, our genius himself provides us the means to repatriate!"

And truly, if one were to tell Pencroff and Nab that a three-hundred-ton ship was waiting for them in Shark Gulf or at Balloon Port, they would not have even shown a hint of surprise. In that line of thought, they expected anything.

But Cyrus Smith, less confident, advised them to return to reality, and this was particularly relevant regarding the construction of a vessel, a truly urgent task, since it was necessary to deposit a document at Tabor Island as soon as possible indicating Ayrton's new whereabouts.

With the Bonadventure no longer existing, at least six months would be needed to build a new ship. Now, winter was coming, and the journey could not be made before next spring.

"We thus have time to prepare for the beautiful season, said the engineer, who was discussing this with Pencroff. Therefore, my friend, since we have to rebuild our vessel, it would be preferable to give it larger dimensions. The arrival of the Scottish yacht at Tabor Island is quite uncertain. It might even be that, having come several months ago, it has already left after unsuccessfully searching for any trace of Ayrton.

Wouldn't it be wise to build a ship that, if needed, could transport us either to the Polynesian archipelagos or to New Zealand? What do you think?— I think, Mr. Cyrus, replied the sailor, I think you are just as capable of building a large ship as a small one. We have plenty of wood and tools. It's just a matter of time.

— And how many months would it take to build a ship of two hundred fifty to three hundred tons? asked Cyrus Smith.

— At least seven or eight months, answered Pencroff. But we must not forget that winter is coming, and in the extreme cold, wood is hard to work with. So let's count on a few weeks of downtime, and if our ship is ready by next November, we should consider ourselves very lucky.

— Well, said Cyrus Smith, that would be exactly the right time to undertake a significant crossing, either to Tabor Island or to a more distant land.

— Indeed, Mr. Cyrus, replied the sailor. So make your plans; the workers are ready, and I imagine Ayrton can give us a good hand in this situation.

The settlers, consulted, approved the engineer's project, and indeed, it was the best thing to do. It was true that constructing a ship of two to three hundred tons was a big job, but the settlers had confidence in themselves, justified by many successes they had already achieved.

Cyrus Smith then set to work on the ship's plans and specifications. Meanwhile, his companions busied themselves with cutting down and transporting the trees that would provide the curves, frames, and planking. The forest of the Far-West yielded the best varieties of oak and elm. They made use of the clearing already made during the last excursion to create a passable road, which was named Far-West Road, and the trees were transported to the chimneys, where the construction site was established.

As for the road in question, it was whimsically traced, influenced somewhat by the choice of woods, but it facilitated access to a significant portion of the serpentine peninsula.

It was important that these woods be quickly cut and processed since they could not be used while still green, and time was needed for them to turn hard. The carpenters worked hard during the month of April, which was only disturbed by a few violent equinox winds. Master Jup skillfully assisted them, whether by climbing to the top of a tree to secure the felling ropes or by offering his strong shoulders to carry the trimmed trunks.

All this wood was piled under a large wooden shelter built next to the chimneys, where it waited to be put to use.

The month of April was quite lovely, often like the month of October in the Northern Hemisphere. At the same time, the agricultural work was vigorously pushed forward, and soon all traces of devastation had disappeared from the Grande-vue plateau. The mill was rebuilt, and new buildings rose on the site of the barn. It had seemed necessary to reconstruct them with larger dimensions as the volatile population was increasing significantly. The stables now housed five onagers, four of which were strong and well-trained, allowing themselves to be harnessed or ridden, and one little one that had just been born. The colony's tools had been augmented by a plow, and the onagers were being used for plowing, just like true Yorkshire or Kentucky oxen. Each settler divided up the work, and hands were not idle. What great health these workers had, and how they brought cheer to the evenings in Granite-House, making a thousand plans for the future!

It goes without saying that Ayrton fully shared their common life, and he no longer talked about moving to the corral. However, he remained sad, somewhat uncommunicative, and joined in more on the work than on the pleasures of his companions. Nevertheless, he was a hard worker, strong, skilled, clever, and intelligent. He was respected and liked by all, and he could not ignore it.

However, the corral was not abandoned. Every other day, one of the settlers, driving the cart or riding one of the onagers, would go take care of the flock of sheep and goats and bring back the milk that supplied Nab's kitchen. These trips were also opportunities for hunting. Thus, Harbert and Gédéon Spilett—Top leading the way—ran to the corral more often than any of their companions, and with the excellent weapons they had, they never returned home without cabiais, agoutis, kangaroos, wild boars for big game, and ducks, grouse, woodcock, jacamars, and snipe for small game. The products from the wilds, those from the oyster beds, some tortoises that were caught, and a new catch of excellent salmon that again swam into the waters of Mercy, the vegetables from the Grande-vue plateau, the natural fruits of the forest, were riches upon riches, and Nab, the head cook, barely managed to store them all.

It goes without saying that the telegraph line laid between the corral and Granite-House had been restored, and it worked whenever one or the other of the settlers found themselves at the corral and deemed it necessary to spend the night there. Moreover, the island was now safe, and there was no risk of aggression—at least from humans.

However, the event that had occurred could still happen again. A raid by pirates, or even escaped convicts, was always a possibility. It was possible that some of Bob Harvey's accomplices, still detained in Norfolk, had been privy to his plans and might be tempted to imitate him. The settlers thus remained vigilant, watching the landings on the island, and every day, their telescope swept over the vast horizon that closed off Union Bay and Washington Bay.

When they went to the corral, they examined the western part of the sea with equal attention, and climbing up the hill, their gaze could cover a wide sector of the western horizon.

Nothing suspicious appeared, but it was still necessary to stay on guard. Thus, one evening, the engineer shared with his friends his plan to fortify the corral. He felt it would be wise to raise the palisade and to flank it with a kind of blockhouse where, if necessary, the settlers could defend themselves against an enemy troop. Granite-House, being considered impregnable by its very position, the corral, with its buildings, reserves, and the animals it contained, would always be the target for any pirates landing on the island, and if the settlers were forced to lock themselves in, they must be able to resist without disadvantage.

This was a project that needed to be pondered, and its execution, in any case, would have to be postponed until the following spring.

Around May 15, the keel of the new ship was being laid on the building site, and soon the bow and stern, mortised at each end, rose almost vertically. This keel, made of good oak, measured one hundred ten feet in length, which would allow for a width of twenty-five feet at the main beam. But that was all the carpenters could do before the arrival of cold weather and bad conditions. During the following week, they also set up the first pairs at the back; then it was necessary to suspend work.

During the last days of the month, the weather became extremely bad. The wind blew from the east, sometimes with the force of a hurricane. The engineer had some concerns for the construction shelters, which, after all, he could not have set up anywhere else close to Granite-House, since the islet only imperfectly protected the shore against the fury of the open sea, and in great storms, the waves would directly crash at the foot of the granite wall.

But fortunately, these fears were not realized. The wind rather pulled from the southeast, and under these conditions, the shore of Granite-House was completely sheltered by the front of the wreck's point.

Pencroff and Ayrton, the two most eager builders of the new ship, continued their work as long as they could. They were not the type of men to be bothered by the wind messing up their hair or the rain soaking through to their bones. One hammer strike is as good in bad weather as in good. But when a sharp cold succeeded this humid period, the wood, whose fibers had hardened to the toughness of iron, became extremely difficult to work with, and by June 10, they had to definitively abandon the boat construction.

Cyrus Smith and his companions had not failed to notice how harsh the weather was during the winters on Lincoln Island. The cold was comparable to that felt in the states of New England, which are roughly at the same latitude as it is from the equator. If, in the northern hemisphere, or at least in the parts occupied by New Britain and the northern United States, this phenomenon can be explained by the flat topography of the territories bordering the pole, where no elevation of land opposes the hyperborean winds, here in the case of Lincoln Island, this explanation did not hold.

"It has even been observed," one day Cyrus Smith said to his companions, "that at equal latitudes, islands and coastal regions are less affected by the cold than Mediterranean lands. I have often heard it claimed that the winters in Lombardy, for example, are harsher than in Scotland, and this would be due to the sea releasing the heat it received during summer in winter. Islands are therefore in the best conditions to take advantage of this release.

— But then, Mr. Cyrus, asked Harbert, why does Lincoln Island seem to escape the general rule?

— That is difficult to explain," replied the engineer. "However, I would be inclined to admit that this peculiarity is due to the island's position in the southern hemisphere, which, as you know, my child, is colder than the northern hemisphere.

— Indeed, said Harbert, and floating ice is found at lower latitudes in the south than in the north Pacific.

— That is true," replied Pencroff, "and when I was a whaler, I saw icebergs around Cape Horn.

— It might indeed explain," said Gédéon Spilett, "the severe cold that affects Lincoln Island, the presence of ice or ice floes at a relatively close distance.

— Your opinion is very valid, indeed, my dear Spilett," replied Cyrus Smith, "and clearly, it is the proximity of the ice floe that accounts for our harsh winters. I would also point out that a completely physical cause makes the southern hemisphere colder than the northern hemisphere. Indeed, as the sun is closer to this hemisphere during summer, it is necessarily farther away during winter. This explains why there is an excess of temperature in both directions, and if we find winters very cold on Lincoln Island, let us not forget that summers there are very hot, on the contrary.

— But why then, if you please, Mr. Smith, asked Pencroff, frowning, why is our hemisphere, as you say, so poorly divided? It's not fair!

— My friend Pencroff," replied the engineer, laughing, "whether it is fair or not, we have to accept the situation, and here's where this peculiarity comes from. The Earth does not describe a circle around the sun, but rather an ellipse, as the laws of rational mechanics dictate. The Earth occupies one of the foci of the ellipse, and thus, at a certain time in its orbit, it is at aphelion, that is, at its greatest distance from the sun, and at another time, at perihelion, i.e., at its shortest distance. Now, it happens that precisely during the winter in the southern regions, it is at its farthest point from the sun, and therefore in the conditions necessary for those regions to experience greater cold. There is nothing to be done about that, and men, Pencroff, no matter how knowledgeable they may be, will never be able to change anything about the cosmic order established by God himself.

— And yet, added Pencroff, who showed some difficulty in resigning, the world is very smart! What a big book, Mr. Cyrus, one could make with everything that is known!

— And what an even bigger book with everything that is not known," replied Cyrus Smith.

Finally, for one reason or another, the month of June brought the cold back with its usual violence, and the settlers were mostly confined to Granite-House.

Ah! This confinement seemed hard for all of them, and perhaps more so for Gédéon Spilett.

"You know," he said one day to Nab, "I would give you, by notarized document, all the inheritances that are supposed to come to me one day, if you would be kind enough to subscribe me to any newspaper! What I miss most for my happiness is to know every morning what happened elsewhere the day before, outside of here!"

Nab started to laugh.

"Truthfully," he replied, "what occupies me is the daily work!"

The truth is that, both inside and out, work did not lack.

The colony on Lincoln Island was then at its peak prosperity, and three years of sustained effort had made it so. The incident of the wrecked ship had been a new source of wealth. Not to mention the complete rigging, which would serve for the ship under construction, supplies and tools of all kinds, weapons and ammunition, clothing and instruments now cluttered the stores in Granite-House. They had even no longer needed to resort to making heavy felt fabrics. If the settlers had suffered from the cold during their first wintering, now that the cold season could come without them dreading its harshness. They also had ample linen and cared for it with extreme attention. From the sodium chloride, which is nothing but sea salt, Cyrus Smith easily extracted soda and chlorine. The soda, which was easy to convert into sodium carbonate, and the chlorine, from which he made chlorinated lime and others, were used for various domestic purposes, especially for bleaching the linen. Moreover, they now only did laundry four times a year, as was practiced in the old families of the past, and it should be mentioned that Pencroff and Gédéon Spilett, while waiting for the postman to bring his newspaper, became distinguished laundresses.

Thus passed the winter months, June, July, and August. They were very harsh, and the average thermometer readings did not exceed eight degrees Fahrenheit (13.33 degrees Celsius below zero). It was therefore lower than the temperature of the previous winter. Also, what a good fire blazed constantly in the chimneys of Granite-House, whose smoke stained long black streaks on the granite wall! They did not spare the fuel, which grew naturally just a few steps away. Furthermore, the excess wood intended for the construction of the ship allowed them to save on coal, which required a more laborious transportation.

Men and animals were all doing well. Master Jup, it must be said, showed himself to be a bit sensitive to the cold. Maybe it was his only flaw, and they had to make him a nice, fluffy bathrobe. But what a servant! Skillful, eager, tireless, not nosy, not talkative, and one could rightfully suggest him as a model for all his biped counterparts from the old and new worlds!

"After all," said Pencroff, "when you have four hands at your service, it's the least you can do to get your work done properly!"

And indeed, the intelligent four-handed creature did it well!

During the seven months since the last searches around the mountain and during the month of September, which brought back the nice weather, there was no mention of the island's genius at all. His influence made no appearance whatsoever. It's true that it would have been unnecessary, as there were no incidents that could put the colonists under any strain.

Cyrus Smith even noted that if, by chance, communication between the unknown and the residents of Granite House had ever been established through the granite massif, and if Top's instinct had sensed it, that was no longer the case during this period. The dog's growling had completely ceased, as had the orangutan's worries. The two friends—because they were friends—

no longer hovered around the opening of the internal shaft, they neither barked nor moaned in that peculiar way that had alerted the engineer from the start. But could he be sure that everything had been said about this mystery, and that he would never have the answer? Could he assert that some circumstance would not arise again, bringing back the mysterious figure? Who knows what the future held? Finally, winter came to an end; however, a fact with potentially serious consequences occurred precisely during the early days marking the return of spring.

On September 7, Cyrus Smith, having observed the peak of Mount Franklin, saw smoke billowing above the crater, with the first fumes being expelled into the air.

15

The colonists, alerted by the engineer, had suspended their work and were silently observing the summit of Mount Franklin.

The volcano had awakened, and the fumes had broken through the mineral layer piled at the bottom of the crater. But would the underground fires provoke some violent eruption? That was a possibility that could not be prevented.

However, even assuming an eruption did occur, it was likely that Lincoln Island would not suffer much as a whole. Volcanic discharges are not always disastrous. The island had already undergone this trial, as evidenced by the lava flows that streaked the northern slopes of the mountain. Moreover, the shape of the crater and the indentation drilled at its upper edge should project the ejected materials away from the fertile portions of the island.

Nevertheless, the past does not necessarily dictate the future. Often, at the summits of volcanoes, old craters close and new ones open. This phenomenon has happened in both worlds, at Etna, Popocatepetl, Orizaba, and on the eve of an eruption, one can fear everything. It only took, after all, an earthquake— a phenomenon that sometimes accompanies volcanic outpourings—for the internal layout of the mountain to change, creating new paths for the burning lavas.

Cyrus Smith explained these things to his companions, and without exaggerating the situation, he made them aware of the pros and cons.

After all, there was nothing to be done about it. Granite House, unless an earthquake shook the ground, did not appear to be in danger. But the corral would have everything to fear if a new crater opened on the southern walls of Mount Franklin. From that day on, the fumes never stopped shrouding the peak of the mountain, and it could even be seen that they were increasing in height and thickness, without any flames mixing with their thick curls. The phenomenon was still concentrated in the lower part of the central chimney.

However, with the nice days, work had resumed. They pressed on with the construction of the ship as much as possible, and by using the waterfall, Cyrus Smith managed to establish a hydraulic sawmill that processed tree trunks into planks and beams more quickly. The mechanism of this device was as simple as those found in rustic sawmills in Norway. A first horizontal movement applied to the piece of wood, a second vertical movement given to the saw, that was all that needed to be achieved, and the engineer succeeded with a wheel, two cylinders, and pulleys, suitably arranged.

By the end of September, the skeleton of the ship, which was to be rigged as a schooner, stood upright at the construction site. The framework was almost completely finished, and since all these frames had been held together by a temporary support, one could already appreciate the shapes of the vessel.

This schooner, narrow at the front and very open at the back, would obviously be suitable for quite a long crossing, if needed; but fitting the planking, the internal cladding, and the deck would still take a considerable amount of time. Fortunately, the fittings from the old brig had been salvaged after the underwater explosion. From mutilated planking and frames, Pencroff and Ayrton had pulled out the dowels and a large number of copper nails. That was a saving for the blacksmiths, but the carpenters had a lot of work to do.

Construction work had to be interrupted for a week for harvesting, haymaking, and gathering the various crops that abounded on the Grande-vue plateau. Once this task was completed, every moment was now dedicated to finishing the schooner.

When night fell, the workers were truly exhausted. To avoid wasting time, they had adjusted meal times: they had lunch at noon and only had dinner when daylight failed them. They would then return to Granite House and hurry to bed. Sometimes, however, the conversation, especially when it revolved around some interesting topic, delayed their bedtime a bit. The colonists allowed themselves to talk about the future, and they eagerly discussed the changes that a voyage of the schooner to the nearest lands would bring to their situation. But amidst these plans, the thought of a later return to Lincoln Island always loomed. They would never abandon this colony, founded with so much effort and success, and which communication with America would give a new development.

Pencroff and Nab especially hoped to end their days there.

"Harbert," said the sailor, "you'll never leave Lincoln Island?"

"Never, Pencroff, especially if you decide to stay!"

"I'm all in, my boy," answered Pencroff, "I'll be waiting for you! You'll bring me your wife and children, and I'll make merry little rascals out of your kids!"

"It's settled," replied Harbert, laughing and blushing at the same time.

"And you, Mr. Cyrus," resumed Pencroff excitedly, "you will always be the governor of the island! Well! How many inhabitants can it support? Ten thousand, at least!"

They chatted like this, letting Pencroff carry on, and from one topic to another, the reporter ended up founding a newspaper, the new-Lincoln Herald! Such is the nature of man. The need to create something lasting, something that survives him, is a sign of his superiority over all living things on this earth. That's what has established his dominion, and that's what justifies it throughout the world.

After that, who knows if Jup and Top didn't also have their little dream of the future?

Ayrton, silent, was thinking he would like to see Lord Glenarvan again and show himself to everyone, rehabilitated. One evening, October 15, the conversation, launched through these hypotheses, had lasted longer than usual. It was nine o'clock in the evening. Already, long yawns, poorly concealed, indicated the hour of rest, and Pencroff had just headed to his bed when the electric bell, placed in the room, suddenly rang.

Everyone was there: Cyrus Smith, Gideon Spilett, Harbert, Ayrton, Pencroff, Nab. So there was no colonist at the corral.

Cyrus Smith stood up. His companions looked at each other, thinking they had misheard.

"What does that mean?" cried Nab. "Is the devil ringing?"

No one answered.

"The weather is stormy," Harbert pointed out. "Couldn't the influence of electricity...?"

Harbert did not finish his sentence. The engineer, towards whom all eyes were turned, shook his head negatively.

"Let's wait," then said Gideon Spilett. "If it's a signal, whoever is making it will repeat it."

"But who do you think it is?" shouted Nab.

"But," replied Pencroff, "the one who..."

The sailor's sentence was interrupted by a new ringing of the bell.

Cyrus Smith moved towards the device and, sending the current through the wire, sent this request to the corral:

"What do you want?" A few moments later, the needle, moving across the alphabet dial, delivered this response to the guests of Granite House:

"Come to the corral quickly."

"Finally!" exclaimed Cyrus Smith.

Yes! At last! The mystery was about to be unveiled! Faced with this immense interest that would push them to the corral, all fatigue of the colonists had disappeared, and all need for rest had ceased. Without saying a word, within moments, they had left Granite House and found themselves on the beach. Only Jup and Top remained behind. They could do without them.

The night was dark. The new moon had disappeared at the same time as the sun.

As Harbert had pointed out, large storm clouds formed a low, heavy ceiling that prevented any starlight. A few heat lightning flashes, reflections of a distant storm, illuminated the horizon.

It was possible that in a few hours, lightning would thunder over the island itself. It was a threatening night.

But the darkness, however deep it was, could not stop people accustomed to this path to the corral.

They climbed the left bank of the Mercy River, reached the plateau, crossed the Glycerin Creek bridge, and advanced through the forest.

They walked briskly, filled with intense emotion. For them, there was no doubt, they were finally going to learn the long-sought answer to the mystery, the name of this mysterious being, so deeply entwined in their lives, so generous in his influence, so powerful in his actions! Wasn't it necessary, indeed, that this unknown had been intertwined with their existence, knowing all its smallest details, hearing everything said at Granite House, for him to have always acted at just the right moment?

Each one, lost in his thoughts, hurried along.

Under this canopy of trees, the darkness was such that the edge of the path was not even visible. No noise, moreover, in the forest. Quadrupeds and birds, influenced by the heaviness of the atmosphere, were still and silent. No breeze stirred the leaves. Only the colonists' footsteps echoed in the dark on the hard ground.

Silence, for the first quarter of an hour of walking, was interrupted only by this comment from Pencroff:

"We should have brought a lantern."

And by this response from the engineer:

"We'll find one at the corral."

Cyrus Smith and his companions left Granite House at nine hours and twelve minutes. At nine hours and forty-seven minutes, they had covered a distance of three miles out of the five that separated the mouth of the Mercy from the corral. At this moment, large white flashes burst above the island and outlined the silhouettes of the foliage against the dark. These intense bursts dazzled and blinded. The storm was clearly about to break loose. The flashes gradually became quicker and brighter. Distant rumblings rolled through the depths of the sky. The atmosphere was suffocating.

The colonists walked as if they were being propelled forward by some irresistible force.

At nine fifteen, a bright flash revealed the fenced area, and they had not yet passed through the door when the thunder crashed with formidable violence.

In an instant, the corral was crossed, and Cyrus Smith found himself in front of the dwelling.

It was possible that the house was occupied by the unknown since the telegram must have originated from it. However, no light illuminated its window.

The engineer knocked on the door.

No response.

Cyrus Smith opened the door, and the colonists entered the room, which was deeply dark. A spark was struck by Nab, and a moment later, the lantern was lit and moved to all corners of the room...

There was no one. Everything was as they had left it.

"Have we been fooled by an illusion?" murmured Cyrus Smith.

No! That was not possible! The telegram had clearly said: "Come to the corral quickly."

They approached the table that was specifically dedicated to the telegraph service. Everything was in its place, the battery and the box containing it, as well as the receiving and transmitting device.

"Who was the last person to come here?" asked the engineer.

"Me, Mr. Smith," replied Ayrton.

"And that was?

— Four days ago."

"Ah! A note!" cried Harbert, pointing to a piece of paper left on the table.

On this paper were written these words, in English: "Follow the new wire."

"Let's go!" exclaimed Cyrus Smith, realizing that the dispatch had not come from the corral, but rather from the mysterious retreat connected by an extra wire, directly linking it to Granite House.

Nab took the lit lantern, and they all left the corral.

The storm was now raging with extreme violence. The time lag between each flash and each clap of thunder was noticeably decreasing.

The meteor was about to dominate Mount Franklin and the entire island. In the flash of intermittent light, one could see the summit of the volcano crowned with fumes.

There was, in the entire portion of the corral that separated the house from the fenced area, no telegraphic connection. But after passing through the door, the engineer, rushing straight to the first pole, saw in the light of a flash that a new wire dropped from the shelter to the ground.

"There it is!" he said.

This wire lay on the ground, but along its entire length it was surrounded by an insulating substance, like that of an undersea cable, ensuring the free transmission of currents. By its direction, it seemed to be heading through the woods and the southern foothills of the mountain, thus running westward.

"Let's follow it!" said Cyrus Smith.

And sometimes by the light of the lantern, sometimes amid the flashes of lightning, the colonists set off along the path traced by the wire.

The rumblings of thunder were continuous then, and their force so great that no words could be heard. Besides, there was no time to talk, but to move forward.Cyrus Smith and his companions first climbed the foothill between the corral valley and the waterfall river valley, crossing it at its narrowest point. The wire, sometimes stretched on the low branches of trees and sometimes lying on the ground, guided them securely.

The engineer had thought that this wire might end at the bottom of the valley, and that there would be the unknown hideout.

That was not the case. They had to climb the southwestern foothill and descend onto the arid plateau that was bordered by the strangely piled basalt wall. From time to time, one or another of the settlers would bend down, feel the wire with their hand, and adjust its direction as needed. But there was no doubt that this wire ran directly to the sea.

There, no doubt, in some depth of the igneous rocks, was the dwelling that had been so vainly sought until now.

The sky was on fire. Lightning followed one after the other. Several struck the top of the volcano and fell into the crater amidst thick smoke. At times, it seemed that the mountain was belching flames.

At a few minutes to ten, the settlers arrived at the high edge overlooking the ocean to the west. The wind had picked up. The surf roared five hundred feet below.

Cyrus Smith calculated that he and his companions had crossed a distance of a mile and a half since the corral.

At this point, the wire ran through the rocks, following the steep slope of a narrow and whimsically carved ravine.

The settlers entered it, risking triggering a landslide of unbalanced rocks and being thrown into the sea. The descent was extremely dangerous, but they were not counting on the danger; they were no longer in control of themselves, and an irresistible attraction drew them toward this mysterious point, like a magnet attracts iron. So they almost unconsciously descended this ravine, which would have been virtually impassable even in broad daylight. The stones rolled and shone like flaming meteorites as they passed through the light zones. Cyrus Smith was at the front. Ayrton was bringing up the rear.

Here, they went step by step; there, they slid down the polished rock; then they would rise and continue on. Finally, the wire, making a sharp angle, touched the coastal rocks, a true mass of reefs that would be battered by the large tides. The settlers had reached the lower limit of the basalt wall.

There developed a narrow ledge that ran horizontally and parallel to the sea. The wire followed it, and the settlers engaged with it. They had not taken a hundred steps when the ledge, sloping down gently, reached the very level of the waves.

The engineer grasped the wire, and he saw that it plunged into the sea.

His companions, halted nearby, were stunned. A cry of disappointment, almost a cry of despair, escaped them! Did they really have to plunge under these waters and seek some underwater cave? In their state of moral and physical excitement, they would not have hesitated to do so. A reflection from the engineer stopped them.

Cyrus Smith led his companions under a crevice in the rocks, and there:

"Let's wait," he said. "The sea is high. At low tide, the way will be open."

"But who can make you believe...?" asked Pencroff.

"He wouldn't have called us if there weren't means to get to him!"

Cyrus Smith had spoken with such conviction that no objections were raised.

His observation was logical. It had to be assumed that an opening, passable at low tide, which the tide was currently blocking, lay at the foot of the wall.

They had a few hours to wait. The settlers remained quietly huddled under a sort of deep portico carved in the rock. The rain began to fall, and soon it poured as the clouds shredded by lightning condensed. The echoes reverberated with the crash of thunder, giving it a grand sound.

The settlers' emotions were extremely heightened. A thousand strange, supernatural thoughts crossed their minds, and they evoked some great and superhuman apparition that alone could respond to the idea they had of the mysterious genius of the island.

At midnight, Cyrus Smith, taking the lantern, went down to the beach level to observe the arrangement of the rocks. The sea had already been low for two hours.

The engineer had not been mistaken. The arch of a vast excavation began to become visible above the waters. There, the wire, bending at a right angle, entered this gaping mouth.

Cyrus Smith returned to his companions and simply said to them:

"In an hour, the opening will be passable."

"So it exists?" asked Pencroff.

"Did you doubt it?" replied Cyrus Smith.

"But this cave will be filled with water to a certain level," Harbert pointed out.

"Either this cave completely empties," Cyrus Smith replied, "and in that case we will traverse it on foot, or it does not empty and some means of transport will be made available to us."

An hour went by. They all descended in the rain to the sea level. In three hours, the tide had dropped fifteen feet. The top of the arch traced by the archway was at least eight feet above the water's level. It was like the arch of a bridge, under which the waters, mixed with foam, flowed. Leaning over, the engineer saw a black object floating on the surface of the sea. He pulled it towards him.

It was a boat, tied with a rope to some inner protrusion of the wall. This boat was made of bolted sheet metal. Two oars lay at the bottom, under the benches.

"Let's board," said Cyrus Smith.

A moment later, the settlers were in the boat.

Nab and Ayrton took to the oars, Pencroff at the helm. Cyrus Smith at the front, the lantern placed on the prow, illuminated their progress.

The very low archway under which the boat first passed rose sharply; but the darkness was too deep, and the light of the lantern too insufficient, to recognize the extent of this cave, its width, height, or depth. Amidst this basaltic substructure, an imposing silence prevailed.

No outside noise penetrated there, and the flashes of lightning could not pierce its thick walls.

In certain parts of the globe, such immense caves exist, natural crypts dating from its geological time. Some are submerged by sea waters; others contain entire lakes within their sides.

Like Fingal's cave in the island of Staffa, one of the Hebrides, like the caves of Morgat on the bay of Douarnenez in Brittany, the caves of Bonifacio in Corsica, those of the Lysefjord in Norway, like the immense Mammoth cave in Kentucky, five hundred feet high and over twenty miles long! In several parts of the globe, nature has carved these crypts and preserved them for man's admiration.

As for this cave that the settlers explored, did it extend to the center of the island? For a quarter of an hour, the boat made its way, taking detours that the engineer indicated to Pencroff with a brief voice when, at a certain moment:

"More to the right!" he commanded.

The boat, changing its direction, immediately aligned itself with the right wall. The engineer wanted, rightly, to ascertain whether the wire still ran along that wall.

The wire was there, attached to the rock's projections.

"Forward!" said Cyrus Smith.

And the two oars, dipping into the black waters, propelled the boat.

The boat continued for another quarter of an hour, and since leaving the cave opening, it must have covered a distance of half a mile when Cyrus Smith's voice was heard again.

"Stop!" he said.

The boat stopped, and the settlers saw a bright light illuminating the huge crypt, deeply carved in the island's interior.

It was then possible to examine this cave, which no one could have suspected the existence of.

At a height of one hundred feet, a vault rounded above them, supported on basalt columns that seemed to have all been cast from the same mold. Irregular fall-offs and whimsical ribs leaned against these columns that nature had erected by thousands during the first eras of the planet's formation. The basalt pieces, fitted one into the other, measured forty to fifty feet in height, and the water, calm despite the external turmoil, came to bathe their base. The brightness from the light source, noted by the engineer, caught every prismatic edge and sparked them with points of fire, as if penetrating the walls as though they were diaphanous, turning the least protrusions of this substructure into so many sparkling cabochons.

Due to a reflection phenomenon, the water reproduced these various gleams on its surface, so that the boat seemed to float between two sparkling zones.

There was no mistaking the nature of the radiation emanating from the light source, whose rays, sharp and linear, broke at every angle and every rib of the crypt.

This light came from an electrical source, and its white color betrayed its origin. This was the sun of this cave, and it filled it entirely. At a signal from Cyrus Smith, the oars fell again, scattering a true rain of sparks, and the boat headed towards the bright source, of which it was soon only half a cable away. At this point, the width of the water expanse measured about three hundred and fifty feet, and beyond the dazzling center, a massive basalt wall closed any exit from this side. The cave had therefore widened considerably, and the sea formed a small lake within it. But the ceiling, side walls, and head wall, all these prisms, all these cylinders, all these cones were drenched in electric fluid, so that this glow seemed to belong to them, and one could say of these stones, faceted like high-priced diamonds, that they sweated light! At the center of the lake, a long fusiform object floated on the water's surface, silent and motionless. The glow emerging from it escaped from its sides like two mouths of a furnace that had been heated to white. This device, resembling the body of a massive cetacean, was about two hundred and fifty feet long and rose ten to twelve feet above the sea level.

The boat approached slowly. At the front, Cyrus Smith had stood up. He was gazing, gripped by intense agitation. Then, suddenly seizing the reporter's arm:

"But it's him! It can only be him! he exclaimed, him!..."

Then he fell back onto his seat, murmuring a name that Gédéon Spilett was the only one to hear.

Undoubtedly, the reporter knew that name, for it had a tremendous effect on him, and he responded in a hushed voice:

"Him! A man beyond the law!

"Him!" said Cyrus Smith.

At the engineer's order, the boat approached this singular floating device. The boat docked on the left side, from which a beam of light burst through a thick glass.

Cyrus Smith and his companions climbed onto the platform. An open hatch lay there. They all rushed through the opening. At the bottom of the ladder was an inner corridor, lit electrically. At the end of this corridor was a door that Cyrus Smith pushed open. An elaborately decorated room, which the settlers quickly passed through, adjoined a library, in which a luminous ceiling poured a torrent of light. At the back of the library, a wide door, also closed, was opened by the engineer. A vast salon, a sort of museum where treasures of mineral nature, works of art, and wonders of industry were piled high, appeared before the settlers, who must have felt they were magically transported to a dream world.

Lying on a rich couch, they saw a man who didn't seem to notice their presence.

Then Cyrus Smith raised his voice, and to the utmost surprise of his companions, he pronounced these words:

"Captain Nemo, you called for us? Here we are."

⁂ 16 ⁂

At these words, the man lying down sat up, and his face appeared in full light: a magnificent head, high forehead, proud gaze, white beard, abundant hair swept back.

This man leaned his hand on the back of the couch he had just left. His gaze was calm. One could see that a slow disease had gradually worn him down, but his voice still sounded strong when he said in English, in a tone that expressed extreme surprise:

"I have no name, sir."

"I know you!" replied Cyrus Smith.

Captain Nemo fixed a burning gaze on the engineer, as if he wanted to annihilate him.

Then, sinking back onto the cushions of the couch:

"What does it matter, after all," he murmured, "I am going to die!"

Cyrus Smith approached Captain Nemo, and Gédéon Spilett took his hand, which he found burning. Ayrton, Pencroff, Harbert, and Nab stood respectfully aside in a corner of this magnificent salon, whose air was saturated with electrical influences.

Meanwhile, Captain Nemo had immediately withdrawn his hand, and with a gesture, he invited the engineer and the reporter to sit down.

They all looked at him with genuine emotion. There he was, the one they called the "genius of the island," the powerful being whose intervention had been so effective in many circumstances, this benefactor to whom they owed such a large part of their gratitude! Before their eyes, they had only a man, where Pencroff and Nab believed they would find almost a god, and this man was ready to die!

But how was it that Cyrus Smith knew Captain Nemo? Why had he risen so sharply upon hearing that name, which he must have believed was unknown to all?

The captain had resumed his place on the couch, and resting on his arm, he was looking at the engineer, who was seated near him.

"Do you know the name I once bore, sir?" he asked.

"I know it," replied Cyrus Smith, "just as I know the name of this wonderful underwater device..."

"The Nautilus?" said the captain, half-smiling.

"The Nautilus."

"But do you know... do you know who I am?"

"I do."

"Yet it has been thirty years since I have had any communication with the inhabited world, thirty years since I have lived in the depths of the sea, the only place where I have found independence! Who could have betrayed my secret?"

"A man who never made any commitments to you, Captain Nemo, and therefore cannot be accused of treachery."

"This Frenchman whom chance threw on my board sixteen years ago?"

"Himself."

"That man and his two companions did not perish in the Maelstrom where the Nautilus had entered?"

"They did not perish, and a work titled Twenty Thousand Leagues Under the Sea, containing your story, has been published."— It's just my story from a few months ago, sir! replied the captain quickly.

— That's true, Cyrus Smith replied, but a few months of this strange life have been enough for you to know...

— As a great criminal, no doubt? Captain Nemo replied, a haughty smile crossing his lips. Yes, a rebel, perhaps cast out from humanity!

The engineer did not respond.

"Well, sir?

— I have no right to judge Captain Nemo, Cyrus Smith replied, at least regarding his past life. I don't know, like everyone else, what motivated this strange existence, and I cannot judge the effects without knowing the causes; but what I do know is that a benevolent hand has constantly reached out to us since our arrival on Lincoln Island, that we all owe our lives to a good, generous, powerful being, and that this powerful, generous, and good being is you, Captain Nemo!

— It is I, replied the captain simply.

The engineer and the reporter stood up. Their companions had gathered closer, and the gratitude overflowing in their hearts was about to be expressed through gestures and words... Captain Nemo stopped them with a gesture, and in a voice more emotional than he perhaps wished:

"When you have heard me," he said.

And the captain, in a few clear and hurried phrases, shared the entirety of his life story.

His story was brief, yet he had to concentrate all his remaining energy to tell it to the end. It was clear he was battling extreme weakness. Several times, Cyrus Smith urged him to rest, but he shook his head like a man to whom tomorrow no longer belongs, and when the reporter offered his help:

"It is useless," he replied, "my hours are numbered."

Captain Nemo was an Indian, Prince Dakkar, son of a rajah from the then-independent territory of Bundelkund and nephew of the hero of India, Tippo-Saib. His father, from the age of ten, sent him to Europe so that he could receive a complete education, with the secret intention that he could one day compete with those he viewed as oppressors of his country. From age ten to thirty, Prince Dakkar, exceptionally gifted, both in heart and mind, educated himself in everything, excelling in sciences, literature, and the arts.

Prince Dakkar traveled all over Europe. His birth and fortune made him sought after, but the temptations of the world never attracted him.

Young and handsome, he remained serious, gloomy, consumed with the thirst for knowledge, bearing an unyielding resentment in his heart.

Prince Dakkar hated. He hated the only country he had never wanted to step foot in, the only nation whose advances he constantly refused: he hated England, and all the more because he admired it in more than one respect.

This Indian embodied all the fierce hatreds of the defeated against the victor.

The invader could find no grace in the invaded.

The son of one of those sovereigns whom the United Kingdom could only nominally ensure the subjugation of, this prince, from the family of Tippo-Saib, raised in the ideas of reclamation and vengeance, with an inevitable love for his poetic country burdened with English chains, never wanted to set foot on that cursed land, to which India owed its servitude.

Prince Dakkar became an artist deeply moved by the wonders of art, a scholar for whom nothing in the high sciences was foreign, and a statesman who grew amidst European courts. To those who observed him incompletely, he perhaps appeared to be one of those cosmopolitans, curious to know but disdainful of acting, one of those wealthy travelers, proud and platonic minds, who roam the world and belong to no country.

Nothing could be further from the truth. This artist, this scholar, this man remained Indian at heart, Indian in his desire for revenge, Indian in the hope he harbored of being able to reclaim one day the rights of his country, to drive out the foreigner, to restore its independence. Thus, Prince Dakkar returned to Bundelkund in 1849. He married a noble Indian woman whose heart bled like his own at the misfortunes of her homeland. They had two children whom he cherished. But domestic happiness could not make him forget the servitude of India. He awaited an opportunity. It presented itself.

The English yoke had perhaps become too heavy for the Hindu populations. Prince Dakkar took on the voice of the discontented. He instilled in their minds all the hatred he felt towards the foreigner. He traveled not only through the still independent regions of the Indian subcontinent but also through areas directly administered by the English. He recalled the great days of Tippo-Saib, who died heroically at Seringapatam defending his homeland. In 1857, the great rebellion of the sepoys broke out. Prince Dakkar was its soul. He organized the immense uprising. He put his talents and wealth at the service of this cause. He put himself in danger; he fought at the front lines; he risked his life like the humblest of those heroes who rose to liberate their land; he was wounded ten times in twenty encounters and had not found death when the last soldiers of independence fell under English bullets.

Never before had British power in India faced such danger, and if, as they had hoped, the sepoys had found external assistance, perhaps the United Kingdom's influence and dominance would have been finished in Asia.

The name of Prince Dakkar became illustrious then. The hero who bore it did not hide and fought openly. His head was put to a price, and if no traitor was found to deliver it, his father, mother, wife, and children paid for him even before he could know the dangers they had run because of him...

Once again, right fell before might. But civilization never retreats, and it seems to borrow all rights from necessity. The sepoys were defeated, and the land of the former rajahs fell back under the tighter domination of England.

Prince Dakkar, who could not die, returned to the mountains of Bundelkund. There, alone now, filled with immense disgust for everything that bore the name of man, filled with hatred and horror for the civilized world, wanting to forever flee from it, he liquidated the remnants of his fortune, gathered twenty of his most loyal companions, and one day they all disappeared.

Where then had Prince Dakkar sought that independence which the inhabited land denied him?

Under the waters, in the depths of the seas, where no one could follow him.

The man of war was replaced by the scholar. A deserted island in the Pacific served him to establish his shipyards, and there, a submarine was built based on his designs. Electricity, of which he had learned to harness the immeasurable mechanical force by means that will someday be known, and which he drew from inexhaustible sources, was used for all the needs of his floating device, as a driving force, illuminating force, and heating force. The sea, with its infinite treasures, its myriad fish, its harvests of seaweeds and sargassum, its enormous mammals, and not only everything that nature maintained there but also everything that men had lost there, amply sufficed to meet the needs of the prince and his crew — and this was the fulfillment of his most fervent desire, since he did not want any communication with the land. He named his submarine the Nautilus, he called himself Captain Nemo, and he disappeared beneath the seas.

For many years, the captain traveled all the oceans, from pole to pole. An outcast from the inhabited universe, he collected marvelous treasures in these unknown worlds. The millions lost in the Bay of Vigo in 1702 by Spanish galleons provided him with an inexhaustible mine of wealth of which he always disposed anonymously, in favor of the peoples fighting for their country's independence. Finally, he had not communicated with his kind for a long time when, during the night of November 6, 1866, three men were thrown aboard. They were a French professor, his servant, and a Canadian fisherman. These three men had been cast into the sea during a collision that occurred between the Nautilus and the United States frigate Abraham Lincoln, which was hunting it down.

Captain Nemo learned from this professor that the Nautilus, sometimes mistaken for a giant mammal of the cetacean family and sometimes for a submarine vessel containing a crew of pirates, was being pursued across all the seas.

Captain Nemo could have returned these three men to the ocean, who were thrown into his mysterious existence by chance. He did not, he kept them prisoners, and for seven months, they were able to witness all the wonders of a journey that continued for twenty thousand leagues under the seas. One day, on June 22, 1867, these three men, who knew nothing of Captain Nemo's past, managed to escape after seizing the Nautilus's boat. But at that moment the Nautilus was carried towards the coasts of Norway, into the whirlpools of the Maelstrom, and the captain had to believe that the fugitives, swallowed by those horrible eddies, had met their death at the bottom of the abyss. He did not know that the Frenchman and his two companions had been miraculously washed up on the shore, that fishermen from the Lofoten Islands had rescued them, and that the professor, upon returning to France, had published the work in which seven months of this strange and adventurous voyage of the Nautilus were recounted and given to public curiosity.

For a long time, Captain Nemo continued to live like this, roaming the seas. But gradually, his companions died and were laid to rest in their coral cemetery, in the depths of the Pacific. A void was created in the Nautilus, and finally, Captain Nemo was left alone among all those who had taken refuge with him in the depths of the ocean.

Captain Nemo was then sixty years old. When he was alone, he managed to bring his Nautilus back to one of the underwater ports that sometimes served him as refuge points.

One of these ports was excavated beneath Lincoln Island, and it was the one currently sheltering the Nautilus. For six years, the captain had been there, no longer navigating, waiting for death, that is to say the moment when he would be reunited with his companions, when chance made him witness the fall of the balloon carrying the prisoners of the Southerners. Clad in his diving suit, he was walking under the waters, a few fathoms from the shore of the island, when the engineer was thrown into the sea. A good move propelled the captain... and he saved Cyrus Smith.

At first, he wanted to flee from these five castaways, but his refuge port was closed, and due to a rise in the basalt caused by volcanic actions, he could no longer cross the entrance of the crypt. Where there was still enough water for a small boat to cross the bar, there was no longer enough for the Nautilus, whose draft was relatively considerable.

Captain Nemo thus remained, then, he observed these men thrown without resources on a deserted island, but he did not want to be seen. Gradually, when he saw them honest, energetic, linked by a brotherly friendship, he became interested in their efforts. As if against his will, he penetrated all the secrets of their existence. With his diving suit, it was easy for him to reach the bottom of the inner well of Granite-House, and, climbing up the rock protrusions to its upper opening, he heard the colonists recount the past, study the present and the future. He learned from them about the immense effort of America against America itself to abolish slavery. Yes! These men were worthy of reconciling Captain Nemo with humanity, which they so honestly represented on the island!

Captain Nemo had saved Cyrus Smith. He was also the one who brought the dog back to the chimneys, who rejected Top from the waters of the lake, who brought ashore the crate containing so many useful items for the colonists, who sent the boat back into the current of the Mercy, who threw the rope from the top of Granite House during the monkey attack, who revealed Ayrton's presence on Tabor Island through the message in the bottle, who blew up the brig by the impact of a torpedo set in the canal, who saved Harbert from certain death by bringing the sulfate of quinine, and finally, he who struck the convicts with those electric bullets whose secret he kept and which he used in his underwater hunts. Thus were explained so many incidents that would have seemed supernatural, and which all testified to the generosity and power of the captain.

However, this great misanthrope thirsted for good.

He still had useful advice to give to his protégés, and, on the other hand, feeling his heart beat again for himself in the face of approaching death, he called, as you know, the colonists of Granite-House, through a wire that connected the corral to the Nautilus, which was equipped with an alphabetical device... Perhaps he would not have done it if he had known that Cyrus Smith knew enough of his history to greet him with the name of Nemo.

The captain had finished recounting his life.

Cyrus Smith then spoke; he recalled all the incidents that had had such a beneficial influence on the colony, and, on behalf of his companions as well as his own, he thanked the generous being to whom they owed so much.

But Captain Nemo was not thinking of claiming the price for the services he had rendered. A last thought stirred in his mind, and before shaking the hand offered by the engineer:

"Now, sir," he said, "now that you know my life, judge it!"

By saying this, the captain was clearly alluding to a serious incident of which the three strangers thrown aboard had been witnesses — an incident that the French professor must have recounted in his book and whose repercussions must have been terrible. Indeed, a few days before the professor and his two companions' escape, the Nautilus, pursued by a frigate in the northern Atlantic, had crashed like a ram into that frigate and sunk it mercilessly.

Cyrus Smith understood the allusion and remained silent.

"It was an English frigate, sir," Captain Nemo exclaimed, momentarily returning to Prince Dakkar, "an English frigate, do you hear me! It attacked me! I was trapped in a narrow and shallow bay!... I had to pass, and... I passed!"

Then, in a calmer voice:

"I was in justice and in right," he added. "I did good wherever I could, and also the harm I had to. Not all justice lies in forgiveness!"

A few moments of silence followed this response, and Captain Nemo pronounced this phrase again:

"What do you think of me, gentlemen?"

Cyrus Smith extended his hand to the captain, and at his request, he responded in a grave voice:

"Captain, your fault is having believed that one could resurrect the past, and you fought against the necessary progress. It was one of those errors that some admire, that others condemn, of which only God is the judge, and which human reason must absolve."Those who make a mistake with an intention they believe is good can be challenged, but we don't stop valuing them. Your error is one that doesn't exclude admiration, and your name has nothing to fear from history's judgments. History loves heroic foolishness, while condemning the results they lead to."

Captain Nemo's chest rose, and his hand reached towards the sky.

"Was I wrong, was I right?" he murmured.

Cyrus Smith continued:

"All great actions come from God, for they originate with Him! Captain Nemo, the good people here, whom you've helped, will mourn you forever!"

Harbert had moved closer to the captain. He knelt, took his hand, and kissed it. A tear slipped from the dying man's eyes.

"My child," he said, "be blessed!"

17

The day had arrived. No light penetrated this deep crypt. The sea, high at that moment, blocked the entrance. But the artificial light streaming through the walls of the Nautilus had not faded, and the water around the floating vessel still shone brightly. An extreme fatigue overwhelmed Captain Nemo, who had fallen back onto the couch. It was unthinkable to transport him to Granite-House, for he had expressed his desire to remain amidst the wonders of the Nautilus, worth millions, and to await a death that could not be long in coming.

During a long spell of weakness that left him nearly unconscious, Cyrus Smith and Gédéon Spilett attentively observed the state of the sick man. It was evident that the captain was gradually fading away. The strength that once defined this robust body was now lacking in the frail shell of a soul that was about to escape. All of life was concentrated in the heart and head.

The engineer and the reporter consulted quietly. Was there any care to give this dying man? Could they, if not save him, at least prolong his life for a few days? He had said there was no remedy, and he was calmly awaiting the death he did not fear.

"We can do nothing," said Gédéon Spilett.

"But what is he dying from?" asked Pencroff.

"He is fading," replied the reporter.

"However," the sailor continued, "if we took him outside, into the sunlight, perhaps he would revive?"

"No, Pencroff," replied the engineer, "nothing is to be attempted! Besides, Captain Nemo would not agree to leave his vessel. He has lived on the Nautilus for thirty years; it is on the Nautilus that he wants to die."

Surely, Captain Nemo heard Cyrus Smith's reply, for he raised himself slightly and, in a weaker but still understandable voice, said:

"You are right, sir. I must and I want to die here. Therefore, I have a request to make of you."

Cyrus Smith and his companions moved closer to the couch and arranged the cushions so that the dying man would be better supported.

They then saw his gaze pause on all the wonders of this salon, illuminated by the electric rays filtered through the arabesques of a luminous ceiling. He looked at, one after the other, the paintings hung on the splendid tapestries of the walls, the masterpieces of Italian, Flemish, French, and Spanish masters, the marble and bronze sculptures rising on their pedestals, the magnificent organ backed against the wall, and then the showcases arranged around a central basin, in which expanded the most admirable products of the sea: sea plants, zoophytes, strands of pearls of immeasurable value, and finally, his eyes stopped on the motto inscribed above this museum, the motto of the Nautilus: mobilis in mobile.

It seemed as if he wanted one last time to caress with his gaze these master-pieces of art and nature, which had limited his horizon during so many years spent in the ocean's depths!

Cyrus Smith respected the silence that Captain Nemo maintained. He waited for the dying man to speak again.

After a few minutes, during which he likely reviewed his entire life, Captain Nemo turned to the colonists and said:

"You think, gentlemen, that I owe you some gratitude?..."

"Captain, we would give our lives to prolong yours!"

"Very well," continued Captain Nemo, "promise me to carry out my last wishes, and I will be repaid for all I have done for you."

"We promise you," replied Cyrus Smith.

And with this promise, he committed his companions and himself.

"Gentlemen," the captain continued, "tomorrow, I will be dead."

He signaled to Harbert, who wanted to protest.

"Tomorrow, I will be dead, and I desire no other tomb than the Nautilus. It is my coffin! All my friends rest in the depths of the sea; I want to rest there too."

A profound silence welcomed these words from Captain Nemo.

"Listen well to me, gentlemen," he resumed. "The Nautilus is imprisoned in this cave, whose entrance has been raised. But if it cannot leave its prison, it can at least plunge into the abyss it covers and keep my mortal remains there."

The colonists listened intently to the dying man's words.

"Tomorrow, after my death, Mr. Smith," continued the captain, "you and your companions will leave the Nautilus, for all the riches it contains must disappear with me. One memory will remain with you of Prince Dakkar, whose story you now know. This chest... there... holds several millions in diamonds, most of them reminders of a time when, as a father and husband, I almost believed in happiness, and a collection of pearls gathered by my friends and me from the depths of the sea. With this treasure, you will be able to do good things in the future. In the hands of you and your companions, Mr. Smith, money cannot be a danger. I will thus be, from above, associated with your works, and I do not fear for them!"

After a brief rest, necessitated by his extreme weakness, Captain Nemo continued:

"Tomorrow, you will take this chest, you will leave this salon and close the door; then, you will go back up to the Nautilus's deck, and you will lower the hatch, securing it with its bolts."

"We will do it, captain," replied Cyrus Smith.

"Good. You will then embark in the boat that brought you here. But before abandoning the Nautilus, go to the back, and there, open two large valves on the waterline. Water will enter the tanks, and the Nautilus will gradually sink beneath the waves to rest at the bottom of the abyss."

And, with a gesture from Cyrus Smith, the captain added:

"Do not fear anything! You will only be burying a dead man!"

Neither Cyrus Smith nor any of his companions thought to object to Captain Nemo. These were his last wishes, and they had no choice but to comply.

"I have your promise, gentlemen?" added Captain Nemo.

"You have it, captain," replied the engineer.

The captain nodded in thanks and asked the colonists to leave him alone for a few hours.

Gédéon Spilett insisted on staying close to him, in case a crisis occurred, but the dying man refused, saying:

"I will live until tomorrow, sir!"

Everyone left the salon, crossed the library, the dining room, and arrived at the front, in the engine room, where the electrical devices provided heat, light, and mechanical power to the Nautilus.

The Nautilus was a masterpiece that contained masterpieces, and the engineer was in awe.

The colonists climbed onto the deck, which rose seven or eight feet above the water.

There, they lay near a thick lens that blocked a large eye from which a burst of light emerged. Behind this eye was a cabin that contained the steering wheels and where the helmsman stood when guiding the Nautilus through the liquid layers that the electric rays illuminated over a considerable distance.

Cyrus Smith and his companions initially remained silent, deeply impressed by what they had just seen and heard, and their hearts tightened as they thought that the one whose arm had helped them so often, this protector they had known for only a few hours, was on the brink of dying! Regardless of the judgments that posterity would cast upon the actions of this nearly superhuman existence, Prince Dakkar would always remain one of those strange personalities whose memory cannot fade.

"Now there's a man!" said Pencroff. "Is it believable that he has lived down there in the ocean! And when I think he may not have found more peace there than anywhere else!"

"The Nautilus," Ayrton then remarked, "could perhaps have helped us escape from Lincoln Island to reach some inhabited land."

"A thousand devils!" exclaimed Pencroff, "I would never dare to guide such a ship. Sailing on the seas, fine! But beneath the seas, no!"

"I believe," replied the reporter, "that maneuvering a vessel like the Nautilus underwater must be very easy, Pencroff, and we would quickly adapt. No storms, no risk of collisions. A few feet under the surface, the sea is as calm as a lake."

"Possible!" retorted the sailor, "but I prefer a good strong wind on board a well-rigged ship. A boat is made to sail on the water, not beneath it."

"My friends," replied the engineer, "there is no need, at least regarding the Nautilus, to discuss the question of submarines. The Nautilus is not ours, and we have no right to dispose of it. Besides, it could not help us in any situation. Apart from the fact that it can no longer exit this cavern, whose entrance is now blocked by rock formations, Captain Nemo wants it to sink with him after his death. His wish is explicit, and we will fulfill it."

Cyrus Smith and his companions, after a conversation that continued for a while longer, descended back into the Nautilus. There, they took some food and returned to the salon.

Captain Nemo had emerged from the state of prostration that had over-whelmed him, and his eyes had regained their brightness. A smile seemed to form on his lips.

The colonists approached him.

" gentlemen," the captain said, "you are brave, honest, and good men. You have all selflessly devoted yourselves to the common cause. I have often observed you. I have loved you; I love you!... your hand, Mr. Smith!"

Cyrus Smith extended his hand to the captain, who affectionately squeezed it.

"This is good!" he murmured.

Then, continuing:

"But enough about me! I need to speak to you about yourselves and Lincoln Island, where you have found refuge... Are you planning to abandon it?"

"To return, captain!" Pencroff quickly replied.

"Return?... Indeed, Pencroff," answered the captain with a smile, "I know how much you love this island. It has changed through your care, and it truly belongs to you!"

"Our plan, captain," then said Cyrus Smith, "would be to make it a territory of the United States and to establish a naval station that would be conveniently located in this part of the Pacific."

"You think of your country, gentlemen," replied the captain. "You are working for its prosperity, for its glory. You are right. The homeland!... that is where you must return! That is where one must die!... and I die far from everything I have loved!"

"Do you have any last wishes to convey?" the engineer asked quickly, "any memory to give to friends you might have left in those mountains of India?"

"No, Mr. Smith. I have no friends left! I am the last of my kind... and I have long been dead to all those I have known... but let us return to you. Loneli-ness, isolation are sad things, beyond human strength... I die because I believed one could live alone!... You must do everything possible to leave Lincoln Island and see the land where you were born. I know those wretches have destroyed the craft you had built..."

"We are building a ship," Gédéon Spilett said, "a ship big enough to take us to the nearest lands; but if we manage to leave it sooner or later, we will return to Lincoln Island. Too many memories tie us to it for us to ever forget!"

"It is here that we came to know Captain Nemo," said Cyrus Smith.

"It is only here that we will remember you in your totality!" added Harbert.

"And it is here that I will rest in eternal sleep, if..." replied the captain.

He hesitated and, instead of finishing his sentence, merely stated:

"Mr. Smith, I would like to speak to you... Alone!"

The engineer's companions, respecting the dying man's wish, withdrew.

Cyrus Smith remained only a few minutes alone with Captain Nemo, and soon he called back his friends, but he told them nothing of the secret matters the dying man wanted to share with him.

Gédéon Spilett then observed the sick man with extreme attention. It was evident that the captain was now sustained only by a moral energy that could soon no longer counter his physical exhaustion.

The day ended without any change manifesting. The colonists did not leave the Nautilus for a moment. Night had fallen, although it was impossible to notice in this crypt.

Captain Nemo did not suffer, but he was declining. His noble face, pale from the approach of death, was calm. From his lips came almost inaudible words referring to various incidents from his strange existence. It was felt that life was gradually withdrawing from this body, whose extremities were already cold. Once or twice, he spoke to the colonists gathered around him, and he smiled that last smile which continues even into death. Finally, shortly after midnight, Captain Nemo made a final movement and managed to cross his arms over his chest, as though he intended to die in that position.

Around one in the morning, all life had solely retreated into his gaze. A final flame shone within that eye, from which so many flames had once burst forth. Then, whispering the words, "God and country!" he gently expired.

Cyrus Smith, bowing at that moment, closed the eyes of the one who had been Prince Dakkar and who was no longer even Captain Nemo.

Harbert and Pencroff cried. Ayrton wiped away a furtive tear. Nab knelt beside the reporter, transformed into a statue.

Cyrus Smith, raising his hand above the head of the dead man:

"May God have his soul!" he said, and turning to his friends, he added:

"Let us pray for the one we have lost!"

A few hours later, the colonists fulfilled their promise to the captain, carrying out the last wishes of the dead man.

Cyrus Smith and his companions left the Nautilus, having taken the only memory their benefactor had bequeathed to them, this chest that contained a fortune. The wonderful salon, always flooded with light, had been carefully closed off. The metal door of the hatch was bolted, ensuring that not a single drop of water could enter the chambers of the Nautilus. Then, the colonists descended into the boat, which was tied to the side of the submarine. This boat was taken to the back. There, at the waterline, two large valves opened that connected to the tanks meant to control the immersion of the device. These valves were opened, the tanks filled, and the Nautilus gradually sank, disappearing beneath the surface of the water. But the colonists were able to follow it still through the deep layers. Its powerful light illuminated the clear waters, while the crypt became dark again. Then, this vast outpouring of electric effluence finally faded, and soon the Nautilus, transformed into Captain Nemo's coffin, lay at the bottom of the sea.

18

At dawn, the colonists silently returned to the entrance of the cave, which they named "Dakkar crypt" in memory of Captain Nemo. The tide was low then, allowing them to pass easily beneath the arch, where the waves battered the basalt support. The metal boat remained in that spot, positioned so that it was sheltered from the waves. As an extra precaution, Pencroff, Nab, and Ayrton pulled it up onto the small beach on one side of the crypt, to a spot where it was safe from danger. The storm had ceased with the night. The last rolls of thunder faded into the west. It was no longer raining, but the sky was still filled with clouds. Overall, this month of October, the beginning of the southern spring, did not look promising, and the wind had a tendency to shift from one point of the compass to another, making it impossible to rely on settled weather. Cyrus Smith and his companions, leaving the Dakkar crypt, resumed their route to the corral. Along the way, Nab and Harbert made sure to clear the line that had been stretched by the captain between the corral and the crypt, one that could be used later. As they walked, the colonists spoke little. The various incidents of that night of October 15 to 16 had made a strong impression on them. This unknown figure whose influence had protected them so effectively, this man whom their imagination had turned into a genius, Captain Nemo, was no more. His Nautilus, along with him, was buried deep in an abyss. Each of them felt that they were more isolated than before. They had, so to speak, gotten used to relying on this powerful intervention that was now absent, and Gideon Spilett and even Cyrus Smith himself could not escape this feeling. Thus, they all maintained a deep silence as they followed the path to the corral.

Around nine in the morning, the colonists returned to Granite House. It had been agreed that the construction of the ship would be pushed forward very actively, and Cyrus Smith devoted more time and care to it than ever. No one knew what the future held. However, it was a guarantee for the colonists to have a solid vessel at their disposal, one capable of withstanding even rough seas, and large enough to attempt, if necessary, a longer crossing. If, once the vessel was complete, the colonists did not decide to leave Lincoln Island for either a Polynesian archipelago in the Pacific or the coasts of New Zealand, at the very least they should make their way to Tabor Island as soon as possible to drop off the notice relating to Ayrton. This was an essential precaution to take in case the Scottish yacht reappeared in those waters, and nothing should be neglected in that regard.

Work resumed. Cyrus Smith, Pencroff, and Ayrton, aided by Nab, Gideon Spilett, and Harbert whenever some other urgent task did not require their attention, worked tirelessly. The ship needed to be ready in five months, meaning by the start of March, if they intended to visit Tabor Island before the equinox storms made the crossing impractical. Thus, the carpenters wasted no time. Besides, they didn't have to worry about making rigging, as that from the Speedy had been saved intact. So, it was primarily the hull of the ship that needed to be finished. The end of the year 1868 passed with these important works, almost to the exclusion of all others. After two and a half months, the frames had been set, and the first planks were adjusted. It was already clear that the plans given by Cyrus Smith were excellent and that the ship would perform well at sea. Pencroff brought a relentless energy to this work and didn't hesitate to grumble when one or another would abandon the carpenter's hatchet for the hunter's rifle. It was necessary, however, to maintain the supplies of Granite House for the coming winter. But regardless, the brave sailor was not happy when the workers were absent from the yard. In those instances, and grumbling, he would — in anger — accomplish the work of six men.

This entire summer season was poor. For several days, the heat was overwhelming, and the atmosphere, saturated with electricity, subsequently discharged only through violent storms that deeply disturbed the layers of air. It was rare for distant rumblings of thunder not to be heard. It was like a low, persistent murmur, much like that found in the equatorial regions of the globe. January 1, 1869, was even marked by a storm of extreme violence, with lightning striking the island multiple times. Large trees were hit by the force and broken, including one of those enormous gum trees that shaded the henhouse at the southern tip of the lake. Did this meteor have any relation to the phenomena occurring in the earth's core? Was there some sort of connection between air disturbances and the troubles of the planet's interior? Cyrus Smith was led to believe so, for the development of these storms was marked by a resurgence of volcanic symptoms.

It was on January 3 that Harbert, having gone up at dawn to the Grand View plateau to saddle one of the onagers, saw a huge plume rising from the summit of the volcano. Harbert immediately alerted the colonists, who quickly came to observe the top of Mount Franklin. "Hey!" exclaimed Pencroff, "these aren't vapors this time! It seems to me that the giant is not just breathing anymore, but that it is smoking!" This image used by the sailor accurately conveyed the change that had taken place at the mouth of the volcano. For three months already, the crater had been emitting more or less intense vapors, but these had only come from an internal boiling of the mineral materials. This time, thick smoke had succeeded the vapors, rising in the form of a grayish column, over three hundred feet wide at its base, and spreading like a giant mushroom to a height of seven to eight hundred feet above the summit of the mountain. "The fire is in the chimney," said Gideon Spilett. "And we cannot put it out!" replied Harbert. "One should really clean out the volcanoes," observed Nab, who seemed to be speaking quite seriously. "Goodness, Nab," exclaimed Pencroff. "Would you take on that cleaning job?" And Pencroff burst into a hearty laugh. Cyrus Smith was observing closely the thick smoke emitted by Mount Franklin and even listened as if he wanted to catch some distant rumble. Then, returning to his companions, with whom he had strayed a little: "Indeed, my friends, a significant change has occurred, we must not hide that from ourselves. The volcanic materials are no longer just boiling; they have caught fire, and we are certainly threatened by an imminent eruption! "Well, Mr. Smith, we'll see the eruption, shouted Pencroff, and we'll applaud if it is successful! I don't think there's any reason for us to worry! "No, Pencroff," replied Cyrus Smith, "for the old lava routes are still open, and, due to its shape, the crater has poured them towards the north until now. And yet..." "And yet, since there is no advantage to be gained from an eruption, it would be better if it didn't happen," said the reporter. "Who knows?" replied the sailor. "Perhaps this volcano will spew out some useful and precious material that it will gladly relinquish, and we will make good use of it!" Cyrus Smith shook his head as someone who expected nothing good from the development of a phenomenon that was so sudden. He did not look as lightly as Pencroff at the consequences of an eruption. If the lavas, due to the orientation of the crater, did not directly threaten the wooded and cultivated areas of the island, other complications could arise. Indeed, eruptions are often accompanied by earthquakes, and an island like Lincoln Island, composed of such diverse materials — basalts on one side, granite on the other, lavas to the north, and loose soil to the south— which, therefore, could not be solidly linked together, would run the risk of being disintegrated. Thus, if the outpouring of volcanic substances did not pose a very serious danger, any movement in the Earth's structure that shook the island could lead to extremely grave consequences. "I think," said Ayrton, who had lain down to place his ear on the ground, "I think I hear deep rumblings, as if a cart loaded with iron bars were passing." The colonists listened with utmost attention and could confirm that Ayrton was not mistaken. The rumblings were sometimes mixed with underground moans, creating a sort of "rimordzando" and gradually fading away as if a violent breeze passed through the depths of the globe. But no actual detonation could be heard yet. One could conclude that the vapors and smoke found a free passage through the central chimney, and that, with the valve being large enough, no dislocation would occur, and no explosion would be feared. "Well then!" said Pencroff, "are we not going to get back to work? Let Mount Franklin smoke, roar, groan, and spew fire and flames as much as it likes, that's no reason for us to do nothing! Come on, Ayrton, Nab, Harbert, Mr. Cyrus, Mr. Spilett, everyone needs to pitch in today! We're going to set the edges, and a dozen arms won't be too many. Within two months, I want our new Bonadventure — for we will keep that name, right? — to float on the waters of Balloon Harbor! So, not a moment to lose!" All the colonists, whose arms Pencroff demanded, went down to the construction site and proceeded to set the edges, thick planks that form the belt of a ship and securely connect the frames of its hull. This was a large and laborious task, which everyone had to participate in.

Thus, they worked diligently throughout the day of January 3, without worrying about the volcano, which they couldn't even see from the shore of Granite House. But once or twice, large shadows obscuring the sun, which traced its daily arc across an extremely clear sky, indicated that a thick cloud of smoke passed between its disk and the island. The wind blowing from the sea carried all these vapors to the west. Cyrus Smith and Gideon Spilett noted these passing darkenings perfectly and talked several times about the progress of the volcanic phenomenon, but work was not interrupted. It was of high interest, from all points of view, that the building be completed in the shortest possible time. In light of potential eventualities, the safety of the colonists would be better guaranteed. Who knows if this ship might one day be their only refuge?

In the evening, after dinner, Cyrus Smith, Gideon Spilett, and Harbert went back up to the Grand View plateau. Night had already fallen, and the darkness should allow them to see if, among the vapors and smoke that had accumulated at the crater's mouth, there were either flames or incandescent materials being projected by the volcano. "The crater is on fire!" shouted Harbert, who, being quicker than his companions, had arrived first at the plateau. Mount Franklin, about six miles away, then appeared as a gigantic torch, at the summit of which a few sooty flames twisted. So much smoke, so many cinders, and perhaps ashes mixed in that their glow, very muted, did not stand out brightly against the darkness of the night. But a sort of tawny glow spread across the island and vaguely outlined the wooded mass in the foreground. Huge whirlwinds darkened the heights of the sky, through which a few stars twinkled. "The progress is rapid!" said the engineer. "That's not surprising," replied the reporter. "The awakening of the volcano has been going on for some time now. You remember, Cyrus, that the first vapors appeared around the time we scoured the mountainside to discover Captain Nemo's retreat. That was, if I am not mistaken, around October 15?" "Yes!" replied Harbert, "and that was already two and a half months ago!" "The underground fires have smoldered for ten weeks, continued Gideon Spilett, and it's not surprising that they are now developing with such violence! "Do you not feel certain vibrations in the ground?" asked Cyrus Smith. "Indeed," replied Gideon Spilett, "but that doesn't mean an earthquake..." "I'm not saying we are threatened by an earthquake," replied Cyrus Smith, "and God forbid! No. These vibrations are due to the effervescence of the central fire. The Earth's crust is nothing more than the wall of a boiler, and you know that the wall of a boiler vibrates under the pressure of gases like a sound plate. That effect is happening right now." "The magnificent jets of fire!" cried Harbert. At that moment, a sort of bouquet of fireworks shot from the crater, whose vapors could not diminish its brilliance. Thousands of luminous fragments and bright points projected in opposite directions. A few, surpassing the dome of smoke, pierced it with a rapid jet and left behind a real incandescent dust. This outpouring was accompanied by successive detonations like the tearing of a battery of machine guns. Cyrus Smith, the reporter, and the young boy, having spent an hour at the Grand View plateau, went back down to the shore and returned to Granite House. The engineer was thoughtful, even troubled, to such an extent that Gideon Spilett felt compelled to ask him whether he sensed any imminent danger, for which the eruption would be the direct or indirect cause. "Yes and no," replied Cyrus Smith. "However," resumed the reporter, "the greatest misfortune that could befall us would be an earthquake that upheaved the island, right? Now, I do not believe that this should be feared, since the vapors and lavas have found a free path to spill out."— Also, replied Cyrus Smith, I'm not afraid of an earthquake in the usual sense of ground convulsions caused by the expansion of underground vapors. But other causes can lead to great disasters.

— Which ones, my dear Cyrus?

— I'm not quite sure... I need to see... visit the mountain... I'll have more clarity about that in a few days."

Gédéon Spilett did not press further, and soon, despite the booming of the volcano, which was growing louder and echoed throughout the island, the residents of Granite House were sleeping soundly.

Three days passed, the 4th, 5th, and 6th of January. Work was still ongoing on the boat's construction, and, without explaining further, the engineer was doing everything he could to speed up the work. Mount Franklin was then shrouded in a dark cloud with a sinister appearance, and with flames, it was spewing incandescent rocks, some of which fell back into the crater itself.

This led Pencroff, who wanted to view the phenomenon only from its amusing sides, to say:

"Look! The giant playing with a ball! The giant juggling!"

And indeed, the materials ejected were falling back into the abyss, and it didn't seem that the lava, pushed up by internal pressure, had yet risen to the mouth of the crater. At least, the opening to the northeast, which was partially visible, was not pouring torrents onto the northern slope of the mountain.

However, despite the urgency of the construction work, other tasks required the colonists' attention at various points around the island.

First, they had to go to the corral, where the flock of rams and goats was kept, and replenish their feed supply. It was decided that Ayrton would go there the next day, January 7th, and since he could manage the task alone, which he was used to, Pencroff and the others were somewhat surprised when they heard the engineer say to Ayrton:

"Since you're going to the corral tomorrow, I'll accompany you.

— Hey, Mr. Cyrus! exclaimed the sailor, our work days are limited, and if you leave too, we'll have four fewer hands!

— We'll be back the following day, replied Cyrus Smith, but I need to go to the corral... I want to check on the eruption's status.

— The eruption! The eruption! replied Pencroff with a dissatisfied air. Something important that eruption, and it doesn't worry me at all!"

No matter what the sailor thought, the exploration planned by the engineer was confirmed for the next day. Harbert would have liked to accompany Cyrus Smith, but he didn't want to upset Pencroff by leaving.

The next day, at dawn, Cyrus Smith and Ayrton, riding in the cart pulled by the two onagers, took the road to the corral and trotted off at a brisk pace. Above the forest, thick clouds passed, constantly supplied with sooty materials from the crater of Mount Franklin. These clouds, rolling heavily in the atmosphere, were obviously made up of heterogeneous substances. They were not just heavy and dense because of the volcano's smoke. Ashes in the form of dust, such as pulverized pumice and ash as fine as the finest starch, were suspended amidst their thick spirals. These ashes are so fine that they have been known to remain in the air for months. After the eruption of 1783 in Iceland, the atmosphere was filled with volcanic dust for over a year, barely allowing sunlight to penetrate.

But, most often, these powders settle down, and that's what happened on this occasion.

Cyrus Smith and Ayrton had barely arrived at the corral when a sort of black snow resembling fine hunting powder fell and instantly changed the appearance of the ground. Trees, meadows, everything disappeared under a layer several inches thick. However, the wind blew from the northeast, and most of the cloud dissolved over the sea.

"That's strange, Mr. Smith," said Ayrton.

"That's serious," replied the engineer. "This pumice, this pulverized volcanic rock—this mineral dust, in short—demonstrates how deep the disturbance is in the lower layers of the volcano.

— But can't we do something?

— Nothing, other than keep track of the phenomenon's progress. So, attend to the corral, Ayrton. In the meantime, I'll go up beyond the red creek springs and examine the state of the mountain on its northern slope. Then...

— Then...? Mr. Smith?

— Then we'll pay a visit to the Dakkar crypt... I want to see... finally, I'll come back to pick you up in two hours."

Ayrton then entered the corral yard and, while waiting for the engineer's return, took care of the rams and goats, which seemed somewhat uneasy given these first signs of an eruption.

Meanwhile, Cyrus Smith, having ventured onto the ridge of the eastern foothills, circled the red creek and arrived at the location where he and his companions had discovered a sulfur spring during their first exploration.

Things had changed significantly! Instead of a single column of smoke, he counted thirteen shooting out of the ground as if violently pushed by some piston. It was clear that the earth's crust was undergoing horrific pressure at this point on the globe. The atmosphere was saturated with sulfur gas, hydrogen, carbon dioxide, mixed with water vapor. Cyrus Smith felt the volcanic tufts scattered across the plain, which were nothing but pulverized ashes that time had turned into hard blocks, but he still didn't see any trace of new lava.

The engineer was able to confirm this more fully when he observed the entire northern slope of Mount Franklin. Whirlwinds of smoke and flames escaped from the crater; hailstones of scoria fell to the ground; but no lava flow was occurring from the neck of the crater, which proved that the level of volcanic materials had not yet reached the upper opening of the central chimney.

"And I'd prefer it that way!" Cyrus Smith said to himself. "At least I'd be certain that the lavas have resumed their usual path. Who knows if they won't pour out through some new vent? But that's not the danger! Captain Nemo sensed that well! No! The danger is not there!"

Cyrus Smith advanced towards the enormous roadway that framed the narrow shark's gulf. He was able to sufficiently examine the ancient stripes of lava from that side. There was no doubt for him that the last eruption had occurred a long time ago.

Then he turned back, listening to the subterranean rumblings that spread like a continuous thunder, interspersed with loud detonations. At nine in the morning, he returned to the corral.

Ayrton was waiting for him.

"The animals have been fed, Mr. Smith," said Ayrton.

— Good, Ayrton.

— They seem anxious, Mr. Smith.

— Yes, their instincts are speaking, and instinct does not deceive.

— Whenever you want...

— Take a lantern and a lighter, Ayrton, replied the engineer, and let's go."

Ayrton did as instructed. The onagers, unhitched, roamed in the corral. The door was closed from the outside, and Cyrus Smith, leading Ayrton, took the narrow path towards the west that led to the coast.

Both walked on ground muffled by the pulverized materials that had fallen from the cloud. No quadrupeds appeared in the woods. The birds had fled as well. Occasionally, a passing breeze raised the layer of ash, and the two colonists, caught in an opaque whirlwind, could no longer see each other. They were careful then to cover their eyes and mouths with a handkerchief, as they risked being blinded and suffocated.

Cyrus Smith and Ayrton could not move quickly under these conditions. Furthermore, the air was heavy, as if its oxygen had partially burned away and had become unfit for breathing.

They had to stop and catch their breath every hundred steps. It was therefore after ten o'clock when the engineer and his companion reached the crest of the enormous pile of basaltic and porphyritic rocks that formed the northwest coast of the island.

Ayrton and Cyrus Smith began to descend this steep coast, more or less following the dreadful path that had taken them to the Dakkar crypt during the stormy night. In daylight, this descent was less perilous, and moreover, the layer of ash covering the polished rocks allowed for a more secure footing on their sloping surfaces.

The embankment that extended the shore, at a height of about forty feet, was soon reached. Cyrus Smith recalled that this embankment sloped gently down to sea level. Although the tide was low at that moment, no beach was visible, and the waves, soiled by volcanic dust, came directly to crash against the coast's basalt.

Cyrus Smith and Ayrton easily found the opening of the Dakkar crypt, and they stopped under the final rock that formed the lower landing of the embankment.

"The metal boat should be there?" said the engineer.

— It's there, Mr. Smith, replied Ayrton, pulling towards him the light vessel sheltered under the archway.

— Let's get on board, Ayrton."

The two colonists boarded the boat. A slight undulation in the waves pushed them deeper under the very low arch of the crypt, and there, Ayrton, after striking the lighter, lit the lantern. Then he took the two oars, and once the lantern was placed on the prow of the boat, projecting its rays forward, Cyrus Smith took the helm and headed into the darkness of the crypt.

The Nautilus was no longer there to illuminate this dark cavern with its lights. Perhaps the electric radiation, still sustained by its powerful core, was spreading beneath the waters, but no glow emerged from the abyss where Captain Nemo rested.

The light of the lantern, although insufficient, allowed the engineer to advance, following the right wall of the crypt. A sepulchral silence reigned under this vault, at least in its front portion, for soon Cyrus Smith distinctly heard the rumblings that emerged from the mountain's depths.

"That's the volcano," he said.

Soon, along with this noise, chemical reactions were revealed by a strong odor, and sulfurous vapors gripped the engineer and his companion by the throat.

"That's what Captain Nemo feared!" murmured Cyrus Smith, whose face paled slightly. "But we must go all the way.

— Let's go!" replied Ayrton, who bent over his oars and pushed the boat towards the far end of the crypt.

Twenty-five minutes after passing through the opening, the boat arrived at the terminal wall and stopped.

Cyrus Smith then got up on his bench and swept the lantern over the various parts of the wall that separated the crypt from the central chimney of the volcano. What was the thickness of this wall?

Was it a hundred feet or ten? It was impossible to say. But the subterranean noises were too perceptible for it to be very thick.

The engineer, after exploring the wall along a horizontal line, fixed the lantern to the end of an oar and again swept it to a greater height on the basalt wall.

There, through barely visible cracks in the ill-joined prisms, acrid smoke seeped, infecting the atmosphere of the cave. Cracks striped the wall, and some, more sharply drawn, extended down to within two or three feet of the waters of the crypt.

Cyrus Smith remained thoughtful at first. Then, he murmured again these words:

"Yes! The captain was right! There lies the danger, and a terrible danger!"

Ayrton said nothing, but at a sign from Cyrus Smith, he took up his oars again, and, half an hour later, the engineer and he emerged from the Dakkar crypt.

❧ 19 ❧

The next morning, January 8th, after a day and night spent at the corral, everything being in order, Cyrus Smith and Ayrton returned to Granite House. Immediately, the engineer gathered his companions and informed them that Lincoln Island was in immense danger that no human power could avert.

"My friends," he said—and his voice betrayed deep emotion—"Lincoln Island is not going to last as long as the globe itself. It is doomed to a more or less imminent destruction, the cause of which lies within it, and from which nothing can save it!"

The colonists looked at one another and at the engineer.

They could not understand him.

"Explain yourself, Cyrus!" said Gédéon Spilett.

"I will explain," replied Cyrus Smith, "or rather, I will only relay the explanation that Captain Nemo gave me during our brief private conversation."

"Captain Nemo!" exclaimed the colonists.

"Yes, and this is the last service he wanted to render us before dying!

"The last service!" cried Pencroff! "The last service! You'll see that, despite being dead, he will render us more still!"

"What did Captain Nemo tell you?" asked the reporter.

"Let me tell you, my friends," replied the engineer. "Lincoln Island is not in the same conditions as the other islands in the Pacific, and a particular arrangement that Captain Nemo informed me of will sooner or later lead to the dislocation of its underwater structure.

"A dislocation! Lincoln Island! Come on!" exclaimed Pencroff, who, despite the great respect he had for Cyrus Smith, could not help but raise his shoulders.

"Listen to me, Pencroff," the engineer continued. "Here's what Captain Nemo observed, and what I myself confirmed yesterday during my exploration of the Dakkar crypt. This cryptextends under the island to the volcano, and it is only separated from the central chimney by the wall that closes its head. Now, this wall is lined with fractures and cracks that are already allowing the sulfur gases developed inside the volcano to pass through.

"And then?" asked Pencroff, whose forehead was furrowing violently.

"And then, I recognized that these fractures were widening under internal pressure, that the basalt wall was gradually cracking, and that, in a more or less short time, it would allow the sea waters, of which the cave is filled, to come through.

"Good!" replied Pencroff, who tried to joke once again. "The sea will extinguish the volcano, and it will all be over!"— Yes, it will all be over! replied Cyrus Smith. The day the sea rushes through the wall and floods through the central chimney into the core of the island, where the eruptive materials churn, that day, Pencroff, Lincoln Island will jump like Sicily would if the Mediterranean poured into Etna!»

The colonists didn't respond to this very definite comment from the engineer. They understood what danger threatened them.

It's worth noting that Cyrus Smith was not exaggerating in any way. Many people have thought about possibly extinguishing volcanoes, most of which rise along the shores of seas or lakes, by letting in their waters. But they did not realize that this could risk blowing apart a part of the globe, like a boiler suddenly pressured by a fire. Water rushing into a closed space with temperatures that can reach thousands of degrees would vaporize with such sudden energy that no container could withstand it.

Thus, it was clear that the island, facing an imminent and terrifying dislocation, would last only as long as the wall of the Dakkar crypt held up. It was not even a matter of months or weeks, but days, or perhaps hours!

The first feeling of the colonists was one of deep sorrow! They did not think about the direct danger threatening them but about the destruction of the land that had given them refuge, the island they had nurtured, the island they loved and wanted to make flourish one day!

So much effort spent in vain, so much work lost!

Pencroff could not hold back a large tear that rolled down his cheek, which he did not try to hide.

The conversation continued for a while longer. The chances the colonists could still cling to were discussed; but in conclusion, they recognized that there was not a moment to lose, that the building and fitting out of the ship had to be pushed with tremendous activity, and that there, right now, was the only hope of salvation for the inhabitants of Lincoln Island!

Therefore, everyone was called to work. What good would it do now to harvest, to gather, to hunt, to increase the supplies of Granite-House? What the store and the offices still contained would be enough, and more than enough, to provision the ship for a crossing, however long it might be! What was needed was that it be ready for the colonists before the inevitable catastrophe occurred.

The work resumed with feverish urgency. By January 23, the ship was half-finished. Until then, no changes had occurred at the summit of the volcano. There were still vapors, smoke mixed with flames, and incandescent rocks escaping from the crater. But during the night of January 23 to 24, under the pressure of the lava that reached the first level of the volcano, it was stripped of the cone that formed its cap. A dreadful noise echoed. The colonists first thought the island was breaking apart. They rushed out of Granite-House.

It was around two in the morning.

The sky was on fire. The upper cone — a mass over a thousand feet high, weighing billions of pounds — had been thrust down onto the island, causing the ground to tremble.

Fortunately, this cone tilted towards the north and fell onto the plain of sands and tuffs that stretched between the volcano and the sea. The crater, now widely open, projected such intense light towards the sky that, by mere reflection, the atmosphere seemed incandescent. At the same time, a torrent of lava, swelling at the new summit, poured down in long cascades, like water escaping from an overfilled basin, and a thousand snakes of fire crawled down the slopes of the volcano.

"The corral! The corral!" cried Ayrton.

Indeed, it was towards the corral that the lava flowed, due to the orientation of the new crater, and consequently, it was the fertile parts of the island, the sources of the red creek, the jacamar woods that were threatened with imminent destruction. At Ayrton's shout, the colonists rushed towards the onaggas' stable. The cart was hitched. They all had one thought! To run to the corral and release the animals contained within it.

Before three in the morning, they arrived at the corral. Terrible howls indicated quite clearly what horror terrified the rams and goats. Already, a torrent of incandescent materials, liquefied minerals, was falling from the slope onto the meadow and eating away at this side of the palisade. The door was suddenly opened by Ayrton, and the panicked animals bolted in all directions. An hour later, the bubbling lava filled the corral, vaporizing the water of the small river that flowed through it, igniting the habitation, which burned like thatch, and devouring even the last post of the fenced enclosure. There was nothing left of the corral!

The colonists had wanted to fight against this onslaught, they had tried, but foolishly and in vain, for man is defenseless against such great cataclysms.

Day had come — January 24. — Before returning to Granite-House, Cyrus Smith and his companions wanted to observe the final direction this flood of lava would take. The general slope of the land dropped from Mount Franklin to the east coast, and there was a fear that, despite the thick jacamar woods, the torrent would spread all the way to the Grande-vue plateau.

"The lake will cover us," said Gédéon Spilett.

"I hope so!" replied Cyrus Smith, and that was all he said.

The colonists wanted to go as far as the plain where the upper cone of Mount Franklin had fallen, but the lava was blocking their way. It followed, on one side, the valley of the red creek, and on the other, the valley of the waterfall river, vaporizing these two waterways along its path. There was no way to cross this torrent; they had to retreat before it instead. The decrowned volcano was unrecognizable. A sort of flat area replaced the old crater. Two chasms, dug at its southern and eastern edges, were constantly pouring out lava, creating two distinct flows. Above the new crater, a cloud of smoke and ash merged with the vapors in the sky, gathered above the island. Loud thunderclaps burst forth, blending with the rumblings of the mountain. From its mouth erupted fiery rocks, hurled over a thousand feet into the sky, exploding in the clouds and scattering like shrapnel. The sky responded with flashes of lightning to the volcanic eruption.

Around seven in the morning, the position became untenable for the colonists, who had taken refuge at the edge of the jacamar woods. Not only were projectiles beginning to rain down around them, but lava, overflowing from the bed of the red creek, threatened to cut off their escape route to the corral. The first ranks of trees caught fire, and their sap, suddenly turned to vapor, burst them open like firecrackers, while others, less moist, remained intact amid the inundation.

The colonists had retraced their steps toward the corral. They walked slowly, almost backward.

But due to the slope of the land, the torrent was quickly advancing eastward, and as soon as the lower layers of lava hardened, other boiling flows immediately covered them.

Meanwhile, the main current in the valley of the red creek grew more and more threatening. This part of the forest was ablaze, and enormous columns of smoke rolled above the trees, whose bases were already crackling in the lava.

The colonists stopped near the lake, half a mile from the mouth of the red creek. A question of life or death was about to be decided for them.

Cyrus Smith, accustomed to assessing serious situations, and knowing that he was addressing men capable of hearing the truth, whatever it might be, said:

"Either the lake will stop this flow, and a part of the island will be preserved from total devastation, or the flow will overrun the forests of the Far-West, and not a tree, not a plant will remain on the surface of the earth. We will have nothing left in sight on these bare rocks but a death that the explosion of the island will not keep us waiting for!

— Then, cried Pencroff, crossing his arms and stamping his foot on the ground, it's useless to work on the boat, right?

— Pencroff, replied Cyrus Smith, we must do our duty to the end!"

At that moment, the river of lava, having carved a path through the beautiful trees it was devouring, reached the edge of the lake. There was a slight rise in the ground that, if it had been higher, might have been sufficient to contain the torrent.

"To work!" cried Cyrus Smith.

The engineer's idea was immediately understood.

This torrent needed to be constrained, so to speak, and thus forced to spill into the lake.

The colonists ran to the worksite. They brought back shovels, picks, and axes, and there, through earthworks and felled trees, they managed, in a few hours, to raise a three-foot-high dam along a few hundred feet. It seemed to them, when they finished, that they had worked for only a few minutes!

It was time. The liquefied materials soon reached the lower part of the embankment. The river swelled like a river in full flood looking to overflow and threatened to surpass the only barrier that could prevent it from consuming all of the Far-West... But the dam managed to hold it back, and after a minute of terrible hesitation, it rushed into Lake Grant in a twenty-foot drop.

The colonists, breathless, without moving a muscle or uttering a word, then watched this battle of the two elements. What a sight this struggle between water and fire was! What pen could describe this scene of marvelous horror, and what brush could paint it? The water hissed as it evaporated upon contact with the boiling lava. The vapors, shot into the air, swirled to immeasurable heights, as if the valves of an enormous boiler had been suddenly opened.

But, however considerable the mass of water in the lake was, it would eventually be absorbed since it wasn't replenished, while the torrent, feeding from an inexhaustible source, continually rolled out new waves of incandescent materials.

The first lavas that fell into the lake solidified immediately and accumulated in such a way that they soon began to rise above the surface. On top of them slid other lavas that turned to stone, but moving towards the center. A jetty was thus formed, threatening to fill the lake, which could not overflow, as its excess water was dissipated in vapors. Hissing and sizzling sounds tore through the air with a deafening noise, and the mist carried by the wind fell back to the sea like rain. The jetty extended, and the blocks of solidified lava piled up on one another. Where once peaceful waters spread, there now appeared a huge mound of smoking rocks, as if a rising of the ground had brought forth thousands of reefs. Imagine those waters disturbed during a storm and then suddenly solidified by a chill of twenty degrees, and you have the appearance of the lake, three hours after the irresistible torrent had burst through.

This time, water was to be overcome by fire.

However, it was a fortunate circumstance for the colonists that the lava spill was directed towards Lake Grant. They had a few days of respite ahead of them. The Grande-vue plateau, Granite-House, and the construction site were temporarily safe. Now, those few days had to be used to finish boarding and caulking the ship carefully. Then, they would launch it into the sea and take refuge there, planning to rig it when it rested in its element. With the threat of an explosion poised to destroy the island, there was no longer any safety in staying on land. This retreat to Granite-House, so secure until now, could close its granite walls at any moment!

For the six days that followed, from January 25 to 30, the colonists worked on the ship as much as twenty men might have done. They hardly took any rest, and the glow of the flames erupting from the crater allowed them to continue day and night. The volcanic outpouring continued, but perhaps with less abundance. This was fortunate, as Lake Grant was almost entirely filled, and if new lavas had slipped over the old ones, they would have inevitably spread over the Grande-vue plateau, and from there to the shore.

But if the island was partially protected on this side, it was not the case for its western portion. In fact, the second flow of lava, which had followed the valley of the waterfall river, a broad valley where the terrains sloped down on either side of the creek, would find no obstacle. The incandescent liquid thus spread through the Far-West forest. At this time of year, when the trees were dried out by a scorching heat, the forest caught fire instantly, causing the blaze to spread both at the bases of the trunks and through the high branches which aided the progress of the conflagration. It even seemed that the flow of flames advanced faster at the tops of the trees than the flow of lava at their feet.

Then it happened that the animals, panicked, both wild and domestic, jaguars, wild boars, capybaras, koula, game of fur and feather, took refuge toward the Mercy and in the marshes of the tadorns, beyond the road to Port-Ballon. But the colonists were too busy with their own tasks to even notice the most fearsome of these animals. Moreover, they had abandoned Granite-House; they hadn't even wanted to seek shelter in the chimneys, and were camping under a tent near the mouth of the Mercy.

Every day, Cyrus Smith and Gédéon Spilett ascended to the Grande-vue plateau. Sometimes Harbert accompanied them, but never Pencroff, who did not want to see the island he loved so deeply in its new, devastated state!It was indeed a heartbreaking sight. The whole wooded part of the island was now bare. Only a small cluster of green trees stood at the tip of the serpentine peninsula. Here and there, some blackened and branchless stumps grimaced. The spot where the forests had been destroyed was drier than the marsh of the shelduck. The encroachment of lava had been complete. Where this wonderful greenery once thrived, the ground was now just a wild heap of volcanic tuffs. The valleys of the waterfall river and the Mercy no longer poured a single drop of water into the sea, and the colonists would have had no way to quench their thirst if Lake Grant had been completely dried up. But fortunately, its southern tip had been spared and formed a sort of pond, containing everything that remained of the drinking water on the island. To the northwest, the foothills of the volcano rose sharply and vividly, resembling a giant claw pressed into the ground. What a painful sight, what a terrifying aspect, and what regrets for these colonists, who, from a fertile domain, covered in forests, watered by streams, enriched with crops, found themselves suddenly transported to a devastated rock, on which, without their supplies, they wouldn't have even found a way to live!

"It breaks my heart!" said Gideon Spilett one day.

"Yes, Spilett," replied the engineer. "May heaven give us time to finish this building, now our only refuge!"

"Don't you think, Cyrus, that the volcano seems to want to calm down? It is still spewing lava, but less abundantly, if I'm not mistaken!"

"It doesn't matter," replied Cyrus Smith. "The fire is still burning hot in the bowels of the mountain, and the sea can rush in at any moment. We are like passengers whose ship is consumed by a fire they cannot extinguish, knowing that sooner or later it will reach the powder magazine! Come, Spilett, come, and let's not waste an hour!"

For another eight days, that is to say until February 7, the lava continued to spread, but the eruption remained within the indicated limits.

Cyrus Smith feared above all that the liquefied materials might spill over onto the shore, in which case the construction site would not be spared. However, around that time, the colonists felt vibrations in the island's structure that worried them greatly.

It was February 20. They still had a month before the ship would be ready to sail. Would the island hold until then? Pencroff and Cyrus Smith intended to launch the ship as soon as its hull was sufficiently watertight. The deck, the rigging, the interior setup, would come later, but the important thing was that the colonists had a secure refuge outside the island. It might even be wise to take the ship to Balloon Port, as far away from the eruptive center as possible, because at the mouth of the Mercy, between the islet and the granite wall, it ran the risk of being crushed in the event of a collapse. Thus, all the workers' efforts were focused on finishing the hull.

They reached March 3, and they could count on launching the ship in about ten days.

Hope returned to the hearts of these colonists, who had suffered so much during this fourth year of their stay on Lincoln Island! Pencroff himself seemed to emerge somewhat from the dark mood that the destruction and devastation of his domain had plunged him into. He was no longer thinking about anything but that ship, on which all his hopes were focused.

"We will finish it," he told the engineer, "we will finish it, Mr. Cyrus, and it is time, because the season is advancing, and we will soon be in the midst of the equinox. Well, if necessary, we will stop at Tabor Island to spend the winter! But Tabor Island after Lincoln Island! Oh! The misfortune of my life! Would I ever have believed I would see such a thing!"

"Let's hurry!" replied the engineer invariably.

And they worked without wasting a moment.

"Master," Nab asked a few days later, "if Captain Nemo were still alive, do you think all this would have happened?"

"Yes, Nab," replied Cyrus Smith.

"Well, I don't believe it!" murmured Pencroff into Nab's ear.

"Me neither!" Nab replied seriously.

During the first week of March, Mount Franklin became threatening again. Thousands of thin strands of glass, made of flowing lava, fell like rain upon the ground. The crater filled again with lava that spilled over all the slopes of the volcano. The torrent ran over the hardened tuffs and finished destroying the meager skeletons of trees that had survived the first eruption. The flow, this time following the southwest bank of Lake Grant, went beyond the glycerin creek and flooded the Grande-Vue plateau. This last blow to the colonists' work was terrible. From the mill, the farm buildings, the stables, nothing remained. The birds, startled, vanished in all directions. Top and Jup showed signs of great fear, and their instincts warned them that a catastrophe was imminent. Many of the island's animals had perished during the first eruption. Those who survived found refuge only in the shelduck marsh, except for a few who had taken shelter on the Grande-Vue plateau. But this last retreat was finally closed to them, and the river of lava, overflowing the ridge of the granite wall, began to pour its fiery cascades onto the shore. The sublime horror of this sight is beyond description. During the night, it looked like a Niagara of molten metal, with its incandescent vapors above and its boiling masses below!

The colonists were forced into their last stronghold, and although the upper seams of the ship had not yet been caulked, they decided to launch it into the sea!

Pencroff and Ayrton therefore began preparations for the launch, which was to take place the next morning, on March 9.

But during the night from the 8th to the 9th, a gigantic column of vapor burst from the crater, rising amidst terrible detonations to more than three thousand feet high. The wall of the Dakkar cave had evidently given way under the pressure of the gases, and the sea, rushing down through the central chimney into the fiery abyss, vaporized suddenly. But the crater could not provide enough of an outlet for this vapor. An explosion, which could be heard a hundred miles away, shook the layers of air. Pieces of mountains fell back into the Pacific, and in minutes, the ocean covered the spot where Lincoln Island had been.

20

An isolated rock, thirty feet long, fifteen feet wide, emerging barely ten feet - that was the only solid point not engulfed by the Pacific waves.

It was all that remained of Granite-House! The wall had been toppled, then dislocated, and some of the rocks from the great hall had piled up to form this high point. Everything had vanished into the abyss around it: the lower cone of Mount Franklin, torn apart by the explosion, the lava jaws of Shark Gulf, the Grande-Vue plateau, the islet of salvation, the granites of Balloon Port, the basalts of the Dakkar crypt, the long serpentine peninsula, so far from the eruptive center! From Lincoln Island, there was nothing left to see but this narrow rock which now served as a refuge for the six colonists and their dog Top.

The animals had also perished in the catastrophe, both the birds and other representatives of the island's fauna, all crushed or drowned, and the unfortunate Jup himself had, alas, found death in some crevice of the ground!

If Cyrus Smith, Gideon Spilett, Harbert, Pencroff, Nab, and Ayrton survived, it was because, gathered under their tent, they were hurled into the sea at the moment when the island's debris fell from all sides.

When they resurfaced, they saw nothing but this pile of rocks half a cable's length away, towards which they swam, and upon which they finally came to rest.

It was on this bare rock that they had been living for nine days! Some provisions salvaged before the catastrophe from the Granite-House store, a bit of fresh water that rain had pooled in a rock hollow, that was all the unfortunate ones possessed. Their last hope, their ship, had been destroyed. They had no means of leaving this reef. No fire and no way to make one. They were destined to perish!

That day, March 18, they had provisions left for only two more days, even though they had consumed only the strict minimum. All their knowledge, all their intelligence could do nothing in this situation. They were completely in the hands of God.

Cyrus Smith remained calm. Gideon Spilett, more nervous, and Pencroff, filled with a smoldering anger, paced back and forth on the rock. Harbert did not leave the engineer's side and looked at him, as if asking for help that he could not provide. Nab and Ayrton had resigned themselves to their fate.

"Oh! Misery! Misery!" Pencroff often repeated. "If only we had, even a nutshell, to take us to Tabor Island! But nothing, nothing!"

"Captain Nemo did well to die!" Nab said once.

In the five days that followed, Cyrus Smith and his unfortunate companions lived with utmost frugality, eating just enough to avoid starving. Their weakening was extreme. Harbert and Nab began to show some signs of delirium.

In this situation, could they even hold onto a glimmer of hope? No! What was their only chance? That a ship might pass by the reef? But they knew from experience that vessels never visited that part of the Pacific! Could they hope that, by a truly providential coincidence, the Scottish yacht might come at this time to search for Ayrton at Tabor Island? That was unlikely, and besides, even if it did, since the colonists had been unable to leave a notice indicating the changes in Ayrton's situation, the yacht's commander, after searching the islet in vain, would return to sea and head back to lower latitudes.

No! They could not hold any hope of rescue, and a horrible death, death by hunger and thirst, awaited them on this rock!

And already, they lay on the rock, lifeless, no longer conscious of what was happening around them. Only Ayrton, with a supreme effort, still lifted his head and cast a desperate look at this deserted sea!...

But then, on the morning of March 24, Ayrton's arms stretched out toward a point in the distance, he rose up, first onto his knees, then to his feet, his hand seemed to make a signal... a ship was in sight of the island! This ship was not just wandering the seas. The reef was a destination for it, towards which it was heading straight, forcing its steam, and the unfortunate ones would have seen it for several hours already, if they had still had the strength to observe the horizon!

"The Duncan!" murmured Ayrton, and he fell back, motionless.

When Cyrus Smith and his companions regained consciousness, thanks to the care lavished upon them, they found themselves in the cabin of a steamer, unable to understand how they had escaped death. A word from Ayrton was enough to tell them everything.

"The Duncan!" he murmured.

"The Duncan!" replied Cyrus Smith.

And raising his arms to the sky, he exclaimed:

"Oh! Almighty God! So You wanted us to be saved!"

It was indeed the Duncan, Lord Glenarvan's yacht, then commanded by Robert, the son of Captain Grant, which had been sent to Tabor Island to look for Ayrton and bring him back after twelve years of atonement!...

The colonists were saved, they were already on their way back!

"Captain Robert," asked Cyrus Smith, "who could have suggested to you, after leaving Tabor Island, where you found no sign of Ayrton, to sail a hundred miles to the northeast?"

"Mr. Smith," replied Robert Grant, "it was to look for not only Ayrton but also your companions and you!"

"My companions and me?"

"Of course! At Lincoln Island!"

"Lincoln Island!" exclaimed Gideon Spilett, Harbert, Nab, and Pencroff together, in the utmost astonishment.

"How do you know about Lincoln Island?" asked Cyrus Smith, since this island isn't even shown on maps?

"I knew it from the notice you left at Tabor Island," Robert Grant replied.

"A notice?" cried Gideon Spilett.

"Of course, and here it is," replied Robert Grant, presenting a document that indicated the longitude and latitude of Lincoln Island, "current residence of Ayrton and five American colonists."

"Captain Nemo!..." said Cyrus Smith, after reading the notice and recognizing it was in the same handwriting that had written the document found at the corral!

"Oh!" said Pencroff, so it was he who took our Bonadventure, who ventured alone to Tabor Island!

"To leave that notice!" replied Harbert.

"I was right to say," cried the sailor, "that even after his death, the captain would still do us one last service!

"My friends," said Cyrus Smith in a deeply moved voice, "may the god of all mercies receive the soul of Captain Nemo, our savior!"

The colonists uncovered their heads at this last phrase from Cyrus Smith and murmured the captain's name. At that moment, Ayrton, approaching the engineer, simply said to him:

"Where should I place this box?"

This was the box that Ayrton had saved at the risk of his life, at the moment when the island was sinking, and he was now faithfully returning it to the engineer.

"Ayrton! Ayrton!" said Cyrus Smith with profound emotion.

Then addressing Robert Grant, he added, "Sir, where you left a guilty man, you find a man whom atonement has made honest, and to whom I am proud to shake hands!"

Robert Grant was then informed of the strange story of Captain Nemo and the colonists of Lincoln Island. Then, taking stock of what remained of this reef that would now appear on Pacific maps, he gave the order to change course.

Fifteen days later, the colonists landed in America, where they found their homeland at peace, after the terrible war that had brought triumph to justice and rights. Most of the wealth contained in the box bequeathed by Captain Nemo to the colonists of Lincoln Island was used to acquire a large estate in Iowa. Only one pearl, the most beautiful, was taken from this treasure and sent to Lady Glenarvan, on behalf of the shipwrecked ones repatriated by the Duncan. There, in this land, the colonists called for work, meaning for wealth and happiness, from all those they had planned to offer hospitality on Lincoln Island. A vast colony was established there, named after the island lost in the depths of the Pacific. There was a river called Mercy, a mountain named Franklin, a small lake that became Grant Lake, forests that became the forests of the Far West. It was like an island on dry land.

There, under the skilled hands of the engineer and his companions, everything thrived. Every former colonist from Lincoln Island was present, as they had sworn to always live together: Nab, where his master was, Ayrton ready to sacrifice himself at any occasion, Pencroff more of a farmer than he had ever been a sailor, Harbert, whose studies were completed under Cyrus Smith's guidance, Gédéon Spilett himself, who founded the New Lincoln Herald, which became the best-informed newspaper in the world.

There, Cyrus Smith and his companions received visits several times from Lord and Lady Glenarvan, Captain John Mangles and his wife, sister of Robert Grant, Robert Grant himself, Major Mac Nabbs, and everyone involved in the intertwined stories of Captain Grant and Captain Nemo.

There, finally, everyone was happy, united in the present as they had been in the past; yet they would never forget that island where they had arrived, poor and naked, that island which, for four years, had met their needs, and of which only a piece of granite, battered by the waves of the Pacific, remained, the tomb of the one who was Captain Nemo!

Printed in Great Britain
by Amazon

54443350R00290